PETROLIO

PETROLIO

PIER PAOLO PASOLINI

Translated from the Italian by Ann Goldstein

PANTHEON BOOKS

NEW YORK

Library of Congress Cataloging-in-Publication Data

Pasolini, Pier Paolo, 1922–1975.
[Petrolio. English]
Petrolio / Pier Paolo Pasolini ; translated from the Italian by
Ann Goldstein.
p. cm.
ISBN 0-679-42990-5 (hardcover)
I. Goldstein, Ann, 1949– . II. Title.
PQ4835.A48P5813 1997
853'.914—dc20   96-27303
CIP

Random House Web Address: http://www.randomhouse.com/

Book design by Jo Metsch

Printed in the United States of America
First American Edition
2 4 6 8 9 7 5 3 1

TRANSLATOR'S NOTE

The manuscript of *Petrolio,* including the system of typographical annotations described on the following pages, was prepared for publication by Graziella Chiarcossi, Pasolini's cousin, and Maria Careri, under the supervision of the literary critic Aurelio Roncaglia, who was a friend of Pasolini.

The manuscript was found in a folder on Pasolini's desk shortly after his death. It consisted of 521 pages, most of them typed (but some handwritten), with handwritten corrections and additions inserted at different stages (blue and black ink, red and black felt pen). In addition to the Notes making up the novel, the folder contained a "Project Note," describing Pasolini's conception of the ultimate form of *Petrolio;* a plot outline of the novel; a letter, not sent, to the novelist Alberto Moravia, a longtime friend of Pasolini; and various pages of notes, all of which are included in the present volume. The pages were left in the order in which they were found, and, since the manuscript was truly a work in progress, there are repetitions, transpositions, and gaps in the numbering of the Notes. Many of these are the result of changes in the text or rearrangements of the pages made by Pasolini, following which the numbering was not always adjusted.

"I have started on a book that will occupy me for years, perhaps for the rest of my life. I don't want to talk about it. . . ; it's enough to know that it's a kind of 'summa' of all my experiences, all my memories," Pasolini said in early 1975. According to interviews and letters, he had projected a novel of two thousand pages; what we have is thus little more than a quarter—"a discontinuous series of fragments, some more extensive, some less, some mere crumbs, telegraphic ideas, even bare titles," Roncaglia has written. He goes on to point out that the novel's incompleteness is "evident not only in the quantity of what is lacking but also in the quality of what exists. The degree of refinement of the Notes, even of the most coherent, varies significantly. In some cases the draft, although not definitive, has a sustained flow and seems stylistically polished. In others . . . there is no shortage of formal imperfections: redundancies, approximations, roughness of style and in a few cases even of syntax." There are also numerous internal inconsistencies, which Pasolini would presumably have eliminated in a definitive draft, and many obscure references, even for an Italian reader.

The translation does not attempt to address any of these issues or solve any of the problems; its aim is to present the reader with the contents of the folder on Pasolini's desk in as readable a form as possible. Pasolini himself insists that the work is not a novel in the conventional historical or linear sense; he is, he says, constructing a form that consists of "something written." Early in the novel he writes, "I am *living* the genesis of my book," and so, too, is the reader, who in a sense becomes the author of this "poem" (as Pasolini often refers to it), not perhaps as Pasolini intended but surely in a way that the author of *Petrolio* would have appreciated.

Ann Goldstein
August 1996

NOTE ON THE TEXT

For this edition, we transcribed the manuscript page by page (including pages of handwritten notes), in the original sequence, eliminating—without any indication in the text—words, sentences, and passages evidently deleted by the author (crossed out or with an explicit note). The transcription thus corresponds to the last wish of the author as documented by the materials of the novel as he left them. Obvious typing mistakes have been corrected, as have other small mistakes; the spelling has been regularized; the often variable writing of names, abbreviations, etc., has been made uniform according to current editorial practice. On the other hand, the numerous irregularities in the sequence and numbering of the Notes have not been interfered with.

Because the novel was not finished, we have had to adopt certain typographical symbols to let the reader know, in an economical and reasonably complete manner, the condition of the text. The meaning of those symbols is as follows:

xxx	Series of "x"s used by the author as a reminder to insert words, often proper names, left temporarily undecided.
< ... >	Signifies the handwritten mark V, used by the author to indicate additions or integrations not carried out.
<?>	One or more indecipherable handwritten words.
<text>	A word, sentence, or passage crossed out by the author and not replaced but essential for understanding the context; if a passage is of more than one line, it has been further highlighted with a broken vertical line along the margin.

/text/   A word, sentence, or passage highlighted by the author (underlined, circled, marked in the margin, etc.) in anticipation of revision; if a passage is of more than one line, it has been further highlighted with a broken vertical line along the margin.

\text\   Alternative variant inserted by the author in the space between the lines, preserving the preceding version.

reduced type   Hand- or typewritten notes containing plans, outlines, and reminders relative to the novel but not incorporated by the author into the main text. Those notes are intercalated into the manuscript, on separate pages or at the end of the Notes (less important notes, written in the margins or in the space between the lines, are instead described in the Notes at the end of this volume); in the typographical arrangement an attempt has been made to reproduce, as if photographically, the physical aspect of the manuscript.

†   See Notes at the end of this volume.

PROJECT NOTE

All of *Petrolio* (from the second draft) should be presented in the form of a critical edition of an unpublished text (considered a monumental work, a modern *Satyricon*). Four or five versions of that text survive: they correspond in some respects and not in others, some contain certain events while others do not, etc. Hence this edition makes use not only of a comparison between the various surviving manuscripts (of which, for example, two are apocryphal, with variants that are bizarre, exaggerated, ingenuous, or "revised in the manner of") but also of the contribution of other materials: letters from the author (concerning whose identity there is an unresolved philological problem, etc.), letters of friends of the author who know about the manuscript (and disagree among themselves), oral testimony reported in newspapers or elsewhere, songs, etc. There are also some illustrations for the book (probably the work of the author himself). These illustrations are of great help in the accurate reconstruction of missing scenes or passages, and, since they are graphic works on a high level, although purely mannerist, in addition to the literary version there will be a critical figurative version. Furthermore, to fill in the vast lacunae of the book, and for the reader's information, an enormous quantity of historical documents that have some bearing on the events of the book will be used, especially regarding politics and, in particular, the history of ENI.[1] Such documents are: journalistic (features from magazines/supplements, *L'Espresso,* etc.), in which case they are quoted in full; "recorded" oral testimony, in interviews, etc., of high-ranking characters or in any case of witnesses; rare

---

[1] *Translator's note:* ENI, or Ente Nazionale Idrocarburi, is the Italian state oil-and-gas company.

cinematographic documentaries (and here there will be a critical recon-struction analogous to the figurative and literary ones—not only philo-logical but also with respect to style and attribution, e.g., "Who is the director of that documentary?"). The author of the critical edition will therefore summarize, on the basis of these documents—in a flat, objec-tive, colorless, etc. style—long passages of general history to link the "fragments" of the reconstructed work. Those fragments are to be arranged in sections in an order determined by the editor. Sometimes the fragments correspond to entire original chapters (that is, there are chapters whose text corresponds in an *almost* identical way in all the manuscripts except the apocrypha, which continue to suggest curious variants). The fragmentary character of the whole book ensures that, for example, certain "narrative pieces" are in themselves complete, but we can't be certain, for example, whether they are real events, dreams, or conjectures made by one of the characters.

Spring 1973

LETTER TO
ALBERTO MORAVIA

Dear Alberto,

I'm sending you this manuscript so that you can give me some advice. It's a novel, but it's not written the way /real/ novels are written: its language is that of essays, of journal articles, of reviews, of private letters, even of poetry; rare are the passages that can be called /definitely/ narrative, and even then they are narratively so bare ("but now let's move on to the facts," "Carlo was walking . . . ," etc., and besides there is also a symbolic citation in this sense: "He traveled . . .") as to recall the language of treatments or screenplays rather than that of classic novels; that is, they are "true narrative passages" made "purposely" to evoke the novel.

In a novel the narrator usually disappears, giving way to a conventional figure who alone can have a real relationship with the reader—real precisely because it's conventional. In fact, outside the world of writing—or, if you like, of the page and of the structure as it appears to one of the party—the true protagonist of the reading of a novel is, precisely, the reader.

Now, in these pages I address the reader directly and not conventionally. That means that I have not made my novel an "object," a "form," thereby obeying the laws of a language that would secure for it the necessary distance from me, < ... > almost to the point of abolishing myself, or through which I would generously negate myself, humbly putting on the garments of a narrator like all other narrators. No: I have spoken to the reader as myself, in flesh and bone, as I write you this letter or as

I have often written my poems in Italian. I have made the novel an object between the reader and me, and I have discussed it (as one can do by oneself when writing).

Now, at this point (here is the reason for this letter) I could completely rewrite this novel from the beginning, objectifying it; that is, disappearing as the real author and putting on the clothes of the conventional narrator (who, < ... >, is much more real than the real one). I could do it. I am not without ability, I am not deficient in rhetorical skill, and I do not lack patience (not, of course, the unlimited patience that one has only in youth); I could do it, I repeat. But if I did it, I would have before me a single road: that of evoking the novel. That is, I would have no choice but to go to the end of a road on which I had naturally set out. Everything that is novelistic in this novel is so as an evocation of the novel. If I gave substance to what is here only potential, if, that is, I invented the writing necessary to make this story an object, a narrative machine that functions by itself in the reader's imagination, I would necessarily have to accept that conventionality which is, ultimately, a game. I have no further desire to play (truly to the end; that is, applying myself with utter seriousness); and for that reason I am happy to have written as I did. And here is the advice I'm asking: is what I have written enough to express in a worthwhile and poetical way what I wanted to express? Or should I rewrite it all in another key, creating the wonderful illusion of a story that unfolds on its own, in a time frame that, for every reader, is the time in which life is lived and left behind intact, revealing as true realities those things which had seemed simply natural?

I would like you to realize, in advising me, that the protagonist of this novel is what he is, and, aside from the similarities of his story to mine, or to ours—similarities of background or psychology that are mere existential wrappings, useful to give concreteness to what happens internally—he is repugnant to me: I have spent a long period of my life in his company, and it would be very tiring to start again from the beginning for a period that would presumably be even longer.

Certainly I would do it, but it must be absolutely necessary. This novel is not very useful anymore in my life (as are the novels or poems

that were written in youth), it is not an announcement, hey, men! I exist, but the preamble to a testament, testimony of the little knowledge
that one has accumulated, and is completely different from what one
expected \imagined\!

Yours,
Pier Paolo

PETROLIO
(Novel Outline)

A man and his double, or twin. The protagonist is now one, now the other. If A has a double, B, B has a double, A, but in that case he himself is A.

It is the schizoid dissociation that divides a person in two, bringing together in A certain characteristics, in B others, etc.

A is a wealthy, cultivated bourgeois, an engineer who works in the oil industry; he is among those in power, he is integrated (but cultivated, to the left, etc., all of which is implicit).†

B, the man with the "bad" character, serves A, the man with the "good" character; he is his servant; that is, he is employed in the most menial tasks. Between the two there is perfect agreement. A true balance.

With the situation reversed, A, the man with the bad character, makes use of B, the man with the good character, to vindicate himself before society and ensure his safety from the police, the magistrates, etc.

Leaving on an official trip—with the head of government, who is going to a country in the Middle East—A the good leaves B the bad in Rome: but just before leaving he realizes that B is a woman. (<?> him through castration complex/anxiety before the youths of '68.) He cannot put off his departure.

B, the man with the bad character, who is, furthermore, a woman, remaining alone in Rome, devotes himself to performing menial tasks, but he no longer looks for women (sisters, mothers, etc.); instead he looks for men, male sex organs. He proceeds, by this route, into the experience of no limits, into anomie.

Protected by solitude and by total liberty—signified by his Double's so-

journ in the East—he succeeds in degrading himself without any limits. He
now desires to have sex with twenty men, neither more nor fewer. Naturally he
succeeds. The affair, once arranged, takes place in a field, in the mud, while
sometimes it rains, etc.

The twenty young men who have had sex go off, one by one or in groups.
They go to the places where their lives customarily take place (realistically indicated), but around a bend, at the end of a street, in the darkness of a courtyard,
in a doorway, etc.—that is, where they disappear into their lives, to be present
no longer, as if swallowed into nothingness—they are killed in different ways,
all of them monstrous: symbols of the true reasons that people die in the modern world (a question of physical death or another kind of death).

Returning from the Middle East (public duties, journalists, economic and
scientific results), A, the good man, can no longer find B, the bad man who has
become a woman. A loses his equilibrium and must himself see to the menial
tasks he had assigned to B; it is degrading; with his physical presence and his
consciousness he confronts those situations from which he had always kept
himself apart.

Naturally he cannot continue. He must choose to be "public" only, and
therefore "holy."

Politically and socially the result is that he moves much farther to the right,
almost as far as to make an implicit alliance with the Fascists. In the meantime
he, too, has become a woman and has sex with a young Sicilian Fascist who
forces him to perform acts that only his Double could, and that he is unable to
tolerate, etc.

After having sex with A, the Fascist goes home, and he, too, dies, devoured
by a Monster.

Constrained by the circumstances, A has overcome his shame, the bond with
his bourgeois conscience, which kept him from being B: and he wants to repeat the act that the young Fascist taught him, once and for all. By this route
he reaches the experience of no limits, anomie—which B arrived at innocently.

He, too, must have sex with at least twenty young men, to reach extreme
degradation, etc. He arranges the meeting with twenty young men, etc., in a
filthy cellar in a slum. He has sex with them all.†

When the sex is over, the young men head for their homes: but they all live in the same area: one of them has decided to throw a bomb in the / Central Station/†. It's unclear if he is an anarchist or a Fascist. The others, drunk, and inspired by Monsters like those which devoured their contemporaries, follow him.

The bomb is set off: a hundred people die; their corpses are strewn in piles in a sea of blood, which floods among shreds of flesh, benches, and tracks.

B (we do not call him A only because it would be too confusing) has a profound nostalgia for the conscientious, secure life that A guaranteed him. From the wretched little apartment in the outskirts where he has settled to the unlimited enjoyment of his solitude, he goes in search of A.

But A's nice apartment, in the center, is deserted. B himself calls in vain. He does not find him. He wonders how to find a substitute for A. The Church and the Communist Party are no longer of any use. For B the only thing left is to make Petrolium the ideal of his life; alone, he castrates himself. And he takes A's place in the office, where the Fascists, with whom A had begun a tacit politics of alliance, have secured for themselves a larger share of power. The Fascists, however, cannot have a friendly, respectful relationship with a castrated man. With their usual vulgarity they hire a girl to tempt B, the castrated man, so that they can mock him publicly (and blackmail him in order to eliminate him).

But while poor B tries to defend himself from the blandishments of the Fascist girl, devouring Monsters arrive, their horrible breath bringing a plague on the Fascists, making them half putrefied, infected, covered with pustules and pus. In this state they can no longer mock the castrated B: in fact, they must adapt to life with him, in the great edifice of Petrolium research.

A, meanwhile, has gone to live in the country, in an old farmhouse, where he sees no one. In the Middle East he had been initiated (by a Westerner) into the mysteries of an Orphic religion: he goes beyond this initiation; becomes a saint; communicates with God, from whom he asks the good of all equally.

God hears him.

Unknown to all, an angel sent by the God of A arrives at the Petroleum Building, during a meeting at which even the Minister of Government Shares is present: the castrated B and the putrefied Fascists have given a marvelous impetus to scientific research and the economic system. Everything is proceeding under full sail, in spite of the tragedy. The angel heals them all. B becomes a man again and the Fascists human beings. Now that they are cured, they have to decide what to do. They decide to continue as before.

PETROLIO (NOVEL OUTLINE)

Spring or summer 1972

My eyes fell by chance on the word "Petrolio" in an article in, I think, *L'Unità,* and the mere thought of the word "Petrolio" as the title of a book spurred me on to think of the plot of that book. In less than an hour this sketch was conceived and written.

More Notes

Sequences for Carlo the First:

Visit to Pope John (a day in 196 . . .) to be described, etc. Balducci and the objection of Conscience (Don Milani) Mattei uses him for his contacts with the Fascists (precisely because he is unassailable as an anti-Fascist and a Catholic of the left) The Sicilian Fascists—for this reason—blackmail Carlo when the moment comes to murder Mattei, and Carlo becomes an accomplice (although only in silence). Concerning the Mafia.

Carlo the First as a woman:

When he decides to do what Carlo the Second was doing, he recalls, from the time of *Il Mulino,* the sex life and prostitution connected to youthful intellectual experiences.† That brings to mind the male prostitution on the hill. He goes there to organize the encounter with twenty boys analogous to that of Carlo the Second.
The bomb is placed at the station in Bologna. The slaughter is described as a "Vision."

Notes for Carlo the Second:

The twenty boys who later disappear are guided by benevolent (traditional) Monsters even though they are "modern" (consumerism, continuous struggle, etc.). Death as oblivion and loss of self has archaic and benign characteristics: the tragedy is pure, etc. The Monsters are later identified with the little lights of Campo Verano. Their sparkling in the night. Essay on the old dead of the Verano.

Names of Indian *devils* for the Communist spirits

NAMES OF THE FASCIST DEITIES
White Wolf
Roll
Pragma
Porsche
Jerk-Off
Fridge
Forty-three
Musket
the Bernabei
/Denunciation/
/the Take/

—Each one advises one of the assailants (veterans from the Fascist cunt); and in a group they divert the police at the Bologna station, creating an unspoken complicity, etc. The assailants all have names of Fascist officials or martyrs but are all very modern (some will have names of music-hall singers).

FORTE (8 September 1973)

Notes 8–9
Devoted to careers of oil industry workers, among which Carlo's is outlined.

Notes 9–20
The two Carlos separate (tacit agreement). Tetis's Carlo goes to Turin. On a train trip, the first sordid exalting, etc., feminine adventure. His house. Fragmentary reconstruction of his life, education, development, early career, etc. His family. Seduces and makes love to his elderly mother (from the odious agrarian bourgeoisie, but she herself is a forward-looking Catholic, as one could be in the fifties), then one by one he seduces and makes love to his four sisters, one of whom is thirteen; the servant; various girls in Turin; finally, in the country, to his grandmother and her little southern servant. He is inclined toward poor girls, especially from the South. Ends at the Pensione Sicilia. [everything *as if seen* by a spy]

Notes 20–40
First, *initiatory* journey (Argonauts)
At this point he is chosen, precisely as a man of the left (it is in return for having what he wants later), for an operation of the right, the extreme right: complicity in a crime (the killing of Mattei, dated to the late fifties?) that puts him in contact with the CIA and with the Mafia. But he lives all this as if in a dream. Like an ideal accomplice, he understands and sees nothing. The criminal operation takes place at the Pensione SICILIA, in Turin.†

Notes 40 and following
Tetis's Carlo has a first great love: it lasts around two years. It ends tragically. He returns to poor girls, this time in Rome. For five or six years. Until we get to 1969. [Story plagiarized from Kafka—letters to Felice]

Notes 40 and following (alternating with the preceding)
Carlo's career reaches a pinnacle. (Stories about Power, inserted into the novel and, in part, one inside the other.)

Note 50 (current 25)

Trauma of '69, sex change of Tetis's Carlo, etc. Great love (unrealized, of Polis's Carlo, which bursts forth at the death of Tetis's Carlo) {plagiarized from *Manon?*} and it continues until a little before the Vision (Medieval Garden— current Note 65)

June 1973

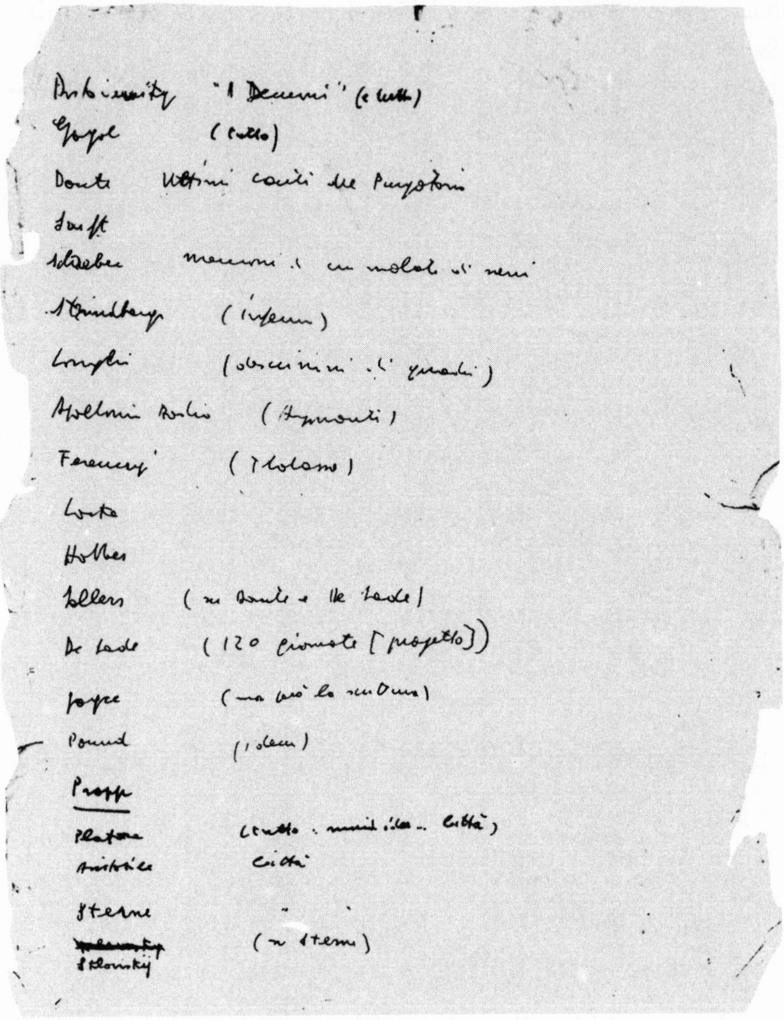

Dostoievskij "I Demoni" (e tutto)
Gogol (tutto)
Dante Ultimi canti del Purgatorio
Swift
Schreber memorie di un malato di nervi
Strindberg (Inferno)
Longhi (descrizioni di quadri)
Apollonio Rodio (Argonauti)
Ferenczi (Thalassa)
Locke
Hobbes
Sollers (su Dante e De Sade)
De Sade (120 giornate [progetto])
Joyce (ma solo la scrittura)
Pound (idem)
Propp
Platone (tutto: mondo idee.. Città)
Aristotele Città
Sterne "
~~[illegible]~~ Shklovskij (su Sterne)

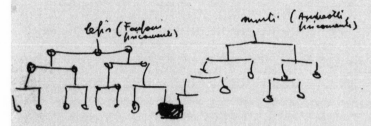

App. 6 ... ... : CARLO SECONDO

Se un uomo è uguale a un altro uomo, tanto uguale da essere lo stesso, quale
dei due è quello vero? Qual'è quello a cui l'altro assomiglia, meglio, con cui
l'altro si identifica?Qual'è il primo, in quanto termine di riferimento?
Chiamare Carlo secondo la persona che è praticamente il "doppio" di Carlo primo è
ingiusto: perchè protrebbe essere benissimo Carlo secondo a essere nominato per
primo e quindi a essere colui al quale l'altro viene assimilato.

Probabilmente l'ingiustizia di questa gerarchizzazione, Carlo primo e Carlo secondo – anche se si giustifica con l'essere puramente numerica o di comodo – è una
ingiustizia di carattere sociale. Carlo primo è infatti, come abbiamo detto, un inge-
gnere, lavora ai vertici di uno dei principali Enti dello stato italiano, fa parte
del "potere silenzioso" ma non per questo meno prepotente, ansi!, proviene da una
famiglia ricca, perbene, religiosa ecc. ecc.; mentre per Carlo secondo, anagrafica-
mente, non si potrebbe adoperare nessuna delle forme di identificazione sociali che
ho adoperato per Carlo primo. La graduazione è quindi sociale. Ma nemmeno Carlo
secondo, evidentemente, sfugge alla socialità: ma il suo modo di appartenervi, come
racconterò, è, appunto, sfuggire. Sosia perfetto di Carlo primo, dentro di sè contiene
il vuoto al posto del pieno sociale che rende Carlo primo ciò che è e ciò che
essere definito. E questo vuoto è riempito da qualcos'altro, che tuttavia si esprime
attraverso tutte le regole di comportamento sociale che caratterizzano la socialità
che riempie e fà agire Carlo primo. In altre parole, se un testimone fosse presente
alle azioni di Carlo secondo, non potrebbe poi riferirle, a un eventuale giudizio,
che a Carlo primo. E così un poliziotto, sorprendendo Carlo secondo a fare qualcosa
di illecito, di contrario alle regole borghesi e, più semplicemente, al codice, non
potrebbe che arrestarlo in quanto Carlo primo: consultando i documenti di Carlo primo, informandosi sui suoi dati anagrafici, su ciò che, per opposizione, come in un
sistema linguistico, lo colloca nel contesto sociale.

Carlo secondo è così, nella gerarchia sociale, inferiore a Carlo primo, pur
essendone identico, così identico da non distinguersi particamente da lui. Ma la sua
inferiorità non è controllata da Carlo primo.

Carlo secondo, come tutti gli umili privi di autorità sociale – un po' come

RACCONTI COLTI

A proposito di "cultura popolare", per introdurre personaggi totalmente
diversi dai protagonisti borghesi, in una ix riunione intellettuale si
raccoytano e si commentano (vedi "I fratelli Karamasov), le sxeguenti
storie:

L'acquisto di uno schiavo (a Kartum) – andata e ritorno (andata schiavi-
                                        sta – ritorno osmosi tra le due
                                        culture, attraverso il sesso)

La storia di una famiglia indiana i cui membri muoiono a uno a uno di fame
                                        (cfr.Appunti per un film sull'"India")

La distruzione della popolazione del Bihar (x Bianchi cercano di distruggere
                                        i 30 o 40 milioni di affamati e xxixxxx
                                        colerosi, dapprima buttando dall'alto
                                        "pacchi" di viveri avvelenati, poi addi-
                                        rittura bombardando a tappeto città e vil-
                                        laggi. Ma la popolazione non muore: appena
                                        uccisi, massacrati, tutti risuscitano.

Lo scambio di esperienze tra un giovane israeliano e un giovane arabo (tutti e
                                        due muoiono in un battaglia sul Golan ecc.
                                        e ognuno dei due rimane nel corpo dell'al-
                                        tro, vivendone le esperienze culturali: l'a-
                                        rabo vive l'industrilaizzazione e il cosmo-
                                        politismo industriale di Isareale (a Betsa-
                                        bea), e l'israeliano vive l'esistenza pre-
                                        industriàle, contadina, magica di un villag-
                                        gio del Libano povero. La storia finisce coi
                                        due funerali veri.

La rifondazione della religione dei Kota

UNa storia che si svolge nel momento in cui la Sicilia è riromanizzata (Arabi e
                                        Siciliani)

Discussioni ixx sui rapporti tra cultura popolare,(poesia popolare, tradizioni reali ecc.) e cultura dominante (il cattolicesimo borbonico ecc) in un paese Lucano.
Storia di un emigrante greco o andaluso in Germania, *nel nei fra tin ami sessanta*
ali nello ini '65 (ocum onoletamente infosril)

To the world of power I was only childishly chained
—OSIP MANDELSTAM

PETROLIO

NOTE I
Facts preceding the story

. . . .
. . . .
. . . .[2]

[2] This novel does not begin.

NOTE 2
/The First Rose of Summer/†

The apartment that Carlo had rented—and where he lived alone, waiting for his father to rejoin him—was in the Parioli, a neighborhood that still had the prestige it had gained in the preceding decade but was already /becoming melancholy/ the way places in decline do, with old gardens that have had too many owners, and an architecture that is /out of date/ even in comparison with the shabbiest lower-middle-class neighborhoods.

But in that May of 1960 Neocapitalism was still a novelty much too new, it was the term of a culture still too privileged to change the feel of reality.

Carlo's apartment was in a gray building, with a garden in front that also seemed to be made of stone; always in shadow, or in a /gray/ light; at the end of an unintended geometric funnel, formed by the corners of the other houses, themselves shut in hermetic silence: corners that were often rounded, in keeping with the style of Fascist-era bunkers. . . . Carlo lived on the fourth floor; the railings of the balconies, which were the dark red color of strawberries, stood out against the rather bleak, worn gray of the old stucco.‡

Carlo was standing on one of these balconies, as if to explore the theater of his new existence. It was morning. Warm clouds were racing across the sky, brooding over the earth, < ... > the dampness of the rain that, a little earlier, they had sorrowfully unloaded. It was as if the life of the city had been interrupted. As usual, Carlo was overwhelmed by /anguish/; having nothing to do except take care of the house—with the certainty in these things that men have at thirty—he was obliged to be alone with himself, like a shadow; and therefore to play that scene of solitude before the panorama of Rome (which from there appeared to be a city like Athens or Beirut). A depression (of distant origin) was taking away his strength and his will. Life appeared to him—before him—as an inevitable failure, and he saw it, moreover, with the most /absolute/ lucidity, etc. The series of failures that for some years had followed one upon another in his life as an engineer who wished to take his place in the society he had renounced was perfectly logical; but what that logic depended on, Carlo was unable to \couldn't\ understand. On neurosis, perhaps? That is—in short—on that Weight which for his whole life he had felt within himself ("in his chest") and from which he had never, not for a single instant, been able to feel relief? So all of a sudden he saw his own body fall. On the balcony, on the dreary cement floor, were empty vases, containers, hoses (because it was probably also used as a storage space for discarded things); and there was his body, lying among those cast-off objects, as if in the bare back room of a shop; alone, with only the sky spreading over him.

In the defenselessness of an abandoned body, a body deprived of consciousness, an observer can read freely and pitilessly all its features and characteristics.

Thus Carlo observed his own body lying supine at his feet: the pale, almost white or yellowish face of an adenoidal, the forehead of an intelligent and obstinate person under smooth, colorless hair, which, in the disagreeable circumstances, was somewhat ridiculously disheveled; the round eyes had dark circles under them, and, not protected by the glasses (which had come off his nose when he fell and were lying nearby, with their thin /metal/ earpieces), they appeared naked and too expressive; the face was long, and smooth as a baby's, the skin tight around the slightly turned-up nose; the mouth, with lips curled like a hen's ass, was half open, because of the long, protruding yellow teeth, or perhaps because of the nose, which was evidently one of those noses that are always stuffed up, forcing a person to keep his mouth half open in order to breathe; and the long, thin body was that of someone who is weak but well cared for, and was clothed in a rather worn gray suit, a white shirt, and a tie (of a color so discreet as to be unnoticeable).

Carlo was well aware of all the events that had brought him to that point[3]—birth, childhood, education, early experiences of life—and so

---

[3] That is, lying there on the floor, on the apartment balcony.

he understood that this fall, too, was included in the logic that, irrevocably and justly, directed all his acts. /The total passivity of a man who suffered that type of execution, who was shot or starved to death, appeared—by the obedient immobility of his body, almost by the offering of it, by its blindly passive, almost infantile availability—to sanction the work of his executioners: like the poor pathetic bodies of the Jews at Dachau or Mauthausen. The ultimate logical act was that the body of a petit bourgeois intellectual who was incapable of offense and fated to be a coward should offer itself for punishment./ Everything that he was proud of, as of a privilege not flaunted—his white skin, the fabric of the suit, those socks that could be seen under the pants, which were unattractively pulled up around the calves because of the fall—was now a rather repugnant object of pity, and that was all. Not even the absence of life was enough to cancel the stigmas of birth; in fact, it exposed them even more brutally.

NOTE 3
Introduction of the /metaphysical/ theme

< ... > /And now/ Carlo sees two beings arrive beside that supine body, beings who have probably descended from the sky—or come perhaps from the depths of the earth, < ... > not human, certainly; but anyway this seems natural, fitting into the logic of the Vision. They sit down, one on either side of the Body, their feet level with its head, and begin to speak. Although their language is not human, Carlo understands it; not only that, but the human language in which he grasps it is a miraculous one. Every word has, in fact, a revelatory clarity; thus, understanding is not \is not limited to\ simply understanding but also the joyous recognition of understanding. One might say, in short, that those personages speak in verse or music. The effect, certainly, is of a visionlike dream, because, taken out of context, <their conversation revealed their

nature without the mystery that Carlo's education could \was able to\ furnish them with and was reduced to an exchange of opinions, to ideological bickering that was quite up to date (as the reader, however, will see).

The first of the two disputants had an angelic look, and Carlo knew that his name was Polis; the second, on the other hand, had the mean look of a devil, a wretch; and his name was Tetis.

It was Polis who had begun to speak: "This body is mine, it belongs to me. It is the body of a good man, an obedient man . . ."

"Yes, but, on the other hand, the Weight that he has inside is mine . . ." Tetis retorted. Polis looked at him and smiled with his heavenly blue eyes, sure of himself. Again he began to speak, patiently: "If this is the Body of a man who has loved his mother within the proper limits, and has struggled against his father, yes, but as he should, knowing how to distinguish within himself his own faults from his father's—this Body is mine."

"All right," the devil replied, obstinately, "but the Weight that's inside him is mine . . ."

Not for nothing was Polis angelic; therefore he did not lose his nonviolent and pedagogic attitude but struck up a new argument in tones of an enchantment heard only in dreams: "If this is the Body of a man who has criticized the world into which he was born with the goal of improving it and has not made of its destruction an alibi for being able to live there with greater merit—this body is mine!"

"Very true," said Tetis, "but the Weight that's inside him is mine . . ."

A shadow began to descend over Polis's face. "Try to realize," he said, "that the Good pursued by the man whose Body this is was not a formal Good, because he lived it in his existence, making it real. Therefore this Body is mine!"

"I don't believe it can be yours," Tetis answered, "this shell, if the Weight it contains is mine.">

< ... > "This is the Body of a man who reproduced his father not through unconscious obedience but through the tragedy by which the

7

father himself reproduced, in his turn, his own father, that is, in his eternal state of being a son: therefore this Body is mine."

"No, because the Weight that is in it is mine," /Tetis insisted harshly, < ... > stuck in a stubborn conviction, which seemed unyielding in the face of anything in the world/.

Polis stands for a moment in silence, looking at the ground. Certainly, he thinks, he could say a thousand more sentences like those he has said; but since they are all analogous \similar\, like the beads of a rosary, none of them would get results any different from the ones he has already offered. He is a saint, this Polis, so he is willing not only to talk—with a being so different from him—but in fact to collaborate: it is impossible to understand this in words. The unique demonstration of real goodwill is common action, even—all the more—if it's scandalous. "/All right/," Polis says in the end, coming to terms with the Irreconcilable. "/Then what do you want to do?/"†

Tetis, who is certainly even more pragmatic, like one who wishes to do evil and is happy with the evil he can do immediately—because there is always plenty of time for the other kind—answers without hesitation: "You take what's yours, and I'll take what's mine/." "Which is?" the angel, tolerant, inquired. "You," answers the devil, "you take your Body. And I'll take the other Body that's inside there."

The devil's proposal is reasonable! Polis looks at him in fascination. Silently he looks at him. And as he looks at him silently, a smile rises up from deep within, slowly, like a sky from which the wind sweeps away the clouds, slowly rendering it perfectly serene and luminous, /until the smile,/ called forth by the devil's proposal but perhaps justified by more profound calculations, /is transmuted into words/ < ... > : "I accept," said Polis. "You take the other Body."

Tetis does not make him repeat it twice: he pulls a knife out of his filthy pocket, inserts the point of it in Carlo's stomach, and makes a long cut. Then with his hands he opens it and from the guts extracts a fetus. Passing one hand over the bloody lips of the cut, he heals the wound and makes a scar; with the other hand he raises the fetus to the sky, like a midwife pleased with her work.

Immediately, in plain sight, the fetus grows. And, with tremendous amazement, Carlo recognizes it as it grows; it is himself as a child, then a boy, then a young man, then a thirty-year-old, just as he is now, a man with a cultivated and alert appearance, ready for life.

When the fetus has become an adult and stands on the terrace beside its owner, Carlo sees that the body lying on the ground, deprived of its senses, is also beginning to come alive again, as a newborn. He sees him slowly open his eyes and look around, lost; put his glasses back on and, planting his hand on the ground, raise himself until he is upright, on his feet, next to Polis, to whom (it seems) he belongs.

And in exchange for his devotion he would protect him. Tetis's Carlo and Polis's Carlo are the same. /And in fact they are identical./ < ... > They take a little step toward each other, as if to better scrutinize each other. And Carlo sees them in profile, immobile, like Christ and Judas in the Giotto painting: they are so close that they look like two people who are about to kiss. And meanwhile they stare at each other so intently that their eyes appear to have turned to stone. In the depths of that gaze is an obscure sentiment, which unites them, as if binding them in an exclusive tension that draws them toward each other.

While Carlo is observing that gaze of one who divines the future and is silent, and is unable to detach himself from the source of the revelation—foreseeing, at the same time, the whole long chain of future acts which that recognition contains—he does not notice that the angel and the devil have moved away. He is just in time to see them disappearing, conversing amicably and holding each other by the arm like two old friends who share life \have performed a comedy\. < ... >

NOTE 3 A
Postponed preface

It was an extraordinarily beautiful day. After those "mythical" clouds I have already mentioned passed over, clear skies returned and the sun shone freely, with nothing interposed between its light and the city. Now, the extraordinary thing was precisely this very light. And I'm say-

ing so not just < ... > to be poetic but because—in this particular case—
the beauty of the light is /in some way of its own/ related to my story. It
often happens, actually, that the light is so absolute, quiet, and profound—making the sky a perfect blue yet slightly veiled, pale like the
sea—that it gives the impression of belonging not to the present but
to a past that has miraculously reappeared. <The light of the
myth that returns and is repeated, if I may so express myself; but in
this case the myth remains indefinite, it does not belong to any concrete moment of the return of the seasons, is not bound to any divinity of any sort of religion; no: we were at the height of summer, and
the season seemed never to have had a beginning; we were in the heart
of something—that is, silence, blue, fullness—whose passing didn't
count but, rather, its fixity: which is exactly what happens with remembered days. In the mere thought of summers of the past, the
light of any one of those days is "so absolute, quiet, profound." And
that is the reason that my description of this light, however brief, is
valuable not in itself but in relation to my story.> It < ... > in fact
shone gloriously in just that way on a morning in the late fifties or early
sixties, and this is the relevant fact, full of significance.

In this light (magic precisely because it is so profoundly anonymous
and daily: the light of any beautiful summer day) the two persons came
out of Carlo's house and slowly walked together as far as a small square.
Around it were some low apartment buildings, very new at the time,
and the wall of a small /ugly/ church and a row of saplings along a thick
hedge; and flower beds amid which was a brightly painted refreshment
stand, and many people were sitting at its little tables or standing
around on the edges of the square, in spite of the hot and blinding time
of day.

NOTE 3 B
Postponed preface (II)

"It was a very ancient opinion that from time to time the Gods let themselves be seen by men," wrote Giacomo Leopardi in 1815, in one of the three hundred dense pages "on the popular superstitions of the ancients," anticipating, in addition to *The History of the Human Race,* other works of his, among them *Concerning Ancient Myths:* but does the qualifier "ancient" derive from *antiquus* or *anticus*? Everyone knows what *antiquus* means; as for *anticus,* the opposite of *posticus,* it refers to the South, the hour of the South (as a great modern hermetic poet in search of "indeterminacy," that is to say polyvalence, notes). Are the myths in question ancient or from the South? One of the Sage's most beautiful passages is entitled "Concerning Midday," and it takes as its subject the hour in which "the sun itself seems to darken with its own heat." It's true that the gods usually appear at night; but it's at this hour that their apparition is most terrifying and sublime. The anonymous authors of the Psalms also knew it: *"Non timebis a timore nocturno; a sagitta volante in die, a negotio perambulante in tenebris, ab incursu et daemonio meridiano."*†

/How true that is—if it matters—was demonstrated by the appearance of our two demons from the South at the refreshment stand in Piazza xxx/: high school students and, disdainfully aloof, university students—with what at that time would have seemed an intolerably vicious sneer at society but today /would seem only/ an inoffensive little petit bourgeois smile, merely disagreeable—suddenly felt the hair stand up on their heads. And even the barman, who had come humbly that morning from Prima Porta and so was not without \lacking < ... >\ experience of grim climates or unacquainted with sloth or sluggishness, felt his forehead bathed in icy sweat when the two ordered an apéritif. Meanwhile the light burned supreme and the heat was turning everything brown in the peace of that midday which is so present and which we know belongs to the past.

NOTE 3C
Postponed preface (III)

Here the outline of a journey is introduced. Its means, its "found" rhetoric, its metaphoric plan, its narrative process, and its demonic technique (consisting above all of the exclusion of toponymy) will be taken up again farther on in the course of this work. We are at the inaugural moment, that of the "founding." Since I intend not to write a historical novel but only to create a form, I must inevitably establish the rules of that form. And I can establish them only *in corpore vili*—that is, in the form itself. There lies the reason for this "outline of a journey." It serves as a matrix or, rather, as a precedent, to which the reader will be referred when he is faced with an analogous, more fully developed example.

NOTE 3D
Postponed preface (IV)

Tetis went on foot to a nearby square with a low wall beyond which is a deep valley that splits the city; beyond the valley rises a wooded hill that has been converted to a public park: it is silhouetted against the plain to the north of Rome, with the smoke-blackened yellow of stubble fields, the woods veiled in heat, < ... > the blotches of whitewashed villages. There he stops and waits at a bus stop. It is not a neighborhood familiar to him: the summer becomes foreign to his eyes, like a phenomenon lived elsewhere. The people are fairly well dressed and as reserved as civility allows. Students, for example, and professionals, nursemaids, middle-class women, as well as a sedentary crowd of those who work for them. The bus Tetis is waiting for will carry him far from there, to the opposite end of the city. After a while it arrives, half empty. Tetis barely has time to climb on before it suddenly departs. The bus eats up the space of that strange neighborhood, where only a Piedmontese would settle. It follows the broad curves of a tree-lined avenue, which leads to another avenue—this one is straight—and then to a /large/ square, where the asphalt bubbles in the not-to-be-forgotten heat from the clear sky; this square adjoins the wasteland along the shores of a river. A river whose steep banks are full of garbage, which gives off a sharp stench. At least it's organic garbage: there's no plastic and polystyrene yet. Still only paper and shit. The bus comes out on the Lungotevere and speeds along; there is little traffic, although in that long-ago year the Lungotevere had not yet become one-way. The façades of the neighborhood on the other side of the river pass by against the light: it looks residential but still Fascist. Then a mixture of styles begins (while sun, rotten vegetables, wastepaper, and shit remain, unchanged): Art Nouveau and the twentieth century first; then the seventeenth century, and the fifteenth, and the Middle Ages. Behind the mass of buildings—always against the light, in the motionless heat—a hill rises, with tall trees, pines, and balustrades among which are glimpses of the houses of the wealthy and a mansion that has become a college, perhaps for American priests. The bus turns onto a bridge that crosses the muddy river. At that moment, in the very middle of the current, a urinal flows by. Below the steep bank (a landslide of garbage), there is a bathing establishment. On a float, with its vases of flowers, wobbly tables, and cats, ten or twelve boys are stretched out in the sun with their caps over their noses and their necks unprotected, their heads shorn or covered with short curls. A line of seminarians crosses over the bridge. Soon the bus is at the top of the hill that was visible from across the river. It continues on along wide, deserted streets bordered by gardens (seemingly abandoned) where there's no lack of red-blooming bougainvillea. On the other side of a very small old seventeenth- or early-eighteenth-century gateway, the bus turns onto a street lined on one side by a long row of modern apartment blocks and on the other by a wall of tufa, grand and ordinary at the same time. It is an irregular street, built, perhaps, on the remains of an older street: one sees the traces: a small seventeenth-century church, also made of that light and porous tufa; some balustrades of white marble, stained by time; the verges of an old meadow, still full of chicory and chamomile (dry in summer). Halfway along this street, at a stop where no one is waiting, Tetis gets off. He sets out toward the row of apartment buildings with their little gardens, then turns onto a fairly wide street that goes downhill (on one side of the street is < ... > a construction site, where some boys in red sailor hats are playing ball). At one of the buildings at the end of the street—a building like all the others—Tetis stops. The entrance has a shabby aristocratic elegance, with gilded xxx. He goes in, takes the elevator, gets out on the fourth floor, rings the bell of one of the many apartments. An old woman comes to open the door; she has the air of a child and is wearing a faded, rather dirty dress; she has soft eyes, a little frightened by the presence of this stranger, whom she evidently feels incapable of responding to. She answers his questions with a hesitant look; her responses are confused, and she is distressed at her inability to be more precise. Her heavy Venetian accent accentuates her bewilderment at saying even what she does know: that is, that the person the stranger seeks is not at home; in fact, is not even in the city; is away in a distant region; in /Syracuse/. Her bewilderment increases with every new fact, and at the same time her regret that the stranger has not found the person he was looking for (who appears to be so dear to her: all that she has, and in whose absence she feels lost). She manages to add the name of a hotel, though she garbles it, where the person who is sought is probably staying. Then she smiles at her bad pronunciation. In that smile one reads her true nature: that of a woman who is intelligent, sensitive, and courageous. She is ageless: she could be very old or still a girl. Tetis goes away, accompanied by her /apprehensive/ smile. He returns to the bus stop and waits. The boys playing ball do nothing but curse, with an almost oppressive violence; but every so often from their laughing, tender mouths comes a witty phrase, swift as an arrow. The bus arrives and retraces, in the opposite direction, its previous route. But just before the bridge over the yellow river on which the urinal flowed by, Tetis descended and waited for another means of transportation. This time it was a tram. It arrived, oddly, quite soon, and it, too, was half empty. It was called "Black Circle Line." In its turn it crossed the bridge, and then < ... > along the river road, passing first through old neighborhoods laid out in no order—now around an odd-shaped square, now at the top of a low rise, with wooded /summit/ and slopes littered with the usual garbage, now right in the river, on an island around which the yellow current broke in a dirty white foam. Then, leaving the river road and heading inland, first among parks full of ruins and then through a populous Art Nouveau neighborhood, it arrived at a train station, also built in the early twentieth century, with a noble yellow façade.

Tetis entered the station and went to the old ticket window to buy a ticket. He had a couple of hours before the train. In the waiting room, the people, exhausted by the heat, had ancient, starved faces, /crushed by the habit of poverty/. In the youths, on the other hand, an insolent beauty was bursting—but it was also ingenuous, and ready for novelty and amusement. All the faces were ancient—some "with fierce cheekbones,"† some with a kind of /clerical/ plumpness, etc. Patiently they waited for their train. The light outside gave no sign of /diminishing/. It was almost five but still seemed to be midday. When Tetis got on the train—full of those poor people dressed in work clothes (the young ones, more elegant, had on cheap caps)—and the train, between long whistles and stops < ... > reached < ... > the outskirts and the countryside—among whitewashed villages with layered-stone walls and foul cottages—the same sun of a few hours earlier reappeared. The same dry blue, the same light charged with the ultimate and most explosive form of life. On the day that had no end they passed deserted countryside on the right and on the left stone-veiled mountains. The villages were infrequent and poor, clustered around the church and the biggest /house/. The only new houses were nothing but cheap villas or little white cubes. Slowly a city appeared, heralded by a chaos of peeling walls, open sewers, hovels, newly constructed factories now in disuse—roofless, their twisted iron skeletons and xxx against the ever more intense and blinding light—the remains of medieval towns among apartment blocks without a thread of green, discolored and stained as if by a devouring tropical humidity—a city without end. In the background the sea was shining. The air was heavy with an elusive stench: of shit, gas, sewers, but also of earth fertilized by gardens, lemons, sulfur, and something lost, suffocating, xxx which was nothing /but the dust of poverty/.

A long twilight began: gold and blood red verging on bronze— lighter and lighter, like a rain of xxx, piled up on the strip of sea that was growing dimmer. They passed formless, anonymous towns, where it seemed impossible that huge modern structures, gray and bare like barracks or prisons, could bury something so vital and xxx, aggressive as that land. But on the other hand even the ancient structures, built of yellowish blocks of xxx, squat, with porticoes and outside stairways, were imbued with melancholy \mourning\, as in certain places in the North. The chaos and the misery restrained the violence of physical life, which managed to break out only in the gardens, overflowing with succulent vegetables and the red bushes of a particular type of almost crudely exotic salvia.

Night came, and everything was swallowed in darkness. Soon, however, the moon appeared: a heavy milk-white moon that shed an intense light. The coasts and the mountains were outlined in black in that milky, almost oily glow.

In the middle of the night, the train stopped in a vast station, where storage lockers, lamps, warehouses, underpasses, sordid hovels for the workers, cement /palisades/, /pits < ... > of/ gardens—everything was scattered in an indescribable disarray, upon which the silence of the night exerted its gentle pressure and xxx. The train began to make lengthy maneuvers with melancholy clanking noises, interrupted from time to time by rancorous voices or the muted baying of dogs, but also by distant songs. The moon obscured the stars and illuminated that station as if it were day.

The result of all the comings and goings of the train was that it ended up in the belly of a ship. The smell of the sea flooded in, mixing with the light of the moon. Most of the people /poured/ onto the deck of the ship. From there one saw an arm of the sea, like a dead thing, where life appeared, uncertain, only on the coasts—off the prow and the stern—in a mournful trembling of little lights. On the deck of the ship, however—on its two big decks and along the xxx—suddenly, though it was still the middle of the night, a kind of joy exploded, a collective awakening. Groups of young men, with short hair or with long curls like a halo over their foreheads, joked and laughed. One group, in which soldiers and sailors mingled, was even gayer: in its midst a boy was playing a guitar, serious as a saint but with laughing eyes.

On the other side of the strait, it was the same thing. Little by little, the joy of the young people, who were both tough and naive, spent itself, and the silence returned, the clattering darkness of the train, the light of the moon stinking with sea dampness.

At dawn the city where Tetis was to get off—and where the train "died"—appeared. It was a formless expanse of small yellowish houses, with a few luxurious mansions and Baroque churches bearing witness to a long history of the absolute dominion of power and of poverty. That was in the gray light of dawn. But soon the sun appeared and /spread/, and at five in the morning there was already a < ... > midday light. Boys and young men, in all their joy and sensuality, were already walking along the streets.

Tetis headed for the hotel that he knew only by its garbled name. But the inhabitants of the city were able to point it out to him (perhaps, by chance, they pronounced its name just that way). There was an old fountain, Alexandrian or Roman, with papyrus in the middle and half-naked boys around it. Nearby was a long avenue from the time of the Bourbons, with < ... > fragrant plants growing amid dirt and garbage; and right in the center of this avenue, which < ... > in a turn-of-the-century bourgeois sumptuousness, was the hotel with the exotic name. The grand entrance—despite the poverty of the materials, it was almost monumental—did not succeed in concealing the rather pathetic simplicity of the family management. < ... > The person Tetis was looking for was not there: at that hour she was out. And no one knew when she would return. Tetis prepared to wait patiently. He settled himself outside, near the entrance, amid the heavy fragrance of the plants, assuming that the person in question would arrive around midday for the noon meal. Instead he had to wait until evening. But the evening was pale, luminous, as if it were /the continuation of the/ day. < ... > The person he was waiting for arrived unexpectedly, on foot, on a street beside the hotel. She was not alone: with her was a tall, pale boy, with a thin mouth slightly twisted by shyness, like that of a paralytic, and an excited smile. His voice, when he began to speak, was high and jarring, and he repeated, in a simplistic way, the sorts of refined things intellectuals might say. She, the person sought by Tetis, was, on the other hand, gentle, humane, the master of her own thoughts, though her nature could be passionate, visceral, tempestuous. She, too, was ageless, and certainly she appeared much younger than she was. Her hair was a light chestnut color, < ... > wavy and abundant like that of women twenty years earlier. Her eyes were blue, like those of some cats, and oblique: now peaceful—even too peaceful—now flaming but unstable, with a neurotic, intellectual aggressiveness. Their light illuminated her entire head, which she held erect and which resembled the heads of Sicilian boys photographed at the beginning of the century by /cultured/ German tourists. Her mouth was small, above a small, weak chin, below which the wrinkle that /would divide/ it was visibly drawn. There were also some wrinkles on her throat. Nevertheless, her face taken altogether was the face of a young cat. As Tetis approached, her eyes shone with a furious hostility; but immediately, suddenly, they relaxed into an equally exaggerated smile. /When/ Tetis spoke to her, saying that he had some important secrets to confide to her, the smile became a happy, dangerous laugh. The boy who accompanied her also laughed, though at first he had dutifully assumed the air of a defender, not without fanaticism and adulation. Right at that moment, in a neighborhood not far from the hotel, the first violent bursts of summer fireworks sounded, coloring a whole slice of the sky green, violet, and orange. The fireworks had such a powerful attraction for the woman and, consequently, for her companion that, no matter how important the secrets Tetis had to communicate to her, everything was put off until the next morning.

But the next morning the woman, whom Tetis evidently wished to invest with a duty < ... > /of the highest importance/, < ... > had already made another engagement: she had to go to the house of a child she had met the day before, who was extremely poor and ugly, although she considered him beautiful—and perhaps rightly: he was desperately poetic because of the tenuousness of what kept him, wan and /needy/, alive. The woman, it seems, was to take the child to buy some gifts in the city, the impoverished city in whose impoverished outskirts he lived with a mother overburdened with children, like a cat, and a blind father. The morning, and also part of the afternoon, passed in that occupation. In the evening, the festival that had begun the day before in the neighborhood behind the hotel started up again; this time there was also a show in a little circus that had pitched its tents near the ruins of an ancient amphitheater surrounded by two-story yellowish houses festooned with colored lights. /Enough./ Tetis did not succeed in communicating his important revelations to the woman, not even on the second day; not even, to make it brief, during the entire time he spent in that city. They took the train back together. But so many extraordinary things happened on the return trip that there was never any time to speak seriously or at length, because there was always something better to hear and to see.

It was very probable that the person Tetis had chosen as his confidante—that is, as the repository of a secret that, once revealed, would be of enormous public value—would have had the courage, or rather the extreme daring, to make good use of it; but she evidently did not want to. < ... > Fifteen years passed, and Tetis remained near her. She, however, by the course she had chosen, or, as one says in our horrible jargon, by her ideological choice, had by now decided not to listen to him. During that period she went to live in a featureless neighborhood at the edge of the city, where construction had begun in the time of the Fascists. Her house was right next to an enormous church—a sort of fake, all-white Saint Peter's. In front of it stretched the ravine where the dirty yellow river full of urinals flowed. There was a village in the distance, on the other side, above some bare heights, and a few huts below, amid the vegetation that grew, probably dirty and dust-covered, /near/ the river. Then gradually the city began to encroach, to loom: with long /ugly/ rows of apartment blocks; with the construction of new factories, among them a huge xxx of the automobile industry from the North; with an invasion of cars and of people who were better dressed and more refined, even if, at the same time, they were vulgar, almost odious, repugnant. Never, therefore, during this entire historically important period, did the person chosen by Tetis as the repository of a secret /that we might well call/ historic wish to hear it. Even though < ... > she was

< ... > evidently more and more courageous and more and more capable of meeting the responsibility, in that she had put herself in the position of having essentially nothing to lose. She < ... > did not wish to know something dangerous and revelatory that she alone would be able to make public. And since she who had been uselessly sought and implored by Tetis was a writer, one can easily deduce that the books of that writer, no matter how full and complete in themselves they were, in reality lacked "something": and were destined, as a result, to a fatal ambiguity.

NOTE 3 E
Second part of the postponed preface:
Mercenary swords

NOTE 4
/What is a novel?/
\The prefatory folly continues: prefatory parenthesis\

Carlo is my father's name. I choose it for the protagonist of this novel for an illogical reason: in fact, between my father and this "split" engineer \technician\ whose story I am preparing to tell there is no possible comparison; my father was an Army officer whose adulthood coincided with the Fascist period and who was an adherent of Fascism (although in the rivalry that arose between Fascism and the Army, he was on the Army's side): his character, which was ready to accept Fascism <—for as a boy < ... > he had been a daredevil and a delinquent, from an aristocratic family—had been modified by it:> there is nothing more united than disorder and order. There is a photograph of my father at seventeen, a little before he left as a volunteer for the Libyan war: he is a handsome boy, strong as a bull, elegant, with the sort of depraved elegance of the son of a rich and decadent family—indulged and crude at the same time; in his black hair and eyes there is something /cruel/: it's his sensuality that looks violent and makes him too severe and almost /fierce/. The purity of his youthful cheeks, < ... > the perfection of his body (he was, however, short in stature, a short man) was that of a man who has a big cock. And yet all this, together, expressed an antagonistic will, almost the extreme defense of one who, though boasting of his violent rights over the present, foresees a future tragedy, which will transform his rights into degradation. < ... > /He had a family and he terrorized it. Then he went to Africa to fight his third war; he was a prisoner for some years and reappeared in Casarsa, my mother's hometown, the "inferior town," which he had always despised, by this means making up for his unreciprocated love for my mother—and he began to drink, as men do. It's clear that he had never thought about his destiny, just as he had not thought about politics./

The Carlo who takes his name from my father is, on the other hand, a man divided and (as Lukács says) problematic: he is my age, not my father's. In fact, in speaking of him I use the present indicative because he is alive today, at this time, indeed, at this moment.

As I said, he is an engineer; that is, if he is enough of an intellectual to experience the social and political contradictions of our time, he is not enough of one to experience them with that consciousness which ensures the unity of the individual, making of the /schizoid/ state a natural state and of ambiguity a way of being.

Because of a profound, unsophisticated honesty, Carlo (like my father) could never accept this compromise, for which only political or literary specialization provides the alibis, the abilities, the tools. If the time in which he is fated to live (he was born in 1932) is a time in which the class struggle produces a division that is present in every aspect or moment—even in the most profound intimacy of the individual—he can only accept this division (just as my father accepted unity, making a mistake and then paying atrociously for it). As my father would never have accepted being split in two, would have been capable even of murder—as the Fascists murdered—to defend his unity, so Carlo, on the contrary, would never agree to pretend to be one if in reality he was /split in two/. He would be able even to let himself murder, just to be consistent with this reality of his.

He is a Catholic who, because of the character I have described here in /its/ outline, couldn't help being pushed to become a Catholic of the left. His childhood, from 1932 and 1945, was spent in a city in Romagna, Ravenna (the city of my father). And I do not see what substantial differences there could be between the Ravenna of the first years of the century and the Ravenna of the years immediately before and after the war. Thus a period in the life of the protagonist of this novel was spent in a world that coincides perfectly with that of the preceding generation and, I would say, of all the preceding generations. Children behaved the same way with their parents; the houses were the same (no television, no refrigerators, no waste of consumer goods; heat provided by a stove in the important rooms; not, for example, in the bedrooms, where we were kept warm with quilts or bed warmers, etc.); the food was identical; identical the smells along the street on the way to school, on pavements laid with care and the artisan's imprecision of the previous century; identical the reappearance of the seasons, with the smell of earth or of something burning, mingling with the perfume of wisteria in spring, a /sharp/ odor of /odorless/ stone or of frozen earth in winter; identical the schools, bare, poor, old; identical the people whom children, in their view from below, see as small, pathetic giants who know what life is and are transported by it elsewhere, in a variety of relations unimaginable to /small/ children, whose time is all so well organized and whose life therefore has a single consciousness.

The authorities, too, were exactly the same, at least until 1944—that is, the Fascists: the petite bourgeoisie that expressed, without restraint and without, any longer, the alibis of a bad conscience, all its own worst qualities: which are, however, mixed up with the good ones. Meanwhile, all the qualities that for centuries, perhaps for millennia, we have been accustomed to consider good were expressed by the people: uncontaminated by either the peasant revolution or the first industrialization and therefore utterly faithful /to themselves/.

Carlo, who belonged to a wealthy family, lived this whole part of his life exactly as my father might have lived it, or, more simply, as his own father might have. (He had died prematurely: he was a titled landowner who lived on the income from land and real estate; an income fatally condemned to shrink.) So Carlo's Catholicism was a habit, tightly linked to his childhood and to a period of history.

One could therefore deduce \infer\ that his moral honesty, his innocent wish not to oppose his own dissociation—real, necessary, historical—might also be one of the many positive forms that that negative behavior which is hypocrisy can take: yes, the old Catholic hypocrisy, Counter-Reformational. I mean that the dissociation could also derive, classically (and class-consciously), from a mechanism for preservation, as is well known, and could then come to coincide with that "real, necessary, historical" dissociation I was talking about. Catholic hypocrisy would preside over the first dissociation, and it would occur outside the domain of conscience. The honesty of the old world (by coincidence Catholic) would preside over the second dissociation, and it would occur not only in the domain of conscience but by the very will of conscience.

/The fact is that there is not just one Carlo but two./

NOTE 5
The prefatory folly continues: Carlo the First

<Carlo was born in Turin on March 6, 1932. He attended elementary and middle schools in Ravenna; he studied engineering at the University of Bologna and graduated in 1956. At school he always did well and was one of the first in his class; but he was good in all his subjects, and so in his intelligence there was evidently something mechanical that functioned well. He resembled his mother, who, after his father's death, had taken in hand the reins of the family—so to speak—and not only had ensured the continuation of its solid economic status but had in fact improved it. His younger brothers, under her protection (closed off, like a separate world), followed in

Carlo's footsteps. As soon as he graduated, he looked around (because until that moment his world had been exclusive) and was immediately confirmed in the excellence of his ideas: that is, his "existential" Catholicism, his enlightenment, his slightly anxious moderate's sadness, his essential pragmatism, which accepted class integration (at the time, it was not so called) in order to be fulfilled and to obtain results that went beyond the interests of the class that he had become part of, subsumed to that unity which is the good of man.†

He immediately became interested in petroleum research; but this does not mean that he had chosen decisively to pursue it or that he was thinking only of his career. (In fact, he did not marry and is still a bachelor.) He continued to do his job at ENI, < ... > also as an intellectual meditation. Bologna was a Communist city; in the fifties the Communist culture, or, generically, the culture of the left, tended to be hegemonic, and besides, there were no real alternatives. Carlo also had friends who studied literature or political science; he had taken part in the culture of commitment and had followed it, as young men follow whatever is popular, the code. < ... > Some of his friends were among the founders of the review *Il Mulino* and he continued to see them; that is, his nonspecialist culture developed there. He knew right away about the new American sociology and the new forms of social Catholicism; right away he knew the new psychoanalysis; right away he knew the first texts of the Communist dissidents. When the sixties arrived, he was ready.> In fact, that was his moment. That was the moment in which he became /a Catholic of the left/, and this enabled him on the one hand to differentiate himself, to stand out, from those in power and, at the same time, through his particular, specialized work in that technological vanguard which was ENI after the death of Mattei, to insert himself boldly (and never ostentatiously) into the "space" where real power is found.

In Carlo the resistance to dissociation functioned when he was confronted by his conscience on a moral plane, which, as we will see, coincided in large part with sexuality, rejected or accepted; it did not function—and in pragmatic times, which, after slow preparatory centuries of Catholicism, pass quickly, this was natural—when he was confronted by choices of action, pragmatically. Pragmatism resolves its contradictions by itself /axiologically/.

He traveled. Although he was still almost a boy, in '61 he went to America; in '62, as we will see, he got to know all the Arab countries, /and he went as far as Tanzania, always on behalf of ENI/. Thus Italy early on appeared to him, almost naturally, as a very particular world, one of many parts of a whole and not among the most important. That it was the center of the world, the navel of the world, seemed to him at a very young age a fable, although he had felt it deeply in childhood. But here, too, a contradiction must be noted. At the same moment that Carlo was detaching himself from Italy, recognizing its ancient and poetic characteristics, he was specializing in that peculiarly Italian science which is sharing in power. He was perfectly free to desire power—power not mentioned, not named, defined only empirically—even if he was without vanity and almost, I feel the urge to say, ascetic and without ambition. Certainly there was a marvelous freedom, which sterilized guilt, made evil unproductive: a freedom as if born of itself and endowed with such real force that a whole part of the historical universe could be rendered immune from the curiosity of conscience.

NOTE 6
/The prefatory folly continues: Carlo the Second/†

/If a man is equal to another man, so equal as to be the same, which of the two is the true man? Which is the man whom the other resembles or, rather, to whom the other is identical? Which is the *first* of the two, in terms of reference?

To call Carlo the Second the person who is practically the "double" of Carlo the First is incorrect, because it could very well be Carlo the Second who was named first and is therefore the one to whom the other is put in relation.

Probably the injustice of this hierarchy—Carlo the First and Carlo the Second—even if it is justified by being purely numerical or convenient, is a social injustice. Carlo the First is in fact, as I have said, an engineer; he works at the top levels of one of the principal Italian state agencies, ENI, he is among the "silent powerful" but not for that reason any less powerful (on the contrary!), he comes from a rich, respectable, religious family, etc., etc.; while for Carlo the Second—whom from now on I will call Karl—in terms of vital statistics I could not use any of the social forms of identification I used for Carlo the First. Classification, however, is social. Not even Karl, evidently, avoids society; yet his method of belonging to it, as I will recount, is precisely to avoid it. The perfect double of Carlo the First, he has inside himself a void in place of the social whole that makes Carlo what he is and which is definable. And this void is filled by something else, which nevertheless is expressed \manifested\ through all the rules of social behavior which characterize the social sense that makes Carlo act. In other words, if a witness were present at Karl's actions, he would then be able to attribute them, in any trial, only to Carlo. And thus a policeman, surprising Karl in some illicit act, something contrary to the rules of bourgeois behavior or, more simply, the law, could arrest him only as Carlo: consulting Carlo's papers, determining his biographical data, the data that, as in a linguistic system, place him in the social context./

Thus Karl \the second Carlo\ is, in the social hierarchy, inferior to Carlo in spite of being identical, so identical as to be practically indistinguishable from him. But his inferiority /is not controlled by Carlo the First/.

The second Carlo, like all poor people, < ... > who have no social authority < ... >—rather like dogs—is good. Social inferiority and goodness coincide. Yet it is in Karl that the bad aspects of Carlo are concentrated, while it is in Carlo that the good aspects of Karl are concentrated.

Karl is a servant; Carlo a master. But, as I will recount later on, Karl (perhaps) is free, while Carlo certainly isn't.

Karl's freedom has unclassifiable characteristics, and there is no connection between it and what is free outside of reason: that is, noncultural, nonsocial reality (which exists only theoretically, however). Although Karl is his servant, Carlo cannot succeed in controlling him. He leads him on a leash, like a dog, but he doesn't know to what degree he knows him or even to what degree he exists, outside of action, of his physical, factual presence.

Karl is above all a good man who would never change; he, too, was born in Alessandria, studied in Turin, lives a life physically of this society and of this moment, yet seems to come from a culture completely different from Italian or bourgeois culture. Being in the service of another is certainly not typical of the Italian bourgeoisie (whose servility is of quite another nature); perhaps he comes from the Italian "people"—that is, from a different and forgotten history—and this would perhaps explain his graciousness as a servant. /Just as there are servants who are profoundly courteous and have no sense of guilt, certain policemen or young soldiers from poor families of the South; just as certain peasants—or, rather, laborers—of the Romagna are ingratiating and dignified, etc./ Although Karl is also burdened with performing vulgar actions, as /I will relate/—vulgar not in themselves but in the bourgeois or petit bourgeois spirit that imbues Carlo culturally—he remains untouched and uncontaminated: and not only in the first years— those of Ravenna and Bologna—thanks to his youth (as with the < ... > policemen or the < ... > laborers) but also now, when he has /graying hair/ and /is a mature man/, although he has the air of a teenager. What protects him is that he possesses nothing and belongs to nothing. To be defined <by a> society that gives him the means to live, including the superfluous, but that he <?> and rejects as the pure do: /the regurgitations and the swallowings that the class struggle, internalized, produces in Carlo's soul are in Karl the *flatus vocis,* lacking not significance but sense./

Beirut, May 5, 1974

—On the first trip to Turin he is followed by a spy. It comes out in a brief scene between two people, one of whom speaks a sentence in Sicilian at the end.

—Everything Carlo does in Turin is seen *as if by him* (one of his projected stories fills the emptiness; the story is done in a crude style, like a report, but I, the narrator, translate it into an artful style, etc.)

At the time of the first *return* trip to Turin (mother, sisters, school friends, mythical places [reconsecrated]) Carlo II makes his first trip to the Orient as (he is at the beginning of his career) a subordinate.

His trip is arranged by two other persons who are among the powerful: not rough Sicilians but cultivated men (who exploit the Catholicism of the left, Carlo II's solid secularism)

*

The journey

It is the voyage of the Argonauts toward an *elsewhere* barely mapped (by the voyage of Hercules)—analogy with all the other journeys undertaken by heroes (<?> scientific-cultural) [which is stated clearly in an introduction by the author]—

—The journey is completely invented; that is, dreamed (the reality is fragmentary, visionary, etc.) [youthful journey, etc.]—

Thus the second trip that Carlo II will make, when he is "powerful," is a repetition of the first. Now *everything is mapped* (above all, because of Oil)—A single corner remains unmapped (in the desert, by chance). It is in that unmapped place that Carlo's <?> begins (cf. the fall of Damascus); he will reconvert to a mystical religion (Italian style, etc.)

The third trip [to Edo] is a third repetition [besides the mapping—cultural—mental]

Notes 6a, etc.

—Where are Polis and Tetis going to end up after their intervention (disappearance analogous to that of Carmelo and the Twenty Spirits)

*(midday apparition of the God—more to be feared, cf. Leopardi's *Superstitions of the Ancients*)

NOTE 6B
The sources (preamble)

/Certainly up to this point the reader will have thought—as is natural and, on the other hand, inevitable—that everything written in this book "refers to reality." Only slowly, as he advances in his reading and follows the author's path, will he realize that the book refers, rather, to nothing other than itself alone. It also refers to itself, of course—why not?—through reality: which is familiar—conventionally and in common—to reader and author. When eventually the premises of an internal logic are set up—a logic whose operation is based entirely on the "movement" that established it—a "movement" completely arbitrary and also, I admit, but for reasons that will become clear later, a bit foolish†—the reader will be able to move more securely among narrative traps "which explain one another." For now, I realize, he must overcome his repugnance, which results in a false transposition of reality: false because in effect it doesn't < ... > exist. I am therefore compelled to ask the reader to overcome, as far as he can, his natural repugnance toward the "masquerade" and, if nothing else, to trust in the positive effect of the pure and simple accumulation of material.

I say all this because I am preparing to set out some already established facts, or anyway some facts that it's absolutely necessary to know; this indeed has the appearance of a direct and almost chronological reference to reality—seen, however, in relation to our story, as a long and somewhat shadowy prehistoric incubation./

NOTE 6 *BIS*
The characters "who see"

It's strange that in the beginning the true "facts" of this story are, so to speak, arranged, experienced, by imaginary characters. But, as will be better understood later on, this was inevitable. The reader is thus free to imagine "where" such characters meet. /We are, naturally, in Rome/, the Rome of the late fifties. To tell the truth, my total \hopeless\ lack of experience of every scene that is set in the realm \sphere\ of power prevents me from imagining the street, the building, the apartment where the meeting—so important for the fate of my protagonist—takes place. It's difficult for me to imagine even the physical types of the people who are meeting, discussing Carlo's case, etc. And not through coyness. /(But the reader does not trust me.)/ It's true that a certain mental laziness suggests to me the image—visionary because of the absence of reality—of a house in the Parioli not far from the one rented by the young Carlo. And also the image—awkward, hard, vaguely common, even if, under the skin, too rigidly bourgeois and proper—of our /shadowy/ characters. I imagine, too, a certain jargon they have, the way they change the subject (always in a strictly economical spirit, except for certain insignificant /digressions/ of a southern and forensic character). But for me a person who is within a certain circle of power (when it's not a question of a dictatorship, because then everything is much simpler) can only be an apparition.

Our imaginary characters meet, then—this /is the essence/—in the apartment of the one with the most authority (not an official but, so to speak, a /head assassin/). The object of their interest is Carlo. What they decide is to follow Carlo, to spy on him, and to take note of everything he does. Charged with this delicate mission is a young /catechumen/ just starting out, though already trusted (a young fellow, an honorable fellow). There is no doubt that he will perform his duty scrupulously and even passionately. He is a youth of about thirty with a square neck, thick, short black hair, a very dark, almost Arab face, a /profile from a coin/, sensual < ... > almost like a teenager; except that, as happens for example in some policemen, the naive innocence, the /bursting/ physicality, is as if worn out and xxx, like a kind of ascetic grayness.

Everything Carlo < ... > does will be "as if seen" by this hit man who does not judge. What I will say on the subject is only the /essence/ of the report—oral, and so partly in dialect—that this Pasquale (as he is—comically—called) will make.

NOTE 6 *TER* †
Old tales

/Innocent/ Carlo leaves the same evening of his birth, so to speak. He leaves for Turin by train. In that May at the end of the fifties, Italy is still intact, and only critical souls note, with a negative judgment by which they gratify their own narcissism, the first signs of the new era that is about to disfigure for eternity the old cities and the old countryside. Carlo's sensibility classified him by natural right among these elect \the critical souls\; but he was good, and the feeling of oneness that through sex bound him to the world—outside his own particular Ethics—was stronger than the aesthetic sentiment. /He was searching—but in the world, among bodies—for the most absolute solitude./ And there was no break between what he intended on that journey—immediately, in the very act of entering the station, buying a ticket—and the intimate pleasure of visions more disinterested and purer than reality, in whatever aspect, human or natural, etc., etc.

It is late afternoon; a ripe, sweet light, the light of catastrophe, illumines the edges of things. The old Central Station disappears, to the monotonous and fascinating rumbling of the wheels of the train over the track (divine noise of infantile sexuality); and, as the houses of an old-style suburb grow sparse, the old countryside appears, shining as if in a Caravaggio *en plein air:* expanses of wheat, of a greenish yellow, /creep/ in irregularly, like wild grasslands, among the plump, bursting acacia bushes; the lime trees are in flower; the grass is overgrown everywhere, washed by the rain, made sweet-smelling by the sun that dries it out. /Irregular hills covered with oak woods and long, curving solitary valleys inhabited by a rushing stream, perhaps the Tiber, swollen to the height of its banks, so that it brushes the big trees, full and shining, along the clean shores./†

NOTE 6 *QUATER*
Carlo's secret life in the light of the sun

Nothing is < ... > easier than to spy on the life of a man like Carlo. He completely, even if not foolishly, gave up a good reputation. He debased himself. If he had thought it was immoral, he probably wouldn't have done it. On the contrary, he considered his degradation profoundly moral. And furthermore, he considered it his right. The purpose of it all was nothing other than the pleasure of the senses, of the body—in fact, to be precise and unequivocal, of his cock. Having to obtain what by convention is called pleasure—and in reality is an unequaled and indeed indescribable happiness—he did not rebel at all against the repressive Power[4] that denies permission to such "pleasure" and in fact harshly condemns it. By rebelling, he would have ruined everything. He would have called attention to himself, would have made a spectacle. His rebellion was much more profound and, as it would be expressed a decade later, global. Everything that pertained to power had *really* lost all value and had crumbled around him, lying like an enormous forgotten ruin. In carrying out his plan for complete, rigorous, xxx, *global* disorder, he had ingenuously adopted the techniques of or-

[4] E.g., the Italian government.

der. He did what he wanted, and that was it: that was his purpose. Externally—except for a certain formal abandonment of the rules that made him a man of the haute bourgeoisie and his behaving, as a result, like one of so many petit bourgeois types, wounded, repressed, perhaps unsuccessful, but sensitive and dignified (and in shabby clothes, which were perhaps a little too youthful)—externally, I repeat, nothing would have revealed the true quality of Carlo's life, Dr. Jekyll that he was. If something had revealed it, it would not have mattered at all to Carlo. He simply didn't care either to hide or to reveal what he really was and what he sought in life. That's why I was saying that there is nothing easier than to spy on a man like Carlo. Not only does it not occur to him that anyone would spy on him—and know about him, put his life on record—but even if, by chance, he did learn that someone was spying, he wouldn't care about it in the least. So much the worse for the spy. Unless, of course, it was a spy from the carabinieri or the police, because in that case Carlo would be terrorized to the point of agony < ... >. /He would be afraid that something/ might keep him from continuing to do what he wanted to do and which alone in life had meaning. And, besides, his love for those dear to him \his family\—who would suffer in any legal disgrace, any scandal—was a real love, originating in infancy, etc.; there wasn't anything conformist or, so to speak, ideologically contradictory in it.

So Pasquale Bucciarelli, on his first important job, does not find himself faced with particular difficulties; it is for him almost a little game. It has gone well for him. He will be able to look good in the eyes of his superiors, offer xxx for his career, already tasting, in his impenetrable heart, the pleasures it may get for him, money, car, women, and all those goods which men like Carlo enjoy so naturally and unconsciously.

NOTE 6 *QUINQUIES*
A few words on this Pasquale
(The story of Pasquale—Picaro—Smerdyakov)†

NOTE 6 *SEXIES*
The suitcase with the report in it

I repeat: nothing is easier than to follow, observe, spy on Carlo. Pasquale, with a talent that could not be unconnected to his vocation, had understood this immediately.

He therefore prepared to carry out his task, to accomplish it with the utmost care and with a result that would be most satisfying for the State (!) and for himself, Pasquale. An aspiration and a plan that < ... > were realized punctually.

At this point, however, I must anticipate the facts and get to the end of this part of my story, which has to do with Carlo's return to Turin.

It is already nearly autumn, everything has happened, and Pasquale is returning to Rome (the day before Carlo himself). He is on the train, in a second-class compartment. He is visibly satisfied; as soon as he can, he starts a conversation with his fellow passengers; and he is sincerely one of them, one who thinks like them < ... >. Then, at Genoa, the compartment empties, and Pasquale remains alone with his suitcase (the so-called xxx were not yet in use; it was one of those cardboard suitcases which had continued to serve Italians faithfully, without a break, from before the war until after, from the Resistance to the beginning of prosperity). Inside that suitcase was Pasquale's treasure, that is, his report. During that whole period, in fact, he had taken notes, in language that was precise, bureaucratic, at once verbose and stripped down, on everything he had "discovered" about Carlo's life. That was the report he would offer, as a real masterpiece of diligence and obedience, to his superiors. And now in Genoa a new traveling companion entered his compartment. Pasquale immediately realized that it was going to be difficult to start talking to this man and have one of those pleasant conversations, full of good sense and mutual respect, which gave such satisfaction to his policeman's heart or, rather, his heart of a failed police officer. In fact, it was a question of a young man his own age, perhaps a little younger. But clearly an intellectual. At that time, an immense gap divided the bourgeoisie from the lower classes, intellectuals from workers. A glance that took into consideration the pure and simple physical presence, *the body,* was enough to distinguish them without the slightest possibility of a mistake. Pasquale, a man of the people, immediately understood that he was in the presence of a bourgeois intellectual, and this bourgeois intellectual understood immediately that he was in the presence of a man of the people. Nothing, to tell the truth, objectively gives me the right to know who he was and what he thought, this intellectual who had entered a compartment of the Turin–Catania train on that early autumn day in 1961, yet I believe that I can confirm with some certainty that he was an intellectual of the left; in fact, the suitcase that he was carrying with him and had with difficulty placed on the rack above was full to bursting with books, and he had chosen one of them to read during the journey: a book by Shklovsky on Sterne (in Russian; the title in fact sounded comical, *Sterna i teoriya romana*). Thus, precisely as an intellectual of the left, this young man, pale, impersonal, and a little /parochial/, could only feel sympathy for that "worker" (that it was a question of a subproletarian was for him irrelevant; evidently, like all his peers, he *did not want to know* that subproletarians existed). And he was therefore polite to him—in the few words they exchanged. The sympathy was not, of course, reciprocated by Pasquale, who instantly saw in him a fanatical Communist \"Red"\ and immediately confused his personal class hatred with his professional anti-Communism. It disturbed him no more than that. He was in the best frame of mind. He prepared to pass the time as agreeably as possible, perhaps having a good sleep. He looked with deep complacency at the suitcase containing the report, next to which there was now the intellectual's twin suitcase, full of books.

The journey was long, eternal. Twilight came, night descended. Other travelers entered, sat down, and disappeared along the way. Sleep finally, suddenly, and almost at the same moment gathered the two young travelers; this time, it was a sleep almost unsought, unwanted: the profound sleep of an infant.

When the two awoke in Rome, nearly at dawn, they both had a shock that shook them to the most impenetrable depths of their souls: their two suitcases were no longer there. They were truly not there; their disappearance had something fatal about it: it gave the impression that no disappearance had ever left behind, on those racks, an emptiness more complete, profound, and, one would be tempted to say, prophetic.

Now, I prefer to tell the reader right away that this motif of the "stolen report" is secondary to my story. But not for that reason will its effects be of minor relevance, nor, on the other hand, of course, will its disappearance be total \definitive\: at the right moment, this motif of the "stolen report" will be diligently taken up again < ... >.

For now the thing has only one meaning. Pasquale could not exhibit his perfect report, /perfectly/ exhaustive concerning the facts, to his principals. Grievously wounded in his pride as an efficient, trusted subaltern, he would have to make some notes and then report the facts in /large part/ orally.

That cannot but be reflected in my story. Which belongs by its nature to the category of the "illegible," so its legibility is artificial: a second nature no less real, however, than the first.

To recount, drawing on Pasquale's "report," what Carlo did during his stay in Turin would have made the balance of the story hang fatally on the side of "legibility." Instead, my duty as a writer is to lay the foundations of my work from the beginning again, and not through a decision already made but through a true compulsion that I am unable to oppose in any way. Even if I had not determined it, willed it, this writing necessarily had to be a "new game"—even if not, perhaps, lexically and formally; everything in it, in fact, is heavy allegory, almost medieval (that is, illegible). I cannot fail in this undertaking. And may the reader forgive me if I annoy him with these matters, but I am *living* the genesis of my book.

NOTE 7
The mother's turn

The Vallettis' country house is in the Canavese:

> *With its wild garden, vast rooms, beautiful*
> *balconies, seventeenth-century, garnished with greenery . . .*[5]

As soon as he arrives, Carlo goes right up to the attic: he has caught sight only of his mother, who, not expecting his arrival, is amazed. She is a very beautiful woman, tall, like her son, but plumper. She is getting ready to go into Turin for one of /her parties/. Carlo, barely glancing at her, has embraced her, lowering his hands down to the top of the large gluteals swathed in silk. Then he goes up to the attic, where as a boy he spent hours and hours. It was there he got to know the crickets and the little owl; the buzzard; the sound of the bells, matins or angelus: the entire life of the country. Here he is, then,

> *in the seventeenth-century oval attic,*
> *with its small-paned windows, where the warp*

---

[5] *Translator's note:* Guido Gozzano, "Totò Merùneni."

of the glass deformed the panorama
like an ancient, unnatural enamel.

Not true to life (yet lovely), as in an enamel
with four sections, the Canavese appeared:
turreted Ivrea, the hills of Montalto,
the straight Serra, the trees, the churches . . .[6]

Alone in the attic (on a day that already has a certain September cruelty; tired from the long train trip and a sleepless night spent in a hotel in Turin), Carlo unbuttons his pants, /pulls it out/, and begins to masturbate. It has a dry and dusty feel; stinging a little, and /splenetic/; the erection is invincible, but that masturbation is determined by the desire of a mind transfixed by the return of childhood, and by a knowledge of the country world with its tremendous purity. Except for the servants, he and his mother are alone in the house. A bell begins to ring, from xxx. It's late morning, who knows why it's ringing; perhaps in joy, for the next day. Along with the dusty morning dryness there is already a hint of evening, soft and wet, in the air. Why? is the day already ending? In that melancholy graying of the sky that is too blue? Carlo interrupts his masturbation but not, as he usually does, in order to start again. He puts his member—hard but empty, slightly damp, /dejected/, and perhaps a little smelly at the tip—back in his pants and rebuttons them. He goes down from his childhood observatory, which he alone knows and where he became acquainted with the world: the peasant world seen by a rich, sickly boy. He goes down the stairs that seem to echo—they are so old, indeed so worn (mentally; because in reality they seem brand-new, smelling of bourgeois wax and lavender)—they seem to echo a single thing, as they did fifteen or twenty years ago: "masturbation, masturbation," hot flesh of the hard, sore penis, excited and squeezed, inside the uncomfortable trousers thought of by the family as refined. He goes down through the empty house (there is a new young maid) and enters his mother's room without knocking. She is turned toward the mirror, her bare back to whoever enters, intently putting on her makeup for the party she is going to. She is an older

[6] *Translator's note:* Guido Gozzano, "La Felicità."

woman—of fifty—and hasn't many alternatives for spending the day; she keeps up with the literary Tuesdays, the Fiat shows, and the whole long worldly entourage at these events and others like them. In the early sixties women like her still /behaved/ naturally. She is blond (and at that point would not have had much gray), with a big wave over one eye, as if she were fifteen years younger. Also, her bosom is partly uncovered. Although it's the middle of the morning (the party she is going to is at noon, in a skyscraper, a kind of Terrazza Martini[7]), the room is invaded by a shadowy evening light, by a sense of the end of the day, of depletion, of terrible proposals for withdrawal and repose, as God commands. The mother's bosom is half uncovered, and of course her whole throat, her drawn and wrinkled throat, is covered with cream. Under the light robe her broad thighs are visible. Carlo approaches and gives her a kiss. It was an old habit from a long period of Carlo's early adolescence. Emma (as in Bovary) is astonished. And she laughs, a hoarse laugh, all on the *o:* "Oh, oh, oh!" and resettles herself, like a hen after the rooster's attack. She tries to speak about Carlo's life in Rome. But her eyes remain on the mirror, and there she sees the figure of Carlo, standing with one hand clutching his crotch as if seized by a frantic desire to pee that has immobilized him. Emma raises her eyes to Carlo's face, pretending it's nothing and continuing to say calmly, as if detached: "Oh, oh, oh!" But she lowers her eyes—it was impossible for it not to happen this way—and this time in the mirror they see Carlo's hands rubbing his crotch and slowly unbuttoning his pants < ... >. Emma concentrates on her makeup, and puts some powder on her face. Carlo leans over her neck and kisses her again; not only that, he licks her back. Emma says, "What are you doing?" like a girl or a whore. Carlo answers (it's the climax): "Be quiet, Mama." She is quiet and starts again with her powder. Naturally nothing happens. Her eyes, however, she cannot command, and again she lowers her gaze in the mirror and sees, without any possibility of mistake, Carlo's penis, straight outside his pants, extended, hard, pointed at her. Emma is frightened and starts to get up from the stool she's sitting on, half undressed. Carlo does not

---

[7] *Translator's note:* The Terrazza Martini is a hall on the top floor of a modest skyscraper in Milan that is used for various literary and other gatherings sponsored by Martini & Rossi.

stop her, but when she is on her feet he grabs her under the arms and pushes her toward the bed (in the meantime the robe she had wrapped around her body—it wasn't tied—has fallen off), saying to her, "Come here!" Emma says, "But Carlo, Carlo," and although she is as strong as a cow, for the moment she cannot succeed in freeing herself from the embrace of that thirty-five-year-old little Narcissus, dry as an adolescent. Carlo manages to throw her on the bed and mount her, after tearing off her underpants.

NOTE 8
Continuation

After such a beginning, everything Carlo is destined to do in the house in the Canavese and in neighboring Turin can only be pale in comparison. But that's how things go, what's most interesting doesn't always come at the end. Emma went to her party; she undoubtedly arrived a little late, but that was of no importance. Since she was gone, Carlo ate alone. The new maid, a peasant from xxx, served him. At that time, as in the preceding centuries, servants could still be found in the neighborhood. She was a woman of about thirty. Carlo immediately began to look at her in a special way, like a master who is too polite, and with some insistence, not only in his gaze but in his demands about the food, etc. When she brings the bowl with the soup, she finds him with his hands clasped on his lap; she cannot avoid looking at him, while he, on the other hand, keeps his eyes lowered. Then, when she brings him the chicken—delicious chicken, with delicious vegetables—his pants are unbuttoned; she tries not to notice, but this time Carlo keeps an eye on her and sees that her glance has fallen on the white strip of undershirt that shows beneath the open row of buttons on the pants. And so, while she serves him, he puts one hand inside that opening and grabs his penis, clutching it violently. But meanwhile he stares at the woman with his misty blue eyes that seem to inspire pity and at the same time demand submission, and begins to ask questions that compel her to give respectful answers, as a poor woman who is paid to serve: "Are you married?" And she: "Yes, sir." "For how long?" "Oh, for a long time, it's been fifteen years now . . ." "You've been married since you were a child!" "Oh, yes." "And do you have children?" "Yes, sir." "How many?" "Three." "Boys or girls?" "The first is a girl, the other two are boys." "How old are they?" "The oldest is fourteen, the second is thirteen, and the last is still a baby, fourteen months." "Ah." During this dialogue, which forces the woman to stand still and answer diligently, Carlo, still holding his penis in his fist as tight as he can, has taken it out of his pants. "And what's the name of the little girl, the oldest?" "Viola." The woman has finished serving; she stands there with the tray in her hand, like a housewife, all practicality, no grace. Carlo opens the fist that is holding his penis to pick up his knife and fork; the penis remains outside his pants, naked, erect, swollen. Lowering her eyes, the woman goes away. Thinking of Viola, Carlo cannot resist, and as soon as he is alone he /masturbates/ rapidly and soon reaches ejaculation, he is so excited. He gets his whole hand dirty. He goes to the bathroom to wash.

Having closed the parenthesis of the servant, he went to his room. Immediately he stretched out on the white coverlet of xxx and unbuttoned his pants. Although his penis was not, of course, erect, he took it in his hand and began to move it, as if he were masturbating slowly— as he always did on any occasion when he was alone. The shadowy light was terrifying, and though its other face, outside, was the strong light of the burning sun—by now, however, no longer truly hot (on the vines that seemed enameled against the sea-blue sky, against the hills)—it weighed on his heart like lead. It was not as in his youth, when the anguish of that shadow (decreed by God) had been unbearable, but still, despite its familiarity, it continued to pain him. The light penetrated from the window as in the summer that had just ended, and a kind of paleness announced that the world had turned, the weather from the South was returning, with its obligations. Carlo was completely outside it; during the winter he would go back to Rome; perhaps he would even go to Sicily. His only occupation was the tremendously pleasurable one of satisfying his sex: the one that he held in his hand and all the rest. He thought of his mother, and immediately his cock, although empty of semen, dry as a reed, began to swell. It was a new code, observed and applied for the first time. Carlo's mother in Turin, in her city house, just after eating, alone, sweaty, tired, returning from one fashionable social obligation and already preparing for the next (that is, the tea at the house where a select few would celebrate the guest or guests for whom the slightly vulgar public festivities had been organized), was now an image of his repertory, one of the /many repertories/ of Carlo's imagination, by means of which he could have an erection and masturbate—but without ejaculating; that is, for as long as he wanted. The motion of masturbation—as if he were rocking his penis—regularly brought on a profound sleep, which dropped like lead on his eyes. At night he fell asleep definitively after the habitual masturbation; at other times he slept for a short while, in a /fierce/, blind sleep. It had even happened there, on the bed of his childhood. When he woke, after five minutes, the penis was frozen in the fist that clutched it. A stronger ray of sun entered through the cracks of the old shutters and the heavy, D'Annunzian curtains. Hearing voices outside, Carlo got up, still clutching his penis; he went to the window and opened it, but just enough so that he would eventually be seen (a by now mechanical calculation). Carlo's three sisters, Chiara, Natalia, and Emilia, were talking, in loud voices. With them was a girl of thirteen or fourteen, whom they called Viola; so she must be the servant's daughter. Carlo, looking at all those girls, held his penis in the unbuttoned pants even tighter, stricken with anguish. His sisters and the girl disappeared into the house. The garden was empty. He could see a strip of it, which included the trees of the countryside beyond, /poplars and maples/. Within, boxwood hedges, conventional and charged with a sense of age-old wealth; white gravel paths; expanses of flowers, purple and orange but as if dusty or faded, food for /celestial/ bees, in that weak yet fiery \strong\ sun. Carlo threw himself onto the bed again, his legs spread, and began again to think of his mother, masturbating his sex, which had suddenly lost the hardness of erection. He had decided to get up and go to Turin. But he allowed himself five more minutes, or maybe ten, to masturbate, there, on the bed, his head burning with erotic images that would be realized in Turin in a few hours. Meanwhile—as often happened—he was distracted by questions that had nothing to do with those images. For example, he wondered insis-

tently how his family could have a style of life so wealthy and so powerfully normal: a big house in the Canavese, an apartment of seven or
eight rooms in the city (a penthouse in Via xxx), the necessary servants,
here and there; cars for all, or almost all, the members of the family.
Every gesture made in that family universe, so solid and old-fashioned,
had to cost a river of new money, money that had not been directly accumulated by the grandparents (the landowning industrialist grandfather). Disturbed by these thoughts that had nothing to do with him,
Carlo buttoned his pants and, without changing or washing, went out.

His mother was not at home. He didn't find her until nearly evening,
at a third party. It had been difficult to learn where she was, because he
didn't have the courage to ask openly and simply, as a son would for his
mother. Now the timidity and fear through which sexual satisfaction is
reached had also inserted themselves in the relationship between Carlo,
his mother, and the others. The fact that Carlo had decided once and for
all to occupy himself exclusively with sex, the source of pleasures
unique, sublime, and inexpressible each time, does not mean that his
life was devoted to pleasure. The timidity was in fact anguish rather
than simply timidity. In this Carlo had remained the same as when he
was a boy. To telephone someone and ask, "Do you know where I could
find my mother?" now that he wanted her not, obviously, for ordinary
organizational reasons, froze him in an unconquerable anguish. He had
to maneuver like a delinquent to find out that his mother was at the
Oddones', at that third party. When he saw her he told her to go to the
bathroom, but he had to repeat it two or three times before she obeyed
and went down to the bathroom on the floor below. As soon as Carlo
was certain she had gone in, he followed her. The bathrooms at the
Oddones' were all white, in seventeenth-century-style majolica; under
the smell of powder and other cosmetics lay the smell of urine mixed
with that of menstruation, which, precisely because it was faint, took
the breath away. It was, of course, the first time that Carlo had been in
that sanctuary. His erection was so powerful that he was bent double, as
if from a sharp pain. There was a woman in front of the mirror in the little anteroom. Carlo had to pretend to have made a mistake, and he took
refuge in the hallway, where he was in danger of being seen by another
woman. The plot began, the plotted wait, in which the cosmos was at

stake. Either it went according to plan or the disappointment was intolerable, worse than death. He had to wait until the woman inside came out, keep his mother from doing so herself, pay attention lest other disturbers arrive. In fact, a maid was approaching. Carlo felt faint, cursing inside, desperate as a boy. As if pushed by Carlo's will, the maid took another route, went down a narrow stairway that led to the kitchen, goddam whore. That other goddam whore (if I may be allowed a brief interpolation of free, indirect discourse) was, on the other hand, still there. How to find out the way things stood without peeking and thus being seen again? The plot required absolute immobility; and a cigarette. But Carlo, that innocent, didn't smoke. Now, when he was about to lose his senses and his nerves were an inflamed clot of tension, the whore, as if sucked outside by his will, left, gliding toward the upper floor like a shadow, faded by five minutes in that place apart. Like a madman Carlo entered where she had come out; of the three stalls, two had open doors, one was closed. Carlo knocked, saying in a low, altered voice: "Open it before anyone comes." His mother, inside, opened it. Just in time, because in fact two, or perhaps three, women came in, chatting about things they had begun discussing upstairs. His mother's face was smooth, almost without wrinkles. It was excitement, overtiredness (three parties in one day). Inside, the stink of female urine was really sharp. "What do you want?" said Emma. She was a modern woman, she knew Freud through the popular books of the Italian psychoanalysts, but what was happening to her was beyond all limits. Certainly she thought her son was mad to do those things which to him, on the other hand, seemed so natural. "Be quiet, you whore," he answered. And he clasped her tight around the chest. Her soft, heavy breasts moved him almost to tears: "My whore," he added, with the disgusting tenderness that makes men sadists. "My sweet, lovely whore." His hand descended to the tops of her buttocks, like two bulwarks or two cupolas; the wrinkled silk did not prevent him from feeling her underpants beneath the swelling, indeed, their stitching and embroidery. Carlo violently turned his mother toward the toilet bowl, put one hand on her head to force her to lean over, and, hushing her, slowly performed the /act/ that at that moment seemed to him impossible to delay: he raised her slip and pulled down her underpants, uncovering her /ass/. Below, in the antiseptic shadow of the bathroom at the Oddones', I mean below the ass, between the thighs, a tuft of hair stuck out. Carlo grabbed it, from behind, in his fist.

Chiara, whose voice had first echoed in the garden that afternoon, was the youngest sister, born when he was already sixteen or seventeen, and she was now a little older than Carlo had been when she was born. They barely knew each other. But two or three years before, when he had left for Rome, he had seen her kiss a puppy that at the time was the pet of the household (it was no longer there, who knows what had become of it). Chiara was speaking to xxx (that was the name of the dog) in dialect, and while she was speaking, her voice low, her breasts had become completely uncovered. All that was part of the /perfect/ picture of the past. But Carlo, the day after he got home, thought he ought to rest, sexually. So he stayed in Turin to spend a day of contemplation.

———————

—Happiness of the day, etc. (September sun—friends)—hopes, etc.
—Midday anguish
    Station (?)—House
—Awkwardness of the sisters (nonconfrontational relation with adults)—
    Grandmother
Description of family assets—change of tune (the other family)
—Mother's poetry (metalinguistic annotations in functional psychology)
—Pensione Sicilia
Relationship between men and Carlo
—Financial relationship with Carlo I (love money and houses)
—The note from the carabinieri
Objectively the mother has a son in Rome
Father at table

8 September 1973

The reasons for his decision caused him to sleep late in the morning, which for him meant nine or ten. Suddenly he *felt* the sun. He did not have to open the windows to know that the light of that sun, just barely faded at the edges, was flooding through the streets and squares of the

city. That it had a whitish, marine transparency in the sky that appeared
between the roofs at the ends of the streets. And that the light of the
sun, although warm, already had in it an emptiness, a lack of strength,
and from it emanated, along with the joyous purity that foretold an un-
changing series of equally blue-skied days, a kind of desperate melancholy, without pain (like all forebodings). He went out into the street a
little before noon, and it was in fact one of the hottest days of the summer, if not the hottest. And yet people had already returned from vacation, and the traffic was the same as in winter. Already in that long-ago
1960 the city was full of southerners. It was they who above all crowded
streets that had once been empty. They gave the city the air of a hospice,
a hinterland full of convalescents. The cafés in the center were crowded
with middle-class Turinese who were drinking apéritifs. Before the
sparkling bar, or in private rooms furnished with solid, well-maintained
nineteenth-century antiques, were the young heirs of petit bourgeois
professionals along with the scions of industrialists.

> . . . . *Casa Ansaldo*
> *Casa Rattazzi, Casa D'Azeglio, Casa Oddone.*[8]

They had the leer, in some cases timid and in some vulgar, of provincial young men. They all said "frequently" instead of "often," and their
world seemed to them the most natural of all possible worlds. Their
habits made everything else alien to them. Moreover, the understanding
among them in turn alienated anyone who had the least suspicion that
what that understanding fixed was not the absolute. Carlo had had such
a suspicion his whole life. That fact had not escaped the others, who had
immediately inserted the knife of their natural fierceness into the crack
opened in the consciousness of a sensitive friend and had widened it.
This situation of unspoken hostility /had, however, eased/ by then, following the early successes of Carlo's career in Rome. That had ended the
discussion. Carlo saw his friends again at the café with /a sincere/ joy.
Their habits, which made them such natural exemplars of a quality of
life identified with the only truth, were well known to Carlo, and his

[8] *Translator's note:* Guido Gozzano, "Totò Merùmeni."

knowledge transformed them. Precisely because he saw them in their totality and complexity, to their distant roots, they appeared to Carlo precarious and unstable, like all the patterns of life by which those young men considered themselves sheltered. To a stranger their code might seem unassailable, firmly rooted in existence; to one who knew it, was involved in it, it seemed a cobweb painted on a veil.

But this only increased Carlo's pleasure, because those young men who were now old, who had been the masters of everything in life, were thus rendered shadows in history and appeared to their school friend, who had been a slave to the want of everything, inoffensive. That morning with his old friends was for Carlo an occasion that rendered them on the one hand vaguely epic (the petit bourgeois schoolboy epic of an aristocratic city of the provinces) and on the other almost comic.

The apéritif was a "golden liquor that makes one sweat"; golden was the light, golden the following day. Carlo's heart was overflowing with happiness. He didn't have to think of anything but his sex, and this in itself contained indescribable pleasures, the only truly sublime pleasures of life. Of course, they would cost anguish and terror, too, and to reach them he would have to cross zones of death, of true death— through fear, anxiety—but the idea of all the possibilities of sexual joy put together and isolated from the rest of life brought a profound happiness: the sense of navigating a sea that became always more peaceful, blue, and luminous.

Carlo ate in one of the restaurants that all fortunate novel readers know and, precisely for that reason, there is no point in naming in a novel that, besides being nonrealistic, is heading, rather entertainingly, toward /the/ <...> Visions; and then he went home, along the porticoes frequented only by southerners and a few distracted Turinese. He slept again for a while. He woke up, and it was already late afternoon. He went out again. Although it was still as hot as the middle of summer, the day was now declining. In the shadows lengthening in the heat there was a tragic suggestion of time renewing itself in ancient repetition.

Carlo was seized by terror. He felt a real physical pain, a fierce spasm from his throat to his chest. He would have liked to vomit or cry, cursing. That sudden *taedium vitae,* certainly justified for reasons that Carlo did not wish to know (he preferred to hold on to things just as they were), made everything meaningless; or, worse, full of tragic meaning. The dream lost its colors and became reality. A reality, certainly, that was also dreamed, because it, in turn, was too far removed from dreams: seen as duty, grief, privation, agony, boredom. There was the terror of being alone, fear of the future, disgust (not at all purifying) with the present. Nothing in Carlo's plans or his situation had changed, with regard to the morning. He would continue to devote himself to an infinite series of sexual fulfillments, piling up the possibilities before him, endlessly, filling his entire life. And yet although this idea remained wonderful and he had not thought, even distantly, of letting go of it or of questioning it, here, suddenly, was the discouragement that made his knees go weak and caused him to cry out within himself, keeping his face unchanged so as not to be noticed by passersby. He cried out senseless phrases, among them complaints addressed to the old God and even to the Madonna. He was raving, singing to himself these blasphemous invocations mixed with scatological interjections. He was lost, nothing could ever save him, the world around him was a surface that was painful to touch or even to look at—the more so the more it remained the same, with the summer sun setting.

He returned to his friends—to those disinterested conversations of intellectual young men in a café far from the center of town, near the high school they had attended fifteen years earlier. But he stopped and, hurling Roman curses at them, turned in the opposite direction. He went toward the banks of the Po, to an unfamiliar park (but even this he had known as a high school student). There was something crude about it, as if it were in a provincial city or even a small village. Behold the grand prospects of sex! the marvelous possibilities of meetings with creatures whom sex points out as exceptional! Behold places not thought of, and so naturally ready for great occasions! The knolls in meadows deserted in the sun, which look dusty yet are so green; the big trees of city parks, a little too widely scattered; benches for people with poor and empty lives; a public urinal modestly surrounded by hedges; across the river the roofs of the city, grazed by the sun.

But coming along the central avenue (on which there were also cars) was a little girl and her mother. Carlo calculated that if he hurried he could arrive at the urinal at the same moment the little girl would pass in front of it. He had not even seen what she looked like. She was a nice, dark-complexioned little girl wearing cheap clothes, that was all. Carlo moved, almost running, toward the urinal, praying to God that the mother would be distracted, would look in some other direction. He prayed to God with all his soul, like a boy /in class during an exam/. And he moaned to himself, grinding his teeth at the idea that instead things might not go as he wished. A kind of fiery knife was planted in his chest, paralyzing him. He was in front of the urinal, the girl was about to go by. The mother was looking ahead, into the distance; but so, too, was the daughter. Carlo put his hand on his crotch ostentatiously but as if he had the right, looking insistently at the girl (and suddenly noticing her too high cheekbones and unattractive mouth) to get her attention. Half inside, half outside /the little temple/ of concrete, he unbuttoned his fly. The girl, like the mother, had now passed by without looking. But Carlo continued to stare at her shoulders, hoping his gaze would make her turn around; it was a piercing hope, a matter of life or death. The girl didn't turn. Carlo, crying and cursing like a /boy/, rebuttoned his fly without peeing, because he hoped to have /to pee/ in a little while. He went and sat on a bench in front of the urinal, looking at the two as they grew distant, cursing and calling them whores with the rage of a young boy.

He wandered from one bench to another, looking for mothers and /girls/ or, by some divine intercession, /girls/ alone. In the whole park he did not find a single one. Besides, the afternoon was becoming darker in its brilliance, announcing days equally brilliant to come. And the park would soon be completely empty even of old people and the few mothers with strollers. Carlo took a taxi and instinctively went to the station. After all, it, too, was full of benches. In his inexperience, Carlo had not foreseen that it was precisely at the station that he would find paradise and that for him it would be like the first time he smoked hashish, a habit he would be unable to break for his entire life, just because it was shameful, dangerous, and divine.

Chiara, Natalia, and Emilia all had one characteristic in common: they seemed poorer than Carlo and their parents. Above all Chiara. There was in her a coarseness and a physical deference whose origins were difficult to understand. Probably the wealth of Carlo's family was in reality limited: the three younger sisters had been the ones to suffer for this. Naturally they had lacked nothing, they had gone to the best school in Turin, they had learned to play musical instruments, etc. And yet one felt they were a little neglected, that wealth had not polished them and, so to speak, "spiritualized" them, as it had the other family members, the truly rich ones. The awkwardness of their bodies was not disguised. A lack of taste made them choose clothes that were not suitable for hiding their flaws; and a tendency toward saving probably inculcated in them since childhood—probably even if it was never verbalized or made conscious—led them to shop in the less fashionable stores, unlike the mother, the father, and the firstborn. They felt this slight physical inferiority, but in their innocence they believed it to be deserved. And thus they had looked for attitudes proper to that deserved inferiority, which <?> pretended to conceal it or, indeed, did conceal it. They considered themselves wise and practical, destined to a life of action—daily domestic action. They ended up avoiding the fashionable places frequented by their mother. At first through an instinctive timidity, because they simply felt not so "refined" by their social position as their friends, who were identified with that social position. Then because they ended up feeling excluded and unworthy. They compensated by assuming a brisk manner, which was somewhat crude and masculine, without feminine weaknesses; it substituted practicality for grace and culture for sophistication. But their culture, like their attitude toward life, was without taste, without real capacity to discriminate. This, too, they felt. Thus beneath their efficient appearance they were eternally insecure, torn by an incurable intellectual timidity. They had taken on the role of one who knows how to pronounce the right judgments, being hopelessly on the side of culture; and yet no one was more insecure in pronouncing judgments. They ventured them with childish trepidation, which their staging never managed to hide. On the other hand, all this made them extremely affectionate, attached to the feelings and values of a family—which in reality had created around them a somewhat sinister and melancholy emptiness. They also liked to be protectors, full of wisdom (that was why, for example, they always had Viola with them, and other children of the servants or peasants).

Consequently, they were socialists. (Besides, it was a family tradition, originating during the Resistance. The mother, /fashionably/, frequented the cultural world of the left.)

NOTE 9
At the station†

One can move from reality to a dream; but it is impossible to move from a dream to another dream. Carlo is sitting on a shabby black bench. The ceiling is high above him, almost dizzying; around him the space of the station is immense. The trains whistle, with their /unchangeable melancholy/. They go and they come, from the countryside or from the South, and swarming through the halls of the station, making it echo inside its broken windows, are crowds of poor people, instinctively following their destiny. Carlo is consumed by the fear that a little girl sitting on a bench on the other side of a large glass wall, in the waiting room, is looking at him. But in fact she is shut in her own sexual reverie, which includes waiting, purity, carelessness, distraction— and the most complete ignorance of sex itself (at least in that faraway 1960). In Carlo's dream, on the other hand, she had to be looking at him and interested in what he was doing; that is, in the violation of her modesty that he is committing, holding one hand above his sex, ready not only to grab it in his fist through the pants in case the girl should look at him but even to unbutton his pants, to slip his hand inside and grasp the living, hot flesh of the erect penis, letting it be glimpsed, even for an instant, in the livid whiteness of its pigment. The people around must be the spectators of the risk. Their modesty, too, must be violated, along with that of Carlo and the girl, sitting between her younger brothers, a comic book clutched in her hand. She would have to raise her eyes and rest them first on Carlo and then on his crotch. If that did not happen, Carlo might even die because of the tension that is shattering his nerves, that has half killed him already. At the same time, this pain of a dying man who is waiting to be restored to life by a look is an immense joy that fills the station like light in that melancholy twilight hour. It's a joy because the world and its meaning are reduced to the wait; there is no limit to this unique hope and activity. The whole day that precedes and follows that hour is devoted to this waiting \search\ for a look, or to other, similar things, attempts, successes; still to be attempted, still to succeed. The fearful wait into which homicidal anxiety is transformed gives him a boundless sense of possessing the future, of sweetness and benevolence in a repressive, punishing world that nevertheless secretly permits the fulfillment of countless undertakings such as Carlo, in his impetuous yet almost calm joy, dreams of.

NOTE 10
The station (continued)†

For many weeks Carlo continues to hang around the station, the home of innumerable sexual possibilities. The girl who will be the fulfillment of his search doesn't matter to him, as long as she answers certain general requirements of the code that for Carlo has split the female world in two; it is not a matter of blond hair or brown, of fat bodies or thin bodies; of petit bourgeois or working-class behavior. There is something that Carlo immediately recognizes, that he has learned in part to predict, before which the miracle is repeated. A miracle that can end with the most extravagant of his satisfactions (the eyes of the girl are resting on him, they have witnessed the unveiling of his secret, and the intoxication of this unveiling, which, together with a long series of strict preliminaries, sometimes leads him to ejaculate in public) or that can end instead in tragedy: at the best part, something takes the girl away, the girl who finally was found and cultivated—leaving him alone, prey to an incurable disappointment, nearly a wish to die, and to the terrible discovery that reality cannot be reconciled with the dream. Dozens and dozens of girls were found or lost. All this represented a period of his life that would then end up coexisting with new periods but would never disappear. The search for exhibitionist satisfaction (which was not the only one, because, if he could, he also attempted relations that were less possible and less easy; that is, having the girl touch him, forcing her to be aware of her own raw and unconscious exhibitionism) did not keep Carlo from observing the world around him; that is, in this case, the ambience of the station. In a fragmentary and anxious way he managed to discover a whole series of facts, of presences, of habits. All of that was taken into the sphere of joy. When he left the house to go to the station (he had nothing else to do in life), he thought of what awaited him with joyful palpitations, full of gratitude for the divine malleability of the world; he included in this image not only the moments of sexual maneuvering and orgasm but also his entire surroundings. And these surroundings were objective. They were part of his dream, but also part of reality. And not the harsh and horrendous reality that appeared to him in moments of unease, in which God, Morality, normality seemed to be right, dissipating the veil of illusion; but a natural reality, seen, for example, through the bright, sharp eyes of a realistic writer. And above all a new reality because, for the bourgeois Carlo, it was the reality of the people, seen, moreover, in an especially low moment, < ... > truly outside bourgeois life and experienced by poor people in their bodies; that is, in an inexpressible way. There were many southerners. They sold contraband cigarettes; they were protectors of the whores who walked the streets around the station; many were probably thieves and made plans there in the midst of that crowd that came and went in the bitter dust of the station. They were almost all young; many were very young, practically boys, who had just arrived from towns in Calabria or Sicily.

NOTE 10 *BIS*
An expense of spirit

With equal joy and pain, Carlo, reversing Shakespeare's lines from

> *All this the world well knows yet none knows well,*
> *to shun the heaven that leads men to this hell,*

to

> *All this the world well knows yet none knows well,*
> *to shun the hell that leads men to this heaven,*

returned to the country house. Shattered, terrorized by emotions that, the moment he escaped them, he couldn't wait to recapture, he felt his heart constricted with anguish at the very moment it was expanding, as if swelling with gratitude for the enormous quantity of things he had begun to experience. A violet evening made the Piazza di xxx, where he got off the bus, terrifying (in those days he was still a man of average income, who did what all men did). The swallows flew high; people were going home, turning their backs to the light, which, however, persisted, a burning fossil that lighted up the olive-green sky. Like a sleep-walker, secretly gasping and groaning inside, trying to keep his step and his face impassive, Carlo walked to his father's house. It happened that the northern night was still bright: < ... > the olive was indigo, it looked like a canvas spread against the blinding light of the Third Heaven. The flowers in the garden /absorbed/ the light, became piercing \cruel\ in shadow that hurt the eyes. At home, Carlo hoped to meet his three sisters, or at least one of them, right away. < ... > Instead, there was an unnatural silence in the house. The servant appeared—her eyes had completely submerged the memory of what they had seen the master's son do—and she told him that Natalia, Chiara, and Emilia were at their grandmother's. The grandmother's house was not far (it was a farmhouse where for many years she had been living in seclusion). Carlo, bleeding from the wound caused by the distance from the places where his sex could "through hell reach heaven," hesitating because of the sadness that emanated from the persistent light, caught hold of the only possibility of salvation. To do with Chiara (or with Natalia or with Emilia) what he did with the girls in the park or the station. He had to do it immediately. He went out of the house and took the unpaved road, flanked by two rows of tall poplars, which led to his grandmother's farmhouse. He found himself again in the evening shadows illuminated by the crystalline light of the cloudless sky, rising from behind the barrier of the mountains. The heat was terrible \unnatural\: walking along the grassy edge of the road, he seemed to be walking in air heated by just extinguished bonfires. Yet now, suddenly, Carlo was happy. A sexual goal transfigured the evening, which, no longer a theater of renunciation—of an ancient family life devoted to purity and matrimonial love, imposed like a duty that the heart feels as a deadly humiliation— had suddenly become the theater of a maneuver that would defy every decency and every reality, giving his heart the palpitations of blind joy that had to be reached even at the cost of death. Although he was not walking quickly, Carlo was covered with sweat. And that seemed to him wonderful, like the night around him, in which some stars now began to shine, unnaturally, and in the distance dogs began to bark, frantic yet barely perceptible. When he was in sight of the farmhouse, the gate of the threshing floor, which had been transformed into a kind of patio, opened, and the three sisters appeared, with their bicycles. Behind them came the grandmother and, holding her by the hand, Viola. The women (who certainly had not seen Carlo, who was standing in the shadow of the poplars) said good-bye lightly, in mysterious \indecipherable\ voices—one could not tell if those voices were happy or sad, as with the distant dogs—and parted. The three sisters got onto their bicycles, skidding a little, and, laughing among themselves, went off along the road, taillights gleaming and bells ringing in foolish joy. Seeing them coming toward him, Carlo threw himself into the ditch that bordered the road, just behind the smooth, odorous trunk of a poplar.

Everything there, against the earth, was strong-smelling, as if it had just rained. But the ditch was dry. The three sisters passed him, pedaling awkwardly, and soon disappeared at the end of the road, disappearing and reappearing along the row of thin poplar shadows, their taillights shining in the last light of the sunset, which had persisted into the first depths of night. The grandmother and the child remained at the gate, watching them go. And there they stayed for a while, in silence. Then, exchanging further incomprehensible words, they withdrew. A dog inside on the patio began to bark enthusiastically. Carlo remained crouching in the ditch. He had to stay there until his sisters got to the end of the little avenue, turned onto the paved road, and entered the house. Only then would Carlo be able to say to his grandmother that he had arrived without seeing them and would never have to tell them that he had been, that night, at the grandmother's farmhouse. The nerve-shattering tension began, the interminable struggle with time that innocent events, always unpredictable, have. To calculate the time it would take the three sisters to get home was literally impossible for Carlo. An exhausting anxiety prevented him; a minute to him was eternity. And yet he could not make a mistake. Mechanically, lying as he was in that dry ditch no more than a foot deep and thick with fragrant grass, he unbuttoned his pants and, to pass the time, since he was already excited, < ... > took his /cock/ in his hand and began to masturbate, as he always did when he was alone and secluded. But it did not become erect; his anxiety was too great, it suffocated him. His mind was completely taken up in imagining the journey of the three sisters toward home. In his agitation, he could not even manage to concentrate on the acts for whose sake he was carrying out the whole plan. What would he say to his grandmother to justify his presence at the farmhouse? There was no justification. Yet there was no need for one at all. Carlo, in a frenzied torment, had both the need to find one and the fear of not finding one. He tried to concentrate on masturbating, which should have comforted him, bringing back to prominence the unique sensation both of the evening (so marvelously and miraculously promising) and of his entire life, and anticipating the happiness to which everything was subordinated. But he didn't succeed; his penis remained soft, just barely swelling and reddened by the hand that was tormenting it. Certainly too soon, Carlo buttoned his fly and got up. With trembling legs and clouded eyes he approached the innocent gate of his grandmother's house and rang the bell. Immediately, from within, voices reached him, echoing brightly in the resonant heat, and immediately died away into the rooms. A moment later the gate was opened, and Carlo entered, greeting with excessive cordiality and guilty calm the old servant who had come to let him in, unsuccessfully hiding his amazement, and went casually into the house. The windows were all open, and a forlornly cheerful reddish light fell glancingly onto the patio, with its vases of beautifully arranged flowers, its big \heavy\ tables and chairs of pale wood, the leather-covered chaises. Near the door, which was also open, a little bench stood on the terra-cotta pavement that sparkled gaily in the light, and there sat Viola. She was holding in her hand a box painted like a merry-go-round. It was probably the Gioco dell'Oca.[9] She was silent, leaning against the oven-hot wall of the house, her eyes in shadow. The grandmother appeared in the doorway in a white old woman's dress, and she made no effort to conceal her surprise. Carlo in the meantime had thought of the most natural excuse, that is, the wish to see her, to pay her a brief visit, since he had come from Rome and would have to leave again soon. The grandmother's surprise passed quickly, and she invited him to have dinner with her. This fit in with Carlo's /plan/ exactly, and an overwhelming, glorious /satisfaction/ flooded him. Peace possessed him. And, waiting for dinner to be ready, while his grandmother was busy, he stretched out on a chaise opposite Viola, who was now sitting on the rough-hewn doorsill. Carlo, lying there, could not help looking up at the stars. They filled the whole space of sky above the old threshing floor, with its symmetrical sides and ancient terra-cotta tiles. Now it was truly night; the light had disappeared, leaving in its place an unnatural darkness. There were no streetlights for many miles around, and the moon had not yet risen. But the stars remained. The wonderful stars of youth, because one scarcely looks at them anymore, while they continue to shine, their light grainy and restless, even in the extraordinary calm. Their insistent twinkling

[9] *Translator's note:* The Gioco dell'Oca is a board game using dice that resembles snakes and ladders.

< ... > /was/ like a language. And to it was suddenly joined the fraternal language of a concert of crickets, close and yet infinitely far. Both languages seemed to want to repeat, without stopping, a single, limitless idea. It would be too easy to think that it alluded to sadness and death; it was something much more: it was pure knowledge, an idea extremely significant but without purpose. Carlo was not troubled by it; he was happy simply to enjoy for a few moments that fixed imminence of the firmament above him. None of it mattered to him; it was only the frame, sublime frame. For years and years, for entire decades he would enjoy it. What truly mattered to him was Viola. He couldn't really see if the girl was looking at him or not. Nevertheless, he slowly let his hand fall onto his lap and held it there firmly, there, in the /place/ that for a girl is mysterious and shameful. But now, when dinner was likely to be ready, he heard an unexpected ringing outside the gate and a male voice calling "Viola!" The servant went to open it, as if this were customary, and a very thin man, astride a bicycle, appeared, dressed like a peasant (in the pants and shirt that peasants wear in the evening, after work, after washing in the cistern in the courtyard). Viola immediately got up and ran to him. Carlo's grandmother appeared at the door in her white dress and with an air of reproof turned to Viola, who had run away: "You're not going to say good-bye?" She spoke with the accent of the dialect, exactly like Viola—who, barely turning, said, "Good night, Signora Emilia"—and her father, who added: "Excuse her, Signora, good night, see you soon!" "Good night, Vito," the grandmother said, her voice still a little irritated, and she went back inside. Carlo remained alone on the chaise under the stars. An entire dinner awaited him < ... > now, < ... > when he would be alone with his grandmother.

NOTE 10 *TER*

The grandmother had some excellent, privately made Barolo. They both drank enough to become completely drunk. It must have been habitual for the grandmother. Besides, confronted by a good Barolo, really good, it's hard to resist. At the end, to finish up with, she also /brought out/ a bottle of xxx, a wine that was completely unknown; it didn't belong to a special vintage and was not at all valuable, yet if it had been for sale it would have cost around <thirty or forty thousand lire a bottle>. In fact, it came exclusively from a hill on Carlo's grandmother's estate, and the name itself was known only in the family and a few of the houses of the peasants who made it (in addition to a small group of privileged friends in Turin). It was nothing special, but it seemed /divine/, because of its utter purity and also because of the quality of its extreme old age, which had maintained an infant freshness through centuries and had reached the perfection of its *ingenuum* almost at the end of a human cycle. Its modest but refined fascination consisted in the fact that it was neither dry nor sweet, as if in ancient times there had been no reason for the distinction: it was wine in its purest state, and not very strong, which was how the ancients liked it. The grandmother's inebriation had strange manifestations. If Carlo's impressions had to be set forth, one might say that she revealed a past that was enigmatic because it could no longer be judged. On the one hand, she showed herself to be a rough peasant, a landowner as crude as her farmhands, with no interest in any aspect of life that her social position offered. Perhaps she had been a prostitute, one of those "cocottes" whom landowners of the early twentieth century, following a nineteenth-century tradition, brought home from the city, causing great scandal, and then integrated into the solid family context. (These women turned out to be good administrators, with a steady conservative spirit.) Perhaps her drunkenness brought out that origin. Sitting on the leather sofa with her legs spread, the glass of xxx in her hand, she was gossiping like a peasant about nothing, as one might have gossiped fifty years before, still *within* an epoch that was now ending, whose standards were now \at this point\ useless except as quotations, when suddenly she began to speak of Shakespeare's sonnets. In the haze of her drunkenness what kept her obstinately interested was a problem of gardens. She was unable to extricate herself from it, like a fly in a spiderweb. Having made an observation, she would stop for a moment and stare at Carlo questioningly, her lips moving nervously and her eyes wandering in a desperate smile, like a beggar's, and then, without waiting for any comment from the person to whom she appealed so intensely (and from whom certainly she expected nothing), she returned to beat her head against the wall of the problem of those gardens. She spoke English perfectly. Was the "flower" of the sestina of Sonnet 94 the young friend or not? Or was it, rather, one part of the whole—that is, not a flower but a garden? And was it then to be identified with lilies, of which it is said a little later, "lilies that fester"? On this subject, Hallet Smith suggested that the lilies of the last verse are one of the innumerable echoes of the Sermon on the Mount . . . but no, no: that last line is definitely taken from *Edward III,* and it's not a question of lilies with no thought of tomorrow, heedless, modest, and pure in their natural state; the negative connotation of "husbandry," introduced in the preceding lines, cannot but refer to them. Moreover, the Evangelist speaks of lilies *of the field,* while here it says explicitly lilies *of the garden.* And Shakespeare was well aware of this opposition, see Sonnet 54, in which against the dog or wild rose, the Canker-bloom, he sets—the garden rose. It is the roses or lilies (the flowers) of the garden that are delicate and are defended against the weeds that make them wither, die, *fester!* Like Richard II, a weak man, devoured by the very "weeds which his broad-speaking leaves did shelter," thus allowing—during the War of the Roses!—that King-Rose /to be supplanted/ by the "wild rose Bolingbroke." The comparison of the two gardeners in *Richard II* proves that the State is nothing but a garden (is this what must be proved?): "Our sea-walled garden, the whole land, is full of weeds, her fairest flowers chok'd up"! So says, to be exact, the gardener's servant. The servant's servant! And in this idea of the Garden—an idea beloved of the very servants—the ideas of the two archetypal Gardens converge (as Peter Ure documents in his edition of *Richard II*): the Garden of Eden and the Garden of Arcadia. But these ideal Gardens tend to be driven back into utopia, /they abandon/ the real State-Garden to the threat of abandonment! It is the new commercial-Puritan civilization that is breaking out, and Shakespeare himself cannot ignore it. Queen Elizabeth is dying . . .

It was not in any way plausible that the grandmother had ever had relations with the high aristocracy. The Vallettis were very rich, yes, but not so rich as to weep at the death of Queen Elizabeth as if they had been with her on the yacht of mutual friends. The grandmother, who was a peasant and also an academic endowed with the best kind of humanistic and philological knowledge—that of the good old days—was at the same time something else: she was a bourgeoise, an ordinary, satisfied Bovary. And that was the worst obstacle to Carlo's plan. But luckily she was now completely drunk. And the moves, this time, did not cost Carlo any real anguish. He too was drunk. Joking, laughing vivaciously, he did everything as if there were no tragic aspect to it—like < ... > Lyudmila with Sasha < ... >. The wine had smoothed and lit up the grandmother's skin, which was not very old anyway. Carlo joked about this. And then, beginning to tickle her while she again took up the subject of the State-Garden, he began to joke, laughing sincerely, about the freshness of her skin, under her arms, at her waist. He really wanted to see her legs, which were already uncovered; and he drew the skirt up above her thighs, laughing. It was at this point that he realized, happily surprised and very pleased, that doing all this had excited him. He really wanted his grandmother to observe the phenomenon with her own eyes, even if she didn't want to believe it. He, too, uncovered himself, unbuttoning his pants with an even louder and happier laugh, and he took one of her hands and made her hold it tight around his penis, which was proudly erect, like that of an infant. The grandmother's weak and bony hand, though willing, moving up and down, was not able to make him reach orgasm, so he detached her hand from him, making her place it on his thigh, and finished rapidly by himself, ejaculating on her and staining that lovely white old woman's dress.

NOTE 10 *QUATER*
The cosmos

/When all that wild laughter was behind him, along with the interweaving of the acts of the body, the things, the light and darkness of a family evening and its customs and transgressions (and those, too, seemed to be recorded in a household account book), and on all that

oblivion had fallen, Carlo inevitably found himself alone again on the
lane of poplars in the middle of the countryside. /

The night was advanced, there were no more interruptions. All was
silent, even the dogs. In the meantime, the moon had appeared, so bright
it seemed detached from the sky, and stood out against mountains black
in the clear air; and thus the stars resumed their discourse more faintly,
endlessly repeating their sorrowful communications, trembling and
imperceptible. The crickets, on the other hand, were imperturbable, the
crickets of that region of the Piedmont at the end of a /sultry/ summer;
they became hoarse repeating their indecipherable message, which
seemed to have an extremely meaningful curve: here, nearby, it had almost the sense of a thirsting love, humanly insatiable, alive; while far
away, fading into the /unthinkable/ distance, it became a lament that
could neither say nor signify anything, so great was its melancholy.

Carlo stopped and sat down. He looked around, as if that were to be
the final look of his life. A night in the Canavese: so perfectly repeating
itself that its thousand past forms faded, canceling one another out, and
so perfectly present that it loomed like an apparition made of a thousand apparitions, each one as enchanting as it was doomed to exist and
that was all: the pure intention of the necessity \mind\ of the world. But
that presence was so strong that the heart, even while rejoicing in it
with its entire capacity, rejected it. Struck by both devotion to all that
silent beauty and fear of it, Carlo was observing the night with a smile
of happiness: the kind of smile that, when one is alone—and the only
embarrassment is what one feels in front of oneself—becomes slightly
mad; despite the scenery, it was the highest and most beautiful moment
of his life, which had been devoted exclusively to sex, in the most complete isolation from every other form of human interest. It was in just
such rare moments of complete suspension, and in the frequent moments of fragmentary suspension mixed with acts of love and with his
long searches—after he had filled the world (in the present and, even
more, with even more desperate happiness and gratitude, in the future)
with this exclusive sexual passion—that his happiness reached its highest points, until he felt safe from death forever and from every form of
ending, while accepting the /final/ and distant culmination as life's
marvelous lack of limits.

Set against all that external becoming, being, and dissolving of the cosmos was the body—now sitting in the hot air where it felt as though a fire had just been put out and there was not a breath of wind—in which life really began: a life that still had everything to give.

NOTE I I
The new day

After a little while (however beautiful relations with the cosmos are, they are of brief duration: they are of little use and cause one to lose other things—time, sleep, etc.—that are reasonably necessary. The sincerity of relations with the cosmos is soon exhausted: they tend to be transformed immediately into an act of homage, into a dutiful concentration, from which man seeks to free himself, hypocritically repressing his impatience, like a child in religion class), Carlo set out again, returned home, undressed, got into bed. Immediately, according to his inviolable rule, he took in his hand \grasped in his fist\ his soft penis— it was still a little wet from the recent ejaculation (Carlo never washed at night)—and began to rouse it to get it hard. After a while he succeeded and began to masturbate. His imagination recalled, with the fervor with which a general recalls the moments of a victorious battle, the pleasure he had enjoyed that evening, but he did not limit himself to recalling it; he looked forward to a future repetition, with variations as exalting as they were easy (in imagination, which lacked the obstacles of reality). But there was also one thought that troubled him. The loss of Viola's presence. So much so that slowly his imagination became completely fixated on her. Masturbating, in a long, uninterrupted ejaculation, Carlo thought of what he would have done in front of the girl if she had not so unexpectedly been "saved" by her father, that thin, lifeless man on a bicycle with the deep voice of an old Po valley artisan. As always, masturbation brought on a sudden, heavy sleep, which reabsorbed him into a mossy gorge just as imagination was painting before his closed eyes acts that went well beyond every real possibility, and yet he was certain that, even if it was through renunciation, anguish, and danger, he would end by fulfilling them. This, and nothing else, was the purpose of his life.

NOTE 17
The Wheel and the hub

Everything Carlo did during that period passed into Pasquale's memory in a completely objective way. There was, however, one thing that did not undergo the same fate as all Carlo's other actions and was not, there-fore, recorded, or, rather, reported, by Pasquale. It was a dream. And precisely the following dream.

Carlo was bound to a wheel. It was one of those wheels that are re-produced in illustrations portraying the tortures of the holy Inquisi-tion, etc., and that—not closely observed—return to memory deformed < ... >, placing themselves in space according to our fantasy or our un-conscious will. Thus the wheel in the dream was enormous, bigger than the wheels of the illustrations, however monumental and baroque; moreover, it was meticulously and elaborately finished, so that it re-sembled the chariot wheel of a Divinity, or the Wheel of Fortune, or even the Wheel of the Zodiac. < ... >

The wheel was suspended in the void. In what void? The void of the cosmos, of course. That void was also, however, a "cultural space": per-haps the background (endless) of a ceiling or an apse, or even simply the sky, but pervaded by a melancholy, freezing light, with some faint clouds painted on the indigo < ... >.

Carlo was bound naked to the wheel. But, as happens in dreams, his being there bound and naked was both an action and the contemplation of it. Carlo *was* bound naked to that wheel, and, at the same time, *he saw himself there.* Not only that, but someone was speaking to him (as if sug-gesting to him, or, rather, teaching him, with a patience similar to the

/unappealable severity/ of parents and childhood teachers in the act of /instilling/ a duty). It was a "humble immemorial serene"[10] chorus that, although intermittent, with lengthy pauses, and lost every so often in the nothingness, was telling Carlo what he himself was experiencing at that moment, and not only that but what he was observing.

The Wheel was turning; whether it was turning fast or slowly was a relative concept, which in that dimension was meaningless. The important thing was that Carlo always returned to the same point (as the "humble immemorial serene" chorus led him to observe). But what was this point? Lacking any reference in that brown, desertlike evening space, Carlo could not recognize any particular point. All the points were exactly the same as one another with respect to the utter bareness of the space, and they were, naturally, all the same with respect to the center, as is the case with every self-respecting circumference. And yet, in effect, *there was a point.* And when Carlo arrived *at this point,* he not only knew it—finding himself there with his body—but saw it, as if he were a spectator of himself; and furthermore the chorus, becoming perhaps a little less "humble immemorial serene," did not fail to let him know. It had been *at that point,* for example, that, in the beginning (?) of the dream, Carlo had seen /exactly, perfectly/ in the center—that is, in the hub of the Wheel—the first scene he was called on to contemplate. It was two serpents in a knot (also enormous, baroque)—down where the spokes of the Wheel ended. The two seemed to form a single serpent twisted back on itself, with dry, violet scales, which had a strange prominence in the colorless air. When Carlo, pulled along in his course, returned for the second time *to the point* and looked, the two serpents had detached themselves from each other and were lying on the ground, in the abstract space of the Wheel's center, as if lifeless; they had also got smaller, had become simply two dead grass snakes dried out by the summer sun. But a woman was standing in their place. She was a savage. She had a low forehead: the roots of her hair reached almost to her snub nose and fell bristling, smeared with some repellent oil, behind her short neck onto scrawny shoulders. She was standing the way pregnant women stand, straight, with her slightly distended stomach

[10] Sandro Penna.

forward, and in her eyes and on her broad lips was a sort of shameless smile. But the curious thing was not that barbaric look, as someone simpleminded and unfeeling, or the strange, ironic consciousness that emanated from her entire ugly little body, but the fact that an enormous penis was hanging from her stomach: it was a penis—flaccid, since, evidently, it was not erect—but /full of the same obscure force and sprinkled/ with the same black pigment that /one imagines/ in priapic men or in beasts, asses, mules. The obscenely beckoning \allusive\ smile in the woman's eyes sprang \originated and grew\ from her possession of that penis. But she was not alone: the "scene" also included (unnoticed at first) a man standing beside her, in her shadow, if one could put it that way (in that world there was neither light nor shadow). He was incredibly small: a cherub, a rag doll that children play with, an elf, a dwarf. However, if viewed alone, in himself, he was perfectly proportioned. His expression was virile and mild at the same time; he had the look of a young father who has only just got married and is still a boy himself. His penis, too, was hanging down above his legs, but it was a normal penis, and in the natural modesty of his nakedness one didn't notice it. But a little above it, on the other hand, in the groin, a long cut, a deep black wound, was clearly visible. The man, bending over himself, held it a little apart with his fingers, as if he wished to display it, and he gazed at it, raising his eyes every so often with a patient, protective smile. Carlo knew, and the chorus—from the < ... > internal spaces of that universe—confirmed it for him, that the deep cut in the man's groin was the vulva. At the next turn of the Wheel, the Scene in the center from which the spokes radiated changed again. The serpents were no longer there, nor was the woman or the man. There was himself, Carlo; but he was dead (or perhaps, although he was in the world, he had never been born). His body was perfectly rigid, like a rock; rather, it was really the body of an ancient stone monument. The chorus let him know, from the depths, that that was joy and there would never be a greater joy.

But now Carlo understood the rotation of the Wheel, and he also knew that the "point" was almost at the top and to the right of someone looking at the Wheel. So now, beginning its rotation again, it would go down, would plunge into the gray vastness, in order then to climb back up and arrive at the top, on the right, and from there he would have the marvelous possibility of contemplating a new scene. And meanwhile he was enjoying the rotation of the Wheel in space with the same excitement (and butterflies in his stomach) that a child feels going up and down in a swing. Soon he returned to the "point," and from there he looked in the direction of the hub of the Wheel. The monument of his own body stiffened by death was now a Penis, an enormous stone Penis; a Lingam; and next to it was a grand old man with a white beard and gentle, suffering eyes: an old saint, who must be extremely good but also, one saw, extremely intransigent and certainly capable, if it should be necessary, of remaining absolutely untouched by pity.

Once again the Wheel plunged into space, rotated on itself, and again Carlo returned to the Point. This time, there, in the center < ... > he was a boy on the shore of the sea, where a boat was rocking; all around, a population of barbarians watched while a man (whose face could not be seen) covered him with marks; finally this man gave him a stick on which there was an enormous spiral shell; and although he cried like a child who has to leave its mother, the man shoved him violently, with his barbarian's hands, toward the boat, which was ready to leave for distant places. The Chorus told Carlo a very odd thing: "Look, you have been born for the second time."

The Rotation began again: on the Wheel's hub there was now a small, normal, ordinary old man for Carlo to contemplate: neither more nor less than a petit bourgeois in a modern-day gray suit; Carlo recognized him immediately: it was his father. Next to his father was an unknown young man, without a face but with an enormous penis, powerful, obscure, like that of the woman in the First Scene. The manner of Carlo's father was not the one that Carlo, awake, had for so many years habitually ascribed to him: it was completely new, as if full of a radiant newness.

THE NEXT ROTATION OF THE WHEEL†

< ... > /In the next rotation/ of the Wheel, Carlo understood immediately that the spectacle would no longer unfold for him in a regular suc-

cession of Scenes, in the Center of the Wheel; from now on the spectacle would unfold outside, in the surrounding space. /Which/ was no longer the naked cosmos but the desert.† And in that desert, in fact at that moment, the sun was rising. Its long, slanted rays grazed the sand and the rocks, scoring < ... > with long shadows.‡ In an oasis or near a ford, where there were some thorny bluish plants, two young men coming from two opposite parts of the desert met: first they looked at each other with fear and hatred, then they came closer and, although continuing to look at each other with distrust§, shook hands. Then other young men, naked and strong like them—and all with the prominent, bestial, powerful penis of that woman of the First Scene—began to arrive, some alone, some together, in that place in the desert (where a tall, pointed rock—Carlo saw it now—in the shape of an obelisk or a stairway rose). At first they looked at one another with the hostility of strangers; then—as it seemed—they decided instead to become friends, to embrace in a pact of alliance. They had already lighted a fire, and some—for all that it may seem anachronistic—were singing and drinking wine. "They are brothers and orphans," the humble immemorial serene chorus announced. That pierced Carlo's heart with an inexpressible sadness.

At that point he woke up. But for a moment the dream continued, though he was awake; the moment necessary for him to become conscious (a consciousness prompted, from a now indescribable distance, by the chorus) that among those "brothers" a new character was arriving, something like a "Devil," a "Spirit of Evil," provided with a name—Polis, or something like that—as Carlo had time to think, or, rather, to find out.‖

NOTE 18
Things irrelevant to Pasquale

Carlo's dream had a little appendix at the lunch table. The same day, his father, who had been away on business during that whole time, returned. Thus the entire family was present at lunch that day. This fact was incidental (because < ... > for twenty years /it had not had/ the least importance); nevertheless, it did /have/ < ... > a certain significant solemnity. The father was sitting at the head of the table. And it was curious because he was just as Carlo had seen him the night before in his dream. Wearing a dark suit and unattractive eyeglasses with tortoiseshell earpieces, he had a rather efficient, youthful air that made him somewhat ill at ease.

Suddenly, looking at him, Carlo remembered a part of his dream—or was adding to it now, as if the dream were continuing.

"You return," said the immemorial chorus, "you return." And it meant to say "You return *to that point*"; but, in this case, the point was no longer "at the top on the right" but at the bottom in the center, where the cosmic abyss deepened like a chasm, and where (this knowledge, too, was absolute but utterly unfounded) the shadows of the characters who had appeared in the Scenes at the center of the Wheel were projected.

When it was time to serve the fruit, the father—becoming a little more talkative—always with that slightly /disgusting/ youthfulness, and perhaps because of the same wine the grandmother had—made a witty remark about some political event of the moment (1960–61, I remind the reader). At those words of his father's, Carlo felt another internal, or prophetic, agitation. It seemed to him that he had never in his life considered the burden that persons of his own and his father's sex, that is, males, represented for him, and above all (but this had not reached the threshold of consciousness) young males; and he thought

that sooner or later he would have to know about their existence, with
the same physical brutality with which he now confronted the presence
of his father: his old father.

NOTE 19
Balance sheet

In conclusion: during the period of his return to Turin, as it remained
\was\ scrupulously noted in Pasquale's "stolen report," Carlo had complete sexual relations—and for the most part repeatedly—with his
mother, with his four sisters, with his grandmother, with a friend of the
last, with the family servant, with her fourteen-year-old daughter, with
two dozen girls of the same age and even younger, with a dozen women
in his mother's "set." In addition, he had exhibitionist relations (which
did or did not conclude with a certain sort of complicity or with an incomplete sexual relation, such as, for example, masturbation) with at
least a hundred underage girls and as many older (but in any case under
twenty); he made use of half a dozen pimps and masturbated—infinitely delaying ejaculation—practically every time he found himself
alone, even if in public.

I have reported all this, with great difficulty, "as seen" by Pasquale,
that is, /through < ... > his report/. Now Pasquale had finished his assignment. And we can release ourselves from him and his linguistic restrictions. Because, let it be immediately clear, Carlo would continue to
behave during the following years and decades as he had behaved during that sojourn in his native city: and even worse.

NOTE 19A
A discovery at Porta Portese

It was a hot morning in June. Summer had arrived suddenly. The asphalt and the paving stones were scorching, and mixed with the stench of garbage burned by a sun unimaginably pure and bright was the odor of wild plants bursting forth everywhere: amid the hovels of the shantytowns, amid the old blocks of seventeenth-century buildings, amid the little factories massed along the banks of the Tiber, and especially on the edges of the Tiber, which carried into the city the rampant, rank vegetation of the nearby countryside. But under that /immemorial/ sun, in whose transparency—so intense that there was something thick and milky about it, especially in its /depths/—it seemed that only the slow and profoundly silent actions of the ancient life of the old neighborhood could unfold, there was instead a deafening, indescribable hubbub. Automobiles, trucks, delivery vans, bicycles, pushcarts rushing; and the crowd: /immense, apprehensive, shouting/. A great holiday and a busy workday seemed to be mixed together, which got everyone excited, especially since that crowd was made up mainly of boys and young men.

Perhaps because the sun penetrated things and from within they xxx its deep, dry splendor, the crowd that was mingling under the arches of Porta Portese and down along the avenue, xxx, was a southern xxx crowd. The light oozed from thin brown limbs, from bony faces, from eyes that gleamed with eager blackness, from shorn necks, and from the voices themselves, hoarse with the shouting and joking that had begun at dawn, when it was still dark out.

The Venetian literary man with the surname ending in -*on* was \was walking\ in the midst of that crowd; though he was not the only intellectual there, in the middle of that proletarian /crowd/, he was all alone. Through the pushing and shoving he walked in his elegant blue summer suit, from stall to stall, with an air of curiosity and availability. Although he was alone, he was clearly performing a social act; he knew it, and he did not at all suspect the conventionality of it; in fact, if anything, he was proud of it, and his glance wandered in search /of the "discovery"/ that was always possible, in the expanses of useless objects, < ... > /which seemed to be staring wildly, emerging from the darkness of shops and cellars into all that blinding brightness of the morning sun/. He looked, he stopped, he pondered before some object, dismissed it ironically, passed on to another. The same thing happened before a stall poorer than the others—if it could even be called a stall. In fact, all the wares were spread on the ground, on the bare dust. Behind them, grazed by the feet of the crowd that walked along past the open doors of the shops, were the sellers: three young men between fifteen and thirty, whom the excitement and a night spent in the open (sleeping on the ground, just where they were now) had reduced to silence: an extraordinarily expressive silence, however. Not a single part of their bodies was still, from their slobbery mouths to their cheekbones that seemed to have been struck and disfigured by a hammer, from the sparkling eyes to the thick hair that seemed to glow on ears that stuck out like tufts. And yet there was in their eyes and their gestures a sort of indifferent happiness, which made them like sphinxes who had landed there, filthy and xxx, from far away. The three were thieves, or fences at least, like, moreover, most of their colleagues; and they were Neapolitan. Thus the things they were selling were nothing to them, had no significance or real value: books, old manuscripts, yellowed portraits of famous people, records of twenty or thirty years before, little Art Nouveau or nineteenth-century *objets* for library or boudoir. . . . Our literary man stopped in front of that shop laid out in the dust and began to observe distractedly, with a slight nervous yawn fixed on his half-open lips; wrinkling his forehead, he looked at that worthless stuff, already prepared to continue on his exploration, when, for some reason, his attention was attracted by a suitcase full of books sitting next to a portrait of no less a personage than General Graziani: some of the books had in fact spilled out, and it was the title of one of these which had caught the attention of our Venetian intellectual; it was a title that to an Italian sounded comical: Shklovsky's *Sterna i teoriya romana*. And with this the reader will have understood what suitcase it was. Faintly curious, since at first glance he had realized that it was a matter of a real, /very coherent/ little library, our intellectual began to pick among the books and leaf through them. The first book that came into his hands was a cheap edition of Dostoyevsky's *The Possessed:* completely underlined, one might say, from the first line to the last; almost stuck to it, /as if/ it were a single volume, was *The Brothers Karamazov,* much less thoroughly underlined but with more decisiveness and almost violence: certain pages had even been torn by the point of the pen. Then an edition, also a cheap one, of the *Divine Comedy,* in which there was only one mark: a big corner of the page where Canto XXIX of Purgatory began was turned down. Whereas the pages on Dante (and also those on de Sade) in a little French volume, *L'Écriture et l'expérience des limites,* by Philippe Sollers, were heavily underlined. There followed, in no order, all of Swift, all of Hobbes, all of Pound. Very heavily underlined and even annotated was all of Propp. Next to Propp, evidently /not by chance/, was Apollonius Rhodius, *The Argonauts.* And Ferenczi's *Thalassa.* There was Plato's *Republic* and Aristotle's *Politics:* read, certainly, but not much underlined. And similarly Schreber's *Memoirs of a Neuropath* and Strindberg's *Inferno.* The presence of Roberto Longhi right there in the middle aroused his curiosity: *Piero della Francesca,* < ... > which evidently had already passed through many hands, and a whole pile of various writings, mostly magazines. In the center of the suitcase, as if in a "place of honor," were the following five books: *Don Quixote, Tristram Shandy, Dead Souls, Ulysses,* and *Finnegans Wake.* Amid another pile of books (the Old Testament, the poetry of Belli, and a dozen volumes of linguistics) that had fallen out of the suitcase. /There was < ... > also the report of Pasquale Bucciarelli. They had been stolen together./ The intellectual began to skim it a little, amused, while there below, crouched beside their goods, the three silent Neapolitans, in their excited happiness, eyed him, waiting for him to decide; they did not, however, give him the satisfaction of exhibiting the least anxiety, remaining there in the attitude of thieves, /marked/ by fatigue and by the sun, with their darkly shining eyes above the cheekbones of starving wolves.

↑

—quote some of the more significant underlined passages
—give the editions with some philological information

Note in pen on a page of the *Argonautica* (Greek-English): "Pay no attention! Every great writer writes only to fill the blank page with marks" and in smaller letters: "Every great writer loves centones above all. The culture of every great writer is medieval."

NOTE 20
Carlo—as if in a novel by Sterne—
abandoned in the act of going to a Reception

While that Carlo whom I am unfortunately forced to call "the Second" or to distinguish by giving him a nickname like Carolus or Karl, which reeks unpleasantly of literature, was living his "Poem of Return" in Turin, the Carlo whom for symmetry I should call "the First" and who in effect is the Carlo par excellence (in the sense of social privilege) was also about to make his leap forward. Popularly, the word is "career." In reality, however, it is a question of something else. We should never accept the language of our enemies; a man's self-fulfillment has no moral limits of any kind. For now, this Carlo No. 1 was satisfied to seek protectors, through whom he would later be able to fulfill himself completely and consistently by himself in historical life, in the life of the City: which was something more than his right.

There is an inevitable symmetry in the beginning of the two stories that constitute the subject of my work; thus the story of Carlo No. 1 also starts not far from the house he had rented in that then stylish neighborhood. This story concerns the salon of Signora F., but a series of digressions will expand it enormously. I do not mean to say, however—I insist on being precise—that the symmetry I'm speaking of is at all unbalanced; in fact, behind the setting and the imaginary persons who presided at the beginning of the story of Carlo No. 2 there is a long perspective that transcends them \goes far beyond them\, even if it's the wretched swarm of anthropologically inferior men who proclaim their right to history by blackmailing us in exchange for their servility: who come from the parts of the nation that are in every sense the lowest.

It was an evening in the middle of spring, mysteriously damp and cold but also, and just as mysteriously, dry and warm. What filled it with mystery \such ambiguity\ < ... > might have been a storm gathering—but in silence, with neither thunder nor wind—over that grand neighborhood, or, on the contrary, perhaps sky and earth were opening wide toward the /peace/ of fine weather, the still stormy fringes of the clouds lit up by the /solemn/ starry sky.

Taking deep breaths of the mysterious air, as if it were his own future made cold or warm on that evening full of forebodings, Carlo had just left his house and was walking with long strides, his overcoat open and flapping heavily, being an xxx made of English rubber (and thus making a realistic contribution to the Oxymoron that presides over this passage of our story).

Beside Carlo—breathing the /icy-hot, dark-sparkling/ air less deeply—and proceeding with less urgency along the streets of the Parioli, toward the house of Signora F., in that /calm-stormy, lifeless-seething/ neighborhood—walked a man of his age and almost identical to him.

He had the same youthful shock of hair, though it was now a little thin, that danced like a wing on his forehead, the same dark coloring of face and hair, the dark coloring of Italians of the North, the same athletic build hidden in a body that appeared frail, the same slightly ape-like walk. The shape of the face differed a little: the cheekbones were a little rounder where Carlo's were pronounced, the chin weaker where Carlo's was strongly molded; the expression more ironic and abstracted where Carlo's was full of a childish seriousness and as if numbed by a kind of terror composed of both anxiety and hope.

The rules that preside over the exposition of my story, even if they are not yet explicit and autonomous—and so are relative only to themselves—oblige me to wander into a parenthesis regarding this friend of Carlo's. It doesn't matter if, after this crucial moment, he is destined not to reappear in our story. Look, then: he's a school friend of Carlo's, Guido Casalegno by name. Not having had Carlo's problems, he was much farther on in that self-fulfillment which is called a career. Neither il-lusions nor de-lusions had distracted him from that "lusion," from that <...> "ludic" <...> construction that does not disappoint expectations and that is in substance, if I may continue to express myself in this fashion, col-lusion with whoever plays best and for the longest time: the power. In the present case, the great agency ENI. Casalegno had been a friend of Carlo Valletti's in high school. At university they had lost sight of each other. By family tradition Casalegno was enrolled in law, while Carlo, having no such tradition, had chosen, as we have seen, engineering. Upon graduating, however, Casalegno had not followed a traditional career. His learning was eclectic (in addition to the law, he knew literature and sociology), and it was eclectic at the exact moment when the boom of specialization was exploding. Where it was logical to expect a specialized "executive," a technician, he offered the figure of a "jack of all trades," although essentially honest. Now, while ENI was an agency, it was also a /topos/ of power, which is too well known for me to dwell on explanations. The suture between these two forms or modes of being could not absorb, in its concrete historical aspect—that is, in the fluctuating reduction and expansion of staff and nearly nameless offices—regular specialized personnel. And so it was in this mixed, suture-like terrain that Casalegno had made his way. There had been in those years (when these maneuvers had not yet come to light; they were considered innocent, ordinary administrative moves) an obscure shifting of pawns in an area important to an organism of power that, like ENI, is of the government and at the same time not of the government: the press. For example, in Milan the new *Avvenire* came out, originating in a merger of the Bolognese Catholic daily and the Lombard daily of the same name and published by Nuova Editoriale Italiana S.p.A. ENI had a particular predilection for this journal, which was not limited to special advertising. The salaries of the editors and the contributors went up so much that the envy of *Il Corriere della Sera* was roused; the number of pages was increased, features, reporting, etc. Indeed, some journalists from *Il Corriere* were hired—for example, the assistant editor in chief of the sports pages—along with editors from ANSA and *Panorama;* not to mention other, more unusual types, such as, for example, the former editor of *Ciao Big;* the former editor of *Kent,* the monthly for men only; the former editor of *Sí* (an affiliate of ABC); and the former editor in chief of ABC itself. The president of Nuova Editoriale Italiana S.p.A., Ettore Zolla, becomes one of the top directors of ENI: he is, in particular, Troya's right-hand man. I would like to call the reader's attention to that point: in fact, Aldo Troya, the vice president of ENI, is destined to become one of the key personages of our story.[11]

The vice president of Nuova Editoriale Italiana is, at this moment in our story, Guido Casalegno himself. His rise had been extraordinarily rapid. He had begun in SNAM, under Bonocore, the president of ENI, when SNAM literally signified National Methane Pipeline Company: destined, in its time, as we will see, to be liquidated by Troya in order to be relaunched with the same name but without its old functions. In the first version of SNAM, Casalegno was employed in an administrative job, and there he distinguished himself through particular and, as regards us, quite fictional merits. Indeed, President Enrico Bonocore was so taken up by the whirlwind of his activities—those of a founder, and belonging to a mythical era—that he could not find the time even to sign the hundreds of *ordinary* letters (for the more important letters, he used an autograph seal): it was therefore Casalegno—I repeat, a man essentially honest—who signed the ordinary correspondence of Enrico Bonocore: signing in full, with an admirable imitation of the Head's genuine signature. As a result of that unlimited manual patience, Guido Casalegno at present held the job we have mentioned, in addition to being administrative director of SNAM and manager of the Segisa Division, thus controlling, both administratively and financially, *Il Giorno;* and he had begun to be part of the small, fluctuating oligarchy of the so-called empire of the Troyas.

So it was along with this powerful friend that Carlo was going to Signora F.'s salon, in a state of mind that was dramatic and ambiguous

---

[11] *Translator's note:* Troya—the name resembles an Italian word for "bitch"—is Eugenio Cefis, who took over as head of ENI after the death of his predecessor, Enrico Mattei (here called Bonocore), in a mysterious plane crash. David Ward writes, in *A Poetics of Resistance,* "It is now generally accepted that under Cefis's stewardship, the State Oil Company ceased to be controlled by its managers as it had been under Mattei, but fell into the hands of Italy's rapacious political parties. In other words, this was the moment when corruption in the shape of the huge kickback scandal that has rocked Italy's political foundations found its first systematic form."

at the same time. The most diverse expressions crossed his face in a tumultuous, unbecoming way: now there was almost a smile, as of one who is possessed by the ecstasy of a life that appears suddenly full of intense and profound promises, even if yet unknown, indeed unnamed; now there was dismay, both at an inevitable debacle, preordained by his own nature, and a premature anguish for the sort of "cosmic" vanity of every possible self-fulfillment on earth. There was, too, an almost vulgar and servile expression toward his friend, who, though he had not spoken of it, was tacitly giving him his protection for a first xxx xxx; but at the same time he had that thuggish sneer of disdain that provincial young men—just because they are young—<have> in the name of culture, <...> for events like the one that awaited him that spring night in the salon of Signora F. (whose house, all lit up and with cars moving in front of it, already stood out at the end of a small, sloping tree-lined street in the heart of the Parioli).

Carlo was free. What had until that moment kept him from throwing himself headlong into life (which, being "social" life, is /marvelous and agonizing/) had separated from him, like a ballast that reins in flight. Separating from him, it had begun a story of its own, parallel to his: and he, in fact, was living the first moments of his freedom. Not only his joy but also his fear. And this was not the only contradiction, because, as we have seen, the one who, in detaching himself, had freed him had experienced a total freedom of his own—absolutely oblivious of every duty and even social convention—and had in turn arrived at the limit beyond which not even the most total freedom can go. That, too, can be known. Rather, it cannot not be known. Such a knowledge of freedom means the possibility of its end. Perhaps because behind him, consciously or unconsciously, there was this inextricable knot of freedom gained and lost, unconfined and guarded, Carlo looked at the sparkling house of Signora F. with an arrested, openmouthed expression, as in a snapshot taken unexpectedly, his step impetuous and at the same time uncertain—as if he had been suspended in an act of conquest by a metaphysical doubt—that "fixed" the folds of his flapping xxx in the style of a mannerist painting. . . .

NOTE 21
Flashes of light on ENI

NOTE 22
Troya's so-called empire: Troya himself

Troya himself is a man of about fifty, but he looks younger. The first
thing that strikes one about him is the smile. It's striking first of all because one feels immediately that it is a smile that has become a /stereo-
type/. He is a public man, so he is obliged to smile, apparently; but his
smile, instead of being < ... > reassuring, shining, in fact radiant, the
smile of "an average man," who, being a good family man, a likable
worker, a devout Catholic, has nothing to reproach himself with: /not
even/ of course, his smile, /which shows all his teeth,/ and declares that,
at heart, he doesn't take life too seriously, given that life is already, in itself, wonderful, worth living, and in just that way. No. It was not a
smile of that kind, so common \widespread\ among public men. Troya's
smile is instead a smile of complicity, almost conspiratorial: it is definitely a guilty smile. With it Troya seems to wish to say to anyone who
looks at him that he knows very well that the one who is looking at him
considers him a despicable and ambitious man, capable of anything, absolutely without weakness, in spite of his demeanor of a former penni-
less boarding-school boy and ass-licker: and he would also like to say, to
anyone who considers him such a man, that < ... > that person may
< ... > go ahead and do so, and that if, by chance, there should be ac-
counts to settle on this point, the matter was, objectively, postponed in-

definitely (that is, until the day when Troya would no longer hold power). Not only that, but every settling of accounts with the powerless and idealistic "simple citizen" who had formulated a judgment on the /disgusting/ truth about him—which he himself admitted—was always in some way put off by something more urgent, more publicly urgent. And it was this "secret of something more urgent" that, above all, was hidden by Troya's smile. In the end, this smile also expressed another message, an essential message, indispensable and I would say almost sacred in Italy: the shrewdly smiling Troya wished it to be known, without an interruption or break in continuity, and by all, that he was shrewd. Therefore he should be left alone, for pity's sake, because he "knew certain things," "had urgent business of national importance" (which someday or other would be known), because he "was so capable and shall we say even crafty" that he always managed things in the best way and in the best interests of all. Naturally, being a smile of complicity it was also an imploring smile; that is, it sought compassion for its evident guilt. As if to confirm everything that smile meant to say—not without a kind of affability, as from one intellectual to another, if not, indeed, from one citizen to another—his head was continually drawn back between his shoulders, so much so that it gave the impression that Troya was slightly hunchbacked. And in fact, if you like, his head was somewhat like the head of a hunchback: round, with a protruding forehead, smooth hair, a small, weak chin. As for his eyes, behind the glasses, they were round and, because of the continuous movement of that conspiratorial guilty smile, expressive. They stuck firmly to anyone who observed him, only to flee immediately. He < ... > walked < ... > quickly; the impression of speed was intensified by the fact that he was always holding under his arm magazines, folders full of papers, and even books, which made him appear very busy.

It is known that he was born in Sacile—a town in the province of Pordenone (but Udine when he was born)—in 1921. His father was the steward of a patrician Degano family, landowners (in a manner of speaking), impoverished and scattered early on, even before he finished his studies. His father, an old Catholic and an anti-Fascist if ever there was one (but then Fascist until 1943), became, on the other hand, quite wealthy (always, however, a peasant wealth, local). In spite of this wealth, the Troyas continued to live in the old, modest house near the church square: an old house in the Venetian style, like all the others, with gray porticoes and charming wrought-iron pergolas. Not far away—that is, behind the church—ran the Livenza, green and deep, on whose banks, it /seems/, the little Troya went to play with the other boys of the parish. This is all that is known of the first part of his life: a dull, obscure legend that Troya never cared to make clear or xxx in any way. He did not like any form of publicity whatsoever. By the very na- ture of his power, he had to remain in shadow. And there in fact he did remain. Every possible "source" of information about him mysteriously as well as systematically disappeared. No anecdotes were told about him, not even a joke. And that was extraordinarily un-Italian, in con- trast to his "shrewd" smile; but it was not, as we will see, without a cer- tain logic. It was known that he went around in a car, a green Citroën xxx, not registered to him (therefore he did not own even a modest Cit- roën); and it was known that he collected white ceramic objects (which made some small tables—certainly not rare antiques—in his house and also in his office look like little cemeteries). That was all that was known at present about his person. Business was the language in which he expressed himself, and so to interpret him I ought to be a business- man as well as a detective. I have done the best I can, and you'll see what I found out.

NOTE 22A

The so-called empire of the Troyas:
the branches closest to the mother company

Troya, who emigrated to Milan in 1943, was not /unexpectedly/ unpre- pared for his choices, as it seems, from the end of Fascism and the beginning of the Resistance. In fact, he took part in the Resistance (this, as we'll see, constitutes the *scandal*). There was a mixed group of De Gasperians and Republicans (the *mixture* started immediately, as we'll see) who fought in the mountains of the Brianza. The head of that partisan group was the current president of ENI, Ernesto Bonocore. (Neither Troya nor Bonocore, as the reader must have noticed, is a northern name; it was in effect a question of immigrants. Their mothers were from the North: Troya's a certain Pinetta Spríngolo from Sacile and Bonocore's a certain Rosa Bonali, from Bescapè (xxx).) As regards the anti-Fascist undertakings of the partisan group led by Bonocore, which were unexceptionable and respectable despite the *mixture,* I have already alluded to them in the section entitled "Flashes of Light on ENI," and to that I refer anyone who wishes to refresh his memory. Mine is a /novel/ not "on a spit" but "in a swarm,"[12] and so it's understandable if the reader remains a little < ... > disoriented. What I would like to underline is the following: in the partisan group Troya was the *second in command.* And the role had seemed to fit him magnificently ever since. I don't want to mythicize, but Troya did not believe in being first merely to be first. He was something more than ambitious. Therefore he did not have the weaknesses of the ambitious; his life, his look, his behavior were gray, or, to be more precise, ascetic. They always had been. As the "second" (second in command or vice president), he could more fully realize his ascetic tendency to "produce." Probably he hadn't calculated it but limited himself simply to piling up and constructing his own destiny according to his own nature. He did not advance, he accumulated. He did not rise, he expanded. It would take too long and would be impossible for me, besides, to follow the whole slow story (two decades) of this accumulation and this expansion. I will therefore confine myself to a panorama, such as might present itself to an observer /at the moment < ... > of/ our story. The < ... > incongruities < ... > between the gray and ascetic character of Troya and the "fictional" physical portrait I have given of him: but that is part of the swarm, or vortex, /which is the/

---

[12] *Translator's note:* "On a spit" and "in a swarm" are literal translations of *a schidionata* and *a brulichio.* By "novel on a spit" Pasolini seems to mean a narrative form that follows a conventional, progressive cause-and-effect logic, as represented by the *schidione,* or long metal spit on which meat is roasted. By contrast, the "novel in a swarm" seems to mean an openended, digressive, nonlinear narrative, as represented by the word *brulichio,* which generally refers to the swarming, teeming activity of ants. (See Ward, pp. 108ff.)

structural model of my tale; and the reader must take it as an enter-
tainment.

Thus, Troya is at this time vice president of ENI. But this is merely
an official position, preliminary to a further leap forward, due not so
much to an ambitious will as to the objective and massive accumulation
of the forces commanded by that will. For now the true power of Troya
is in his private empire, if such a distinction is possible. Troya has always consistently \instinctively\ acted under the sign of *The Mixture*. So
there is really no line between what is his and what is the public's. Nevertheless, at least one of the fiefdoms of his so-called empire is definitely,
in the classical sense, his own; it is, however, a fairly distant fiefdom,
across the ocean, in Argentina to be exact, on the immense plains near
Mar del Plata. Here he has an actual little "domain," whose feudal lord
has apparently been for many years his brother Ivan. A brother who
went directly from Sacile to Mar del Plata, transplanted there with the
ease that, in whatever latitude, the earth gives to one who cultivates it.
Ivan was the very image of Pinetta Spríngolo, his mother. He was completely Sacilese; or, rather, proto-Sacilese (the substratum of Sacile is
Friulian, while the bourgeoisie, which also imposed itself linguistically,
is from the Veneto). He was a Solomonic and stooped peasant with a red
face, especially the nose, and he inevitably wore a creased hat with a soft
brim. This Ivan will never appear in our story again. The other principal foundation of Troya's empire was the Società Immobiliari e Partecipazioni (?), registered to Amelia Gervasoni. This Amelia Gervasoni was
one of those women who are found only in Milan, although they are of
provincial origin. She had already passed forty, she was a spinster (or at
least she thought \conceived\ of herself in that antiquated term) of
unimpeachable morality, a pure moralist. She had preserved in her thin,
bony features a sense of inferiority: as a woman (and a spinster) and as a
petite bourgeoise (and a provincial). But these weaknesses were also her
strength. Objectively, in fact, they kept her from having unattainable
ambitions and in consequence made her ascetic, like her powerful
brother-in-law. She was the sister of Troya's wife, a Gervasoni who came
from xxx. She therefore knew very well that she was a < ... > figurehead,
but, precisely because she was not ambitious, she made herself useful,
not only in name; and although a subordinate, she efficiently played a

role in the business. That's also why we will often find her name in the continuation of our somewhat . . . swarming "dossier." Amelia Gervasoni had even become an elegant woman, with a perfect Via Montenapoleone elegance; she had ended up somewhat resembling, through antiphrasis, Camilla Cederna: Camilla Cederna "by not being Cederna." Nevertheless, /even/ < ... > her hairdresser, the best, was discreet; her scarves were not showy, nor were her skirts, < ... > or her shoes. Except that all these "discreet" things put together ended up becoming a little bit indiscreet and revealing their origin: an origin that included something "antique" as well, which, contrasting with her efficiency, made her if not sympathetic at least not antipathetic. Enough. From Immobiliari e Partecipazioni eight more companies, or corporations—I don't know what the hell to call them—were born, arranged, so to speak, in two ranks. In the first rank: La Aronese, Inv. Imm., S. Floreano, DBDI; in the second rank: Spiritcasauno, Spiritcasadieci, Cen-Mer, and SIL.

The reason for the two rather "swarmlike" names of Spiritcasauno and Spiritcasadieci is simply that at the present time Carlo Troya was living in Via Santo Spirito in Milan. Let's begin with the first rank. Aronese: a limited partnership simply for acquiring, operating, and owning and managing real estate. Formed in March of '59. There are two partners: the first is a Mrs. Donata Bandel Dragone, who is Aldo Troya's secretary, and who, in contrast to Amelia Gervasoni, is only a figurehead (and in many instances, as we will see). Since she accepts that function to the letter and so doesn't care at all about the business, she can allow herself to be an extremely vain woman, but only outside the Troya universe (where she is ascetic). The other partner in Aronese is the General Lake Investment Trust of Coira.

Inv. Imm.: Investimenti Immobiliari. Limited partnership that invests in industrial and commercial businesses, real estate and money management, buying and selling of real estate. Among the partners Donata Bandel Dragone figures again, as I noted, but this time Amelia Gervasoni is added, as well as the usual General Lake Investment Trust of Coira.

San Floreano: limited partnership real estate company (formed somewhat more recently) for investment in industrial and commercial businesses, management of personal property, buying and selling real estate. The first partner is the eternal Donata Bandel Dragone, the second this time is Ladina Établissement of Coira.

DBDI: that is, Donata Bandel Dragone Immobiliare: real estate management. A limited company formed in March 1949 (when Donata Bandel Dragone was very young; it was her first test as a mythical figurehead, still, historically, in the ambience of the Resistance). The detail that characterizes this branch of the Troyan empire is that the famous aforementioned bottle-green Citroën is registered to it.

Now let's go to the second row of offshoots.

Spiritcasauno: limited company for the acquisition and management of real estate, founded in February of 1951 but taken over by Troya ten years later. A single director: Donata Bandel Dragone. Troya's office in Via Santo Spirito is also listed under her name.

Spiritcasadieci: (un)limited company, founded in '51, also taken over by Troya about ten years later, for acquiring and managing real estate. A single director: Donata Bandel Dragone, who is said not to have known it.

Cen-Mer (Centro-Meridione): limited company for buying, selling, and managing real estate, formed in '58 but taken over by Troya later, in '60. Sole director: Donata Bandel Dragone.

SIL: Società Immobiliare Lombarda, limited company, for the sale and management of real estate. Sole director: Donata Bandel Dragone.

NOTE 22B
The so-called empire of the Troyas:
another important branch

Aldo Troya had a third brother, Quirino, who was midway between Aldo and Ivan, that is, between Ciociaria and Sacile, between sandals and clogs, although he was the oldest: he had the thin face and narrow nose of Pinetta Spríngolo, or rather, as they say up there, "Spríngola," but the round head and the shrewd yet slightly ill-at-ease eyes of father Troya (the elder Troya had always felt guilty about his progression as a southerner to the Veneto). To Quirino was entrusted the shuttle between Milan and Coira, almost a Ladin destination and, moreover, buried in time, at least in Sacile. Beside him, however—and he commuted with the religiousness of a peasant who has become a worker—was an old friend who, as for Ladinity, could boast a lot of it, untainted: pure almost to /purism/. In fact, he was from Cividale, Civitas: the City of Friuli; the Florence of Friuli: a certain Erminio Cossut, who had not only, probably, the surname of a Slav but also the long yellow < ... > slanted eyes. After playing *coram montes*—hills now bare and almost grim, now divinely idyllic, /producing/ very good white wine \grapes\—and along the banks of the Isonzo, with its divine little currents, the color of turquoise in any weather—he devoted himself to studies that would have made him a modest businessman if he had not become a school friend of the very Catholic Troya. The trips to Coira, however, were Quirino's infinitely least notable activity, even if probably the most delicate. In general he presided over relations with the international partners in other, non-Ladin tax havens, like Liechtenstein, Luxembourg, and the Principality of Monaco: it was a matter of partners functioning as limited partners, such as Pentavalor Trust Reg. of Eschen (?), Universoil Investment Trust of Coira, Abat Finance Établissement of Triesen (?), Iskra Finance Établissement of Triesen (?), Samko Trade Trustreg, VAI of Schaan (?), Tech Finanzanstalt of Coira, Filil Anstalt of Triesen (?), Monasvir Finanz und Industrie Anstalt of Triesen, Nauticwarn Holding AF of Mendrisio, Sosmel of Vaduz, Walalla Établissement of Balzers (?): all companies that had been started precisely as limited partners for third-party guarantees and third-party bonds or to permit greater real estate acquisitions and industrial and commercial investments—also, it should be noted, on behalf of third parties—in other Troyan companies, as we'll see.

N O T E 2 2 C
The so-called empire of the Troyas:
brother Quirino's most important business

But brother Quirino's most important business was Informatica Applicata and its activities, which were directly under his control. Informatica Applicata in turn generated three /subsidiary/ companies. Lignea of
Quirino Troya & Co. Sas, located not far from Santo Spirito, in Via Manzoni; company capital: L. 100,000, but the silent partner was that Pentavalor Trust Reg. of Eschen (?) which I've already mentioned. SDN, also
part of Quirino Troya & Co.—capital in this case L. 1,200,000—also in
the neighborhood of Santo Spirito (Via della Spiga). Activity: the usual
real estate investment and management. And finally Pattern Italiana,
which /has a little/ history /of its own/. It had been started some years
before with the name Am.Da. and had been introduced to ENI to offer
its skills and its cooperation in the area of subsidiary services; as with
the other companies, moreover, Troya secured for this one a partner
with a limited partner function, in Hong Kong. Am.Da., Amminis-
trazione Dati, S.p.A., also has its headquarters in Via Manzoni, near its
secret sister companies: its activity, unlike theirs, is "start-up and administration of data processing centers for third parties and itself, rendering services, etc." At the start there was an honest Milanese in
charge, a Cremonese, in fact ("honest" meaning a little too conservative), and so he was soon replaced by another Lombard, that Beolchini—Virgilio Beolchini—whom we find in the same position, chief
executive officer, at the aforementioned SDN. He came from the wife's
side, from the matrilineal branch xxx. As for her, Camilla xxx, the wife,
she had done nothing except give Aldo Troya two children, a boy, Vin-
cenzino, and a girl, Pinetta: two unhappy children, who, since they
were physically xxx, not to say attractive and in good health, might in
other circumstances have been reasonably happy. Besides having those

two children, Camilla xxx Troya also had the virtue of knowing how to feel perfectly at her ease in church, especially at funerals. And it was a real pity, in this regard, that her husband did not have greater ambitions—for example, to become a government minister. A year later, Am.Da. was taken over by Li.De. (Lineamenti Demografici S.p.A.), whose purpose was "printing and sending letters and correspondence, filing systems, etc." With the increase of the initial capital from one to fifteen million lire, the purpose became better defined: "programming businesses for data research and collection, processing and diffusion of information, consulting and services for electronic data processing."

In short, something technically like a small SID[13] (which in a few years would be put to use so profitably by Troya, who had gone on, as will be seen, to another /government job/). Besides, the cultural moment of this Li.De. foreshadows interests that Troya is not completely indifferent to, and, at least initially, those interests have a direct bearing on our story.

Then Li.De. moves to Rome, with a board of three members, until the Troyas' faithful notary (a figure whom I have until now unjustly neglected; his name is Eugenio /Tramontin/, he, too, in terms of class, is a man who speaks Venetian in a Friulian environment) announces that the company's capital is three hundred million lire. One member hands in his resignation. He is replaced by another. And the company takes the name Da.Off., Data Office S.p.A. But only for a little while, because soon the aforementioned Virgilio Beolchini replaces the member who had replaced the member who resigned and the other members as well, who are only now dismissed; and the company is again called Am.Da. It is at this point (capital: nine hundred million lire) that Quirino Troya is named president, and the company, diversifying, expanding, takes the definitive name of Pattern Italiana (Beolchini leaves, one of the dismissed board members returns, and Evelyn Lane, the man in Hong Kong, is added). Pattern Italiana is precociously (for the years I'm speaking of) Americanized: it can offer the ENI of the early sixties the most advanced technology in the field of "computer letters," of compiling "mailing lists," in the problems of "direct marketing."

---

[13]*Translator's note:* SID, or Servizio Informazioni Difesa, is a government intelligence agency.

NOTE 22C
The so-called empire of the Troyas:
the flea speaks ill of the louse

At the head of the two other principal branches of the Troyas' empire are two perfect symbols of the Lombard-Venetian pact that constitutes (though with some shadowy southern roots) the base of that empire. One is Erminio Cossut, of Porpetto, whose physiognomy and childhood days we have already discussed, as well as his association with Troya's older brother, Arduino. As for the other, he, too, had played in the mountains, but it was the lofty xxx foothills of the Alps, not the dark hills of Venezia Giulia; he, too, had wandered along white-graveled shores beside pale blue currents, but of the Oglio, not the Isonzo. He came from xxx, a solidly industrialized small town between the provinces of Bergamo and Brescia. He therefore belonged to the system of the xxx, which was feminine in character: Ermenegildo xxx. For whatever reason, there had always been between Erminio Cossut, of Porpetto, and Ermenegildo xxx, of xxx, a mysterious rivalry, which <...> however <...> exhausted itself in malicious remarks that the two were unable to resist. At this point, Arduino Troya usually intervened with a set formula of sure effectiveness: "The flea speaks ill of the louse." Erminio Cossut was in charge of direct oil production, Ermenegildo xxx of indirect methane production.

From both these matrixes, which do not lack their own modern epic aspect—if not of Homeric proportions, then certainly of Hesiodic— descended, in orderly fashion, new /offspring/; as a trunk forks off into branches and then a tangle of leaves.

Let's begin with direct oil production, for the simple reason that it is with indirect methane production that, in the interest of our story, we must end.

The reader must not forget—I /eagerly/ beg him not to—that this "whirlwind" excursus has an end, and its delaying elements are, in essence, merely "suspense," pure and simple. Following the Troyas' empire in all its branches, we must necessarily end up at a final little branch, the last offshoot, which, being of a double nature, is marked by a dramatic question mark: as we will see, in fact, it lies at the intersection between one universe and another, half here, half there; half in one domain, half in another. And the meaning of the story of Carlo and his choices will be based on that very ambiguity. Enough: at the proper moment, the reader will have a clear idea of this. So let's not anticipate.

However, let's proceed a little more quickly, since precedents have, I believe, been established in the reader's mind for a clear understanding of what follows.

Offshoots of direct oil production: three: MCCC (combustible compressed methane fuels), of which that same Cossut was the director; Usi Meta (use of methane for industrial and civil purposes), also headed by Cossut; and finally, International Petrochemical Instrument Co. (?) : /cisterns, pipes, tanks/; naturally, good investors /are needed/ not only for methane and oil but for materials and drilling infrastructure, both for storage and for processing. Its technological director is xxx xxx (a Lombard), the commercial director xxx xxx (a Venetian), the administrative director xxx xxx (a Lombard), and the director for supplies xxx xxx (a Venetian). This time Erminio is in charge in Iran, the Land of Plenty < ... > so to speak. Naturally, even though I have not /said/ so before now, Erminio Cossut has a brother—how could he not?—Mariano; and so Mariano Cossut (who started up the Cormons project on his own) is the site manager. (But he is also the president of a company, Làssem, that is outside the boundaries of the Troyas' empire but on whose board of directors we find the Lombard xxx xxx and the Venetian xxx xxx.)

We have reached the crown of the leafy tree, and I would like to confine myself, following a device that has the noblest literary precedents, to "lists." But I will linger for just a moment on one of the eight companies, arranged in two rows but not /ranked/, as an example. It is the first one in the first row: Fratelli Panzini, STI (Italian Thermoplastics). Half a dozen years ago, its capital was nine million lire; at the time of our story it was three hundred million (declared). The fact is that Aldo Troya got into it as a member of the board, together with Leone

Panzini, one of his faithful, who was also in Stiem (ENI) and in the press agency Information. Then Troya became president of this marginal company that "molds plastics and related materials"; and naturally under Troya's presidency the range of its activities broadened: not only molding but also the manufacture, production, and sale of objects made of plastic materials and synthetic resins, in particular technical products, housewares, stationery, electrical and plumbing fixtures, religious articles. The first row continues: Fecit, Italo-American Prentice (?), Industria del Legno A. Bortotto. In the second row, SRM, Po-Petrol, Stilgraf, Calzificio Lombardo L. xxx. On the boards of directors and in the management of all these companies we always find the same names, mixed in, of course, with the local, regional ranks of what is vulgarly called the public trough.

NOTE 22D
The so-called empire of the Troyas:
the louse's branch

De Sade teaches us that one must not "require too much of the reader." Going on to indirect methane production, whose head is Ermenegildo xxx, I will therefore try to be considerably briefer and to adopt almost exclusively the "technique of the list."

Three main branches grow out of the trunk of indirect methane production: the Alpha Group, directed by xxx xxx (a Lombard), the Beta Group, directed by xxx xxx (a Venetian), and the Gamma Group (directed by a Tuscan, xxx xxx, the grandson of Gioacchino).

In the lower rank we have the usual teeming /efflorescence/: Fiorani Fabbriche Rinnile, Banca xxx, Linea Società Pubblicità Italiana, xxx Produzioni Cinetelevisive, Tazio Giubertoni, Società Trasporti Speciale, Fibre Tessili Artificiali.

And finally a company or entity or anonymous enterprise that cannot be indicated by anything other than a question mark: "?"

NOTE 22F
The salon of Signora F.: her artistic activities

This Signora F., to whose house Carlo, as a /poor, ironic/ initiate, was going that spring night, was completely round and dwarflike. Her hair was little more than a tuft, a blond brush, usually gathered into a pony-tail; her eyes were large, simpering, and a little mad; her complexion was white and spread with a rather anachronistic layer of baby fat; her nose and mouth were small, too small, especially the mouth, which was hardly more than a faded cherry; her face, naturally, was round, like the rest of her. She was Neapolitan and lived /mainly/ in a villa on the slopes of Vesuvius, above Castellammare. Her husband had left it to her, finally making himself useful by dying. With the Vesuvian villa (not far from where Leopardi spent his last days, among the same *ginestra,* /naturally/), her husband had left to Signora F. a wonderful collection of paintings, whose core consisted of a rare stock of Bamboccianti (authenticated by Roberto Longhi). All of which constituted a great source of pride for Signora F., an inexhaustible font of satisfaction: practically, her "special" place in society. In Rome she owned only the small apartment toward which Carlo was heading, with who knows what hopes—dark, confused, humiliating, and deeply agonizing—in his heart, but that small apartment was a center from which culture veritably radiated. Signora F., in fact, invested her initiative in cultural undertakings. Not only did she organize almost weekly Receptions (like the present one), at which literary types, journalists, scientists, and politicians met, but she also devoted herself to a more specific activity: a small theatrical school and workshop, a center for "audiovisual" research. For this Signora F. needed financing, even if minimal: some few million lire: let's say twenty million for the year. Who was funding it, if one < ... > may speak of funding? Well, apparently the funding came to her totally out of friendship, from that agency or company "?" that I mentioned just above; since the hand that, concretely and physically, "held out" the little sum to Signora F. was the hand of a certain Eleonora Ciaffi or Cioffi, a friend of hers, connected to her by complicated relationships (her husband's family, the paintings, a certain "fishiness" involving the illegal foreign export of some paintings, and, in addition, money and, further, ties to the Florentine literary world), Signora F. only vaguely attached a political meaning to her financing. First of all, because of her character—a character that tended to artificially heighten the cynicism innate in a femininity perceived by xxx ideology as that of a courtesan if not a prostitute—rather as certain priests are absolutely unembarrassed about begging or collecting stuff even if it's a little shady, in order to maintain their orphans or their asylums; second, because of the particular cultural mentality of those years, when everything was vaguely pioneering and consecrated by a sort of "establishment" of the left, the Communist cultural hegemony, which included great masses of intellectuals who remained bourgeois nonetheless. For that reason, a man like Troya or—named with slightly worshipful respect, almost in a low voice—Bonocore, having been in the Resistance, seemed absolutely above suspicion; on the contrary.

NOTE 22G
Continuation of the preceding

Signora F. had something "superior" to pursue. The contradictions of both the ends and the means were left in that particular state of unconsciousness which is reasonableness. Obviously, certain men are esteemed without regard to their political color: and then, above a certain level, important and successful people are united by a certain equivalence that—as if in a hallucination, because their respective "rhetorical structures" are identical—is identical to a kind of pact or alliance.

Signora F.'s salon, I repeat, was a salon of the intellectual left. But in Signora F., as well as in the culture of those years, there was a certain ecumenical and conciliatory tendency. I don't mean that Signora F. was similar to the "Governoress," Julia Mikhailovna, of *The Possessed* . . . but then why not? In her heart, she did love to surround herself with young men and to flatter them in order to be flattered; the purpose of this reciprocal adulation was, further, precisely to "keep the young men (who eventually were not of the left) on the edge of the abyss"; or anyway to make them less dramatic and render them presentable, because of their intelligence and their inclination toward art, in a salon of the left. We will see in what follows what I mean by all this and what I mean, above all, by my reference to *The Possessed.*

Around a dozen million lire was therefore lavished by "?," the last of the last branches of the Troyas' empire, by now entirely contained within the universe of power, in spite of the long-ago acquisition of democratic values through the Resistance. Then (as would still be the case for many years) anti-Fascism was not even discussed as a "virtue."

I would like to remind the reader that among the branches or twigs immediately above "?" there was the advertising company Pubblicità Italiana (and everyone knows how close, in that period of "discoveries," the links were between intellectuals and advertising, which was considered almost a literary genre), but, most important, there was a xxx Produzioni Cinetelevisive, which speaks for itself. Thus, it was through these branches that did not explicitly have to do with oil that *half* the financing necessary for Signora F.'s artistic initiatives flowed into her salon. But where did the *other half* come from?

NOTE 22H
Outline of an elementary *puzzle* and its ludic pleasure

I don't want to pry into anyone's financial affairs. I couldn't do it in the "contemplative" spirit of one who vanquishes and kills in himself interest in such things, as Balzac did; nor can I do it, evidently, with interest; that is, spurred by my own love of money. So I am able to do all this only on the condition that I take it as a game, as entertaining as possible. I say this because in a little while we will manifestly be forced to play. Therefore, the fact that half the financing for Signora F.'s salon came from Troya (who probably knew absolutely nothing about it) through the subsidiaries was quite well known, or anyway it *could* be known. And because of, or thanks to, Signora F. herself. Not that Signora F., our little Governoress of Piazza Buozzi, did not know how to keep a secret. She simply forgot to. Above all, when the temptation to reveal a secret was particularly and sweetly irresistible. But the revelation would never have occurred, perhaps, if there had not been a special mechanism in Signora F.'s behavior that favored it and made it seem natural. This mechanism was a linguistic mechanism. In fact, over the years Signora F. had gradually constructed a language of her own that had almost paranoid characteristics: a real little linguistic system in which things were named by means of rhetorical (or, rather, oratorical, because the "Iroquois" of Madame F. was exclusively oral) devices that made them utterable through their placement in particular syntactic-phonological folds that no other system of known signs possessed. As in certain languages spoken in China (but also among the North American Indians) the intonation was enough to change the sense of a sentence: not in the nuances (Jakobson heard about sixty different "intentions" in the way an actor pronounced, in Russian, "Good evening") but, rather, in the literal meaning. It was precisely in one of her linguistic seizures that Signora F. had "revealed" the name of her Second Financier, who therefore in her salon merged with the First, although that was, as we will see, ideologically impossible.

The Possessed, p. xxx.†

NOTE 221
Continuation of the *puzzle,* etc.

But in order to explain this, I said we would play. It has not been easy for me to make this "superfluous and excessive" decision, which in substance is nothing but is also so much. If an author resolves (as is the case with Petrarch) never to use, in a linguistic system, the word "foot," which is in itself meaningless, then the moment he uses it he has created /a scandal/. Thus I had decided not to use in my story any device that would interrupt a normality that I would call almost severe, not to say even austere.[14] But an absolute demand for clarity urges me to transform my text for a moment into the "superfluous and excessive" page of a puzzle magazine. Let the reader therefore observe this diagram. Rectangles that represent the various Companies or Agencies of the Troya empire are drawn; the drawing represents a figure, that is, in this case, the firm's capital, declared and actual. The last little rectangle is only half drawn. It represents Signora F.'s "Cultural Initiatives," and the source of only half of its financing is known.

NOTE 23
Second part of the *puzzle*

To fill in a little sketch, which goes from right to left rather than from left to right—that is, in order to know where the second half of Signora F.'s financing comes from—we must do exactly what is done in some word puzzles; that is, symmetrically retrace a route already taken, but from left to right rather than from right to left, and, at the same time, in this case, from bottom to top rather than from top to bottom: as if descending and then reascending two contiguous staircases whose bottom step is the same.

Handing over, always (in symmetrical fashion) personally, that is with a small hairy hand of flesh and blood, Signora F.'s other annual twelve million was . . .

[14]"Austere" in the sense in which the word is used by Aristotle and Thomas Aquinas, cited by the sociologist Ivan Illich in *Conviviality*. In effect, working on this book I experience "the joy in the task of the convivial instrument." I have come to know *convivencialidad* or *Mitmenschlichkeit*. Therefore I am austere. "*Austeritas secundum quod est virtus non escludit omnes delectationes, sed superfluas et inordinatas: unde videtur pertinere ad affabilitatem quam Philosophus, lib. 4 Ethic. cap. VI amicitiam nominat, vel ad eutrapeliam, sive jocunditatem*" (*Summa Theologica*).

The reader who is even slightly acquainted with the little-known sociologist Ivan Illich will understand that it is not without reason that I cite him in this first series of Notes of my work.

NOTES 20—30
History and background of the oil problem

↓

FLASHES OF LIGHT ON ENI

*

Notes 20–25, approximately (previous history): *The sources*

Notes 25–30, approximately (the plot): *Appendices on yellow paper*

*a novel not so much "on a spit" as "in a swarm," or perhaps a "shish kebab"

↑

All this is an enormous digression à la Sterne, which leaves Carlo in the act of going to Signora F.'s reception and picks him up again when he enters.

—Summary of the ENI empire, later Montedison

—Summary of the Monti empire
   according to this outline

Cefis (physically Fanfani)   Monti (physically Andreotti)[15]

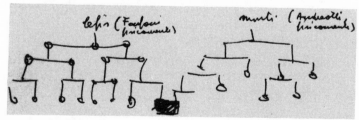

—The woman at whose house the reception takes place is the official head of a Cultural Agency financed (for reasons of friendship or kinship) by both Ce-

---

[15] *Translator's note:* Fanfani and Andreotti were both Christian Democratic politicians; Monti an industrialist.

fis and Monti (Fascist)—The salon, however, is an intellectual salon of the left.

—On this occasion *Carlo* is observed and taken on by one of the two big firms: but, rising through the ordinary *petrochemical* subsidiaries, he will become a big shot (vice president or nominal president, like Beolchini) of the other

* The story that leads to the *crossroads* of the Signora's salon is made up entirely of business news and information and relationships, etc. (Notes 20–30). But also at the crossroads facts concerning business affairs, interests, intrigues, patronage that prepare for Part II are recounted <?>
↑

At this precise historical moment (POLITICAL BLOC I) Troya (!) is about to be made president of ENI: and that implies the suppression of his predecessor (the Mattei affair, moved forward chronologically). He, with his political clique, needs anti-Communism ('68): *bombs attributed to the Fascists*

(we get to know Restivo in Signora F.'s salon)

POLITICAL BLOC II will be characterized by the fact that the same person (Troya) is about to be made president of Montedison. He needs, with the clique of politicians, a Fascist virginity (*bombs attributed to the Fascists*)
**insert Cefis's speeches, which serve to divide the novel into two parts in a perfectly symmetrical and explicit way (a bit like the two episodes of the twenty boys, etc.)

(October 16, 1974)

—In both crimes Carlo takes an active part:
in Bloc I *unconsciously* (in an abnormal relationship between the Ego and the Id) becoming an active member of the conspiracy
in Bloc II hallucinatorily (making the in fact visionary bomb explode at the Turin station)

(Oct. 16, 1974)

NOTE 31†

In my story—on this point I must be brutally explicit—psychology is forcibly replaced by ideology. So the reader should not be deceived: he will never come up against characters who mysteriously appear and develop, revealing themselves to the other protagonists and to the reader, while events—of which they are the cause or by which they are manipulated—force them into a dramatic coherence. And thus—in my story— there are not even extras of this type. So there is no reason to describe receptions and no pleasure in it. And that is a good excuse, I don't deny it, not to describe something I don't like and of which, therefore, I have no real experience (which is above all linguistic experience). /But there is still something else/ to justify all this: in psychology there is always *something else* and *something more* than psychology. And so, too, in a social figure there is *something else* and *something more* than the social figure. Note carefully that I have said not "outside" or "above" psychology and the social figure but in them. I cannot say that I am not familiar with— perhaps even with the help of psychoanalysis—psychology. < ... > /But knowledge/ of the human spirit is, in fact, something more and different. Analogously I could say—perhaps this time also with the help of Marxist culture—that I know the "sociality" of an individual quite well. But in that case, too, knowledge of the human spirit is something more than social knowledge. What is this human spirit? < ... > It is a presence; a reality; that's all. It looms within the individual to whom it belongs and over him, like his double—monumental and at the same time elusive. That "looming figure" (which in some mysterious way is also physical) *is only there where it can be.* It has the property of bodies. Thus I will never, in my story, practice psychology; but surely my knowledge of the human spirit will prevent me from putting psychology in the service of ideology incorrectly. That is, I feel certain that every character "will be" and "will act" only as he could "be" and "act," even according to the deductions of the most classical psychology; no one will be out of place, the reader can be assured.

Still, there are some "imaginary characters" who will set in motion the story or action. At that reception, which takes place partly outside, in a small narrow garden, and partly inside, in the delightfully warm and brightly lit apartment—in the idle and pleasant coming and going of at least a hundred people—it's evident that these "imaginary characters" have little in common socially and psychologically with the "imaginary characters" who made the decision to put a spy on Carlo's heels in order to find out about his entire life; yet—as the continuation of this story will in part, and irregularly, very irregularly, *perhaps* explain—there are some analogies and some links between the two groups of "imaginary characters."

NOTE 32
Provocateurs and spies (in 1960)†

/À *la recherche comme à la recherche:* I remember those receptions of the late fifties and early sixties (a phenomenon that will not fail to appear very poetic someday, wrapped in the mystery of time past) with a mixture of loathing (of which I have spoken) and compassion. I am moved by a certain ingenuousness in the way such things were experienced by young men like Carlo. And I am moved, too, by the willful, hardened, monstrous ingenuousness with which old men, already feeble then and now decrepit, experienced them; or men and women who were old but at the height of their professional activity, the peak of their social power./ Whether their faces were marked by folds of fat or were unhappily thin and drawn, they all *believed.* They believed as the dead believe. There, in the eternity of an evening reception in midsummer, with lights blazing in the coolness of the evening on the stunted grass of a little garden stuck in among luxurious apartment houses, where from time to time a breeze agitated the shiny leaves of the lemon trees, those people remained as if untouched, with smiles glued to their lips, glasses or pastries in hand; and with, above all, that faith, that hope, that carefree lack of charity. The problems were the problems of that moment, the truth was the truth of that moment (and every person there evidently numbered himself, without the slightest doubt, among the privileged repositories of that truth; there was not a gesture, a smile, a wink that did not allude to this). The sparkling of the light, like a festive ship anchored in a dark port, mingled with the "light" of that so profoundly and sincerely felt truth: and the red of certain velvets or wallpapers, the green of some woman's daring dress, the glitter of gold and pearls: it all remains there, in that living corner of the world of the dead. I remember the groups, carried here and there as if by the choppy sea of good humor and the general conciliatory, almost fraternal mood (it must be remembered that this was in the early years of prosperity: society had "taken off," to the great satisfaction of all and with their secret personal hopes); some settled themselves around a low table xxx, sitting on a slightly worn, silk-covered divan or in the matching armchairs, while those who couldn't find seats squatted casually on the carpet; others were standing against a bookcase loaded with precious little objects—they were all men and were speaking of particularly "serious" problems; still others gathered in their host's bedroom, open for the occasion, wide open and blazing with light: some sat right on the heavy satin bedcover, and these were for the most part young men, whose predetermined contribution to the evening was foolishness and gaiety; still others gathered in the garden or, rather, between the living room and the garden, sheltered from the coolness. The men's jackets, navy blue or midnight blue, over dark gray flannel pants, like a uniform, and the women's dresses, also similar to one another, following a model that was /an absolute model/—that neckline, that skirt length, that type of jewelry—stood out with a particular prominence there, between the bright light of the salon and the weaker, fainter light of the little lawn (mingling with a third light, that of the slender moon, carved in the blue sky between the Parioli and Villa Glori), whether they were gold or reddish violet, mauve or a bold turquoise.

I remember the people who were conspicuous in those groups (and whom a journalist, full of blind faith in an "establishment" that was "taking off" beyond everything, would have noted first on his list). Anyone who didn't know them—and, like the young Carlo, was seeing them for the first time—after hurried introductions gazed at them from afar with the same look with which one might look at the daily life of gods.

There was an intellectual who had been around for many years and was therefore celebrated and venerable, yet still had the youthful air of someone who believes in nothing but is interested in everything; his hair was white and very short, his nose prominent, his mouth sunken, as if he had no lips, his chin sharp; his eyebrows were very thick and wild, and beneath were the bright and forever distracted eyes of someone who is a little deaf. Whatever position he took, sitting or standing, he was constantly restless, almost violently restless. Although he was a perfect outsider at receptions of this sort, he was at his ease there, he fitted perfectly into the picture: he was far removed from it, but since he was there he accepted the game and did not withdraw for even a moment from the pressure of his intelligence. Every word was a critical word: grandfather and grandson, he was in the middle of that eternally stranded fleet, like the prow of an old ship that has plowed all the seas, but in an adventure more intellectual than poetic; it had become poetic, however, because of an intellectual rigor that never for an instant /slackened/.

Another intellectual, fifteen years younger, was in another corner of the room, far more timid and so more aggressive; his aggressiveness— mixed with the natural sweetness, almost gentleness of his character— seemed part of a role he had been forced to accept. He did not seem to feel at all at ease; if anything, he seemed to feel he had been placed there by his success and his stormy reputation. He looked like an adolescent, thin and pale, with almost exotic cheekbones and bewildered chestnut-brown eyes. An obscene sensuality dripped from his body, which was nevertheless ascetically and rigidly devoted to a completely intellectual adventure, like his older friend's; his socks, besides, were short and his clothes a little too flashy.

There was also a politician—he had been a minister for ten years and would be for another fifteen—sitting in a red armchair, with a round, catlike face drawn back between his shoulders, as if he had no neck or were a hunchback; his broad intellectual's forehead formed a contrast to his sly smile, which had in it something indecent; that is, he wished to demonstrate, with cunning and contempt, the knowledge of his own cunning and contempt. Indeed, if the idea of life as a "game," as a "bet" to lose or win and therefore based on action and behavior, had in him its real champion, it was a model of life that was followed more or less unconsciously by everyone at that reception, including those who mocked it, even presumptuously (for example in the columns of *L'Espresso*).

And of course there was a Communist from the Central Committee of the Italian Communist Party, still burdened with the look "of the people" that a militant had to have in those days and, in addition, with the illusion of hegemony that Marxist culture still had then. His mode of expression was laughter: everything became a laugh. As if to exorcise the foolish fear of Communism (which no one there appeared to have). It happened in him naturally, because laughter and good nature (moralistic, of course) were inherent in his character, the sympathetic character of a man who has remained a boy. And, besides, everyone called him by his first name rather than his last name. And the name was a diminutive.

And all around were the faces of men and women, almost all of them old (the few young people made a group of their own, under the benevolent gaze of the fathers): faces as deeply, monstrously branded, stained, hollowed, swollen by time as they were well preserved, cared for, breathing ease, prosperity, and brotherhood in the truth. Among these people were also the "imaginary characters" who had given their attention to Carlo the Catholic of the left (Catholic of the left in the accepted meaning of the phrase during the Papacy of John XXIII). To anyone observing him, Carlo manifested an essential characteristic: that of being interested in everything and of remaining perfectly /unchangeable/. Just as a subordinate should be unchangeable, should have no feelings. But at the same time this unchangeableness was that of a manager, who, in contrast, must not reveal his feelings, being above them. Carlo, lacking the habit of power, had, it's true, the look of a sacristan, of a provincial just come from a college of priests: and his thickset body, with the gray pants and black jacket that made his soft, heavy, awkward figure stand out even more; his round head, where the black hair was already, prematurely, falling out in the middle, leaving a clear empty space similar to a monk's tonsure; the face round, too, with two big sad eyes in the middle, almost weeping but at the same time full of tension and an obstinate will, which was also priestlike—everything about him was reassuring as to the high quality of his hypocrisy and an honesty not without a Machiavellian side, that is, the capacity to silence conscience for the purposes of good.

Among these "imaginary characters" there was, in addition to a top director of ENI and a politician (of the same faction as the minister I mentioned above), etc., a young intellectual, perhaps even younger than Carlo, who was also from the provinces (he was from the Veneto and had a peasant last name that ended in -*on*), with large eyes, black and burning—rather handsome for a literary man. In his conversation, in the acquaintances he had, in the quality of his thought, he did not visibly differ—at least in terms of the "category"—from the other intellectuals, even of the first rank, who were also present at the reception. Apparently, he had written some books, respectable but hopelessly mediocre; although he was young, it was clear that he was not destined ever to become, literarily, a revelation. He would never go beyond the limits of the work that had gained for him the interest of editors and a fairly warm welcome from the critics. He was made of the same stuff as the other intellectuals and literary men who were prominent in those years. Yet there was something else about him. For example, his relations with some politicians and businessmen. The same ones who were busy with "that Carlo Valletti" and who, to be precise, had, /just then/, at that party, decided to put him to the test, /while Carlo was there, present-absent, deferential, authoritative. The test for employment by a big agency like ENI, which, as we have seen, was something other than a simple agency, even if it was a government agency, was almost purely a formality: it was a job of a bureaucratic nature, which would require a trip to the Orient./

With this I would have completed the point of this little chapter of my poem: a trip to the East is not an everyday event, the real explanation of its meaning is found in myth; it is the repetition of one of those "inaugural acts" of man (/if/ such a thing can be evaluated). However, if the reader will patiently bear with me, I have something more to add.

At the not so distant time, then, when that evening at Signora F.'s house took place, Italian "culture" was very uniform, in the accepted historical-ethnological sense of culture (De Martino was writing his fine books at the time), in its particular bourgeois and academic sense, and finally in the sense of being an /élite/ culture, embodying the hierarchy of values that placed it at the top in the country. The cultural hegemony of the left still dominated, just as it /had coming out of/ the Resistance, and while sociology and the technological myth were beginning to advance, it was as a "renewal" that, on the one hand, put the old Marxist intellectual in crisis and on the other revitalized him. But anti-Fascism and progressivism were still the unifying force in an Italy made up almost entirely of peasants. The young men plotted their happy reinventions in the shadow of their fathers (who, as I have said, watched them benevolently, in a traditional relationship). It worked well. Italy had never known cultural activity more fervid, intense, and virtuous than in that period. There was still room for scandal, because power was /tightly held/ by the Christian Democrats, whose obtuse brutality made the cause of anyone who opposed them so much more noble. In conclusion, the roles assigned to all were distinct: a worker was clearly distinguishable, *by his physical presence alone,* from a bourgeois; and similarly an apprentice mechanic from a student; an intellectual of the left from an intellectual of the right; an academic from a writer. Confusion was not possible. Never, for example, would an overambitious literary person belonging to the subculture (in the hierarchical sense) be confused with a literary person *of value,* that is, one who belonged to the culture. His very physical presence would betray him. Now, the question the reader should ask at this point is the following: whether it was possible in those years to have provocateurs and spies. Well, yes—I would answer—for all that it is contradictory, irreconcilable with the "idea" that we rightly have of that historical moment—it's possible that even in those years there were provocateurs, spies.

NOTE 33 †

NOTE 34 *BIS* ‡
First fable on Power (from the "Plan")

"I will tell you the story of an intellectual"—began the storyteller, who, as in the *Thousand and One Nights,* was not omniscient but modestly intended to "report" only what he himself had heard—"I will tell you the story of an intellectual, but be warned that choice and selectivity will dominate my story and that linguistically it will be impoverished: universal and therefore generic!

"So much for the beginning. I will not even tell you the name of this intellectual; nor will I tell you his exact work, his age, his habits, the city where he lived; it may in fact be that he was not even born in our country.

"What I must deal with instead—strictly as a function of the story— is the clinical portrait. Neurotic. And perhaps more than neurotic, mad.

"In his corpulence (he was not obese but round and puffy, with crazy yellowish flesh) there were grim signs of psychic degeneration. /On his face/, which was completely round, as if made of concentric circles, he had round eyebrows and, beneath, round eyes, round cheeks (although he was only thirty-five, they were already caving in), a round chin, a round mouth. This last lost its rotundity when he spoke, and assumed irregular but always indefinite and imprecise shapes and thus a certain repulsiveness—the kind that viscous things have. His forehead was also round, with a receding hairline and a crown of thinning pale hair— vaguely ascetic, like that of a country priest, a provincial lawyer < ... >.

The roundness gave his physiognomy a childish look; but the child he resembled was a rather repugnant child. However, he behaved just as an adult should behave.

"He did not yet know—at the beginning of our story—what the real purpose of his life was. He was like a worm inside a cocoon. Yet potentially he was already what he wished to be; and, in consequence, the maneuvers /(which I would define, not objectively, as despicable)/ of one who wishes to reach goals for which he was not made /were/ already visible in his behavior—in his life and his work (although in a certain sense merely to conceive grand or noble goals ennobles one who is not worthy of them). He was precise, indefatigable, discreet, always efficiently in his place; and at the same time he was calculating and sycophantic. Since he was not yet well known, no one realized /it/, but in reality he was a repellent /monster of passionate servility/. He would be capable of the basest acts to obtain a person's /favor/. At the same time he also cultivated the myth of his own innocence. The fact is that his desire to prove himself and get ahead belonged to the category of clinically anxious desires; and it was therefore the "malady" that took care of preserving innocence, as a primitive condition of grace, while at the same time excusing all petty violations of it.

"Our intellectual thus appeared destined to fulfill himself in the most common way: with some satisfactions obtained not only by means of his mediocre talents but, in addition, by moves calculated in the depths < ... > of his conscience.

"But one night, while he was lost in the light slumber of the unfortunate who—without admitting it—suffer from insomnia, he was awakened by a voice calling him.

"He opened his eyes, sat up, and indeed something, a Presence, was standing at the foot of his bed (/the neurosis, or his predestination to madness/, had accustomed him to accept such phenomena meekly, and /meekly/ he immediately accepted this, too). The following brief moral dialogue occurred between the man and what for now let's call the Dark Force, sitting at the foot of his bed.

< ... > "'What is it?'

< ... > "'Do you know what the purpose of your life is?' /asked the other/. The intellectual opened his eyes wide and swallowed, diligently

preparing himself to give a judicious answer, which <?> his essential innocence:

< ... > "'Like everyone, I want to make a position for myself in the society in which I live,' he said, 'but in the capital instead of in this provincial city.'

< ... > "'Good, good,' /the Dark Force admitted/. 'But this is one part, or phase, of the true purpose of your life. Question yourself more closely, go deeper into your conscience' (a brief benevolent laugh concluded this last, /priestlike/ sentence).

< ... > "'It's the greatest effort I can make, sincerely.' (He did not in the least intend to go deeper than this, interrupting the now so well established direction of his life. On the other hand, he did not know that he himself, so abject and impotent, and above all so lacking in every virtue, /had managed/ to create for himself the possibility of a destiny of greatness.)

< ... > "'Then if you don't want to say it I will tell you: the purpose of your life is Power.'

"At that word, the intellectual sharpened his gaze in the dim light thickened by the gloomy provincial night in his rented room; and he succeeded, in effect, in seeing more distinctly the one who was speaking to him. His hair stood up on his head, and he froze with terror.[16]

"Trembling with a fear that /unhinged him/, and covered with a cold, deathlike sweat, our intellectual in fact saw before him, sitting on the edge of the bed, none other /than the Devil in person: the Devil, with two/ little horns sticking out of his white head, and a small toothless face, fiery red, like that of a drunkard, who knows he is repulsive; his lips were tightly closed in a kind of pointed smile, which was at the same time a smile of /obscene/ pity for himself and resigned ill feeling toward whoever looked at him. His vileness was like a crust scattered over the unhealthy redness of his face, over the skin on his head, under the unruly tufts of dirty white hair. He gave off the /unbearable/ stench of one who has slept in a dusty corner or on a pile of rags in some waiting room or storeroom without taking off his clothes and shoes.[17]

---

[16]Simple past tenses—that is, finite tenses—are dedicated to heroes.
[17]Nothing terrified our intellectual more than the extreme aspects of misery failure leads to.

"Although he had frozen and his hair was standing up on his head, he understood that the Devil had /spoken/ the truth. Power was in fact the purpose of his life, he admitted, preserving by his reticence a possible way out for himself.

< ... > "'If you say so . . . '

< ... > "'I am here to help you.'

< ... > "'But how?'

< ... > "'Ask me for the means by which you wish to reach Power, and I will give it to you.'

< ... > "A flash of intelligence gleamed in the eyes of the intellectual, lighting up for an instant his feigned torpor of a bloated child; and what he finally said, after some seconds of concentration, of hesitation, and, I would say, of inspiration, was surprising.

"He could have /named/ a thousand ways of reaching power, swift and secure: /literary/ fame, won by writing literary works, or works of sociology and essays, to which perhaps he was better suited: fame that would have to be crowned, let's say, by the Nobel Prize (it would be easy for the Devil to help him in Sweden); or he could have asked to become an employee of one of the great firms that are traditionally inclined to steer intellectuals to technical work (obtaining excellent results): in that case, too, it would be very easy for the Devil to have him rise rapidly in the company, until he was directly alongside the top management of the /immense/ < ... > /indeed/ international firm; or still, finally, he could have asked to have an openly political career, becoming a member of a large and powerful political party, perhaps the largest: and here it would have been /extremely easy/ for the Devil to control the exchanges of favors, the opportunities < ... >, which (/joined/ to the innate, even if still potential, demagogic capacity of our provincial intellectual) would conduct him to the real and formal summit of power: he would become a minister, in fact Head of State, perhaps of a semi-dictatorial government of the right.[18]

---

[18]The father of our intellectual had been a well-known Fascist in his provincial city, but the intellectual did not confine himself to hiding this in the larger provincial city where he worked; rather—a definite sign, this, of his malady—he had made his father pass for a heroic anti-Fascist.

"No, our intellectual did not propose to the Devil any of these 'natural' means of reaching Power; they would have been impure and inauthentic, and that quality would have been reproduced in the Power obtained through them, devaluing it before his conscience. This, perhaps, our intellectual thought in a flash, before responding. /Finally/ he said \spoke\:

<...> "'I wish to reach Power through Sanctity.'

<...> "'Why not?' answered the Devil. 'You will obtain Power through Sanctity, good!' <...> Again he gave his reassuring smile and disappeared.

"Perhaps the Devil, caught, so to speak, off balance, behaved a little carelessly, or perhaps, who knows, everything had been prearranged by him through some complicated calculation; the fact remains that the next morning our intellectual began his new life as a saint, and in the most natural way lived a true contradiction in terms.

"He was one of those people who <?> have always known perfectly well 'how to be saints': just as delinquents in juvenile prisons know perfectly well how 'decent' people behave, and if they don't know it, it's the first thing they learn, so that when they come out it is through this very knowledge that they become true delinquents, who are no longer innocent.

"So, naturally, he had no doubts: he had to be a Catholic saint; sanctity should not be made scandalous.

"He started his training in silence and secrecy: the right hand never knew what the left hand was doing. (Someone else knew, of course, and, not being a saint, did not in the least propose to observe the rules of silence and secrecy; in fact, in human fashion, he loved to gossip and above all to appear informed, to be in the know about matters that were still mysterious <...>, etc., etc.)

"He spoke of Faith and Hope: and that could only be public. In private, on the other hand, he practiced Charity, which if it is announced loses its nature, becoming, instead, the work of the Devil (!).

"He took care not to interrupt the Church's traditional separation between Faith and Hope on one side and Charity on the other. He abandoned in the name of this last the goods of the world (that is, his government job). He lived in pure poverty (near a very popular convent at the center of his native city). He began to devise a plan that, although not in fact heretical, was nevertheless innovative with respect to the ecclesiastical tradition. He approached, in moderation, the Catholic movements of the left, always proclaiming, however, with contrition and humility, his loyalty to the Vatican. All sexual contact was forbidden, and 'the love of woman,' which had had such importance in his previous social life, proving to be the condition necessary to all progress, was supplanted by chastity.

"While all these operations were /progressing/ toward the ultimate point, signs of power began to manifest themselves. Around our holy intellectual an atmosphere was created first of prestige, then of respect, then of profound and silent veneration, and finally of exalted, rapturous expectation.

"But it was just when everything reached the final result that the situation < ... > was turned upside down.

"Attracted by the odor of Sanctity, a group of young Catholics surrounded our intellectual in the courtyard of the monastery (which was new, built in Art Deco style with money from a big industrial firm); the occasion of the meeting was the city's weeklong film festival, and the monastery was in charge of hospitality for the young people participating in the conference. It was right after Easter, a Sunday—one felt the warmth and clear weather of spring: violets and primulas came out on /sunny/ banks; the dry streambeds gleamed with the roiling blue of waters flooding down from the mountains. The desolate brown Appennines, lost in the still unsettled sky, rose behind the city, while before it the plain stretched down to the banks of the Po swollen with floodwaters. Salimbene seemed to have just passed through there; or, at least, it seemed as if grazing in that fragrant hemp were the horses of some small population of barbarians, destined to measure their own old age against the great Newness of the Church . . .

"Our intellectual was at the center of a peaceful discussion, while somewhere bells rang out joyfully. He could gauge what point his popularity had reached at that moment: he had not yet 'taken off,' but there was around him the solemnity charged with expectation that precedes the ascent of exceptional men. He was really the center of the whole gathering, and the monastery was swarming with guests only because of him: a few days still, a few weeks, a few months, and his case would explode before the nation. His fame, his prestige would have no limits. He perceived all this with the capacity for internal calculation that /had always distinguished him/; his dark pessimism had never kept him from analyzing good news when the moment came.

"But instead of freely exulting in the glorious future that began to open before him, he suddenly felt a shadow fall on his eyes, a wintry cold froze him, a < ... > desperation constricted his throat and made his knees go weak.

"His eyes, terrified, stared at the void, charged with a grief that was full of a consuming sense of truth—and of nobility: because every 'comic' element had fallen from tragedy, there remained only the sublime style; and the eyes of the 'saint,' staring into the void—under the thin hair disheveled by the May wind, his neck twisting like that of a person who looks to one side or behind, trying to flee, but in reality remains immobile where he is, as if petrified—reflected the light of this sublimity.

"To stick to the facts, /to things/, what had flashed on him was /how radical/ was the theoretical division in which he lived, preparing for sanctity. Suddenly, in a whirl, Faith and Hope deprived of the Charity from which they had been separated became inconceivable to him (as if it were a matter of Idealism or Nazism!). Every kind of innovation in religious thought turned out to be unthinkable, except heresy. The Catholicism of the left seemed irreconcilable with the Vatican. But all these were only pretexts or < ... >.

"Our intellectual, stunned and trembling, was staring at the simple form of the Truth—to which he was now prey—when at the far end of the monastery courtyard /< ... > he saw the Devil pass by < ... > and look at him with a smile of complicity, as if winking at him, red as a drunk. Certainly, < ... > he had kept his word: it was Sanctity that he had brought him to; Sanctity, not the pretense of Sanctity. Poetry, not Literature./

"Possessed by real Sanctity, he realized that that real Sanctity was a gift from the Devil; that the Truth in which he was suddenly living had been the work /of a Lie/; that the Good which he /suddenly/, ineffably enjoyed was the product of Evil; that the Revelation /had come about through/ his worst sentiments. But all that, thus set forth, was only the letter. Under the series of rational and banal oppositions ran another series of oppositions, not only unspeakable but not even intuitable except as a Joke, /the Theft of the cosmos. Our intellectual gave a shout and fell to the ground <...>. The Devil took advantage of this to open \to make sure that\ on the palms of his hands were two long, bloody stigmata . . . /

"He was carried in delirium (or in rapture) to his bed; and those who had the good fortune to hear him speak in those hours could /report/ that it was in a style of the highest level, that of Ecclesiastes or the Apocalypse, or the presumed lost true texts of Saint Francis: but they could not, of course, report or reconstruct it.

"During the night, while he was delirious in his bed, the body of the saint was transported somewhere else.[19]

"/There/, in the light, appeared a /stronger/ light, which called him by name. By analogy with the Dark Force, /we will call/ this new presence the Luminous Force.

"The saint fell on his knees before it, because he believed he could logically deduce that it was God.

"The Luminous Force called him by name.

"The saint raised his eyes to him and in fact recognized the features of the Divinity; he recognized, to be precise, and to stick to the subject, Power, reduced to /physical/ semblances; but he recognized the authority, the knowledge, the peace, the goodness: unlike the drunkard's face of the Dark Force, immediately recognizable among thousands, the Luminous Force—God—had an anonymous face <...>. The following dialogue ensued:

<...> "'God!' /murmured the saint/.

<...> "'Yes, He,' /answered God/.

<...> "'I am not worthy . . .' /stammered the saint; and he well knew why/.

"(God began to smile lovingly. The saint, astounded, looked at him: was it a joke?)

---

[19] /Presumably to a desert (as we will see), but this was only a first stop, because from there—far from indiscreet glances—he was taken up into the Third Heaven./

< ... > "'Yes, I am not worthy,' /he insisted, ready for a full confession/.

< ... > "'I know, I know,' /said the Lord, always with kindly cheerfulness/. 'But do you really believe this story of the Devil? Do you really believe it?' (He stared at him, gently laughing at him . . .)

< ... > "'What?' /the saint stammered again/.

< ... > "'It really seems to you that the Devil can have led you to Sanctity, true sanctity?† /In that there would be neither logic nor lack of logic. Evil is merely a transitory experience: it is not at the beginning or at the end. You have to pass through it in the middle, that's all. Therefore if the initiative did not come from the Devil, who is only an accident, from whom did it come?/ Whose plan is it \can it be\ to use you, who are among the most abject of sinners, to /redefine/ sanctity? Who can have needed extreme cases to make the living /negative/ extreme sink all the way to the /positive/ extreme?'

< ... > "'You!'

< ... > "'It was a Joke. The Devil is not a person but simply an aspect. /I put it on my face,‡ and I appeared to you, in the wretched house of the wretched city of the wretched world where you live. I had to use the worst to bring about the best and an arbitrary contradiction in terms to make the absence of contradictions triumph./ Now go, return to earth; go and bear witness to all this. There is only one condition that I place on you . . . '

"(Here his joy diminished a little to make room for the solemnity of the inscrutable Will.)

< ... > "'Tell me,' /said the saint humbly/.

< ... > "'In going away from here, you must go straight, without turning back to look at me.'

< ... > "'I will do it,' /said the saint firmly/. God's words had been a dismissal, and so the saint, after prostrating himself yet again before Him, rose, turned his back, and walked on with his head slightly lowered, looking straight in front of him, determined not to turn around.

"But he had hardly gone twenty steps when an irresistible curiosity took possession of him; it was a new seizure that swept him away as if he were a straw: he could not, literally, contain /a force/ at his neck that obliged him to turn around and cast behind a last look at what he had been forbidden to look at. The rushing return of base sentiments—

which, evidently, are not overpowered by lofty ones but continue to co-exist with them—was like a < ... > law of nature; and he turned around for an instant, a single instant.

"The Luminous Force was there. < ... > But he no longer had the face of God. < ... > He had the face of the Devil: a three-quarter view, with the little shining eye, the high cheekbone lighted by a lurid redness, the smile < ... > of a mendicant, < ... >.

"Immediately, at that sight, our intellectual-saint, like Lot before him, turned to stone. He became a heavy mass and fell like lead from the Third Heaven.

"Some geologists found the mass in a melancholy little valley in a desert lost in the middle of another desert. In the middle was, in fact, the stone that had fallen from the sky: it was divinely beautiful, like a conch shell or a Moore statue. All the tints of the desert seen from a distance were concentrated in it: the paradisiacal rose, the veining of a sublime orange red, ocher, violet—an indefinable violet, similar to the luminous indigo of tropical evenings when the sun has just set. The geologists loaded that precious find into their Land Rover as well as they could and carried it to the civilized world to analyze it. But they did not succeed, and today that stone remains a pure enigma. The infinite variety of its soft colors corresponds to an infinite variety of materials, but none of them have really been identified, because each mineral presents contradictory characteristics, both in relation to itself and in relation to the other minerals with which it is amalgamated or compounded; it has not been possible to distinguish in that rock what appeared precious from what appeared to be worthless or even /toxic/; it has not been possible so far to determine if the analysis is impossible and the contradictions absolute, because the fact is, the research, which has never been suspended, always gives good partial results."

* other stories follow: the people and power (as they were up to or before '68), and as they began *to be no longer* [and this is the reason for the discussion]

May 1974

NOTE 34 *TER*
The end of the reception

At the end of the reception, quote sentence of a schizophrenic patient (Roheim cited by Brown)

NOTES 36—40
The Argonauts

"Mythical" journey to the Orient, reconstruction of Apollonius Rhodius. Unmapped place (where the figure of the Hero who has gone before appears[20]). Series of "visions" reconstructed on the Myth of the Journey as initiation, etc., mixed with realistic visions of true journeys (without names or precise information, as in dreams, etc.)

↓

Write it all in Greek (with the translation summarized telegraphically but exhaustively in the titles of the sections)

↑

Understood as an initiation, the basis of the second journey—but also as the passage of time for the maturation of a "political era": bringing the situation to an end through the substitution of Troya for the president of ENI and therefore the assassination of the latter. The arrival of Carlo from a "dreamed" trip to the Orient puts him like a dreaming automaton in the hands of the assassins.

---

[20] Centaur (?)—coincidence of ancient Greece with Africa.

NOTE 36
The Argonauts. Book I

Departure by jet—An interminable dawn—A young porter with a military-style beret on his head—Greek newspapers—Low mountains of white stone, sheer, with no beach, above the sea made blue by chemical waste—Appearance of the Giants—Their gentleness and the enormous size of their penises—Their flight toward the clouds massed above Mount Dindyma—Waking up—American breakfast (xxx xxx xxx, good French "champagne")—Landing in Tehran, with snow—Traces of heroes who passed in the preceding centuries through the first /mapping/ of the world—Appearance of Heracles—His gentleness, enormous size of his penis—His lingering at a great distance—Heracles takes the road again—The Tehran Hilton—The son of Umberto II, Victor Emmanuel, at the bar—Orpheus sings of the first part of the journey—Operation of the teletype machine.

(Greek text)

NOTE 36B
The Argonauts. Book I (Continued)

Reception at the palace of the Shah—Crossing the city covered with snow—Thousands and thousands of big concrete buildings set on the desert covered with snow—Broad avenues recall the Boulevard Périphérique—The Shah's palace at the edge of the city, in the direction of the rough, jagged, formless mountains—In the midst of a group of low hills that seem to be a newly reforested park—Part fort, part bath complex: very simple and forbidding—The pavilion for the Reception: isolated among artificially massed trees with tall trunks—Style vaguely Art Nouveau—Interior with large rooms. Somewhat reminiscent of the White Hall of Julia Mikhailovna's party in *The Possessed,* except that the carpet is not red but, naturally, consists of enormous Persian rugs that seem fake—Honors of the house by the Shah's sister—About fifty, youthful, but her hands tremble, she has a lot of facial tics—She is frightened, filled with uncertainties and at the same time vaguely despotic, like all multimillionaires—A huge amount of ordered-in food is served.

(Greek text)

NOTE 36B
The Argonauts. Book II

Via Melli at night—Drunks in a little courtyard—Hovels dug out of old cellars and a pile of rubble—a drunk knifed in the back while he sleeps on his stomach on a filthy old blanket in all the shit—Flight of the murderers into the big square xxx xxx—A lot of police, little comfort—National soccer team at the Hilton—Story of the Kurd xxx xxx exactly identical to the one told by xxx xxx (the only difference: xxx xxx is a soccer player rather than a soldier)—Episode of Jaffar: oddly similar to that of < ... > in Voltaire's *Zadig*—The desert: a plateau that extends like a milky ocher barrier, containing in the center a dry salt lake, very white—On the road an interminable line of cars heading for the (modern) mosque at Qum—Still the desert: big conical violet mountains with asymmetrical scaly slopes, like fjords, which enclose sandy valleys and boulders that seem to be of metal, veined with sulfur—Appearance of Apollo—his adoration—Appearance of ceramics, turquoise blue, both in the cone-shaped cupolas among the ocher-colored clay houses and in the objects made by artisans <In> a small town that, like a beehive, incorporates all the houses, and in the middle of a street shut in between high clay walls broken by the doorways of the houses, which have half vaults (dome-shaped vaults, with the edges of the xxx xxx bordered in blue) and stone seats on either side, a tin of canned meat or perhaps of fruit juice sticks out, painted a turquoise color that looks extremely different on tin than on tile or terra-cotta—Arrival on the plain near the Persian Gulf.

(Greek text)

NOTE 36C
The Argonauts. Book III

The mosques of Isfahan, azure, turquoise, and blue—Reception at xxx xxx, where the Shah's brother is staying, very informal—The head of the expedition explains his plans to the Argonauts—Arrival in Abadan—Arrival in Kuwait—The wind covers the city with sandstorms—It's like Milan on a foggy day—The palaces of the sheikhs are like tents in the desert—The sumptuous entrance halls are full of dusty shoes in disarray, and also of not very clean socks—On all the televisions, of which there are hundreds, the same interminable song of Ramadan is sung—Old Arabs, thin as boys, are singing, and boys with their heads shaved, in gray pants and white shirts, all at the top of their lungs—Jason's plans for getting possession of the Golden Fleece are in reality intentions, pure and simple—Long afternoons in the pool of the xxx xxx where the wives of diplomats of the second rank, who, of course, boast of knowing Medea, come to exhibit their weaknesses, whether they are uterine or snobbish is unclear—One of these diplomats of the second rank, with a Roman accent, speaks of the trouble caused by the death of some fellow—The young soldiers, of Palestinian or Jordanian origin, guarding all the palaces, with red-checked scarves under their military berets—Return to Abadan—Evening at a nightclub with young Iranians who are exactly the same as Italians, especially southern Italians—

Madness of Iran: they are all mad—Central squares of the city, the flower beds ringed with Conchs and Cupids—The taste of mint tea (the coarse mint is like a pile of algae in the glass)—Return to Isfahan— Jason meets the Shah's brother—A funeral passes: some young men carry the black bier at a rapid pace, while other young men, in the lead, hold a dozen enormous black fans made of feathers, perhaps peacock feathers.

(Greek text)

NOTE 36D
The Argonauts. Book III (Continued)

Return to Kuwait—Forced landing in Dubai—Unbelievably white sand, perhaps the most beautiful in the world, with clusters of very tall palms—Camels wander freely, unused, returned to the wild state— Complete ingratitude toward them and their centuries of service to man—An English nymphomaniac at the hotel xxx xxx at the port—She has a pronounced jaw, blue eyes that look at the crotch of every man she meets—An obscene and challenging smile—The harbor is full of old Persian ships—Squat, round, with carpets on the decks, the toilet like a little wooden cage hanging above the stern, a long wooden beak on the prow—At night the rowers drink tea and play their instruments— Return to Kuwait—The world of the diplomats: reception including many of those women with their uterine and snobbish tensions, possessed and as if dehydrated by their fever—Medea's love for Jason, on the lips of all—As for the Golden Fleece, it shines /in shreds/—with an oily and barely trembling red light, here and there throughout the desert.

(Greek text)

NOTE 36E
The Argonauts. Book III (Continued)

Meditation of Orpheus—The true birth is the second birth—Initiation; cultural birth, <?> Orpheus—The true journey is the second journey— The first is sleep (in a cave, under a tree: it's all inside the mother's womb)—The second journey is the true one because it is realistic—It couldn't be if it didn't have the "dream foundation" of the first—We go in the footsteps of Heracles, who dreamed our journey—We do what Alexander did, what many others have done—The moment will come when the dream space of the journey is filled—It will take only the <...> space of the journey—We are perhaps the last, and in fact our dream is very close to reality: to the /banal mapping/ of every place— /We are "late," we are corrupt Alexandrians, we are cultivated men/ who still have, no one knows why, the possibility of initiation—Death of Orpheus (malaria)—Burial of Orpheus—At twilight on the outskirts of the city, near the sea, two young men who have just returned from work spread a small faded carpet on the sand outside a little house—They leave their shoes on the sand—They sit on the carpet, legs crossed, and begin to play their instruments (a drum and a kind of very crude man- dolin, with a round, swollen belly, like the Persian ships)—They are two workers, immigrants, with very dark skin; two Sudanese.

(Greek text)

NOTE 36F
The Argonauts. Book III (Continued)

Aeetes' plans against the Argonauts—Medea promises Calciope to help
her children and her companions—Journey by car to Bassora. At the
border with Iraq it is the middle of the night—A truck stop, with
stores, cafés, barracks—In a dilapidated structure with a porch, opposite a /small store/ whose lights sparkle as if for a peasant feast but immediately die out on the sand, two young workers prepare to sleep,
spreading their carpets on the uneven floor—They look around for a
long time, tall young men with mustaches and childish, lined faces—
In the courtyard of one barracks, the soldiers have carried their beds out
into the open—Against a high chipped wall there is a television screen,
where an American film is being shown—Some eighteen-year-old soldiers stand guard—Others go to sleep—Two sleep together, embracing
and smiling, in the same bed—There is no moon—There is a strong
odor of the stagnant sea—Between the huge, shining branches of the es-
tuary of xxx appears the oasis of Bassora—There are squat, thick palms,
covered with dust—They stretch to infinity—From time to time a
muddy channel cuts through them—A big boat, half rotten and all encrusted with salt and mud and painted with pitch, is pushed through
the water by the black arms of an old man who with all his strength
braces himself against a long oar that fishes for the muddy bottom—On
the threadbare carpets in the one big hotel in Bassora, which is owned
by the government and is immense, damp, and noisy, Jason has a conversation with some bureaucrats, who seem to feel perfectly at ease in
that Balkan hotel—Return to Kuwait—Preparation of Jason, who sacrifices to Hecate—Appearance of Hecate—Appearance of a group of
sons of multimillionaire sheikhs, young men of around thirty, who sit
in the open space in front of the hotel xxx xxx and play cards like beg-

gars or prostitutes—Hecate disappears—The moon hangs over the Persian Gulf, which is flat and hot, like a lagoon.

(Greek text)

NOTE 36G
The Argonauts. Book III (Continued)

The will of Orpheus—There is a point in the journey where one begins the return—Alexander is not only Alexander, he is also Sikandar—It is Sikandar who knew how to pluck that miraculous moment, which precedes the return by an instant—The end of every journey is Zulmat (the Land of Obscurity)—One turns back by chance—One leaves the interior, returns to the light—But is it worth the trouble?—Advice to the tourist Tenelo and the observer Linceo—In order not to remain excluded from the myth—Recall that the serpent found in the desert had been killed *the day before* by Heracles—One has only to sharpen one's gaze and his figure will appear, remote, at the edge of the desert—His footprints, then, which mapped the land, are still fresh everywhere—Because he had sung its origins (Orpheus has written in his will), the journey was possible—The myth is literary; but it is always myth—But now, having arrived at the climax of the journey, if you realize it stay there—Just let everything at Zulmat be shadowy and arbitrary: pure folly, in fact grotesquerie—You have the head of Buzug ibn-Sachriar, who sees portents and that's all, without any connection, any sense—If in order to turn back you must make sacrifices, don't do it—Remember what a poet tells you from the grave (near an oil well): you are not "late," you are not "later"; you are the "last"—If you turn back with the new news, no one will ever again be able to travel as you have (that is, laying a foundation in dreams for later realistic journeys)—Impregnate monkeys with serpents' heads or the feet of baby ducks, not Medeas—

Remain in the miracle under the light of the Purple Cloud—Do not come and tell Propp and Blanchot anything—Embarrassment and discomposure of the crew at the reading of the Will—No one feels he has the nature of a Gordon Pym or of a "Divine Rascal."

(Greek text)

NOTE 36H
The Argonauts. Book IV (Continued)

Brief trip to Damascus—The city piled up like an enormous mass of bunkers on the ruins of souks and Arab villages, on bare dusty hills inhabited by baying dogs—The Minister of Foreign Affairs, xxx xxx, in his shabby little study, with heavy furniture that seems to have been bought from a junk man—He is melancholy—In the evening < ... > invites him for cocktails, there the wives of the diplomats /do not even have the/ energy of anxiety, either sexual or arriviste < ... >—The poor women are silent, melancholy—A young pianist plays a score by an anonymous, unpublished Italian master of the seventeenth century quite well—A popular motif, which recalls Neapolitan songs—Perhaps the general lack of energy is the result of the visit, a week before, of the Italian Foreign Minister—The government offers a tour to Palmyra— Triumph of Tenelo and Linceo—Bitter cold—In the morning one's nostrils are completely black, all the way to the throat, because of the emissions from the little oil stoves in the hotel—Ruins of Palmyra— Desolate appearance of Heracles on the horizon—Return to Kuwait.

(Greek text)

NOTE 361
The Argonauts. Book IV (Continued)

Flight of Medea from the palace—Meeting with Jason—Gift of the Golden Fleece—Departure of the expedition for Eritrea—Stop in Aden—Stop at the burning-hot airport from which one cannot depart—Entrance "visa"—The enormous group of jagged, violet volcanoes at the foot of which the /wretched/ city extends on an infinity of peninsulas, isthmuses, lagoons, piers, islands—Signs of struggle everywhere—Walls of the workers' houses pitted by bursts of machine-gun fire—Here and there signs of bombardment—Rubble—The big abandoned warehouses, the empty port (some ancient Persian sailing ships lie overturned on the mud)—The roads continually blocked by tangles of rusty barbed wire—Roadblocks manned by emaciated Yemenite soldiers—The former colonial hotel, deserted—The English club on the sea, deserted—The deafening croak of ravens—Formal reception in the grim hotel lobby, given by an undersecretary, or something similar, in a gray suit and dusty pointed-toe shoes that will break your heart.

(Greek text)

NOTE 36L
The Argonauts. Book IV (Continued)

Scenes of Medea—Apocalyptic crises of complaints, recriminations, threats, explosions xxx of hatred—Jason's plans— "Excursion" to a fishing village, with rows of sharks lined up where the waves break and flocks of birds flying around—Two hours in a jeep along the beach—The "savage woman" is abandoned there, after becoming intoxicated by "whiskey"—Precipitate departure from Aden—Appendix to the Will of Orpheus (found among his papers at the embarkation)—Identification of the death with the real goal of the journey—For our Sikandar, the Land of Obscurity, or Zulmat, would be, curiously, Kuwait—The intuition he would have during an evening spent in a neighborhood of the old city, overflowing with innumerable squalid cafés and small hotels—Large dusty squares swarming with people—Turbans, robes (Kuwait is very traditional), and blue jeans—The even more crowded streets, all without paving stones or asphalt—Ancient dust everywhere—Apparently, at the passage of Orpheus all the young men who crowded the cafés (there was not a single woman) *turned,* with a joyful and possessive smile, to look at the stranger, as in the stories of the *Thousand and One Nights*—This would be the sign.

(Greek text)

NOTE 36M
The Argonauts. Book IV (Continued)

Arrival in Asmara—Meeting with the Ethiopian authorities—Object: plan for oil exploration along the coast, in the area of Hassan (?)—Meeting with the commander of the guerrillas in the neighborhood of Agordat (the object of the meeting is the same)—Long journey to Agordat across Keren—The pretext is hunting warthogs—Arrival in Agordat at twilight—Curfew: the impoverished town, entirely white, sits on a foot of dust—Big empty rooms with little beds like cots and torn curtains of a flowered material—Carlo's prophetic dream—Interior of a Coptic church, where some young priests are singing—They stand in an oval at the back of the roughly square church—The Sanctum Sanctorum is at the center: another rough square covered with garish naive pictures telling stories of the Archangels—There is nothing clerical about the priests who are singing—They are boys whose hair is between curly and kinky, very thick, and sticks out behind over their necks and in front over their foreheads—They have thin noses, fleshy mouths, the dark, wounded eyes of herbivorous animals—The old men are like them, and just as youthful—Their hair, between curly and kinky, has become white—All sing the sacred song with great joy, leaning forward with their bodies, offering them almost sensually, as if drawn by the music—In their smiles, however, there is something sweetly shrewd and familiar—Some accompany the song shaking sistrums with regular movements; others beat little drums—The old men are leaning on bishops' staffs, which are T-shaped and end in a handle of worn precious metal—One of these old men has a radiant smile—The dreamer approaches him, until the eyes of the white-haired old man rest on him—It is a penetrating and revelatory look—That old man "knows everything" about Orpheus and his relation with the Third World—"Knows everything," as well, about the poor deceived native woman whose bones grow white among the sharks (unless she has become a beggar in front of the porch of the little mosque).

(Greek text)

NOTE 36N
The Argonauts. Book IV (Continued)

"When one writes without thinking that one is revealing a secret, that is, sincerely, one realizes one has revealed a secret one did not know one had"—"To die before abjuring these people"—"But also to communicate cheerfully to others what one knows of these people"—Last notebook of Orpheus—Departure for Tel Aviv—Stops at Cairo and Nicosia—Arrival in Tel Aviv at twilight—Rapid vision of a nineteenth-century Levantine city—On the beach not far from the hotel, some poor boys spend the night, lighting fires for themselves—A bar, farther on, big, empty, and bright—Morning "reveals" a city full of soldiers— Something stupefying, mysterious, sad—Transfer to Jerusalem—The climate of revelation continues, but it leaves the most important thing regarding this nation obscure and in suspense—Night—The sparkling entrance to a cinema—A group of boys and girls stand in front, in the empty street, with idle uncertainty—Permissiveness and timidity—A boy stands precariously, a little neurotically, on the edge of the side-walk—He is the most beautiful creature in all the land—Perhaps he comes from Spain—With his big strong body, which nevertheless still seems that of a boy, he leaves the sidewalk, in a flash, capriciously, sud-denly—Runs away—Reaches a deserted alley behind the cinema— Here there is a rather decrepit white majolica urinal—The brown-skinned boy goes to pee there—But he pees standing far away from the little chipped cup—The pee is a long, shining jet that traces a bold yet innocent arc in the shadow—The brown boy, grabbing his cock in his two hands, sticks out his crotch, spreading his solid ado-lescent legs—He's not afraid of being seen—It doesn't even cross his mind to be modest, or, at the same time, that he is making an exhibi-tion of himself—His is a boy's game—But at the same time that pee is possessive—It's strange that an introverted Jewish boy pees like that— Certainly no Arab boy pees that way: he hides, slightly embarrassed, perhaps squats—There is no desire for affirmation in his peeing, though it's innocent (and only a little depraved socially), as there is in the Jewish boy.

(Greek text)

NOTE 37
Something written

At the end of my "Argonautica" I feel I owe the reader some explanation in reference to what I was saying in Note 221 about the stylistic oddity of a novel that proposed to be austerely normal. There it was a question of inserting a "graphic," here of inserting a long Greek or neo-Greek text (or, more precisely, the literary neo-Greek used by Cavafy). Well, these printed but illegible pages are intended to announce my decision in a way that is extreme—but is then established symbolically for the rest of the book; that is, not to write a story but to construct a form (as will become clearer later on): a form consisting simply of "something written." I do not deny that certainly the best thing would be to invent an alphabet, perhaps of ideographs or hieroglyphics, and to print the entire book that way. In fact, xxx Michaux (?) has done this recently, creating an entire book, line by line, through the infinite, patient invention of non-alphabetic signs. But my cultural background and my character prevent me from using similar methods to construct my "form"—extreme, yes, but also extremely boring. That's why I have chosen, for my self-sufficient and pointless construction, materials that are apparently meaningful.

NOTE 40
The art that gladdens the human heart

"Obscurity and solemnity are completely out of place in the study (even the most rigorous) of an art originally intended to gladden the human heart:

> Gravity, a mysterious carriage of the body to conceal the defects of the mind
> —Laurence Sterne"[21]

We have reached in a swift and concise manner the end of the first of the three parts that make up this poem; it was not simply a matter of a long prologue or a long foreword (that's why I have been able, relatively speaking, to move rapidly). Looking back, however, I cannot at this point keep from making an observation that seems to me somewhat inconvenient. In what context, under what cultural "umbrella," do the relations between the Ego of our protagonist and his Id occur? From the pyschoanalytic point of view, both orthodox and heterodox, both Freudian and Jungian, both Frommian and Lacanian, such relations are so free that they can permissibly be defined as arbitrary and in fact provocative. Concepts accepted "obediently" rarely seem to be played with so disobediently. In fact, the repression by which Carlo's Ego frees itself, classically, from responsibility for the slaughter with which the first part of the poem ends obeys laws that are completely invented. I have no other explanation to give except that the stories are rough. And so dividing Carlo's ego in two /fixes/ /the/ relationship between a Half-Ego and a whole Id in reality every time. The repression is half classical repression, scientifically analyzable, and half simply a dazed state simi-

---

[21] Ezra Pound.

lar to that of certain paralytics in whom only half the brain functions. This is neither obscure nor serious, it must be admitted; and all the eventual allegorical implications < ... > can only be < ... > amusing. At least I hope so. And with this hope I pass to the second part of the poem, which in reality, then, is the true first part.

COLLECTED STORIES

Concerning "popular culture," in order to introduce characters totally different from the bourgeois protagonists, the following stories are recounted and commented on at an intellectual gathering (see *The Brothers Karamazov*):

The purchase of a slave (in Khartoum)—journey there and back (going: slave trade—coming back: osmosis between the two cultures, through sex)

The story of an Indian family whose members die of hunger one by one (cf. *Notes for a Film on India*)

The destruction of the population of Bihar: the whites try to destroy 30 or 40 million people who are starving and sick with cholera, first throwing from the air "packets" of poisoned food, then carpet-bombing cities and villages. But the population doesn't die: as soon as they are killed, massacred, they are all revived.

The exchange of experiences between a young Israeli and a young Arab: both die in a battle on the Golan, etc., and each is reborn in the body of the other, having its cultural experiences: the Arab experiences the industrialization and the industrial cosmopolitanism of Israel (in Bathsheba), and the Israeli experiences the preindustrial peasant magic of a poor village in Lebanon. The story ends with two real funerals.

Three stories about Trapdoors
—in Morocco (Rabat) the world behind the trapdoor: the same, thanks to a King (dying, plague-ridden)
—in Nigeria (Kano) a depraved world, with the old woman in a cage
—in Algeria (?) the world of Paris, where the boy becomes a street sweeper, *truly* degraded and servile

The refounding of the Kota religion

A story that unfolds the moment Sicily is re-Romanized (Arabs and Sicilians)

Discussions on the relations between the culture of the people (popular poetry, real traditions, etc.) and the dominant culture (Bourbon Catholicism, etc.) in a Lucanian town.

Story of a Greek or Andalusian immigrant in Germany from the early sixties to the threshold of '68 (still utterly unforeseen)

NOTE 41
The Purchase of a Slave

"Our hero," he said < ... >, "could not be Italian and would also ring false if he were French, /let's say he's Anglo-Saxon/; and for the fun of it (because it doesn't have to do with anything) /let's call him/ Tristram. /He is a type who might resemble/ the film critic of a large daily that wanted to rejuvenate its staff. Blond, adolescent, stupid, clever.[22] He is endowed with the usual 'middlebrow culture.' But he has been 'initiated.' And this transforms his middlebrow culture into a social qualification that allows him to be integrated into bourgeois society and at the same time avant-garde. To write for *The Guardian* (?) and to mock the establishment (which is extremely gratifying) in a nihilistic tone, disdainfully (like those rebellious youths encountered in Russian novels from Dostoyevsky to Bulgakov). Good, I'm saying all this \that\ for the pleasure of the telling, which, of course, always sins through excess (anyone who decides to tell a story immediately has the possibility of describing the entire universe).

"But now I will be schematic. This Tristram *would be* puritanical and inhibited, if his middlebrow culture expected him to be uninhibited. Therefore his conscience finds a way of accepting his classical, Victorian, etc., sadism. Naturally, the moment that sadism is accepted it is also modified—it goes without saying. And furthermore, on the ideological plane our Tristram has arrayed his anti-authoritarian and anti-colonialist

[22] See Mr. Walker (the critic, in fact, of ". . . .").

progressivism on the vaster canvas of a Eurocentrism that constitutes his real, and much deeper, inextirpable racial prejudice. However, one day a friend says to him that in certain places in the Sudanese region, that is, the south Sahara, slave merchants still exist. Every year, for example, throughout the Islamic world, pilgrimages to Mecca are organized. People leave from Morocco, from Mauritania, from Senegal and go dutifully to pay homage at the tomb of Muhammad. (Then, it seems, they have the right to wear a green turban.) Let's take a group of young Mauritanian peasants: black Muslims. They wish to go to Mecca. But they are poor—impossible to be poorer. They have never seen more dinars at one time than it takes to buy a pair of pants at the souk. But someone will provide for them, that is, for their thirst for devotion. Their journey is arranged: they will pay for it by working rather than with money. They leave in a truck that is rickety but gaily painted in the brightest colors. They say good-bye to their mothers, to their many friends, to their village, and go off. The journey to the other end of the desert, across the entire Sudanese region, lasts three or four years. I will not describe to you such an odyssey. The work of the pilgrims is, of course, hard labor. And the trip is organized so that they work on the plantations, and perhaps also at some construction sites, according to a regular schedule. Of course, they have no protection and the work is practically < ... > /unlimited/; but they have no alternative. Either they work like slaves or no Mecca (and also no return home). The oldest and the weakest die on the road. Those who reach the Red Sea, at Port Sudan or, more likely, some small, solitary place on the coast, may finally embark and hope to be at the end of their calvary. But as soon as they have got to the other side of the Red Sea, around Jedda (because it is not actually considered necessary for them ever to reach Mecca), they are seized, chained, and held as slaves.[23] Well, all this is little more than an excursus, too bizarre, perhaps, to be truly 'real.' . . . But don't forget that your narrator is a journalist. What counts in our little story, whose 'reality' is symbolic, is a detail that is a kind of /excursus within the excursus/. Some of these 'pilgrims,' along with other young men and girls of the Negro race, whose provenance /escapes me/ (perhaps the pagan

[23] Our narrator was telling this story around 1965–66.

south of the Sudan?), are in fact seized and sold as slaves even before they reach the other side of the Red Sea. This happens on the outskirts of Khartoum, probably in Abadan, the old city (that of xxx xxx), which still has its low, ocher-colored mud houses, its long walls jealously enclosing the almost religious intimacy of the peasant dwellings, its wide, dusty open spaces blinding in the sun, against a background of brilliant bougainvillea or red acacia. . . . Those slave merchants are at the margins of the law, but under the regime of Abboud[24] they are more or less tolerated. In short, anyone who wants to can succeed in finding a way of arriving surreptitiously at the slave auction and buying a girl or boy for a figure corresponding to, I believe, about three or four hundred thousand lire. Tristram was struck (ironically) by this story. And he decided (always ironically) to set out on a trip for Khartoum to buy a female slave. He was, apparently, heterosexual. Thus began what we have the weakness to call his 'anabasis.' It was a matter of setting out for a definite but, to our traveler, unknown place (the Middle East and the Sudanese region) and, at the same time, of leaving behind him a known place—rather, THE place par excellence: England, Europe (Western civilization—I beg you, banally, to note). Now, our clever Tristram had always 'known' of the existence of another universe, and he did not hesitate, as a progressive, to give to that universe the same value as his own. . . . But 'knowing' is one thing, 'knowledge' another. Especially as Tristram's cultural milieu was, evidently, a very aristocratic, empirical, and pragmatic one that believed only in 'field' research (even though Tristram had been 'corrupted' by ideologies originating on the Continent—utopian, dogmatic, crudely rational). During the anabasis, which goes relatively slowly, despite his traveling by plane, our Tristram's consciousness acquires what it deems socially acceptable but what in his heart (and precisely for social reasons) he rejects: the reality of another universe. It is one thing to think of the sun in Khartoum and another to live it, to accept in one's body <...> its silence <?>, etc. It is one thing to think of the person who can put you in contact with the slave merchants, another to meet him in flesh and bone (a tall man, fat, soft as a child, with two big mustaches; wrapped in a white robe, with

[24] See preceding note.

a pair of black European trousers underneath, and wearing shoes hardened by the dust that permeated everything). The sale of slaves took place /in secret/ in a small hotel that also had a bar on the ground floor (a big empty room that stank because of the toilet next to it, where urine was overflowing from the hole). The rooms opened onto a small white interior courtyard, with massive wooden galleries eaten away by the humidity. Inside the rooms were some grayish cots, a few chairs that were also massive and half rotted, a rag at the sink. The slaves, grouped in threes and fours in these little rooms, were all bathed in sweat (because there weren't even fans, like the ones that turned desperately and almost uselessly in the bare room with the bar). Tristram was expecting to see them naked. Instead they were all modestly clothed. When he asked his xxx if it was possible to see the female slaves naked so that it would be easier to choose, he immediately saw that he had caused a serious embarrassment, which was followed by confusion. Tristram understood that he had made a gaffe, and, following the dictates of his philosophy, he adapted instantly and ironically to the situation. There was a moment of agitation: if the puritanism of the blacks and the Muslims, taken together, had to be violated, it could not be without dismay. But—power of the white man!—immediately afterward Tristram was led into another small room, similar to the others but with a big fan, and here the slaves were brought in in turn and, as if they had received an order, began to undress. This did not happen without some amusement on their part. They smiled the way peasant women smile, flashing their teeth, and looked at the buyer with a certain mocking impudence (that is, as if from the heart of their blackness they considered this white man "other," exactly as he at heart considered them; the estrangement was so great there was no possibility of a meeting, not even a meeting of a morally negative character, dramatic, scandalous, as between the one who buys a human being and the one who is bought! Evidently those women felt so different, so *distant* from the man who was buying them that his act became nonexistent, or at least did not concern their real life). Observing those smiling, provocative faces, Tristram thought of prostitutes. It often happens, in fact, that prostitutes have with their clients that extreme (indeed, mocking) look of defiance. And the thought of prostitutes was immediately linked to the thought of decep-

tion. Those women were merely prostitutes who had lent themselves to
the game of selling slaves, organized by that fat black man with the
mustache, who was therefore nothing but an audacious swindler
(/bound/, of course, to his own trickery by a tenacious and frightening
relationship \chain\). Tristram understood immediately that it was impossible to make direct accusations, and, philosophically angry, smoking his pipe, he limited himself to saying he didn't like any of them.
And they, meanwhile, continued to smile, looking at him, as if making
fun of the deplorable weakness he had shown in asking to see them
naked. But the *background* of their smile was so remote and so hopelessly
foreign that Tristram wondered if he should < ... > be upset. Just at that
point, however, he freed himself from the unpleasant situation (the broker already had a kind of mean, stubborn veil of complaint in his eyes)
with an idea that was surprising even to him. He asked to see the male
slaves; perhaps he would buy one of them. The broker and his thugs,
who, innocent and apprehensive, were young men of an indefinable age,
suspended all judgment. They threw themselves into satisfying the
wish of the buyer; and immediately a dozen male slaves had been
brought to another little room, and as soon as Tristram entered they
hurried to undress, according to the same directive given to the women.
They did it without laughing and without mocking the stranger. Some
of them, in fact, smiled gently, with sympathy, devotion, and obedience. Most, however, were serious, their eyes dull or else open in a stu-
por of uncertainty and fear. Some, perhaps of Ethiopian origin—and
perhaps not Muslims—were prey to a dramatic sense of offended modesty (bound to who knows what /desperate/ taboos). If Tristram, instead
of standing there filled with reluctant understanding toward those
black 'brothers,' about to commit an arbitrary guilty act, had held a machine gun in his hand, like a marine, or one of his old military forebears,
to threaten them and take them by force rather than money, the effect
would not have been different. In fact, it would have been exactly the
same. That crowd of young men with their modest cocks dangling were
from the opposite shore and had no relation to Tristram except existentially (and in that sense they could just as easily have been poor European peasants); while their cultural xxx remained lost in xxx distances.
The very advanced < ... > Tristram Walker was therefore in danger of

being unable to have any experience: either private (sadist) or social (knowledge of a different world, which at that time was beginning to be called the Third World). It was from the immorality of the first that the authenticity of the second was to be derived. And what was expected was a confirmation of Tristram's democratic progressivism. Remaining what he was—instead—and disappointed by the fact that that 'other' world had not opened its arms wide to welcome him to its breast, not even if provoked, that is, assaulted by a desire perceived as real because it is scandalous—Tristram went out again into the gallery, followed by the thugs, in whose eyes shone desperately and ominously the frank hope of a reward even for a transaction that had not been concluded. But in the gallery Tristram saw an apparition. It was a girl of about twelve or thirteen, but perhaps even younger. She had a beauty so perfect and inhuman that she appeared almost metallic (apart from the color of her skin): a mask from Benin, with /pure/, carved plantlike features. Her dress was that of an impoverished peasant: a faded pink flowered rag, tight around the chest and wide at the bottom, hanging down to the middle of her knees. When Tristram saw her, the child made a pirouette and disappeared. But Tristram had made up his mind: it was she he must buy. He immediately said so, loud and clear, to the broker. He, as usual, fell into a state of confusion but, after consulting with his thin adolescent accomplices, ended up conducting Tristram decisively to a third little room, where the boys were gathered. She was there among the others but in the first row, submissive and at the same time proud as a soldier. Perhaps she had understood everything and, with steady, shining eyes, was declaring that she was willing to be bought as a slave, and by that very master. The business was quickly (relatively quickly) concluded, with great satisfaction on all sides.

"Tristram had rented a little house with a garden on the other side of Khartoum, in the upper-class, European neighborhood along the Nile. Here it usually felt like a hot summer day *au bord de la Seine*. In the privacy of his villa, where he could tranquilly 'give free rein to his desire'[25] since no one would report on the conduct of a citizen of the Commonwealth, he got busy writing the articles with which /he had calculated/

[25] *Translator's note:* Dante, *Inferno*, Canto V.

he would pay for the trip and began the practical application of the *'philosophie du boudoir.'* For example, all the time he was at his table writing, Giana, the little Negro slave, had to stay under the table with her master's penis in her mouth, even if it was not necessarily erect. Any infraction of this rule would be followed by a punishment that had been determined by legislative judgment and was based on lashes: two if the child—seized by some bodily necessity or girlish distraction—abandoned her master's penis for a single instant; a number that would naturally increase in proportion to the gravity of her disobedience. Thus Tristram passed the last three hours of the morning and all the late afternoon (the periods of the day when he worked) with his prick in Giana's mouth. Any punishments were marked down in a notebook and given together in the evening. The girl found all this natural and did not bat an eyelid at any demand or any xxx; for her, being a slave was an idea that was rooted in her consciousness. And the more she accepted with total passivity the servitude, the pain, the torments, the blows of her /inscrutable/ master, the more that master, on his side, was /charmed/ and implacable. He realized, besides, that the child accepted in the most natural way his changes of humor and behavior. In fact, Tristram was naturally kind, gentle, and good to /her, except/ when he decided to engage in sadistic practices. A transition that /he made without/ any violence, by means of a simple but irrevocable summons. And the girl, in fact, did not wonder why 'the master' went so suddenly from a gentleness and understanding such as she, certainly, had never known to the most /ruthless/ demands, with /equally ruthless/ punishments attached. Observing that he had done this made Tristram immediately /behave again like a master/, or, rather, with ceremony. But /just as/ the girl accepted violence and punishment as natural, with equal naturalness she accepted Tristram's kindness and polite favors; she did not have any gratitude toward him for this—as, on the other hand, she felt no rancor for the pain he caused her. During the sexual rituals, which she performed diligently, the way children do homework or carry out tasks, with self-confidence and a desire to do well—it was not clear what was passing through her mind. She was less beautiful than she had first appeared in the gallery of the National Hotel, she had become darker, smaller, more pathetic; and this was all that leaked out, indirectly, of her feelings. When she was punished she usually shrieked and cried, only to stop immediately. When her master treated her well, in normal times, outside the rituals, she betrayed no feeling. Only when /she was eating/ did a greedy happiness shine in her eyes. < ... > Tristram finally realized this, too. And so 'dispensing food to the slave' came to be part of the rituals. The first time it was a great pleasure for Tristram. In fact, she was completely innocent and was preparing, that day, to eat the good things that are eaten in the houses of the rich, with her usual calm happiness. As soon as Giana was on the point of starting her meal, Tristram—as he had calculated, abominably, to himself—took it away from her, with a severe look, like Jove 'arcanely just,'[26] as a supplement to the punishments she had earned that morning. One of her duties was to wash him scrupulously, all over, in the big bathtub of the colonial 'toilette'; and that very morning she had shown some carelessness in cleaning Tristram's penis and anus. For the first time, Tristram, taking away from her her bitch's meal, was able to make out on Giana's face a desperate disappointment and an almost tortured look at him from head to foot. From then on, food, too, depended on the inscrutable will of the master, and Giana, as with all the rest, resigned herself to it.

"This story lasted only a few days. Tristram, as you have understood perfectly, was by nature lacking in grandeur. So he had decided on a very brief trial for his sadistic experience, intending to remember it for his whole life, with irony—that is, without nostalgia regarding the first part, the slavery, and without the least sentimentality regarding the second part, the liberation.

"He had decided to free Giana in the best way; but there was not, to tell the truth, much choice. In fact, there was a single possibility—to leave her at a mission. /There was/ in Khartoum only one Catholic mission, and it was run by a Dutch father, xxx by name, a young man around thirty, with an enormous mass of hair and an enormous red beard and, in the midst of all that hair,† eyes that were eternally and madly smiling. When Tristram brought Giana there to hand her over to him, it was nearly evening, the heat was atrocious, the bougainvillea and the red acacias hung inert in the peacefulness of the African night,

[26] Dante, *Purgatory*, Canto XXIX.

with the sound of a distant drum but not a single voice rising from the pink or ocher mud houses in that immense part of the city: covered by a foot of soft dust. The mission was a small villa, something like the one Tristram had rented by the Nile, but infinitely /poorer/. As soon as Father xxx—who already knew of Tristram's decision and expected him—saw him arriving, he /immediately/ began to make large, exaggerated beckoning gestures with his hands—in fact, with the whole of his long arms. These gestures usually ended with his long bony index finger at his lips and a flash of a pleased smile in his /candid/ eyes: it was more than obvious that Father xxx wished to make Tristram understand by this that he must be silent. Then the broad gestures underwent a change, also solidly underlined. This time they clearly /indicated/ that Tristram was to follow /him, still in silence/. Thus Tristram found himself, with Giana tight by the hand, in a room (which must, of course, be the sitting room) with the doors wide open onto a veranda that overlooked a dusty garden, forbiddingly thick with xxx and palms. The heat was atrocious, the darkness profound. Nevertheless, on the floor of the sitting room, in which there was almost no furniture, forty bodies could be seen; they were the bodies of sleeping children. Sleep had come upon them in the most diverse and disorderly positions. If it hadn't been for the profound peace and a certain modesty in their shabby white garments, they would have looked as if they had been shot. Father xxx, with his hands folded, contemplated them, as if a little moved and certainly much amused. His eyes, which, intensely and ingenuously /glittering/, stared at his guest, /led one to understand why Father xxx/ had found the sight so comical. Having shown Tristram his organizational masterpiece—made in all simplicity of spirit and Christian poverty—Father xxx whispered to Tristram to follow him into his study. It was a suffocating little room, because of the /heavy/ fabric of the divans and chairs gathered around a small desk overflowing with papers. Here occurred briefly what was, in practical terms, the second sale of Giana, who uncomprehendingly watched the two masters speaking. Until the new buyer took her by the hand, preparing to lead her out into the dormitory, with the others. But first he accompanied Tristram to the door. Tristram caressed Giana's head, shook hands with the father, and, with his ironic smile, like that of a young, prematurely wrinkled American marine, took his leave. With his usual exaggerated and happy pirouette, the father turned toward the interior of the villa. Giana followed him, and although Tristram stood unmoving on the /soft/ carpet of dust that covered the wide dusty street, watching her, she did not turn, not even for an instant.

"A sickle moon had risen over the <...> /Islamic/ countryside. The night was indigo-colored. Not a voice could be heard. Some American music sounded in the distance.

"The catabasis began: not only less clear and less, so to speak, 'expressive' but also much longer than the anabasis. Tristram went by plane, it's true, as far as Cairo (where he visited the city), but then he went by train to Alexandria in order to return to Europe by sea. Alexandria is a city with some traditions of culture, and not only /archeological/. Writers (for example, Cavafy) have been born and lived there, and there are some cultural circles. Wandering through the center as he waited to embark, Tristram went into a bookstore, and, curiously, the first book he happened to pick up was a small anthology from Marx's *Capital,* in some edition or other. Tristram had never read it, having been a snob both at Cambridge, where he had studied, and in London, where he lived his intellectual's life. Besides, there were many books Tristram did not know. Being an 'initiate'—that is, belonging to the most culturally prejudiced élite in his country—gave him a way of reading practically nothing except newspapers and magazines. In fact, the truth is that after Cambridge he had not read any books except some stupid monographs on Eisenstein and Hitchcock; he did not know a word of the history of religions, of linguistics, etc., and in anthropology he had read only a few pages of Lévi-Strauss, at the time when /he was absolutely fashionable/. As for Fanon (because he was equally fashionable), he knew him only by name. He imagined, however, that behind the mystery of Giana and her sellers there was a 'magical world,' but instinctively, through pure ignorance, he denigrated it to an ultimately insignificant and refutable fact. For him, as a progressive, the magical world was nothing but superstition (about which, in truth, he knew only the four banal facts that everyone knows). The 'otherness' of the world of Giana, *who had not turned around,* evidently included the magical world, but it was not there that it was expressed; in fact, Tristram instinctively attributed to Giana, at least in an extremely rough and only potential way, his own feeling of condemnation toward it! < ... > the negative judgment of a modern man who interpreted the Third World as a mythic confirmation of his own reformist progressivism and as the mythic march toward the future that encouraged the New Left in its just struggle. But, even interpreted that way, Giana's Third World was a total frustration, without any glimmer of reasonable hope; and in fact at the inevitable moment of their parting, each going his own way, it could not be said either that Tristram had integrated his culture with Giana's or that Giana, for her part, had integrated her culture with Tristram's.

"But the only possibility of a democratic relationship between people like Tristram and people like Giana was in the integration of these two cultures. There was no other solution in the world for living together in a civilized and reasonable fashion. That this had not even minimally occurred wore terribly on Tristram's nerves. Nevertheless, it was already an important thing (for an impartial observer like me) that the crisis had begun and that he had wished to put off his return home indefinitely. The problem was: to save his own conscience in the relationship between two cultures that could not be integrated with each other and that in fact, in spite of all the goodwill, remained completely alien.

"The solution < ... > was unexpected. The ship on which Tristram was to go to England, on an endless return voyage, made a stop of a day or two in Naples. Tristram naturally disembarked and devoted himself to exploring the city (although he had been there before). In a certain little /irresistibly/ filthy garden, where some children were bathing in their underwear in a fountain, as children had been doing twenty years before, he saw a dark, ragged urchin, standing unsociably apart:

xxxxxxxxxx

xxxxxxxxxxx

"There was no doubt, she resembled Giana. She was almost her sister. She belonged to the same 'culture.' One that gave the same physical quality (in spite of the purely accidental differences) to those street children of Naples who were diving into the fountain and to those of Khartoum who were sleeping in Father xxx's dormitory. The material /of their flesh/ was a material different from that < ... > of the dominant culture < ... > ; < ... > which could integrate the popular culture only by making it its own, that is, by forcing it to degenerate, to remain at the lowest levels of consciousness, as it had remained, for centuries, at the lowest levels of society.

< ... > "And Tristram < ... > let himself fall on the rank grass of that little garden in Forcella: 'fall,' I say, like Saint Paul on the road to Damascus. He had suddenly been converted to Marxism < ... > ."

< ... > "An extraordinary story, also because it's /disappointing/," said one of the listeners.

< ... > "Yes," said /the Reciting Voice/, "but the story of Tristram is nothing compared with the story of xxx, xxx, and their three children."

"And what is this story of xxx, xxx, and their three children?" asked the same listener.

"Pour me a drop of whiskey, and I will tell it to you," said the narrator, his face alight.

—experience of slavery (<?> symbolic, etc.)

—Liberation of the slave

—indifference of the slave both to slavery and to freedom. Her disappearance without trace, nonexistence. What is different does not exist. Enigma not posed, besides not resolved, etc., etc. [left at a Mission—*she does not turn and look back*]

—failure of cultural mixture and integration: in her and in him

—Catabasis: passage for Naples (by ship)—Neapolitan child—Fall in Damascus—Impossibility of a real, living [democratic] cultural integration—Unique possibility of approaching the problem to safeguard one's conscience and then not give a damn about it. Tristram's enrollment in the Communist Party (conversion to Marxism)

May 26, 1974

NOTE 42
The story of xxx and xxx and their three children xxx

NOTE 43
The story of the city of Patna and the region of Bihar

"The city of Patna," began the narrator, "as you all know, is the capital of Bihar and is situated on the banks of the Ganges. The night on which our story begins was an ordinary night. At nine in the evening the silence was already profound, but many people, as is customary in India, were still awake \even though\ < ... > . Huddled in corners, /against the shanties, beside the fetid drains, among the bushes on the edges of the endless open spaces, which were all marshy at this time of year, in front of the harshly lit hotel entrances. There were also crowds of bicycles silently coming and going/. In contrast to the voices of the people, which were so restrained as to be more like whispers pronounced in a sacred place (but with the tranquil, idle sound of people who have known one another for a long time and meet every night to gossip), the lights, on the other hand, /contrary to the voices/, seemed to have no restraint: in festoons, as if at some abandoned festival, they glittered white and fierce and were reflected in the wells and in the mud (the rainy season had just begun). In a place where these lights shone with a grimmer and more naked violence, right in front of the xxx Hotel, which was the most important hotel in the city, the band of nocturnal gossipers was more numerous and denser than elsewhere. In fact, all the 'coolies' out there—in the muddy open area /in front of/ the hotel, some

run-down houses, and the endless /space of the/ marshy, moonlit parade
ground—had lined up their bicycle-drawn carriages. Some, having
rolled themselves up in the same long rag that, wrapped around their
sides, served as a garment and now was stretched lightly, like a shroud,
had already gone to sleep on the seats of their carriages, which were also
<...>. But generally the ones who did this did not really manage to
sleep and gave <...> their attention to the conversation of their friends.
Then, some were completely devoted to preparations for sleep: they
parked their broken-down, mud-encrusted carriages, performed their
ablutions in a puddle, dried themselves with a rag fished from the bottom of xxx, made sure to fill with water a mysterious little brass am-
phora, which everyone in the city carried. And these preparations put
whoever was making them in a particularly cheerful frame of mind; and
if in the quiet talk that followed, and sounded like a whisper under the
immense humid cloak of the tropical night, /every so often a cry arose,
or a call, or a louder laugh, it was one of those getting ready to go to
sleep who was guilty of it/. The xxx Hotel was about to close. The red
door, pierced by peepholes, as in a nightclub, and with a halo of lights
around it, had already been closed; inside there were only one or two
customers, who were dining in the big underground rooms, and the
porters circled and recircled with an unfriendly, absorbed look, like
priests repeating their useless gestures, of which even the symbolic
meaning is lost. The waiters, as they finished their shift, went out, and,
before going off on their own business—that is, to sleep—most of them
stopped to have a word or two with the group of "coolies" and the old
night walkers, whose bedroom, moreover, was visible nearby, faintly illuminated: it was a bare floor of beaten earth, with a bench, two or three
rags, and, in front of the entrance, a stinking puddle. Only those who
worked at the hotel were dressed European style, and very approximately besides: they wore a pair of very light white pants and a shirt of
the same material. For this reason, they did not fail to assume and maintain an air of hauteur. The others, as I said, had a single piece of cloth
wrapped around their sides, and some wore a faded old shirt on top.
Around ten, the last customers, all Indians, left the restaurant. That
night no foreigners were passing through, and the rooms of the hotel
were empty, their enormous fans idle and the doors open onto the long,

forbidding, dark wooden galleries. After those last customers—who left in a car—came Sardar, one of the waiters in the restaurant, perhaps the youngest but also the nicest and the strongest. He was in fact a native of the mountainous region at the Nepalese border. He had an air of being satisfied with his work, he was very elegant in his black pants and his European—or, rather, American and flowered—shirt and his pointed shoes (hardened by the dust and dry mud, perhaps, but a sign of great luxury /there/ where everyone was barefoot). His eyes—which looked as if they had been made up, so deeply was their oblique outline carved into the socket and so thick were the eyebrows—shone with an irrational joy, like an animal's; in fact, they were not really distinguishable from those of all his contemporaries who were gathered there, in that corner of the world. As his hair, smooth, straight, gleaming, and black, was indistinguishable: the black of a blackness so pure that it evoked the plumage of birds; and gleaming with an equally pure gleam.

"Sardar went off in silence, on foot, in front of the group of street people; he did not dare to interrupt their conversation, but he was smiling and sympathetic. It was both timidity and pride. Timidity because he was more refined than the poor coolies, masters of the street; pride because he felt socially superior to them. But timidity and pride canceled each other out, leaving only the bright and silent smile of their most agreeable side.

"His less fortunate and coarser contemporaries—if it's possible to speak of coarseness in those creatures as delicate as lambs, fragile, with their innocent eyes—continued to discuss among themselves the subject of that evening, with their rapid speech, and they had just noticed, as something perfectly natural and irrelevant, the presence of Sardar. Indeed, Sardar himself was pleased with the inattention; he wished to stay there just a little while because he was a boy, life always had many attractions for him, even if it was the common evening gossip of coolies, he did not feel like going home right away—it was some distance—to sleep. He enjoyed simply being there, being part of that little circle (the only authoritative waking community in the immense wet desert of sleeping Patna), to know, on the one hand with respect, on the other with a certain irony, what was behind the scenes, both the casual quarrels and the jokes. There was in him a deep purity, such as all boys have who are without any sense of guilt and are at the same time humble and respectful; that purity seemed to be reflected, glowing, in his skin and in his eyes.

"When suddenly something unexpected happened. Unexpected probably more to a casual Western observer than to a citizen of Patna. Nevertheless, we all know that when these things happen, there is always something new and sacred about them. It's the fulfillment of a fate that threatens us but that we always believe belongs to others or to tomorrow. When it happens to us, today, we remain stunned, prey to a religious terror.

"And that was what happened also to the innocent young coolies and to the old porters who were standing around idly, on that hot night in the rainy season, in the square in front of the xxx Hotel.

"All at once they stopped speaking, and in their eyes, until a moment before full of a loquacious and optimistic /peace/, /was/ the < ... > gleam of fear.

"The cause of all this was Sardar. Suddenly, his clear face was covered with inflamed pus-filled sores, and his pure black eyes, which had been full of a happy light, were reduced to two horrible fissures, because the flesh around them was < ... > swollen. Very quickly the spots on his skin were transformed into wounds, and the swelling around the eyes cracked, becoming livid, trachomalike. Pus flowed from the wounds, streaking Sardar's neck and his white shirt with a repugnant and oily yellowish slime, while from the cracks in the swelling around the eyes blood flowed, which then became mixed with the pus. While the blood and pus rolled down along Sardar's body, you could see that his whole body as well was covered with wounds and swellings, from which streams of pus and blood were draining.

"Sardar, who had just time to perceive, with a shock, what was happening to his body—casting a last glance, a silent plea for help—fell down in the mud. And there he remained like a horrible pulp, emitting an unendurable stench. Everyone ran away, shouting and yelling. Immediately even those who were sleeping awoke and came to the doors and windows of their hovels. All the lights of the xxx Hotel were relit. Now the people had something definite and urgent to speak of. And soon one could see that those passing by on bicycles—who had seemed so few—were in reality a crowd, which in a short time had gathered there, but at a distance from the place where Sardar's body lay, infecting the air.

"Deep into the night the agitation and the noise continued; until dawn, in fact. The whole neighborhood was teeming as in daylight, hungry dogs wandered here and there, children cried or played. Not until the sun was already high did an ambulance arrive to take away the body of Sardar, who had begun to moan.

"Sardar's disease very quickly infected those who had been nearby: first the doorman of the xxx Hotel, who gave himself so many airs, poor hoarse old man, because he had been chosen as a soldier under the English; then the dishwashers in the kitchen; then the coolies; then at random all the inhabitants of the surrounding neighborhood. In short, an epidemic had broken out, not of smallpox or cholera but, rather, of an unknown disease, < ... > /which reduced/ men to a bloody pulp.

"The epidemic, let's call it, did not erupt and spread only in Patna: but the next day, simultaneously, many other places besides Bihar had their turn."

—slaughters, etc.
—the only happy story, <?> etc. (resurrection as the impossibility of destroying a value [popular, poor])
—the one note of sadness is that the only one not reborn, dead forever [innocent victim], is Sardar (?), of whom one thinks with tears in one's eyes.

*

N.B.

in one of the last stories conclude with the metalinguistic note "The delirium is exquisite, the pedantic, etc."—The work *as a joke*

For Part II

*The love of Carlo the meek for the Communist young men of the people— which transforms him into a woman, makes him their slave—turns into hatred in the Carlo with Power, who in his anti-Communist role participates (unconsciously, however, in a psychoanalytically anomalous way) in the slaughter.

*After the slaughter he feels the remorse of the whole Italian bourgeoisie for being *bloodily* anti-Communist (a nightmare of blood). That remorse lays down the prerequisites for an analogous anti-Fascist action (which *restores* a democratic conscience—naturally false)

October 1974

NOTE 41
A significant dream

"Ten years have passed. Carlo is in his bed < ... >, and he is dreaming."

*Carlo dreams about blood; but the red of the blood is *Red* (that is, Communist). It is a premonitory dream, for which all the rest of Part II is only a flashback. This dream is a) the terror of blood; and b) the indifference to blood.
The terror is the terror of the entire anti-Communist Italian bourgeoisie, which, however, has an unhappy conscience because of it
The indifference is the historical indifference of the Italian bourgeoisie, insensitive to everything, politically apathetic, because of a rampant pragmatism.
From this dream of blood and the consequent regret are born the anti-Fascist turnabout and the series of slaughters of Part III.

Oct. 30, 1974

NOTE 42
Clarification

< ... > Appearances to the contrary, this poem is not a poem about dissociation. Dissociation is nothing but a conventional motif (and an homage to the great bourgeois narrative initiated by Cervantes). On the contrary, this poem is a poem of obsession with identity and, at the same time, its destruction.

Dissociation is order. The obsession with identity and its destruction is disorder. Therefore, the theme of dissociation is merely the narrative rule that ensures the limitedness and legibility of this poem; which, on account of the other, truer theme, the obsession with identity and its destruction, would by its nature be limitless and illegible.

But the contrary is also true: that is, since the order of the novel is based on the first theme (that of dissociation), the symbolic-allegorical idea of the novel is also based on it; and this makes it in practice, therefore, unreadable. While it is the second theme (that of obsession with identity and its destruction) that gives birth to the bursts of life and the concrete details, however mad and aberrant (it could not be otherwise, without undergoing the xxx of convention), that make legible the pedantic, vertical, inhuman ....,
the sign of impotence (needing the help of literature) and evidence of the end of the novel.

So while our Carlo, whom on certain occasions, for clarity, I am compelled to call Carlo the First, or No. 1, was having these "dreams of blood," the Carlo < ... >, I sometimes call Carlo the Second or No. 2†

NOTE 43 †
Flashes of light on *Linkskommunismus*

"The ideal way to present the next section of this booklet would be to give the quotations WITHOUT any comment whatever. I am afraid that would be too revolutionary. By long and wearing experience, I have learned that in the present imperfect state of the world, one MUST tell the reader."[27]

In an early draft of this text the various chapter titles were followed by the heading: "From the Mystery" or "From the Plan." The texts belonging to the category "Mystery"—that is, the pages perfectly completed (at the time of that still very fragmentary first draft)—were very few; in consequence, the real chapters, those, that is, belonging to the category of the "Plan," were preponderant. The whole work was in every way conceived as a living coexistence of the "Mystery" that was to be and its "Plan." In fact, the two words "Mystery" and "Plan" were also, provisionally, the subtitle of the novel. Then I yielded to the exigency Pound had had to yield to. Every author is a dictator, of course. But a gentle dictator. He is a dictator always ready to repent, to go backward, even to let himself be killed. He is a dictator who doesn't miss a chance to prostrate himself before the least of his presumed subjects. He is a dictator who goes begging for < ... > the attention of his court. So I hurried to get rid of the coexistence of "Mystery" and "Plan" as soon as I realized that the "Mystery" was too difficult because of its completeness and the "Plan" was similarly difficult because of its incompleteness. I mixed them up, pedagogically canceling them out.

The first pages of this second part would undoubtedly belong to the "Plan" section; and, in fact, they are purely informative, or, again, introductory. That can be explained as follows. In this work the point of

[27] Ezra Pound, *The ABC of Reading.*

view is always at the peak. Things are caught at a moment of actuality so extreme that they appear crystallized or petrified. Everything is a series of friezes or statues, at the height of expressiveness and at the same time linear, as in Theological Works or Allegories. Yet this heightened point of view does not disdain to consider from time to time (quite often, in fact) the depths of the abyss; not only that but, indeed, to observe how things formed down in the abyss slowly rise up until they emerge and are crystallized into peaks; in sum, to capture them exactly, in their movement, in their evolution, in their history. But—between the peak and the abyss—there is still a third alternative; that is, the "middle road." Well, the medieval verticality of the work does not disdain even the middle road, which is typically modern. If a diagram of the work consists of a series of "leaps" between peaks and abysses, it also— and with some continuity—consists of a regular line, which is precisely that of the middle road. The initial portion, destined for the "Plan," has been reduced and is identical to this "figure of the middle road."

↑

the story of the revolution of '68 and its historical significance follows. (cf. also *Linkskommunismus*)
The theme is that "Communism of the Left" has revived the fear of Communism in the bourgeoisie.

"I do not admit youth. They are all proclamations" (said by Governor Lembke, *The Possessed*)

*Cf. p. xxx of *The Possessed*.

NOTE XXX
Evening encounters

Every evening the first and second Carlos met. < ... > They had nothing in common except the Ego itself. Which, /it might appear/ < ... >, is a lot. But not enough, it seems, to furnish a particular number of subjects to discuss or create a particular mutual affection.

It's true, there was always in their encounters something intimate, moving, and at the same time solemn; because, in those encounters, life was being celebrated. And, it should be added, a personal life; that is, a life that had come into being of itself and in itself, as something unique and objective, although destined to be easily lost (a possible reason for the consuming feeling of the memories). Anyway, the two Carlos experienced, in these meetings, intimacy, emotion, and solemnity, but as if automatically, in an /ordinary/ dream in which events have become habitual, are managed routinely, and have gradually lost all significance.

In other words, intimacy, emotion, and solemnity were experienced by the two Carlos in the depths of themselves (waiting to be unleashed someday or other); while on the surface, or, to be more exact, in practice, they were ignored.

But regarding the utter normality, in fact /banality/, of these meetings at which the two Carlos exchanged experiences, and, /so to speak/, *reconnected* them, there is a perhaps still more important observation to be made (and certainly important as far as the organization of our story).

The experiences that the two exchanged had nothing special or dramatic about them; they never transformed the encounters into disputes.

And the fact that my present poem is what it is depends on this.

I mean that if Carlo the First had lived a century ago, or perhaps even fifty years ago, he would have been a hero in whom I, his contemporary, believed. That is, I would have believed in the value and the objectivity of his social anxiety. In his being guilty of that anxiety there would have been, in consequence—just because it was historically < ... > /petty/— something grand. The sin /offense/ of getting rich, of possessing, of advancing, of achieving: all things that always turn tragically against one's own conscience and the freedom of others. And that take for granted the reality of wealth, the reality of possession, the reality of advancement, the reality of success. A society that has recently invented and put into effect its own laws is /profoundly/ unitarian, stable: to the point where it confuses its own unity and its own stability with those of the history of man, if not the universe. No one ever doubted for an instant then—or even, thanks to the authoritativeness of the story, now— the imperatives of a Balzacian hero and his relations with his patrimony; and therefore of his personal psychology.

I could say the same thing for Carlo the Second. His sexual freedom was, at heart, only the affirmation, reiterated a thousand times, of a right in the face of a shriveled-up repressiveness, reiterated in its turn. /In this/ < ... > stubborn, infantile, and ultimately humble reaffirmation of his own right to commit a sexual /transgression/, there was in essence only a little anarchy and a lot of idyll. It's true that in his infinite reaffirmations of the right to sexual transgression (and the consequent pleasure) Carlo the Second experienced what is called a totality: he had pledged his whole self, once and for all (and we all know what an immensity a man is). Anyway, that totality—even if rightly understood as a martyrdom and a radical alternative—was in the end only anarchic and idyllic. Think of the sins of Stavrogin, and you will understand me better. Through his sins, Stavrogin had the same idea of his own society that those who accepted it and took part in its conquest had. Won or lost, a virtue is always a virtue. Also, our Carlo the Second did not lack that little dose of the demonic needed to smooth for himself the road to degradation. But since the virtue he lost in this way was modest, the losing of it was also modest. Besides, since the standards of petit bourgeois virtuous behavior were mediocre, so, too, the shameful behavior of this /renegade/ petit bourgeois was mediocre. Carlo the Second would never have left one of his two young daughters to hang herself in a closet while he was observing a little red spider. He did not know the \the true\ abysses of infamy and perversion, exactly as Carlo the First did not know presidential or dictatorial temptations.

Certainly, one might ask at this point (since I have brought up my /method/) why I did not choose, in that case, to write a poem about Troya or Spigulin, who are, in their way, heroes just like the heroes of Balzac and Dostoyevsky; that is, they possess greatness both of integration and of crime. But to that question—if it had been asked—I would respond that it is not possible to write a poem about people who are boring. And they are boring because they are exceptions and as such do not fall into the sphere of daily experience. Once upon a time, when psychological works could be written, there were no Troyas or Spigulins; but everyone was a Troya or a Spigulin, more or less exceptional.

At the evening encounters—in the hour that follows dinner and precedes the depths of night—the two Carlos "celebrated life," exchanging news of their reciprocal experiences (experiences that, from the psychological point of view, for the reasons I have mentioned, had nothing interesting about them) in that low voice, monotonous and /natural/, which is used for practical everyday communications in the recesses of a house. In reality, it was Carlo the Second who was speaking, since it was Carlo the First who was to be made a participant in the joys he had renounced. For Carlo the Second, on the other hand, the two or three items < ... > of a "social" character that Carlo the First gave him in order not to lose contact with "society" were enough; but already at his companion's first syllables he began to yawn. Rather, anguish came over him. Besides, it was the time when the last shows ended and the city came alive again. The Sex was hungry: a dry, blind, feverish, spasmodic hunger on account of which Carlo nearly began to tremble. Nothing could have kept him seated a moment longer than necessary in the intimacy of the house, whose silence and tranquillity he found literally unbearable.

NOTE 43A
The continuity of daily life

So Carlo, having gone home for a little while, went out again and lived his night. A night that was rigidly codified; and notwithstanding was always open to chance. It's true that sometimes—in fact, fairly often— Carlo had organized it, with an appointment or a series of appointments. But in general the appointments, too, were open to chance; everything that had been arranged might go up in smoke, and Carlo was alone in the night, with the whole city before him, starting all over again from the beginning. If on the other hand the appointments worked out, then they were merely repetitions. Carlo found himself in the same room, usually dirty, with the same woman or the same girl, and he did again what he had done some evenings earlier. Sometimes, it's true, instead of the room it was a field, some shrubbery, full of garbage and shit, old and new. Both before and after the encounter, as we know, Carlo, with his hand in his pocket, was somehow, even on the street, holding his cock and masturbating. But the successful appointments, that is, the repetitions, never satisfied Carlo, not before, while he was waiting, although he waited in an agony, or after. The anguish and the existential misery were tied to the anxiety of the expectation of pleasure and to the pleasure itself. Moreover, the whole thing was, in turn, tied to pitiful negotiations about money and to an economic world made dangerous and elusive by poverty. At the time, Carlo had not understood what an intimate and supreme bond there was between poverty and the body: and how the body had benefited from it, thus preserving in itself, as it did, the "raw material" of the people, which was health, innocence, crudeness, crime: everything except banality, vulgarity, and a sense of guilt. This Carlo would discover later. In reality, at that time he loved the bodies of bourgeois women and girls and was forced by necessity to repeat the scene of his sexual passion every evening, to make his arrangements in the world of work and poverty. Anyway, the setup (the appointment, the room, the bed, the woman or girl already trained and obedient) was an atrocious anti-aphrodisiac: because it suppressed the deep and desperate joy of the *true* repetition, which is a miracle, with its risk that is perhaps even mortal, or almost. Now, when the night was completely deserted, that is, around three in the morning, Carlo went home and slept until eleven or twelve. At that hour the other Carlo had already gone out for business, in his historical world . . .

But although my work belongs to the category of "Acroamatic works" (whose vulgarization Aristotle had been blamed for by Alexander the Great), I would like to make an observation at the end of this chapter.

It is the first time, here, that I have used, in narration, the inchoative imperfect (but the reader may also recall a part analogous to this throughout, that is, the "poem of return," approximately Notes 7–17). The inchoative imperfect signifies the habitual repetition of an action, generally for quite a long period of time (in our case it would be a matter of about a decade).† Well, then, using that imperfect is a mistake on my part. My narration should always be in the present, according to the spirit of my work and the rules that this spirit, in getting established, has issued. It's true, I can grant myself the historical past tense, which is a present removed in time, by means of a pure mythic fiction. But both the present and that historical past are powerful evidence of a will, which conceives the story as singular and linear, the action and the characters lined up as in a gallery or a series of niches or altars. The inchoative imperfect, alluding to the passing of time and of life, proclaims instead the thickness of the story: presents it as a vast, deep lava flow; or, rather, a boundless, bottomless river that runs /in that imperfect, which/ from the flow chooses a detail that is repeated, or a habit, really, and notes it, but purely in outline (which the reader feels is filled in by an infinity of things and sensations). In that imperfect, in sum, *c'est la vie* (threateningly ripe to become a memory).

On the other hand, what I have said by using that imperfect is what I consider appropriate and sufficient to say about the relationship between the two Carlos in the "continuity of life."

NOTE 50
How young men were supposed to be in '69 (from the "Plan")

One November evening—it was around six and already dark—Carlo was walking in the neighborhood of the Central Station. In those days he was looking for a /duplicate of/ Rita. < ... > Sexuality went in cycles; it was now Rita's moment. The female sexual organ had acquired the characteristics of Rita's sex. It was like a fresh light that was projected over old material, renewing it. And it was strange how this newness presented itself as objective, as if there were a great number of women and girls who lent themselves to the role of Rita: they had her small, slightly downy stomach, her thin thighs, they held their head bowed, their sighs were stifled by timidity, yet they did not for that reason lose the courage to speak, to respond, they blushed more in childish obedience than in shame, and the blush made their lips and cheeks fuller and brighter, etc. His dreams at night, his waking in the morning, his perception of the day, all were preoccupied with the idea of this Rita and the infinite series of her variations, which presented as new and consuming to the point of delirium an old desire destined, by itself, to fill a human body forever.

/The idea of Rita was therefore a formal idea and, as a form, determined existence, gave it meaning, order, and also that particular "selective" or "tonal" light which is part of the figurative inspiration of a poet. In fact, in a certain sense Carlo was a poet, even though the idea of writing verses was far removed from him. Like many people, he wrote living poetry. He was a bourgeois, it's true, and so theoretically it was not possible; because only a poor person can sometimes express himself poetically by his actions and his physical presence, especially in moments of joy. Carlo, however, in being obsessed, had been pushed outside his class. As an old man he might very well become a tramp. Now, in any case, he was on the edge, he lived like a criminal, outside the law. Thus, as he was drawn through the streets of the city, far from every idea of duty, of work, of the future, lost and alone in his sexual research, the inner light that revealed the life around him, choosing the forms of it with precision (the role of Rita), was exactly the light with which a poet illuminates the "detail" that at that moment thrills him as the unique physical truth./

So there was a sexual excitement in the traffic around the station at that hour; the human dust that, as if dragged by the wet wind, heavy and warm, whirled below the brown walls of the houses, around the windows of the bars and little shops; the lines of cars ridiculously backed up in the narrow streets, at signals strangely bright in the evening obscurity: /everything was as if determined by the idea of Rita, in everything was her sex, her flesh, with its slight odor and its tenderness/. And so the surrounding world, swirling with bodies, each one drawn into the chaos, seemed the accomplice of Carlo's solitude. Solitude, which he sought through the search for sex, and where he lost himself with an inner happiness to which nothing in the world was equivalent \could compare\.

Suddenly he heard singing.

Was it a radio turned on, a television, a group of recruits under the station marquee? He did not understand. Obscured by the noise of the traffic, powerful and uninterrupted, the song sung by those distant voices could not be made out. But they were male voices. That extraordinary thing, which occurred at six o'clock in the wet, dark air of a November evening, launched a kind of panic. The traffic seemed about to crash; the fixed, meticulous, and tight \melancholy\ daily rhythm of restrictions, interruptions, /through streets/ was broken. <...> Heads leaned out of the windows of buses. Smiling faces appeared behind the windshields of hedged-in cars. On the sidewalks people looked around. In the doorways of the shops young men and old appeared in their smocks or overalls. Boys ran here and there, uncertainly, in different directions.

The evening came to a halt, as if /a flag had been unfurled/ over it, which made it /exceptional/ just because it was suddenly happy (released from its duties and its grayness, which were poetic only in the depths of Carlo's solitude).

Suddenly the song drew near. From Via xxx, turning off Via Cavour, which was swallowed up in the gloomy confusion of the shadows, first one truck appeared, then another and another—among the black /and gray puppets/ crowded there, some hostile, some joyfully curious and infectious; and behind the trucks was a row <...> of motorcycles. On the trucks red flags were unfurled: so many flags jumbled together, soaked with rain, blackened by the evening light; and beneath the flags so many heads, these, too, soaked with rain, whether they were bare or were covered by those little berets that only young men know how to wear, pulled down over their eyes or set at the back of their heads, above the neck. It was they who were singing. Massed on those trucks like beasts led to the slaughter or soldiers transferred from one barracks to another, /unable to do anything about it, putting a good face on/ a bad lot. But instead of being silent, ashamed or passive or ironic, they were showing off, crowding along the edges of the truck, and those who were not in the first row /stuck/ their faces between the dark heads of their companions. The journey bore them away. Their smiling eyes were visible. /And the sheaves/ of clenched fists. They were swallowed up in the gray obscurity of evening, among a /thousand/ lights, hopeless in the rain. And what had been an excited panic at their appearance—the revelation of their fundamental happiness in being alive—became an incurable disappointment at their disappearance. What had brought them forth was as gray and harsh as what was swallowing them up. Other places in the city and in the nation. Where things are born; where things end in order to continue. A definite will wanted them there at that hour, meteors who knew everything about themselves, who offered themselves to view, who imposed their glorious song. They were poor boys; laborers, housepainters, plumbers, elevator men, delivery boys, carpenters, it was easy to see. It was the end of November 1969. /All those young men seemed to have just been reborn in a new form. They were anticipating something that was about to happen: even in their way of being, their young men's bodies. Their shaved necks and the hair that fell over their foreheads were those of the obedient sons of all the preceding decades and centuries. But their attitude held something new that filled them, irrationally, with happy surprise, with anxiety about the future, and also gave them a part in the new events./ These were not students but workers. In the murk of the impalpable hostile rain, they were singing a partisan song. A song that had never been heard before, that they alone knew, and who knows how they had learned it or where. It was like an announcement of the Kingdom, which suddenly vanished at the end of Via Nitti, near the church of Santa Maria Maggiore. Those divisions of an immense army perhaps mysteriously camped on the outskirts of the city, toward which the trucks were evidently headed, were dressed in cheap work clothes, but of a new style: the pants were tighter than usual, < ... > and /many wore/ short tunics and gray-green American jackets. They all had red handkerchiefs at their necks. All had knotted them in the elegant, carefree fashion of bold, sensual boys. They sang their song, they clenched their fists, and they disappeared. Their youth, even physically, was an apparition. It was as if they had not had a childhood, a growing up. /But they had been ready, just like that, in that new form of youthful virility, forever. And suddenly the obscure will of the country, or of the people, had offered them, lost in sleep, to the gaze of the citizens, sending them forth from distant reserves—from those < ... > barracks on the periphery.

What was new in their youth was the rediscovery < ... > of being young men, as if that were in itself something new. Something new that threw into a panic anyone who was no longer a young man. With such sudden force life renewed itself, and for now that virile sensuality was ready, and ripe, to sow—in loves re-created for them and become mysterious again for those who had already experienced love—a new seed, the consciousness of which was swallowed up by the authority of the song that passed through the agitated city. Political force and the force of the body were one./ And someone had foreseen it, that /identity/; someone knew there would be this sudden changing of the guard, someone had directed this new horde faithful to him. Certainly not Carlo, lost in his solitude.

He was on the sidewalk watching, like the other citizens present at the Apparition, silent, pitifully happy, a participant. The first truck passed before him like a shadow, and he saw only smiling eyes and clenched fists; and the barrier of flags above, very familiar to a man like him. The second truck passed before him just as quickly; the third, on the other hand, slowed down slightly, until it came almost to a stop very near him; but so close to the sidewalk that his gaze, from below, could not take the whole thing in. What he could just see, immediately above his head, was a row of legs and groins. The pants that covered those legs and those crotches, all in a row, seemed even grayer and shabbier in the wet air: the folds of inexpensive cloth, the rips, the loose buttons or cheap zippers, the belts with big buckles pressed against the lower abdomen, the seams of the threadbare material, worn or discolored at the knees or crotch, where the bulge of the penis stuck out, now neglected, buried, and forgotten in the manly song of struggle. Thus the song seemed suspended and detached, like a spirit, above that pedestal of bodies cut off at the height of the row of penises, poor, humble, all equal, but at the same time aggressive and glorious like their possessors. An earthly spirit, of course, born in the places where the fathers, in greater poverty, had been born and had lived, in the /most ordinary/ tradition, < ... > a variant of the most /trite historical Nous/ of humble Italy, felt a thousand times; yet stronger than any logic or memory. The truck resumed its journey with that burden, it was in the shadowy throat of Via xxx, disappeared into the /wide spaces/ behind Santa

Maria Maggiore, with its \among its\ cornices and roofs shining in the
rain. Life resumed its course. But in its profundity an /irreversible/ event
had occurred, with the announcement of a new youth.

NOTE 51
First fundamental moment of the poem

/Carlo's chest grew heavy. It was an unnatural weight, a mass that
crushed him as it rose. At the same time, his lower abdomen became
light and empty. Awareness of his penis, which in Carlo was a "basso
continuo," a note without end, vanished. Never for a single instant,
never, had he forgotten that flesh in which desire was urgent as a bubble that cannot evaporate: desire < ... > , a mixture of sweetness, ex-
haustion, a burning sensation: an indefinable circle in the soft flesh
around the tip, which continually needed caresses, pressure, stroking
to obtain a relief that it would never get naturally.

An unexpected chastity overwhelmed him. The vision that reduced
him to an entity in which only sex counted (that day, sex almost without the flesh of a girl) suddenly vanished from the world. Carlo, as if
driven out of the unfamiliar reality that chastity had re-created in the
world—and that must be the real reality—took a taxi and returned to
the house in the Parioli. The "other" was not stingy with money or
any of the bourgeois comforts./

For Carlo gradualness did not exist. The gentle outlaw that he was
did not know (like Des Esseintes!) /stopping places/ < ... > in the middle; he had no experience of feelings that were equidistant from the extremes.

He went straight to his room and undressed, looking at himself in
the big plain mirror < ... > of virile intimacy. Suddenly he saw what had
happened to him. Two large breasts—no longer young—hung from his
chest; and below his belly there was nothing: the hair between his legs
had disappeared, and—only by touching it and pulling apart the lips—

did Carlo, with the clear gaze of one who from his experience as an out-law has learned the philosophy of the poor, see the little fold that was his new sex.

NOTE 5 1 A
Bullicame

Acqua Bullicante with the field at night, as it was in the late fifties and remained for another year or two. Its description ensuring (swear-ing to) its authenticity. The infinity of types and episodes of the noc-turnal pit of Hell. Carlo's passage through these, where he dares only to observe.

Then Carlo takes the tram and arrives at the Central Station, there, as if expecting him, is Tonino.

NOTE 5 2
Young prick (The story of Tonino)

NOTE 5 2 A
Move to Via xxx xxx, in Quadraro

NOTE 52B
The Negro and the Redhead

NOTE 54
The real journey to the Middle East

The previous journey to the Middle East, when the engineer Carlo Valletti had been a member of a commission and, at the time, the "low man on the totem pole," had ended in partial failure. Through COMIP, ENI had invested between 12 and 15 billion lire in Morocco; but not a drop of oil had been found there. And that was before our engineer's journey. Indeed, on the journey in question things had not gone much better. In the Sudan < ... > another vast number of billions, and not a drop of oil there, either. In Eritrea precisely ten billion was invested—around five million a day for operating the drills—without the slightest positive result. In the Persian Gulf, on the other hand, oil—the new Golden Fleece, according to our jargon—was found: and Scarabeo, ENI's famous floating platform, was triumphantly started up. Unfortunately, however, in that same period, all that had been won in the Persian Gulf was lost in the mountain massif of Zagros: a useless year of drilling to a depth of 3,350 meters. Now, about ten years later—let's repeat it—the engineer Carlo Valletti returns to the Middle East; but this time he is not the low man; rather, he is the head of the Commission. Besides, just because he is in possession of "dream fundamentals," as the reader knows, he can be considered an expert in things of the East: one who *has already seen.* He returns to places that he recognizes and evaluates: and where he therefore moves freely, without the "delay" due to amazement at their appearance.

NOTE 54B
Sikandar

—Arrival in Damascus—Reception by a diplomat—Story of one of the spectators: Sikandar:
Alexander the Great, his journey through Iran, as far as India.
The transformation of the world: destruction of traditional, real cultures, replaced by a new, alienating, approved, etc., culture. In the villages various events unfold (from traces of popular local stories, Persian, Nepalese, Indian) which *are interrupted* by the passage of Alexander—just as the courtly life of the villages and fields was *interrupted*—emptied and contaminated by the new civilization, which covers them with garbage, refuse, man-made objects, etc., etc.

(Twenty stories)

(3 December 1974)

NOTE 55
The field beside Via Casilina

When they had come to an agreement, Carlo took a few steps forward into the field, without turning back to see who had decided to be first. He looked around to choose a suitable place. But here were too many holes and small mounds, there too many stones (mixed with shards and garbage), farther on no grass, just dusty earth; then, in fact, there was a nice little place, covered with dry grass, level, but it was too high and exposed to the view of those who were waiting; even farther on was a hollow, but it was too deep and, besides, was full of thistles and nettles. Just beyond that hollow was a small open space that looked as if it would do. The others, who had remained behind in a mass, began to get impatient and let out a few whistles. The reason for that impatience remained mysterious. They felt too exposed in the middle of the field, perhaps; or it annoyed them to have to cover all that distance, coming and going; or they wanted to be able to see the "fuck" of the friend whose turn it was. These, at least, were the "bourgeois" suppositions of Carlo, who felt some anxiety about it. But that small space he had spotted beyond the hollow definitely seemed all right. He reached it, slipping and stumbling; it was almost as high as the previous place, but it was screened from indiscreet looks by three or four piles, or "dunghills," of earth and crushed stone, mixed with the usual broken glass, the usual garbage. The grass in that place was thick and dry, like stubble, but soft; probably it was all xxx, xxx, or chamomile. It had a piercing fragrance.

From there, all around, only three or four /things/ could be seen. The immense, irregular expanse of the field, and at the far end a barrier of houses with twinkling lights (apartment buildings on one side, a stretch of small denticulated houses with drystone walls on the other); the sky, with a few clouds lightly brushed across its deep indigo; the red moon, in the middle of the sky, whose light was becoming cool and very clear; and, beside it, just as luminous, the small faithful evening star. This whole scene—where there were no shadings, except perhaps at the phosphorescent edges of the piece of sky illuminated by the moon—was filled with a single, intense fragrance of wild fennel. The whole cosmos was there, in that field, in that sky, in those barely visible urban horizons, and in that intoxicating odor of summer grass.

At this point, reader, the poem <...>. I beg you to let yourself be transported without putting up too much resistance. Begin, meanwhile, by not smiling at the nod to the cosmos, which, even if it was made with a perhaps unsuitable seriousness, was not, you must admit, truly excessive. The fact is that I do not wish to laugh or joke about my material. Laughing and joking, distancing me from it, would actually be a great help to me, given the roughness of that material—or, rather, its mass. But Carlo's heart was pure, despite the tension of his nerves: a tension due, among other things, to a sexual desire so strong and exclusive as to be, in the end, tragic, or at least to impress itself as such. On the other hand, all twenty of those boys there, standing out against the sky (stupidly crowding on top of a mound, where they could be seen from the street), were poor.

Besides, I realize that my notes about the landscape are "applied" like elements of a stage set, rather than of reality; but the very movement of my writing requires it.

Anyway, the first to come up behind Carlo was Sandro. Carlo, squatting on the hard dry chamomile plants, turned to look at him. He looked at him without expression, like one preparing to perform a duty that has been reduced, if I can put it this way, to pure technique; that, besides, has already been determined and agreed on in advance. All that remained was to /carry it out/, so to speak. In vain did his heart within his breast perceive the miracle /before him/ ("feeling," all around, that field shading into the crystalline solitude of the sky, that moon brightly distant from its faithful evening star); his heart was cruelly filled—in fact, as one says in cases like this, overflowing—with this consciousness. But Carlo's looks and actions—from the beginning, with the first one < ... >—gave no sign that he was a participant. In sum, one immediate feature of Carlo's behavior was an imitation of the hurried services of a prostitute, who must not admit to doing what she does for pleasure, in addition to the money. If she revealed her pleasure, she could no longer ask for money. Thus Carlo, almost without having planned it, went down on his knees before Sandro and waited, expressionless and as if detached, to perform the acts that were of such importance to the boy; and to perform them diligently, and also with a complicit thoughtfulness. Sandro was, for his part, a little shy. But at that time boys had a code of behavior in common, even for a feeling as private and personal as shyness. There was a smile for shyness, there were words for shyness, there were gestures for shyness. Of course, it was a slight shyness and therefore easily masked. Sandro, however— who was a head taller than Carlo and quite strong—must have been much younger than he appeared: he was perhaps barely sixteen; and in fact in his eyes sparkled the smile not only of a boy but of a boy who practices the good manners his mother has taught him: a mother from the people, for whom a good upbringing is naturally an instinctive, deep-rooted politeness. This maternal politeness was betrayed in all of Sandro's gestures and movements. It had remained attached to him like a smell. Moreover, his clothes, too, the simple pants and plain shirt, had the appearance of having been bought at some market stall by him and his mother together, with money from the family. Seeing Carlo motionless, waiting obedient and docile like a sheep, not taking the initiative, Sandro, with the "codified" gestures of his timidity, began to unbutton his pants, hiding his embarrassment—this, too, was very slight—behind a kind of gruff and rather overbearing haste. At first all he did was unbutton his pants and thrust his hand into the opening to pull out his cock, evidently squeezed too tight, crushed inside the dark blue briefs; then, since he couldn't manage to get it out, he unbuckled his belt and pulled his pants down to the crotch, with a movement even rougher and quicker. Then he was able to get his cock out of his briefs. And the reason that he had been unable to do so at first was simple: it was erect. That was cause for a slight new embarrassment for Sandro, who had thus shown the ingenuous desire of a boy. But for this, too, he had a smile and a remark "ready": he smiled cheerfully and said, "It's already erect," and at the same time he reached out a hand and just touched Carlo's neck to make him come closer. Carlo's heart was in tumult at the sight of that cock, big, /pale/, almost luminous in its pigment < ... >, with the skin drawn over the tip, which was just barely red, and slightly chapped because of an odorless down, a sign that it was some time since Sandro "had come"; and moreover the weight of semen and desire was visible in a kind of palpitation of the whole cock—clean, pale, but knotty, the veins on the surface—which was pushing out and up, uncovering ever more desperately the clear, dry, pinkish tip. At this spectacle, I repeat, Carlo's heart was in a tumult; but he let nothing show on his face, while mechanically he prepared to do what Sandro had showed that he wanted. He merely raised his head and looked for an instant into Sandro's face, murmuring happily and somewhat affectedly "My love," to ingratiate himself. In that instant he had time to see Sandro and to contemplate what he was in that moment of his life. The smile on the wide, fleshy mouth almost Negroid, while the shape of his face was of a pale, almost blond type; the round eyes, made smaller by the smile; the ears sticking out a little under the thick down of light chestnut hair, like that of a recruit who has been made to shave it by a cruel sergeant; the slightly squashed nose and the broad cheekbones; and, suffusing everything, the mother's good manners. Furthermore, from Sandro's clothes came the good smell of flour. He must be a baker. Carlo leaned over his cock with infinite tenderness, almost delicacy. He almost didn't dare to touch it with his hands, and he brought his lips close, brushing it. He wished, in short, to delay as long as possible the moment when he was allowed to touch it, feel it. But Sandro was not of that opinion, and he said, "Come on," and tried to push it against Carlo's mouth in such a way that he would begin to do a more substantial job. Docilely Carlo obeyed. In the "work" he tried to make Sandro feel his diligence and his humility, which almost gave him a lump in his throat; to make him feel, that is, that he was serving him. And from the beginning he did it mechanically, because that was precisely an aspect of the behavior of the "prostitute," who forces the client to be content with the mechanicalness of the act she is paid to perform. But then, as if more and more /enamored of/ that infantile yet already overbearingly paternal penis with its knotty hardness and its tenderness, he began to /"put more feeling into it"/. Which gave him the overwhelming joy of hearing Sandro, slightly bent over him, say, "Bravo." This word threw him into an abyss of tenderness, and tears nearly filled his eyes. Also because Sandro was pushing it in as hard as he could, choking him, in fact, which was making him cry. It was fatal that at the end Sandro's hand came to rest on Carlo's neck: it was the heavy, callused hand of a tall boy who from birth had been accustomed to work. Exaggerating slightly, Carlo imagined that he felt on his neck the paw of a large animal, and he became even more tremulous, almost consumed by a feeling of gratitude, when that giant hand began to exert a light pressure on his neck, which gradually became stronger and more powerful. After a while, Sandro's other hand was raised and came to rest on Carlo's shoulder, squeezing it. Thus he was now Sandro's prisoner, the slave of his xxx will, apparently. Half suffocated, his eyes filled with blinding tears, Carlo was no longer moving his head up and down; it was Sandro's hand that was making him do it, and with a violence and a rapidity that would have seemed impossible to imagine. Finally Sandro stopped, suddenly silent. Carlo felt his cock swell and < ... > /contract/, as if relaxing. He made an attempt to detach himself from it: but Sandro was silent and his hands were a vise on Carlo's neck and shoulder. Only after the last drop of semen was squeezed out did Sandro loosen his hold and free Carlo's head. Carlo pulled away and looked at Sandro's cock, a few inches from his nose: in that condition, already a little soft, it seemed even bigger; and then there was the translucence of the semen and the saliva, which gave a kind of bestial and obscene lividness to the color of his skin; and yet there was something sacred in that oily liquid. Carlo raised his eyes to Sandro's face again for an instant. It was another instant equal to a century of contemplation. The smile had faded somewhat from Sandro's features: the game was over. This time the new embarrassment (slight) was due to the moment of disgust that follows orgasm. But even that had its ritual: a certain brutal hurry and an uncertainty about where to put his hands to clean himself off. Carlo smiled at him and murmured another "My love," as simpering as xxx. And he hastened to clean that /trunk/ greasy with semen, which had not yet decided to surrender \give up\ and was hanging almost erect; as he cleaned it off, Carlo saw it in profile—it was really enormous—against the background of field and sky. But while he was contemplating it, delaying for a moment, Sandro suddenly took it away from him. Carlo saw him running off, up and down the little hills, smiling as he buttoned his pants, returning to his friends. From the group of them the shadow of another boy detached itself, running; he came straight toward Carlo, crossing paths with Sandro. He was wearing a mechanic's overalls of a very dark blue. They were covered with black stains, and he smelled strongly of iron and motor oil. The name of this second boy was Sergio. He was different from Sandro, he was serious; or if a faint smile strayed into his dark eyes, it seemed to split his face in half, like a wound. He took hold of the clasp of the zipper—which he called a shutter—at his throat and with a clean cut opened it down to the bottom of his crotch. The overalls covered a pair of gray pants and a shirt the color of strawberries that was black with grease. Sergio immediately unbuckled his belt and with a decisive gesture pulled his cock out of his briefs, where it nestled amid the thick curly hair. It was almost, but not quite, erect. And although it was not erect, it was already even bigger than Sandro's. So, still a little soft, it hung there, powerful and heavy, as, /a moment before/, Sandro's had. Beside himself with excitement, Carlo put his face a few inches from that /surprising/ cock and gazed at it close up—as he had done moments before with Sandro's—against the background of the field and the sky above the distant trembling lights of the houses, which disappeared into the pale blue light of the moon. Thus Sergio's cock became erect before his eyes, as if it were a living being. And it was ready, erect and /turned up/, < ... > like that of a prepubescent boy, its rich, delicate skin drawn up over the tip, which was thus revealed as pinkish, hard, the skin around it dry and dense, covering the veins and making the cock powerfully cylindrical. This time, too, Carlo looked up at Sergio for an instant and observed him. His smile was not pure and shining: there was something awkward and tight about it; the light in his eyes was motionless, a little hostile, and a kind of pallor suffused the whole of his brown face, the kind one sees in men who are weak and therefore faithless. But it was only a superficial impression, because ultimately that smile was also the smile of a boy destined to follow a normal and, all things considered, honest life. Perhaps he had begun to be unhappy, with the unhappiness that comes to all when first youth, innocent and generous, passes. His hair clung close to his head, like a thick black crust: black as pitch. Perhaps if he let it grow it would be wavy. As it was, compressed, it stuck to his beautiful head as if to the head of a statue with a splendid neck. The beauty of his hair, simple and luxuriant as a tenacious climbing plant that cannot detach itself from the rock or tufa it clings to, corrected the imperfection of his somewhat sharp and defensive smile. "My love," Carlo said to him also, to congratulate him on that marvelous <instrument> of his. Sergio intensified his smile, and his black eyes narrowed, becoming cloudy and almost myopic. In response he, too, grabbed one of Carlo's shoulders with one hand—which was, however, small and nervous—and pulled him to his crotch with ostentatious force, almost rudely. Carlo bent his head, surrendered willingly to his fate, and prepared himself for the first, purely mechanical moment of his work. He opened his mouth and with difficulty was able to get Sergio's cock in it; he had just begun to move, saving up to do it with more spirit and pleasure in a while, when he felt the cock swell, as if becoming painfully stretched, and immediately afterward he felt it move rapidly in a series of precipitous contractions that filled his mouth with an enormous quantity of a thick, sweet liquid; meanwhile, Sergio had clasped his hands behind Carlo's neck and had pulled him to him with all his strength. Unlike Sandro, he didn't even wait for the last drop to come out. He took it out of Carlo's mouth and turned to leave, buttoning his pants. "Wait, so I can clean it off for you," Carlo said, with a consuming desire—/become/ suddenly terrible—to have that cock in his hands. But without listening to him Sergio shrugged his shoulders and ran off toward his companions, this time laughing out loud. At his first departing steps, another boy, also running, detached himself from the waiting group. It was Claudio, one of the three from Nettuno. In fact, yet another boy had also been ready to run toward Carlo. But Claudio had gone ahead of him; the other had begun to remonstrate in a loud voice, and Claudio had responded in the same tone. For this reason he now arrived joyfully, with a roguish smile printed slyly on his wide mouth, the mouth of poverty. That smile was uncontainable and had to do with something from which Carlo was excluded. But Claudio appeared to understand that exclusion and as he arrived said kindly to Carlo, in his rough voice, and with a certain euphemistic complicity: "Hi." Thus he made his turn personal; just barely, the minimum needed to place a certain emphasis on himself, differentiating him from the others. In his heart, perhaps, it interested him; while on the surface it was merely something slight and negligible. With the wide mouth in his small, fair, delinquent's face still smiling, he stopped a few steps from Carlo, on the edge of the open space; he unbuttoned his pants and quickly took out his cock. Not to enjoy himself right away with Carlo, however, but simply to pee. He concentrated for a moment in silence, while the smile faded from his eyes, which remained, in a sly way, cheerful, then he began his long pee. He held his cock, still small and slack, with two fingers. And he peed right in the direction of Carlo, while in his smile there was now an insolent expression, challenging, openly full of a sort of equivocal demand: it seemed that he wished to make Carlo watch while he peed. Unless it was a silent request to pee on him. Anyway, that pee was offered to him. In those long moments Carlo observed it. Claudio, now with his head bent over the little cock held proudly between his fingers, now pointing it directly at Carlo and staring at him, was erect, thin, tender as a child. But his whole body gave off an air of virile decisiveness, mixed with that light and careless availability of children from poor families where harmony does not reign and they have been left alone. His hands were red and swollen: he was a laborer. But he could have broken off his work at any moment to leave home and become a thief. Perhaps it was one of those moments. His head was long and his ears stuck out, and the blond hair that made a thick mane on his forehead, round and smooth and shiny as silk, seemed the /seal/ of his fate: too common and at the same time too fantastic to be that of an ordinary boy. On the contrary, however, everything else about him was common and betokened for him a destiny like any other: the long nose, the irregular oval of his smooth face, the chestnut-colored eyes with their slightly stupid, delinquent's smile, the wide mouth. When Claudio had finished peeing, he took a few steps toward Carlo, grabbed him by the head without much ceremony, and stuck that little cock, still soft and dripping, in his mouth. This time, the technique of a good whore was explicitly demanded of Carlo. The job of giving the cock an erection, something that falls within a norm better covered /by the rules/, apparently, than that of the two preceding cases. Carlo therefore tried to demonstrate his patient skill. This time, too, his heart was in a tumult, because the cock always appeared in the form of a miracle: as soft as the cock should be of one who, taking turns with twenty others < ... >, has recourse to the skills of a whore. Carlo therefore /resorted/ to all the devices of the amatory art that he had learned during those months, recognizing the peculiarities of every cock. He sucked it hard, slowly and deeply, or rapidly, holding only the tip, and at the same time rubbing it with his tongue. He also used his hand, alternating with his mouth. But Claudio appeared not to want to get excited. Detaching himself for a moment to spit, Carlo threw him a quick glance. The boy was leaning over a little, but he did not look at all preoccupied or indifferent; his eyes continued to display < ... > his complicit < ... > peasant irony, charged with expectation. Reassured, Carlo continued his work with a will; and in fact soon afterward came the first results: the cock began to swell and harden. This phase, too, however, lasted quite a long time. It was a while before it became, so to speak, "big." And then Carlo started to rejoice again. He had been afraid, seeing it soft, that it was one of those disappointing little cocks that cause so much frustration and annoyance. But no. Claudio's was nice and big; if not like Sandro's and Sergio's, /almost/. It may not have been as large but in compensation was perhaps longer. Finally it got completely hard; and it was, unexpectedly, the hardness of a stone, /of a club/. And in fact it was immediately evident that Claudio thought of his cock as a weapon. He stuck it in Carlo's mouth violently, making it penetrate to the back of the palate. And he repeated this gesture, each time pulling out the whole thing and each time seeking Carlo's mouth again, as if to contemplate, from above, his power < ... >. With a painful thrust < ... >, he finally stuck it down his throat, giving Carlo a horrible sensation of suffocating and causing him to retch. And Carlo naturally, yielding and docile, let him do it. But then, partly because it was really too much, perhaps partly to excite Claudio to do still worse, he planted both hands against Claudio's wide-apart thighs in an attempt to keep him from going so far inside. With a nervous start, Claudio took the hands off his thighs and pushed them away, almost behind Carlo's back, holding them there for a moment firmly as if to make him understand that they were to remain in that position. Then, with his tender adolescent right hand curved like a bowl, he seized the nape of Carlo's neck and began again with his calculated and violent thrusts. The tip of the cock went in right up against the roof of Carlo's mouth, with such force that it bent slightly. Two or three times Carlo was on the point of vomiting, his eyes full of burning tears; and several more times, against his will, from his mouth < ... > groans and belches or retching sounds, so loud that the twenty < ... > over there must have heard him; indeed, they were laughing. The number of times Claudio repeated the movement that so excited him was, relatively, /infinite/. Then suddenly he moved a step away from Carlo, holding his cock in his hand as if to hide it from Carlo's sight, and in his rough peasant's voice he said: "Turn around." Carlo understood /in a lightning flash/, and, docile, almost distressed, he turned; pretending not to /understand/ what he still had to do. In fact, he felt

Claudio's hands on him, trying nervously, almost angrily, to pull his pants down along his sides. Then he murmured, with the air of a patient victim, "Wait," and, unbuckling his belt, /took care of/ pulling down his pants himself. Claudio was on him, and, with some difficulty, and not wanting Carlo to help, he began to enter him. He gave three or four heaves with blind force; but, as he had done < ... > he wanted to take it out completely; he tried that and then was unable to enter him again. Then he ordered Carlo: "Lie down on the ground." Carlo blindly < ... > obeyed. Claudio was immediately on top of him. And, groping a little with his hands, he managed to enter him and began a dense hail of blows that seemed as though they would never end. The smell of grass was stupefying, but at the same time the hard stalks stuck Carlo in the stomach, in the neck. The cosmos viewed with eyes glued to the ground was even more absolute: a single flat expanse divided from the luminous strip of the sky by an almost perfect line. The moon was behind him. Carlo was able to think about this while on him Claudio, as if he did not exist, tried whatever he felt like doing. Now, in addition to the dry and penetrating thrusts, he had found another way to experience pleasure: to push with all his strength, grasping with his fists the dry stalks of grass in front of Carlo's face, until he plunged his sex so deep into the /woman's/ belly that he could not go any farther unless he expected the impossible: and in fact he had made Carlo slide several feet along the stubble, face down. The act lasted longer than any imagining. And when, finally, Claudio, also silent, came, and the two, dazed and in disarray, got up again, the moon seemed much higher in the sky; its light seemed to have changed, becoming more transparent, purer. Claudio smiled. He had an air of wanting to be pardoned for his excess, but at the same time he seemed to be making fun of his victim: an *a priori* and infantile fun, but in the manner of one who, in a different situation, might behave \might have behaved\ < ... > like a criminal. As Carlo, still with his victim's expression, was busy cleaning off Claudio's cock, Claudio said to him, "Put it back in your mouth." Carlo, without a word, obeyed. And again he began to gently suck the cock that only a few seconds ago /had been so violent with him/. Immediately the cock, which had not become flaccid while Carlo was cleaning it, started to get hard again. Which Carlo would never have expected, since /before/, the first time, it had taken so long. The fact is that Claudio's cock was soon completely erect again, and he took it out of Carlo's mouth, as if to threaten him with seeing it again. "No, that's enough," Carlo said; and that was enough for Claudio, who, this time grabbing him by the hair on his forehead and holding him so tight that it hurt, again found his mouth with his cock, sticking it in with such force that Carlo made a hollow sound, as if he were about to vomit up food. The twenty friends in the distance began to laugh again; but someone also started whistling impatiently; and a cheerful voice rose up, saying, "Come on!" But Claudio continued impudently. Until suddenly he said, "Do a hand job." Almost relieved—although Claudio continued to hold him painfully tight by the hair on his forehead—Carlo grasped the cock in his fist and began to masturbate it. This time, too, it took longer than any possible imagining. This time, too, the mournfully shining moon, with its small companion, seemed to have shifted visibly in the vault of the sky. At the end Claudio threatened: "Put it in your mouth," and quickly stuck the cock down his throat, holding him so tight by the hair that for a moment Carlo did not cry out. When Claudio had discharged the remaining semen in Carlo's mouth, to the last squirt, he calmed down, but not so much that he did not order him peremptorily: "Clean it." Which Carlo hastened to do thoroughly. "Ciao," Claudio said at the end before going off. His sly smile had become gentle and almost kind; and before turning his back he gave Carlo's cheek an affectionate pat. Meanwhile the second boy from Nettuno, Gianfranco, was arriving, running lightly up and down among the little hills: a bit bourgeois, as his name implied. In fact, he was a hairdresser, a women's hairdresser. He was very good-looking: well proportioned, his face perhaps a little too round, but with a lovely full mouth, a small, regular nose, big black eyes and thick eyebrows, the hair on his forehead like a crest, shining, wavy, and soft, which fell back, flowing over the ears in long, capricious undulations that ended in soft curls on his schoolboy neck. His trousers and shirt were neat and clean (while Claudio had on a pair of filthy pants and a red-and-white-striped T-shirt that barely covered his navel). In spite of all his attractive qualities Carlo did not much like Gianfranco and perhaps for this reason—since in fact he deserved it—welcomed him in a more friendly manner than the others, saying more distinctly, "Love" and "Come here, lovely boy." Gianfranco approached; and < ... > not for nothing was he, too, from Nettuno. Besides, he had probably seen from a distance what his friend had done. So, in contrast to the sort of feminine sweetness of his face, as soon as he was close to Carlo he said, "Come on, get down." Carlo, for all that he was skeptical, as usual was willing to obey. He heard Gianfranco struggling above him. Certainly he didn't want to get his pants dirty. When, finally, he seemed to be ready, Carlo felt him fall on top of him, his belly pressed against his sex, so that he looked, as his friends would say, "like a sheep." But still Gianfranco didn't seem to be comfortable. His hands were planted on the ground, which might be fine as an athletic exercise but certainly not for having a fuck in peace. Then with an impatient jump Gianfranco got up again and, as Carlo, looking out of the corner of his eye, was able to observe, pulled down his pants and his briefs to his ankles; but in that glance Carlo could also see that at the bottom of Gianfranco's white belly there was, yes, a thick bush of black hair; but the cock was barely visible. Anyway, Carlo, obedient with this new client as with the others, let him alone. Gianfranco stretched out again, floundering a little, on top of him, and began to rub his lower abdomen against the flesh with a sort of rotating motion. He was quiet, anxiously quiet, trying to concentrate. "Why don't you let me suck it?" Carlo dared to propose. But Gianfranco's only response was a blow to the shoulders as if to arrange Carlo better beneath him, and he began to rub against him more heatedly. After some minutes, although to Carlo it seemed impossible, he felt the hard cock searching and pushing between his thighs, blindly /searching for/ the opening, like a dog. And like a dog, in fact, Gianfranco /possessed him/. With quick thrusts, breathless yet regular, all the same; at the end he fell on him and he was the first who, ejaculating, let Carlo hear a kind of moan, or at least a louder drawn-out breath. He remained like that for a moment, as if to gather his strength; and finally he got up, preoccupied mainly with his pants. He pulled them up, examining them to see if they were wrinkled or dusty, concentrating on closing his complicated belt buckle. Meanwhile, Carlo, with the handkerchief as usual, was cleaning him off, and thus he finally saw his secret. It was a handsome medium-sized cock, straight and well proportioned; and, since it was getting soft, it also appeared grosser, heavier, more powerful. As Carlo gazed at it, a sudden feeling of /love/ seized him, as if pouring down on him from the cosmos, mixing with the sharp, fermenting odor of the wild grasses and the heat of the summer night. In that so ordinary penis, which, still swollen and greasy with sperm, was becoming flaccid, he saw those he had lost forever, of Sandro, Sergio, Claudio, while a consuming desire seized him for the sex of those who were still to come. It was as if he had only now awoken from a kind of sleep or artificial form of hypnosis or apathy. Desire had finally become the desire for depravity, for obscenity, for excess. "Pee," he said to Gianfranco. "I don't have to," the boy answered. And then immediately added, "Wait." He seemed to have a moment of inspiration, and then, first in a thread, and then in an irrepressible jet, the pee came out of his still bulging cock. Carlo contemplated brushing with his lips the thick skin of Gianfranco's cock; while, < ... > he was hurrying to sheathe it again in his fine pants, tight at the hips, high-waisted, and had already /turned/ his smiling face toward his companions. He darted away, barely directing a timid smile at Carlo < ... > /and without/ the courage—given the weakness of character which had kept him from exposing himself—to say the rough "Ciao" of his friend and leader, who, unlike him, had been able to allow himself some friendly intimacies. Gianfranco crossed paths not with the third boy from Nettuno but with a dark-haired boy who, on the contrary, lived nearby. "Me and my friend gotta go, or we're gonna be late," he told Carlo when he got close to him (/there is no need to say/ that he, too, arrived at a run). "Who is your friend?" asked Carlo, and those quick and affectionate confidences did not make his frenzied desire less fevered or, so to speak, dirty. "He's that blond, with the part on the side," said the dark one, imprecisely but making himself understood right away. Over in the group of twenty—some of whom had sat down—a blond head was distinguishable immediately, at first glance, under the now almost solemn light of the moon, which had reached <its zenith>. "If we get home after midnight our mother will kill us," added the dark-haired one, whose name was Fausto (while his blond friend was called Gustarello, that is, Augusto). Fausto, too, was wearing overalls. "Wait," he said confidentially and good-humoredly. Carefully he pulled down the "shutter" and with equal care unbuttoned his thin pants of a delicate blue, under which the brutal, livid bulge of his cock, that of an adolescent who is already a man, made a contrast that brought Carlo's xxx heart to his throat. "Wait," Carlo said. "Wait before you take it out." He wanted to look at the violent swelling under those light, delicate summer pants, slightly yellowish, or bluish, over the bulge. And Fausto was just the boy with whom these things could be done; docile, obedient, and curious as he was, he was at least as strong and virile. He was curly-headed. His hair was very curly, but, perhaps ashamed of it, he had cut it short, and he combed it with a clean, straight part on one side. Under those thick little curls, which, despite being so well trimmed, formed on his forehead a sort of bold forelock, the face was the honest face of a laborer; happy in nature, serious in purpose. "What is it?" he asked, smiling. And he looked questioningly at Carlo, who, in turn, was looking as if xxx at that bulge under his pants. It was a powerful swelling that Fausto was usually a little ashamed of, because it declared his naiveté and his inevitable boy's chastity, as well as his deplorable weakness in being so excited the first time. He must have been containing that bulge in his cheap, thin trousers from the start, ever since they had reached the field. There was something bestial and, in fact, obscene about it. Fausto was not really very tall; and that club, which was pressing against his pants as if it would split them—now that they were unbuttoned and not quite so tight—had something excessively /priapic/ about it. Carlo observed it /like/ xxx; then slowly, in order not to waste even an instant of that /ecstatic/ occasion, began to take it out of Fausto's pants himself. It wasn't easy, because that cock was too big for the little opening of the unbuttoned fly. "Hey, you're pulling my hair," said Fausto, laughing; and the more innocent he was, the more that "beast" that he had in his crotch, monstrously gross, massive, and dark, made Carlo tremble in agony. Finally Fausto's cock was outside his trousers and extended in the open, caressed by the warm perfumed air of the summer night. It was, /as Carlo's friends/ /would say/, perfectly "bareheaded": and it seemed fragrant, too, like the wild grasses. Carlo stood staring, observing it, wishing the moment would never pass. "What's up? You're staring," Fausto asked, still cheerful. "Yes," Carlo answered. And he stood immobile, with his eyes fixed on that boyish cock, powerful and still pure. "What is it? You want to stand here till tomorrow morning?" Fausto said, smiling. "My love!" was Carlo's response; and, as if unable to resist any longer, seized by an infinite yearning, he took Fausto's cock in his hand and pressed it against one cheek and then against his lips. But Fausto pulled it back, and with hands that smelled of the shop took Carlo's hands off it. Carlo looked questioningly at him. But it was simple. "Gimme a fuck!" Fausto said. Carlo felt a new rush of overwhelming gratitude, and he kissed it again and began to suck it. "Let me do this a little first," he said. Fausto let him for a little, then insisted: "I wanna fuck!" Carlo stretched out on the ground. And the dry-grass fragrance of the cosmos assaulted him more violently than ever. Fausto knelt on him, then mounted him; with his own hands he looked for the /eternal/ orifice, which he found quickly. Slowly, delicately, he stuck his enormous cock in, perhaps thinking that it wouldn't be able to fit; and when, to his satisfaction, he had entered, he stretched out happily on top of Carlo, trying to find the most comfortable position while holding him tight in his arms. At one point he even brought his mouth to Carlo's neck, under his ear, and while he was "fucking" he clasped him still more tightly, his mouth glued to his neck. He came as if transported in ecstasy, letting go inside Carlo's body and spilling his seed perhaps for one of the first times in his life. "You got a nice ass," he said at the end, getting up. He let Carlo clean him off well, without hurrying. And at the end he turned toward the group of his companions and let out a deafening whistle, like a shepherd. At that whistle the "blond" jumped to his feet and came running. Fausto didn't move. "Pay us first," he said, "cause we gotta go." Carlo understood: he took out of his pocket four thousand lire; he gave two thousand to Fausto and two thousand to Gustarello, who had meanwhile arrived, fresh as a rose. "Thanks!" Fausto said, going off and leaving his place to his friend. It was not clear if the pleasure of /sharing/ something beautiful and useful /with this/ friend of his was more profound and "natural" on his part or if his regard for him was more profound and "natural" since he knew that, like <him>, he would carry out his masculine duty with the most absolute xxx. Gustarello's head was a true masterpiece of nature. His blondness was gold, but a pale and well-polished gold. It was a little dark at the roots, but on the surface it was of a blinding brightness. He, too, had a part on one side; but the hair was much longer and more abundant than that of his curly-haired friend, and the two masses of hair divided by the part were like wheat sheaves ruffled by the wind and grazed by the light of the setting sun. His head was oval, so that those masses of hair, capriciously waving, extended from his low forehead to the nape of his neck, which was prominent and narrow—as it often is in southerners, especially Sicilians—thus showing off all the brilliant beauty of the hair. The hot evening breeze had disheveled it a little, and above the two dense sunbursts that on either side of the < ... > careful part went from the forehead to the nape of the neck, a kind of down or fleece had formed in which the gold was really white and was like a light emanating from the thickest vortexes and knots of the hair, which had been combed in such a wild and at the same time /meticulous/ style. To tell the truth, nothing else about Gustarello was on the same level as his head. His face was rather thickset, with prominent cheekbones, a sort of potato nose, a fleshy mouth, and eyes of an indefinable pale color: the forehead and cheeks were reddened by the sun; as a blond of that type, Gustarello must have delicate skin; and yet he did heavy work. He, too, was a laborer, with a construction company. His body was coarse and rather squat, like his face; but that did not in Carlo's eyes constitute a defect—on the contrary. Less lighthearted than his friend, his clouded eyes fixed, as if a little alarmed, on Carlo, he unbuttoned his pants as if he were an automaton. Like his friend, he, too, was ready. His penis, hard as a rock, sprang out of his pants and was extended in the air. It wasn't very big: it was of a normal /size/. In compensation, though, it was hard in a /very/ particular way and full of knots and veins, which didn't alter its perfect form: the skin enclosed the tip, wrinkling over its pinkish < ... >, dry but not rough. Carlo uncovered it; and, as always, looked at it against the background of field and sky with an insatiable yearning. Gustarello said nothing, so Carlo was able to remain in that state of contemplation, just rubbing it a little with his hand, as long as he wanted; which was not long, because a yearning even more profound than that for contemplation consumed him. He began to kiss it, suck it, touching it and measuring the substance of it, the reality, of its hardness, its weight, its size, which included an entire way of being < ... >: a gift that would soon, however, be taken away from him.

Gustarello's silence and his otherness made it possible for Carlo to have a relationship with his sex as if he did not exist. But desire was urgent. He lay down on the dry grass and said to Gustarello, "Come on, do it." Gustarello, ready, mounted him, without discussion. Self-contained and having decided to go to the end, whether it was now Carlo's desire or not, he was physically strong like his friend Fausto, hardened by work; it was a game for him to bend over, to grab Carlo without any awkwardness or difficulty as if he were /a straw/, clasp him in his arms, mount him with the precision of a stud animal. He was— as Carlo's friends used to say—"strong in the gut," this one. But the duration of coitus didn't involve the slightest effort. In spite of the heat of the summer night, the blond didn't sweat at all. He did everything he had to do calmly, with concentrated violence, with obsessive regularity, which nothing in the world could now interrupt. When he came, he squeezed Carlo so hard in his young worker's arms that Carlo's bones nearly cracked. He remained motionless for a moment, in a silence even heavier than before. Then he got up and, silent, legs apart, stood waiting for Carlo to clean him off. Which Carlo did with the care and respect one has for a mature husband. "Where are you from?" Carlo asked at the end, curious about the blondness of his hair and thinking he was from the North. "From Rome," said the blond. "But your parents, your grandparents?" "From xxx xxx," said Gustarello, and that was all; he was a little undecided, as if waiting to be dismissed, then he silently turned and went away. While the one whose turn it was approached ("Next!" cried the usual cheerful voice in the group), Carlo stood watching what Fausto and Gustarello were doing, since they had said they had to go home. Instead they were still there, among the others—some standing, some squatting, on top of their mound. Twenty! They were a little army, and even seen from afar each of them had his masculinity, his innocent way of hiding in his pants (and mostly they were American pants) his own /animal/ secret, which to him was merely a happy animal endowment. In fact, they were arguing among themselves, with their jokes, as if they were in the local bar or at a < ... > /social/ gathering. Smiling, they looked at the one whose turn it was and then resumed their discussion, now excited, full of ardor, now tranquil, almost good-natured. In that "sociality" their sexual reality dissolved, < ... > —hypocritically—as if it were secondary. Yet even among themselves they liked to display /the violence/ of their cocks inside the American trousers, which were stiff and tight, almost chaste; or the powerful oblique swelling inside thin, light-colored or even white trousers, a swelling marked by the almost livid, indecent discoloring of the material < ... >. It was useless to pretend, among themselves, that that point in their pants did not exist or that it was normal, so normal that it disappeared in the "special" atmosphere of a relationship among equals, all poor, who knew very well how to act smart. /They knew/ perfectly well what each one brought down there behind those bushes at the end of the perfumed field where someone was waiting for them. Their lightheartedness about this was, it is true, part of their way of being—carefree, thoughtless, without a real destiny—but it was also a tacit hypocrisy, and if they had realized it they would have laughed at it with another type of laugh—now ready < ... >— quieter yet open. The one who arrived next—the sixth: so there were only fourteen more!—was the third from Nettuno. His poetic peasant parents had named him Erminio. He was the first to approach slowly. In fact, he was not a boy. For one thing, he had on a jacket, a jacket of the same color as his pants; and a shirt instead of the usual T-shirt. And then his body was /solid/ and massive, full of a threatening dignity. He could not have been more than nineteen. But it was his character that made him more adult. In him, perhaps only a year or two earlier, the irrevocable decision had been made to be a young man, a man and not a boy. His hair was thick and reddish; though you would not have called him a "redhead," if anything a "blond," with that lion's mane. And reddish, too, were the freckles on his peasant's face, whose beauty could not be comprehended at first glance, as with Fausto or Gustarello. It was the beauty of a man, shadowy, secret, irregular. Above all, that face expressed malice and threat; clearly no one would ever try /to bully him. His strength seemed to have been established once and for all at the beginning of adolescence; but perhaps even before, when he was a boy. Indeed, his strength seemed to have been established generations before, when his race developed. His eyes were expressionless, that is xxx at a smile: they were a gilded chestnut color and also reddish, as if injected with blood. And the shape of his face had the beauty that realist

painters without mannerisms or aestheticism are able to characterize:
the fine nose with slightly flared nostrils, the chin accentuated under
ruddy cheeks; and those evil, almost ferocious eyes. He was a mason. It
was impossible that anyone had ever bothered him since he started
working; nor had he, perhaps, troubled others. In fact, he was serious
but gentle, almost gallant. He said nothing to Carlo when he appeared.
And yet Carlo felt protected by him rather than threatened. He stopped
at the edge of the little space and, turning /modestly/ toward the far
side of the field, began to pee. At the same time he took the last drags
on a cigarette reduced now to an almost invisible stub between his big
fingers. He threw it away with an almost rude toss and, without putting
his cock back inside his brown trousers, came over to Carlo: the cock
just bouncing along with a self-assurance that bordered on indifference.
His particularly fierce look at that moment was intended to say to
Carlo, "Come on, you've got a job to do." And Carlo understood and
obeyed, nearly collapsing at his feet; the emotion took his breath away.
That cock he had dreamed of while the first boys were giving him
theirs—as if of something so far removed from reality that it constituted the sole reality, /violent/, carnal, /brutal/, all contained in that irregular cylindrical form and in that hairy sac—was before him in the
totality /of an unmistakable apparition/. Erminio's cock, dangling outside his pants, was already swollen, but in a way peculiar to itself; and
the brown pigmentation was peculiar, peculiarly brutal. Carlo took it in
his hand, caressing it a little < ... >, and then into his mouth, to excite
it. His work had to be efficient and without sentimentality. The anxiety
that was by now nearly making him faint had to be kept inside, silent.
Besides, Erminio's silence was perhaps equally xxx. Soon the cock
swelled, extended. Perhaps it was no larger than Sandro's or Sergio's,
but it seemed twice the size. In its erect form covered with small knots
of veins, but solid, potent, up to the half-uncovered tip, and fragrant,
with the scent, finally, of both urine, the stream that had just been
spurting into the field, and concentrated semen: or maybe not, Erminio
was not the type to masturbate, and it must have been a while since he'd
/had a fuck/, so great was the power and swelling of his penis; perhaps
it was the odor of the semen held inside; and < ... > with it was mixed
the smell /of sex/, hot, intense, almost perfumed, sharper around the

balls, which were strong and tight inside the hairy skin. It was the hair itself that was fragrant. It was the fragrance of the sex of a very /strong and healthy/ man, whose cock is so virile that it has lost any memory of its infant tenderness. So it was to become: enormous, potent, hot, and odorous. Carlo continued his work, even though the task was by now completed. If it had been up to him, he would have continued all night and perhaps even the next day. But there was the other anxiety which continued /to devour him/. So on the one hand he was overwhelmingly grateful to Erminio, who was letting him continue, without saying anything to him, as if pitying his weakness; on the other, he waited in an almost hysterical frenzy for him to give an order: /that is/, the only possible order, to /lie down/ under him. And now, in fact, just at the right moment, Erminio put his hands under his armpits and, lifting him a little, almost delicately, turned him and laid him down on the grass. Then, after undoing his belt and uncovering his belly, he climbed on top of him. First he clasped him /firmly/ in his arms, calmly, trying to find the right position for himself and for his victim. His arms were strong, powerful, even if for now they wished to be delicate and almost affectionate in their embrace. An embrace from which Carlo could never possibly have freed himself. Then with his sex Erminio looked for Carlo's. He would have found it immediately if he had wanted, violently thrusting that stake of his inside the opening. But before reaching that point, Erminio evidently wanted it to feel good to Carlo, sliding it between his thighs, pressing it against the tender flesh of his buttocks. Then slowly /he thrust/ it into the hole and pushed. If he had wanted, with his strength he could immediately have had the upper hand over the slight physical resistance offered by the skin of Carlo's sex. But he did not wish to use that strength. Instead, he detached Carlo from that embrace which, tight and invincible, seemed to have been /fixed/ forever and murmured his first words since he had been with Carlo: "Lick it." And he leaned toward Carlo, whose head was on the ground, with his whole penis extending out from the hair of his naked belly. Carlo obeyed, turning his head like a pathetic crushed snake; and smelled again that strong /clean/ odor of athletic sweat. Conscientiously he bathed Erminio's cock with his saliva, and Erminio, calmly, again took his earlier position. First of all he embraced Carlo again, still more, almost suffocating him, and, with his hands crossed under his chest, grabbed Carlo's breasts with sudden violence; then he looked for the hole with his cock and shoved it in. Carlo cried out with pain, and this must have touched Erminio, because he clasped Carlo's breasts more forcefully between his fingers, which were hard, like stones; and began slowly to go up and down. Suddenly Carlo understood that Erminio wasn't thinking only of himself; of the pleasure of his own cock, of his own quick ejaculation. Erminio—it was clear—was thinking also of Carlo's pleasure. In fact, he penetrated him gently, thrusting in such a way that, by his calculation, Carlo would feel it inside himself with xxx xxx pleasure. And after he thrust it in he withdrew it slowly, as if to make Carlo feel its whole length; in order, then, to thrust it in again, but harder, knowing that the female flesh is weak and he had to be indulgent of that weakness. He also began to rotate his penis inside Carlo's belly < ... >; then began once again to go up and down with slow thrusts of his hot, tense cock, which must have been at least six inches long. At a certain point, gradually, and with an almost exasperating slowness, he took it out completely; surely so that he himself—and Carlo, too—might again experience the pleasure of feeling it reenter. Then he moved up along Carlo's back; with his mouth he reached his ear. And he bit it, lightly. In that position the penis was more perpendicular to Carlo's sex, and it was painful when he moved it up and down. Carlo cried out again, but this time Erminio had no compassion; rather, he wanted to go on for a while and, with gentle domination, make him suffer < ... > : he knew that this, too, was part of the pleasure. But evidently Erminio had reached the limits of his capacity to control himself; he went back to his original position, /so/ that his cock went into Carlo in the normal way and began to go up and down more quickly and /regularly/. He came as if in a dream, < ... > continuing to go up and down. Carlo felt in his guts the penis contracting in quick palpitations, each one of which poured into him a burning stream of sperm. When the last drop had come out, Erminio did not immediately withdraw his cock; but he stayed awhile to let Carlo feel it, now perhaps enjoying that slit, that deep wound, which the anxiety of orgasm, evidently, had kept him from enjoying to the end with a /clear/ conscience. Now it seemed that it was he who felt pleasure in the fact that that six inches of cock flesh, hot and already becoming tender, was rubbing against such soft and welcoming walls. He took it out suddenly, /evidently/ having decided he was finished. He waited, squatting, for Carlo to get up as well and clean him off. And Carlo did so, /delaying/, because the sight of that cock, already soft but for that very reason unspeakably large and powerful, again made him nearly faint with desire. As Erminio went off, he overcame his slight embarrassment < ... > by saying to him: "I'll send you another!" Carlo was almost breathless with grief at having been permitted to share with Erminio once and for all the pleasure of his cock, so natural and therefore, for him, so overwhelming: natural for Erminio, but if it was also natural for Carlo it was in the sense that Carlo had suffered, like a silent slave whose destiny it was, without Erminio's having even remotely asked himself the question. There he was, going away, having done what he desired, with no obstacle opposing his desire, and having therefore used Carlo, like a thing. He went away with his back turned and the firm and steady step of a man who is like an animal. "Come on, whoever's turn it is!" cried the usual voice, cheerful and somewhat jarring, which was unable to resist, at every change, repeating the customary remark; nor were the others able to restrain a short laugh. The "new one," removed from an intimacy that was sociable and lighthearted (unless they were having a more serious and complicated discussion), detached himself from the group, /taking the path that led to the person who was to be used because of his own desire, which was painful and violent, without the least consideration for this person and making a careless claim that was, in the end, saintly/. This new one answered to the common name of Gianni; and in fact he was common, like his name. But it was precisely in this commonness that his extreme beauty consisted. Objectively, indeed, he was the most beautiful of them all. First, he was much the tallest; then, he had the narrow waist, broad shoulders, and long, muscular legs of a soccer player, or anyway an athlete. His hair was very short: a compact black fleece, though on both his neck and his forehead there were straight, bristling tufts. His face was tanned, so deeply that this Gianni seemed to be a colored man: his tan had something yellowish about it that made him look Brazilian. Not to mention that his eyes were big and black, large and sparkling like two butterflies; his nose straight and thin, his mouth very wide, with the same sparkle as the eyes. But the head, observed closely, looked sort of like the shaved head of a recruit (that is, as if it had been shaved in a humiliating way, in military school or prison); so if < ... > it had been cropped for athletic reasons, it made him somewhat bourgeois. His face, in spite of that dark, wild coloring, had something weak about it, especially in the chin; and in the sparkle of his eyes and teeth there was something false. He arrived with his tall, athletic body clothed in a pair of gray pants with little checks and a white shirt, and he stood smiling in front of Carlo, legs apart, leaning forward slightly. As with Gianfranco, Carlo, precisely because he was less attracted to him than to the others, said a few kind words: "Hello, love!" And then: "What a nice body. How old are you?" "Nineteen," answered Gianni in a voice that made Carlo's heart throb: it was deep and virile, and he spoke completely, almost harshly, in dialect. Anxiety, dry, obsessed, feverish, again clutched Carlo's stomach: like a fist that squeezed him as if /to make him blurt it out/. "I'm going to be a soldier," Gianni added simply. "When?" Carlo asked just to be polite, for what now interested him was Gianni's cock, made more precious—so that Carlo nearly fainted—by the /voice of its possessor/. "I don't know, they have to make two divisions . . ." Gianni tried to explain; it must seem to him on the one hand complicated and on the other completely natural. He had no objection to being called to military service by the State, as if in those years nothing had happened and nothing were happening. Military service, being part of life, transcended and made pointless every other political argument, old or new. This was what Carlo, for whom such simplicity was almost "holy," and made Gianni's sex even more /precious/, thought. "Come on," said Carlo as if it were his duty, almost putting himself in the place of those who were waiting. Gianni's pants were taut and smooth over his crotch, as if it were completely pure. Carlo unbuttoned them, nearly trembling. But the secret reason for that absence, that excess of chastity, was immediately clear. The underpants that covered his crotch were extremely tight athletic briefs. With difficulty, and helped almost lovingly by him, Carlo pulled it out. As a result of all that manipulation, performed just for the purpose of getting it out, the cock was half "hard"; and in a few moments it was erect. Meanwhile, from those briefs that had been so laboriously breached came a rush of scent, an odor identical to Erminio's; although Gianni's cock was smaller than Erminio's, it was also one of those with a strong but good smell of healthy sweat, an unmistakably warm and intimate odor, wafting, so to speak, from the pores of strong, manly skin and hair. In fact, Gianni's abdomen was flat, almost concave, completely dry and hard, and below the groin began the powerfully muscled thighs. At the first moment, as that odor evaporated from the briefs in which it had been closed for so long, it was too strong, a stench. But immediately it became the perfume of healthy sweat that it was, mixed with the semen which that cock must be full of.

With a kind of delicacy, or respect, Gianni placed his big, agile hand on Carlo's head and there exerted a light, inviting pressure. Carlo looked up into his face. As if that gesture had been a question, Gianni answered Carlo with a look of consent, accompanied by a small movement of the head that meant: "Yes, yes, go on." And with his hand he pressed more forcefully on Carlo's neck. With a kind of feminine calculation in which his victimization, serious, honest, and sulky, almost moved him—so closely did he identify with what was nevertheless manifestly a game for him—Carlo resisted the pressure of the boy's hand. In fact, he knew very well that Gianni was, or at least could be, innocent enough to believe that his victimization was serious and therefore, as a result, to seriously believe that his own domination /was to blame/. What moved Carlo was Gianni's incapacity to resist the voice of conscience that obliged him to stop his pressure and his demand; that is, Gianni's weakness in the face of his own flesh. And in fact Gianni was pushing, although he knew how to take advantage of his strength and his youthful rights. He pushed Carlo's head hard against his desperately erect cock, the edge of the foreskin reddened by desire. Carlo, of course, could not presume to resist too much, and his head yielded. But still he let only his cheek be crushed against Gianni's cock. Gianni, for a few moments satisfied with this, rubbed it against his cheek, pressing down hard with his hand. But then, predictably, he began again to maneuver to get what he wanted. He pushed Carlo's head back and then brought it close to his cock so that he could direct the cock to his mouth. But Carlo kept his mouth closed, as if refusing, in the last desperate gesture of protest of "a girl who has fallen" but does not want to get as far as that. And Gianni, ingenuously, believed he had to struggle against a real resistance. He did it forcefully but also with grace; rather, he was bewildered, though it was clear that he would not for anything in the world give up making Carlo do what he desired with his whole being. After trying two or three times to thrust his cock between Carlo's locked lips, he resorted to the other hand, which until that moment had hung, abandoned, at his side. With it he grabbed Carlo by the jaw, and as he violently, now almost angrily, pushed his cock against Carlo's mouth, he squeezed him so hard it hurt. Carlo suddenly yielded and opened his mouth. The cock entered, went in as far as the throat. But Carlo didn't move; it was as if, having obeyed, he were stunned, like a violated girl, and no longer knew what he was supposed to do. It was Gianni, then, who moved it slowly up and down in Carlo's mouth. Carlo remained immobile, as if hypnotized by obedience, dazed by the novelty; and in fact it was true. These were his real feelings. He in effect had to obey Gianni; that was a fact. Besides, it was as if that enormous penis, soft and hard at the same time, which, insatiable, filled his mouth, were the first that Carlo had ever known and felt. And it would never be different, even if there had been not twenty boys but a thousand. That powerful rod of hot, soft, yet agonizingly hard flesh penetrating him was a true miracle; seeing it happen was for Carlo, yet again, something hopelessly new. But Gianni had moved his cock, slowly and, so to speak, attentively, up and down in Carlo's mouth barely ten times when Carlo felt it precipitously release: contracting, it became a sweet hot liquid, of a viscosity that resembled no other. In the spasm that tore that vital fluid from him Gianni had leaned his hands on Carlo's shoulders and bent his knees: it was as if not only his penis but his whole self had been released inside Carlo. Then with a little sigh he suddenly took it out of Carlo's mouth. And in the light of the moon the penis still appeared powerfully swollen and dripping. And after Carlo had cleaned it off, sadly, as if for a definitive, painful farewell, Gianni, too, felt it his duty as he went off to give a brusque caress to the head of one who had served him and complied with his desires. He ran away, with his athlete's stride, toward the others.

Pietro† came forward from the group; Carlo recognized him by the overalls, a pair of those very wide, dark blue overalls made even darker by oil stains. It was as if Pietro were packed in, although the "gate" was completely open, down to the crotch; underneath, a red T-shirt was visible, also darkened by grease from the shop. Pietro was approaching very slowly, smoking a cigarette. When he reached the little open space where Carlo was waiting on his knees, he quickly took the last drags and, as usual, threw it away almost irritably. He undid his pants under the overalls: the hook of the fastening shone between Pietro's legs, just where he was now ingenuously groping with his hands to pull out his cock. The fact that he was having a hard time—because his cock, now almost erect, was stuffed into a pair of tight briefs (this was the principal reason for his difficulty), which in turn were inside a pair of pants, which in turn were inside a pair of overalls—caused a small embarrassment for Pietro; but he didn't want to show it and remained sullen, his face pale and absent. At the same time, the gesture a boy makes when he is alone—in order to pee against a bush or a wall or any solid structure < ... > as the rules recommended < ... > xxx xxx xxx xxx—was made with completely natural care. Thousands of times that gesture < ... > /is/ hidden, removed from all profane curiosity, out of sight of the stare of strangers, men or women; and now in a situation so different it remained perfectly the same < ... >. Carlo saw an edge of his undershirt gleaming against the mysteriously dark skin of his abdomen, and there was the cock, outside at last, grasped in his fingers. To get it out, Pietro had leaned over, drawing his stomach in < ... >; < ... > now he stood erect, legs apart, belly thrust forward. And the fact that, with the overalls, he was doubly clothed made the nakedness of the cock that was sticking out seem even more naked. It was one of the largest Carlo had seen all evening. The foreskin /was not drawn back/ to uncover the entire tip; only part of it emerged, a bright and livid pink, from the circle formed by the wrinkled skin. But the part covered by the skin pointed \pushed\ forward, large and knotty, like a little fist. Once again, Carlo was as if hypnotized. But this time he would never have had the strength to play the game of < ... > /balkiness/: Pietro was certainly less good-looking in the social sense, so to speak, than Gianni. His face was /pale/ and almost greenish: perhaps he had worked indoors too long on that summer day. His forehead was low, and all the features were slightly irregular. His eyes had a hostile expression; nor did his mouth seem capable of smiling. His hair was thick, black, dusty, un-combed, and had not been cut for a long time. But Carlo knew that that irritated and vaguely venomous expression was due < ... > /to libido/. It was the manifestation of that pale, rather unhappy boy's desire to ejac-ulate. All the casual violence practiced on Carlo by the others—until now, at least—was nothing in comparison with that silent desire. He was sure Pietro would not raise a hand to force him to do what he wished. But Carlo felt his violence in the very fact that he remained im-mobile, waiting, filled with hatred toward anyone who forced him to /reveal himself in that way/ and, moreover, made him wait. Choked by desire for that cock, just as he had been a few minutes before with Gi-anni—and in the same way—Carlo did not wait to be asked; and he immediately leaned against Pietro's belly, taking in his mouth that tip, with the thick skin covering it, and the little pink, pale circle in the center, which seemed of another material, light as silk and bathed by the grease of the sperm that had already come out of the little hole above the taut frenulum. Carlo was just in time to feel in his mouth, with his tongue, those shapes so charged with xxx and to catch not only the scent of sperm, which was like a perfume, but the odor of metal and oil from the shop which suffused that penis, when Pietro released it in his mouth, as Gianni had a short time before. < ... > He did not make a move, did not let out a sigh; he did not give Carlo the least satisfaction, as he would have put it. Carlo, bewildered and disappointed by the rapid conclusion of that encounter, waited for the entire long ejacula-tion to end, trying, of course, to enjoy it to the last drop. Pietro, having finished, did not have the same delicacy as Gianni: to get his cock out of Carlo's mouth, he gave him a slight push. Thrown backward, Carlo, on his knees in front of Pietro, who was standing, cast up at the boy an unhappy and suppliant, although resigned, look. However, Pietro was not looking at him: he was looking intently at his own cock, which was all greasy, an irritated grimace on his pasty face with its shadows of dirt from the shop. He was slowly wiping it off with his hands, holding it tight in the left while the rough palm of the right ran over the uncov-ered little circle of the /tip/. But the penis showed not the slightest sign of swelling. "Come on, I'll do it," Carlo said; and Pietro was persuaded to leave it in his hands. Carlo slowly cleaned it off, with the usual handkerchief. He took, as usual, more time than necessary, every so often kissing it. Strangely, patiently, Pietro let him do it. The cock was just slightly softer than when Pietro had taken it out, but as Carlo's hands cleaned it, it showed signs of becoming as hard as before. Carlo, timidly smiling, glanced up at Pietro, as if in admiration but also to spy on him. Pietro's face did not show the least expression: it was looking down, as concentrated and hostile as ever. Then, besides kissing it, Carlo also began to put it back in his mouth, as if in gratitude, feeling again with a concentrated and almost religious devotion those heavy and massive shapes: the knottiness of the tip covered by the thick hair, the delicacy of the uncovered part with the taut frenulum, and its odor of sperm— dry sperm from the day before and the still fresh sperm of just now— mixed with the smell of grease and metal from the shop. He began to move his mouth up and down again, as if it were all still to be done. Carlo kept being afraid that Pietro would give him another shove and push him away; instead the boy brusquely put one hand and then the other on his neck, interlocking them and hugging Carlo's head to him. With this gesture he expressed his consent to begin again and, even more than consent, demand. As if obeying, Carlo got to work conscientiously: he was exultant, but this time it was he who was ashamed. The more happiness gripped his heart like anguish, the more steady and diligent was the work Pietro required of him.

> *S'ils n'ayment fors que pour l'argent*
> *On ne les ayme que pour l'heure.*[28]

Something like this was what Carlo was thinking as he was leaning over to "satisfy" the boy: if they love only for money, one loves them only for that hour. But perhaps, he thought with pleasure—which did not eliminate the other pleasure, which he felt intensely in that act, trying not to be distracted—it was not true. Perhaps one loves them forever. An hour is a hole. Where time that is not consecutive accumulates. He did not love Pietro only for that gigantic piece of flesh that he had in his mouth, smooth and hard, with its shapes that were as if /created/

---

[28] Villon.

by a mold, although they were so overwhelmingly themselves, new, /never/ seen: with their heat, their odor, and that lividness, almost abjectness—that is, something not innocently animal—which oozed out. He loved that boy also for what he did not give him and could not give him; for example, that he, Carlo, was unable to enjoy the act completely—without /other thoughts, which sought/ the reasons for his enjoyment. That he was there only for the time purely necessary to obtain that pleasure which to boys seems so important and which they cannot resist. That he was about to leave and disappear forever, taking away with him all that he had given. As soon as that piece of flesh had come out of Carlo's mouth and, still swollen and dripping, had been put back sideways inside the briefs and then closed up inside the pants that would be buttoned up tight again, he would become that untouchable and mysterious thing he was by nature, by the decision of society. Pietro's return, soon, to his own life was the resealing of a social pact. And what he returned to was poverty, the world of work. For this reason Carlo liked in him, besides his naked, powerfully revealed sex, the smell of grease from the shop that he had about him, the absolute, innocent casualness of his clothes, the expressive force of those overalls, and, especially, the fact that he was there for a short while, that he was ready to disappear; because all this, in spite of being so obvious and irrelevant, so transparent in itself, was on the other hand the symbol of a profound social difference: the world of the other class, which was almost the world of another life. It was that which made Pietro, and all the others, dear; and their love of money, even if money was only a pretext, derived from a whole way of life, a whole economy. And there was also the fact that they had no way to relieve themselves—in an hour analogous to that one, and in general in their whole life of poverty—other than going to a prostitute and paying her. This, more or less, was what Carlo was thinking—trying to be distracted as little as possible from the profound pleasure that holding Pietro's cock in his hand and his mouth gave him—when Pietro came: almost suddenly and with such abundance that he would never have believed that he had come five minutes before. Pietro felt this almost as a weakness and somewhat embarrassing. In fact, he took his cock out of Carlo's mouth quickly and impatiently let it be dried. He tried not to reveal any feeling on his face except what derived from the conclusion of something. He did not stay long enough even to pull up the "shutter" of his pants. He did it as he ran away, in a rush, toward the little group of his companions. He ran easily, in his overalls, up and down the slopes of dry earth and the blond fleece of the grass, over the great field struck almost violently by the silent /enormity/ of the moonlight. Pietro had evoked for Carlo < ... > his Penates, his Lares of dust, dry wood, a few household goods, a bed or cot made up in the kitchen, perhaps, or the entranceway < ... >. But he also felt the presence of subterranean Gods, Demons, as if in sacred /league/ with these Gods for the night; it was clear: that night, so profoundly penetrated by the odor of dry grass and fennel, so rooted in a lunar light that seemed inexhaustible, that had fallen from the sky to create an eternal summer <night>,† was demoniacal: but these were not Demons belonging to an Inferno where the damned atone; rather, they belonged simply to the Lower World, where everyone ends up. In short, poor Gods, who go around leaving behind the smell of dogs, cunning and rough, /threatening and comradely/; who, coming out of their effigies of tufa, xxx xxx, or of wood eaten by sun and rain, make the entire nocturnal world, and the cosmos, melancholy. But without grief or pain: since the fragrant, silent, white, and hopelessly quiet and happy form of the nocturnal city, of the meadows, and of the sky consisted in being melancholy. Naturally the Gods of the Lower World, going around in that night without dampness, dry and fragrant as midday, were above all attracted by the group of their fellows standing on top of a low rise in the enormous field; they had evidently gone to mingle with them, it was clear, divine protectors, Spirits or Genies, but at the same time humble, dependent, and faithful as dogs.

NOTE 60
The return from the second trip to the East
(from the "Plan")

Italy appeared to be in reality the Arab East. It was only the sixteenth or seventeenth of March 1972, but the spring was so advanced that it already seemed midsummer. The hills < ... > of the Syrian desert or the bare Lebanese slopes looked like the pale backdrop of an almost Nordic landscape, familiar to French or German crusaders, compared with the savage light that invaded Italy; and in fact central Italy, not just Naples or Sicily. Carlo had landed in Milan and had traveled to Rome by car. In Milan, it's true, the weather was gray, although in the car it was hot enough to sweat. But here the "East" assumed other forms; a few days before, there had been a battle between extraparliamentary groups and the police (while the Fascists had calmly held their meeting, I believe, with Birindelli and Almirante). The extraparliamentary groups had organized what would later be considered the first real clash of "urban guerrilla warfare" in Italy; everything that had preceded it was casual and dilettantish. The youths of Communist Struggle were well armed and organized, almost like a little army, etc. Milan still showed the signs of that clash; and the smoke of the tear-gas bombs, of the bombs, did not yet seem to have dissipated. Then there had been the news of the death of Feltrinelli:[29] the image of the pylon at the foot of which Feltrinelli had died overwhelmed whatever other real images the continuation of life immediately began to offer as a comforting alternative (succeeding \and it would succeed\ in the end). But on the day of Carlo's return from /Syria/ none of the details of Feltrinelli's death were known yet; it was known only that the dead man was he. And there had been

---

[29] *Translator's note:* Giancarlo Feltrinelli, a left-wing editor who died in mysterious circumstances.

the hasty statement signed by a group of intellectuals declaring that he had been assassinated by the Fascists—or rather, probably, by an organization that was not Italian; that is, the CIA—in order to create a climate favorable to the right in the coming elections. /Carlo's own immediate interpretation was that Feltrinelli had been murdered alone, playing the guerrilla; that if he had been poor or simply some petit bourgeois, he would already have been in a clinic, or even an asylum, for some years; that, in short, he was a madman who had met the end of an idiot; there was no contempt in this interpretation; in fact, there was a certain compassion—certainly there was no pity./ Thus it was the death of Feltrinelli that gave Italy an Oriental, almost Palestinian look, in actions, things, bodies, aspects of life, the air; but at the same time threw on it a new and crazy light: a newness that Carlo at once felt unable to resist, was overcome by.

But I want to get to the flowers. It was just the season when, in the space of a night, flowers appear /en masse/; and they are the first flowers of the year, large daisies of an almost grayish white, deservedly without any commercial value but also without that poetic value which neglected, noncommercial things have. And those yellow flowers that have still /less value/, so little that no one even knows their name, although they appear punctually every year, thick and healthy, to color the meadows of Italy yellow, which, in turn, are green, an /immoderate, ugly/ green on which the sun casts a /pitiless/ light, blinding and /unpoetic/, an illumination that makes everything look the same. Add the almost violet lilac color of certain fruit trees (almonds, I believe) in rows on those so brutally green fields, with clusters of other trees, still bare, and the fences, the enclosures that bear witness to work that is now without hope, that is done, in fact, only by the old.

To Carlo's heart (since we are in the realm of /pure sensiblerie/), which must have been hardened by the pride of success—as confirmed by the last trip, in regard to the past, and now definitively open to the future, as an established value—that Oriental sun, those fields, that countryside of central Italy, so carefully maintained, so neatly divided, and so well /kept/, piece by piece against the sorrowful hills, along irrigation ditches surrounded by gray and reddish clouds of willow, and over it all a /dully/ clear sky, with some old, unmoving clouds—this brought an unbearable, unreasonable grief. He was helpless in the face of it, except to note its most acute moments, which nearly brought the wish to die. Because /although/ everything was the same, everything was different. All around was the sense of the end of a world, at least of the world of agriculture; and at the edge of every old village was a row of horrible new houses, with fake red bricks or bare yellow walls, which made them /all the same/. The people on the streets were horrible, too: the young men with hair like whores, with ponytails and curls, and on their faces forever stamped a sneer of satisfaction and presumptuousness; the girls bundled into those awful < ... > maxicoats, which gave them a suppliant look, like homosexuals in search of humiliation. The old people nearby were like ghosts, /set aside/, silent, shut in the grief of their < ... > exclusion.

It's well known that the light of three in the afternoon is painful and that one should never go out at that hour: it's no wonder everything hurts then, grabs you by the throat, and life appears a place of internment, where madmen believe they are free and spend their day as an entitlement. But the evening? The gentle < ... > evening? The hour when the cruel, too pale clouds of days of good weather begin to turn pink, when the green of the meadows, fiercely mottled by harsh yellow or white, begins /to turn brown/, to crumble into the great < ... > of the sunset that opens silently in the sky from one horizon to the other? When the towns on the hillsides or the ridge tops assume their ancient shapes, kneading into the cool darkness the new shapes that distort \debase\ them? And the people seem to revive, at least if seen from a distance, with the old spirit that made of every place an "other" place, to be experienced in its individual profundity, its originality, which ennobled whoever was not part of it but knew it, or wished to know it, or even only imagined it?

/Yet the evening, that evening of the eighteenth of March 1972, brought Carlo's heart nothing but terrible, insupportable pangs of grief. Is it possible that to a man like Carlo a change in the world mattered so much? Had he himself not contributed to that change? Or, if his contribution to that change had been accidental and insincere, had he not fought to possess that world, whatever it was? Indeed, did not such a change guarantee him work and success?

Instead, the fact that things were no longer just as they had been ten years before seemed to him a tragedy. < ... >

It was not his good taste that was offended by the wretched world of progress, the world of prosperity, of sexual freedom, of struggle against oppression, of the end of the power of the Church, of the disappearance of the old landowners, of reforms, of restlessness that guaranteed the tireless struggle for freedom; it was not even merely nostalgia for the past whose repressiveness had created things so marvelous, men so gentle; it was a true sense of tragedy.

He had decided to sleep on the way, at Florence or perhaps Orvieto; instead, he was so terrified by the world as it appeared on that afternoon, in that twilight, that he arrived in Rome, traveling as fast as possible in that lousy car rented from Hertz at Malpensa. It was already night. Although he was tired, at least an idea smiled at him: he would meet Karl, he would charge him, as usual, to go away, out into the night, so that he, at least, might enjoy as much solitude as possible. And Karl—gentle and good like the men of old, like them moral, and, like them, capable of violating the law for a purely inner or vital necessity—would obey him. And as for solitude, he would experience it thoroughly, without regrets, and without any guilt at his own intoxication; because if he had felt a sense of guilt at his own intoxication, that would have served only to make his intoxication still greater and more overwhelming, the only real good in life./

NOTE 61
Karl is gone

/His rich and handsome house in the neighborhood of Via Cassia, which had become fashionable among the wealthy in the early sixties, was pleasantly deserted. No one knew of his arrival. He was so eager to get to his den that he didn't even put the car in the garage. The liv-

ing room was silent and in order; yet Carlo immediately felt that
something was not right./

Carlo went on without Karl for some months as if nothing had happened. Every form and figure in his life, every aspect, it's true, continued in itself to pain him. Strangely, he would feel anguished in front of
a glass door opening xxx, or at the faces of four employees in an elevator
or a line of cars stopped at a traffic signal in the light of a summer Sunday. But that is natural in an "ideal" phase in the life of a petit bourgeois
intellectual. /It is neurosis./ It can be experienced along with everything
else in life. And perhaps Carlo would have gone on in that way indefinitely if he had never met, bought, and used Karl, that poor dog who
had now gone astray, no one knew where. The pretext for cutting short
this situation, which, moreover, was destined to be cut off, /came/ from
/historical/ circumstances: the position Carlo had reached in the ENI hierarchy xxx

his power xxx†

in a few months they were being divested: thanks, it's true, to Carlo
himself, who was working toward his own disgrace, through pleasure in
the pain that everything in the world caused him but, above all and
specifically, through the unexpected and, until a few months before, inconceivable competition from a Fascist colleague of his (or, at least,
someone who was suddenly revealed as a Fascist). This man, no doubt
put forward by the Fascists as a political reward, was now ineluctably
destined to take the place held by that Catholic of the left and Communist sympathizer who until that moment had been, or seemed to be,
Carlo. It is true that Carlo was offered another job xxx xxx; but this was
clearly a diversion: even if the level of power (measured in practical
terms) was about the same as that which Carlo had operated at *before,* it
was not the level he had reached *per gradus,* it did not have the sacred
characteristics necessary to true power. This had begun to emerge and
take shape in Carlo's life with the appearance of that poor dog Karl
and began to diminish and come to an end with Karl's disappearance.
And this was objectively. That subjectively, too, Carlo now desired its
diminution and its end is something that for the moment is only potential and will be realized only after a long and tortuous subterranean
course, much farther on in his story.‡

NOTE 62
/In consequence of Karl's disappearance/
\Imitation of the other Carlo (from the "Plan")\

But let's return to that March 18 of '72, when Carlo < ... >.

Desperate, obliged to live rather than to live in expectation of the other Carlo but always hoping that sooner or later he would reappear alive, Carlo prepared to spend the evening in the way he had forgotten. What to do? What he was doing while he was delegating his real existence to Karl? But that truly had the feeling of being a pretext, a practical way of filling the void. And, in any case, when news arrives one always believes for a moment that it can be rejected, so that one may go back and confront it prepared; thus one doesn't immediately give oneself up to the real sense of it, one experiences a moment of detachment or even of skepticism, sometimes almost smiling; also because news— even the most hopeless—is always an unthought-of enrichment of life, something that fulfills, reveals. /And therefore something vital./ Carlo felt simultaneously that there was no hope of Karl's return, that he was finished with Karl forever, but that nevertheless what now was a tragedy would not fail to give some other value to his life. That is, he understood at once everything there was to understand.

The grief he had felt in the face of pure and simple aspects of life on that afternoon of a day in March 1972 was a grief explicable exclusively in terms of himself; that is, it was already outside life; it was pathological; indeed, it had taken shape and crystallized, as almost always happens, in a moment of particular well-being or even existential triumph. It was nothing other than the forewarning of Karl's disappearance, rather, *it was* Karl's disappearance.†

The first solution Carlo could come up with was the most natural: to gather his courage, reopen the door of his house, get back in the car, start it up, leave.

Perhaps because of the "novelty" of the matter he was full of spiritual fortitude; and the rapidity of his resolve revived him. He was bringing to his private life the virility and the capacity for action of his public life! Thanks to his social successes, he had not for some time now felt like the provincial /Romagnolo/, an immigrant in Rome and marked for positions of command as if by predestination, yet slightly disgusted because he had the timidity of a Catholic, the awkwardness of a traditionalist, the credulity of an intellectual.

The time had come when he could let himself do what until then he had delegated a servant to do—one of the meek. In fact, all in all, he could almost consider what at first had seemed to him an irremediable misfortune to be the just design of destiny. But the reader has already understood that he was deluding himself and was destined for an immediate awakening.

With night, spring had recovered its climate, cool but not sharp; the warmth of the day persisted and especially, odd as it seemed, in the dampness of the grassy flower beds along the great tree-lined avenues.

Carlo knew Karl's routes pretty well; they were, at least a certain number of them, the obvious ones. There was a particular avenue that ran beside a reddish wall on which, rather than moonlight, the /darker/ light of the stars seemed to shine. By day that street was traversed by rivers of cars; not at night; although it was no longer deserted and as if outside the world—as it had once been, until a few years before—it was a place where prostitutes could peacefully wait for their clients. To Karl it was all familiar; familiar the great red wall, opaquely illumined by the night with its mournful warmth, with its /other/ human race; familiar the thin grassy strip opposite the wall, on the other side of the narrow avenue, which bordered a large, irregularly fenced field that was absorbed into the darkness of a cut through which passed some railway line or other; familiar the little fires of the prostitutes with the groups of youths and men around them, almost all in cars now, because for some years the boys had had no more need for those women; familiar the chain of streetlights that disappeared beyond that meadow, against the silent railway bridges, the forests of apartment buildings. But for Carlo it was all new, even if known. And here was the terrible grief that the very presence of things as they were gave him; not so much those things that the darkness rendered the same as they had been in the past as those that were irrefutably new and modern: the automobiles, the clothes and hair of the young men; their gestures, their words; their comings and goings, their being there; life itself.

The first woman who came up to him—one of three who had chosen that strip as their place of business and were heroically, stubbornly attached to it, accepting, too, poor girls, the great decrease in clients with pious resignation—was a girl in a short leather skirt that barely covered her crotch and a red shirt with a high collar; she was shouting incomprehensible words at someone; girl and old woman at the same time, with heavy thighs and her stomach sticking out, reddish hands clutching a purse clasped against it: all that was what Karl and Carlo liked. And yet to approach that girl, speak to her, have her get into the car, like one of the innocent old whores of Carlo's generation who wandered in those places that had definitely now been deserted by boys, was an undertaking that immediately revealed itself to be impossible.

The sharp pain that all day had pierced his guts became, if possible, still more painful; and was transformed into a feeling of nausea, which forced Carlo to accelerate toward a place in the shadows below the wall, where, pretending to pee—something that was against all his principles, in fact /it was the first time in his life/ that he had done it—he vomited; or rather he tried to vomit, but nothing came out. Surely he was not made to take the place of a man of another nature or at least compelled to another experience. His "private" life must undoubtedly be considered over. There remained for him only to choose (?) to be solely "public" and therefore "holy."

NOTE 63
Clarifications and complications (from the "Plan")

The death of Feltrinelli, along with the revolts of the extraparliamentary groups, which were now isolated from the rest of the nation—a nation blackmailed by the events of '68 and therefore inclined to remember them with loathing—had given a further impetus to Fascism, which, in spite of everything, in spite of the desperate efforts of the few honest /and ingenuous/ political forces, had already been tremendously strengthened by the slaughter in Milan and the two hundred other bombs, which had not resulted in any casualties but /were part/ of the same program. The Fascists in all positions of power began their /counteroffensive/, their series of tactical exchanges, /etc./; the Church was finished, the Curia remained, that was enough for a return to a clericalism that could conceive of the Fascists as possible allies: the basis of their possible understanding—which began pragmatically with exchanges of men in the centers of "power"—was simply "power," in and of itself, stripped of every sort of attribute; since a clericalism that desires the power of the Church is inconceivable without the Church; and a Fascism without tradition that wants traditional power is inconceivable. The people were those Carlo had seen—in a terrible flash—on that day in March of 1972 as he rushed by car from Milan to Rome on the Aurelia; those were the people; and they no longer had the old values of the Church or the corrupt values of conservatism: stupid, brutal, sneering, empty, neurotic, anxious, casual, undifferentiated; the young men all wanted the same thing, and it was nothing but the eternal repetition of a model, which made all the contents the same; a civilization was beginning whose center was not a particular man but groups of men; the man-hero, still \however\ modest, like Carlo, was something now inconceivable except to men of a certain age, who still felt respect—respect even for those who did not deserve it—which was therefore in itself something noble, ennobling life.

Though Carlo, like all petit bourgeois intellectuals, knew this, and owed this knowledge to good sense, and had passed judgment—not banally against "the extremist opposition," by means of which the old swindlers of Italian politics tried to surround themselves with a halo of popularity, but desperately against all—yet he had within himself something that, like an eel in a school of eels at the bottom of the ocean that knows how to find the route that will take it back to the tiny source of the Alpine torrent, obeyed a profound call that I do not even dare to name.

NOTE 64
Hesitations preceding sanctity (from the "Plan")

What does it matter if it remained secret not only from public opinion and from the circle of friends and colleagues but even from Carlo's own consciousness?

In the interlude of an existence, which comes between an event's happening (in our case the disappearance of Karl) and its real effect on the course of the life of the one who has been struck by it, there is a moment of inertia in which things go on as if nothing had happened and reason continues to function in the normal way.

There is nothing more innocent than an invitation to dinner; even at the moment when this invitation to dinner begins to seem guilty, the fiction of innocence can be easily and justifiably protracted for a long time. So much more so, besides, when at this dinner nothing can be said, no suggestion offered, no response given, no allusion made; and the dinner remains dinner and that's all.

I can only say that before yielding even a single aspect of power to the direct control of the Fascists (now shamelessly defined as such), the most Catholic wing of the Christian Democrats—/let's take Andreotti—naturally thought about it for a moment/; and not so much because of any scruples or the natural physical repugnance that a Fascist can inspire (twenty years have not been enough to wash the bloodstains from their hands) as because of the natural insecurity that even the most informed and capable man may have in predicting the future; in the future history still exists, and history is confusion; though it may be absurd to imagine, there could always be some imponderable in the immediate future that takes away from the Fascists the success that everyone predicts and they themselves arrogantly expect.

All in all, it's better to push to the right a man already tried—and always, in every eventuality, good for the left—than to take on in his place a man who is definitely of the right, proposed (in fact, practically imposed!) by Almirante.

So there was this dinner (many months before Carlo was to make the "great refusal"[30]). And besides, as we know, Carlo was not new to temptations to corruption. Rather, he had been corrupted. But not publicly. This dinner, on the other hand, could not but presage some publicity about corruption. Even though it remained a dinner and no more.

It remained a dinner and no more. Never was a dinner more ontological. Polenta with stew, Alpine style, was served, with some very good Trentino wine, since the Honorable at whose house the dinner was held was from that region; while, not counting Carlo, two of the other guests were Roman and four were from the south (one Sicilian). xxx xxx

Thus Carlo's shift to the right was *objectified*. He did not say it, did not admit it, never knew it publicly; he said it, admitted it, and knew it in private, but as a fact purely momentary, diplomatic, tactical: Machiavellian.

Yet there remained in the depths of his soul, and in depths not even so obscure, that unnameable cry that united his conscience to the school of consciences.

NOTE 64 BIS
What happened during that dinner (from the "Plan")

/I have made a feeble attempt to "describe" a dinner that includes Christian Democrats of the right (or, rather, available to all) and neo-Fascists, hinting at the presence, as always little spoken of and mysteriously allusive, of mafiosi deputies from Sicily.

This description consists of one or two feeble allusions (a certain dish, a certain type of wine). The minimum requirement of a story that does not want to be completely fanciful. In reality I know noth-

[30] *Translator's note:* Dante, *Inferno,* Canto III.

ing of such dinners; and the allusions are only suppositions. Others could make a "set piece" of the above dinner better than I, with lists not only of the food and wine but also of the guests' clothes, details of their physical and social appearance (ties, rings, etc.); and, in addition, brief digressions on their careers (which, however, I will not fail to do in the continuation of the story). I do not say that all these details, or rather "particulars," are superfluous or purely aesthetic. No. In fact, I would like to be able to describe them, to give the illusion of truth, besides the conceptual truth (which would be enriched by it). I am unable to do so because I would find not only the experience of such dinners repellent but also asking someone for details about them. That is, doing what the novelist I would like to be does. But there is something essential that interests me more, and I would like to keep to a simple denotative reference to this. And precisely, perhaps, for the economy of art./

What happened that was essential during that dinner, which preceded by about a month the elections of May 7, 1972?

First of all, and this the reader has already grasped without my needing to descend to detailed \particularized\ explanations (which, anyway, once they have been made explicit, clear, and, in short, banal, turn out to be false), what occurred was the phenomenon of corruption, even if it was internal and not admitted or was admitted with all the old justifications, calculated, /in global fashion/, to silence conscience.

But this is not the essential thing, at least as regards the facts of this story. The essential thing is something else.

Meanwhile < ... > it was a dinner "among men," or for males only.

This appears, I believe, as an /essential/ symptom of a ritual of corruption, southern (Sicilian) in origin, establishment, and form, that is transplanted to a bureaucratic capital through a party patronage operation.

The absence of women meant an absence of nuances. There was not even a lady of the house, provincial or vaguely Romanized, to act as a mysterious resonance chamber and to bestow on unspoken agreements that particular grace which the great established hypocrisy knows how to attain.

No, neither the robust provincial woman whom the deputy from

Trentino had married when he was a young man, still smelling of the sacristy or, indeed, the seminary but already full of that fierce animal energy which presides over brilliant political careers, a woman who, having grown dumpy <...>, is no longer her husband's equal but is there beside him, looking on, like an Erinys, smiling the smile of Venetian Catholics; nor even the vaguely intellectual wife of superior social standing, married when he was already on in his career, etc., etc. No wives.

To complete the picture, there was a manservant, also from the Alpine slopes, perhaps a former carabiniere, his whiskers still black, with the forehead /of an herbivorous animal/.

Both the Trentini and the Sicilians felt perfectly at ease in that atmosphere of masculine complicity; while Carlo was forced to make an agonizing effort (not since before the birth of Karl had he felt anything like it) to keep up with the situation.

The presence of one or two women would have reassured him, not only because sex binds everything, makes everything recognizable and existentially easy: no, not only that, but because of the infinite capacity of women to lie and not to betray reality, the negotiation (which in a man of action is always there beneath the surface) has an almost hallowed character.

Among all those male faces, between thirty-five and fifty, consumed by lives spent in affairs that were, all in all, disgusting, so that their bodies—in which those affairs had been experienced concretely—had suddenly in a way degenerated <...>, Carlo was like a child among grown-ups. He had to stay at their game (which they knew so well), feigning their good humor, their optimism, and their voracity—and—something no one knew—their repulsive vulgarity (expressed by noses, paunches, wrinkles, thick necks, mouths, pallor, sweat).

<...> Thanks to Karl, Carlo had acquired a profound, disinterested, blameless complicity with his own sex.

/He was in continuous contact with it and followed it all the time, like a thread that was guiding him (perhaps) through life in a dimension that life did not contemplate, etc. It was the gratuitousness, the freedom obtained by violence, without either consent or tolerance, etc. The guarantee of a secret protector, of an internalized "elsewhere," etc. Therefore Carlo always felt that the penis itself had a value that was always physically present and active./

Toward the middle of dinner (at the braised meat with polenta) Carlo suddenly stopped feeling his penis as flesh. The physical /path/ between him and his penis, that is, the underpants and pants, seemed to have suddenly lost their capacity as inanimate intermediaries. They did not tighten or loosen on anything; and the drop of pleasure always vaguely burning at the tip, under the skin—the bubble of pleasure, which requires pressure, a healing grip, etc., even when one cannot manage it— seemed to have evaporated, to be lost like the first mad guilty pleasures of adolescence, etc.

Neither during dinner nor after did Carlo, among all those colleagues and powerful men, have the courage to go to the bathroom and look at himself. And let the reader remember that Carlo was not a sensitive intellectual full of complexes but a man of action and power.

NOTE 65
Prologue to the medieval garden (from the "Mystery")

I feel a deep repugnance toward stopping, with my imagination, in the neighborhood where Carlo lived—Vigna Clara, the new part of the Parioli, which is really Olgiata—in order to be able to write about it. Why? Thinking about it causes a sharp pain in my heart. It's not moralism, it's not a social or class feeling. I have already for many years, in fact, belonged to the world that lives in such neighborhoods. For (nearly) an equal number of years, it's true, I haven't frequented it. But I cannot separate myself from it economically. I did not live in it. I lost it. Willingly, with joy, with liberating satisfaction, with unspeakable relief, but I lost it. Perhaps for this reason it pains me. And add to this a certain pity, but the pity one feels for something that is nevertheless repulsive.

What repels me violently about that environment is the absence of a halo for it to fade into, losing its shape, or, rather, the absence of an open space from which it can be contemplated, analyzed. It is all there before one's eyes and feelings: without <...> /idealism/ <...>. Yes, I repeat, without idealism, without notorious idealism. It is a totality realized by the few but nevertheless expressed by the majority: the fronts of the houses, of the (slightly shabbier) buildings where embassies have their residences, gardens that are in reality /meager/ but still a sign of luxury in that sea of cement, the silence of "private lives" sealed up in houses that respect them, with marble and glass (these, too, all things considered, /meager/), with long strips of sparkling brass bells and the still more profound and almost primitive silence of garages; all that is a "form" without excesses: its meaning is absolutely fixed and consists essentially of the absence of margins and space for "something else." This something else could be the class struggle, or a self-inflicted preoccupation with class entropy, or religious mysticism, or literature, or love of culture. Instead, nothing like that, nothing. The mere idea of this reality takes my breath away; makes my imagination flee in terror. Instead I force myself to remain and even to write a kind of poem whose background is just /this. Meaning there is something that, although it disgusts me, escapes me; and not only the fact that I didn't experience (with all my desire) that world and therefore missed it; but possibly the presence of a form (perhaps aberrant) of idealism, that is, of asceticism regarding that world, which escapes me./ Without that liberation life would not be materially possible. And yet there in Vigna Clara, in the New Parioli, or Olgiata, people live, I know; entire existences waste away, infinitely charged with reality. /I suppose that just as hatred of power is idealistic, so is the desire for power. And perhaps it is superficial to condemn, by choice and without discussion, the desire for power. The form of idealism that gives life to that completely uniform city of the wealthy, or at least of the well-to-do bourgeoisie, with its internal hierarchies, its coteries of snobs, of marginal types who are tolerated, etc., up to those with true power, directors of banks, big business executives, entrenched bureaucrats, government ministers, is a natural and—I must write even this—innocent desire for power./

Those who—as in my case—hate power have, at some moment or other of their life, an inaugural moment, loved it, because that is natural and because it's what later provokes a hatred that—besides being almost religious!—is justified.

Our hero, through all the metamorphoses—as ambiguous and incomprehensible, and perhaps also as arbitrary as one likes—was a man whose life was defined by a "natural and innocent desire for power."

Of grass and plants, yes, I love to speak. Around eleven in the evening a strange warmth was in the air after a day that had been quite cold and a bit rainy—like all of April and May in 1972.

Carlo arrives home as if in a hallucination (due to the wine?), and it seems to him that outside the city are gardens, orchards, etc. Quote almost to the letter the road "behind the city" of Alyosha in *The Brothers Karamazov*: rather than meeting his brother Dmitri, he meets an Angel† who makes him get into the "cart" and carries him in front of the garden of his house. That garden, too, must be doubled: the double is a courtyard or threshing floor, whose description is taken in part from Dostoyevsky (still *Karamazov*), partly from Gogol (*Dead Souls*); while for the description of the divinities or idols refer to Longhi's descriptions of sacred figures from the painting of the fourteenth century (Cimabue, Stefano Fiorentino, "spacious" Giotto)

(May 12, 1974)

/ <...> The grass in the gardens <...> was <...> already thick; and the half-wild plants, like acacias, which in Rome can overflow among the garbage, along crumbling walls or rotting fences, even in the heart of the richest residential neighborhoods, were at the height of their lushness. The rain that had fallen during the day lurked in that uncultivated vegetation, and in the sudden warmth the air became fragrant.

<...> In front of Carlo's house there was a large garden; a city garden, of course, with neatly cut grass, neatly trimmed boxwood, tall pines; yet, as one entered, the surrounding houses of that residential neighborhood (the villas built in the last ten years) could hardly be seen anymore, and one seemed to have fallen into the heart of the countryside./

That countryside, of course, had nothing to do with the country that

Carlo had known as a child and a boy (and that had become THE country); yet, just because of this strangeness, it gave one a sharper and almost painful sensation of being outside the city, lost in a rural world where nature reappeared in all /its mystery/.

Carlo, returning from the dinner that I spoke of in the preceding chapters and going into the house (perhaps a little drunk because of that damned wine from who knows what damned hills with a German name), witnessed a fantastic spectacle; or, rather, he had a vision, < ... > whose protagonist was his father.

NOTE 65 BIS
The medieval garden

His father was sitting in the middle of the garden in a realistic wicker garden chair. The light was not electric light, low and gloomy in its elegant restraint, almost obligatory in a world ruled by /inviolable/ laws: light as it should be in a garden set in a wealthy neighborhood defenseless against the nocturnal silence of a spring night of the past. Rather, it was a universal light, which came directly from the stars.

/The old man was silent, as if everything had been said or as if speaking were superfluous. < ... > As the author and inventor of this Vision, I must say that an Anachronism can regain reality and actuality, but that does not happen by chance./ The fact that the Past must persist in an /arrogant/ modern time makes it eloquent. It's true that it involves a return and an ephemeral rearrangement, yet at the moment at which it exists, it exists. Sitting beside the father, on the grass of that Garden which had regressed to distant times—ephemeral as well, yet endowed with a quality of stability now no longer possible or even thinkable—was Providence.† With the height of oneiric /impudence/, she was not dressed in the fashion of the last years of the Epoch that is ending, that is, the /thirties, or the twenties—but

I would dare to say even the forties or fifties! No: she was wearing a < ... > Romanesque tunic.

In a row in front of her were four little Gods, whose presence brings tears to the eyes—not, of course, to Carlo's, for he was experiencing them in the vision—but to mine as I describe them.

O Gods of humble Italy, whom the peasants saw and used to reproduce in wood carvings, making them stiff, awkward, and childlike yet deliciously precious, as no cultivated poet was ever able to be \do\!/

The light of Intelligence and Reason did not exist in them, no, it's true; and my emotion is not an emotion having to do with the Intelligence and Reason of man. There was only man's Reality, and his innocent way of endeavoring to see it and express it in its perfection, which no language can define except by saying what has been lost and what has remained not spoken and not inherited by the fathers, poor creatures, who lived with such energy, such goodwill, such innocence. The first had a scythe, the second a basketful of grapes, the third an ax, the fourth, who was smiling, a branch with large buds on it.

Standing behind the father was Grace, with her three daughters. Although they were, of course, graceful and sweetly smiling, there was nothing /affected/ about them. < ... > /They believed/ truly in the goodness of others and the objectivity of good; they believed truly in the principles regulating life; but their belief was slow, late, filial, inherited; yet, precisely for this reason—though it may seem absurd—the more perfect and enchanting. Good education had an ideal ancient source that made it natural in the present. Reserve, discretion, obedience, cheerfulness, respect, /submission, and heroism/ were second nature. They were totally lacking in the aggressiveness of those who, at a moment in history, established this source of principles; they accepted them and applied them diligently to living, extracting from them, indeed, grace; with the mother as with the daughters, all were equally ready to accept the sacrifices imposed by nature and by power, which were confused in them not through ideological error but through realism: a realism not thought but experienced in their bodies, in their gentle eyes, in their humble smiles, in their hair, which was marvelous but modest, like vegetation or the fur of beasts, in their rough-hewn features, somewhat stubby but like all those who resemble handsome, flawless mothers and fathers.

Beside Grace stood her sister Parsimony, who resembled her /as one drop of water resembles another/. She had two boy children who were playing /together/. They were playing marbles, and the marbles were the kind that can't be bought but that children somehow dig up; for example, once upon a time they were in soft-drink bottles (/someone will surely/ remember that): they were two normal, innocent boys with dust in their hair, wide, funny smiles, necks cleanly shaved, graceful bodies.

In a circle a little farther back stood Obedience, Patience, Resignation, Pity, Joy, Goodwill, and Health, but also Disobedience, Arrogance, Villainy, Cruelty, Rage, Violence, and Sickness, all facing forward: they were all sisters, they had the same wild and /laughing/ eyes, the same /crude and kind/ gestures, the same light, almost gay feeling of shame for their own presence.

These were all Divinities: the Divinities, evidently, < ... > of the father. Yet their relationship with him was not one of authority; in fact, they seemed to be there not to guide or dominate or defend the life of the father, sitting silently, but to put themselves at his service. Miraculous holiness and humble reality were in them a single nature.

/Beside them/ was a Horse, also a God, I wouldn't know if it was a stallion or a cart horse or a saddle horse; nervous, skittish, and shining, he continued to graze, shaking now his great tail, now his long mane; every so often he raised his head and sniffed the wind. This, too, this marvelous animal, though not a Thoroughbred, was there ready to watch over the father, /serving him/.

Beside him was April, who held in his hand an acacia flower, with its sharp, almost indecent scent of human seed. He wore wool trousers and on his hair a jaunty little cap; he was whistling a song that boys usually sing in chorus.

There was also the white-haired God of Primroses, old /as Methuselah/, with his shoulder blades sticking out on his childlike back; he held a glass in his hand, and, with an ironic look (surely not the look of an old bourgeois but that of a slightly mad peasant), he was reciting a poem of which only the accent could be heard, not the words.

There were some other Gods as well, but the list would be long and boring:† they were all friendly Gods, happy to be protectors, with an air at once majestic and subordinate. But at the back of the garden, in opposite corners—naturally, in a symmetry so perfect—were two other groups of Divinities.

On the left, neglected in the shadows, were the Devil, Adolescence, Tarchet,‡ the Son, the Hermaphrodite, the Anarchist, and Eros, their heads bowed, some even with their wrists bound: all naked and handsome, but without sex. Perhaps their services were useless, their protection unasked for: yet they, too, were part of that humble Celestial Circle.

To the right, /on the other hand/, were Divinities of a completely different type and nature. < ... > They were the First Father, the State, Order, Folly: these divinities did not appear to be at all obliging; on the contrary, they seemed to demand silence and prayer. It was impossible to predict whether or not they would yield. Something—equally impossible to predict—was needed to distract them from the task they were engaged in. The First Father was holding one of Folly's breasts tight in his hand, like an apple, and that had caused him to have an erection; he looked into space with burning eyes, his hair blowing in the wind. Not Romanesque but Art Nouveau, < ... > /to the/ expert eyes of Carlo and the author. Order was intently reading a book from the early twentieth century. The State was /pompously/ consulting some Greek texts: but not classical Greek. Folly, with the nails of her monstrous foot, was absorbed in scratching the head of a Divinity so low in stature that at first it could not be seen: the head was very large < ... > with a jutting forehead above a snub nose. It was Power.

The father was not looking at this group of Gods, perhaps he didn't dare; or if by chance he did turn toward them, it was with a look of complete and total subordination—in essence, of love.

Above this Vision/—as a musical accompaniment—/hovered a song: a song that was something between a national anthem, a liturgical melody, and a pilgrims' chorus. Singing were the Institutions, in three symmetrical rows—the shortest in front, the medium-sized in the middle, the tallest in back.

/That is an almost complete description of the vision. I've done it with a diligence and a simplicity of form that border on coyness, I realize. But there is a reason. This whole description is purely marginal and preparatory; its function is simply to reach, by the greatest possible economy of means—by what is strictly necessary to make myself understood, perhaps hinting or quoting or taking away—what has real importance to the unfolding of the story./

Among all these divinities, whom I—being neither Pizzuto nor Tostao—have summarily represented, there was one I would call an outlaw or anomaly. And it is here that I should, if anywhere, employ my wished-for style: on this divinity who does not have a precise place in the symmetry of the Medieval Garden, who is perhaps not even a Divinity but simply a man—a very young man—raised to a divine nature. Or perhaps he is a fallen Divinity who has left the fixed place entrusted to him by Ananke—an erratic, wandering, vagabond, unstable Divinity; perhaps he is the servant of the gods rather than of men; or was assigned by the gods to serve men directly and is therefore the servant first of the one and then of the other. Servant of all and therefore of none. <...> Made to serve the gods through men. /Therefore *directly* in the service of men and *indirectly* in the service of the gods—and therefore authorized in that case to consider men masters of the second rank and to pretend with the gods to be in the real service of men (as in effect he is) and not of them, the Gods. Etc., etc./

This God who wanders around with his hands in his pockets, /half/ yawning, among those celestial Circles and Semicircles around the father, without finding a fixed place to settle in, through boredom, impatience, disdain for all, or inability to adapt—an inability due precisely, perhaps, to his inferiority—is a dark-skinned young man who looks ordinary and not very intelligent, and not even particularly unpleasant.

Toward him the father does not have the reverent and restrained air that he has toward the Gods on his right (and that he does not let out too much—like a dignified professional, who has nothing to fear from them because his obedience and loyalty toward them has been established *ab aeterno* and *sine die*)—but has the confidential and simple attitude he has toward the Servant Gods. Also toward him the father's *eloquent silence* assumes and expresses mutual trust, the security of their relationship, the certainty of being able to count on the satisfaction of his needs, both private and, above all, public, directed to the public good.

Yet there is a fundamental difference between that young man and the other Gods, both the Servant Gods and the Master Gods; and that difference is evidently social. The Master Gods belong, visibly, to the bourgeoisie, perhaps with aristocratic origins, etc., etc.; they have the /hard/ noses, /weak/ chins, /guilty/ eyes, etc., etc., of bureaucrats, of professionals, of businessmen or industrialists; their aggressiveness is completely social (because even if they are athletic they are physically weak) and is mixed with the sense of guilt that gives rise to it, etc., etc. And even where their weakness is poetic—and their uncertain and therefore ungenerous mode of existence originates in an old, familiar sort of education for which it would be absurd and inhuman not to have some sympathy and even feel a kind of /tenderness/—an incurable vulgarity deforms, consumes, obscures those features, which are marked by a /repulsive/ senility.

But the Servant Gods belong essentially to the same class; their peasant origins are more recent and visible, it's true, and so their lack of responsibility, their brief, rigorous education, their eagerness, with its limited interests, etc., etc., preserve in their physical selves the innocence, health, and grace of the people. When Lenin said that peasants are all potential petits bourgeois, /he was alluding/ to these Gods of ours, who, though they live a bourgeois life, have not completely lost the possibility of human appearances: with smiling eyes, vivid cheeks, features, as I have said, rough-hewn but handsome.

On the other hand, unlike both the Master Gods and the Servant Gods, the young "anomaly" present in that fine company, whose God name is Salvatore Dulcimascolo, does not belong to the bourgeoisie in the least.

He is clearly of the people; and—since physically, even to the most inexpert eye, he appears to be from the South—of the subproletariat. This is the reason he is isolated there in the middle, he cannot join or merge with the other Gods: "marked" by a difference that cannot be eliminated, /etc./.

He is simply accepted, both by the Gods—among whom he was elevated—and by the human father; and he has been able to transform that acceptance into a privilege. He does not hide it. In fact, he exhibits it noticeably, in a gaze that is between threatening and bored, in his thug-like attitudes, which nevertheless have the grace bestowed as a gift (perhaps by other Gods?) on one born in a hovel in the heart of some old, dirty, hopeless southern city. Probably, I would add, Palermo, because if it were some other big, non-Mafia city petit bourgeois contamination might have changed him more profoundly, giving him those character-istics of servility that he does not appear to have at all. He does not for a single instant lose his dignity. If he is accepted in that world, he in turn has agreed to be taken into it. He is not a hired gunman, not he (like, for example, a policeman, persuaded to serve the rich for a little stipend, passively and with no alternatives). No, the god Salvatore Dul-cimascolo has taken but has given; takes but gives: his is an exchange, a pact. As with a man of honor, of course. He makes the most of himself gracefully, through ancient instinct: the firstborn son of a Palermitan mother who is proud of him. As a young man skilled in corruption, he is able to represent for the wealthy who corrupt him something they cannot do without. Therefore either to take or to leave. You give me so much and I give you so much: we are equal. In the circles of the Celes-tials he behaves with the same naturalness as in a neighborhood where poor boys either go to work or devote themselves to crime, choosing their own fate or enduring it as something unique: personal and at the same time common; /therefore tragic/. Besides, thanks to the ancient experience of corruption he is well acquainted with his corruptors; that is, he knows their principal sin, which consists precisely of the act that initiates their relationship with him: corruption (silent, for the most part, but ancient and thus always the same, fatal).

In other words, the God Salvatore Dulcimascolo is economically in the hands of the Gods, who have raised him up among them, but at the same time he has the Gods in his hands; in fact, he could always, at any moment and for any reason, blackmail them.

He does not know the deep reasons for them, the great original sins, but certain little crimes—judged nevertheless with the greatest sever-ity in the penal code—are well known to him, because he has commit-ted them himself on their orders.

How is it that Carlo's father—who was an old anti-Fascist, a De Gasperian Christian Democrat, growing old with a certain dignity, that is, experiencing bourgeois guilt only in the most generalized and innocent way—seemed to find the presence of that young man so natural?

His gaze, if it fell on him as it wandered from the Center of that Vision, did not betray particular feelings of wonder, of embarrassment, etc. It seemed that he had always seen him, known and accepted him, as one of the many usual daily presences of his world.

The lives of fathers always give off a < ... > sense of mystery; and that boy seemed at that moment one of the most enigmatic elements of the mystery. Because, in Carlo's case, his attention had NEVER dwelt on such a personage. Perhaps it was thus that his natural bourgeois racism manifested itself. He had not felt hatred, disdain, disgust, grief, incomprehension, etc., for a similar form of humanity; no, his eyes *had simply never rested on it.* And /it's strange/, because Carlo was a man of culture; a man of science, even if he dedicated himself not so much to science as to applied science; so he should have felt at least once in his life a little curiosity, intellectual, if nothing else, or practical, for people like Salvatore Dulcimascolo, their fathers, their mothers, their brothers, and all those like him. And it's not that he lacked opportunities—precisely because of his work; only recently, he had been in the Middle East \for a short time\ in Iraq, in Iran, where in fact all those around him—with the exception of about ten people, technicians, employees, and two or three ministers—were of the race of the God Salvatore Dulcimascolo, although at the same time gentler or perhaps fiercer. But Carlo's eyes had never really taken into consideration those human presences. /There must have been some good reason: something that kept Carlo's eyes and his capacity for perception from recognizing subproletarian human brothers (I say brothers because he was a Catholic)./ He knew that they existed, yes. And he also knew their problem: as seen above all by the left, since it had always been presented to him, for his whole life, as an *abstract* problem, and *never* once did the powerful élite to which he belonged devote itself to making it *concrete,* putting it on the carpet and solving it. That's why it was a problem of the Communists, the leftists; and so Carlo the democratic Catholic of the left could place it only as such. Never once, I repeat, had he connected his knowledge of that problem with a person who had lived it in his body. And it was from that body in fact that his eyes shrank.

NOTE 66
The medieval garden (continued)

And it was to that body that his eyes were now drawn.

But while Carlo was about to realize it—was, that is, about to become aware of the body, the whole body, of the God Salvatore Dulcimascolo, there, now, present, living, carnal, with its odor, perhaps its stink, with its weight, its heat, with its possibility of attacking or being attacked, of desiring or being desired, like a fruit just ripe and ready to be picked, or rejected, untouchable, reserved for actions that a bourgeois can succeed in imagining /only mythically/—then Heroism and Resignation began to sing. Their song, sharp and sweet, affected (in the popular style), a bit ridiculous even, in its /absolute/ faithfulness to the musical canons that /determined/ it and at the same time consuming—as happens (still sometimes) when a song assails one /suddenly/ on a street along the sea or in an alley among old /crumbling/ houses or in a field of grain or in the mass /of trees/ along a canal submerged in \absorbed into\ the peace of the sun—suddenly /silenced/ the boring, repeated little refrain of the Institutions, who continued to sing into nothingness, undaunted, following a learned canon for many voices, perhaps an old popular motif reworked by some imitator of Hindemith, < ... > by order of some minister (and perhaps /a candidate/ to become the national anthem, I would add, if the Vision aspired to be exhaustive).

That song led elsewhere and to another /time. It revived/ a reality as profoundly forgotten as it had been profoundly lived. Oh, nothing precise: perhaps the countryside around Turin, or perhaps some other place in the Po valley, when the sun sets, the evening is what it is, eternal and without alternative, a rite in which the whole cosmos shares, with the hundred, two hundred, thousand men and women who live in that corner of the world—/and their cottages,/ fences, old reddish churches—

with the light of the sun that is losing its colors and of the stars that are coming out /of the sea/ or from behind a distant row of blue mountains whose cap of white snow separates them from the blue of the sky. At that moment a bell rings, and a voice, melancholy or cheerful, of mother or friend, begins to speak, indistinctly, beyond the house walls or beyond the walls or fences of the gardens, because there is always someone who lingers outside in the air that begins to be hostile and the grass that sadly begins to grow damp.

While Carlo, easy /prey/ to this song, felt his heart tighten—until a tear, not unpleasantly, forced its way to his eyes—the young God Salvatore Dulcimascolo slept. It was partly that he was yawning, one could see he was tired or bored, and that song, which had such meaning for Carlo, for him was merely a pleasant lullaby, and so he went to sleep.

He stretched out on the holy grass, where he had been, with his elbow planted on the ground and his neck resting on the palm of his hand, chewing something in his teeth, perhaps the long light stem of a wheat stalk; now gradually he stretched out completely, with his forearm under his head, and let himself fall into a youthful sleep, the way boys do who think they can go all out in work or in making love and then afterward, at the /first opportunity/, pathetically, innocently, collapse.

The song of Heroism and Resignation—monodic and monostrophic, the song that two friends strike up together in unison, while in reality each one is singing on his own—stopped then as suddenly as it began, and with it there vanished into nothing the vague visions of a world /buried in memory and not even mourned, with its odor of hay, its paths of dirt or white dust, its gardens overflowing with peace, its rising or setting sun, the voices, the cries, the laughs or laments of the people/.

It remained there alone, that sleeping body.

In sleep it was even more corporeal, so to speak. The defenses of being awake—let's call them cultural—had fallen, and only the flesh remained.

Also, it was now easier for Carlo to rest his eyes on him. He had to overcome only his own modesty, /which/ was not simple: yet guiltily, taking advantage of the fact that no one could see him, he for the first time not only set eyes on a human being like Salvatore Dulcimascolo but paused to observe him and /indeed/ to ponder him. He did so without knowing the meaning of it, naturally, although he felt a profound grief, which was manifested in a pressure on his chest and a sense of emptiness in his stomach, as when one feels dizzy.

It was the dream force of the vision that gave abnormal importance to things: a terrifying significance to /insignificant/ and common details. It was not a political or ideological interest that Carlo felt for the first time *in corpore vili,* in the body of that subproletarian. Certainly he was not thinking about how to resolve the southern problem or how to improve the local relations of ENI's plants in the Sicilian region, for example, or similar things; or, if he was thinking about them, he was thinking, so to speak, in a second column that buzzed and vibrated in his desperate and /strangely/ heavy chest.

Salvatore Dulcimascolo asleep had the possibility of drawing Carlo's attention to him as a body, and as the body of a person.

Carlo observed the black hair, its roots so thick they recalled the flooding, overpowering vegetation that in that month of May had been reborn everywhere, as if for the first time in the history of the world; the narrow forehead, the irregular, rather brutish features, almost ugly and at the same time filled with the beauty of health and sexuality inherited as a blessing; the slightly hooked nose, the too fleshy mouth, the cheeks taut over the cheekbones; the body rather tall for a southerner but not long-limbed, its strength feline and solid, that of a dark-skinned boy who as an old man will be consumed by poverty or disfigured by the obesity of the poor; and the belly and the crotch, that part of the body where Carlo's eyes were certainly most reluctant to rest, even to pass over, and where now, more guiltily, because the act was performed in secret, they did rest. In that place was the purity and inviolability that the trousers of poor boys seal up, as if their sex were closer to the grace of creation or, anyway, closer and more nearly identical to the inaugural model /than any other/: /the perfect repetition, by right, of a gift that is with such difficulty granted to the bourgeois (and, if granted, immediately suffered, endured, considered undeserved, corrupt, debased). The perfect repetition of a mechanism, without possibility of error, at the level \worthy of the whole\ of the nature that so designates it and desires it. Between the cultural sexuality of the trousers—fastened by a simple clasp, as if it were a < ... > seal—and the natural sexuality of the body, of which the form conventionalized precisely by the use of pants could be glimpsed, there was a harmonious and perfect relationship: where nothing was for or against modesty;/ immodesty was chaste and chastity immodest, the miracle was brief and vulgar, and the briefness and the vulgarity were miraculous. Now, as he slept on the hard ground covered with holy grass, perhaps because of some dream, some uncontainable youthful sexuality, the member was erect: Carlo's eyes, in theory unskilled, in practice as skilled as those of a whore, immediately saw it, and the perception of the image was expressed in him wordlessly and unconsciously, as usual: just like the observation that it was a penis larger and more powerful than what Carlo imagined to be the average and was therefore < ... > faithful to the mythic image the /ordinary/ bourgeois has, without saying so to himself, of the /proletarian/ sex. /The pants, slightly worn along the fly—the worn part a little dirty, a little discolored, though this was barely perceptible—and the supine body, rigid because of its position and at the same time relaxed by sleep, did not have the indefinable bulge they have when the body is erect, standing, a bulge that is continually changing and mobile, revealing the power of the sex ambiguously and leaving uncertain its true form and size; nor did they have the almost geometric bulge they have when the body is seated or bent, the form of a triangle in the first case, of a cylinder laid out horizontally in the second, and in both strictly unintelligible; now the bulge was formless and undefended: the form < ... > that was hidden was almost perfectly legible in its disarming innocence./ All this Carlo analyzed and grasped in an instant, I repeat, without saying so to himself. He only felt more acutely, and almost unbearably, the weight that pressed on his chest and the sense of emptiness, of shrinking into nothing, in the pit of his stomach. Ignorant of all this, the God Salvatore Dulcimascolo, hired gunman of the Master Gods, slept blissfully, with his head on the grass and his face a little pale, his dark skin transparent-seeming \of ebony or ivory\, framed by the open collar of his black shirt.

NOTE 67
The fascination of Fascism

I said in the preceding note that there is a mystery in the life of fathers.
It's not a profound observation. But for that very reason I would like to
add some variants \considerations\.† The mystery of the life of fathers is
in their existence. There are things—even the most abstract or spiritual—that are lived *only through the body*. Lived through another body,
they are no longer the same.

What has been lived by the body of fathers can no longer be lived by
ours. We try to reconstruct it, to imagine and interpret it; that is, we
write the history of it. But history moves us so much (certainly more
than any other science) because what is most important in it inevitably
escapes us.

Thus \For the same reasons\ we cannot experience bodily the problems of boys; our body is different from theirs, and the reality experienced by their bodies is denied to us. We reconstruct it, we imagine it,
we interpret it, but we do not experience it. Hence there is a mystery in
the life of sons as well; and consequently there is a *continuity in the mystery* (a body that experiences reality): a continuity that breaks off with us.

We know how the phenomenon happens—since we, too, experience
in our body reality, in all its infinite forms; but our consciousness of the
transience of that experience is so strong as to disfigure and debase it.
Thus it appears to us as an experience to be used only to understand the
analogous experiences of others: experiences /so/ endowed with the
quality denied to us, absolute value.

Certainly we know that the existential experiences of others are also
transient, wretched, confused—they have hardly begun before they
end. But this sense of transience becomes an element, one of the many
permanent and absolute elements, of the value of the bodily experiences
of fathers and sons.

/The sense of transience, also innate in future experiences, causes such experiences to appear as already past (since, ideally, they are by their nature)./ Thus the mystery of existential experience is a mystery above all of the Past: not only of the Past as it appears to us in the Present (the mystery of fathers) but also of the Past as it appears to us in the Future (the mystery of sons).

The continuity of the element of transience is identical to the continuity of the Past and its bodily mystery.

That continuity invades all life, is its continuous record.

The stability of the Present, the Institutions, and the Power that defends them are based on this feeling of the Past, as a mystery to live again; if we did not delude ourselves that we refashion the same existential experiences as our fathers, we would be seized by an unbearable anguish, we would lose the sense of ourselves, the idea of ourselves; and the disorientation would be total. All the more since the mystery of the history of fathers /is identical/ to the mystery of the history of sons.

Fascism expresses all this in a primitive and /elementary/ way; thus it gives first place to an irrational philosophy and to action, which are the actual and logical forms of the bodily Mystery. No one of us is exempt from it, undamaged or free. Even when we do not want it, the Past determines the forms of life that we imagine or project for the future.

Fascism is the ideology of the powerful, the Communist revolution is the ideology of the powerless. The powerful and the powerless of the moment, of course. In the historical moment /in which it is current/. The powerful are also torturers, the powerless are also victims.

There is something absolute in the mind of the man of power who wishes /to stabilize/ the Past; while there is something precarious in the thinking of the victim who wishes to destroy the past.

In the man of power there is no ambiguity; similarly in those who decide to obey the powerful and therefore, in return, to benefit from power. Victims, on the other hand, are profoundly ambiguous; their decision to reject the power that is within reach in order to create another in an uncertain, improbable, often idealized and utopian tomorrow cannot but arouse suspicion.

The man of power can be condemned (for his abuse of power, his violence, his aggression, his vulgarity), and so can young men who, having reached the moment of choice, decide to stay with the powerful, to serve them, with the purpose of sharing in power and, a little at a time, becoming truly powerful themselves; but in all this there is nothing suspicious; it is, I would say, natural. In fact, it is difficult to imagine how it would ever enter anyone's mind to make the opposite choice; that is, to renounce the course of life that, putting him in the service of power, with his youthful /self-confidence/, assures him by seniority and old age power and prestige; and to choose instead the life of a victim, excluded from the great paternal banquet of power: the glorious repetition of life as the Past /that goes on forever/.

NOTE 58
Second fundamental moment of the poem

/Here in a few words is how the matter ended./

Carlo went into his room and got undressed, half drunk (the acceptable drunkenness of serious people). The Vision had remained behind, in the Garden saturated by the dampness, which now seemed almost icy, of that May night. The Gods and the other Celestials, looking toward the street and the gate—immobile, facing forward—now turned their backs to the house, where Carlo was undressing with trembling hands. His heart, sucked by drunkenness \which drunkenness had hurled\ down into dark, muddy depths, was overwhelmed by an unknown feeling that, although it was despicable—and /perhaps/ because of this—was exalting, wonderful. In Fascism there is a fascination that no one has ever had the courage to explain.

When Carlo was naked, his eyes fell on the mirror, which showed his reflection; and there, suddenly, the reason for the weight that pressed on his chest and the emptiness that unpleasantly lightened the lower part of his stomach, under the trousers, became clear.

In fact, two enormous breasts were sticking out from his chest; and between his legs, in place of the penis, there was an empty space, covered by a bush of hair: a vulva. But it was in other words—the words used < ... > by the people, which the bourgeoisie has never been able to find substitutes for—except by making them vulgar—that Carlo became aware of /his own sex change/.

NOTE 59
The passage of time

From May of '72 to October of that year there was no sign of what had been predicted simply as an Event. The Fascists got a lot of votes in the elections; in fact, they were very successful, as the reader knows better than I. The Socialists left the Government, which shifted to the right, with the Liberals, and Andreotti became the head of the Government. The old clerico-Fascists grew arrogant again, and an atmosphere of restoration blew over Italy like a sirocco. But, at least for now, it was limited to this. Which was a familiar state of affairs. Reality, moving forward on its own account, as its real laws willed, transformed the Italians through new phenomena of permissiveness < ... >; certain < ... > gains, which, with the Socialists in the Government, had been called Reforms, were by now irreversible. Italy was headed toward the Hedonism of Consumption—if the reader will allow me this superficial definition—whose temple was certainly not the Church. A hedonistic Fascist was a contradiction in terms. Power was caught /in the impasse/ of this contradiction. What direction would its Mind impose, descending, in /this case/, on Head of Government Andreotti? A more decisive turn to the right—as the moralistic /revival/ of the old dying clerico-Fascists in the Magistracy, the Police, etc., superficially demonstrated? Or a *more serious* turn to the right, down the long road of tolerant democracy?

Power is eternally young, malleable, often in doubt and in crisis, /like every human thing/. Now its followers were called into question.

The Opposition had reorganized itself and had regained a certain traditional unity based on the rhetorical idea of Power, traditionally understood as "old, stupid, obtuse, without dilemmas." Leftism had lost the masses, because a subculture of protest against a subculture of power is an antithesis that can end only in the defeat of the former. The masses of youths had enigmatically returned to normal, despite visibly retaining the /traumatic/ signs of the revolt of some years before. That, however, had turned against them. The total, intransigent condemnation that they had pronounced against all the fathers, without distinction, had kept them from having a dialectic relationship with those fathers by means of which to overtake them, to pass them by. Pure rejection is boring and tiresome. And so, by their rejection, the young found themselves stuck in history. Which meant, fatally, a regression. The physical and psychological characteristics of an old, unhappy bourgeoisie reappeared in them, signs that had disappeared, at least in a small way, in their fathers: the faces of old priests were seen again, of guilty lawyers, of vain judges, of corrupt sergeants, etc., etc.: this in the most defenseless youths, of course. In the "mass" there was nothing but discontent, neurosis, ignorance, aggression; integration did not pay for the betrayal.

The approach of the periphery to the center, of the provinces to the capitals, had meanwhile destroyed the varied, particular popular cultures as well. The outskirts of Rome and the poor lands of the South, the small traditional cities and peasant regions of the North no longer produced their own human models, whose origins lay precisely in the old cultures: human models to oppose to those offered by the center, as embodiments of resistance and liberty—even if they were old and poor. There was now only one model: it was that which the center, through the press and television, /gently/ imposed. And since it was a petit bourgeois model, the huge number of poor youths who sought to conform to it were frustrated \humiliated\ by it. The pride of the people no longer existed, < ... > an alternative < ... >. Rather, the extra thousand lire that prosperity had put in the pockets of proletarian young men had made those young men foolish, arrogant, vain, mean. It is only in poverty that the goodness of man is manifested, even if it is illusory. By now there was no young man of the people who did not have stamped on his face a sneer of self-sufficiency, who looked anyone in the eye anymore or did not walk with eyes lowered, like a schoolgirl showing dignity, reserve, and morality. There was no longer any curiosity at all. Everything was already compulsorily known. There was only a nervous anxiety—which made the young men ugly and pale—to consume their own piece of /the pie/. Added to this was long hair, or rather hair styled as if on hideous masks, with long sideburns, ponytails, bangs, curled forelocks: an unrestrained disfigurement that appeared to be the result of indescribable efforts and was in fact a substitute for words. Old prostitutes, young whores of the twenties, or mindless gurus—boys of the people imitated the students in this masquerade, which made them spend the most wonderful years of their lives as /clowns, ashamed/ of the unbearded splendor of their skin, < ... > which was brightened by the old proud, innocent forelocks, by the manly, humble shaved necks of the era of Poverty.

Among educated men there was not one who had the courage to raise his voice in protest against all this. The risk of unpopularity inspired more fear than the old risk of the truth. Furthermore, even specialized culture was worthy of the times; by now its internal organization was definitively pragmatic—intellectual products were products like any others. They were defined by success or lack of success, and their heuristics was in their existence, as things or acts: bets lost or won. Bad faith as an element of being a person of culture, or even a poet, became ideology. Some "Groups"—these, too, psychologically and physically similar to a bourgeoisie that had seemed finished forever—made "literary power" their stated and direct goal, not only doing so without shame but, indeed, at the same time performing a moralistic, terrorist, and blackmailing function borrowed, with unheard-of impudence, from a pitifully defeated leftism.

The only reality that beat with the rhythm and breath of truth was the implacable reality of production, of protecting the currency, of maintaining the old institutions still essential to the new power, which certainly were not the schools or the hospitals or the churches.

NOTE 60
The incarnation of Salvatore Dulcimascolo

Carlo, of course, as a man of power, as a public man, lived through all those months just as enigmatically as the Government to which he had given his technical support in an unspoken, much less written, exchange. He was in a state of suspension. Fascist violence—as a Great Innovation—was succeeded by prudence, which counseled waiting; in order not so much to do something as not to do something: not to make the mistake of overestimating Fascism and readmitting it into the arena of the decisions /of power/. On the other hand, Carlo kept his breasts and his female genital organs well hidden in old suits of grisaille or tweed, which, after some vulgarity in the preceding years, had tended to recapture their classic line, even if hairstyles were not yet really tapered. . . . After the attempt at a change or increase of power, as a "pure proposal," which had occurred in that May of anxieties and which now, as a fact, was irreversible, Carlo had remained in his position: the one he had reached with his trip to /Syria and the other Arab countries/ (where ENI had always preceded the State). In reality nothing had happened: except the irreversible fact of that silent proposal.

Precisely as a consequence of the suspension (which does not mean giving up) and of the possibilities (always open) of that First fact, there occurred—as if by pure chance, with a cordial, light, independent appearance, comradely in the parliamentary way—a Second fact. A second little dinner. This time in addition to the Trentino deputy there was a deputy from the South (Neapolitan) with the dove-white name of Tortora, who was the host. While the rest of the "little company" remained unchanged. The event had originated gaily, casually, in a meeting xxx xxx xxx. Thrown out there, this unimportant proposal fulfilled, by agreement, the firm wish of everyone. Who knows what was passing through the minds of the four Sicilians, the two deputies, and the two not further identified men of power. The fact is that they were invited by Tortora to El Toulà on an October evening: warm, with timorous stars on their guard yet resigned to the worst.

Tortora always had a table reserved at El Toulà; and so the guests sat around a white tablecloth, resting their heavy behinds, clothed < ... > in dark suits, on chairs reserved for the great of the earth, who are capable nevertheless of very modest earthly dinners. They spoke of many things: but certainly not, for example, of Restivo. As it got late, they all became lively and the Sicilians began to caress their table companions, giving them affectionate pats on the cheek. In Tortora, as he received those pats, the expression of /a sacristan/ was accentuated on the round face behind shrewd eyeglasses. They did not dare to give pats or caresses to the honorable Trentino, even as from servants to master; and not even, to tell the truth, to Carlo, with his cold northern hair, blond over a dark forehead, with his equally dark deep-set eyes and his mouth with its large, protruding teeth, from which came his dry conversation, conditioned by the habit of using technical terms. Neither Buscetta nor Vassalla nor Buttitta nor Gallina would ever have been able to imagine that behind that plain clear face of a northerner and under those impeccable manly clothes the body of a woman was hidden, of a female!

This El Toulà, so pompously official and devoted exclusively to political power, was not at that time /such a wonderful place/; it looked out of date and rather gloomy, and everything was a little crowded: the waiters, properly dressed in black tie, the bar, in a narrow space to the right of the entrance, the carefully set tables—all naturally gave a sense of luxury and high privilege; but (how to put it?) in that low restaurant—whose entrance resembled that of a government office building, with two or three steps down, and off to the sides some other small, higher-ceilinged "private dining rooms"—the squalor of everything that has to do with the State, and is therefore the habitation of power par excellence, continued without interruption. Thus the checkroom, too, was narrow and small: the coats were hung in a closet that opened just behind a low desk in a corridor where two or three people would have felt crowded. As he was leaving, Carlo, along with the others, lined up in front of the checkroom, where the waiters pompously paid their respects in parsimonious silence, as if absorbed (while an amused look of ironic complicity strayed into their overexpressive pupils). When it was Carlo's turn to put on his coat—amid the exuberant chatter of the /mafiosi/, already wrapped in theirs, enormous and gleaming with fur and leather—he became aware of a young waiter employed in the place.

First of all, the gaze of that waiter, < ... >, was directed at Carlo, when Carlo became aware of him; it was the look of one who "already knew": not precisely complicitous but ready, immediately or for always, to become so. It was a gesture of willingness, of complicity. Yet it was not servile. It was simply the look of one who—though aware of his own social inferiority—proposes an agreement between equals, and yet will not violate his subordinate position, which means, for example, caring for the superior person, who thus becomes, in a certain sense, protected by him. As a son is protected by his mother: by a mother who, though she has in her head other thoughts, equivocal, ambiguous < ... >, is ready nevertheless to sacrifice < ... > for love of her child, to take care of even the most humble needs, shit, underpants. . . . Yes, the look of that waiter—who, it appeared from his friendly relations with the others, who were already familiar with him, was called Carmelo—was a maternal look, and so were his gestures; at the moment when he helped Carlo on with his coat, he seemed in fact to wrap him in an embrace—a light embrace but overpoweringly possessive: the protective tenderness was also that which the torturer usually shows for his victim. He was not very young, certainly he had done his Army service some years before; his body, which would one day be fat, still had the blooming character of first youth, all suppleness and strength; his face, despite a few lines, was that of a young man, exclusively that and nothing else; and his youth, appearing as a force, had the same function as his maternal attitude, which imposed, with mute violence, its protective tenderness. Thus youth appeared to want to place itself almost by force (silent, of course) under the orders of one who needed it. The only physical defect was the fact that this maternal youth had already begun to lose the hair at his temples, already his head was bare almost to the middle; but there the hair was still beautiful, flowing and wavy, the way it is in virile mama's boys who come from the people /who are the true people/, from the depths of underclass misery, which joins, in an involuntary and consuming sense of tragedy, < ... > sexual destiny and death, military service and delinquency < ... >. With an almost cloying smile, Carmelo helped Carlo put on his coat, looking at him as if he knew him *or as if he knew something about him;* in sum, as if between them there was to be— if there was not already—a particular friendship and /gentle/ complicity.

In those seconds Carlo completely lost his head. His northern fairness became, if possible, still harsher and grimmer, and, as if with ill-contained annoyance and anger (due to better reasons, of another type), he let a big tip slide into Carmelo's hand; which felt large, fleshy, hot, hard, and obliging.

NOTE 61
Going to El Toulà

Although until then he had not been a customer, Carlo began to frequent El Toulà, and the situation immediately became embarrassing. One does not go alone to El Toulà, nor does one go merely to eat. It is difficult to find a table. The Honorable Tortora is part of the family, and to run into him there—without having reckoned on it—is embarrassing: how does one go about showing him that one can be alone, lost in a great city—outside the iron circle of political maneuvers, which require self-confidence, good humor, aggressiveness, and above all company—in front of some international dish, chicken or boiled beef? The Honorable Tortora is here, with his boisterous company of politicians, Christian Democrats from the provinces, who, at the table, demonstrate a boisterous sense of confidence, which is the other face of prudent tastings, < ... > relationships of necessity, etc., < ... > in official places; which, if they have ended in defeat, around the table set at El Toulà are gloriously minimized and mocked; if it's a question of victories, they are enjoyed in a vulgar fashion, /and if the sentence "we kicked their asses" is not always literally uttered, that is the sense of the discussions/. The Honorable Tortora can also—if, in an excess of that confidence, he has lost all restraint—take out the yellow envelope that comes from the Vatican, perhaps directly from someone close to the Pope, in the name (unspoken) of the Pope himself, in which he is congratulated, with the other Christian Democratic leaders, on a courageous struggle in defense of morality, let's say, and for the repression of rampant sexual freedom, etc.

To be alone there is as if to say: "Murder me." But of course the Honorable Tortora and the others filtered everything through the aggression of their triumphant good humor and, /possessed by/ an intoxicating /blindness/, made no accusations.

Naturally the complicity between Carlo and Carmelo had become more intense and, above all, more justified; now the gesture with which Carmelo put Carlo's coat on was a rite, and the thanks with which Carmelo took Carlo's regular tip in his big hand /rather than an "Amen" was an "Introibo"/; but nothing /damaged/ the obliging virility of the young man of honor, who, if he bowed and scraped before power, did it because—I repeat yet again—he had an equal dignity to put into the balance that sooner or later would weigh their giving and their receiving.

NOTE 62
Carmelo: his availability and his dissolution

One evening Carmelo, after silently holding out one hand to take the tip, held out the other with a quick, furtive movement, unfamiliar to Carlo. Mechanically Carlo took what Carmelo offered him. It was a piece of paper. He did not understand; he put it in his pocket with the quick, furtive gesture he had that very moment learned, like a lesson that can immediately be applied. His eye, though it fled like that of a businessman who must put his coat on quickly in order to leave in a hurry—and who does not, of course, know the coat-check man—managed to pick up in Carmelo's face something unexpected: a light blush. But perhaps because of Carmelo's skill, innocently bound to his ancient philosophy of poverty, that blush, which perhaps was of shame, appeared to be a blush of satisfaction or, rather, of joy.

As Carlo left, with his coat still flapping, he could not keep from glancing back. Carmelo was busy doing something else, with an absentmindedness that suddenly revealed all his essential mystery, the mystery of a person profoundly strange; but as soon as he became aware of that look from the gentleman, he assumed again his splendid smile, childlike and subproletarian, which had made the brown of his Sicilian skin go lightly red, /so that at the first opportunity he was released/ from the gunman's dark depths or the shining gaiety of the boy \kid\, who laughs without knowing why; and had immediately adopted that manly kindness toward the rich man, as if wealth by its nature could only feminize: a polite and hypocritical kindness, evidently, and alluding \with allusion\ to a /maternal/ tenderness /that, whenever it was asked for/, would be granted.

As soon as he was outside, Carlo gave a quick, furious glance at the note. There was only a number: a telephone number.

It was not easy for one who had been a man for forty years to suddenly behave like a woman. So the days that followed were /terrible/ for Carlo. The telephone became a monstrous mechanism, a window onto an infernal, cosmic darkness. A thousand times he was on the point of telephoning and a thousand times he gave it up, just as in a love story. While—and this should be absolutely clear—love did not enter into the business at all. /It is not true that sex and love are a single thing; rather, they are almost always two completely separate things. Even if it's true that there is always a drop of love. Even in the two minutes it takes to fuck a whore standing up in a field littered with garbage and shit. It was not love, with its calculations and its anguish, that kept Carlo from telephoning./ It was, simply, sexual shame, the terror of admitting that in the lower part of his stomach there was a terrible contraction that took away the breath, that was willing to run any risk— even death—to find peace for a single instant; to receive in the pain-racked emptiness the healing fullness, manna, gift of God; Carmelo's penis, surely swollen with virility, blindly \obtusely\ extended toward fecundity (though he was ignorant of that function \end\ because of his youthful recklessness and egoism).

It is incredible that against such desire, so consuming as to make one long for death, cold reason, which safeguards its own dignity, could have power: reason that wants at all costs to make others believe that for certain things one does not suffer, one does not even dream of suffering.

These are things that seem to be happening during the time when Forster was writing *Maurice,* in England in 1914, rather than in Italy at the end of 1972. But for Carlo (if the reader even needs /these justifications/) everything began from the beginning, and he knew nothing about this type of relationship, absolutely nothing: just as when, a plump and vaguely eunuchlike boy, he had left his native Alessandria to go to Turin; where he would learn nothing more. To telephone Carmelo meant not only revealing to him and to himself his unseemly desire but also putting himself in the hands of a stranger: perhaps a murderer, perhaps a blackmailer, or anyway a repository racially different from the secret itself, which was a bourgeois tragedy.

/Enough of that./ Naturally Carlo ended up telephoning Carmelo, at a time when he supposed he would be home, breakfast. Carmelo's voice sounded for the first time in Carlo's ears: it was a voice much more Sicilian than he had imagined, and also much more common. He was able to express himself in Italian only by pronouncing his Sicilian more distinctly and slowly: for example, instead of saying "ing" he said "in'," pronouncing it almost elegantly, or for "enjoy" he said, a little quickly, perhaps because he felt something was not right, "*ín*joy." Carlo—as in a naturalistic novel—had a kind of dizzy spell and "felt faint"; while the other, /soothing/, continued to talk, making exact arrangements for an appointment without any meanness, any vulgarity.

/They met on a "corner," which for Carmelo was < ... > the most open, natural, and innocent place in the world: at an angle to that corner was a wall that ran along a former boulevard, now absorbed by the city, which, according to Carmelo's information, led to a place called Casal Bertone./ /It wasn't clear/ what was behind that wall, a warehouse, an abandoned factory, who knows. Night dominated. At the corner was a traffic light, and there the former boulevard intersected with a street called Via Prenestina. The traffic on that street, at that moment, was indescribable. An endless line of cars was stopped at the light, like a drainage canal whose source was in the center of the city (which seemed to Carlo cosmically distant). On one side of the street beyond the traffic light were small dark fields and the ruins of some sheds, and, behind, the tarred walls of apartment buildings lost in a sky filled with a transparent, cold bluish mist. In the middle of a broad square opposite /those buildings/, on an ill-defined plot of land where a Circus (yes, a Circus) had pitched its tents, there was a small, solitary pink structure: it was a bar, sparkling with light, and since it was right at a tram stop, it was full of people passing through, old and middle-aged, except for a /small crowd of habitués/, young men with long, filthy hair falling over thin, stunted shoulders or obesely /fat/ ones. Still farther on was the end of a bus route, with a crowd of buses, a cinema—in short, hell.

Carlo had stopped his car next to the sidewalk, where there was a no-standing zone, given the proximity of the traffic light. But what to do? Next to him was a urinal, a flower seller, and a newsstand, not to mention another, less busy bus stop, under an old tree that had survived who knows what sort of times; thus there was a lot of coming and going around Carlo's car. The place was perfectly suited to one who wished to be alone, to sink into the center of the earth. Carlo's wish to be possessed by Carmelo was a matter of life and death; still, although the probability was great that in a little while this would come true, Carlo was as if stiff and frozen; <...> the gestures of possession his fantasy held out to him were extremely meager. Yet when Carmelo appeared, or rather was revealed by the appearance of his body at the corner of the street, everything again became so mysterious and complex, so frighteningly rich, that Carlo was about to faint. Carmelo, on the other hand, seemed to treat everything very naturally. Who knows how many times he had got into a car that waited for him at some corner. Who knows how many times he had performed those erotic movements, un-buttoning his pants, pulling it out, etc., which <...> to Carlo seemed so extraordinary.

"Ciao," he had said to him as he got into the car. He spoke familiarly. "Where shall we go?" he said then, pronouncing distinctly his pathetic Sicilian, which, however, corrected by his physical presence and his vaguely unctuous smile, had lost some of its purity. Where to go? But Carlo thought Carmelo would know. That Carmelo was ready to go anywhere on earth, to whatever place the gentleman had in mind, was

another reason for Carlo, who did not know, and would never have suspected, the existence of such availability, to marvel. For all that the boy
was, /presumably, protected and settled/, it was incredible that he had
kept so intact that freshness of a poor man available for everything.
That he had no logistical difficulty to put in the way, no psychological
resistance. He came with Carlo like an animal, a young beast so uninterested in the human world that even to be led to the slaughter is a
thing that seems to have nothing to do with him; and lays everything,
therefore, on the conscience of man. It's just a manner of speaking.
Carlo, like a woman, had imagined that Carmelo would take the initiative. That he would know where to lead him: perhaps to murder him or
blackmail him and do to him who knows what.

/Instead Carmelo put himself in Carlo's hands. Apart from the fact
that Carlo hadn't the least idea where to go (and may the reader excuse
me for this new interpolation of real conversation). To a hotel? His
hair stood up on his head at the mere thought of it: entering under the
eyes of the doorman, the cashier, the porter. . . . The identity card!
Some dubious small hotel? Carlo did not know any and had besides a
terror of such places that kept him from even considering the possibility. Going to his house meant that he would automatically make of
Carmelo, and with no possibility of relief, a murderer or a blackmailer
(not to mention the neighbors)./ He tried to say these things to
Carmelo, in a cracked voice that suddenly became more northern than
he remembered: he was pronouncing certain words in the Piedmontese
accent used by the characters in the comic /legends/ of the region.

Carmelo immediately adapted to these difficulties. He really had an
awful innocence. He said: "I know a place. A good place. Let's go!"

/A kind of fog had descended. < ... > It congealed around the traffic
signals, in the middle of the avenue, and in the infinite rows of streetlights along the roads that intersected it. But also every one of the innumerable red or white lights of the congested throng of cars had
around it, like a halo, wisps of that fog. The lights in the windows of
the houses, arrayed against the sky, without views, massed, row upon
row, some very high, some very low, above corners still dark and
muddy, were all veiled in black. No one paid any attention. The fog
united them, submerged them in a single world, where the insolent

and the confident groped blindly. The virgin Carlo was as if terrified by it. But the "naturalistic" palpitations that hammered in his brain, flooding it with blood, were still stronger than the terror that rose around him like a thick wall of fog./ His eye fell on Carmelo's body. Carmelo, taking a cigarette out of his pocket, had slightly disturbed the neatness of his outfit, a splendid new stiff white raincoat that came to just above the knees and had a wide sport collar that framed his Sicilian neck; one flap of this coat was elegantly folded back, leaving uncovered one thigh (in a pair of Scottish plaid pants), while the other flap, stretched tight, remained over the leg down to the knee. /Thus, under the stiff raincoat, open in that way, the point where Carmelo's thighs met could be seen; but everything was sunk in a deep, impenetrable darkness. The raincoat whitened over the thighs clothed in a virile fabric too colorful, actually, to be truly Scottish; but there was only enough light to dimly touch the more exposed of those two thighs, while the crotch was in darkness, protected by a hellish obscurity that Carmelo, in his innocence, had no consciousness of. But as soon as the car moved, pulling away from the sidewalk with its gloomy urinal, the light penetrated that darkness impalpably, and a particular bulge in the smoothly ironed fly of the pants—nor did Carmelo, in his innocence, have the least consciousness of this—was for a few seconds illuminated by a strip of light that had somehow penetrated that cave where Carmelo guarded the innocent naturalness of his manhood, legs apart, one hand every so often resting in the middle, large, hard, heavy, a cigarette between the fingers./

They took a long road, neither old nor new, over which arched an infinite series of strings of colored lights \little lamps\ in the shape of pediments, with outlines of crosses or other religious symbols in the center. They came to another traffic light, similar to the previous one, but the street, which came from the center of the city, was narrower and sloped down, and was even more /jammed/ with cars. They went along this street, heading away from the center, among old houses mixed in with some new, jutting structures, whose lights seemed to be shining on empty interiors; and old streets, to the right and the left, which were lost in the darkness, as if amid the ruins of a countryside reduced to a muddy mass. Farther along, the street widened, and the streets that ran perpendicular and were lost in the darkness were also wider, with low walls and chain-link fences. The stucco on the houses was the old-fashioned kind, dark brown or light blue. /And over all this the fog blackened./

"Go on, go on," said Carmelo, calmly, making a gesture with his hand that no bourgeois would ever have known how to make; and which had to be obeyed. Beneath the fog, the street had widened; on the left, here and there in the darkness, rose large factories, schools, or plant nurseries, on the right opened the empty immensity of a dark meadow-land where the fog was clearing, allowing distant glimpses of a view of another part of the city, crowded with apartment buildings. And there, on that stage set like a pale concrete wall with reddish windows along the horizon, the moon appeared in an oblong tear in the fog. The edges of that tear were as if bleached; and the light of the new moon was nearly an ashen violet, of a corpselike whiteness. At the end of the de-serted street beside the field rose the dark shapes, strewn with the faintly luminous holes of windows, of yet another, older part of the city; from there a tram approached, rattling, which, in not very reassuring contrast, was /brand-new/. In front of the tram shelter, which was also new, suspended in the emptiness between the old, unused debris-covered street, < ... >, and the new avenue, which had just been built, Carmelo, with a look of irritation, however, made a sign to stop the car.

On the embankment in front of the enormous field, dark and dripping in the infernal mist, was a long row of little pine trees; and a dozen of them were lying on the ground, on the asphalt of the street. Among these abandoned trees, imbued with the sadness of their moun-tains and with the still more intolerable \depressing\ sadness of the small run-down apartments of those neighborhoods—when they should have been festooned with lights and colored balls—a little fire was burning; it shone weakly, like the prostitutes' fires /along the edges/ of /similar/ streets. Around this fire were some dirty, /ragged/ children, black as miners. They were standing still, looking out toward the street. One was nearly adolescent and, perhaps for that reason, because he al-ready knew life with its humiliations, and the place each one must take, stood apart, with the distant look of someone doing his job. The two others were younger, still children. And for that reason their eyes were turned to the street, bright with ill-concealed curiosity, expectation. They were dressed in rags, in very light summer pants <?> and woolen shirts from whose high loose collars their dirty necks stuck out, tender as those of the weakest animals. Their faces appeared transparent because of a congenital weakness, and while one had in his eyes the virile, dangerous light that would make him a thief or a delinquent, the eyes of the other were lost, as if he were a child of the bourgeoisie trying to save his dignity. They stared at Carlo's car, immobilized in the position they had taken the moment they turned. The flashing fire lit their smoke-blackened faces, in which the eyes gleamed, sidelong, unmoving, inexpressive. There was also a fourth, unnoticed at first. In fact, he was stretched out on some sacks piled up near the fire, on the damp weeds, and was /wrapped/ in a blanket. From that bed only his face stuck out, pale, almost yellow, and round. His eyes, too, looked at Carlo's car; but sleep overcame him, and the eyelids descended over pupils that grew dim as if blinded.

"Turn around," said Carmelo, distracted yet with the confidence of a guide who, having taken a close look, realizes that the trail is no good and he has to find another one. Carlo, obedient as a tourist, obeyed. He started the car and, with blind obedience, made a U-turn in the street <...>, following it back in the opposite direction. A few hundred meters farther on, Carmelo again ordered: "Turn left." And Carlo, as if suffocated by the pleasure of blindly, submissively obeying him, turned onto a narrow street that, behind a group of apartment blocks, all exactly the same, headed into the darkness, probably following another side of the immense field skirted by the avenue. In fact, that was the case: after two or three sharp turns the narrow street went over a bridge, passed a group of shacks, and then turned right toward the jagged-looking neighborhood with the big cupola and the long wound in the clouds above the horizon—which had first appeared on the right, at the end of that /meadow as big as an airfield/.

Here, too, along the edge of the field fires sparkled on mounds bristling with winter grass, piles of garbage, of dirt. At a distance from one another, like the signals of sentinels. Beside the first, one could make out, in a halo of colorless light and a billow of black smoke— from burning tires—the prostitute, with her short red skirt that ended above the thighs and her black purse. Beside her was a client, his back turned, wearing an old man's shabby clothes that fell loosely over his bent body. Near the other fires, too, dark figures could occasionally be discerned.

"Stop here," Carmelo said calmly. They were in the space between the first two fires, along a /dark/, high part of the bank, behind which stretched the rotting mounds. Carlo stopped the car near a half-open gate in a long fence. < ... > Behind it was the empty space of a playing field. Beyond this was a broken hedge, ravaged by winter but still leafy; and, farther on, another neighborhood. This one had low structures, shacks, and /some/ three- or four-story houses put up by contractors, bare, gray, unstuccoed. But this neighborhood, too, was immense and, with its darkly lighted windows, /rose/ against the part of the sky where the sun, which had set sometime \many hours\ earlier, had left a mysterious, irremediable trail of light.

Carmelo got out of the car and like a young hood adjusted his elegant white trench coat with its turned-up collar. His eyes were smiling. Carlo followed him, feeling as if he were naked out in the strangely warm air of that quarter, which reminded him of the cities of the Middle East, Damascus or the outskirts of Cairo, where, indeed, he had been a stranger, condemned to feel everything around him as exotic, separate from history. He followed Carmelo over the low bank and into the field, which stretched as far as the eye could see toward other distant lights. The blind pleasure of obeying took away all the bourgeois anxieties of a man who of that entire world knows only that it exists; but takes great care not to deepen his knowledge of it in any way. On the other hand, the mystery of greater virility and richness /of life/, which he attributed—as a racist—to the quality of life in those poor neighborhoods, was the same that he attributed to Carmelo; and so in his presence he felt inferior (and, at the moment, happy to be so). < ... > Carmelo turned toward him and gallantly held out his hand to help him up and down the muddy mounds, bristling with rocks and clumps of dirt-caked weeds. At that sudden gallant—if a little showy—gesture of help and protection, Carlo entered something like a trance; he said nothing, he showed nothing; obedience had to be blind, total. Carmelo's kindness was not only the proof of his strength. His wish for possession used that chivalrous and ceremonious gesture—which concealed the true grace of the people—to subjugate still further the willing victim, whom he protected in this way as if to reassure and soothe him. All this provoked in Carlo an emotion so powerful that he started to tremble and almost cry, in a strange, exalting kind of gratitude. Eagerly he followed his guide, who gently led him—with his large hand, whose strong grasp he was unaware of—through that rough place familiar to him and /experienced by Carlo for the first time/.

Beyond the line of the prostitutes' fires, which became sparser in the direction of the new neighborhood shining in the distance, above the fog, like the crenellated wall of an ancient city, the mounds ended and the ground became more level. Carmelo let go of Carlo's hand and moved more quickly. After a few hundred meters, they reached a high chain-link fence that was torn in places. Here were some hollows in the ground, where the grass was thicker and cleaner. They were near the center of that vast expanse, and all around, in the distance, against the different skies, shone the lights of the various neighborhoods. (Even the hills of the Castelli were visible, slightly thicker shadows in the black-blue of the sky, because the moon, in the long, thin tear in the clouds, shone more brightly now, as if victorious over the /fog/ that covered the earth.)

"Here," said Carmelo. And he stretched out on his side on the ground, leaning on one elbow. He looked at Carlo with a sort of irony, which was, however, affectionate and partly directed at himself as well.

Carlo, careful and silent, lay down beside him with his head lowered. His heart beat inside him like the thunder of a great waterfall; and the emptiness in the pit of his stomach was a contraction that nearly gave him a < ... > spasm, < ... > yet he wished it would last forever. Carmelo, however, did not perceive things that way. And Carlo's heart again throbbed with joy. The joy was almost unbearable; and could not be revealed. Silence had to be strictly observed. Carmelo then had another demand, other than leaving Carlo there to suffer agonies as he waited. In fact, with a deepening of his ironic smile—which he concealed, perhaps a little embarrassed this time—he took Carlo's hand, as if afraid of showing a lack of respect, with the delicacy one shows a victim and, drawing it slowly to himself, so that the force or strength with which he did it was not evident, brought it under the white edge of his trench coat, which still tightly covered his crotch, between legs spread as if he were stretched out on the grass. First he rested it there lightly, still holding it tight in his own, as if he were afraid of doing something improper—even he was /weak/ in the face of his own need. Then he released the grasp of his fist, continuing, however, to press the back of Carlo's hand with the hardened palm of his own. /At first/ the pressure was /very light/ and almost uncertain, /for all that it was/ insistent. Carlo's entire body was infected by that contact, /which/ had /no/ intention of stopping, in fact it slowly became stronger, then brutally, almost suddenly, forced Carlo's hand to touch the /mass/ of flesh that was crushed down over the crotch by the tight pants. The strong pressure that Carlo now felt on the back of his hand, and spreading < ... > throughout his whole body, had brought his /unendurable/ anxiety /to the limit of/ endurance; a /rapture/ of happiness and gratitude shook him completely (in his exhausted silence), almost like the symptom of an epileptic attack. His eyes were dim, almost blinded by it; and he did not dare to raise them to Carmelo, who was surely, with his ironic smile—now less calm and less capable of masking his distinctive man's emotion—staring at him. The pressure on the back of his hand was almost more exalting than the pressure that, in turn, his hand was forced to put on Carmelo's crotch. It was the first time his hand had fondled a man's sex, but the violence that made him do it was still more exalting than that discovery; again Carlo wished the moment would never end. But again—according to a kind of calculation that to Carmelo must be familiar—the boy revealed a new demand. He made Carlo spread his hand, which he was holding crushed, and by now numbed, against his groin; he spread the fingers, to make them /take hold of/ that flesh which the trousers so tightly clothed. Carlo could not yet distinguish its simple shape with that random grasp; perhaps his hand was grabbing the end of the penis, between the testicles < ... >. Then patiently, sure of himself, Carmelo helped him, moving Carlo's hand against that secret known to him alone. First he pushed the hand of his prey down toward the end, above the testicles, soft but /as if slightly hardened/ by the tightness of the pants, then, very slowly, he pulled it up, making him grasp the /hard/ part with his fingers. To Carlo it seemed that he would sink into the ground with the wonder of it: what his fingers were touching was not what he expected. /He expected < ... > a penis like his own, or like those of his schoolfriends, which he had only caught glimpses of in bathrooms or in the locker rooms of playing fields. This instead was much bigger < ... > and as if of another material; it was another sex, precisely that which the myth of the people had made Carlo imagine, but abstractly, not concretely./

And, moreover, from that massive protrusion, at once tender and hard as a rock, emanated a /profound/ warmth, which through Carlo's fingers, grasping it, invaded his entire body yet again, flooding it with a joy that thirsted /for death/. And still it was not over. Carmelo, victorious, continuing to maneuver Carlo's hand, now drew it down so that the full measure of his penis could be taken, in accordance with his man's need and with the carnal pleasure the grip of that obedient hand gave him. Surely it was a matter of a few seconds to cover the entire length; but to Carlo it seemed an eternity, because this time, too, its size was beyond his imagining. If boys of the people were supposed to have penises bigger and more powerful than those of their masters, who are farther from nature, then that penis confirmed a common and current conviction; yet the confirmation was more astounding than if it had been an unexpected discovery: because reality, as we know, is always larger than any idea we have of it. The edge of the trench coat, meanwhile, had slid down off the knee of Carmelo's raised left leg: and the groin, which had until then been wrapped in thick shadow, was visible. The moonlight that flooded the field reached it; the legs, with those long thighs, moved apart gracefully, and, where they were joined, Carlo could see his own hand, held by Carmelo's, touching the untouchable, yet leaving it as if strangely inviolate and pure. Suddenly Carmelo— now completely master of himself—took his hand off Carlo's, leaving it alone. He planted his own on the ground and made himself more comfortable, spreading his legs still wider. The embarrassment had disappeared from the affectionately ironic, complicit smile with which he regarded Carlo; and his desire was now brutally plain. Carlo was to do it alone. Again submissive, obedient, clearly without any will of his own, moved almost to tears, head lowered, Carlo satisfied him. He began to move his hand by himself up and down along that warm penis constricted by the pants. Mechanically he continued to do what Carmelo had impelled him to do the first time, that is, to take its measure from top to bottom. And every time he felt the initial emotion: the sense of its immensity. In fact, repeating the gesture—< ... > that is, conscious of what he was doing with that gesture: taking the measure of something that seemed to him immeasurable—increased his pleasure even more; and now his guts seemed to collapse and he was drawn into the maelstrom of passion.

But a sudden start by Carmelo frightened him: the boy had suddenly pulled back, as if in anger. Carlo was overwhelmed by the fear that someone had arrived and had seen them; or that Carmelo had suddenly, for some mysterious reason, decided to stop the game; or even that he wanted to hurt him, throw him on the ground, steal his money, kill him. But Carmelo had drawn back so quickly, with such impatience, only to unbutton his pants. He unbuttoned them completely, carefully, he even unbuckled the belt, and with an effort he pulled down his white briefs, uncovering his entire belly. Carlo was just in time to see the apparition: the member proudly erect, wildly extended to reach who knows where, emerging from the dry tuft of hair that vanished inside the pants. Perhaps it was a little less immense than it had seemed to the touch, under the material of the pants; but still it was enormous and, above all, perfect, as if fashioned by a /marvelous/ craftsman: white in the light of the moon yet gilded by a livid brown coloring, the tip uncovered and almost the same color as the rest, only pinker, a pinkish brown, and the skin—that covered it when the penis was not erect— was stretched tight, revealing its shape completely: it looked not only just washed—which would have been humiliating and prosaic—but as if it had been clean and pure forever. Carlo, I repeat, was just in time to see the apparition before Carmelo's hand came to rest on his neck.

Again it was a question of pressure. That is, the presence of the force of another body on a part of Carlo's body. This pressure signified command and possession. It signified that Carmelo had no intention of letting his prey escape, now that he had him in his hands, and, though it might be with respect and delicacy—almost with gallantry—he would admit of no contradiction.

If the pressure on his hand had been disturbing, almost paralyzing—like that of a master on the domesticated animal—the pressure on his neck was nearly enough to make Carlo lose his senses. What did that broad, massive hand want, resting on the delicate neck of a man of the bourgeoisie who had always been weak, had always seemed absurd to himself because of his complexes and his obligations? It was as if his entire history no longer existed; the force of a body exerted on him with so much overpowering delicacy by that callused palm reduced him to a body as well: a body given new value by the fact that it could be the source, however poor, of pleasure. Moreover, the neck revealed itself as a point infinitely more sensitive than the hand and reacted to the pressure by causing in Carlo a kind of weakness so overwhelming that already he felt despair at the idea that it would soon end, and even now he lamented it as something lost forever. . . .

It should be noted that Carlo continually resisted the consuming naturalistic sentiments to which he was, objectively, prey by force of circumstances. Rather than a late-romantic character described in "the writing of 1880," he was a character out of de Sade—a presumed de Sade—in whom a subtle but persistent vein of ironic fatuity profanes the most atrocious sexual act, that act being nothing but the realization, rationally predictable, of a plan: a realization so predictable that the act becomes in a certain sense boring, perhaps inspires a certain ironic temptation to yawn, that is \in other words\, to become separate from the prosaicness and banality that characterize the realization with respect to reason, which plans it.

Now, in reality, nothing that happened to Carlo that night—in that hollow in the ground, on the grass and earth, beside that broken chain-link fence, under that moon which shone brighter as its pallor became more deathlike—was for him predictable. In fact, it was above all infinitely superior to what he had imagined.

Yet a thread of irony, almost a sense of the comic, never abandoned Carlo completely to the extraordinary and dramatic experiences he was having.

A kind of comic satisfaction coexisted in him along with the marvelous giddiness and the obedient slave's overpowering contrition compelled by the pressure of Carmelo's hand on his neck.[31]

Thus Carmelo's hand pressed on Carlo's neck, throwing him into a state of confusion that, if protracted, would have verged on hypnosis or delirium. Carlo believed he was to interpret that sign as Carmelo's wish for him to touch his now living and naked sex. He reached out his hand and grasped it. Awkwardly, that is, mimicking with unconscious shrewdness the inexpertness of the woman, who, not having one, does not know the sensations of the masculine sex organ; furthermore, and again unconsciously, Carlo mimed the desire of the woman to do what the male asks, not for her own pleasure but to give him pleasure.

But the fist, grasping Carmelo's member through pure obedience, that is, conventionally, could not help feeling the reality of it <...>. And it was a new plunge into marvelous martyrdom. Now he held in his hand the naked sex; the miracle was completely fulfilled. There was no longer anything that divided Carlo from his desire, which until now he had always considered unrealizable. Carmelo's sacred trousers were unbuttoned, the briefs had with difficulty been pulled down below the testicles, and his penis was out in the open, in the cold evening air, which was at the same time warm, under the dark light of the moon: more naked than nakedness itself.

The heat of that flesh proved to be still more intense: it was almost burning. And its tenderness proved even more tender; and its hardness harder. But what thrilled him, above all, so that he trembled was its utter nakedness.

Carlo repeated with that naked penis the movement he had made before, when it was covered by the pants; that is, he caressed it from top to bottom, taking the measure every time of its length, as if it were a fact one could not grow tired of \convince oneself of\. Moreover, his in-

---

[31] I apologize to the reader for the essayistic—perhaps somewhat Proustian—/"*ronron*"/ of my descriptions: it is that "comic" detachment which compels me. Carlo is not a character who experiences existence fully; and his sexual encounter with Carmelo cannot be anything but a succession of facts whose rhythm is certainly not realistic. But surely the reader has already understood that.

satiability was aggravated by the pressure on his neck, by which Carmelo drew him to himself.

Carmelo's hand persisted in that pressure, which forced Carlo to remain with his head lowered, as if continuing to express a desire that he hesitated to show openly.

Carlo's head resisted the pressure that drew him toward Carmelo's belly; but in fact it drew him delicately, as if it were merely force exerted with unconscious determination, a sign of possession that admits of no resistance. There was now something mechanical in the pressure of the hot hand, which remained heavy and inert on Carlo's neck. And it was perhaps mechanically—as if in place of something else, which a certain amazing considerateness on Carmelo's part kept him from doing—that he began to move his hand up and down along Carlo's neck, caressing it. At first it was a normal caress, almost instinctive, the usual pressure becoming lighter, then heavier; a pleasant variation. But then it was a close succession of real caresses, which fell heavily and with equal pressure on Carlo's poor neck. They were mechanical, dull, repetitive, hurried: surely they continued to be a substitute for something else.

Carlo was swept away, this time truly on the point of losing consciousness and falling to the ground, like the lovers of the *Thousand and One Nights;* but a greater ecstasy, more unbearably wonderful, was still to come. In fact, Carlo, though in a tremor that seemed to be destroying the roots of his being, continued to analyze the situation, as if with a profound interior smile. And he wondered what the real character of those caresses was; for the moment it escaped him, like a well-known name that one cannot manage to recall, though it hovers on the threshold of memory. The revelation—as usual in such cases—was sudden, like a thunderbolt.

Carmelo was caressing Carlo's head as one caresses the head of a dog; rather, of a bitch.

For a few seconds Carlo contemplated, so to speak, the situation: Carmelo caressing him as one caresses a bitch. Then suddenly he could no longer contain himself, he let his feelings overflow as if seized by a sudden current that /carried him away/ into its vortex: two tears, as big as raindrops, rose in his eyes, rolled down his cheeks, and were immediately followed copiously by more tears, which flowed down uncontrollably and abundantly, /totally/ bathing him, /in fact washing/ his face. But he wept silently, with lowered head. He was like wax that, hardened for centuries, was now melting. He hoped that Carmelo would not notice; but at one point he had to sniff (again, and certainly without wanting to, mimicking a woman), and Carmelo, compassionate and paternal, heard him. Yet he did not console him at all; in fact, just at that moment he found the strength to do what until then he had evidently expected but hadn't made clear. With a violent tug, he pulled Carlo to him brutally, a hand on his neck, and crushed his face against his cock, shoving it so hard that Carlo couldn't breathe and was about to suffocate. But the boy did not seem to be at all aware of this; indeed, it must seem to him that nothing was impossible when it was a matter of doing for him what he had the right to have done, for his pleasure.

And while Carlo was half suffocated and still wet with tears, though they were drying, Carmelo ordered him, /commanding/ but still with his usual respectful timidity, barely murmuring: "Suck." He addressed him formally.

Carlo hurried to obey: with the feminine haste of one who thinks that if he does not it will be the worse for him. He opened his mouth and the enormous tip went in: it was perfumed, it had the taste of an infant, and not only the tip but the skin below, darkly brown, seemed of silk.

With his usual awkwardness—certainly natural, but at the same time a calculated faking of inexperienced femininity—Carlo remained unmoving, his mouth open, filled by that sex. But still Carmelo was certainly not satisfied with this. Giving Carlo's head a shove, he made him swallow as much as was possible of that burning cock, which, as if frenzied by its erection, went so far down Carlo's throat /that he/ pulled back choking, retching. But Carmelo grabbed him again and with another thrust made him swallow it again, almost to the end. Carlo's eyes were rolling, and again tears rose and bathed him, this time because he was suffocating. Carmelo, not yet satisfied, now grabbed Carlo's head with both hands and began to move it up and down with such violence that Carlo was frightened and shaken by continual retching. He was like a straw at the mercy of a hurricane, yet determined not to fail in the rule of obedience. But it was not enough: still using both hands,

Carmelo pulled Carlo's head away from his cock and threw him to the
ground, on his back; then, at the level of Carlo's chest, he knelt on top
of him, planted his hands on the ground, and again stuck his cock into
Carlo's mouth with a violent up-and-down thrusting motion, and
/shoved/ it to the back of Carlo's throat as he writhed, choking. Carlo
was convulsed by a new storm. Carmelo possessing him in that way, furiously—but where did he want to go? He was already beyond the possible, yet surely he didn't realize it, he must consider the satisfaction of
his pleasure an absolute natural possibility—suddenly, with almost
rude anger, he ordered: "Don't bite me." Stupefied, but immediately
obedient, Carlo opened his mouth still wider, as wide as he could, letting the fury that was moving up and down penetrate still farther into
his throat, though it was not humanly possible to bear it; and surely
Carlo would have choked, or would have < ... > failed in the rule of the
most absolute passivity, if Carmelo, even more rudely and impatiently,
hadn't repeated: "Don't bite me!" and hadn't then grabbed him by the
shoulders, lifting him off the ground, and, dragging him along, gone to
lean his back against the chain-link fence.

Carlo barely had time to see him standing there in the moonlight
that illuminated his belly under the white undershirt, making the fuzz
of hair even more shadowy, and, in the middle of it, /coming out of/ the
open pants, the penis, still more enormous and perfect, like a little
monument; because Carmelo had seized his head and had again stuck
the penis in his mouth, had again begun to choke him by demanding
that the whole thing enter his mouth, as if it were a vagina or an anus,
and to go up and down furiously, even more intensely than before, if
that was possible. But then suddenly, as usual, he grabbed Carlo under
the arms and pulled him to himself, as if Carlo were a child, and looked
him in the eyes for a moment, with a dim smile. A moment: then
hugged him against his chest, squeezing with his hands spread; Carlo
felt both palms of those big outstretched hands as they grabbed whatever part of the back they could, squeezing him hard, almost to suffoca-
tion, but at the same time with great and deliberate delicacy, a
protective and affectionate delicacy, like a mother's embrace.

/<To leave> those two embracing, in the middle of that immense,
shining meadow (for the lips of the wound in the clouds that extended

along the entire horizon had separated, leaving open a long strip of sky, blue as the sea), where things stood out with a hallucinatory clarity, would certainly be the most poetic resolution.

But the function of my story is different and requires me to remain with the subject.>

Carmelo held Carlo clasped to his chest for a moment with the palms of his hands taking in his whole back, as if to gently measure the entire /extent of the flesh/ that rouses affection \tenderness\, as one does with a sacred thing entrusted to one's protection, and then, after that long maternal embrace, Carmelo put a hand on Carlo's shoulder and, in his usual overpowering way but as if restrained by some delicacy, he began to push Carlo back. And since Carlo still did not understand—like a child who needs to be guided—Carmelo gave his shoulder quick, repeated taps, to make him understand that something new was beginning and that he was to assume another position, do other things. It was the same tap the masseurs in the Turkish baths in Damascus or Cairo (where Carlo had once wanted to go with some friends) give when, having finished massaging the chest muscles, they inform the client, just so quickly and mechanically, that the time has come to work on the back and he must turn over. There was in that hurried and respectful tap of Carmelo's a kind of frenzy, an obvious orgasm that he was unable to contain; to obey was urgent, definitely urgent. And since Carlo did not understand (or, continuing in his unconscious mimicry of a woman, pretended not to understand), Carmelo leaned over him and, groping wildly, undid the belt of his pants, unbuttoned them, and carefully pulled them down to the knees. Then, with a gesture that he believed to be gentle but was in reality violent, as of an animal that does not know its own strength, he pushed Carlo to the ground, on his back, climbed onto him, and with blind fury found the vulva with his penis. While he was doing this he uncovered Carlo's breasts and began to bite them desperately.

The possession was rapid: Carlo did not even have time to feel the terrible pain of the penis that frantically entered his flesh—or to think that he would never have been able to resist—before Carmelo had already fallen on top of him, immobile, almost without heaving, as if merely the narrow passage of the vulva had been enough for the penis to dissolve in semen, /like a stick/ of wax. He took it out still dripping—and even larger, because, no longer completely erect, it was hanging down—and forgot Carlo and began to clean himself off.

Everything, then, was finished. Carlo found himself unprepared in the face of this completed and in some way tragic act. Fortunately the rule of silence and contrite obedience still seemed valuable. Thus, like an unhappy woman who has yielded to sin, incapable of resisting the dominant male, he rebuttoned his pants and straightened himself.

Carmelo, having become almost estranged, distanced, /sealed/ in his mystery, lighted a cigarette with an elegant gesture and an elegant sneer, elegantly threw away the match, and, wrapped in his immaculate white trench coat, took the first drag and prepared to cross the meadow toward the street. And Carlo followed behind like a dog. Or, rather, like a bitch.

The fires of the whores continued to glow, melancholy and vivid; even more so now that the moonlight had darkened again and the black fog had thickened over the earth. /They disappeared/, those fires, one after the other, at almost regular intervals, with their billows of black smoke, along the curve of the street, toward the neighborhood that loomed in the distance and the metallic-looking cupola. They were like sentinel fires < ... >, calm and ancient signals that announced the daily, normal facts of late evening, unconscious of their tragedy:

(lines from the beginning of the *Oresteia*)

Carlo, defeated, with new tears in his throat, wondered if now Carmelo would turn to gallantly offer his hand, as before, to get over those muddy mounds, those trash heaps that separated them from the street. <...> And yet—contrary to his bitter prediction—Carmelo did turn, stretched out his hand to help him with the same real, if slightly ostentatious, kindness as before. Only this time the gesture was a little less delicate and /hesitant/ than before and had acquired characteristics of normality; as if Carmelo, now the master—fiancé or husband or official lover, anyway—wished to establish the ritual of proper courtesy.

They got back in the car, Carlo, silent and sullen, made the customary U-turn; and as they retraced, in the opposite direction, the route taken a short while before, suddenly strings of Christmas lights appeared, hanging at regular intervals on a street that headed straight on into the neighborhood of old houses and squalid new apartment buildings, everything vanishing into the dry dust, the mud. The stillness was the stillness that follows a /bomb/ or an /earthquake/. The chaos was fixed forever, in layers: broken sidewalks, chipped asphalt, banks of mud against wrecks of cars, crumbling cornices, walls where door and window frames were encrusted with the dust of a lifetime, awnings over stalls, shutters, smashed and rusting gates, a series of lighted stores, rows of old clothes hanging on balconies that projected from shiny new walls. And in that scene of disorder that had become fossilized and everyday, thousands and thousands of human beings of all ages, alone or in groups, walked, ran, met, called out, stopped, crossed the street, exchanged greetings, and parted, dressed like poor puppets, frenetic and noisy.

Festoons of lights from a parish festival shone above them, with rows of little bulbs in pale shades of green, pink, yellow making geometric designs that contained symbols of the Church in the center, one after the other, in an infinite perspective, to the end of the long street.

/Carmelo had passed on to other subjects/ <...>.† With some hesitation, despite a confiding and amiable tone, he asked Carlo if sometimes he could bring along a girl, whom he would satisfy first and then him. But, at Carlo's shocked reaction to this suggestion, Carmelo immediately drew back, as if he had said nothing. Then he asked if Carlo by chance knew of a lotion or cure for making hair grow back.‡

Thus they reached the place where they had met, but on the opposite side of the intersection. Carmelo asked Carlo to stop, saying he could get to the center by going straight, on the Prenestina, all the way to Porta Maggiore. He himself was getting out, and it was just a short walk to that Casal Bertone where he lived. He held his hand out ostentatiously to Carlo as if to say good-bye, but also as if there remained between them something unsaid or unfinished. Even in Carmelo's eyes, which gleamed with a slightly stereotyped, too pleased smile, there was this sense of a vague question, the consciousness of something suspended, and at the same time of a complicity between him and Carlo concerning something pleasant and easily comprehensible. Carlo did not understand. Carmelo then made a decisive move to get out of the car but had just put his hand on the door to open it when, instead, he sat back on the seat, looking at Carlo with smiling eyes. "You're not going to leave me anything?" he asked. Carlo knew that there was this detail to resolve, he expected it, he expected even worse, but by himself he did not know what to do. He was grateful to Carmelo and, overwhelmed by confusion, by a sort of anxiety of repentance or fear, hastily pulled out his wallet and gave Carmelo everything in it, perhaps a hundred thousand lire. Carmelo looked at that to him fabulous amount and took it, full of amazement; but then his smile became paternal again. "No, it's too much," he said. "Some money to pay the rent is enough, I'm broke." He took, somewhat indecisively, twenty thousand lire and, with a smile now gentle and friendly, got out of the car after shaking Carlo's hand with the warmth of a friend.

Carlo watched him from behind as he went off along a street bounded on the right by a mass of hovels in some stinking, garbage-strewn fields, on the left by a long wall that edged the silent night, and at the end by an overpass with a few scattered lights on it. Soon he was far away, at the end of that street that was taking him wherever, with his resolute, bow-legged walk and that raincoat he had put on for perhaps the first time that night, to go to his appointment.

Carmelo soon reached the overpass at the end of the wide street. Anyone following him would have seen him light a cigarette, pausing a moment—in the shadow of the overpass—cupping his hands in front of his face, then throwing the match away with his elegant gesture of impatience. His eyes had an absorbed expression; every mask had fallen and his face was his ordinary, true one; the one he had with himself. And, as if he were no longer joking or knew, through ancient wisdom, how it is to be alone, he was absorbed in something distant—a thought \a flood of thoughts\ that, following him from his origins, was what now formed the wellspring of his life.

So, back turned, he went along toward his immediate destination; and anyone following him would have seen him going down the long avenue/ with a row of /stunted/ pines in the middle, towering warehouse walls, and the dark, denticulated mass of Casal Bertone, sprinkled with faint lights, against the window of the sky; a little farther, on the left, was an alley that skirted the high embankment of the railroad and was littered with mountains of trash and with wrecked cars, piled up in the courtyards of small, run-down workshops. He would turn that way toward the house where he had < ... > a room < ... >. While he slowly made his way home, the fog thickened, lit behind him by the moon, now high and swollen in the sky. Casal Bertone disappeared from view, and also the high stone walls of the warehouses and the empty expanses of the fields. In the shadow of a tall concrete building that cut off the street along the railway a voice was heard < ... >: "Hey, Cammelo!" And another, laughing. < ... > Two mushrooms of fog were suspended against the darkness. The impartial moon outlined them like the few other objects emerging from the milky shadows. They met, those /two Spirits/, just at the point where Carmelo would turn and disappear into places known only to him, where his fate had placed the stairs he would climb, the little room he lived in, his bed, his suitcase, /the things of his body/; in short, where his existence unfolded.

Anyone following him—violating the secret that would be revealed, in all its humble pathos, around that corner—would have seen him stop, look at those two Shades, and, at a nod, as from old acquaintances, < ... > follow them down toward the muddy street, along the walls of garages and auto repair shops. He was in the middle in his immaculate white raincoat, and on one side and the other, like two guards or old relations, were those two companions, indistinct in the steaming black /fog/: dark backs and white collars and above them the necks, the tough necks and tight ears of beasts of burden, buffalo or bulls: /because they were not adolescents, like Carmelo, spotless in the mud, but two old Spirits, hardened by life. < ... >

They went on, as if pushed by a common desire that united them in life and in death.

Here—before the eyes that had violated it—the disappearance of Carmelo would take place! The simple disappearance of one who turns a corner and heads for the neighborhood where his house is, lost among thousands of other houses, going as he does every night to sleep the sleep of his body. < ... >/

Seen thus, from behind, it was impossible to tell if there was an understanding between them, an agreement; or if Carmelo accepted the situation as something new, unexpected—but certainly not, anyway, unforeseen. They were silent, as happens when an appointment has been agreed on among accomplices or when there is a relationship, irrevocably fixed, between victim and persecutors who belong to the same world and are therefore interchangeable; the one knowing the mind of the other. Perhaps those two, with their massive, workmen's shoulders, were two colleagues from El Toulà, porters, dishwashers, bodyguards, or perhaps they came straight from Sicily. There did not seem to be any other alternative. They got into a car depressingly stopped in the middle of two endless lines of cars at the corner of a street called xxx xxx. After a while the car, with a sinister rasping sound in the silence of that place lost like an island in the cosmos, started off, in no hurry; it reached the end of the street, turned down another street, whose name, muted in the silence, sounded xxx xxx; and reached a wide avenue (the same one Carmelo had turned off of beyond the overpass, to lose himself in the slum). There were big lumberyards here and there; broken hedges and, behind them, the empty spaces of abandoned construction sites, the plowed and fragrant earth of gardens, with irregular rows of fat cauliflowers or favas, and wild figs; and, behind them, an immense wall of distant skyscrapers, their lights burning in nothingness. That road, which was now in the country or the extreme periphery, led by a roundabout route /to Tiburtina/, still in the heart of the city, < ... > with traffic signals whose breathless yellow lights blinked on and off; < ... > and they passed hysterical cars returning from the movies; and even a group of soldiers, returning from leave, who were hurrying with their packs to the barracks at Forte di Pietralata.

A little before Tiburtina, the fog suddenly dissolved; and the world reemerged as clean as if from a bath. The apartment buildings rose clearly above the chipped asphalt. The closed kiosks, the rows of lowered shutters, the sawhorses and lumber piles of work in progress—all had the excessive clarity of apparitions. The car entered Tiburtina and continued on, leaving the city behind.

The figure of Carmelo could be seen in the rear window, sitting almost stiffly on the seat with his white raincoat; while the outlines of the other two were visible in the front seat; they were silent; their motionless backs were charged with an impenetrable meaning.

At the top of a bare hill, into whose sides caves, of a sort, for little workshops had been dug and beyond whose outline other barriers of darkly sparkling buildings could be seen, the car left Tiburtina and turned onto a road bordered by vast expanses of land and the ruins of houses that had just been torn down; their shapes, all alike, were visible. A few walls remained standing; and in the rubble bits of lime showed white, or a toilet bowl. Soon the houses began again; these, too, were all the same and still standing; the street rose briefly, then descended, turned to the left among the derelict cottages that had survived the destruction of the slum, and turned onto another country road, < ... > between immense fields planted with alfalfa and old trees abandoned to their fate; a gas storage tank, dazzling in its extreme cleanliness, appeared, with tall pylons around it. In the distance (where tiny lights twinkled in other silences) rose the first foothills of the Appennines, limpid and dark against the limpid darkness of the sky. The car turned to the right along that country road, then, after crossing a narrow bridge over a railway track set between banks overgrown with intensely fragrant vegetation, again to the left (pointing toward those distant hills). And here again was the city: a completely deserted slum, with its pitiful hovels one on top of the other, with streets that ended in the chaos of construction sites lost in country darkness.

As they left that slum—again on a narrow consular road that pointed toward the hills—a dog flung himself at the car: a little dog who, wandering alone in those places, represented life, perhaps. He believed that he recognized a hostile presence in that car, and he attacked it, barking loudly. Even when it was far away, he kept barking for a while, though he was weak from hunger, with the feeble breath he had in his lungs; when he had given his final rebukes, he was still, and soon resigned himself. In the calm night there were other things for < ... > the travels of a night wanderer, who had lost the regular rhythm of life but recognized its old mysterious warmth.

The consular road that headed toward the luckless hills of the Ciociaria joined, by means of a short connecting road, a big new four-lane highway set between high embankments. /There/ the car began to go at a more /sustained/ speed. A short ascent led that trunk of highway up toward the hills and level with the great plain, its reddish lights in groups here and there under the setting moon, which had suddenly reappeared. Along with the moon, a big used-car lot appeared, on the right, below the embankment, illuminated as if by the blinding white light of a village festival; in the middle was a shed from which radiated an even stronger white light (in the emptiness and silence), and all around in the asphalt parking lot, surrounded by a high chain-link fence, were long shining rows of Fiats, Alfa Romeos, Volkswagens, Citroëns, BMWs. Difficult to distinguish in all that light and that orderly chaos of cars, but just beside it, was a little Shell station, which added its yellow light to that sea of lights between the highway lost in the plain at the foot of the mountains and an immense suburb of small gray, unwhitewashed houses densely crowded together in the moonless part of the sky.

The car slowed down, brazenly backed up where it was not allowed to, and, going down the ramp in the wrong direction—the ramp for getting onto the highway, not off—reached another narrow consular road, perhaps the Casilina.

But the will of the three men shut in that car, in the expressionless hard shell of their backs and necks, had decided this; besides, it was presumably in their nature to do so. Thus the car came to a stop in front of a gas pump. The attendant was enclosed in his glass booth. He came out. No expression showed on his face. Surely he had found the irregular maneuver of his nocturnal customers natural, they who, besides him, were the only living and waking human beings in those parts. He went silently to the pump and served them, with his bright, blind-man's eyes turned toward the xxx where the little numbers clicked; he examined them intently, with the look of a beggar. Then he went meekly to the window and put in his pocket the money that a large, hairy hand, powerful and impatient, held out to him. He said good-bye, touching his hand to his cap, and stood watching the car go off, then paused, with his thin peasant body, in the middle of all that light in the cold and damp of the night. This was not the hour that counted for him; and the indecipherable intensity with which he stared at the car that was returning to the ring road, as he carefully put the three stinking thousand-lira notes into his greasy wallet, seemed to pronounce a judgment neither negative nor positive on the meaning of the night shift. His pale blue eyes and his long blond beard showed that already the day had been exhausting.

Carmelo, with his white back, remained erect in the backseat; he let himself be carried by the car moving toward its goal, letting no sign betray whether he knew it or not: if this was a night journey to be expected, of common occurrence in the life of a boy, or if it was the near-solemn fulfillment, although unknown to all, of his fate. From certain slow gestures, illuminated by the whiteness of his raincoat, one could see that he was smoking now, absentmindedly, the cigarette rendered smaller and lighter by the size of his fingers.

At the end of that long highway on the plain beside the hills, another interchange appeared, this time with scenic curves (beneath a moon that was near death). There in the countryside, lush with grass, with dense thickets of acacia and elderberry and tall oaks petrified in the motionless light, each leaf distinct, as if sculptured, were immense ruins, towers and aqueducts. The new consular road that the car turned onto as it left that interchange was busier and wider than the others. All around could be felt the majesty of a long decline, which the plants and their scents—with an impudent, almost sexual freshness—had survived: for example, the almost obscene fragrance of the lime trees (although it was winter!). The warmth hovered, threatening, over that no longer abandoned and proletarian countryside and made one feel that even there—where the mind of man and his ancient civilization appeared to dominate in its slow work of consuming itself—true reality existed: a springlike Christmas, an absurdly precocious May. And the blind sleep of the men, the workers, in those villages, in those cottages.

After a dozen kilometers, a smaller road went off to the right and vanished between fat, still leafy hedges. With continual wide turns, that road ended in one that was similar but wider and straighter; until it became completely straight and at the end of it appeared a horizontal mass of low white houses, with a few taller buildings, most of them under construction. The air was, if possible, even calmer, and the silence

more profound. Even the warmth was more intense: now it really
seemed a night in midsummer.

Close up, the village looked like one big construction site; even most
of the finished houses were unplastered and were crowded together
\lined up\ haphazardly one after another with shoddy little walls in
front, or gates, pretentious but just as shoddy. There was work in
progress everywhere, the little gardens in front of the houses were un-
planted or had only a few small, stunted /pines/; rows of terraces and
balconies, thousands of them, displayed their closed shutters. There was
no laundry. /There were/ few cars in front of the houses, and those
seemed to be abandoned. There were restaurants and bars, one after another, all hermetically sealed, every so often with an untidy grass
canopy. The sidewalks either were of beaten earth or had just been /laid/
and were already chipped. No light filtered from the houses. Only the
strong light from the street revealed the squalidness of that district,
which was not a place where poor people lived but a kind of abandoned
encampment, with window and door frames of polished wood and walls
bright with whitewash.

Soon they came to a rotunda; beyond it was the sea—pale, gray,
muddy, and motionless as a lake. But above it opened a sky infinite in
its darkness. The extraordinary clarity of the air had again vanished; and
over all a tepid mist, a fog, had descended.

In front of the rotunda, where the car had stopped—though no one
got out; the three could be seen motionless in their places—a night pa-
trolman passed on his scooter. He stopped at the corner, in front of a bar,
and, leaving the scooter near the sidewalk with its motor running, fid-
dled /with the gate/: in silence, turning his /back to the world/. He
stayed there for a long time; then went to another gate (there were wide
porticoes in front of the shops, on both sides of the rotunda). His footsteps echoed in the warm, veiled, infinite stillness of the night. Then silence fell again. He /fussed/ some more, bent and patient, in front of the
< ... > gate, then, with sudden decisiveness, but still extremely slowly,
turned toward the scooter that faithfully awaited him and left the
shadow of the porticoes, revealing a broad face, that of a < ... > family
man, hair sharply tapered in an outmoded style and a longish black

beard with not a hint of gray in it. He did not look around, did not observe the car. He grabbed the scooter by the handlebars and got on, lifting his heavy, father's leg, getting comfortable as if in an easy chair, and vacantly, without any interest in anything, went on his way with his motor crackling, and the sound soon disappeared.

The car resumed its course, in the opposite direction /from the cop/. The houses became more scattered and, if possible, shabbier and more unkempt. Enclosures and reed huts for parking cars became more frequent. And even more frequent was the sight of the sea through the spaces between one group of houses and another; until, after a bridge over a putrid canal, the houses stopped and there was only the beach, like an enormous garbage dump full of dried-up garbage.

The car stopped in front of a xxx bush; and, < ... > as if they had to attend to a need, the three got out, lazily slamming the doors. Thus they disappeared behind the bush: the two men on either side and Carmelo in the middle.

Only in appearance was the sea motionless. In reality, on the beach, among the blackened trash, it moved as always, rolling with unceasing persistence, wave after wave, tumbling, indolent waves, whose /supremely/ graceful foamy edges were an apparition too brief every time, in that human filth, that melancholy world. The continuous splash of the sea ended in a kind of white column of light humidity rising above the breakers, which remained suspended like the shadow of a ghost in the mist that covered the whole length of the beach.

Perhaps it was no longer night and dawn was beginning; and that was the reason for the unnatural whiteness.

NOTE 63A†

/Now/, on the sea's far horizon, rows of lights were visible, as if on an island or a peninsula joined by a thin and invisible isthmus to land (was it Ostia? Fiumicino? Anzio? or still more distant, one of the first towns

along the sea in Campania or Tuscany?). But the distance was so great
that they seemed a single light, made up of an infinite twinkling, at the
horizon of the sea or the sky. And strangely, though the air was all white
with dampness, that little clot of light was of a reddish or pink color. As
if filtered through an atmosphere of twilight. Now, although there was
a very faint, perhaps only imagined, hint of dawn, it was still the depths
of night, the very middle of the night, lost in itself and in silence. That
distant twinkling of lights was the only sign of life in the whole world;
over there people lived, there were houses, streets, the silence of sleep
and the passing of cars, perhaps music, love: all without relief, all gray,
all melancholy, everything had already happened, of course. Yet those
clotted reddish lights at the edge of the darkness bore witness that at
least all this was existence. Yet why, if it was so, did they hold nothing
that was happy, that gave the least /comfort/, that called one back to
them; and why in fact did they seem to say: "Don't come here," /al-
though with the sharp pleasure of deeds now sadly done/, like funeral
candles?

Their work completed, their task performed, the two who had accompanied the body of Carmelo up to that point evaporated. And it was
over there, in the small melancholy brazier /that was the city at the sea's
horizon/, that they took shelter. Each of the two spirits < ... > was quivering, just perceptibly, like its colleagues, in one of the little lights
whose desperate flickering made up a language whose meaning was monotonous and terrible, though it was barely whispered and from such a
long way off.†

Following paragraph (or the same):

    embarkation in a little motorboat
    The Three Old Men
    the crew—Sicilian surnames
    journey one day and one night—<?> lightly on the sea

    Arrival in port, around evening —(Palermo)
    walk through a city—cemetery (Palermo cemetery)

                    [quote Dante—Charon's boat]

*

Previously:

faced with the chthonic deities (Andrí and or the Mothers)—the characters—the gas pump attendant, the night watchman feel a shiver in their
spine, their blood freezes, etc. (greater death and "mystery" suspense in the
journey)

(August 1974)

NOTE 63B
Embarkation, journey, new lights in the night

Beyond the clump of xxx xxx bushes flattened on the sand, within the
tall column of mist suspended over the breakers, there was a little shed
that wasn't visible from the street. Opposite were two or three huts and
perhaps also a row of half-smashed cabins; and farther on a concrete
structure that must have housed toilets. <...> In the middle ran a channel with blackish water, as in a drain or sewer, between two high concrete piers, fittingly chipped and crumbling. There were some boats in
this channel, under the xxx and tall winches of the fishing rods. They
were small boats, wrecks of boats, barges, a few motorboats, probably
unused since the previous summer; alone, at the end of the channel,
rocking gently against the open sea, was a big white motorboat that appeared to be empty. It was to this that Carmelo, escorted by Andrí and
xxx, had come down from the street <...>. And there some others no
less trusted than they awaited them: four or five boys Carmelo's age and
three Old Men. Carmelo got onto the boat, jumping from the jetty
alongside, and disappeared behind the bulwarks with the others. Very
slowly, without any noise and without any hurry, the sailors began to
loosen the moorings; they exchanged a few words in an undertone, and
those brief words, in dialect, were the only testimony to their presence.
Their bodies were not visible; one leaped for a moment onto the little

bridge of the prow but immediately disappeared again. As usual, the maneuvers for weighing anchor were lengthy and complicated and were performed calmly and thoroughly: someone started whistling; someone else rebuked him harshly, perhaps one of the three Old Men. There on the boat, < ... > they seemed to be walking back and forth as if to use up time, for some unknown reason. It seemed a miracle that finally the motor was started, and its deafening sound mingled with that of the undertow. It still took a while for the boat to move away from the concrete jetty and, gliding slowly and extremely carefully, begin heading for the open sea. The little light at the top of the mast remained swinging for a long time, in that xxx xxx, before disappearing beyond the < ... > bank of white mist suspended along the entire coast.

But just a few hundred meters farther from land, the air was bright and clean. There was no moon, but the stars were luminous, so that the darkness of the sky was clearly distinguishable from that of the sea. The sea, however, was smooth, and on its surface swelled mysterious clear, oily patches that seemed to reflect the light of the starry sky. The boat proceeded slowly, it's true; and anyone who observed the light at the top of the mast, curious to see it grow distant, would have had the exasperating impression that it was almost motionless. Yet after a few minutes the boat had glided some distance, had reached the open sea, and was already vanishing toward the point on the horizon to which its course /destined it/.

For some time now, the night had seemed about to end, and just at the moment when it was darkest. On dry land—to the east, that is, behind the boat that moved off—the sky was changing color. A /terrible/ < ... > gray < ... > that reached as high as the stars replaced the deep blue or indigo of the night. At the same slow pace, but also with the same speed, at which the boat was vanishing farther and farther into the open sea, that gray began to be tinged with pink.

On the boat everyone seemed to be asleep. Except for one of the three Old Men, who, being at the helm, naturally gave some signs of life. But he, too, appeared to be dreaming, barely touching the tiller with his knotty black hand. Who can say what he was thinking about. Only the eyes, sunk in the bones of his face, in the white hair of his beard, burned black as coal, gazing at the distant horizon that had begun to lighten.

Soon dawn came, and then the sun rose.

It was a clear day, almost warm. By midday, the sky and the sea were so blue that it seemed to be midsummer, or at least spring. And if the blue was just a little faint or faded, that seemed due to the heat, not to the weak force of the winter sun.

In the immense deserted expanse of the sea, only the engine could be heard, loud, strong, solid; and that increased the peacefulness and the silence. On board each one kept to himself, finding a way, despite the confined space, to be enclosed in his own solitude. Some, perhaps, were sleeping. Two were playing cards and, speaking every so often in low voices, called each other, oddly, by their surnames: one was Aneli, the other Scafili. The youngest of all, a boy dark as a Moroccan, who couldn't be more than eighteen, was sitting by himself on the bridge, contemplating something; what he was carefully examining was his identity card, and in particular his photograph, beside which his name was written: Sapienza, Saro. The name of another of the group was shouted out, with the usual imperious irritation, by one of the three Old Men: "Agatino!" in a voice so harsh, in the accent of the dialect, that Agatino seemed no longer the name of a person but an exclamation or a threat. And in fact the name was followed by an equally irritated and terse exclamation: "You dickhead! xxx xxx xxx."

Around one o'clock they ate, and for this occasion they gathered on the bridge (excluding the three Old Men, < ... > who ate on their own in the cabin, served by that Saro Sapienza who was the youngest of the crew). As they greedily ate rolls with some oily vegetable in the middle, which made their mouths greasy, they all became happy, chattering to one another in their innocent, sinister, and incomprehensible language. "You prick, xxx xxx xxx."

Afternoon, and the first shadows descended with the same illusory slowness with which the sun had risen and spread its light. And with those first shadows—which cast their coldness on the sea—land appeared. It was a dim outline of flat-topped mountains, against which were visible the darker outlines of islands and the coast, with its irregular plains and cutoff hills. Then the < ... > city could be distinguished, an immense semicircle, but with long spurs that went off along the coast and into the interior. It was an /inextricable/ < ... > mass of white houses, all stained with the fog of dusk. Only by coming still closer could one distinguish any shapes in that xxx xxx. To the right of the boat the light < ... > of the sunset turned red; but just at the last moment, before disappearing behind the sea, the sun came out of the mists, striking, grazing the city with its light; then indeed the shapes of buildings appeared, dove-colored < ... >, with their barbaric xxx and windows with pointed arches, but rounded, as in an exotic, decaying, oriental world; there were also large cupolas and heavy seventeenth-century balconies suspended among the palm trees; and in the midst of a green garden, which must have been an orange grove, the sun illuminated a small Romanesque church, whose domes were bright red xxx. Soon, however, the sun was obliterated by the thick winter mists, and in place of its grazing rays a cold shadow fell on the city and the sea beside it.

When the boat reached the harbor, all the lights were already lit, as was the light hanging at the top of the mast. Close up, the houses that pressed around the small curving harbor revealed all their /crumbling/ wretchedness; not only the new ones but also the old ones, which were in ruins, besides, reduced to garbage heaps and toilets, where in the warm evening boys were playing amid the stench. The old harbor smelled not only of shit but of spoiled fish and rotting vegetables; and also of orange blossoms and perhaps mulberry. The maneuvering of the motorboat as it entered the harbor was, as usual, interminable. By the time it docked the evening was advanced; and that meant, in that city, the middle of the night.

The three Old Men, followed by the crew and by Carmelo, disembarked and went toward the city center, along alleys that wound among ancient empty houses reduced to garbage heaps and toilets. But suddenly they came upon a beautiful avenue, paved with big xxx of xxx, on which, along with the old houses, rose occasional churches or mansions, with grand entrances of xxx; farther on was a square, in which there must have been a fish market; but at that moment it was all neat and clean; large bucketfuls of water had bathed the pavement; it was not yet dry and shone with all its xxx distinct irregularities. On the other side of the square, the street that the three Old Men and their company took consisted of a narrow stairway that had also just been washed, under a baroque shrine without a statue—which led to a higher part of the city.

NOTE 63
Was it a deviation?

Carlo woke early the next day. The light between the slats of the venetian blinds was still gray. Like a Flaubert hero he thought of the night before, of what had happened. Surely it was a miracle. Something like a feeling of glory vitalized him. He felt like raising his face and his eyes to heaven but without thanking God: the joy he believed he had had was stronger than whoever had given it to him. It existed for him alone, as if for an atheist, who has no other horizon than his own life.

He trembled with impatience to see Carmelo again that evening at El Toulà. A new chapter of his life had begun. It was to be lived day by day. And to do so he needed nothing but that telephone number (still written on the crumpled piece of paper), a telephone call now simple and almost /ordinary/, an appointment in that hellish place, which had become the /symbol of the strange kindness/ of fate.

Everything that separated him from the moment when he would see Carmelo again—young, boyish, in spite of that balding forehead by which someone or something had mysteriously decided to make him vulnerable, to wound him with an untimely revelation of his inevitable future, perhaps in punishment for his innocence, because surely in that future only misery awaited him, since the one thing he possessed was youth and never in the world would he possess anything else—everything that separated Carlo from the moment of seeing Carmelo again was for him /a void/. The gestures and words with which he had to fill that void repelled him. They repelled him so much that he could not face them. Had he perhaps entered that *taedium vitae*† which leads very slowly, or sometimes suddenly, to a change in life? Career, ambitions, power (as the reader knows), everything seemed to him /stupid and without/ any value.

The epoche,[32] perhaps, the epoche was coming to pass.

And it was not even love that had suddenly called into question and made vain all that in life, until that moment, /as if through the Anonymous,/ had been *reality, value.* Or perhaps, yes, there was also a drop of love (in the poetry of Carmelo—which, however, the bourgeois Carlo did not understand); but in effect it was a question of pure < ... > /sex/. Yet sex by itself could fulfill a life and give it meaning; the acts and words of sex could be infinite, always new, always filled with anxiety and terror; Carmelo could have an erection ("I've got a hard-on," he would say, as if to say, /"It's raining, sir" or "It's hot, sir"/) and every time this would be an overwhelming miracle, to experience first in thought and then in memory—with one's heart in one's throat. Because the injury that that erect penis—so naturally on its part—would inflict on Carlo's flesh was decisive every time; and while for Carmelo it would be a momentary desire to kill, immediately soothed by the ejaculation of that day's white, fragrant Sicilian semen, for Carlo it would be the fulfillment of something opposite, /the background/ of his desire for death. He remembered when he had been a man, when he, too, had had a penis like Carmelo's. He remembered the rapid mechanics, preceded by an immense, fabulous mythology of female sex. But all that was nothing in comparison with the vastness of his expectation as a woman, because to possess is nothing in comparison with being possessed, to do violence is nothing in comparison with suffering violence. And so, thus conceived of and arranged, sex could indeed fill a life. But to do this he needed solitude, the most absolute solitude. A solitude in which even Carmelo, in some way, was superfluous and cumbersome, at least at those moments when his body was not simply an instrument. A solitude that gave Carlo, already practiced in the experience he had just begun as a passive apprentice, all the time /to rejoice/. < ... >

But in a little while he had to get up, to go to the ENI building in EUR! It was a distant, colorless, cold world, motionless as the Pole; he

[32] *Translator's note:* "Epoche," from the Greek, is a philosophical term meaning "suspension of judgment on the reality of things."

felt like laughing at the thought of it. Yet, still, he would go. In fact, he got up right away. With a shudder he looked in the mirror at his breasts and his /cunt/, feeling as if he were dying, consumed, at the idea that this would again be a meal for Carmelo, blindly eager to fertilize, believing—in his innocence—that he was only fulfilling the desire of his erect penis. He bathed and dressed and found himself in front of the statue of Salvatore Dulcimascolo. "But is Carmelo," he wondered, "truly the incarnation of Salvatore Dulcimascolo?"

NOTE 64
Factors contributing to the clinical portrait

A bourgeois does not really know how to appreciate innocence that is not taught in schoolbooks or in the unwritten code of society. In fact, he feels for that innocence a certain repugnance, which has a racist character. He has invented rules in order to condemn the innocence that does not know them. Especially since innocence is often linked to delinquency; and so if it is outside the culture it is also outside the law. The bourgeois always feels a sense of fear in the face of innocence and, even in the best case, judges it an inferior product of his own way of life, not knowing or wishing to imagine the terms of another way of life, to which it belongs. Thus, attaching it to his own history, he can free himself from it, wash his hands of it, escape it, /cut the cord/ to the places to which it has been exiled.

Now, since even when a life is not symbolic everything in it is arranged according to the obscure design of our will, all of that remained to be revealed to Carlo.

For example, it was evidently part of the obscure design of Carlo's will that near his house—in the Parioli, at Vigna Clara, or Olgiata; it's up to the reader to decide—there was a school, a high school.

This school, this high school, had for some years been the scene of assaults, of demonstrations, of brawls, etc. And in those days the Fascists took punitive action against democratic students who were demonstrating on behalf of what was undoubtedly a good cause.

Carlo left the house, and as he was opening the door of his car he saw a group of these Fascists. Or rather glimpsed them. They were at the end of a street and immediately turned their backs, taking a street parallel to the one they were on, and broke into a run, seized by an excitement that, however much it may diminish, appears exalting, blissful to the one who is excluded.

He saw those faces for some moments. By chance, the ugly ones— with their vulgar long hair, cut and styled like that of their enemies on the left, the /round/ or oblong Italian faces, in which hunger and an unhappy conscience were revoltingly blended—passed by more quickly than the others or stayed in shadow; because on that November day a tropical sun shone. The handsome ones remained for some seconds almost isolated (the rapidity of the action permits this lightninglike schematization, which then becomes the truth). They, too, were Italian: young Italians of seventeen, eighteen, nineteen, and they were Italian in an almost exaggerated way, according to a formula, as if from a laboratory. They were not very tall, of course, but they did not have short legs or low asses; their height was a little above the average but enough to make them seem young athletes. They had square, severe shoulders. And the pants they wore, very tight across the pelvis but wide in the legs and especially at the bottom, with big bulky cuffs over the shoes, accentuated that look of slim yet solid young men. They, too, had rather long hair, but a sort of ancient restraint kept it from falling obscenely over their shoulders, like that of whores and, in those days, of subproletarian youths in the slums; it stopped at their necks, black, wavy, abundant, like grass bursting forth in spring, with thick, strong roots.

They were running, and in their fists they held bars, or poles, around which black cloths were rolled; it was not clear whether these were banners or arms, an elementary question but one that was part of the mystery of urban guerrillas. As they ran, their virility, forgotten with respect to sex yet aroused by their undoubtedly monstrous civic passion, was revealed almost shamelessly. The pants were so tight at the crotch that the genitals could be seen entire, penis and testicles, but all crushed into a single soft block with a mysterious shape, bulging on both sides of the fly, as if that sex would not assume \appear in\ the usual animal form but were a pure weight, a quality or attribute infinitely more functional than its function, quite humble in the end. They were ignorant of all this. Not only was such a thought inconceivable at that moment; but perhaps they had never thought it and never would. They carried that massive weight of their own virility, crushed by the tightness of their pants, as an obscure threat, something that for the moment was superfluous yet was everything, was at the center of their body and therefore of the world they wished to be masters of.

For a moment Carlo's breasts were as swollen as those of a cow that has not been milked for days; he needed to give nourishment, a need that was yearning, tormenting, uncontainable: a need to nourish until he became nothing and died starving, there on the ground, on the humble asphalt. They, those young masters—descended to earth from who knows where and already so determined to live here, so familiar with it—had to suck on him—because they had the right—even if in doing so they took his life. But this delirious frenzy of the breasts was nothing in comparison with that of the womb, which was the same yet opposite. It was another need of those young masters that was to be satisfied: the need they had, in their turn, to give and to die, even if they did not in the least realize it and what they desired was merely to find a particular pleasure that they alone knew. That the desire to realize this pleasure betrayed an arrogance as fleeting as it was fierce, and that the knowledge of all this was no more substantial than a puff of wind, did not diminish but, rather, increased Carlo's need to put himself at their service, to please them, to let them do anything with as much brutality and as little tenderness as they liked. It was their natural carelessness, their hurry, that most fascinated him; even if they were young bourgeois. Furthermore, their political choice, too, was careless, hurried, natural, and arrogant.

/Carlo looked at them as Hierophants. Where did they come from? What had led those young Italians to become Fascists? What series of circumstances—connected by what means—had so unfailingly led them to appear on that street (and on countless others)?

In what Heuristics did their actions originate, actions that seemed so perfectly organized?

Anyway, this much was certain: that they appeared as masters and had seized for themselves the rights of masters. They would possess and sow their seed only if they wanted to. But their will was as uncontrollable as their advance: it could not be bought./

NOTE 64
The last evening at El Toulà

As usual, Carlo enters El Toulà very early, when there is still no one there, and the governmental squalor of the restaurant appears in all its clarity, illuminated by nauseating, weak lights. He does not see Carmelo's face at the long window of the checkroom, his short balding forehead and his full lips, his gray eyes that have always known everything, his smile not of inferiority but of complicity. He must be inside, busy with the coats of the only two customers, foreigners, sitting at a table. Carlo sits down and eats, attended to by a group of waiters from the North, who feel toward him the ironic mistrust one has for someone alone and unprotected, outside the rules, but at the same time show a certain kindness because of their common regional origin. Slowly the restaurant fills up, and here—inevitable, fatal as an Erinys—is the Honorable Tortora with one of his usual groups, in full parliamentary behavior. Carlo finishes eating, pays, gets up, goes toward the checkroom. Carmelo is not there. In his place is a new woman, expressionless, yellowish, with a Venetian accent. Carlo feels faint. At that moment, he turns automatically toward the interior of El Toulà to hide his disappointment, his tragedy; and for an instant his eyes meet Tortora's. It's true that Tortora is talking to a distant fellow diner, at the other end of the table, and so his lawyer's witticism is almost shouted, his attention on the table; still, his eyes, which must be laughing or at least excited, rest on Carlo and the window of the checkroom, as if they were detached from his face and from the reality he inhabits at that moment; as if they were two other eyes, standing by themselves, opaque and expressionless. It is, of course, what one calls an instant; and the Honorable Tortora is again talking with his brothers who have come down from the North or up from the South. Exactly like certain girls, who, while they are walking and talking absorbedly with a girlfriend, know how to look right into the face of a passerby who interests them, as if he were made of air, and continue to talk with utter and total unconcern for the person they have absentmindedly looked at. Carlo realizes this and appropriates that look. But at the same moment he realizes that Carmelo's absence is not an affliction, no, it is a liberation. The solitude in which he suddenly finds himself is the \the new\ state he needs to make the world his.

NOTE 65
Confidences with the reader

What kept Carlo from feeling the profound grief that was logically predictable at the loss of Carmelo? What kept him from despair, from weeping for such a "cosmic" deprivation?

The analysis of his inner life lies outside the task I have undertaken (which, in truth, does not even provide for the objective existence of that inner life). All I can do is resort to a change of tune. And promote a moralistic analysis in place of a psychological one: I, the omniscient manager of this story. But no one can tell all, that is, be totally honest \pure\; there is also a mafia \mystification\ in the structure, universally accepted, by tacit consent. What is said is ruled by what is not said; testimony by reserve; civic sentiment by a conspiracy of silence. The form is based only on what is not the form. And the exclusion of form is always planned, calculated. Unfortunately, to "tacit consent" I oppose the verbalness of my guilt: I don't know how to pretend to create an object, a mystery. But it /will be re-created, I hope/, in the mind of the reader, and just now I beg him to accept my confidences.

Carlo had always grasped the meaning of possession: < ... > his Piedmontese great-grandparents were landowners, who, around 1850, had founded a textile mill and hired as workers boys who were under twelve, possibly orphans and already ill, so that low wages were /established/ naturally < ... >. /But this "infamy"/ of Carlo's great-grandfather (a right-thinking Catholic) is nothing \an episode\, if you consider that before that, before the Napoleonic invasion, before the French Revolution, /on the eve of the bourgeois era/, the long line of his ancestors, who were already rich, or even if they were still poor, had always had a sense of existence based solely on possession. This sense of possession /(whether of a small field, a farm, or a textile factory)/ was actually depicted in Carlo's physical aspect. His puffy, babyish face, below the thinning blond hair, was as if /dulled/ by the shrewd decision to do nothing rash, to stick precisely to the education that had been imparted to him from infancy; and the awkwardness of his body—as of one who still pees on himself, like a handicapped child—was made up for by the skill and the knowledge of a Boy Scout, who knows how to get out of a difficult situation better than a virile and innocent boy of the people; in short, the physical appearance that made Carlo a /"foreigner"/, that is, an inelegant fool, /wearing/ a gray suit that was too big and a name-brand but absolutely anonymous shirt—all this was nothing but a barrier of ingenuousness, honesty, and stupidity raised around Carlo to defend and mask in him the reality of being a master. A master who directs and possesses by a privilege so thoroughly inborn that he is not even aware of it. This duty to define himself and to silence the sense of guilt had, so to speak, /pruned/ all Carlo's feelings. His emotional world was maimed, truncated.

The other Carlo, his milder brother, was the contradiction of this. He < ... > had no need of a gradual passage, as constituted by Carmelo, to reach extremes. Extremes: the area forbidden to those who, having cut-off or atrophied feelings, become first theorists, then blackmailers, of "moderate feelings," of the philosophy of the "just middle," and, as a consequence, of "gradualness."

I know that in a "Mystery," in a "Miracle play," gradualness is inconceivable, like a dim petit bourgeois element; there cannot be experiences that go off course and are therefore left suspended. In that context, every cause has a corresponding effect: the effect that logically follows. It is in this that the sublimity of fate consists. The mistakes due to a numbed spirit are not tragic. And therefore its hesitations and its incapacity to interpret the accumulation of events that happen to him in their fatality is tragic, because it's mathematical.

Carlo had met a body and had experienced the physicality of it. All right. But the fact is that this body—Carmelo's body—inhabited another "quality of life,"† a different social universe. Therefore, it was obvious that *knowing* such a body he also had to *know*—in its historical concreteness—its life. It was obvious that *loving* that body he had also to *love* its world.

This would in fact have happened (had happened) to the other Carlo, who did not even present the problem of extreme consequences and did not hesitate to deduce from a cause the knowledge of its inevitable effect.

Now, in the case of the bourgeois Carlo—who although he was not the most despicable bourgeois, being, as we know, a progressive Catholic with an essentially secular education, /expanded/ < ... > by the experiences of a modern and open-minded job, and not, like his colleagues, entirely without cultural interests or interest in the sociological aspect of his work—this problem is presented: was it his incapacity to love Carmelo that kept Carlo from the possibility of loving his world, or, on the contrary, was it the impossibility of loving the world of the people that eliminated the possibility of loving Carmelo?

If, for example, Carmelo had been one of those Fascists whom Carlo had seen, as if in a vision, as they ran in front of his house in their little armed band, emerging from the dark background of a country that suddenly appeared to expect them, historically, just as they were, mature and complete in their revived presence—would there have been a greater likelihood of Carlo's loving him? Would not the nature of his social world—being the same as Carlo's—have been an obstacle to the expression of his violence against the man who had become a woman?

In this regard it would be perfectly useless to question the dull, negative, hostile body of the engineer Carlo—that head of a bourgeois puppet without physical strength; that cowardly eye lit by fear, by hypocrisy, and by the determination not to lose any of the privileges of a master; that clinging dull blond unhealthy hair, always combed in the same sporty style as when he was in high school in Piedmont; the body itself, which was unattractive but unaware of it, since all that mattered worked and all the rest was an idealized dream, to be left to proletarian narcissists and inefficient bourgeois. Since Carlo's intelligence in understanding the psychology of others, though limited by insuperable racial and class prejudice, was acute and immediately came to the point empirically, he had presumably understood everything concerning Carmelo; but it does not mean that that comprehension had become rational and verbal. More than intelligence, Carlo possessed shrewdness, and censorship had an easy time with that.

Moreover, there is a whole other subject to discuss. Carlo remembered very well—although by now only conceptually—the time when he had a penis. His sense of possessing it was what is called a "basso continuo" or, better still, "ostinato": it was continuous. And it was precisely this continuity that allowed him to make interruptions and detours, even long ones; it was this security that granted the possibility of devoting himself to another. Thus his life was normal. The sexual act was a form of rapid possession, sometimes artificially prolonged. It was an episode, anyway, with a beginning and an end. It's true that that end, being similar to death, "opened" the episode to totality, let's say, that is, to a cosmic "dimension." But this was not what distinguished the act; it was only a background for it. The act remained, precisely, an episode; it was a violent experience, inexpressibly necessary and hence vast, but partial.

The possession of a body implies that the body has a boundary. And also a kind of economic value: it appears as "so much" (wonderful, of course, even if it's a question of an ordinary woman, of little value, of low quality). Certainly, love as the need for protection masked by the desire to protect tends to enlarge the "limited" sense of the sexual act as penetration of the penis into the possessed body for the brief time necessary for ejaculation. But the limit, in essence, cannot be overcome. The possessed body is an entity that is in one's arms; it is measured by a look. It is an instrument that, when one has finished using it, is put aside for the next time.

It's true that next to the "basso ostinato" of the presence of the penis, there was in Carlo's life as an ordinary man another "basso ostinato," that is, an obsession with women. But this was something other than true intercourse. Besides, the man has the right to /his tangent/, which draws him out of the circle and projects him into the infinite! And this tangent was the obsession with the female genital organ, understood as a place where one is lost and dies and for which one lives.

But, I repeat, true intercourse—that is to say, apart from the subject, the most meaningful moment of love—as possession was the possession of something fatally limited. By definition, in fact, one cannot possess the whole.

Rather, being possessed is an experience cosmically opposite to that of possession.

There is no relation between the two. They are not simply the opposite of each other. The one who possesses does not communicate, except illusively, with the one who is possessed, because the experience of the one who is possessed is not comparable; it is of another type, it is, I repeat, cosmically distant from it.

On the other hand, the one who is possessed cannot communicate with the one who possesses him; because the latter does not seem to him a limited entity, an individual. < ... > And one cannot communicate with the whole! *Because it is the whole, precisely, which possesses, by way of the penis and its violence.* The one who is possessed loses consciousness of the shape of the penis, of its limited wholeness, and feels it as an infinite and formless means by which Something or Someone takes possession of him, reduces him to a possession, to a nothing that has no will except to be lost in that different Will which /annihilates him/.

/Therefore on the part of the one who is possessed the one who possesses is felt as a Good, even if that implies sacrifice, pain, humiliation, death. The blow that violates the flesh spreads over the whole infinite face of the flesh, not just a single point. The entire body, whose internal consciousness is unlimited because it corresponds to that of the universe, is drawn into the violence by which the possessor is revealed—who does not know pity, half measures, respect, respite; his desire to possess does not grant limits to the one who is possessed, who must be blindly passive, obedient, and who, even in suffering

and degradation, can at most be permitted only to express his gratitude.

On the other hand, it is beyond dispute that the Possessor is an
Evil, in fact is, by definition, THE Evil; therefore, being possessed is
what is farthest from Evil or, rather, is the only possible experience of
the Good, as Grace, life in its pure, cosmic state. Which nevertheless
comes when it wants and goes away when it wants. But even this
capriciousness is wonderful, innocent, leaving the one who is possessed in a state of expectation that still fills him with gratitude,
pushes him toward a purifying sorrow./

NOTE 70
Nocturnal conversations at the Colosseum

Carlo arrives at the Colosseum on foot. A tram from Prenestino brought
him to the neighborhood. The winter night (in '73 or '74) has abandoned the streets to the cold of the north wind.

The wide avenues of the suburbs with their /big/ irregular apartment
blocks resemble empty corridors; the only thing moving is a dirty scrap
of paper blown here and there by the wind.

The narrow old streets between San Giovanni and the Colosseum
have already been swept clean by the wind; not even a dirty scrap of paper is moving.

If by chance a human being, bundled in an old coat, moves, he seems
to do it furtively, obeying an obscure /destiny/.

Around the Colosseum cars run incessantly; but almost noiselessly,
and with distant goals, to be reached in a hurry.

The whirling wind skims sidelong over the broad expanses of asphalt; and makes the scaffolding set up on the ancient arches tremble
slightly.

From the slopes of the Oppio and the Celio a shadow descends and
falls over that expanse of illuminated asphalt. On a knoll on the Celio

glows a little fire lit by a /prostitute/, who stands motionless beside it, lost in thought, and does not even look at two clients—soldiers, perhaps, who, however, follow their own route and disappear into a narrow street in the direction of the Baths of Caracalla, /like the shades of two deserters/.

Meanwhile the prostitute's fire is twisting crookedly, as if in a whirlwind, because the wind is gusting in every direction and gives not a moment's peace.

The Colosseum is encircled by iron scaffolding and insurmountable fences. Despite this, a small group of regulars has gathered there, beneath a sort of metal cage, near the wall along Via xxx, which rises like a circular track.

A couple of the regulars stand apart. One is /completely bald/; he has an aquiline profile and holds his head proudly erect against the wind.

The cold has made his face almost white, so his stiff black beard stands out, though he may have shaved just a short time ago. His coat is unbuttoned and his arms are folded; one shoulder is slightly raised, in profile, and it is from behind that shoulder that his impassive face is seen, silhouetted, casting proud, cold, arrogant glances.

The other solitary is shorter and round; he is much younger; he has all his hair, it's wavy and hangs to his shoulders, and is obviously his pride.

Self-assured and cautious, he, too, stands with his arms folded, which makes him look cold, like a destitute woman who, going out of her house, regards the world around her with hostility, a deserted world, beaten by the wind, which some duty forces her to venture into.

His eyes, with their dark circles, as if sloppily made up, give an unfriendly glance at anyone who passes by, weighing him idly and suspiciously, as if he were thinking: "Who is this stranger \outsider passing through these parts\?"

The other regulars, however, stood together in a group, five or six of them, and they were laughing. Yes, they were laughing, wide mouths made scarlet by the cold under jaws black with beards, broad cheekbones, temples with thinning hair.

They were long laughs, or shrill or too deep, the laughs of men who are calm and /self-sufficient/. Indeed, if by chance some shadow passed in the distance or a car slowed a little, they did not stop laughing and talking, merely turned toward those intrusions an empty look that stuck there casually, < ... > /while/ their faces were filled with that cheerfulness which flaunts a good-natured but total disdain for life, life already too deeply tasted, enjoyed, /dissected/ to still have anything relevant about it.

In the midst of those who were laughing shamelessly, /however, someone was/ lost, although, as at a society evening, he was trying to keep up with the level of social frivolity.

On his face was the mask of one who once and for all has decided to yield to the blackmail: "Anyone who doesn't play isn't one of us." And a grimace twisted those poor features; a blissful happiness lay deep in the gleam of that desperate eye.

NOTE 70
Conversations at the Colosseum (continued)

A grimy scrap of paper had gusted from an unknown corner, along with a bit of straw: which the wind dragged madly over the surface of the asphalt, crudely lighted by festoons of useless lights.

Following the wild flight of that garbage, interrupted by long pauses, Carlo timidly arrived beside the group—where he was known by sight—and stood with them, apart.

He, too, was soon laughing; on his broad, Po valley face—an unhealthy grandson who resembled his healthy grandfather or his father who had died of heart disease—the dark brown pupils, sunk between the thick wrinkles of middle age, had a sparkle that resembled tears; but it was laughter, a furtive laughter, which pretended complete self-confidence, an invincible optimism that is able to see good everywhere. The floppy brim of his brown cap protected him, though he wore it rather high on his forehead like a vendor in the market; and his cheeks, on either side of his slightly hooked nose, were red, an almost artificial red shading into violet. And in them, above all in their /brightness/, was revealed the eternally renewed gratitude for that little—that very little—which is always able to give life, even in moments of /want/, of emptiness.

His acquaintances were telling stories, as if the plague had burst upon the city and only in that circle, resembling an equestrian circus, around the Colosseum, in the deserted night whipped by the north wind, did there remain any hope of survival, reduced, perhaps, to mere knowing and remembering.

Listening to the words of those poor creatures, Carlo had a *Vision*.

NOTE 7 I
The Shit (Vision: first section)

> I would like to gain all,
> all the favors of the Gods.
> —Marx,
> youthful lines (1836)

/Earlier I used the expression "the material the scene is made of"; it would have been better to say "remade." In reality the scene reproduces, through its style—the material and the light, as I've said—an actual scene: to be precise, the intersection of Via Casilina and Via di Torpignattara and of Via di Torpignattara itself with the first twenty cross streets, to the right and the left, starting from the intersection and moving in the direction of Via Tuscolana.

In this first section of the Vision we see the scene as a whole. It is fashioned entirely of light metal and other transparent and unbreakable materials, at least as regards the essential structures; but there are other materials, too, apparently crystal, alabaster, and xxx xxx xxx, perhaps even plastic. But although the materials are hard and rigid, they are all transparent. In fact, in the Vision Scene there is no light. The light comes from behind and shines through the material the scene is made of, thus taking on different colors according to the shades of that material. As a result the scene is luminous, of an even, diffuse luminosity that has no shadows or half-light but, rather, tones, depending on the intensity of color of the material through which the light shines; and it is, of course, polychrome. For accuracy, the Scene of the Vision is evenly divided into an ordered series of subscenes, or Gironi,[33] each of which has a different color./

NOTE 71A
The Shit (Vision: second section)

In this second section of the Vision we see characters whose movements act as a guide to the Vision itself. There is a young man, The Shit, and his fiancée, whose name, it seems, is Cinzia. At the start of the Vision these two young people are passing the traffic light at the intersection of Via Casilina and Via di Torpignattara. Carlo, the one who is watching, observes them coming /toward/ him: in fact, he is in the middle of Via di Torpignattara, on a cart with cork wheels, exactly like a director on a dolly. And since the two Protagonists of the Vision are, as I have said, coming toward him, the cart is being pulled backward along Via di Torpignattara at the same very slow rate at which they move forward, so that the distance of the point of view is always the same. To turn again to film jargon, there is a long, slow backward tracking shot. Pulling the cart—which is also of a light, luminous metal—are three Gods, whom Carlo, however, sitting on the tailgate, with his back to the shaft, cannot see.

   The Shit is a young man of about twenty-five and so no longer callow; he is short and has a very wide pelvis. In compensation his shoulders are narrow. He is not fat but has, as they say in the slums, a gut. His face is

---

[33] *Translator's note:* The Gironi are the three subdivisions of the Seventh Circle of the *Inferno*, where the violent are punished.

covered with freckles, and his hair and skin are reddish; his face is pink-ish, the color of the freckles, and the hair is more like brown. This hair is thin, dull, and somewhat greasy; but it's long. In back it hangs to his shoulders; <...> wisps of hair emerge from behind his ears, which are covered by locks as greasy and spinachlike as the ones that hang down his back; in front of the ears they form sideburns. The Shit's head is tri-angular: wide at the top (his friends used to say to him: "It would take a year for a louse to get around that face"; but they don't use such ex-pressions anymore) and very narrow at the bottom, that is, at the chin; which in compensation is slightly pointed, below the wide mouth. On the mouth is a "fixed" smile that reveals yellow teeth; this smile ex-presses confidence and satisfaction, and so a certain disdain for every-thing. At the same time it alludes to various reassuring and respectable facts of his life that are not visible here, of course, when he's out for a walk, and clearly have nothing to do with his nickname: The Shit. His eyes, too, are yellow, but more in the /metaphoric/ than the real sense; they are yellow with satisfaction and disdain; but that tired smile, wa-tery and forced, gives the color an unconquerable tinge of envy, bitter-ness, grief, and /entreaty/. All things The Shit does not <...> admit; and so every now and then he yawns slightly, which makes his eyes squint, and then the tongue makes a kind of *"pchak pchak"* sound against the palate. This is a fossil, expressing times past, which now has other meanings and other references.

His girl, Cinzia, is an ordinary girl in blue jeans, with a fat ass and a shirt bought at Standa.

In this entire Apparition the most important and significant fact is that the two are embracing as they walk. That is, The Shit has reached one arm around Cinzia's side so that he is clasping the opposite shoul-der with his hand. Now, since The Shit is a little shorter than Cinzia, he has to hold her bent over him, and so he gives the impression, to an ob-server, of supporting her, as if she were ill or handicapped.

The two advance in silence, concealing in the most casual and xxx way the uncomfortableness of their position: in silence, because be-tween them—in their previous life, only hinted at for now—everything has been said, and as for the others, their presence is enough to say everything.

NOTE 71 B
The Shit (Vision: third section)

In this third section, our attention is directed to the Real Scene that the Vision Scene reproduces: the first scene remains within the second like a "double," completely covered by its reproduction, it's true, but not without a slight displacement that allows us to recognize it and keep it in mind. This "double," or Real Scene, is not contemporaneous, chronologically, with the present view, or Vision Scene. In other words, the intersection of Via Casilina and Via di Torpignattara in Reality—which is "behind" the intersection of Via Casilina and Via di Torpignattara in the Vision—is "that of once upon a time," which is to say, six or seven years ago.

That "sets up" the possibility of a continuous comparison. Without this comparison it would be impossible to interpret everything that unfolds in the Vision Scene: gestures, looks, attitudes, facts, places, and people.

The intersection in the Vision Scene is /made/ entirely out of big blocks of transparent metal and alabaster through which a violent garnet-red light /spreads/ evenly; in the centers of objects (the walls of the houses, sidewalks, store shutters, trees, lampposts, etc.) it is pale, almost white, as if incandescent, while toward the edges it darkens, becoming almost bloody. In an optical anomaly, this monochrome light makes objects and lights of different colors stand out: for example, the orange or green light of the traffic signal, or people's clothes, all bright-colored—blouses, jackets, helmets, denim vests, sneakers, etc.

The scene of the intersection in Reality, on the other hand—which, by means of a slight displacement, is visible behind the intersection of the Vision, but very indistinctly, as if with a casual, hallucinatory concentration of one's gaze—is revealed in all its lost, colorless, ancient /confusion/: the houses are whitish and dilapidated or yellowish (except for some groups of new apartment blocks < ... > in the background), broken-down/ doors open onto dark, dusty entrance halls, the sidewalks are cracked, stunted, deformed trees alternate with the lampposts. People walk in a daze, dressed in gray, almost in rags; only the young men wear slick T-shirts, white or with vivid stripes. A light warm wind raises spirals of heavy, stinking dust (yet /charged/ with those ancient and forgotten laws which have animated history and the cosmos since the world began).

NOTE 71C
The Shit (Vision: fourth section)

In this fourth section of the Vision, The Shit and Cinzia, still closely intertwined—she supported by the man, as if she were "ill or handicapped," that is, practically like a sack of potatoes—are seen arriving at Via xxx xxx, which is the first turning to the right off Via di Torpignattara.

The color that bursts as if from the depths of Euresi—which here has the name Periphery and is part of the Theater of the City—shining and violently monochrome, although as usual paler and more incandescent at the center than at the edges and where the big blocks of transparent material are joined, is, in this case, vermilion red. But at the end of the short, narrow Via xxx xxx, lined with shabby working-class houses built fifty or sixty years ago, this vermilion red fades and becomes lighter and more uniform: becomes almost a dusty strawberry pink, which shades into the sky. Down there, in that pink, is a row of gigantic new apartment buildings, apparently empty.

The "double" has the usual color of the old life, worn out, gray, gloomy, indistinct; in the view a narrow alley, broken window and door frames, faded doors, rusty shutters, signs for old taverns and run-down grocery stores and butcher shops, a few bakeries; and down at the end, in the haze of the heat, the new apartment buildings.

In this wretched prospect, however—along the sidewalks, which are cracked or, indeed, consist of merely a beaten dirt track with a long, disconnected border of stones—some handsome people are walking: fat, disheveled women in dirty black dresses, old men with faces made fiendish because they have either the brutality of old drunken thieves or the meekness of people who have never hurt anyone, which is the same thing; and then the chirping of half-naked snot-nosed little boys with their bellies sticking out, but all the same full of a strange sex appeal (as one said then)—warm and tender as loaves of bread—and already little sneaks; and especially, gangs of young men who are laughing, joking, shouting insults, one in a smock riding on a broken-down bicycle, some sitting like street kids on the doorsteps, in dusty trousers and striped T-shirts that, according to their positions, reveal their backbones or their navels; some lounging on the chairs outside the local bar, the Stab Wound or the xxx, with their hands on their cocks and sleepy eyes that are quick to flash, like knives in the sun.

The most beautiful thing about these bodies is the heads. < ... > The boy on the bicycle has a head black as pitch, the hair shorn high on his long nape with its long groove but thick on his forehead, in waves and in uneven, capricious curls—like grass that bursts forth here and there on a wall in spring; the forelock makes a curve on the forehead, wide and /solemn/ as the wing of a bird of prey, and comes to /an end/ behind the ears in perfect disarray, ruled by a /capricious grace/.

Those who are sitting on the steps of the houses, on the other hand, have short blond manes, with dark roots and light tips, making a sort of halo that becomes smooth and tidy on their necks, which are long and beautifully drawn on the arc of their shoulders.

Those who are sprawled on the chairs outside the bar have small heads that make up a complete pattern book of /ancient, perhaps/ Neapolitan elegance: /the endowment and coat of arms/ of male children, pets of the household. One has thick black wavy hair worn close to his head like a statue, revealing a fine soldier's neck; some instead have abundant, smooth, blond hair, which when they move cascades on all sides but always elegantly, lightly, sliding as if it were silk (and it is always neatly cut behind the ears, on the bare nape, where virility < ... > shines); still others have very short, razor-cut hair, just washed, black as pitch yet, on top, almost clear, it is so thin and glossy: on the back of the neck the razor has worked to perfection, that is, without tapering, so that the hair is compact behind the ears and on the neck, with an almost cruel and xxx perfection. < ... >

But in the Vision Scene things are not exactly the same. Carlo, following the progress of The Shit and his girl in the long backward tracking shot, gives a long, contemplative look at Via xxx xxx in the blaze of its vermilion light; and there he observes practically a /museum of horrors/.

They are all standing still and turned toward him, like wax statues: gestures, acts, smiles, actions, words are insignificant or irrelevant. What is on display, in this Girone, is pure and simple physical presence.

The women—massive and disheveled, though their black aprons have in some cases been replaced by flower-print dresses—are immersed \lost\ in a kind of fog, and < ... > /they are/ indistinct; and so are the old men—both the evil drunks and the < ... > already half-dead pensioners; the older men, too, are immersed in that vermilion fog, which makes them silhouettes without importance, trying laboriously to be seen, to keep up with the situation. Some succeed; for example, there is a "potbelly" with olive skin and a big mustache that droops like a Tartar's, he's wearing a flowered shirt that hangs down outside his pants. And a tall man with watery eyes and the face of an old pimp who is passing himself off as a clerk; he has hair like a saint, already turning gray, which falls in waves down his back, yet he's bald in front, polished as a manhole cover. On the other hand, the young men and boys are lit with perfect clarity by the metallic red-vermilion light of the Girone.

NOTE 71D
The Shit (Vision: fourth section, II)

They all seem to be fleshly brothers and cousins of The Shit, who as he passes by at the end of their street casts a conspiratorial and sleepy glance (while in reality he has to show that his gaze is drawn into the distance, ahead of him—with a distraction no less somnolent and his light, fixed smile of satisfaction—toward other horizons: Tuscolana). But ugly and repulsive as The Shit is, with that hair on the back of his neck and those sideburns, those yellow ratlike teeth, that greasy face covered with freckles that look like fly shit, that expression whose arrogance displays hatred toward everything and everyone, although not /without/ a / (well-concealed)/ anxiety by which he begs for attention— his "equals" and "contemporaries" who are "exposed" in the vermilion light of Via xxx xxx are even uglier and more repulsive.

Because they aren't smiling, don't have an arm around the shoulders of a girl, don't have an attitude, don't look ahead, don't stare at the ground like schoolgirls, don't speak to one another, don't move, are intent on no action; they are there only to demonstrate their ugliness and repulsiveness.

NOTE 71E
The Shit (Vision: fourth section, III)

Since at this point the true contemplation begins—an intellectual contemplation—the three Gods who are pulling the cart, with Carlo's back to them, begin giving explanations: which are really internal suggestions, moving from thought to thought, as in a dream. In fact, only two of the Gods speak. The third is mute. But Carlo cannot see them. Yet "he comes to know" through them—invaded by their inner communication as if by a light—what is necessary in order to understand /what/ his eyes see.

The first thing /he "knows"/ is that every Girone represents a Category, and so each of the Apparitions is partial: it highlights an isolated Element of the new Euresi of Via < ... >. The second /thing he "knows"/ is that all the Elements, which from time to time will be highlighted by a Representation—as if immobile or crystallized—are vivid and articulated when they are mixed with all the others or a good number of the others. And nonetheless (this is the third idea that /is communicated/ to Carlo), all the isolated Representative Elements in reality coexist in people who sometimes reveal those elements in themselves, in their bodies. Anyway, finally—and here is the fourth important preliminary idea—in some of those Representatives the isolated special Element exists in its pure state. In the present instance, Via xxx xxx, it is the Element of ugliness and repulsiveness.

The individual in whom there is no other Element of life but ugliness and repulsiveness is a Model.

But this Model is invisible, because no one could endure the sight of it.

It is buried in the heart of the Girone, in a small marble tomb, which is its tabernacle, and above it is placed a statuette (whose color varies according to the Girone; in this case it's vermilion) that reproduces its features; but it is covered by a cloth, because the sight of it, too, would logically be unendurable.

This "Tomb" or "Tabernacle" of the Model is at the end of the street, where the vermilion shades into the dusty strawberry color, which is faint and almost whitish because of the distance.

That the sight of both the Model and its Statuette is intolerable is /amply/ demonstrated by those who, scattered along the street and facing Carlo, who is observing them, try to imitate it. Imitation (as the Gods say) is the "formal" basis of their code of existence. Thus the people in the Girone of ugliness and repulsiveness imitate the Model of ugliness and repulsiveness: which, however—it should be kept in mind—is one of many Models they imitate, as in a Cult. And in fact they imitate them at the same time. The Model for the Models is in a Tabernacle in a place as yet unknown to anyone < ... >. The two Gods' information regarding the specific, actual meaning of the Model represented in the Girone of Via xxx xxx is somewhat more precise. The information is this: since the first Model, at least first in the physical sense of proximity, is that of ugliness and repulsiveness, it follows that those who are by nature endowed with some ugliness and repulsiveness take the place in life that once was held by the "beautiful," those "endowed with grace"; they are, that is, the living, particular biographical "models" that in some way approximate the First and Invisible Model, which is an object of cult anxiety. It is the defect—being stunted, or obese, having one shoulder lower than the other, having skinny legs or bowlegs, being short or thin, having a long nose or a bony one, or a crushed and disfigured one, having eyes that are expressionless or whose expression is idiotic or frightened or evil or without personality, that is, erased by anxiety or by xxx self-satisfaction, having a misshapen mouth, with a sullen or oily or livid smile, or a wide mouth, the teeth bared by an unjustified, intrusive merriment, etc., etc.—this is what determines how one is placed as a possible model, in one's circle, one's street, one's bar, next to the First Model shut inside its Tabernacle.

In underlining, correcting, amplifying, exploiting, and above all making "meaningful" all these physical defects of the fortunate who have been endowed by nature with a dose of ugliness and repulsiveness, Hair has enormous importance, in the form of whiskers, beards, sideburns, bangs, curls, ponytails, other styles to which the preceding civilization has not given a name. < ... > Some heads have abundant hair, are swelled by hair that has thick roots on the forehead and temples and falls over the neck in a long xxx that gives the finishing touch to the tight waves that stir the whole head as if it had been perfectly set, in the sort of permanent popular in the forties; generally, the ones who have that hairstyle are not particularly ugly and repulsive, their faces are, on the contrary, more or less regular: but gray, anonymous, and so humiliated by that hairstyle "quoted" from a period they themselves do not know as to seem heartbreakingly monstrous. Others, however, unintentionally quote an even more distant era: the twenties or early thirties; they are generally darker-skinned, the hair falls smoothly on both sides of the forehead, while over the forehead are long, straight bangs. Also, these are generally brunets, perhaps with southern features, not ugly but similarly monstrous because of that quotation with its /"faded"/ coquetry, of which they, like horses, are unaware. In some cases the bangs have been replaced by kiss curls. Still others, whose hair has no body, have let it grow wild; but it hangs in stringy black dishevelment: the exact look of a neorealist prostitute of the fifties. And all the more so because these types are usually fat or even obese, with pale cheeks and hooked noses; their asses, besides, are cello-shaped, and their tight pants brazenly emphasize that. In this case, too, the quotation is utterly unconscious, and the ugliness and the repulsiveness have been arrived at with an innocence that makes them even more ugly and repulsive. There are some who quote men, rather than women; they quote, that is, Great Men of the Past who are completely unknown to them: /Christ/, Cavour, a reactionary intellectual of the eighteenth century, a judge drawn by an anonymous neoclassical painter, etc., etc. It's generally boys who are a little older, already twenty-five or twenty-six, who make such quotations. And they seem to have chosen beards, of all types: short, thick beards that cover the whole cheek up to the eye, or long, flowing beards, but with wiry hair, which keeps them stiff; there are some blonds, on the other hand, who have fine hair, and their beards flow in waves, like Art Nouveau apostles (for naturally the unconscious quotations continue to be terribly heartbreaking). Some have both beards and long hair, thus achieving a kind of cultlike "extremism" recalling the gurus of a religion unknown to them, like Hinduism or the old fire-eaters: emphasized by the fact that in general these extremists have pathetic little bodies, are dressed in blue jeans and a Neapolitan boy's T-shirt, and, in short, as they say in Rome, "their asses are hanging out." Then, there are those who have a "constructed" hairstyle; generally it's the ones whose hair is curly or thick and wavy, and who have gotten around this misfortune by letting it grow and then cutting it straight at the neck or into a point on the crown, or even on the forehead, so that the head is almost shaved in the center, with two enormous bulges around the ears: recalling—this time, too, unconsciously and therefore heart-/rendingly/—the hairstyles of certain primitive initiates who disfigure their faces, making them unrecognizable masks. In that sense the best results seem to have been achieved by those who have had the extreme bad luck to be born with curly hair (and in the old days would have been called "Curly") but have had their hair straightened; and so, with artificial hair, have been able to shape it the way they want, completely disfiguring their nature and as a result approximating, in apparently the most satisfying way, the First Model <...> of their Girone: that is, the Model of Ugliness and Repulsiveness. From their greater or lesser approximation to that model derive two more or less satisfied attitudes (but complete satisfaction is by far the more prevalent). The first attitude is the blissful attitude, which is manifested by the peaceful light in the eyes and moderate gestures of one who has fully realized his own dream and no longer has anything to reproach himself for, to ask for, or to expect from destiny. He is completely fulfilled; he is at peace with the society in which he exhibits his \own\ approximation to the Model, that is, the social model, which he considers nearly perfect. Yet that perfect imitation of the Model undergoes in him the typical "reversal" of all perfectly conformist positions; that is, it becomes aggressive and violent. Total devotion to Authority becomes, in short, a demonstration of violence against the minorities who in some way or other do not practice or accept that devotion. And so in one who has given his whole self to realize in his own Body the Dictates of Authority, a grim light of rancor, anger, rage coexists along with the inert, blissful light of satisfaction and transforms the excess of Obedience into near-Anarchy; and the utterly normal into a scandal.

The second attitude that derives from approximation to the Model is silence. The word has become a word of pure physical and mimetic presence: the expression of it is transferred to the Body's way of being, especially the hairstyle; and it's a way of being that is derived from an incontrovertible Model, the imitation of which in itself says everything.

Of those things, at least, the two Gods made Carlo aware.

NOTE 71F
The Shit (Vision: fifth section)

In this fifth section of the Vision, The Shit and his girl—always entwined in that special way which they seem unwilling to abandon for any reason in the world—are seen arriving at Via xxx xxx, the second turning off Via di Torpignattara. This time the Vision Scene is to the right of Carlo, who observes it as the cart moves back. The light is ruby red. As usual it's very bright in the center of the surfaces and darker at the edges. And as usual it vanishes at the end of the prospect of that mean street in the slums, into a mist that contains no more than a faded memory of ruby. But in the almost colorless light no huge new, perhaps uninhabited apartment blocks loom; rather, there are hovels, construction sites, the walls of an Aqueduct. "Behold what was once a great city of the people" /is the idea the Two instill/ in Carlo. And he observes diligently. He sees, in the double—in the hallucination of the displacement (like a printing mistake)—the old populace thronging: in rags, gray trousers, white blouses, colorful T-shirts, and some anomalous articles of clothing, a red handkerchief, a /sailor/ cap pulled down over the eyes, leaving the neck bare.

Now, on the other hand, in the ruby light of the Vision, they all seem to have come out of a clothing store. Objectively there is nothing shameful or distressing here. But it's enough to observe a little: the language of those clothes, which seem to have the price tag still attached and are as good as those of the bourgeoisie, and, in the guise of being "poor" and "patched," are at the absolute height of fashion and good taste in their range of dusty blue colors, turquoise, azure, gray, with sudden blazes of yellow or red, in the impeccable tightness of the pants at the waist and the crotch, and in the equally impeccable width below the knees, etc., etc.—the language of those clothes is no less significant than that of the bodies and the hair. < ... > It, too, imparts < ... > to eyes and gestures a calm, blissful light of satisfaction and fulfillment < ... > and at the same time the rage of one whose bad conscience, deriving from enslavement to the Model, is mixed up with a /heretical and revolutionary/ agitation /that/ inspires him to dress according to a taste that he considers at least as anarchic and outrageous as codified and legitimate. And naturally, because of the untaught innocence through which all this has come to pass, the ugliness becomes more ugly and the repulsiveness more repulsive. But the Element that is isolated and represented in this Girone is not ugliness and repulsiveness but, rather, dress codes and conformity to them. < ... > As I describe the various Elements isolated and represented in the various Gironi, I cannot < ... > keep strictly to the subject, and so in expressing myself I instinctively end up obeying in effect their contemporaneousness. When I'm talking about hair, it's impossible not to talk about asses, and when I talk about asses I can't help speaking of hair. As for conformity in clothes, the thought

communicated to Carlo by the two Gods is approximately the following. It's true that—except for the little purses held tight between
thumb and index finger or under the arm, ridiculous prostitutes' purses
that have the power to humiliate and make painfully ridiculous even
the most good-looking of the young men—the outfits as a whole do not
achieve, objectively, the degree of horror achieved, for example, by the
hairstyles and beards; yet the clothes express with greater and xxx clarity a fact that the hairstyles and beards express too dramatically and repellently to be noted: the intermingling of classes. Those clothes are not
the clothes of the poor—this is the interpretative key to the Vision inspired in Carlo by the two Gods—not because the poor have struggled
to reach (in their clothes) social equality; but because it has been con-
ceded to them. In sum—why /repeat it/?—it's a humiliating and deplorable phenomenon, the intermingling of classes, and that says it all.
And as one looks at those people, especially the young, in the second
picture of the Vision, that's what is heartbreaking and inspires a /pro-
found and inconsolable distress/. And at the end of the street, in the dissolving light of distance and twilight, in the fading of the ruby light
into the whiteness of a dream, where life is repeated and multiplies infinitely, as if outside time (a late spring or a warm winter), everything
becomes fatal: far from sight and also from conscience. Inconsolable.

NOTE 71G
The Shit (Vision: sixth section)

In this sixth section of the Vision, The Shit and his girl, in their tenacious embrace, pass Via xxx xxx to the left of Carlo, who, contemplating them, continues to move steadily backward. Via xxx xxx therefore
heads toward the ring of apartment blocks rising in the colorless mist of
heat or twilight. The dream time does not permit a distinction. The
metallic or alabaster slabs that here reproduce the low houses and small
shops crushed in a long perspective toward the chain of apartment tow-

ers are black-cherry red: bright in the center, opaque, almost violet at
the edges. This violet is slightly sinister. The Girone of Via xxx xxx /is/
different from the others; and its look of mourning makes it immediately suspicious. The Gods clarify this for Carlo. The Girone does not
have a Tabernacle: the usual Tabernacle that is built in the subterranean
crypt where the Idol is concealed. Lacking a Tabernacle, it also lacks,
naturally, the statuette that represents the Idol! So the attitude that is
isolated and revealed in this Girone does not have a Model that would
make it in practical terms historical, actual, concrete: a Model that can
be held up /concretely/ as an object of Imitation, replacing the old one,
which preceded it in earlier centuries and was valid, in fact, until a few
years ago. A glance at the "double," the profound scene of the original
reality that remains in the < ... > of the Vision—and already yellowed,
like an old photograph—leaves no doubt about what the earlier Imitation /and Value/ < ... > consisted of: which have now, apparently, been
overtaken by history. There is a holiday atmosphere, one of happiness:
sun and poverty. The ordinary time is precisely that of the dream. A late
spring, I repeat, or a warm winter. There is no reference point. But
everything is suspended as if it were eternal. Women, old and young,
gossip; girls pass stealthily but full of expectation about what life surely
holds for them. Their complexions have a healthy color; and their
shabby clothes are full of /dignity/. The old men are no longer certain
what life held for them, but, sitting at tables in the bars or on benches
in the little gardens /visible/ in the background, they know at least that
they have lived a life: a unique and irreplaceable life. Their faces have
the impenetrability of statues. Nothing in them is damaged or desecrated. They go toward the end and death, but they do not reveal the secret of what they feel. It seems that they have always known how to
become old and how to be old. The young men and boys have this dignity, too. Careless, they spend their afternoon in the sun, some working,
some doing nothing; but in their hearts glows the certainty that whatever they are doing is right. It is eternal in their illusion and eternal in
the reality that contains them. Their eyes are filled with an intense happiness and reveal that they are at peace with time. Perhaps in those eyes
are other expressions: mean, bad, dangerous, or simple, innocent, and
joyful. But what is common to all is the consciousness that they are fol-

lowing a unique Model: that of their street, their neighborhood, their universe. A unique Model that, although it entails poverty, is the best and most sympathetic Model in the world. That ensures for them, I repeat, inner strength, consistency, and therefore health. < ... >

In the Vision Scene, on the other hand, everything is the opposite: the characters, old and young—who began to appear in their physical and social actuality in the preceding Gironi—here stand as evidence of the absence of a Model and therefore of disorientation and disease. Consider the old and the very old: they have lost the Model, but at least they have had it. Many of them, moreover, are not even aware of having lost it. But the young suffer /atrociously/ from this deprivation; they don't know whom they should resemble, that is, what Model to follow. They have some Models, as we have seen, in the preceding Gironi and, as we will see, in the Gironi that follow; but this Model, which represents certainty in the eternal values of existence, that is, in health, doesn't exist. Thus the color of their complexions is /the color of disease/. They all have an unhealthy pallor, sometimes even bloodless or corpselike. There is no light in their eyes, or it's an exalted light < ... > or a purely physical, crazed light, as in the eyes of certain animals that circle and circle back on themselves as if mad because the ardor persists even though the reason for it has been lost. This pallor of the skin and this /despair/ or apathy of the < ... > are clear symptoms of an illness that has the generic name of Neurosis. It runs from the usual slight cases to almost frightening cases of madness: in which the pallor is ghostly, the eyes fathomless, and drool trickles from pale, twisted mouths.

NOTE 7IH
The Shit (Vision: seventh section)

In this seventh section of the Vision we have reached the fourth street that crosses Via di Torpignattara: there's a little traffic light. The Vision Scene is on Carlo's left. The light is cherry red. The blocks it emanates from re-create a twisting street that heads in the direction of the distant hovels /clinging like chickens/ to the walls of the Aqueduct. Just beyond the corner, there is a small supermarket and a bar with chairs outside. The signal is red. The Shit and his girl stop at the edge of the sidewalk. Everything would lead one to suppose that here, at least for a moment, The Shit would abandon the embrace in which he supports the bent-over bundle of his girl—to rest a little, to relax the arm muscles, which must be stiff, aching, or at least tingling. But not at all: The Shit continues to maintain his position, for which he evidently thinks there is no substitute. In fact, with a patient and almost foolish smile, to hide the tenderness that is usual in these situations, he holds the girl in a tighter embrace, and she, in order not to fail in her part, responds with the smile of a sick person (while it's perfectly clear that she is healthy and strong, with the face of a Gypsy, and that if for some reason she had to smack The Shit she would send him flying to the other side of the street).

Here—as the Gods reveal to Carlo—in the cherry-red light of the Scenography, the Tabernacle is definitely present. But here, too, in fact, is an anomaly. The Model is *outside* his tomb, and the tombstone lies overturned on the street. He is sitting beside it with his legs crossed, displaying his own Statuette, and he is supposed to give spoken advice, like an oracle, to those who have been initiated into the Cult of his Imitation. The Model is thus a kind of Saint who "preaches" the new Word like an apostle. There he is now—beside his open tomb and his cherry-red tabernacle, with the odious face of all priests, though he is dressed in strict secular taste, as we saw in Girone II—speaking to a group of acolytes, who have the same odious faces and the same clothes; the sentence he is pronouncing is: "What, there are still people who go with fags?" The tone is sarcastic, triumphal, full of hatred, /sure/ <...> of having the whole future on its side. The Word preached by the Model of Girone IV is (say the Gods) the Word of Abjuration.

NOTE 721
The Shit (Vision: eighth section)

In this eighth section of the Vision we see Girone V: Via xxx xxx. The light is raspberry red. The barrier of the big apartment buildings in the background has ended, and the antennas of a power plant can be seen. As for the Tabernacle, this time there is one: it's over there in front of a dairy store. The tomb on which it rises is closed in the regular way, and on top of the tombstone is the Statuette, covered with a cloth.

The Shit passes the beginning of Via xxx xxx without relaxing his embrace; it seems to imply great faith and serene complicity with a friendly world, well disposed to admit and to approve. But a patina of sweat begins to cover his face, amiably smiling among the freckles.

The Element embodied in the buried Model—whose appearance would be particularly unbearable (this time, there is no doubt) and is therefore represented in this Girone—is Respectability, at least that's what the Gods call it. /To summarize/: champions of ugliness and re-pulsiveness, /showing miscegenation in their appearance/, disfigured by a neurotic pallor, devoted with odious ignorance to the abjuration of all that they have been, the boys and young men of this Girone tri-umphantly reveal, with a kind of arrogant carelessness, a new feature: bourgeois respectability. They talk to one another about serious things, they keep their distance from chance passersby, they do not exchange a word with anyone they do not know, they make it very clear that their way of life is full of dignity, they show off decent, clean clothes, they leave no doubt of the fact that they do not know anyone who does not follow their rules of /serious/ people, they give serious and sensible guarantees as to their future, they allude unmistakably to the utter self-sufficiency of their life, which illumines them from within like a /reve-latory/ light. Their gaze does not touch even for an instant anyone who looks at them.

NOTE 7 I L
The Shit (Vision: ninth section)

In this ninth section of the Vision the Element embodied in the Model
and offered for Imitation to the Initiates—all young men—is Dignity:
not human Dignity but, rather, bourgeois dignity. This the Gods or
Leaders say to Carlo /in no uncertain terms/ as he moves backward in his
chariot. The Shit advances with his woman: they both know very well
what this dignity is, although, of the Imitators, they are undoubtedly
among the less skilled, in fact, really, among the xxx. Those who are on
display in the Girone of Via xxx xxx—distinct in its visionary form
which is suffused with an intense scarlet light—are, on the other hand,
xxx among the perfect Imitators of their Model, who is closed inside the
newly constructed Tabernacle. This Dignity would be a negligible variation of the preceding Element, Respectability, except that it has been
incarnated in the bodies, rather than remaining a somewhat ostentatious attitude, a flabby and bloodless sense of superiority. No: unfortunately, bourgeois Dignity has somehow become in bodies a new kind of
manly dignity. Abjuration, in this particular application, has been forgotten. The rejected Model—which represented the value of human
Dignity and virile Dignity < ... > in one of its well-codified forms < ... >
strictly of the people—has been replaced by a Model that no longer
even condescends to know it: is ignorant of it. A profound attraction
draws these better-nourished and better-dressed males elsewhere; they
can no longer even conceive of being treated as innocents or as inferiors;
they do not even dream that their virility must be revealed by acting
smart and cocky, by pride in their own dick and their own chastity, by
the poverty and innocence of their appearance, the dominance of the
Underworld with its Seven Cities: no: on the contrary, according to
them, and in complete good faith, virility is displayed—unintentionally—in a certain almost intellectual attitude, a way of dressing, like

daddy's boys, a refinement of habits, a certain xxx of sporting xxx, indeed, a sort of timidity and reserve oddly linked to greater muscular strength and greater physical eminence. As will become clearer at the end of the Vision—and as the Gods have already divulged to Carlo—the street of Dignity thus established is the street by which to arrive at a new form of military pride. In the bleak, whitish scene of reality beneath the powerful scenographic installation of the Vision scene, with its scarlet light—"flesh for the slaughter" is in fact seen. It used to be that the poor were required to be soldiers. Now no one is required to be a soldier anymore. (At the end of Via xxx xxx, where the scarlet fades and turns pale, are two soldiers on leave: in front their hair sticks out of the regulation berets, set roguishly on the backs of their heads; their uniforms are worn like pajamas, all unbuttoned and torn.) But if there must be new soldiers they should be like American soldiers. Or rather—as the Model buried in the Tabernacle evidently suggests to his Adepts—the true militarism that has already been unconsciously adopted is that of the SS. In fact, by whom was the SS "troop" founded? Apparently by young men of the people whom industrialization had only just made bourgeois, like these.

NOTE 71M
The Shit (Vision: tenth section)

In this tenth section of the Vision we see The Shit and his woman pass Via xxx xxx. The Shit, acting as if nothing were happening, with his free hand wipes off the sweat that bathes his wrinkled little forehead.

The Gods tell Carlo that this is the Girone of Cowardice (or even Weakness, or better still Rejection, Unavailability). This is so because the world that throngs /behind/ < ... > is a world where the boys have decided—perhaps without knowing it, because their Model told them to—to be brave and ready for anything. If someone had asked them to follow, they would have said farewell to their neighborhood and fol-

lowed him, to the end of the world; or at least until they got sick of it.
Any change or event was welcome. Their life was pure, absolute, but
not self-sufficient, because it was poor. And so all those thronging that
poor street were ready and willing for other destinies, they who had a
destiny so perfect.

Now instead the Model—< ... > who is buried, < ... > because he is
repulsive, in a crypt under the crypt, and whose ritual Statuette is
wrapped in a double thickness of cloth—says to his Followers that they
are to fear everything and everyone; trust no one, with all the things
that happen; mind their own business, not as they once would have—
when this was a bold and xxx statement—but merely in the literal
sense; that is, they are not to come out of their own shell: their own family, their own fixed-up little house, their own group of friends, their
own work (those who work; but it's the same for those who steal), and
at night are to go to bed early (the single exception in this case being
those who are thieves). Don't speak to strangers, and if someone looks at
you, continue on your way, looking straight in front of you or, rather,
with eyes lowered, like a good schoolgirl, since you, too, have angel hair
and white skin.

The light of the Scene in this Girone is reddish purple. In the background, where the small houses along the street, mixed in with the new
apartment buildings, edge up against the nearby antennas of the power
plant, the purple color becomes a beautiful dusty rose, /which looks like
the work of an ice cream maker/.

NOTE 71N
The Shit (Vision: eleventh section)

In this eleventh section of the Vision, we reach Girone VIII, as will be
clear to the reader who has done a good job of keeping track \accounts\.
The Shit advances. Surely the effort required to hold the girl close to

him, always in the same position, is making him see /double/. Surely the arm has no feeling left in it.

The light is bright orange; and in the center of the slabs or blocks of crystal—where apparently the crystal is not as thick—the orange, exploding with blinding violence, grows lighter, becomes a strange lemon yellow suffused with fire. The orange fades to this color in the background, too, where there is no longer either the barrier of the new apartment buildings or the antennas of the power plant: only the pure and simple emptiness of the sky. The earth seems to sink: perhaps into a deep valley full of drainage channels.

Via xxx xxx, which is Girone VIII, widens in the middle into a small circular piazza, as if in a village. At the center of the piazza is the Tabernacle: orange, the sacred color. But there's something new here, too, although it's not completely unfamiliar. The Model is outside his tomb, in front of his Tabernacle with his legs crossed; but, unlike the Model of Abjuration, this one—who < ... > is the Model of Tolerance—has no face. In its place he has a big egg. A speaking egg, because it, too, is an apostle: it preaches its Word. Although the listeners are strong, sure of themselves, open to the future and its modern words of liberty, < ... > they are agitated, their weak, feminine bodies are seized by a sort of nervous tremor, they are incapable of paying attention, they make irritated, prissy faces. They wish not to know but to be. The words of the Model are already /Law/, and they, born under this good star, are < ... > impatient to fulfill /what/ for them is normality, < ... > that afternoon, that evening, that night, and for their whole future.

NOTE 710
The Shit (Vision: twelfth section)

In this twelfth section of the Vision, The Shit passes Via xxx xxx, Girone IX. Holding Cinzia tight (God forbid she should run away from him), The Shit, white as a sheet from fatigue, walks very slowly and winks at a crowd of his buddies, thronging \massed\ in the street.

In the canary-yellow light that the Vision Scene emits through its massive transparent walls, those "peers" stand out with particular clarity, because blue is the predominant color of their clothes. The Chapel of the Girone's Model, in the background, is also canary yellow; and the Model embodies the Element of Free Love. Free Love, apparently, of a somewhat narcissistic character. < ... > As for the narcissism of the young men's predecessors, < ... > who appear, like shadows, in the "Reality" < ... > buried behind that Vision, it's no joke, either; but it does not contradict their nature as male children suddenly proud—thanks to their mothers—of their own dicks. They dressed and posed to show off to one another, in the background; dressed elegantly, as they might have some years earlier, before the centuries-long era of subproletarian misery ended. Tube pants or hip T-shirts or the "outfit" par excellence—dark, with a white shirt—were made to display their (seven) beauties and their endowments to other boys. The street, and the whole universe of the slums, was a single big < ... >. Where boys were educated among themselves, competing to embody in the most xxx way < ... > the old < ... > Model.

Now, the boys here in the Vision—Girone IX—are in effect obliged to show off their masculinity to women. Here is the reason their narcissism appears to be an anomalous element: < ... > of pity.

They are standing or leaning against the wall or lounging on the chairs in the bars; and all are showing off their sex: indistinctly but not metaphorically. It really is a matter of their cock and their balls. The pants in fact are extremely tight at the waist and the crotch, and whatever they have inside stands out in objectively /indecent/ relief, but the usual "natural" innocence downplays it and makes it sort of grossly painful. Where the swelling, without any mystery, xxx its bulges, the pants are frayed, threadbare, faded to a worn-out, pale /color/. And this accentuates < ... > the display. Sometimes one sees crushed against < ... > a thigh the entire little cock, like the ones children draw in toilets. But sometimes the form is less distinct: on one side of the fly are the balls, like two potatoes, on the other is the cock, like a little cucumber or a tender zucchini. Finally, somehow or other, a few succeed in preserving their mystery a little better, displaying an oblique, livid bulge: always sickeningly innocent in every way. < ... > The Gods let Carlo know this; and reveal to him that there is in the Vision a Novelty, conveyed \heralded\ by that exhibition of < ... > priapism.

NOTE 7 I P
The Shit (Vision: thirteenth section)

In this thirteenth section of the Vision, the journey of The Shit and his woman along Via di Torpignattara leads to Via xxx xxx, that is, Girone X. Here Carlo's eyes half close for an instant, struck by the sudden change in the light. It is now green: pea green, and not even on purpose. In this new light that emanates from the depth of the Vision, the Spectacle is new as well. The males have been replaced by females; this is something that for a few moments remains uncertain, probably owing in part to the sudden change in the light, but after a while it becomes obvious from, if nothing else, the presence of breasts.

According to the Gods, one of the continuous Elements ends here, that is, the Element of Ugliness and Repulsiveness; while all the other Elements more or less continue. For example, even the Element of Free Love continues to coexist with the others: in fact, all the young women and girls wear blue jeans just as tight as those of the males: so tight that below the abdomen the crack of the vulva is visible. There is a minor variation here with respect to the analogous male phenomenon: the cracks are all the same. A minimum of variety is provided by the fabric of the pants: some of the lighter fabrics form a series of horizontal pleats around the vertical cut of the vulva. Those who are not wearing blue jeans have on skirts so short (the two Gods have the linguistic modesty not to give them their current name) that you can practically see their underpants and, beneath the underpants, the familiar bulge. The Elements represented in the Gironi of the Women and embodied in their Models are valid for the males, too, and coexist with all the other Elements of the Vision. Beneath the Tabernacle, closed up inside the crypt in this Girone X, lies the Model of modern Mentality. He is the twin brother of the preceding two—the Model of Tolerance and the so-called Model of Free Love. It's pointless to dwell on this. The body language of all these girls states clearly that they /are modern/.

NOTE 71Q
The Shit (Vision: fourteenth section)

In this fourteenth section of the Vision we see The Shit passing Via xxx xxx. The color is emerald green. The Tabernacle is dedicated to the Model of Imitation of the bourgeois way of life. On this point, too, the girls' clothes, their bodies, their behavior, their expressions speak clearly. The Gods confirm this to Carlo. This Model is imitated not just by the girls—who are dedicated to the cult yet with a slightly more intense devotion—but also by the boys. /To tell the truth, among the girls imitation is a little more fanatical/, and in their relations with the boys they become apostles for this (and have good reasons for convincing them). I repeat: if age-grouping functions, sex-grouping absolutely does not.

NOTE 71R
The Shit (Vision: fifteenth section)

In this fifteenth section of the Vision, The Shit—striking a special pose—passes Girone XII, Via xxx xxx. By now he must be on the point of screaming with the pain in his arm; yet he is still smiling, peaceful, calm, willing, modest, it's as if he were saying a blessing, he feels so at peace with everything and everyone. Only, the ironic smile on his mouth, behind which, as usual, he hides all this, is slightly twisted. The light of the Girone is Veronese green; and again, in the background, where the green becomes light green, the street ends at a group of apartment buildings, much taller than the earlier ones that appeared just beyond Via Casilina; these are real skyscrapers, with a lot of glass and metal, < ... >. Here the Tabernacle is dedicated to the Model of the Lay Spirit. One sees quite clearly, moreover, that the girls are no longer religious and are used to getting the boys to do everything except take them to Mass on Sunday. The Vatican's ignorance has for centuries been the model for the ignorance of the people. It's an ignorance based entirely on practicality, as the Gods suggest to Carlo: a practicality in comparison with which American pragmatism and indeed the most fanatic and provincial behaviorism "are pikers." So though the Vatican itself is /finished/, its ignorance remains, and because of its completely unreligious pragmatism it's easy for the Model of the Lay Spirit, from his Tabernacle, to introduce the Word of hedonism and American-style materialism, a materialism typical of the entire new civilization. In this case, too, the silent Preaching of the Model of Girone XII holds for both females and males. Except that the females are by nature more impervious to its arguments in that they are substantially less compromised by the old Models of the Past, which until a few years ago were omnipotent at Torpignattara; now no one knows where they've ended up.

NOTE 71S
The Shit (Vision: sixteenth section)

In this sixteenth section of the Vision, The Shit passes Via xxx xxx, and here his ironic smile becomes sly and satisfied, although by now the sharp stabs of pain in his arm must be deafening in his head. It is Girone XIII: where the cult of the Model of the New Family is practiced (this, too, is valid for the males). The light is olive green, vaguely sinister. In the background, in the pale green that looks almost sepia, the skyscrapers of the /New/ Quarter reign. It is clear that the New Family, whose spirit is xxx by the Cult and the Imitation of the Model of Girone XIII, has nothing to do with the Christian family, that is, with the petit bourgeois family /formed on the model/ of the old peasant family: the family as /clan/, den, shelter against the horror of an economy based on poverty (say the Gods). All these girls look as though they knew perfectly well that people get married not in order to struggle against poverty but to attain and socially express prosperity. While the family of poverty was blessed by the Catholic Church, which had deposited there its usual criminal ignorance, the new family of prosperity, as we have seen, has freed itself from the Catholic Church, which thus has historically bequeathed it nothing but the above-mentioned ignorance (we are still referring to the words of the Gods).

At the end of Via xxx xxx, the Via of Girone XIII, there is a small semicircular piazza. The houses are small, built some decades ago by the owners themselves, with their hands, and stuccoed in bright colors; behind them are little gardens; two or three of these houses are very old and unstuccoed. They are cottages of tufs from the nineteenth-century, or perhaps older, with outside staircases, doors with lintels, and arched windows. The piazza is paved not with asphalt but with old cobblestones, and there is grass growing between them. In the doorways of the new houses are curtains of thin flowered material. While the old cottages—like small rustic forts, with the old blocks of tufa, their outlines indistinct, their surfaces stained here and there with rust-colored moss—no longer have their solid old doors. Some boards, which in turn have decayed, have been nailed xxx across the doorways, over the dusty glass that looks into the darkness of the interiors. In one of these doorways, certainly unused for many years, a /rose/ bush has grown up from a bit of earth and is /flowering/. Ancient flies, along with some bluebottles and wasps, circle and circle in that corner beaten by the sun. There is also an old woman dressed all in black, bent over some cans reeking of fish or motor oil. < ... >

NOTE 71T
The Shit (Vision: seventeenth section)

In this seventeenth section of the Vision, The Shit passes Via xxx xxx, and if his ironic smile became sly and satisfied as he crossed Via xxx xxx, here it is wide, happy, rapturous, revealing all his eroded little yellow teeth; he immediately makes up for his \for that\ naiveté with a faint yawn of boredom and a glance to the left (that is, to the other side of Via xxx xxx); nor does he fail to give Cinzia another squeeze, as if to reassure her and confirm that she is under his protection. This must cause him horrendous pain, if he feels his arm at all anymore. Via xxx xxx is Girone XIV. And it's the third in which the Model is sitting outside his tomb, in front of his Tabernacle, in order to complete his act of xxx through preaching and the promulgation of standards. This—according to the prosaic definition of the Gods—is the Model of Conformity. Young women and girls, all diligent and well trained, with the appearance of knowing perfectly well what they want even when they are < ... > bitches or sluts, follow the preaching of this Model very attentively. What does this preaching consist of? In codifying, regulating, standardizing, and making ordinary, to a fanatical degree, everything new and revolutionary—with regard to the recent past—that may have been desired and imposed silently (or even, in some cases, as we have seen, by an explicit intervention) by the preceding Models for Living. The Gods do not tire of repeating this to Carlo; although the Model of Conformity has been placed in a visionary scene made up solely of women, the spirit he sends forth and imposes is valid also for males. The Element of Conformity is an Element that coexists in everyone—male or female—with all the other elements. But it's the women who have had special authorization to assimilate and promulgate the spirit of this Model; without the women it would be /experienced/ chaotically by the men, perhaps leaving them with the illusion of the new and the revolutionary: which would be unforgivable and, indeed, inconceivable.

NOTE 71U
The Shit (Vision: eighteenth section)

/In this eighteenth section of the Vision we have reached, along with
The Shit, Via xxx xxx. There is another traffic signal, which is red. So
The Shit, protecting and supporting his beloved, stops. And Carlo's
cart stops, too. The towing Gods take the opportunity to recapitulate
to Carlo what he has seen and review the situation. The New Youths
are ugly and repulsive; consumed by a disfiguring interclass anxiety
(with those prostitutes' purses); pale and neurotic, with drooling, angrily contorted mouths; brutally ready to repudiate everything that
they themselves and their brothers have been; disdainful and aloof in
order to be respectable, in complicity with the wealthy classes; totally
forgetful of every simple smile < ... >, like subordinates, because of a
dignity incarnate in them that is not human dignity but sullen bourgeois dignity; completely taken up in the round of their life, outside
which everything is suspicious or a source of fear; free, with painful
indecency, to take advantage of a sexual <freedom> that in reality
does nothing other than display the weakness of their flesh and their
xxx vulgarity—above all, the New Youths are completely militarized
by the same Conformity (opposite but equal to the Conformity that
for centuries promulgated laws, written and unwritten, in defense of
ancient Values) that has already produced the troops of the SS; and has
been entrusted to the special care of young women, who are thus delegated to restore to a rigid, fanatical normality everything new and
"scandalous" that a new modern mentality, the imitation of the superior classes, a lay and materialistic conception of the family < ... >, etc.,
may have brought to the habits of life.

But that's not all; there is worse to come./†

NOTE 71 V
The Shit (Vision: nineteenth section)

The traffic light turns green. The towing Gods start towing the cart again, and The Shit, easily stepping down off the sidewalk, crosses the street, carefully supporting his poor paralytic girl.

The great scene of Via xxx xxx, that is, Girone XV, is < ... > constructed of the usual slabs of transparent material; in this case, they let through an intense melancholy light of a color between sepia and rust. The Gods are unable to find a name for the Model, who lies in his Tabernacle and is honored with garlands of flowers (plastic flowers: an attention of the cult that is almost certainly attributable to a feminine hand). If the Gods cannot find a name for the Model, they nevertheless hasten to provide the introduction necessary for Carlo to understand the meaning of this Girone XV. The Element of Ugliness and Repulsiveness was suspended, not valid (as we have seen) for the preceding four Gironi, which were populated exclusively by females; here, however, in Girone XV, it returns to currency, indeed, it is especially vivid and effective despite the presence of women.

In fact, Via xxx xxx is frequented only by couples. Young couples, of course; the old are, as usual, not noticeable, semi-invisible in the melancholy sepia-rust color; or, if they are seen, their function is reduced to the pure and simple one of spectators or, to be more accurate, admirers. The couples are of all types; but they all behave in exactly the same way, observing the following rules: 1) They expect the admiration of the bystanders, though they manage, smiling and serene for the most part, not to look at anyone even for an instant; 2) They manifest in the most unequivocal way their utter self-sufficiency and total lack of interest in anything that doesn't have to do with their xxx relationship; 3) They remain—according to the rule, and without departing from it for a moment—tightly embraced: either he clasps her to his side or by the shoulder (like The Shit); or she clasps him (to her side); or finally, by mutual agreement, they hold hands, even if he is grasping her with her tacit consent; 4) They are silent < ... > because of their vividly indescribable relationship, which < ... > they display as if it were provocative (in the midst of hundreds of other couples who are doing exactly the same thing); 5) They speak, when they speak, in a close and intimate way, as if they were speaking a jargon for initiates, barely audible, the understanding between them is so instantaneous; 6) They miss no opportunity to exchange kisses, and they do not xxx a single time to observe their effect (which must be overwhelming) on passersby.

All these rules, and a few other minor ones, are, I repeat, rigidly observed as the couples walk down the street. If, however, they stop beside a wall or on a bench in a garden, the rule is reduced to one, No. 1.

There is also another case that's very common. And Via xxx xxx has a typical example of it. A whole family group is sitting in a pizzeria (this time the old people are in the light): three or four potbellied men with their wives, the old mother in a flowered dress, a young man, a bachelor, fat, pale, with eyeglasses sparkling on his potato nose, "constructed" hair that stands up in a point on his head like an enormous pinecone, and the usual purse under his arm. In the midst of all these guests, in the place of honor, is the couple. Both girl and boy are silent, as if solitary and aloof; but their silence is the official silence of one who is successful and knows it is his turn to be venerated and honored. The girl, in extremely tight blue jeans, so that as usual one can see the crack of her vulva, is silent, sulking, following an old model that has not yet been completely abandoned. He, on the other hand, is exquisitely modern, utterly consumed by the art of making himself admired. He is tall, thin, sheathed in a very simple shirt of dark turquoise silk; < ... > he holds his purse carelessly in his hand; he has long, rather wild hair, which, however, elegantly harmonizes with a face that is, on the contrary, anything but wild: thin, gaunt, smooth, with a red mouth and cheekbones that are delicately pronounced, like the jaw. The eyes have dark circles under them. His silence is due to a sadness that makes him sullen and distant. Perhaps it is his neurosis—which causes repulsiveness and pity—that makes him so < ... > distressed; but he masks all that with the somewhat fastidious silence of one who is handsome and fortunate, who is the object of envy and /has/ all the future before him, in a society that ingratiates itself with him and that he manifestly counts on being welcomed into as a husband and father, < ... > very modern, of course. He leans on the table of the pizzeria with a thin white elbow, which has an intellectual, feminine delicacy. He is not a bourgeois or a student, he is one who lives there, in Via xxx xxx, at the intersection with Via di Torpignattara.

/The ostentatiousness of the love that binds the couples—love fatally and manifestly carnal, as permissiveness allows, in fact requires— clearly reveals that these relationships \loves\ are deeply insincere./ < ... > And this is the reason that even in this Girone, where there are also Women, the spirit of Ugliness and Repulsiveness prevails < ... >. In addition to the couples, Via xxx xxx is crowded with mixed groups of boys and girls, though the girls are less numerous. These groups keep to themselves, establishing despite their size the venerated privacy and self-sufficiency of the couples. They laugh, they joke. Now the women are a little embarrassed, as they try to keep up with a situation they are not yet completely used to, and they hide their embarrassment by wiggling their hips and acting like idiots with shouts and grimaces; now, on the other hand, it's the men who are embarrassed, who laugh with watery or stiff smiles or stand apart like dogs with their tails between their legs, put on the defensive by the intrusiveness and dominance of the girls, who have made themselves masters of the situation and are the center of attention. But these are extreme cases. /Generally the mixed groups of boys and girls, like the one at the end of Via xxx xxx at the edge of some dusty, stunted little gardens, behave as if comradeship between males and females were a thing of ancient date, of immemorial tradition—in the tradition of Torpignattara—and had made them, all of them, happy and content. In reality the presence of women in the bands of men < ... > restrains < ... > them < ... > not only physically—in running, in joking, in < ... > violence—but also, for example, in speaking and, above all, thinking. They are educated together; and given that in such matters women are stronger— because conformity is stronger than any other feeling—education is in reality controlled by the women. And above all they assimilate the

men to themselves. Here are the old cheats and bullies of Torpignattara, who consider their thinness, their fineness, their graceful poses
an advantage as they stand with one shoulder slightly raised and a hip
sticking out, making rather feeble and xxx gestures with their hands./
Their older brothers—whose bodies, strong, poor, and fierce, had been
there only a few years before—<...>/would have/buggered/them/, first
to last, or set fire to them. But probably they would not have believed
their eyes and would have taken them for /hallucinations/.

NOTE 712
The Shit (Vision: twentieth section)

In this twentieth section of the Vision, here's The Shit arriving at Via
xxx xxx; <...> this is no longer a Girone but a Bolgia.[34]

Thus begins a second part of the *Inferno*[35] <...>

The Bolge, which are five, compared with the fifteen Gironi, are characterized by a different type of Model. It is "double," or "two-faced." It
is made up of two physical aspects and therefore has two meanings. It is
ambiguous; but the two natures that make up that ambiguity are like
oil and vinegar: each one, developing autonomously, maintains and af-
firms its own autonomy. And they turn their backs to each other.

Finally, therefore, the Models of the Bolge are a Contradiction that is
not resolved; but it is not an Opposition. They are a single Thing with
two Faces, attached, in classical fashion, at the neck and therefore prevented from knowing each other or, more simply, from looking at each
other.

But these Siamese twins in the form of a Janus herm have two other
characteristics.

First: they are in the throes of death. They are about to die, dissolve,

---

[34] *Translator's note:* The Bolge are the ten ditches, or chasms, into which the Eighth Circle of
the *Inferno,* where the fraudulent are punished, is divided.

[35] Italian: not for nothing do the toponomies make easy and common reference to Dante.

no longer be. History wanted them thus, because at the moment it could do no better and had to be content with the two coexisting forms—competing, perhaps, but not really contradictory.

At the feet of the Deities of the five Bolge, besides the usual sacred statuette, which, so to speak, "crystallizes" their character, there is also an ax. It is the ax with which, not too long from now—in a few years— the Two-Faced Models will be cut in two; and it will be seen which of the two surviving Halves prevails, eliminating its rival.

Second: the Deities of the five Bolge have neither names nor descriptions. And that is for the same reasons that they are temporary and about to die. History produced them, placed them as Models in the streets of the <People>, but found them, so to speak, under its feet. They are the Unexpected and so, for now, the Unrelated. A thousand classifications and a thousand probable meanings can be predicated on them; or they can be defined by circumlocutions and generic terms; but one thing is certain: which is their cohesion and perfect solidarity with the Models of the preceding Gironi. Except that the latter are in some way established and therefore clear; while these are still being established and so are still enigmatic. In any case, the transformation they have brought about—despite /the coexisting doubles/—in the way of being, in the quality of life, /in the bodies/ of their Imitators is established.

So let's go on to the first Bolgia.

Here the Two-Faced Deity could be a Deity who presides over smells; but to say "smells" obviously means nothing: it is a simple metaphoric suggestion, a poetic guide. For lack of anything better, however, we can follow this track.

From the scene of Reality (Via xxx xxx of a few years ago), which, as usual, glimmers and xxx under the Vision scene, odors stream, the odors of the bodies of the young men and boys who are hanging out on the sidewalks and in the bars (as usual, the old people are out of the picture). It's the smell of sweat and dust, of poverty and innocence, that is. Their pants are saturated with these smells (pants worn with style though shabby, threadbare, or bought secondhand in Via Sannio), as are their cheap cotton T-shirts; their hair is saturated with them, and so are their handsome necks, bare and shapely.

The shoes give off a faint stink, it's true, especially if they're made of rubber. But it's an odd, forgivable stink, as old as the world. There is the smell of the shop, the slightly sickening engine grease < ... > /but also/ the < ... > smell of rusting metal. And also the smell of freshly baked bread or of bread dough. A smell that comes naturally from a baker.

There's no need to mention the smell of fruit sellers. But even the fish sellers—although the innate stink of fish is distressing—are not repugnant; on the contrary, they /are/ < ... > likable.

The butchers' aprons smell of blood, and, to tell the truth, it's a little sickening/ /yet no less likable, too. It's the smell of work.

The smell of the grocers' helpers is almost a perfume; the smell of packing paper and pepper. And so on: I could go on for pages and pages.

Also the smell of sex, although not very clean, and in some cases definitely xxx—it's urine or what, at the time, those boys laughingly called *"caciotta"*—it's not repellent; it's the odor of nature and of people.

Now let's see what's happening in the superimposed Vision Scene. And meanwhile the Model is down there, standing on his little pedestal with his two sagging faces that express nothing.

/But his duplicity/ reverberates and xxx clearly throughout Via xxx xxx, < ... >. On one side are the young men and boys who Imitate one of the two Forms of the Deity, on the other are the young men and boys who imitate the other. But they are Imitators: not Disciples or Initiates. The double spirit of the Deity descends on them, subdividing them into two different bands, not only without their wish but even without their knowledge. It's not /untamed/ innocence anymore but total passivity, like that of automatons, entirely played by their destiny, which makes the Model of the first Girone, that of Ugliness and Repulsiveness, particularly < ... > here.

Thus all the young men and boys who appear in this Bolgia have in common the characteristic of being particularly ugly and repulsive, both those on the right-hand side of the street and those on the left, who are separated by their resemblance to the one face or the other of the Patron.

First let's observe the ones on the right.

They stand in picturesque, indeed photogenic, groups, large and small, along the street. They do not look anyone in the face. They speak among themselves, probably of serious matters; or they chat amiably, with sneering irony. Each of them shows off an exemplary little suit: pants with shining star-shaped patches; shirts like reversible vests, blue inside < ... >, a sort of ash-gray turquoise outside; trousers that are very tight at the waist and flared at the bottom; great exhibitions, naturally, of "baskets" (that is, the potatolike or tuberous bulges of the sex). < ... > Everything that does not concern them is a source of irritating boredom and almost of disgust \nausea\ in their pale faces, their dark-circled eyes. When they are not, instead, tanned and muscular, thanks to intense athletic activities. Anyway, they all < ... > seem to wear on their chests the glitter of medals, as it were; /that is,/ < ... > the admiration of all the girls whose hands they have held and whose shoulders they have squeezed, in the neighborhood and outside it. They are < ... > there to be admired; and the presumption disfigures their faces no less than the enormous hairstyles, "constructed," in an attempt to outdo one another, in the most disfiguring ways. The portrait is completed by the purses they hold fastidiously in their hands, with the air of people who are used to a way of life full of refinements that spoil them and, curiously, make them sad and self-absorbed.

Well, then, all of them—and let's not forget that they're ugly and repulsive, even if, in other historical circumstances, they could have been, attractive or handsome—give off a smell of barbers and unwashed bodies.

It's a smell that hovers over them, noticeable only to particularly sensitive nostrils: the specter of a smell; but if by chance it is perceived, it becomes an unrelieved, pitiless moral judgment. It's the smell of the Fascist worker or the church lawyer; of the shopkeeper who gets out of his bath fresh, tan, clean-shaven; of the efficient young executive who uses French eau de cologne.

This smell is also the smell of penises: because they have not been washed thoroughly—and so the soap, mixed with urine, makes the smell of urine a stench; or talcum powder, mixed with sperm, makes the smell of sperm asphyxiating, for that little that xxx. If, however, they have been washed thoroughly, their antiseptic odorlessness makes them disgusting, mere flesh—weak, dangling anatomical organs.

And now we come to those on the left.

The light that emanates from the interior of the large blocks, probably of xxx, that reconstruct, in the Formalism of the Vision,† Via xxx, is bluish: the dirty nocturnal blue in the choreography of an operetta or, if you like, the indigo of a primitive illustration. Therefore it is night. But the hypothetical moon or electric lighting splits the street in two, as usual. The right-hand side is in the light, the left in shadow: the shadow of the "slums," of these old neighborhoods that long ago in the depths of night were isolated from the world, peopled only by those who knew them as they knew themselves: people few and far between, who xxx xxx. So on the left-hand side, in shadow, on the low steps of shops with their metal shutters lowered, or around the streetlights, are groups of boys symmetrical to those on the other side of the street, in the light.

If you sharpen your eyes, however, in this cursed half-light and observe these boys more closely, you end up < ... > making a < ... > disturbing discovery: *these boys are the same ones who are on the other side.* They are their twins or, better still, their "doubles." /In short/ < ... >, a repetition of them: the incarnation of another possible state of being.

This phenomenon will be repeated—as the Gods warn—in the other Bolge. The Doubleness of the Model is not a mere curiosity but a drama; even though it's a drama that doesn't unfold, that's a dead Representation.

The boys sitting on the steps of the closed shops or standing around the streetlights—as in a nineteenth-century illustration—are waiting for something, are ready for something; which escapes the bourgeois observer because this "something" has nothing to do with his life. It is otherness. As if because of an organization of their evening and night that breathes imperceptible passwords and secret signals, they are strangely quiet and /orderly/. The only sign of life, which in a way is too lively and compromising, is a small fire lit at the corner of an intersecting alley, in front of a closed bar. This fire flickers and glimmers without crackling and without making any smoke, as if it, too, respected the rule of order and silence.

The boys here on the left-hand side, in shadow—that is, the duplicates of the boys who are so proper on the right—are < ... > horrible, /victims of/ a degradation that makes them almost bestial: their faces are disfigured by a corpselike pallor, as well as by horrifying hairdos. Their mouths drool. Their eyes are sunken, like those of old men, and stare dully, almost certainly because of some drug.

They give off an odor of the most disgusting and ancient filth. Although their clothes are elegant and stylish, they are evidently the only ones they have, and they wear them for weeks, so that sweat and dirt have saturated them, mingling with the < ... > foul odor of people who have slept all night without undressing and < ... > of course without washing when they get up. Naturally, this smell is strongest at their mouths and feet.

It is intensified in their penises, where it is concentrated; it is no longer the smell of old urine or of xxx, suffocated inside underpants reduced to rags, it is an indefinable smell: the smell of gas combined with onions, rechewed tobacco, vomit.

NOTE 72A
The Shit (Vision: twenty-first section)

In the second Bolgia (Via xxx xxx), the night is even deeper, though the street is still as if split in two by the edge of the light. A /sinister/ deep violet on the side that's in shadow, an equally /sinister/ pale violet on the side in the light.

The Two-Faced Model is sitting on its pedestal, on the divide between light and shadow, like a traffic cone in the depth of night. Its two faces look in opposite directions, into the emptiness.

Here the ambiguous Element that the Model represents is something like < ... > the "new criminality," with its new laws and new characteristics < ? >, apparently in the process of formation and for now entrusted to chance and necessity, which precede consciousness (always the last to arrive, always fatally delayed).[36]

---

[36] "It is not consciousness that determines life, but life that determines consciousness." Marx and Engels, *German Ideology* (1845–46). "It is not the consciousness of men that determines their social being, it is their social being that determines consciousness for them." Marx, Foreword.

Let's pause for a moment at the image of the old Via xxx xxx, as it was before it appeared in the guise of this second Bolgia. The image appears and disappears, like a light that flickers before going out forever. So it's an image that's hard to grasp now. There, it's the old criminals moving in the night silence.

/Briefly/ < ... >: they embody better than anything else the ideal of the poor man in a great plebeian metropolis. With a perfection equal to their ignorance, they apply the language and the code to themselves: to their own bodies. In the heart of the slums they live the tradition of the Seven Cities of the Underworld; and their morality, if it's not love, is honor. They have been taught humanity and respect by their mothers. And though their education is completely urban, they belong to the great world of Masses and tabernacles, of sacred woods and slavery, of poverty and the return of the seasons. Their rustic innocence is secular; but the rationalism that has /rejected/ the Gods (among men but not women) is also a peasant rationalism: like that of the Stoics or of Epicurus. With an endurance inferior only to happiness they face the hardships of an unjust life. From the dominant social class they steal possessions, and, very rarely, when it is really necessary, they murder one of its members. Otherwise they ignore it; in fact, they consider it literally nonexistent. It lives in a meaningless elsewhere that, obeying other (foreign) rules of life, is simply so discredited as to have no meaning or reality.

The criminals of the Vision are a totally different matter. The Model says nothing. But it's clear—and time to say so—that he has been put there to kill and destroy. Someone brought him there. And this someone can declare himself satisfied. The Genocide is complete. All those who were not only < ... > no longer exist. < ... >

Those who are now in their place do not know the rules of the Underworld, neither honor nor humanity. Even their tattoos are quotations.

Let's look first at those on the left.

Estrangement from the wealthy classes has totally disappeared from their bodies. The dough of those bodies, which was kneaded by that estrangement from official history, has remained, it is true, a thin dough, that breathes scarcity and otherness. But a new destiny, together with the old one—now powerless—has devoted itself to the job of kneading that flesh. Rather than butcher it and annihilate it from the face of the earth in a /bloody/ genocide, it has found a much < ... > easier (final) solution: to knead it again. There it is. < ... > Pale and bloodless, < ... > with dull, empty eyes. Furtiveness like a thick cry; the sneer like a prayer for pity, cut off at birth. Expressions, these, which surface on the yellow skin and in the lusterless eyes like the last glimmer of a totally repressed life, so withdrawn from others as to be withdrawn from itself. That such a withdrawal corresponds to the necessity of hiding their criminal activity is not enough to explain the utter naturalness with which these criminals succeed in behaving like perfect professionals, like < ... > arrogant, bespectacled officials if not < ... > university students. The air of disdain and superiority that distorts their faces under the long hair falling to their shoulders, the mane over their reddish foreheads, is the consciousness of a greater social success compared with that of others; nothing else distinguishes them. < ... > Their ideal of life is represented by professionals or officials who rob or steal. Like a canal that, as it drains, reveals banks littered with stinking garbage, the life that has withdrawn from their bodies leaves a space filled by professional, technical, organizational bourgeois dignity, whose Vulgarity, joined to the Misery that in every way still persists in those Bodies, inspires the same holy terror /as a body/ that has been tortured and killed.

Their twins or doubles on the right-hand side of the Bolgia have lost even the appearance of the "power of intellect," however extended to the xxx, and are pure and simple forms of Mad Bestiality (if, in all modesty, I may be permitted to refer to a negative fact of a Past and of a Culture that no longer have real references). This is a Mad Bestiality that, like everything else, is new. Because the genocide victims carried everything away with them. The organization of the underworld as a profession becomes in these Beasts with distorted faces, dripping noses, squashed cheekbones, sunken eyes, brutish mouths that curl at the edges in a sneer of hatred (but for the most part are completely expressionless)— the organization, I say, becomes < ... > dissociation. The organization in fact confirms the criminals in the absoluteness of their function and the invariability of their specialization. Once stealing and killing are established, everything follows from that decision with total coherence.

Bloodthirsty and murderous, they perform their actions deliberately and as if drugged. They go home at night with a scrap of human flesh between their bared teeth, they let it fall, they wipe their mouths with their forearms, but their lips remain greasy with blood, and in their eyes is the light of a vaguely comic exaltation.

NOTE 72B
The Shit (Vision: twenty-second section)

The Shit reaches Via xxx xxx, the third Bolgia. The light is blue-black. Continuing the discourse of the Gods in the most simplified terms—we have, as usual, at the end of the street, the Two-Faced Model, put there by the Exterminators to cause death through transformation.

In its two faces originate the light and dark halves of the street, with the two crowds of Twins and their double Representations gathered on either side. On the left are vulnerable and sensitive young men, who, along with the usual Repulsiveness to which they are condemned, are truly a little pitiful. It's the poetic quality of the happiness and the neurosis in which they struggle, trying to /begin/ the search for that cultured and revolutionary "something" which is put at their disposal. The results of this search are disastrous. Commonplaces, certainties, fanaticisms, moral blackmail, the assumptions of an ignorance enormously increased by the wretched little knowledge that has been acquired—it all falls on their heads. In this context the sneers reappear, the looks not exchanged, disdain, sufficiency, self-sufficiency, etc.; and that trace of sincere pity on the part of one observing them, and of their own confused and rather disgusting poetic quality, is reduced to little more than a shadow.

On the other side of the nocturnal street, their mirror-image bodies look as though they had given up the search and had instead taken possession of the little at their disposal that is cultured and revolutionary, along with much that is deceptively cultured and basely conformist, through which the Assassin Model suggests to them how to reach the level of the sons of the bourgeoisie and the wealthy. The attitude has become so natural that it is ingrained in their bodies. Their relationship to those others is from equal to equal; they are, naturally, unable to see in them any mystery, nor have they any mystery themselves anymore, not since the moment they lost their innocence, the innocence of a subordinate, and their human dignity.[37] Having gained equality (which they don't know is purely illusory) and given up human dignity, in favor of a normality that speaks the "prose" of the bourgeoisie perfectly, they have become totally, ineluctably unpoetic.

NOTE 72C
The Shit (Vision: twenty-third section)

In this twenty-third section we contemplate The Shit as he arrives at Via xxx xxx, the third Bolgia.

The Shit must be practically at the point where he can't continue. He is as white as a dead man. But his arm continues to hold the stocky Cinzia as if he were glued to her. No one must miss the passage of that fatal couple, *entwined exactly in that way.*

Now that's been settled, let's see what this important third Bolgia looks like.

The light is a very dark blood red. At the center of the slabs it looks like coagulated blood; at the edges, like blood that's been washed off with water but not very well.

On the two faces of the Two-Faced Model there is a smile. And he may well smile, and doubly, and even rub his hands, our Assassin, sent there by the Masters < ... > to slaughter; the slaughter could not be more complete. < ... > (And may the reader forgive me if I "let myself

---

[37] ". . . [the bourgeoisie] has made of personal dignity a simple value in exchange." K. Marx, *Manifesto, etc.* (1848).

go" into somewhat /unrestrained/ /registers/, reliving, as I do, the "interior monologue" of the two Gods, which reverberates in Carlo, who is absent because of the trauma.)

On the left-hand side of the street, which is the color of washed-out blood, young men and boys speak animatedly (in the next Bolgia we will see what kind of language it is). "Animatedly" is not the right adverb, anyway; but the right adverb doesn't exist. The discussion is really half affable, half worldly, < ... > with the stereotype of a disdainful sneer stamped on the prosaic faces: as if the object of that discussion and its arguments were already established and indisputable, according to a profound agreement binding those who are talking and those who wish they were. In short, there seems to be an understanding, /with apparently/ a livid < ... > yet rather gentle scorn for anyone who for some reason does not accept the understanding or has the misfortune not to be at the social and intellectual level to accept it and remains excluded. At the same time, however, that discussion is "angry" (not "animated," which would presuppose a certain—intolerable—innocence). The "anger"—undoubtedly—is due to certainty, not innocence. Those who show it seem charged with a duty, < ... > freely assumed; and in the expression of it they invest all the vulgarity they would have invested in making, for example, Fascist statements. The fact that their statements are completely reversed with respect to Fascism only increases their certainty, that is, their vulgarity.

Anyway, the discussion that takes place along that sidewalk is, on the whole, perfectly *comme il faut:* the ideas are exactly the ones people should hold in order to be modern and advanced; some disgust and almost boredom in the faces doesn't hurt, to hide their complacency toward so much progressivism and modernity. The lesson has been learned well, there is nothing else to say. And for this reason one of the two faces of the Two-Faced Idol put there by the /distant Power/ smiles.

And we come to the other sidewalk, submerged in darkness the color of coagulated blood. The doubles that are reproduced here, on this sidewalk, the "fucking little pricks" (as, deplorably, the Gods put it), do not talk at all about social and political problems; in fact, on those subjects their faces express an invincible disgust. Eyes close, mouths form a painful grimace: like someone sleeping with a stomach ache. They don't want to hear, they don't want to speak. And these are the best. The others, who are the majority, do not even know that the problem of refusing to talk about political issues, or even knowing something about them, exists. What fills their faces with interest—faces contorted by a nervous excitement or by floods of "nonverbal expression," like laughs or farts—is quite different. This is why the other face of the Two-Faced Idol is smiling.

NOTE 72D
The Shit (Vision: twenty-fourth section)

But before leaving the third Bolgia, we must cast a glance at the Scene of Reality that survives there, glimmering, about to disappear forever.

In the street called xxx xxx—by now we're at the edge of Torpignattara, approaching the Mandrione, with its high walls, which, as it crosses those poor neighborhoods, cuts them in two, opening up large spaces where the sky plunges down (behind brick-walled cottages, two- or three-story houses, hovels, shanties)—there is the usual crowd of people: a crowd that includes all types, women, old women, men, old men, boys, little boys, teenagers and young men.

These last are wearing red handkerchiefs at their necks: < ... > on their shabby pants and their thin shirts, and, for those who have one, on the beret or cap pulled down so low over the eyes that they have to stick their noses up to see. Their hair is cropped and thick curls cover their necks, which are outlined boldly on thin shoulders or tenderly on square, robust ones.

They are Communists, at that hour returning, perhaps, from a demonstration in the Center. They are happy. Their eyes flash with light. A /black/ light, southern. The poverty and injustice against which they struggle do not dismay them. In their hearts they enjoy life as it is; because they know in their hearts that one day they will overcome and the world, the whole world, will be theirs.

Red flags wave, too. The Communist Party is not a big clean party; it is a big dirty party; but it is dirty with the oil of the shop, with metal, with rust, flour, dried fish, blood, mint, sweat, and dust. What it gives is as grand and human as those who receive. He who hands over the flag and he who carries it are true companions, even if they are as different as an intellectual can be from a worker or a worker from a beggar.

NOTE 72E
The Shit (Vision: twenty-fifth section)

Similarly, in the fourth Bolgia—Via xxx xxx, which The Shit reaches straining with a supreme effort—what remains of the Scene of Reality cannot be ignored.

The shadows of the living who appear intermittently in the wonderful fullness of one of their lost days—on the point of sinking into the oblivion not of yesterday but of millennia—are here endowed with the sublime capacity to speak. Their inventions are not innovations, it's true. They are inventions that break the code, following certain rules suggested by the code so that it can be broken. But the linguistic excitement is continuous: from the frenzy of old women who open and close their mouths in a concert of pure sounds, interrupted by long cries: *"Nadiaaaaa!,"* the *"Na"* nasal, the long *"iaaaaaa"* irritated and complaining; from the quiet repartee of the respected old men, who, in front of liter bottles or carafes, readapt to toothless mouths the old locutions \expressions\ that have brought them so much glory thousands of times a day for thousands of days—to the dry, thundering "shots" of the young men, /haiku/ inspired by some Attic Spirit that has survived slow Italianization, adding "Fuck you"s and "shit"s like sung refrains. Every combination of words is a poem, and every reference to facts is a novel. Hermes Trismegistes still presides over the language, of this there is no doubt; since the hand when it steals does so just as it did two thousand years ago. And I beg the reader's pardon if the discourse of the

Gods, taken up by me, borders at this point on madrigal and the prose of art; but *"je ne fais pas d'ouvrage, je fais seulement des essais en comptant toujours préluder. . . . "*[38]

NOTE 72F
The Shit (Vision: twenty-sixth section)

We are nearing the end of the Vision. How much trouble and anguish it has cost me to describe it, I do not wish to tell the reader; it will be enough for me to remind him that it is terrible to inhabit and know a world where eyes are no longer able to give a look—I do not say of love, but even of curiosity or sympathy. Although I am now "content with the desert," thinking about it I feel the sort of pang that usually prevents one from expressing oneself or speaking politely: only those who love suffer when seeing loved ones change. Those who do not love are not even aware of it. Nothing to do with poor people matters to politicians; nothing about young people matters to intellectuals. And so not only do they not suffer because of the change but, indeed, they do not even recognize it. Furthermore, it's not even a question of a simple but painful, degrading change; rather, it's, as I've said, a true genocide.[39]

The Shit arrives at the point where the Pattern imposed on poor young men, who apparently are now no longer poor, is responsible for the destruction of the Language. Because the xxx logic of this, my modest Vision, assumes that the Elements of Life, and therefore of the Living, are destroyed xxxing one by one.†

Along the sidewalk, charged with the livid light of late twilight or night, those who "have taken the place of those who were to be" are actually speaking. So they possess some linguistic faculties. In fact, their speech has been released, it flows, one might say it knows no obstacles

---

[38] To paraphrase Leopardi (in a letter to an admirer of April 6, 1936).

[39] "The *devaluation* of the world of men increases in direct relation to the *making valuable* of the world of things." K. Marx, *Economic and Philosophical Manuscripts* (1844).

and considers everything speakable. But soon it's clear that they are automatically repeating something obtained for them "elsewhere." Their aphasia is manifested in the mechanical application of a verbalism whose lexicon increases and then becomes fixed forever in that amplification; and so the cognitive amplification required by the lexical amplification is also fixed. There is the illusion of knowing, and hence speaking of, the entire world. Deriving from it are an unconscious uncertainty—the source, as usual, of ugliness and repulsiveness—and a presumptuous certainty: a no less fertile source of ugliness and repulsiveness. One of the two faces of the Model smiles with satisfaction at having spread this national language, which, as the need for it increases \through an increase in the xxx need\, is proportionally diminished, its expressive capacity reduced to nothing. Its speakers leave out feelings (above all naiveté, wonder, respect, interest); but conform rigorously to the monotone of one who knows without further limits himself, the other, and their mutual relationship.[40] Along the right-hand sidewalk, where the livid light of twilight or night becomes shadowy, dialect is still spoken—by those who know how to speak it. But it is also a gray and purely informative dialect, remodeled on the language. It is little more than a pronunciation. It has lost all its expressiveness, and the words of the dialect have fallen from its withered branches like dry leaves. If one of those old brothers—who lived there until a few years ago and have been robbed xxx of their place—could, by a whim of history, reappear and speak in his own language, he could be understood only with the help of vocabulary furnished by a special glossary of slang. But the majority of those who stand on that shadowy sidewalk no longer know how to speak, *sic et simpliciter*. They whine, they push and shove, they make guttural sounds; if they must express wonder, they give an exaggeratedly loud, skillfully exhibitionist shout (imitating a sheep, a hen, a dog \beasts, which they specialize in\); if they have to express joy, they raise their voices in harsh, vulgar guffaws that end in a snort or an epileptic's wheeze, which inspires not pity but horror.

---

[40] ". . . everything sacred is desecrated [by the bourgeoisie] and men are finally forced to consider with eyes free from illusion their position in life, their mutual relations." K. Marx, *Manifesto, etc.* (1848).

NOTE 72G
The Shit (End of the Vision)

The Gods, with as much care as the good Virgil, are already explaining to Carlo the meaning of the Bolgia whose turn it is (and from which comes a noise that—it can truly be said—is infernal), and anticipating the present Inferno as it will continue after the fifth Bolgia, beyond a ditch that, /stinking of shit/, cuts Torpignattara in two—when The Shit suddenly stops.

He is at the corner of the Street that must be Bolgia V, though the sign with its name still isn't visible; rather, lines of vehicles are glimpsed, cars and motorcycles, all running, with the mufflers xxx, and around them awful, helmeted motorcycle racers. But certainly The Shit doesn't see any of this. His eyes are clouded, almost rolled back in his head, in fact, so that the white is visible; a deathly pallor covers his face, and a /patina/ of icy sweat. The pain in the arm with which he embraces his woman and supports her like a sack must be unbearable by now. He tries to smile with a patient and indifferent air; but then, instead, /abruptly/, he yields. A grimace of inhuman pain < ... > flickers on his face, the arm falls off the girl's shoulder but remains stiff, and The Shit, fainting, "falls as a dead body falls."[41]

---

[41]At the time at which the events of the present novel take place, the "couple" is cursed rather than blessed. And increasingly so the more it is adulated, publicized, imposed through so-called sexual permissiveness. But its evident insincerity reveals without any shadow of a doubt that it is criminal. In fact, in the past every child born to that couple contributed to the majority of the living over the dead, that is, it was a necessary good; today it is a real crime against humanity, which is threatened by excessive population increase and therefore by hunger and by the devaluation of the individual.

NOTE 73
Grand finale of the Vision

As The Shit fell to the ground, the Chariot rose. The earth appeared to collapse under Carlo's feet; Via di Torpignattara stretched dizzily to infinity; in the opposite direction, in the background, Via Casilina appeared and, behind it, endless masses of apartment buildings and tracts crowded with the hovels of the poor, along with vacant lots or hollows and the glinting blade of a ditch; everything was turning white and formless under a chalky sun veiled in a dirty fog.

At the front of the chariot the Gods were snickering; and they did not stop until the end of the Vision.

Sucked up in the vortex of the ascent, Carlo was breathless, terrified. And yet it was in those very moments that some thoughts on what he had just seen along the street of the Vision crossed his mind—and were engraved there forever. First /he thought/ < ... > that in all the crowds of young men and boys who populated the Gironi and Bolge of Torpignattara THERE WAS NOT A SINGLE ONE who had had toward someone or something a look, I will not say of love or sympathy, but simply of curiosity. Second, < ... > he realized that if those young men and boys had become that way, it meant that they had had the potential for it; so their degradation also debased their past, /which had therefore been completely deceptive/. Third, Carlo felt intuitively that those young men and boys would pay for their degradation with blood: in a massacre that would render their presumptuous illusion of well-being /fiercely ridiculous/.

/Still accompanied/ by the snickering Gods, the chariot reached its altitude and began to fly horizontally: clearly, it was heading for the Center of the City. Half suffocated by the dizzying flight, Carlo began to observe how, slowly, at his feet, as he approached the Center, true, well-defined shapes began to emerge from the formless mass of sky-

scrapers and ancient buildings. His eyes burning with tears, < ... >
Carlo /observed/ that all the cupolas had been reclothed in new materials and, with their anatomically perfect nipples, unequivocally assumed
the look of breasts, like trompe l'oeil. Similarly, all the squares—both
large and small—had been modified in such a way as to take the shape,
unmistakably, of enormous vaginas. Finally, all the bell towers, which
in Rome are neither many nor large, had been transformed by the same
device into a series of penises of all dimensions. When the Chariot was
at its zenith, above the Center, and had stopped, the whole city could be
comprehended in a single glance: it had the shape—again unequivocally—of an immense Swastika.

↑

Carlo's thoughts (the three points in the visions) are first expressed during
the movement of the cart toward the boundary of the infernal Zone. Here is
the little monument described in Notes 74–74a—with the annotation "in order to laugh."

It is beside this monument, which is a kind of boundary stone or tabernacle
(that is, it marks the boundary of the Inferno), that The Shit faints and falls.

NOTE 74
Last flash of the Vision†

In spite of the almost pyrotechnic finale, the Vision was not to end
there. There was evidently still something left to be expressed, although, as we will see, it was somewhat ambiguous.

/My usual honesty forces me to avoid the rules of ambiguity—which
I should rigorously hold myself to—and warn the reader that what's
left of the Vision also has a metalinguistic significance:/ its meaning is
valid for the "Mysterion," at the exact moment when it's presented, but
is also valid for the general plan of the author's intentions (and no less
ambiguously than in the story).

When Carlo timidly took leave of the men who were chatting under the arches of the Colosseum (and who were not even aware of him or the timid farewell that he risked giving them), the night was already advanced. It still seemed like the middle of winter, though the wind that was blowing was not a north wind but a damp sirocco. Everything was deserted. The wind seemed to have swept away not only the paper and the unimaginable garbage that had collected on the pavement—there was still a bit of straw—but also the men and their phantom selves.

In any case, a tram passed, noisy, lights on, and completely empty. Carlo ran after it and reached it at a stop in front of the lowered shutters of a couple of bars and a newsstand. He was just in time to observe that on the other side of the Colosseum two or three boys were sitting on the fence that kept people from entering the arches. But they were distant shadows and were soon left behind with their /secret intentions/. The tram brought Carlo to the station, and there he waited a long time for another tram to take him to where he lived, that is, Tuscolano in the direction of Cinecittà: to be precise, the Quadraro. His house was far from the tram stop; thus he had to go some way on foot through the deserted windswept streets.

The Quadraro was an old, poor neighborhood consisting of houses build by their owners with their own hands and decrepit two- or three-story apartment houses. There was no stucco, or it was old, flaking. And the sidewalks were little more than dirt tracks beside the houses, separated by an irregular stone border from the chipped asphalt of the streets.

Between the houses were empty lots, untidily taken up by gardens or open sheds crammed with stakes, metal roofing, and piles of equipment abandoned on the hard, foul-smelling ground. The old shutters on the windows were all closed, as were the doors in the crumbling entranceways and the shop gates. Only the streetlights spread their < ... > yellowish and deathlike illumination.

The house that Carlo had rented was, as we have seen, one of those run-down semilegal houses on a street parallel to the main street of the Quadraro, which ran along a railway line; beyond the railway rose the barrier of the seventeenth-century walls of the Mandrione. To reach his street, Carlo had to make a detour through an alley lined with little gardens and warehouses that at a certain point widened into a sort of circular space that looked like a village square (in the distance, punctuated by faint lights, loomed the new apartment buildings of Cinecittà). He was just passing through that wide part, almost at his house—where the bed with the horsehair mattress and the shabby furniture of rooms poorer than a worker's awaited him—when the last Scene of the Vision, detached, appeared to him.

Suddenly the wind fell. In the distance, with a mournful gasp, the whistle of a train sighed, and for a few moments the crying of a newborn could be heard. < ... >

The cottages all around suddenly seemed to break apart and collapse; and above them the sky, thick with stars but moonless, seemed to become more present, intense, luminous; as it is in the desert.

In place of those houses appeared an enormous tabernacle. The pedestal was of brick, and it, too, had been eaten away by time, the way things are in dreams: the bricks were of rustic manufacture, small and red; but the Tabernacle was of wood: four tall, very slender wooden columns, worm-eaten, almost rotted, held up a roof, which was also very rustic but, at the same time, precious, as the entrance to the court-yard of an Oriental palace might be. Its tiles—which could be seen above an elegant architrave carved with little figures and eaves of lead—were black, and they, too, were much xxx by time.

This Tabernacle—whose shape, however, was quite imprecise and dissolved in the sparkling sky—held a large image of a different material: *nefra* or *tumo* (?). The dimensions of that image could not be called gigantic; yet it was grand: three times as tall as a man of normal height. To say that it represented a woman would be inexact, though this was the first impression. /It was/, rather, a monstrous woman, consisting of two stocky legs, and between them, in place of the groin, a huge woman's head was embedded—so that the crack of the vulva coincided with the break in the chin. The hair was arranged like a peasant's, but for a holiday: it was bound by two circlets (one could not distinguish if they were of metal or cloth); so that one part formed a crown over the forehead and one part formed a kind of chignon in the middle of the head. This monstrous woman, moreover, held in her right hand a long stick, as tall as she was; and this stick was, without any possibility of doubt, a long, knotty penis.

In front of that enormous image of dark, porous *tumo,* which blended in with the starry sky behind it, there was a small crowd: distracted or indifferent; yet serious and almost dismayed; in any case, it was—how to put it?—a crowd of dead people, who no longer now had any interest in or curiosity about anything that might appear before them or happen to them in that nocturnal place abandoned by the present world.

The image rested its feet on a kind of high step of *nefro* (?); and, on the vertical part of that step, there was an inscription.

Carlo approached and read the following words: "I have erected this statue in order to laugh."

NOTE 74A
Gloss

I repeat: this inscription is not merely the inscription on the monument that at this moment of the "Mysterion" is of importance and interest. Besides this, it: A) predicts or prefigures a "mystical" act that will occur at the end of this novel: which will be a resolving, vital, completely positive and orgiastic act, and will reestablish the serenity of life and make the course of history resume; B) is placed as an epigraph for this entire work (the "monumentum" par excellence); but its meaning here is diametrically opposed to the one noted above: it is in fact mocking, sarcastic, delusory (but no less sacred on that account!).

"I HAVE ERECTED THIS STATUE IN ORDER TO LAUGH"

I want to add that the "laugh" I allude to—in this archeological citation—has its explanation in a long tradition of mystery cults, which binds it to *apórreta simbola:* real or artificial, like the *olisbos* (the stick used in female onanism); or even mixed, like those of Bacchus—*"Eleleu kore dímorfe!,"* in spite of Aristotle's moralism (which comes quite a bit later, anyway).[42] Moreover, it's well known that one function of the

---

[42] Aristotle made a recommendation to the magistrates, advising them to promulgate laws against obscene language (*"aiskrologhian . . . ospe ti allo"*), against obscene sculpture, painting, mimicry.

"laugh"[43] is to resolve cosmic crises, if it's caused by the display of the "member" or the "vulva."

Furthermore, to cut it short < ... > : "Besides, I sometimes make you laugh, and that is truly precious."

—Insert in the groups of the various Gironi and the various Bolge of the Vision some twenty boys from the Field of Via Casilina, completely transformed and depraved (a little older now, of course)

—Organize the various visions of the Gironi and the Bolge with *episodes* and *situations* that are more narrative and concrete

(16 Oct. 1974)

NOTE 81
Getting f———d

/The Italian bourgeoisie is divided into two categories; one is a majority, a huge majority; the other a tiny minority. Six percent (the statistics say) read a book every so often; the number of those who read regularly, that is, who can be defined as cultured, must therefore be

---

[43] I mean that when the meaning of life changes, it naturally follows the pattern of a cosmic crisis. It is pointless to say that the characters seen by Carlo in his Vision do not know that the crisis they are experiencing is a cosmic crisis, consisting of the passage from the natural "Cycle" of the seasons to the industrial "Cycle" of production and consumption. The first was slow and common to all the members of a community: the grain was sown, the grain was harvested, the grain was processed, the grain was eaten. The second is purely abstract and diachronic. Thus it has no dates, rites, recurrences. Every different product has its own different and, moreover, rapid cycle. Every product requires its own recurring ritual, but according to a rhythm really so decentralized and pluralistic as to be inconceivable. As a further result, "initiations" have disappeared. Children are immediately educated in general to imitate "patterns": they enter society already initiated. Therefore the laugh, among other things, has lost all its revitalizing holiness. So it's not surprising if the characters of Carlo's Vision have, first of all, unlearned to laugh.

around two percent; but among them are the traditionalists, the university officials, etc.; the conclusion is that the real intelligentsia constitutes only one percent of the Italian bourgeoisie!/

In theory, this last should be clearly separated from the society in the midst of which it operates. In reality, it is not.

Many of those belonging to this intelligentsia are in fact conservatives or moderates, who, it's true, take on the role of contradiction—rather, of simple class opposition—to the world as it is. Culture is above all rationality and a critical spirit. But the bourgeoisie is critical and rational as well. And since the practical world includes culture (the application of science, social organization, production, consumption), one cannot say that the culture of the bourgeoisie is not critical and rational in its actions.

The real intelligentsia, which truly contradicts the bourgeoisie and truly is opposed to it, is thus even more limited: a few thousand people scattered in a hundred little (very open) ghettoes here and there throughout the country, in Milan, in Turin, in Rome, and, to a lesser extent, in various provincial cities. If a conservative or moderate opposition, with its necessarily critical and rational characteristics, is in reality not distinguishable—except by its theoretically greater goodwill—from bourgeois society, in what way is a progressive and revolutionary opposition /distinguishable/ from it? Briefly, I would respond: the revolutionary intelligentsia is distinguishable from the enlightened intelligentsia by its wish to put itself outside the bourgeois universe (whose values have autonomous variations) in order to become part of an uncreated, merely projected universe that prefigures a democratic workers' society. That puts it in a state of perennial, /biological/ ambiguity. Its members live everywhere: in the real world—this bourgeois world—and in the ideal world, still to be established, in opposition to the real world, and presupposing its destruction.

In short, what /I meant/ is this: the more advanced intelligentsia is gratified by a clandestine Frondeur spirit that allows it to be separate both from the rest of the moderate (and therefore Fascist!) intelligentsia and from the enormous repellent body of the bourgeoisie, which is simply Fascist. The primary sensation of this intelligentsia is of being in the right. And in fact there's no doubt that it is. This sensation it has of being in the right, however, is accompanied by habits contracted precisely by its having originated in the bourgeois world, from which it then separated itself.

First of all, for example, moralism, in both its highest and most banal expressions (not for nothing has the plan of "free love" been completely abolished in Communist society).

Moralism creates choices, canons; that is, a conformity that unfortunately does not have rules (because theoretically it rejects them) but is not for that reason any less rigid.

In reality its rules could be written; its rites described. It is enough to participate in a cultural meeting of men of the left, one of the groups of the so-called intelligentsia: the choice of names, of books, of sympathies, of what is approved and what is condemned is all perfectly predictable, /from top to bottom/.

A work of culture—chosen to represent the spirit of that minority and to benefit from a curiously uncritical "enjoyment"—is defended with the same formal passion and the same hopeless conventionality with which a mediocre work is defended at the lower or even the lowest level of official culture.

Our protagonist, Carlo, is a man who has experienced all the gradations of being bourgeois: since potentially he has always aimed at belonging to a higher grade. And not formally but in reality. The good bourgeois family of Turin into which he was born and in which he grew up belonged to the enormous bourgeois majority: industrialist grandfather—as we have seen—professional father, etc.; farmland, industry, and professions on the maternal side as well, etc. Thus that bourgeois world contained—in spite of its profound, perfect nature—the potential for self-criticism, made in the name of developing its own critical and purely practical rational spirit.

Thus Carlo, growing up, < ... > automatically became part of the intelligentsia that I have called enlightened; triumphantly he entered the leadership minority of the élite, which has, besides a pragmatic knowledge of power, an ethical one; and which, precisely by means of a critical attitude toward it, /preserves < ... > it/, masking its violence.

Finally, that élite could not but potentially contain, in its turn, as we have seen, the higher élite, more progressive and indeed revolutionary;

because the critical spirit, once set in motion, cannot be stopped (except by an artificial act of will).

Thus Carlo *also* belonged potentially to the second, higher-level élite, the progressive and revolutionary one. And if he did not in fact belong to it (because that artificial act of will, certainly unconsciously, had intervened), *certainly he was acquainted with it.*

All that made him a bourgeois profoundly tied to the bourgeoisie and in fact destined for power; but it made him, at the same time, a man who would contribute to the bourgeoisie and its power a radical criticism (with the attached knowledge); and, moreover, guaranteed it a kind of opening toward the extreme left, without which a modern power is not even conceivable. This "perfection" of Carlo's, which was also reflected in his physical appearance (the stunning white hair cut short but not too short, its pure whiteness framing an /athlete's tanned/ healthy face; the vaguely imploring and slightly intoxicated softness of the blue eyes, which the habit of power from time to time hardened to a metallic gray), this "perfection" of Carlo's—his being a man of power without illusions; that is, without the innocence of the practical man, who has an ancient, infantile idea of power—would save him from even the least impurity of existence: guaranteeing him the absolute irreproachableness of the tolerant man. < ... >

NOTE 82
No longer getting f——d

Meanwhile, the other Carlo, the Carlo of Tetis, felt decisively, < ... > one morning < ... > in that < ... > same spring of 1973, < ... > that he had reached the end of the experience. It was upon waking up. The sun was already high. Carlo the Poor Man did not lead the existence of poor men, and < ... > he slept late, because, in order to be with the poor, he kept very late nights. He returned to his room not yet tired and therefore not yet happy, at the time of night when there is no longer anyone

on the streets, just before the reappearance of people who are going to
work. At that hour the darkness is melancholy, and it is a universal
melancholy, even stronger if the air is clear, if distant outlines of other
parts of the city can be distinguished, with their useless lights, or the
outlines of the hills; /< ... > or if by chance a scent of lime trees or
wisteria lingers after the wind has fallen, < ... > motionless on the dry
sidewalks, on the trampled earth; and < ... > (from the bushes on the
embankment of a railway line or in the middle of an excavation where
no structure has ever risen) a nightingale sings, as if exhumed, yet
strangely intact./

That May 21 was above all a /particular/ day; the light was very intense, but the sky was cloudy, close, white. The sun leaked through that
fog like a whiter circle. It was years and years since dust had been seen
on the streets. Now there it was. Swirled by a gusty wind, it obscured
the ends of the streets, the squares, the open spaces of construction sites;
one seemed to be on the outskirts of an Arab city, near the desert, where
the sand is transformed into a foul, tormenting dust. Even near the Central Station, where Carlo arrived after an hour of traveling on the trams
from the periphery, that absurd barrier of dust hung suspended. It was
a time of poverty, life was stripped to the bone. The traffic continued,
spectrally, but the streets around the station were almost empty. It was
there, in those streets, that everything had begun, on a rainy evening in
1969. Carlo remembered it with the precision of one who has the memory of a poet. Had he been right? Of course he had been right. What
man has the greatest claim to is vacation, evasion, disappearance, solitude. The womb that had produced the last fruits of beauty was rotten.
Look there, two idiots, one with shoulder-length hair, the other with
hair bound behind his neck with a string. They were old, they no longer
interested anyone, they wandered around like survivors. But their story
would slowly end, and a new one would begin, just as slowly, with cor-
ruptions, confusions, regressions, and advances. The fact is that for
Carlo May 21, 1973, a day chosen by chance, marked the end of one
epoch and the beginning of another. Carlo arrived at his house on that
street in the Parioli that the author finds it repellent to describe or even
to name, "guided" by a new spirit in which absolute novelty, that is, a
superficial regard for the world, and a very old feeling of return and sur-

render curiously coincided. Wisdom is probably inevitable and inevitably leads to understanding and forgiveness. But the superficiality of this wisdom disfigures and nullifies it; and understanding and forgiveness end up becoming a game.

The house in the Parioli was empty, the Carlo who had lived there was no longer present; all, however, was in order. It appeared that the change of shift had been foreseen: one returns and the other leaves. The same reasons that recall one expel the other. But if returning meant accepting a negative and degrading situation, leaving did not then mean rejecting it: on the contrary. The reader correctly sees in this a false symmetry. The one who had returned returned from an illusion and accepted a reality that was in turn an illusion for the one who had gone away. Objectively, the first illusion was extremely positive; the second was, with its fascination, a fault. But what was terrible about accepting it became almost innocent in enduring it. A saint accepted it, a guilty person endured it. But evidently an exchange of attributes could not occur; the saint (so to speak) remained a saint and the guilty person guilty. History, once it has determined the facts, can perhaps contradict them, but it cannot change them; it is powerless with its laws and its original decisions, like Allah.

NOTE 82
Third fundamental moment of the poem

Having crossed the garden of the Vision, Carlo enters his empty, abandoned apartment. He feels in his chest a lightness /that does not make/ sense and in his belly a weight that similarly does not make sense. He goes to his room and, in front of the mirror, undresses. In fact, he no longer has breasts, and below his belly hangs the male sex organ.

He dresses again and telephones a clinic not far from his house, near Piazzale delle Muse; he makes the necessary arrangements to be hospitalized the same evening. There would be no need of the head doctor;

any novice would do; in fact, the operation Carlo has decided to undergo is among the most ancient and simple: castration. Freedom is well worth a couple of balls:

> *My life is sweet today,*
> *I know no reason why;*
> *from me has been lifted*
> *what weight I cannot say . . .*[44]

NOTE 84
The game

There are people who have believed in nothing since their birth. That does not remove the fact that those people act, make something of their life, are busy with something, produce something. Other people have, instead, the vice of believing: duties become concrete before their eyes as ideals to be realized.

If, one fine day, they no longer believe—or perhaps gradually, because of a logical, or even illogical, series of disappointments—you see how they rediscover that "nothingness" which for others has always been so natural.

For them, however, the discovery of "nothingness" is a novelty that involves other things; it involves, that is, not only /the continuation/ of action, of intervention, of industriousness (understood no longer as Duties but as gratuitous acts) but also the exhilarating sensation that all this is only a game.[45]

---

[44] *Translator's note:* Guido Gozzano, "Una Risorta."

[45] "O Menippus, Diogenes exhorts you, if you've laughed enough at the things of the earth, come here, where you will laugh even more. Where you are, laughter always had a certain doubtfulness, that doubt being: who really knows what's after life? but here you won't stop laughing with all your heart . . . " (Lucian, *Dialogues of the Dead*).

It's clear that I don't mean those who discover philosophical, cosmic "nothingness." In that case it would be a matter of a conversion, entirely consistent with their preceding illusions and beliefs, and would cause a cutting off from everything; withdrawal from the world; asceticism. No: I am speaking of those who, one fine day, adding things up, come to the conclusion that they have discovered social "nothingness." They do not, then, withdraw from the world; rather, they participate more intensely; and the more intensely, the more in bad faith, necessitated by the lack of alternatives and understood as parody. They are not ascetics; but are interested in a social world reduced to nothing and rebuilt on pragmatism, on the autonomous value of virtue: which is extremely exhilarating indeed.[46]

To identify the social world with nothingness and to be stimulated and revitalized by this; to believe no longer in the values of a world annihilated by a critical and humorous spirit that no fact or argument can resist and, as a result of this, to apply oneself with greater certainty and skill to the practical realization of those values—all this implies, fatally, a regression, a conservative or moderate reacceptance of society— assuming naturally that, *before,* the protagonist of this experience was in some way a revolutionary or a rebel (precisely like Carlo the Meek). But what is the meaning of this return to order? Can it be redefined in the classical terms that are used for the purpose? The state of the soul of one who has this experience of the world—understood ultimately as nothing and accepted again in practice, with enlightened patience—is derisiveness.

Someone who mocks a part of the social world—let's say the conformist bourgeoisie, which, understanding nothing, passes from one phase to another, from peace to war, from /prosperity to massacre/, from the habitual to total < ... > /annihilation/—cannot help at the same time mocking /those who know/ this. Mockery can involve only the whole, entire reality.

And in fact it is the whole, entire reality that—the very moment it is mocked—is accepted again. Reality is not divided into, on the one hand, /conformist society/, which follows the evolution of capitalism,

[46] It is from an experience of that kind that the author got the inspiration for this novel.

and, on the other, those who oppose it through class struggle; reality includes and integrates both these parts, because reality itself is not Manichean, does not have interruptions. The mocking view of it succeeds in reconciling the /integration/ inevitable in order and, at the same time, the most radical and revolutionary criticism. Ultimately it resembles the mechanical gesture of a worker: which is both a gesture in the production he contributes to as ordered < ... > and a gesture charged with revolutionary threat; the ambivalence of this gesture therefore includes all of reality. A bourgeois will never make such a gesture. But the bourgeois can arrive at a point where he accepts social reality as "nothingness" and identifies life with mocking that reality. This mockery is the equivalent of the worker's mechanical gesture; it includes the integration but deprives it of any meaning.

Every preconceived idea of the future < ... >, however < ... >, succumbs to derision; in fact, if there is one thing that causes us to smile inside with greater pleasure, it is precisely the future. The idea of hope for the future becomes irresistibly comic. The resulting lucidity strips the world of fascination. But the return to it is a form of rebirth; the eye of irony sparkles as it looks at events, at men, at the old imbeciles in power, the young men who believe they are beginning heaven knows what.[47] The terrible wound they have inflicted has healed and formed a scar; now they have among them a new collaborator and friend, who is deeply, and with strange lucidity, interested in their problems and helps solve them without too much fuss; they do not know that in his amused gaze they vanish like /scattered phantoms/. (All this, at any rate, with reference to Carlo the Meek, in that May of 1973.)

Notes 90 and foll.

90 Carlo the First in Pisa.

91 Carlo the First in Turin.†
    The twenty, etc., Fascist spirits (Pensione Sicilia?)

[47] "Tell him this: and further, thar he should carry a knapsack containing plenty of lupines/ a lustral egg, and any other little things he finds at a crossroads or from a meal dedicated to Hecate" (Lucian, *Dialogues of the Dead*).

92 they drive to the slaughter: explosion at the station in Turin. Seen as a VISION:
93 the victims seen and analyzed as if it were a matter of living persons in all
94 their wretchedness, stupidity, vulgarity.

95 At the end of the Vision, the Turin station appears isolated in the middle of the world. Through the gaping holes of the explosion one sees the emptiness all around (like the sea or desert). The desert is the wild plain of the Po—in dying it has returned to its origins—Carlo goes out and walks through that desert. Until he reaches present-day Turin (Auden poem).

96 There is a neo-Fascist demonstration. Page of civil poetry. The neo-Fascists appear for what they are: passed over by the history of power. Passed over with them is anyone bound to them by a love-hate relationship (the "fascination" that no one ever expresses and the tradition of the Resistance).
Faced with the knowledge of the Fascist loss and with the new form of power that organizes in a new way not only society but existence, Carlo feels out of the game, in another game.

97 He returns home: he has become a man again.†

98 Choice of sanctity. Ascetic-pragmatic sanctity. Frivolity and industriousness. Ironic indifference and painful impatience. Help for others as if in a dream and withdrawal into the enlightenment that generates and regenerates the idea of nothingness, etc.‡

August 1973

NOTE 100
The Epoche§

NOTE 97 †
The narrators

Carlo made his entrance into the xxx Room around four in the afternoon. He was not the only "powerful" personage to resign himself to
this official celebration, the /goal/ of arrivistes, snobs, secondary figures,
functionaries, and bureaucrats (with their wives). And he was not the
only one to put a good face on bad luck. Drawn up like a fierce beast but
expansive and smiling, as if giving benedictions, like a priest—and
making of the silence a weapon of defense and at the same time the motionless banner of his power—he parted the crowd of his fellow citizens
who were celebrating the Festival of the Republic, unhurried, as if they
all might be, why not?, casual acquaintances of his in the circumstances. In reality he was looking for his equals. Over there, /the un-
moved mover/ was Saragat. But Carlo could and should take his place in
the tighter circle of the Rose

xxxxxxxxx

xxxxx

xxxxxxxxx

Meanwhile, as soon as he entered, pure chaos surrounded him. The
frenetic milling of the "nobodies," those who lead exposed lives, the
usual. The Chichikovs, the Peredonovs, the titular councillors /(which
is the third from the bottom of the fourteen ranks of the tsarist hierarchy)/, like Jakov Petrovich Golyadkin, or even servants, like
Smerdyakov—as my "literal" writing allows me < ... > to say. And also
some literary men. Here Carlo Valletti has to pay the price of democracy. In the eyes of the bystanders shines the demand, unsatisfied. Nor
does he avoid it. But *"fata trahunt."* The main point of the delegation is
"to represent them all" (Hobbes, I think). Besides, "democracy does
not have monuments, does not strike medals. Does not put any-

one's head on the money. Its true essence is iconoclastic" (also Hobbes, *Leviathan* . . . or Locke, *A Treatise on Government*). And, besides, even in democracy the "holy game of kings" continues, and the ceremonial life of royalty has spread throughout bourgeois etiquette . . .

Reaching the Empyrean, one sees a different type of milling. There one is among the actors, not the spectators. There "one does not remove the soul from its own body to put it in a peaceful place for safekeeping" (as Frazer declares about some primitive subjects, adding: "If they discovered a totally safe place, they would be happy to leave their souls there forever"). There—it's better to clumsily repeat it—one is among the actors: with whom the spectators[48] identify bodily, poor things; it is "methexis for them," not "mimesis." As for the actors, they display their whole person as if it were a penis; but exhibitionism, as everyone knows, indicates castration. Thus the heads of Medusas were "cut off." And it was for that reason that they turned everything to stone. Carlo went among the petrifiers to assume his role: to be an exhibitionist, to show off his genitals (in a living theater of mediocrities). Being not at all discouraged by the inauthenticity of the literal interpretation, /I would add, in a commentary no less serious than all the preceding ones, that if the genitals of the "powerful" (the castrated) were displayed, something else remained hidden; but if each one had a secret, it was a secret to all, but not to the SID: and I know the reader will shudder at the metaphoric poverty of that note, in fact—I admit—at its pitiful nudity./ In concentric circles around the Head of State, the mass of worms was an agitation of little heads, some bald, some white, some thick, some thin; but all utterly dignified. They are destined to attain, in the Allegory, the *real* dignity of narrators. But for now they are "realistically" elect souls who weave at the Quirinal Palace a chant that will make the reader's head spin; still, I will not, for that reason, spare myself a description of it, < ... > after all, at a certain point every epic poet feels the duty to describe, to list, the catalogue of the armies. It is apparently an unavoidable topos. The first whom Carlo casually encountered was Mancini; his massive, immobile face was a /funerary stele/ reflecting what was pressuring him at that moment; he was in fact

---

[48] At least according to Lévy-Bruhl, Durkheim, and others.

very interested in the "restructuring of ENI" and in three soon-to-be-created financial groups within ENI that would assume control of ENI's various production sectors < ... >. He would then want < ... > at least one of the presidencies to go to a Socialist Party member but would not be opposed in that case to putting Professor Valletti—that is, our hero—in the job and in that case replacing him in his present position with another Socialist.

And so Professor Valletti paused there, in that little group, making it the center of his observation.

Nearby was De Martino, along with Raffaele Girotti and some of their Neapolitan friends. De Martino was speaking to these Neapolitan friends in a very low voice, confidentially. But it was not difficult for Professor Valletti to guess the theme of that colloquy. Surely De Martino was complaining that ENI, at the moment, not only was not helping him but was doing its best to thwart his victory at the Socialist Party congress. He declared that some journalists with ties to ENI had been invited to attack him. But he was careful about making such declarations because (as Professor Valletti well knew) he was not sure if those directives had come from Girotti himself or from some other "despot of the group."

Another Socialist: Enrico Manca. He was silent, tough and vindictive. A few days before, at a Party meeting, he had accused ENI of failing to keep promises made during the electoral campaign in Umbria—promises used to get votes away from the Christian Democrats. Manca claimed that Engineer Girotti had failed to undertake the construction of a new Lebole factory which was to compensate for the closing of the jute factory, and the new factory for producing plastic pipe. Engineer Girotti would not only have closed the jute factory in Terni but would also have decided to close the factory in Papigno, which employed 540 workers. Nothing was known, according to Manca, of Terni Chemical's plans, since it, too, had moved to the ENI group. In contrast to Manca's "defeated but vengeful" look, the Honorable Danilo De Cocci had a jubilant, if restrained, expression in his gray southerner's eyes. In fact, he was seeking in Roman circles confidential information on the contacts between ENI and representatives of the various factions of the Christian Democrats. According to De Cocci, not one but all of the Christian Democratic factions were getting funds from ENI, IRI, etc. No one knew why the member of parliament "was carrying out his investigation." That was the reason for his look of satisfaction.

Beside De Cocci was Ricucci. Vincenzo Ricucci was silent. He was director general of the Italian Pipeline Company (part of ENI); and he had recently decided to finance the current precongressional campaign of the Nenni faction of the Socialist Party in Civitavecchia (in view of the future ENI refinery). Mancini every so often glanced at him. He couldn't help it. In fact, he was trying to ascertain if the subsidy Ricucci had decided on was his own personal initiative or the wider initiative of "a direct interest" of ENI.

As this point, I must in all honesty[49] warn the average reader that if he wants to, he can skip, so to speak, over all these pages and go on to the next Note. Although this report on one of the many hot spots of humble Italy is very diligent, it's not essential to our Allegory; it can be of interest only to a reader who is either endowed with a deep civic sentiment or particularly malicious.

Since it was the Festival of the Republic, the Communists could not be absent. There was a delegation of them, though they appeared to be looking out for their own interests, dissociating themselves from their immediate surroundings with a look as decisive as it was affable. Moreover, they were from the top rank. In fact, there was Berlinguer himself, with his "honest face": quite relaxed and even a little ironic at the moment. That same morning—with good prospects of immediate and satisfying results—he had ordered the Party's press office to examine all the issues of the weekly *Il Borghese* published since January 1, 1970, and to list the notes and articles favoring ENI and all the ads for ENI and Montedison that had appeared in the pages of the periodical. Beside him, and no less respectable in his entire person, was a minor Party figure, Eugenio Peggio. A member of the economic committee of the Communist federation of Florence, he had undertaken the job of checking and reporting on the "real estate" maneuvers of ENI in the Prato area, above all ENI's acquisition of a ten-hectare lot and the upcoming

---

[49] One should be suspicious of this honesty, precisely because it is sincere.

sale of another lot, on which at present stood a textile factory belonging to the ENI group. Meanwhile, De Martino had approached the circle of Communists, shaking hands with friends and colleagues. Professor Valletti (even with his frozen heart) knew what was behind that cordiality. At a recent Party meeting, De Martino had announced that he was against the government's granting Dr. Cefis's requests. According to De Martino—it appeared—Montedison would have to give up its chemical business, leaving the field entirely to ENI and the other companies "active in that sector." Moreover, at the same time a certain Engineer Nino Rovelli, of the SIR group, had poured "conspicuous" financial aid into the precongressional campaign of the Honorable De Martino's faction in Campania.

All that was well known to Professor Carlo Valletti—and is of direct interest to us—because he was aware that the goal of Alberto Grandi, who had left ENI a short time before to go to Montedison, was to get from Dr. Cefis the job of managing director of Montedison. This opened up for Carlo the possibility of gaining greater power in ENI; especially since he knew that it was ENI, rather than Montedison, that Dr. Cefis continued to hold dear.

Dr. Cefis, who, naturally, was not present at that ceremony <...>, could best offer inspiration for episodes from the life of Zadig or Candide.

/xxxxx—(Greek lines from the catalogue of ships from the *Iliad*
    —or Latin from the *Aeneid*)/

There was /also/ a group around La Malfa, the most numerous and at the same time the most élite.

Beside La Malfa, meanwhile, was Professor Tiziano Federighi, a member of the Party federation and an official of Montedison, who a little earlier had handed over to La Malfa a long, confidential report on the internal problems of the Company (Montedison). La Malfa, however, was instead busy "chatting" with the Honorable Francesco Compagna about the parade of the Bersaglieri: it was to him, in fact, that he intended to entrust the task of asking Jean Louis Lehemann for financial help from Mobil Oil Italy for the Republican Party's electoral campaign. He had high, well-founded hopes. It might even be that La Malfa would be able to give Mobil Oil the guarantees that Ferri had given, regarding him, to Shell; Ferri had, in fact, the very morning of that burning July 2, assured Norman Bain—who on behalf of the "mother house" was asking for information on the orientation of the government's politics with respect to the oil companies after the implementation of the value-added tax—that the present government did not intend to let any tax increase fall on the oil companies (there he is, the Honorable Ferri, his pale, tormented face covered by a layer of sweat).

And there, as if bound to the two by a thin "electoral affinity," was the fair-haired Honorable Mario Zagari, with a glass of whiskey in his hand (although he was abstemious). He had just started a new press agency, called the Socialist Agency, in Via Colonna Antonina, and entrusted it to one of his confidential aides, Giorgio Nardi. That Agency had been established thanks to financial support from, this time, Italian Esso. < ... >

Engineer Renato Lombardi (of Confindustria) was, on the other hand, engaged in a "direct" conversation with Dr. Alessandro Alessandri, of Standa. The two had been friends since their "high school days." Engineer Renato Lombardi was "privy to the secrets" of the Vatican; while Dr. Alessandri apparently held the same position with respect to the Agnelli family. In fact, the former was confiding not yet public information concerning a mutual friend, Vincenzo Cazzaniga.[50] The appointment of this man—already a high-ranking director of one of the companies of the Montedison group—as the new president of UCID was the best proof of the high consideration he enjoyed in Vatican circles. UCID was in fact a "creation" of Italian Catholic Action, bringing together the industry executives who were avowed Catholics.

The ecclesiastical general assistant of the Roman division was Monsignor Casaroli, who was in charge of papal diplomacy.

Thus Cazzaniga, also making use of influential Vatican support, would have greater possibilities for action. (I wish to remind the reader that we are still in 1972, and therefore the Vatican could still guarantee its authority nearly intact.)

In exchange, Alessandri could inform Lombardi that Gianni Agnelli continued to be interested in Standa and its problems, because he would

[50] He has already appeared in the course of this novel under the name of . . .

like to buy the company. And he was ready to make that acquisition and would pay for it with the Montedison shares he held.

There was Cottafavi, the former chief of staff of the Honorable Moro, just named the new ambassador from Italy to Tehran. He is "rather combative" toward the Arab-favoring politics of ENI. As a result he is tied to Attilio Monti instead, and to the oil interests of BP.

And next to him, in a brand-new double-breasted suit worn with natural elegance despite the heat, is Dr. Bozzini, former ambassador to Damascus, who is now chief of staff thanks to Senator Medici. Bozzini is no friend of ENI, either.

There is also Antonio De Bonis, an official of the Center for Italian-Arab Relations, who is charged with preparing a weekly report on ENI's international relations. He has just returned from a trip to Sicily, in company with the Syrian diplomat Hafez al-Jamali.

And there among them, too, is a certain Angelo Berti—who is part of the leadership of the Mario Fani Clubs, a political-religious organization established some years ago by Gedda. Berti is charged with maintaining contact between Professor Luigi Gedda and the industrialist Attilio Monti, who since September 1 has been paying a million lire a month to the National Civic Committee. (I insist on reminding the reader that we are in 1972.)

Impelled, perhaps, by the heat, Carlo went over to one of the windows, where presumably it was even hotter, in view of the burning ray of light that streamed from the utterly cloudless sky. There, scarcely more than outlines in the luminous dust, stood the Honorable Angelo Nicosia and the Honorable Pino Rauti. They were in good spirits, it seemed: they felt at ease. The Honorable Nicosia had met for a short time with the industrialist Monti to illustrate to him the strategy he intended to follow to bring about the appointment of a parliamentary commission of inquiry on CONI. He said he was sure that "big things" would come out, and irregularities that would hit more than one political figure. It emerged that during the conversation he had said these exact words: "For me, Giulio Andreotti and Giulio Onesti are one single person." As for the Honorable Pino Rauti, he had met a few days before with a Bruno Riffeiser. The two had discussed the progress of the judicial inquiries involving Rauti "regarding the attacks of the extreme right" and the accusations that had been made against Monti of having financed Pino Rauti's extremist movement. To judge from his easygoing expression, it seemed, as we have said, that there was nothing in the situation to worry him.

A man dressed all in white stood there, the smoke of his cigarette mingling with the dust of the ray of sun that, Caravaggio-like, broke into the reception room of the Quirinal Palace; a white cap was set above his thin face, like a tiny, aged boy's, now wrinkled as well by a grimace caused by the cigarette smoke clinging to his mouth. It was General Eugenio Henke. Behind the blinding ray of sun a dark chasm seemed to open, in which the scarlet of the hangings, poor and oppressive like everything governmental, was barely visible. Carlo crossed that blinding barrier of light and found himself in a dark, even cool, corner of the reception room, where some fortunate people had found chairs to sit on. They were eighteenth-century chairs, gilt and uncomfortable, to tell the truth, but still they were chairs; indeed, there was even a charming little sofa. These were set around a lifeless hearth (all decorated, stuccoed, gilded). But it was a peaceful corner, outside the hellish throng. There was silence. In fact, all the people sitting there were listening intently to someone who was speaking, like children listening to the old storytelling grandfather. The speaker was, in fact, telling a story, which Carlo, distracted by that unexpected scene and, above all, by the look of those guests, did not hear. They had nothing in common with all the guests described above. They seemed made of a different material. Certainly they, too, were bourgeois Italians; and men of prestige and power, since they were there. But their interests and their culture appeared to be of another quality: more innocent, more idealistic, perhaps duller, but undoubtedly /clearer and more profound/. Probably it was an illusion, because they were nothing more than literary men with their wives. And they were telling stories to pass the time at that official gathering they were obliged to disdain. As Carlo, observing amazed and rather fascinated, looked for a place to sit down among them, the narrator finished his story, apparently passing the word to someone else. This one looked like a big ant dressed as a man in tails (but probably it was some sort of sober black suit), and he lisped slightly, while his large eyes remained curiously fixed and as if liquefied by timidity. Making an effort, this new narrator began to speak with a look of being unable to avoid it but also of being accustomed to success as a witty man. It was the look of a celebrated democratic journalist.

"The narrative art, as you well know," began this narrator, "is dead. We are in mourning. Therefore, dear listeners, in the absence of wine you must content yourselves with *ciceone.*"[51]

NOTE 98
The Epoche: The story of a man and his body

"Mine is not a story but a parable," the voice of conscience began, "and since the meaning of this parable is precisely the relationship of an author to the form he creates, any introduction to what I am about to tell seems to me utterly pointless. Andrea Fago (that is, a man who eats) took, in the ordinary way, Alitalia's DC-9 departing from Rome for Cape Town on an ordinary spring afternoon last year. He was going to Cape Town on business, which has no importance for the story whose protagonist he is. I will not even say if he was tall or short, if he was dark or fair, if he was from Rome or from Milan, if he was from the lower middle class or the upper middle class, if he was an intellectual or an industrialist; I will say nothing about him, not only because it has no importance but because it would cause confusion. All right. The DC-9 took off in the ordinary way, made a wide turn above the sea at Fiumicino, and headed south. Inside the airplane people began to smoke cigarettes and drink orangeade and tea: not, as far as Fago is concerned, champagne; in fact—this time for reasons strictly functional to our story—let's imagine him sitting in the last seat in the tail of the plane. So he was not a first-class passenger. But don't make any inferences \no inferences should be made\ about this. The first stop was Cairo, where everything was normal. The airport in Cairo is the most depressing in

[51] *Translator's note:* A ritual drink of the ancient Greeks.

the world, and one becomes mortally bored there. But never mind. The two-hour stopover, which then inevitably turned out to be three, finally passed, the in-transit passengers were called, and the DC-9 took off normally for the second time. Thank God it did not have to land at Khartoum but went directly on to Kampala. So /there would have been/ a few hours of peaceful and magnificent flight, first over Egypt—the Nile becoming green with palm groves and fields of grain; the villages that were dark ocher masses—then over the Sudan with its endless southern desert, all marvelously pink. The pink color of this desert—I take the liberty of emphasizing—makes an impressive effect; /but more impressive/ still is its immensity. It extends, uninterrupted and always the same, from just after Khartoum all the way to Lake Rudolph and almost to Nairobi (in the direction of Kampala, the forests begin sooner). I do not understand why the immensity of this desert (along with its pink color) is so unknown and underrated. Not because it's important (to me or my story) but for love of the truth. In fact, it makes a greater impression than the Sahara. I do not know the Amazon (that is, I have not flown over it), but perhaps that's what the desert between Sudan and Kenya should be compared with: its idyllicness, its paradisiacal pink color. In reality (this is the point), it's not a true desert; it's a country, or indeed a little continent, made up entirely of an infinitely intricate maze of mountains and valleys without a tree (colored pink) < ... > . The sky, implacably azure, also seems vaster than elsewhere. It's a cosmic sky. And it falls almost precipitously onto the endless horizons (clouding a little with extraordinary hues between azure and pink) of that desert, where mountains and valleys never stop following one another, as if arranged by an imagination capable of every possible elaboration— the most tortuous, the most nitpicking—except that of inventing a different color, a color that is not, ultimately, a shade of that pink. What nevertheless makes that desert frightening (although not completely unpleasantly so) is, I repeat, the fact that it is not a desert but an enormous empty country, abandoned by God and by men. Well, it was right in the middle of this desert that the Alitalia DC-9 crashed. When Andrea Fago reopened his eyes and, with a happiness that I certainly do not aspire to describe, realized that he had survived, the experience was like being inside a surrealist painting. He was sitting in his seat, with the back raised and the seat belt tight across his stomach, in an upright position; in front of him was a charred, grinning skull. Andrea Fago recognized the hostess by the flirtatious little beret, which, surrealistically, had remained in place. A hundred meters farther ahead, on a ridge with well-marked striations, the DC-9 was burning: against a whimsical series of peaks, some conical, others breastlike, but curiously aligned in a perfect perspective and carved in the sugary, metallic perfection of their forms. The plane was entirely black. Only a piece of the tail had been spared by the flames. The wreckage of < ... > that looked like worthless sheet metal was painted yellow with a blue stripe; thus, at last, two different colors, as new as a material, in all that sublime pink.

"But enough joking: the preamble is over. I could begin again from here if I had not needed to establish a social relationship between my protagonist and the rest of mankind. A social relationship so well known to you that it verges on banality; and it is for this very reason that I could not speak of it without joking a little.

"However, I will repeat it to you. The true story I am telling is not this. The true story has to do with the absolute independence of laws that establish a form with respect to the laws of all other forms. Of the *continuity* that unites all the laws that more generally establish a universe (characterized by lack of interruption) there is no doubt, it is a fact. But in relation to the fact that contradicts and refutes it—that is, the break in continuity, the moment of autonomy—it disappears, at least for an 'ideal' instant. The continuity and the autonomy of a form are its contradiction. They do not coexist, cannot coexist. There is either one or the other. Contradiction is only a break in coexistence. Hegel is naturally, if divinely, mistaken. The only true infinity is the one he calls 'bad infinity' (so he knew it!). As a result, the two terms of the contradiction do not defeat each other but proceed into the infinite, exchanging the right to exist at a speed that, since it's supernatural, does not prevent two such coexisting terms from being taken into consideration alternately and therefore being isolated, each one analyzed only in itself. Exactly; our story isolates and analyzes in itself the moment of the autonomy of the form.

< ... >

"Andrea Fago observed the men coming toward him. Ancient men whom he knew very well. He looked at them—rather, recognized them—in silence. Then his mouth widened in an extraordinary smile, which lit up his eyes. That smile, enigmatic because it was too profoundly human, had its origin in the thought: the continuity between me and them, which returns from them to me, is broken: I am a form the knowledge of which is illusion."†

NOTE 98A
The Epoche: The story of the reconstruction of a story

"As he did every morning, Dr. Tomoo Tsushima, having finished his work at the hospital, went out into the city. For some months what appeared to his eyes as he left the hospital had been exactly the same; and moreover all around there, nothing ever, for any reason, seemed to have the least possibility of changing. There had been an 'end of the world' in the beginning, and this, there was no doubt, was another 'end of the world.'

"I add, almost as a preface to my story, that, furthermore, a third 'end of the world' (but this Dr. Tomoo Tsushima could not yet know) would begin in about thirty years.

"/Therefore, with almost logical symmetry, the three elements from which the end of the world could \can\ derive succeeded one another in the history of humanity in the clearest and simplest way. The three elements are: the dangerousness of nature, the dangerousness of man, and finally (and it was this that Dr. Tomoo Tsushima could not yet have knowledge of) the finiteness of nature. This last is something that seems < ... >, of course, to promise a definitive 'end of the world.' For days, for years, for centuries, nature seems brotherly toward man; that is, in reality paternal, maternal (and therefore even in its benevolence already in some way dangerous); nevertheless, in human consciousness it is felt as a brother: a dear, eternal habit. The sun rises, shines, grasses and flowers grow, animals and fish are ready to be killed and eaten; one eats, sleeps, makes love, sings, works, etc., etc. From time to time the element of definitive, moral danger 'is introduced' by the mysterious narrator of our story, through relative dangers (hurricanes, typhoons, earthquakes, plagues, wars): until the absolute danger is explicitly presented for what it is, and there we really have 'the end of the world.'

"Man, as we know, was able to survive the original 'end of the world': with skill, patience, providence; by means of his first pitiful technology. From then on, the 'dangerousness of nature,' as an element of the potential end of the world, was apparently conquered and averted./

"But look at the second element (also 'introduced' by an infinity of relative prefigurations of suicide); that is, the 'dangerousness of man.' The spectacle that appeared before the eyes of Dr. Tomoo Tsushima < ... > was there just to bear witness, frighteningly, to the probability that the dangerousness of man would bring about the 'end of the world.' There was no reason to hope, in those days, that it was not so.

"/As for the third 'end of the world,' the one that has nothing to do with this story because it was yet to come and which, as we have seen, is due to the 'finiteness of nature,' < ... > we will see. . . . / Certainly I do not envy those who are twenty today, much less their firstborn children. Dr. xxx < ... > "

Cult of the dead—reconstruction of scenes of lives—one scene is particularly interesting—from it originate visionary memories of other scenes mysteriously connected to it—through a pure leap of imagination and "visionary" capacity the doctor reconstructs the entire story of a family. It's a mystery story "about power." He is spellbound looking at a person who in turn is remembering the dead; and that makes him suspicious.

NOTE 99
The Epoche: The story of a thousand and one characters

"A premise absolutely necessary to my story is this," began the second narrator with a typical air of indifference, as if he wished to go to sleep. "Everything I'm going to tell you appeared not in the theater of the world but in the theater of my mind, took place not in the space of reality but in the space of my imagination, is finally resolved not according to the contradictory rules of the game of existence but according to the contradictory rules of the game of my reason.

"The first character and, let's say, archetype was one alone. I will call him (for my own personal reasons) the 'God of Saulo.' His oneness was /invisible/, simply because the eye was unable to embrace it all. His identity, /as a result, was mysterious/. There is no doubt that he was good, protective, regularly generous with food, heat, and sun.

"I was coming from death. And, weeping, I had just entered a marvelous Garden. Gradually, thanks to this God of Saulo, I stopped weeping and began to experience the joys of the marvelous Garden I had entered. Anyway, I had already adapted to my new condition and counted on remaining there forever. Instead, he, the God of Saulo, chased me out of there.

"It was at that moment that I became a narrator: the narrator, that is, who is telling you this story. In fact, as soon as I had stopped crying and was no longer desperate because of this second expulsion, and began to look around me for the first time, *I saw him.* he was a /pathetic monster/ (as I reconstructed it later, when /I was able/ to): a poor disgraced monster, small, completely occupied by the business of survival, eating and getting food for the others, working, sweating, waiting for his pay, saying thank you, going back to work again until late, lying down to sleep but never long enough, getting up, starting everything again from the beginning. It was as I was observing this life of his that the desire to write a Novel came over me.

"But a single person, that single one I knew, was not enough to make a story; I needed at least an antagonist. So I did what novelists in general usually do; that is, from one real person whom I knew I made two.

"I would not know how to describe to you the first person, the God of Saulo, who, I repeat, had first appeared to me as powerful and good (something between a bull and a wet nurse); then had appeared to me as hostile and punishing, chasing me away for no reason, for a fault I was ignorant of, from the Place that was as if suspended in air and where I felt so happy; and in the end /had appeared to me/ as a poor devil, both powerful and powerless, authoritarian and beneficent. In sum, I would not know how to describe such a person.

"On the other hand, I know quite well how to describe the two people into which my novelist's fantasy split him.

"The first is a man of about forty-five or fifty, small, with a thin body, but full of an energy that was more than youthful—childlike, a Neapolitan street kid's (my family is poor, southern in origin). His eyes are lively and always as if a little excited; his hair is very grizzled, almost white, but it falls over one ear and youthfully over his eyes. He has a pronounced nose and mouth (the mouth always half open in an expression that the eyes reveal as something between stunned, servile, and excited). Altogether he is a comic figure, and, as if he'd been bitten by a tarantula, he is always a little agitated. His smile is strong and happy, also like a street kid's, or rather like a xxx (because, to be precise, my family is Calabrese); and when he is serious it's unexpected, because one always expects from him an obliging cheerfulness, as from a comic mask. Nevertheless, secretly, like all southerners, in spite of his face— so obviously that of a laborer or a housepainter—he maintains his dignity and perhaps is also a little touchy and cries easily.

"The other person is a woman. She, too, is short, has short legs. But unlike the man she is plump, though she is a year or two older than he; her flesh is bursting out of the peasant dress of unbleached silk she wears on holidays. She isn't fat, but she has that youthful fleshiness, though it doesn't make her heavy. On her face, too, a kind of comic smile is always stamped, which irresistibly touches her overexpressive eyes (of a brownish red color, like the man's). Her hair is white, the nose, the mouth, the cheekbones, also pronounced, are typically southern. She, too, is something of a mask that one always expects to make one laugh or smile. . . . For example, through a kind of atavistic crudeness, or aphasia, she is unable to pronounce except in a very comical way many unusual names; not only that, but even though she has lived far from Calabria for so many years, she has learned very few Italian words; and the few that she knows how to pronounce correctly she pronounces with a refined and ceremonious air; and that causes as much laughter as when she comically mangles, let's say, < ... > the word < 'Claudio Villa' >. Yet she, too, like the man, conceals behind all this a strong sense of dignity; she is stubborn in her ideas and knows how < ... > to make her own < ... > calculations.

"Well, when I found myself with these two characters, invented and therefore objectively distinct from each other, I understood that they were in reality a single character and that, if they were antagonists, their antagonism was in reality an inner struggle.

"Precisely because they were a single character, like Don Quixote and Sancho Panza, they strained irresistibly toward their original oneness.

"In order to endure being separate, they had to represent two opposite symbols of a single reality. Even so, their opposition could only be infinitely repetitive: repeated in a series of episodes all substantially the same.

"Dividing in two a single character who had fallen within the sphere of my experience and interest had guaranteed me a drama: but a symbolic drama—that is, too heavily dominated by logic. < ... > order.

"/Who knows why/, this was not what I wanted.

"Then I repasted the two characters back into one: obtaining, however, only in rough form the by now mythic first person, the God of Saulo. By now he had been irremediably tampered with and, once reconstructed, could not help but carry marks of the historical tampering he had undergone.

"On the other hand, as Melville says: 'Fathers are not in the habit of revealing themselves completely to their sons. . . .' Above all, and with all the more reason, I would add the 'first fathers.'

"Once the figure of the God of Saulo had been reconstructed, I took it and dismembered it. As in certain so-called primitive myths—and <...> later rites—I /scattered/ here and there the limbs torn from the body, burying them like seeds in the earth. Soon those seeds sprouted; and I was surrounded by a whole crowd of people, all of whom had 'something' of that first person: 'something,' therefore, fragmentary, which they had nevertheless developed into something complete, their own. I mean that even if they were common, petty, narrow-minded, numb, maimed (like the majority of men) in that they were fragmentary, still they contained in themselves a potential wholeness that is just as mysterious and infinite as that of the 'God.'

"Now that whole crowd of characters at the disposal of my novelist's fantasy could no longer be called 'symbols.' They were random parts of a whole and had mysteriously become totalities; that is, men. They were part of reality, chaotic, they could be dominated by an organizing mind only if they were abstract and general. They were, in short, Disorder.

"They were there around me to demonstrate with extreme and incontrovertible vividness that in practice historical time never coincides with lived time.

"At this point, however, another urgent necessity presented itself. What to set against that lively disorder? If that crowd—mysterious and full of human dignity, it's true, but still unstable, empty, mad—was the protagonist, what was the antagonist?

"It was simple. I was the antagonist.

"But the moment I thought of myself as the only possible antagonist—that is, as a concept—I realized that I did not know concretely who I was. I could not embrace my wholeness, and so I was practically invisible (just like the God of Saulo earlier, you remember?); and as a result my identity became utterly mysterious.

"But my narrator's mind was terribly fertile. What did I do? From the whole that I imminently was, so to speak, inside myself, I cut out a part. I don't really know what criteria I followed in cutting it. Certainly, at least in appearance, on the surface, they were criteria of convenience: whatever gave me pleasure. At the very moment when this operation no longer seemed amusing to me, I could not go on. In the end, the figure of myself as antagonist jumped out, more or less refined and polished.

And here I am. You see me. A little southerner, northernized, ugly, small, with a prominent nose (somewhere between aquiline and snub, like certain Arabs'), the mouth fleshy and rather disgustingly red, the eyes, in enormous wrinkled pouches, too lively, the forehead balding, the hair artistically long on a collar that's not too clean. Yet something of the eternal adolescent serves as a corrective to all this and makes me almost endearing; I have a ringing laugh, a little crazy but innocent, and it wins for me the goodwill of others, especially women, with whom I am terribly unlucky but also quite lucky, < ... > that entreating look which I conceal so well in my gentle laugh, an entreating look that tends to allow me to be forgiven for my secret. Not only that, but belonging to the world of poverty and even of hunger also plays in my favor.

"All right, but this is only one part of me. < ... > In conclusion, I also brought about a split in myself, a dualism. The same that I had made in the God of Saulo. Saulo also was two. And each of his two parts ended up becoming symbolic. And, with that, giving order to the world (and readability to my possible novel).

"No, this was precisely what I didn't want.

"I didn't want this convenient, quixotic, and bourgeois duality. I didn't want the contradiction conveniently resolved by a synthesis and peaceful progress, even if 'on a spit,' along the unilinear course of the story. No, no, I repeat, the historical can never coincide with the lived, unless *we wish to lie to ourselves.*

"I took myself and dismembered myself. What I had done with the God of Saulo I did with Saulo. After reconstructing myself, I dismembered myself. I had to be all, not two. Not two 'selves' opposed to each other like light and shadow, the complete and the incomplete, the knowing and the not knowing, the unlimited and the limited, inside and outside, and so on, always defending, then, the same thing.

"From my scattered limbs another crowd was born. < ... > As I did not describe to you the crowd born from the scattered limbs of the God of Saulo, I will not describe to you the crowd born from the scattered limbs of Saulo. < ... > It would be pointless. I would merely be making a list. Look out the window and you will see < ... > the crowd born from the pulverization of the Father, the God of Saulo: the crowd that walks along the street or stands there, like a /Gordian knot/ that cannot be untied, big, small, old, young, a gas station attendant, twenty people in their cars, fifteen young men at a bar, a little supermarket with women and children, two policemen on motorcycles; the light is shadowy, it is evening, the clarity of the air is hallucinatory, the first lights are coming on, some boys burst in running, carrying joy, < ... > it's dinnertime. . . .

"If instead you wish to see the crowd born from the pulverization of the character of the son—that is, of Saulo—look around you, in here. < ... > Of course you get only an approximate idea. Things are much more orderly (planned) and confused (superiority of the plan to itself) than that.

"My novel—not 'on a spit' but 'in a swarm'—was ready. I began the first operations, that is, assembling the characters. The two opposing crowds, it is true, made up a duality. But it was a real duality, not symbolic. It was full of the mystery of its origins. I could not say, for example, that the crowd of characters born from the fragmentation of the God of Saulo was 'objectivity,' you understand. Nor, on the contrary, that the crowd of people born from the fragmentation of the person of Saulo was 'subjectivity.' Objectivity and subjectivity were constituent elements of both crowds of characters. At least as regards the individual or interior life. But it was also /the same thing socially/. Could I say that the pulverization of the God of Saulo character makes up a poor or proletarian crowd? No: because the God of Saulo was preeminently the Master. Could I say then that the pulverization of the Saulo character makes up a bourgeois crowd? No: because Saulo was by definition the Inferior. Moreover, both the God of Saulo as /Master/ and Saulo as Subordinate were poor. In short, the same confusion persists in actual class experience as in interior experience. My two crowds are the two crowds of reality: they are at the same time two and one.

"From that my next manipulation takes its meaning. Which is, as I was telling you, the mosaic-style construction of my characters, who were picked out of the swarm only to be introduced into it again. For example, there, in the pulverization of the paternal figures, is a young man with *fair* hair and *black* eyes, which are dazed and a little wild; in appearance he is a subproletarian who occasionally works as a furniture polisher. And there, in the pulverization of the filial figures, is a very thin young man, slightly hunchbacked, with *dark* hair and mildly smiling *blue* eyes; he looks like a student in whom political passion is obstructed by a vague knot of inner fears and anxieties that he conceals behind that adolescent smile of his. Well, I mix the two characters: I transform the fair hair into dark hair, the black eyes into blue eyes, I give the political passion to the young man of the underclass (thereby making of him a figure absolutely exceptional and surprising in the poetic sense of the word), and I leave to the student (who has become short and /fleshy/) his knot of fear and anxiety, with nothing in compensation, nothing to offset it (and look, another poetic < ... > character).

"Therefore, my novel, < ... > was about to take *form*. . . . Form: this is, alas, the word. That form had its own internal laws, which established it and maintained it \dedicated first to establishing it, then to maintaining it\. < ... > And all that created a new order. If the historical did not coincide with the lived, except hypocritically, you see how the lived, overwhelmingly, wished to establish itself as historical.

"For me it was the checkmate, the end of the illusion of liberty.

"I confess to you that I would have adapted, resigned myself; and that I would have continued to write my novel as freely as possible, following the philosophy of the 'lesser of evils,' if at the same time I had not become conscious, so to speak, of another fact.

"Rather, of two facts.

"The first is this. In planning and starting to write my novel, I have in effect accomplished something other than planning and writing my novel; that is, I organized in myself the meaning or function of reality; and once I organized the meaning and function of reality, I tried to master reality. To become master of it perhaps on the mildly intellectual cognitive or expressive level; but, in substance, nonetheless brutally and violently, as happens with every possession, every conquest.

"The second fact is the following. At the same time as I was planning and writing my novel—that is, looking for the meaning of reality and taking possession of it, immersed in the creative act that all of that involves—I *also* wished to free myself from myself, that is, to die. To die in my creation: to die as, in effect, one dies in birth: to die as in effect one dies, ejaculating into the mother's womb.

"In reality this mysterious desire, which, without my realizing it, had accompanied the entire intense, complex, endless labor I have described to you, slowly came to light, victorious, sketched clear and clean in my consciousness. Suddenly, all competing desires were /eliminated/. < ... >

"I left the manuscript of my novel on the table (there was already an enormous pile of notes and fragments) and set out for Calabria.

"I remembered, as in a dream, the sea, which I had seen as a child one Christmas, when my parents had taken me there; I do not know how they could have scraped together the money for that single return to their village.

"The village was really a subdivision consisting of little houses like dice, somewhat crude because of the vivid whitewashing, as in Arab towns; there was just a small, vaguely Bourbon square, like a Neapolitan crèche. It was cut into a slope among wild and desolate mountains. At the foot of these mountains ran the railroad, and behind the railroad, beyond a small stony white beach with small sharp rocks, stretched the sea.

"When I arrived, coming down from the village, it was just as I had seen it as a child. A kind of blue barrier that appeared suspended on the lighter blue of the sky. There was heat and silence. One did not even hear birds singing.

"I stripped and went into the water, walking among the stones and sharp little rocks with difficulty; I wanted to reach the point where one could no longer touch bottom, and so die.

"My decision was calm and absolute, perhaps because it had been made in some way outside myself. To die by drowning in that sea in reality neither pleased nor frightened me; it simply was the only solution that remained to me, a duty to perform without any possibility of /regret/.

"Thus I went on until my feet no longer touched, and, since I don't know how to swim, it was enough, at that point, to take a little jump forward and let myself go. So I did, and I found myself completely immersed in the water.

"What a vision of supreme beauty appeared before my eyes! The light was diffuse and at the same time full of very gentle flashes and whirls, and transparent shadows, which sketched an immense paradisiacal landscape all around. /Thus/ < ... > I was not, as I believed, a few dozen meters from the coast but really in marine abysses; the bottom that the fluctuating lights and shadows hinted at was the unexplored ocean floor. All around me it was warm and softly luminous; and breathing was wonderfully easy and light. In that immensity I went up and down, my body making slow circles, blissfully; I could not say that I was swimming, my slow darting resembled, rather, a flight without wings. . . . There, my story is all here. It—I must say—*desinit in piscem;* but though it is hallucinatory, you must not believe it is any less real."

NOTE 100
The Epoche: The story of four critics and four painters

NOTE 101
The Epoche: The story of a father and his two daughters

"Let's place our story here, on the outskirts of Rome," the narrator resumed. "In fact, we will concern ourselves with a man of the Roman, so-called black or papal, aristocracy. At the time our story begins, he was forty and had two daughters of around eighteen or twenty. They lived together (the wife had been dead for years) in a castle or family mansion in the center of a town in Alto Lazio or Etruria. At that time (ten years ago, although it seems much longer) the town was still intact. Its houses of tufa, with their thick walls and small windows, rose along dark streets that ended at a wall overlooking a bright valley. There were long, wide squares with houses that had outside staircases like an upside-down 'V,' with old cobblestone pavements and, set apart, a tiny Romanesque church—you could not imagine one more ancient—and in the background, incomplete, a < ... > gray seventeenth-century church. The mansion where our protagonist lived—we will call him, not without a touch of parody, Agostino—was also from the seventeenth century. On one side it was wedged among the houses of the town, on the other against a green bank of vines and /olive/ trees, which, just below the house, ended in a stone wall in which a 'naive' sculptor had made a fountain with mythical trompe l'oeil figures, some very small, others gigantic, and all comical. The porous tufa of which they were made, however, gave them a strange authority. An artificial provincial counter-reformism was contaminated by a popular spirit in which the myth was something real. All right. Agostino spent his days in those big rooms, well kept (even in their false disorder and decadent emptiness). He was an intellectual. He read, he studied, he received friends. < ... >

"He had been forced into that sort of exile right after the war. In fact, he had been a Fascist. It should be immediately explained, however, that his Fascism was not at all objective and, so to speak, ordinary. In fact, it was completely aberrant. It was based on the misunderstanding that it \Fascism\ was a great Right. Only when it had fallen (and that coincided with the coming of age of our hero) was it revealed to a retrospective and, at last, historical and cultured gaze as a simple /sinister/ joke. But Agostino was rich and could allow himself to live in an 'affectation,' that is, in exile, paying provocatively and with /extreme/ subtlety for his error. Besides, the world he stayed away from was also, in substance, wrong. A false democracy neither more nor less comic than Fascism. The true great Right was farther than ever from being fulfilled; in fact, it had openly declined. The Center pretended to have progressive aims, even where it was most wretchedly reactionary (Mafia, government patronage, bribes, factional struggles). But of course you know all these things better than I. Agostino loved his daughters very much, but he didn't spend much time with them, so that they had gradually become strangers with whom he played—without even hiding it too much—the scene of family affection. They had meals together, when guests came they gathered together in the living room around the hearth; all their encounters took place there. It was a friend by the name of Tertulliano (this, too, is obviously a made-up name) who warned Agostino about what was happening. This was around the late fifties. It was a matter not of real facts but of inner facts and had to do with the two girls.

"One of them, Laura, was not in fact happy with the life she led with her father in Isola Borghese. < ... > Thus, unknown to anyone, there was a crisis. It was a big thing; the land was silently caving in under their feet, and now the abyss had opened and there was nothing more to do. If it had been a matter of a life, so be it. But it was a matter, as I told you, of a performance; and above all of a performance almost entirely of gestures. Agostino had organized his own life like certain poets (I think of Gottfried Benn) who are convinced they are Nazis and make the 'gesture' of writing Nazi verses (also in Benn's case, anyway—Nazism was nothing but a refined and concise decadent consciousness). Agostino did not write poetry. But, like the majority of men, he expressed himself through his own body, his own behavior, that is, the scenic action of his own life. Saint Augustine says: 'Do not unite with words, unite with the word made flesh' *(De spiritu et littera),* recalling, evidently, Saint Paul: '. . . since it is clear that you are the epistle of Christ, drawn up by us his ministers, written not with ink, but with the spirit of the living God: not in tablets of stone but in the tablets of your fleshly heart' (II Corinthians 3:3).

"Why was his daughter Laura not content with the life with her father in the palace-monastery of Isola Borghese? As Tertulliano informed him, the reason was very simple, I would say almost natural. Laura was a girl of not even twenty. And so it was, really, more than understandable that she didn't like the boring life in the Alto Lazio hermitage. In fact, she dreamed of life in the Capital, with all that it entailed. The point is that her calling in life was an irresistibly worldly calling.

"This offended Adriana, the other sister, who was a little younger and instead declared herself faithful to what we might call her father's stylistic plan, which made of their life a work of art, even if it was necessarily an affectation. In fact, she went still farther beyond the paternal 'stylistic' boundaries, as we will see shortly.

"Agostino, it must be said, confronted the problem of Laura that was presented to him like a coup de théâtre. Moreover, he had not the least doubt about how to behave. He had—from the start—decided to be an authoritarian father, and an authoritarian father he would remain. He called Laura /to him/, and, though it was with the style of a cultivated man, he communicated to her his < ... > repressive decisions. No Rome, no worldly life, no ambitions, no involvements with Italian society. At the origin of Laura's worldly calling there was evidently the same 'theatricality' as the father's (the two in fact resembled each other strikingly); thus she possessed the psychological and ideological elements necessary to accept repression; and to perform that heroic act—which has been a great virtue throughout all the centuries and millennia of human history—of *resignation* and the consequent internalization of her own disappointed aspirations.

"But as soon as the problem of Laura was—or appeared to be—resolved, the problem of Adriana burst forth. This time, too, it was Tertulliano who informed Agostino, who again had been unaware of any problem. Adriana had suddenly felt in her soul, in those very days, an irresistible religious vocation. And, indeed, she had decided to become a cloistered nun. She was certain that her father would approve; yet she was afraid to speak to him about it. In fact, the idea of speaking to him about it filled her with an inexplicable terror.

"On this point, too, Agostino immediately took a drastic stand; no cloister, no ecclesiastical uniform, no involvements with a Church that did not know how to establish itself as the foundation of a great Right (!) and in fact in recent years had devoted itself, if only verbally, to foolish progressive ravings (nurturing in its breast, along with the old cardinals who were as ignorant as cowherds, unbearable Catholics of the left who were no less pietistic and unctuous).

"He was just about to call Adriana and give her the same repressive little talk he had given Laura. When suddenly he had a revolutionary revelation concerning himself, which enlightened him. It was June: a lovely day on which summer had burst forth—though there were clouds brimming with late rain. The drops that fell from the burning gray expanse of sky were like drops of sweat. But often the hot wind opened up large rents of blue sky, and the slanting rays of the sun (it was already late afternoon) gave to the deep valleys, the country villages, the oak forests a splendor that the present, always so sordid, seemed unworthy of. Agostino left the house and went for a walk outside the town, where the silence was more profound and nothing had changed since the < ... > Middle Ages. A wild, Ariosto-like sweetness hovered over the deep canals, over the semicircles of mowed fields against the darker green of Mediterranean woods. Agostino, unlike most of the Roman aristocracy, was not an ignorant man. /On the contrary/, he was very cultured; and this constitutes an anomalous case, so anomalous that it probably /makes/ my story arbitrary. The fact is that Agostino had not only a good classical education but also a fair knowledge of contemporary texts. Besides, even as a dilettante, he had specialized in the history of the Church and the history of religions. He should be able to examine the features of his daughter's monastic vocation closely; identify what type of sanctity she aspired to (Adriana also resembled him, they were like two drops of water; so it was inevitable that if she had a religious vocation its goal could only be extreme, that is, to be exact, sanctity).

"He decided to speak to her for as long as was necessary. Which he did the next day and the following days.

"Questioning Adriana, he also questioned himself, since the revelation about himself that had flashed < ... > (and immediately vanished) had made everything in his eyes so new and 'problematic.'

"The conclusions he arrived at as he questioned Adriana were in a certain sense positive. His daughter's mysticism was of a spiritually high quality, that is, scientifically valuable. The Christian 'cliché' was xxx by good archetypes. Adriana was prey to a real regression, which only her culture and that particular mysterious crystallization which distinguishes the schizophrenia of saints from that of the mad kept from becoming a troubling symptom. She experienced the 'repetition' again, outside the consciousness she had as a reader of the best of the mystical Saint Paul (innocently forgetful of his suspected sex phobia and his antifeminism). The high quality of Adriana's renunciation of the world was taken into consideration. But it also reintroduced the case of Laura. He therefore had to closely examine the worldly vocation of the latter. Which Agostino /did/ diligently. For Laura, too, the examination was positive; indeed, highly positive. Laura's desire to enter the world was not at all a girl's foolish vanity and superficiality. Hers was a wish to be a true presence among men: men of her social level, of course, understood here as cultural level.

"What, then, did the revelation consist of that, on the occasion of the crisis of his two daughters, Agostino had had about himself? < ... > Why—Agostino asked himself—for so many years had he kept himself apart from the world in a state of voluntary impotence? And the answer that had been given, instantaneously, was precisely the substance of his own enlightenment: 'I have kept myself far from the world in a state of voluntary impotence because I desire the world and have a thirst for power.' This question and this answer of Agostino's about himself were modeled on the questions and answers he had been forced to devote to the problems of his two daughters. 'Why does Laura wish to assert herself in the world? Probably, no, certainly because she fears it and detests it.' 'And why does Adriana want definitively to give up the world? Surely because she loves it and is tempted by it.'

"The 'thirst for power' that Agostino had rediscovered in himself—lying like some precious material in an abandoned mine—was /immense/, at least as /immense/ as his thirst for impotence had been. And it immediately erupted in him—as soon as it was recognized and admitted—with a violence worthy of his ancestors.

"His calculation was immediate. To reenter the world and become master of it, asserting /his own/ power. But how? < ... > The occasion had offered itself; and one better than this it was impossible to imagine. He would send his daughters ahead: two extraordinarily beautiful, extraordinarily aristocratic women, and, moreover, endowed with *real* vocations and cultural interests. The moment they achieved the success they certainly would achieve, the one as a woman of the world, the other as a saint, he, the father, would appear. He personally would not have to take a step to reascend the stream of lost time. He would find himself already standing on the best possible pedestal or springboard. It's not important to give the concrete details of his plans for power. The founding of that great Right which he—probably a unique case in a society like Italian society—had so precisely and clearly in his head. And even the inevitable ties with neo-Fascism, which he continued to despise but which, in his strategy, could not be ignored.

"He called his two daughters and again imposed on them his 'repressive' paternal will.† In fact, his fixed, unshakable decision was that they should‡ exchange roles: Laura, the daughter <who had been seized> by a desperate worldly vocation, would have to take the veil and become a nun; while Adriana, the daughter <who had been seized> by an irresistible and sincere religious vocation, would have to go and establish herself in Rome, to fulfill there the most ambitious and xxx plans of worldly success.

"Both Adriana and Laura accepted, bowing their heads before the will of their father. Moreover, for Adriana this was only a measure of her true sanctity; for Laura, on the other hand, it was a calculation that made her worthy of her father, since he had divined her intentions.

"Nearly ten years passed (and thus we have arrived at about our own time). Agostino's predictions had been fulfilled exactly. Adriana, the mystic, became a powerful woman of the world. The rich and cultivated life of Rome was now inconceivable without her. The superficial Laura, for her part, became a nun whose piety immediately attracted the world's attention, and it had increased so much over the years that in the end /the woman was called/ holy. And in effect it would have been impossible, <...> to demonstrate the contrary. From the shadow of his two daughters, Agostino had slowly come into the light; and his authority, precisely because it was still hidden, and legendary, began /to be/ indispensable.

"The day came when—restraining his agonizing desire to reveal and assert himself—Agostino considered it opportune to abandon his by now twenty-year exile and reappear on the world's scene. Everything was ready. Certainly it must not happen without the repercussions and results that Agostino intended, but, at the same time, every form of rhetoric had to be strictly avoided.

"But it is just on the morning of that historic day that our story stops. Or, rather, is folded back on itself, into that inner silence <...> from which it began, even if that inner silence is now profoundly, unspeakably different."

———

—Meeting of sociologists *ecology* (<?> etc.)—With problems and sound points. With humorous language and comparisons—But (<?> of a gag) Dionysus appears and upsets everything.

—The two days of the meeting on the *ecological disaster* end with all the participants drunk (aleatic wine and wine?)
—Dionysus again becomes horrible and criminal.
—They were there to tell the *truth,* but for that very reason they did not say it.

The Epoche:

> The story of the Infant-Shit ———————————————▶
> (child born from a man—a
> bourgeois industrialist—who shits)

NOTE 102
The Epoche: The story of two fathers and two sons

"Let me make an introduction!" said the third narrator. "A cautionary introduction, perhaps even brilliant. . . . In reality its purpose is, as you know, to hide the tragic moment of the beginning, which is always, so to speak, an autotomy. Furthermore, storytelling endangers existence and thus throws it into confusion. The narrating subject, faced with his own opening sentence, enters a state of crisis. And it's a real crisis, typical of relations with the sacred. The story is within the sacred enclosure. And the approach to the enclosure always requires a long, compulsory ceremony. Which is also comic. Savages mock, with great wit, the strictly regulated approach to the place where the Spirit is. They perform clownish little acts, silly gestures. And so do I. My 'brilliant' prologue has to do with the function of the rectum. The function of the rectum, I'm saying, in all of human life, seen in its totality. Meanwhile, as you well know, and as I solemnly wish to repeat here:

"'The rectum teaches the bladder conservation, and the bladder in turn teaches the rectum generosity.'

"Engrave these words deeply in your memory, and perhaps use them as epigraphs to your personal history, if the necessary minimum of civic courage does not fail you.

"Thus there is no urethral eroticism that is not tinged with the anal and no anal eroticism that is not touched with the urethral. Something fundamental for the formation of character. Yet at the same time it should be observed that 'rectum' (or ass) and 'bladder' (or testicles) are entities of late development and definition. The heuristic hypothesis is that these are assigned the principal role in the sexual act not only during coitus but during the whole life (individual or of the species). With that assignment made, we then find ourselves—to make it brief—faced with the double temptation of discharging both the penis and the contents of the intestines: which, in a hallucinatory way, have been identified with each other through their common identification with the child. Our cock is the child I, but so is shit. Furthermore, in conclusion, I wish to recall the phenomenon of parental sexuality: the pleasure, that is, deriving from birth. A pleasure that the man envies the woman and that he tries to get, through mimesis, by shitting (through a whole hallucinatory ceremony either of retention—constipation—or of excessive evacuation—diarrhea). All of that constitutes the preface to my story. But you may very well not realize it, as < ... > of a hypnotic babble. In short, in order to seduce you I have <...> and unfurled the tail. And now I penetrate you.

"There is a part of the Italian bourgeoisie that still goes hunting. And it makes of the hunt a sophisticated ritual. Wealthy industrialists, arriviste professionals, and even some intellectuals meet together at the country house of a common friend and, as the nobles (who, moreover, still mingle with them, and are, in fact \to tell the truth\, much sought after) once did, organize hunting parties. Their wives follow along. All that—I believe I can say—already appears to you in itself potentially comic. And I believe I also know the reason. Thus introduced, these men and women of the solid Italian bourgeoisie (who have to be, with rare exceptions, from the North) present themselves to your imagination abstractly, in a generalized form that fixes them in stereotyped physiognomies, as masks. And the masks, naturally, are comic. When furthermore, attention is directed to Engineer Gianni xxx, that is, to an individual, fixed mask, the muffled tickle of the laugh—attributable to humor that is not without something vicious in it—becomes still stronger and almost irresistible. In the origin of every figure of the Italian bourgeoisie there is something cartoonish, everyone knows it. Well, this Engineer Gianni xxx was in fact as you imagine him: Milanese by residence, from Varese by birth, with a Ligurian tan \skin\ and something Roman in the black of his eyes and his black, slightly graying hair (the gray, for some reason, had something profane, unforgivable about it, it was so unconsciously vulgar). Still, let me be clear, this engineer, of course, could be completely different from the way I've described him. Who he was hasn't the least importance in this ideological story of mine. Anyway, Engineer Gianni xxx was at one of these hunting parties I was telling you about. His group had settled in Countess C.'s stupendous country villa. A villa of glass, wood, and decorative exposed concrete. It rose in a large, round, slightly sloping deep green meadow. Around it was a light, dry frame of deciduous forest, already half stripped, with the last blood reds and the fresh humus of leaves just fallen and trampled. In the recesses of those woods ran a kind of immense aquatic labyrinth formed by the branches of the Oglio: narrow, twisting channels, gray and excessively clear. They disappeared into the wood, which was as dense as an African forest. Then, suddenly, appeared the shores of the main branch of the river, which at that point was set deep between its banks. The banks were dark green, covered with all kinds of grasses, and formed a sort of overhang, almost perpendicular, above the current, which was a deep bottle green. A path ran along one bank, among the bare xxx and some thickets of evergreen, beaded with dew and glistening in the < ... > rays of the sun, with an overpowering odor of bark. The path led on to a point where the wood began to thin out, until suddenly it ended; and the Oglio, rising out of its gorge, spread freely in a thousand streams over an immense pebbly shore that /extended/ toward the horizon < ... > foggy, < ... > pearly. The water had become a clear turquoise, divinely clear. The scattered thickets of the wood became more numerous, thin, reddish, along the shore. And in that patrician /desert/, the autumn birds sang.

"It is at this point that the 'useless fiction' stops and the true representation begins, in which the gestures and facts that speak appear; and Engineer Gianni xxx like the ascetic Pambo—'On sighè retòs epaìdeuse'—made of himself an instructive example by speaking in silence.

"In fact, as soon as he had gone from the tangle of the woods to the broad opening of the shore, Engineer Gianni xxx felt the first stab of pain. <...> He didn't want <...> to pay attention to it and continued on casually, clutching in his hands his precious xxx xxx xxx. But it was no joke. A little later a new pang, inexorable, pierced his bowels, this time becoming a long, steady agony that began to twist his guts. Engineer Gianni xxx, his face pale, covered in an icy sweat, disgusted by his difficulty, brought his hands to his stomach and pressed. In vain. The pangs, <...> which took his breath away, became more frequent and uncontrollable. Already the engineer was looking around with clouded eyes. Before him, the expanse of the shore was bare, open. The first thicket of reeds was far away, beyond a little stream of turquoise water that rippled and whirled. Behind him . . . Behind him was the wood, the high, shaded grassy bank. Into the engineer's searching eyes came a light, comforted expression of relief. He ran toward it, already unbuttoning himself, and there he retired. The place was a true retreat. Blinding green grass pearly with dew, and all around, like the courtyard of a little temple, the dense fragrant bushes of xxx. As if in a state of happiness that caused him to murmur to himself and even to hum (parental happiness!), he stripped, and, as if in contrast to the urgency, he with difficulty, like one constipated, freed himself of the 'contents of his intestines.' When he had brought to term, with a satisfying outcome, that autotomia—which is usually creative only in a symbolic sense—the engineer's eyes again began to look around. In that place there was no paper. There were some lovely leaves, smooth and clean. But while the engineer examined them, a little suspiciously, to choose those most suited to his need, he heard, from an indeterminate place behind him, a faint, bitter cry. It was immediately extinguished, leaving behind an unreal echo; and for an instant the engineer was reassured, safe from surprises that were alarming even to a practical sportsman like him. But only for an instant. Because soon that vague isolated surreal complaint transformed itself into the long, insistent wailing of a newborn infant.

"The word 'engineer' evokes Gadda for me, and a certain style in this presentation derives from that.

"Now, by means of a genealogical logic that is not without its strict reason, I pass to Faldella. . . . With him we are still in the Po valley; in a place analogous to the one just now described. Perhaps a little more in the country, more isolated. But it's clear that this is a northern Italian story and that it could not be anything else. The context in which it unfolds is a context of bourgeois progressivism in which feminism has a fundamental role: a feminism that is not ideological but, although not even named, has for some time been mature and active: modifying reality. While Engineer Gianni xxx was busy with we know what, something historically analogous was happening in a not very distant valley in Monferrato, an area of erratic immigration.

"On the sepulcher of a city, which in Etruscan and Roman times merited the name of Industris (it is indeed Faldella who is speaking), a poor, idle village with the name of Passabiago cracked and slid from the hilly edges of lower Monferrato to the right bank of the Po.

"In a deep, twisting valley, as unexplored as a virgin forest, was a very precious ruin of Christian antiquity; a little temple, whose construction goes back to three hundred years after the birth of Jesus Christ.

"It is said to have been founded by Saint Eutizio. It suffered a Saracen invasion. A scrap of an inscription scratched into the old stone, XI KAL. NOV. ROLANDUS, and a vague tradition let us imagine a visit by Roland in love, who later returned, furious, to recover his lost mind. But, naturally, later structures were layered above the original construction: the last in the fifteenth century.[52]

"At the bottom of the valley, then, almost buried in brambles and dog roses, lay the gem of a little church. Its walls, of blocks of gray stone, were open to a deep wood of centuries-old hazelnut trees, where clearings carpeted with dry leaves /created a space/ equally sacred, even if, naturally, more ancient. The church moreover was held tight in a vise of ferns—besides the brambles and clumps of dog roses. I believe such ferns are extraordinarily rare; they were as big as bushes. And they were

---

[52] There Napoleon I took by surprise a magnificent Cistercian abbey, which boiled capons in white wine and dunked calves in the Po for a moment in order to fish them out and eat them on meatless days as fish. The Corsican emperor abolished the abbey, scattered the abbey priests, and gave its land and buildings to a lively Marshal Bonnelane, who played and lost them at taroc. The Minister Urbano Rattazzi, In the political restoration, the convent was reestablished, with more modest customs. *coul Rataz, fieul d'Cain, fratel d'Caffas, sulle zucche incapucciate a l'à dait un famos crep* whence the guardian father could chant, following the witty Piedmontese song of Brofferio: *Bruta neuva—orate frates—Bruta neuva per dabon.—Babulonys impii patres—portu'l Diau an procession* (*Donna Folgore*, by Giovanni Faldella).

so thick in the space around the ruin—ground that had probably once been a cemetery—that it seemed almost impossible to get through, to reach the interior of the church, of which only the four main walls were standing. Of the ceiling and all the rest not even a shadow remained. Now, the man who was crouched there inside the church, in, if possible, an even thicker tangle of nettles and relentless thorn bushes, must have performed a miracle to get there. The fact is, he was there. He was, as I said, crouching; his pants pulled down so his /ass/ was completely uncovered, his head low between his legs, and, as far as one could tell, his eyes sidelong like those of a convict and his mouth foaming. But everything was seen foreshortened, because the pain that had propelled the man inside there now forced him to keep his head down in a gesture of desperation. Behind him, like a Platonic model and somewhat presumptuous in his 'teaching by speaking silently,' was a fine Saint, the only intact figure of a fifteenth-century fresco—the other figures were all blessedly headless. A beautiful scarlet waistcoat covered our Saint, probably Saint Eutizio; it had puffed sleeves with stripes of white and light green, a faded Veronese green. The trousers were dark, almost black; but they were rather shamelessly undone (almost like those of his distant descendant who was crouching, drooling like a dog, below him). With an elegant gesture of his hand, our Saint Eutizio was pointing to a wound in his thigh, just below the groin. Thus the hand that was demonstrating the \that\ mortal wound, pulling away the trouser leg, was suspended just above the cock; for decidedly and correctly one could speak of a cock regarding that fine figure of a man, a ditty of a peasant whom the anonymous painter must have chosen as a model on the spot. The man who there below him was writhing in some sort of spasms that made him twist his neck, as if he were crawling on the ground, was named Orlando. He was not from those parts; he was a southerner. No one knows how \he had been transported\ he had ever happened into that valley in the outskirts of Passabiago, into the ruin of the church of Saint Eutizio. It is known only that, having emigrated from the South, after a long series of wanderings he had happened on Monferrato by way of certain friendships made in Turin with his 'countrymen.' There he had found a temporary job in a cookie factory; if they can be called cookies. < ... > In fact, it was < ... > Krumiri, a specialty of

Casale Monferrato, founded in 1886. The founder and inventor was a certain Rossi, who had been succeeded by the present owner, E. Portinaro; who still had not introduced (into the packaging; as for the rest, who can say?) any innovation. Krumiri in fact were still offered under the quality label of *'Provv. di S. M. il Re d'Italia e Reali Principi d'Aosta e di Genova.'* This Orlando, so unexpectedly acquired by us, was a man of about thirty, still young. In other times he would have been a laborer or a squat peasant, with a dull but confidence-inspiring face, hair like a soldier's, big ears, and very narrow eyes but of an /electrifying/ blue, like a blind man's. Now, though, it was a grotesque mask, almost /repellent/: better nourishment and greater self-respect \a certain improved idea of himself\ (not to be confused with true dignity) gave him a look of unnatural health that did not connect with his own, natural health. He even seemed a bit Italian American. Moreover, he was a perfect example of mimicry so successful as to be /degrading/. He possessed neither more nor less than an ordinary bourgeois boy in Turin. His hair was a mane that fell to his shoulders, in his eyes was fixed a doltish expression of superiority, not without, however, some consciousness of his own foolishness (absolutely necessary for him to be accepted). Finally, in his big hand, even in his present, hardly aesthetic situation, he held by the corner an /extremely/ coquettish little purse. As for his spasms, even they—like those of the engineer < ... >—were a mixture of 'anguish' and 'pleasure' in the form of the contrast between the desire to hold on and the desire to be free. So, too, was his autotomia, when, finally, it took place, < ... > satisfaction that put the poor peasant—racially inferior but perfectly equal to his bourgeois contemporaries, even if it was a mask—at precisely the same level as Engineer Gianni xxx. Like the engineer, he discharged the object of parental joy, looked around with an uncertain and searching eye. There were only nettles and thorns as long as a finger. Never mind. He was about to pull up his bell-bottom pants anyway and button them with a big buckle, when, he, too, heard behind him a desperate, overpowering wail.

"Both Orlando, therefore, xxx Orlando and Engineer Gianni xxx, experiencing a similar situation, found themselves unexpectedly confronted by what we might call a perception of the divine in the present that becomes the future. The revelation. What one does not want to admit. What above all one cannot admit, and yet all that remains is to admit it.

"The two turned, looked around, explored, went 'Boh!' (or 'Beh!'), pulling their heads between their shoulders, began again to search; <...> until they really had to admit that the phenomenon to be examined was <...> their own <...> shit. Since it really was their shit that was wailing."

NOTE 102A
The Epoche: The story of a cosmic flight

"Have you ever dreamed of flying into the cosmos and looking down from the height of the Moon or Mars?" began the fourth narrator somewhat aggressively; and, an ironic light shining in his wide-open eyes, he continued, "I have. Yes, I have dreamed of it. The impression has remained with me vivid and complete. It is as if I had *truly* flown in the cosmos.

"You will wonder, with this introduction, whether I am not by any chance beginning a science fiction story. Well, no. I would never do that. I think it's impossible for a narrator to base his story on experiences that didn't really happen. What I am preparing to tell has to do with the present. It's a slight story, a little foolish, yes. But our storytelling here either is crazy or isn't. Besides, I could not, by my nature, be other than Mannerist. Thus my story is based on an experience that happened in a dream. If I hadn't dreamed of making a cosmic flight, it would never have occurred to me to tell you, really, this story about it. As for the rest, it, too, is based on real experiences, as you will see. But I will tell it to you flirtatiously (and, again, you will understand the reason at the end). It's part of the narrative flirtatiousness of an anonymous man to make up the names of the characters from beginning to end. In that case a little humor—or perhaps, let's say, coarse humor—is not wasted; it enters into the great scheme of alienation. Enough. My story begins inside a spaceship. Seen from the surface of the Earth, that spaceship could be taken for a flying saucer. But its shape is not circular; rather, it's spherical. And that's why it flies dizzily, at a speed that only mathematicians possess the terminology < ... > to express, certainly not I—because, seen from afar, that sphere looks crushed, like a disk. Inside the sphere that whirls at such a, so to speak, supernatural velocity, there is another sphere, a few millimeters smaller. This sphere is completely immobile: suspended inside the whirling external sphere that moves dizzily through the spaces of the cosmos. The ship left a few seconds ago from xxx xxx and is already some hundreds of kilometers from the Earth's surface. Exactly the height from which I looked at the Earth in my dream. Now, the velocity of the external sphere is such that it practically seems to evaporate and becomes transparent; so that from the porthole of the inside sphere—which is immobile—one can comfortably look out. The Earth is there below. At the bottom of the darkness of the cosmos: tinged with a celestial indigo. One sees its well-known shape: the mass of France, the two peninsulas, Spain and Italy, the latter with its disarming boot shape, etc. But everything, seen materially, in a true flight, at that more than vertiginous and terrifying distance, seems moving and mysterious. Soon the Earth disappears, and there remains only the profound void, without life. This, too, I dreamed, I experienced it completely in the dream.

"Observing the Earth disappear from the lower porthole—almost at their feet—were two very healthy men < ... > of about forty. One was named Klaus Patera and the other xxx xxx. They watched together, in the same position, with the same expression in their eyes. They were, however, not the only members of the crew. In fact, to tell the truth they were not part of the crew; they were two observers, exactly like me, at the moment in which I had dreamed the same event. Except that they were official observers. The interior sphere measured about ten meters in diameter. Thus it was almost as big as a reception room. Inside that 'sphere within a sphere' was placed, in turn, an enormous glass cube, whose four edges were propped against the inside wall of the sphere, so that it was firmly held. It was precisely inside the cube that the two 'official observers' were situated; like the actual crew, as well (made up of half a dozen technicians). Naturally the cube was divided into various sections, and each of these was a kind of little room or cell. The technicians were dispersed in these little transparent cells, in monastic absorption. Each one had his task, which he attended to with silent inspiration. The only two who were doing nothing except observing were the two official observers.

"I will give you at this point a simple series of facts. And—for good reasons, which you will understand at the end—they will be as objective and inexpressive as possible.

"That spaceship, so different from the spaceships we have been accustomed to seeing in these last years, was built not publicly but privately. The gigantic technological effort, involving the almost simultaneous teamwork of some hundreds of thousands of people and some dozens of industries, had not been supported by the State. It had been supported by a private Company. The fact had not been made known; but since the early years, when the State /monopolized/ the construction of spaceships, many private companies had protested, asking that they be granted the right to 'cosmic space.' And since the request was completely democratic, that 'right' had been granted. Similarly, no one can be kept from building cars, planes, or ships, or from starting a newspaper or installing a television transmitter. Public opinion, I repeat, was kept in the dark. Besides, it was thought that granting 'the right to cosmic space' could only be platonic. Instead, it was not, even if—as, moreover, we will see—there are the usual good reasons to believe that the private Company that had built our spaceship was not completely separate from the State. Anyway, this is certain: that technical wonder which was the spaceship now navigating in cosmic space was ruled by two forces, or two powers, at the same time. It was an ambiguous ship, amphibological. It was inhabited by a dramatic dichotomy. The collision between the opposing interests of the two powers that had presided over the plan and its construction was no less violent for being hidden. Whether these two powers were constituted by the State on one side and the private Company on the other; or by

two competing private Companies; or by two different groups of share-
holders in the same Company in a struggle to the death for control; or,
finally, by a legitimate national power against a subversive < ... > foreign power—I don't know. Or at least for now I prefer to say I don't
know, thus making you my collaborators to the end.

"An observation, before passing on to the other facts (an observation
due to the optimism—a bit mannerist, I repeat—of the one who is
telling the story < ... >). Spies are always rather ridiculous; not only in
fiction but in reality. When one reads in a newspaper that a real spy has
been arrested and sees the photograph, one generally finds it deeply and
irresistibly hilarious. The spy is comical. Probably because he is obliged
to play a part. He has to play the part, let's say, of a baronet or a major
in the British Army. But a baronet or a major in the British Army—
which in themselves are comical—become so in an irresistible way *if
they are feigned.*

"In his role, the spy cannot in fact invent, because he has to imitate.
Therefore he can only exaggeratedly be the figure (perfectly conformist,
proper, and perhaps just slightly original) that he pretends to be. The
comic quality, then, is even stronger and more obvious when the spy
is in the end unmasked. Children who do not know how to speak give
their first real laughs when someone hides and then is found. Recognition is the original paradigm of all hilarity.

"But let's continue with the facts. The two forces or powers that
make up the dualism of our spaceship are, as we have seen, in conflict.
The one that wins (that is, becomes absolute master of the spaceship
and of all that can be gained by means of the spaceship) will also
become, practically speaking, ruler of the State. In fact, according to
the calculations made by the experts, it would objectively have available
funds far in excess of those of the State. Which therefore would fall
automatically into its hands. In any case, it would be a matter of one
side's seizing power over all. According to the examples I presented to
you above, we would therefore have: first, a private Company would
take over the State (probably with the basic connivance of the State);
< ... > a private Company would liquidate a private Company and then
take over the State; < ... > a party supported by the analogous party

already in power in another State would take over the power in its own State.

"Klaus Patera and Misha Pila were two spies (and this is the last real 'bare fact' that I will give you). The sense of the comic that has already invaded you is perfectly justified. The two, in fact, were playing the role of two Italian Americans. And they did it with such commitment that never were two Italian Americans more Italian American than they. Vitamins and proteins had erased the more obvious racial characteristics (those due to hunger, buffoonery, the state of mind typical of lying and need) but had left intact the essential characteristics: black eyes and eyebrows, snub noses, distended mouths, bodies plump and xxx, /bobbing/ like indestructible fossils on the amorphous and incomplete physiognomies of middle Americans.

"Now, chance had willed that these two personages be thrown into space and find themselves in the middle of the cosmos: a fact that could not but automatically increase their comicalness, by isolating them, when it isolated them, one before the other and both before the universe.[53]

"But that's not all. I told you, on a purely referential level, that Klaus Patera and Misha Pila were two spies. One a spy for the power that, for convenience, I will call 'Urina,' and the other a spy for the power that < ... > I will call 'Feci.'

"And here is the point: Klaus Patera, a spy for the power Urina, knew that Misha Pila was a spy for the power Feci. *But* Misha Pila, a spy for the power Feci, also knew that Klaus Patera was a spy for the power Urina.

"Not only that; but Klaus Patera, a spy for the power Urina, was playing a double game; that is, he was also a spy for the power Feci.

"And similarly Misha Pila, a spy for the power Feci, was also double-crossing; that is, he was also a spy for the power Urina.

"Now < ... > Klaus Patera, who was double-crossing as a spy for both the power Urina and the power Feci, *knew* that Misha Pila was also playing a double game as a spy for both the power Urina and the power Feci; /while/ < ... > Misha Pila did not; he did not know that Klaus Patera was playing a double game; *he only suspected it.*

---

[53] " . . . we are like two abstract beings on a lighter-than-air craft who meet to tell the truth" (Dostoyevsky, *The Possessed*).

"In a table or diagram drawn by a semiologist of pragmatist or even behaviorist training—a table or diagram perfect in all ways as to typicalness and absolute symmetry—the uncertainty of Misha Pila would constitute, so to speak, a Half-Unknown. Which, even more dramatically than a true Unknown, would make the ambiguity /constituted/ by the duality of plan and power experienced by our spaceship in the persons of Klaus Patera and Misha Pila irreducible to any scheme, even an ambiguous one. The abyss of the sky was wide open at the feet of these two. <...> It's not true that space is dark. Certainly, there is no real light or brightness. But nevertheless 'that' which through the portholes gives way beneath the feet and opens wide over the head—that is, the infinite—has a color, which emanates from itself. The cold and the silence, but also the solemnity, create the special indigo of cosmic abysses, which, at the farthest point visible to the eye, shades into a celestial glow—if I can call it that. I know all this because I saw it in a revelatory dream. Both looking up and looking down, one feels /special/ vertigos, which, grabbing at one's guts and stomach and making one almost faint, clearly demonstrate their intolerableness. The poor human body is not made to bear them; and, turned upside down by the dizziness and feeling that it is on the point, so to speak, of vomiting \throwing up\ itself, it understands that the hour has come when, with a terrifying smile turned just to it, the nothingness it was born to is beckoning. Yet not only is the vertigo endured, but, indeed, the terror it causes has something sweet and exalting about it, like some event of early childhood. In my revelatory dream I understood, once and for all, that the sea is not our true origin, that is, /the original/ maternal belly (which with all our strength we long to return to); our true origin is space. It is there that we are truly born: in the sphere of the cosmos. In the sea, perhaps, we are born a second time. And therefore the attraction of the sea is profound, but that of heavenly space is infinitely greater.[54]

"The planet toward which the /amphibological/ spaceship was hurtling with Klaus Patera and Misha Pila had been discovered recently. Refer-

[54] Perhaps religions were referring to this with the cult of the Ascension. As for the attraction of the sea, cf. in particular *Thalassa,* by Sándor Ferenczi, apparently considered by Freud "the most daring application of psychoanalysis that has ever been attempted."

ring to a casual remark of Saint Paul made in the *Lausiaca History* (which the discoverer was by chance reading in those days), the new planet had been called 'Ta kai ta,' or now, under the agreement immediately established, 'Takaità.' (The sentence in Saint Paul, which, as luck would have it, referred to the Heavens, in the Lausiacan quotation, rang out: 'Autòs gar èleghe Paulos: "O gar karpòs tou pneúmatós esti" tà kaì tà . . .').

"The new planet was extremely far away. The spaceship's journey was to last exactly three years, three months, and three days. Therefore Klaus Patera and Misha Pila had a lot of time ahead of them to observe and, above all, to be observed; following the scheme of that behaviorist semiologist's diagram, which, alas, would have been so wonderfully perfect if it had not been for the unfortunate Half-Unknown due to Misha's uncertainty.

"Anyway, no one, let it be said, through exaggerated, if modest, optimism—neither the men of the crew nor the two main characters, despite the relentlessness of the serious tasks assigned to them by the company, in which they were energetically engaged—could escape the joy of that dive into the cosmos: of that return into the spaces from which everything had come /in an inorganic form/. Joy, I repeat, joy, even though terrifying.

"The three years, three months, and three days passed. The spaceship's supernatural velocity slowed, and it entered the stratosphere of Takaità. Light reappeared. A light that came up as if from a steaming funnel: freezing and ash gray, with distant blue patches that appeared to be holes in another sky, summery and pale blue, and yellowish /banners/ or streamers, fluttering faintly thousands and thousands of kilometers away, probably around the planet. And now in fact the ball of Takaità appeared, half of it lit by its sun (we were no longer, of course, in the solar system). Exciting, familiar globe! They approached dizzily, because the velocity of the spaceship was still vertiginous. Seas and continents were outlined, swampy, magmatic, with frothy lights that were at the same time flat and flowing (in fact, from the height of the spaceship dawn, midday, and sunset could be seen on the globe in a single glance). Immediately the ship was just above the planet, at the distance of a common television satellite; at the distance, that is, from which the outlines of seas and lands became perceptible. And it was at this point that the unimaginable occurred.

"While the ship was approaching the earthly crust of Takaità, Takaità, naturally, was spinning: it went from day to night. And for this reason what appeared to the eyes of the astronauts and the two observers, besides being unimaginable, was also so fleeting as to seem a dream and to leave serious doubts about its reality; in short, the sense of it was suspended.

"What did such a surprise consist of, a surprise so stupefying that it caused the disbelief of a fleeting dream? It consisted simply of the appearance on Takaità's earthly crust of shapes that—even in the anomalous, mad light filtered through other layers of the atmosphere—recalled, with a fidelity that made them in substance identical, the shapes of the earthly crust of our globe. There was the stocky shape of France, below it the equally stocky form of the Iberian peninsula and the 'bootlike' form of Italy. A perfect, I repeat, similarity. Immediately, however, everything was swallowed in darkness; and the lightninglike apparition—thus kindled—seemed, in the darkness, a spectral mirage.

"The ship landed /in the dark/. And there again began—after more than three years—for its xxx the convention of real time. Night was night and only night. And it was a night that normally lasted a dozen hours, including twilight and dawn. The obscurity was profound. Takaità did not have a moon, or if by chance it did, this was a moonless night.

"The operations for disembarking from the ship were lengthy. They would have to last about as long as the night lasted. There is nothing more affecting than the bewilderment of technicians; and there is nothing more heroic than their bewilderment and their sense of duty. Although frankly astonished, they got busy performing their job with the utmost gravity. One could not say that the night was at last completely over when the team was able to come out of the ship. All around, it was still dark; barely visible, all around, were motionless masses, perhaps trees or rocks; only in the east was the sky transformed into an enormous, stunning slab of crystal through which a light, still low, began to shine, transforming the deep indigo into an inky blue without a nuance, but already as if on fire.

"The cosmonauts went out, and, moreover, as the experts had predicted, there was no need for either a heavy space suit full of ballast for walking or masks and oxygen tanks for breathing. One could walk and breathe freely, as on our Earth. Thus the team could go out of the ship in overalls and with their heads uncovered. As soon as the astronauts were outside the ship, another startling thing filled them with amazement and immobilized them, to a silent, alarmed attention: in the distance, in the depths of the darkness, sounded the warbling of a nightingale. But probably—if it was truly the warbling of a nightingale—it was the last of the night. All that could be heard was a final questioning phrase, little more than an echo. It, too, disappeared too quickly to seem real and not the trick of a dream. The night around was warm, summery. But at the same time there was that shiver of coolness that precedes dawn; in fact, their feet were wet with dew. As the plain, endless inky blue slab of the eastern sky, just growing light, began to be streaked with an infinite series of fine shadings, among which an almost hard strip of coral pink was beginning to prevail—other mysterious noises, like /breaths, sighs/, could be heard in the obscurity. Until suddenly, this time without possibility of a mistake, some larks began to trill. Almost as suddenly, the air was luminous. The light was there, ready, a dull and pearly light, still cold. But it revealed all, without /possibility of denial/, in a gray fatality."

NOTE 103
The Epoche: The story of the slaughters

"If I understand correctly," said he who was to be the fourth narrator, preparing to pour his glass of *ciceone,* "in all these stories, explicit or masked, the same story is repeated, which is the pattern, the paradigm, or, if you like, the real, historical *dromenon* that these stories of fiction, *legomena,* give a symbolic dress to and refer to. That 'primal story,' it seems to me, could be entitled 'The Story of a Failed Coup d'État.'

"Now I will tell a story that is not symbolic, not second, not subsequent. It does not refer to 'The Story of a Failed Coup d'État" *but is it.* Whether the failure is a momentary or a definitive failure is a thing I leave you to judge. As I leave it to you to judge whether it is historically possible or not \simply an attempt\.

"You will certainly wonder who I am, an anonymous narrator—in mourning, moreover, and so abstemious—who can tell you such an important 'primal story,' which occurred not in myth but in reality. Well, gentlemen, I am no one. Outis, like Montale. Chance simply wanted me to be the one who knows the facts. Facts that I therefore limit myself to reporting. Among other things I am not even an expert. I am a man who lives on a private income, and I do not practice a profession. I devote my time to cultural research, like a dilettante. And it's that which provided, just by chance, the occasion of my coming to know the facts in question. As it is likewise my economic condition that establishes, almost automatically, by its own necessity, the style of my account. Why? Because I have much to lose—being a rich man—and at the same time nothing to lose—having no job and no responsibility. As a result—as a person who has much to lose—I will give the names neither of the protagonists of these actions nor of the places where these actions occurred; as, on the other hand, a person who has nothing to lose, I will report the facts as they were reported to me, without fear of their terrible truth.

"But first a word on the 'chance' that acquainted me with this story, or rather its essence, reducible to a synopsis of not more than two or three typewritten pages. More I did not learn (but this seems to me enough). I found myself in Katmandu, and I was there because one of my hobbies is collecting folk music. I knew only that in Bhaktapur in those days there was a great popular religious celebration, corresponding closely to our Easter or Christmas. Thus by chance I found myself in a little square in Bhaktapur, in fact following the itinerary of an ordinary tourist; instead of having in my hand an ordinary movie camera, I had a slightly less common   †, that is, a very good Nagra. Besides, it was night; and a camera would have been completely useless; while, as it seemed to me, there was a /beautiful/ atmosphere for my /tape/. The square /was/ unusually animated. And in the distance singing and music could be heard. This was completely normal in the evening in Nepal, because people always gather in the little rooms of the temples to sing, accompanied by two or three ancient instruments. But in the square in Bhaktapur this singing and music, which sounded sometimes close, sometimes far away, had something special about it. Very soon groups of people appeared, holding little torches in their hands, hardly bigger than matches, and small brass plates with a few offerings: red flowers, partly crushed, some dust that was also red, perhaps a spice, half a handful of rice, some peppers, and other indefinable substances, all between orange and crimson in color, strangely damp and seemingly withered, and at the same time <...> precious. The people held those little plates of heavy metal with their offerings, not hiding their excitement, joy, hurry. They were groups of families or friends. Fathers and mothers with their children, or bands of young men. Around their necks they all wore necklaces of red beads or red thread, with a little knot that hung on their chests. Also, on their heads— behind one ear—they had those orange flowers that fade into an indefinable cinnabar red. Then, in the middle of their foreheads, they all had big moles, also of that mysterious color: a gluey paste stuck on with the stroke of a finger. In fact, a joyful old man, his laughing eyes slits between wrinkles and ears that stuck out—followed by a group of young men, also laughing but with /the greater timidity and restraint/ <...> of sons—came up to me and, with a little pressure of his dark index finger, made that reddish mark on my forehead: which excited a general merriment. So much so that one of the young men, small and happy as a boy, came up to me and put a necklace of red beads around my neck. I was now definitely, even if jokingly, one of them. Like a tourist, and that was embarrassing. But I wasn't discouraged; my interest in all that was happening to me was—for a collector of folk music—too moving and real. And then I have never been able to feel any racial differences, or even any social and historical ones. Just by nature. Finally, with that mole on my forehead and that necklace and, above all, those loving smiles around me, I felt perfectly at ease, even if trembling, almost, with excitement and tenderness. My chance companions and hosts did not, moreover, make their graciousness burdensome even for an instant; as the first moment of joy in meeting, with its smiles, was exhausted, they, /untouched/, went on their way.

"It was already dark. The little houses and the larger buildings of red brick, with their stone foundations and their friezes of carved wood, especially under the cornices and around the windows, the repeated outlines of the temples (here in this square was a very old one, very rustic), the groups of tabernacles scattered everywhere on the red-brick paving of the streets with their stone borders, as in our cities, the washhouses in deep, wide hollows at the foot of stone stairways, with their thousand precious ornaments and statues—all was about to be swallowed by the darkness of a moonless night. The groups of people with their little lights were all going toward the end of the square—the last in Bhaktapur, near the countryside—and then they turned onto a marvelous street lined with buildings with wonderful little entrances or wooden balconies, alternating with crowded tabernacles and their exquisite bronze monsters. I, too, went down that way, mixing with the crowd. Soon I reached the end of the street, which opened onto a square full of stupendous wooden loggias, with a rise in the center that was dotted with the usual tabernacles and now, too—like the inner courtyards that could be glimpsed behind the doors and at the ends of the alleys— crowded with rows of red peppers and I don't know what yellow grain, put out to dry. There were still some little temples around, their courtyards crammed with statues, statuettes, and low altars. The square was raised high over the countryside, which could be glimpsed, densely green and muddy, in the darkness. It had become very crowded. Some people stayed in the alleys or the loggias, others in the middle of the square; others, finally, turned onto a street paved not with bricks in a herringbone pattern but with uneven stones, which descended toward the first muddy fields. But the really extraordinary thing, exciting for me, was that everywhere, all around, there were groups of men and boys playing instruments, all at the same time; some groups were small and meager, with rough, primitive woodwinds and the inevitable rustic drum. Other groups, on the other hand, were bigger: real bands. And these had modern instruments, too: even violins and trombones, although they played their old songs. Not always, however; some motifs seemed to me to be European: probably English, assimilated and elaborated during the colonial domination. That so many groups of people were playing at the same time here and there in that open space was already, I repeat, for me an extraordinary and exciting thing. But it was small in comparison with what awaited me a little farther on. All the groups, whether they were playing or simply carrying votive offerings, after lingering a bit, joyfully, went down along the street toward the countryside. I mingled with them. And this time I was literally in the middle of a thronging crowd. On both sides of the cobbled street were ditches full of muddy water that smelled sharply of fresh human feces. Beyond the ditches were the last walls and the last little farmyard enclosures filled to overflowing with piles of straw and manure, of equipment and xxx. Then the country began, and the stinking ditches overflowed onto the muddy verges of the fields. Thus the crowd, in the midst of which I slowly and with difficulty walked, was totally contained on the road that was lost in the darkness of the countryside. And the walk was even more difficult because after a while the crowd began to meet another crowd that was returning (I still did not know from where); and this crowd, too, was made up of groups carrying jars of offerings (now empty) and playing instruments. One heard a refined wild music, closer to Western music than to that of another Oriental country: a music that rose as if by a miracle, dense and joyous, in the middle of the crowd. Quickly it came closer, and quickly, after sounding again, deafening to the ears of those who encountered it, disappeared, in the direction of the city. Quickly, yes, however strange it might seem, given the slow pace at which the crowd proceeded, in two opposite directions. But it was so. I walked, pushed here and there by the throng, holding high my tape recorder. The music arrived, intersected, disappeared. Playing, I repeat, were men, even old men, and boys. But the majority were boys. And they were all smiling, sharing in the general happiness and, as young men always do, wishing to become its champions. They were all young men who seemed boys, with smooth faces, black hair cropped short, dressed partly European style, with plain white shirts, and partly in their traditional garments, consisting very simply of a white or light-colored tunic over pants of the same color. They played their instruments gaily, greeting their contemporaries and then disappearing toward the city without lights, looking forward to who knows what other continuation of the festivities. The street became narrower and more crowded, so that the fields around had become real swamps,

always vaguely stinking of fresh human shit, of children. To walk amid
all that deafening music, and the ever more relentless crowd, was almost impossible. Finally I began to understand more clearly (because I
had by now imagined it) what was happening. People were making a
pilgrimage to a temple or a great tabernacle, which now could be distinguished in the darkness at the end of the street. And it did not look
particularly ancient or beautiful. Which is something that also happens
in Italy with sanctuaries that are the object of pilgrimages. It rose down
there in the muddy ground, beyond a ditch crossed by a dilapidated little wooden bridge. Suddenly, in the middle of a particularly closely
packed group in the crowd—among whom it seemed impossible to
pass, because they were also as if possessed by a kind of orgasm or
panic—there appeared in front of me the marvelous image of a divinity;
in reality it was nothing but a puppet, perhaps of cloth and straw, like
the ones that are burned at Epiphany or Mayday in Europe. But it was
clothed in magnificent garments and a mask was attached to its face.
Neither the clothes nor the mask was truly sumptuous, of precious materials. In fact, they were shabby. The splendor was in the conception,
which nevertheless was completely, purely popular. It was the insidious,
devious, splendid, baroque madness of popular fantasy that reached a
refinement otherwise unobtainable. The predominant colors of the
clothes were two colors habitually brought together by great mannerist
painting: red and green. A vaguely violet, light red and the poisonous
green of newly sprouted wheat. Above all, the streamers, the bows, and
the ribbons were those colors. And they were tied in loops and knots
that, at least to me, recalled the loops and knots of the elegant Alcibi-
ades, as he appears to Socrates in the *Convitum.* That image was carried
by a group of young men; but though they had tried to hold it high, the
crush was so great that it was immediately torn from my sight. I saw it
wave and immediately disappear. But soon another, similar idol appeared, loaded with knots and trinkets of a ragged and baroque sumptuousness, the features of its pink mask impassive. This, too, was
swallowed up by the devout and frenzied crowd. Slowly I proceeded
toward the temple. Since now beside the road there was a fairly deep
ditch, I left the street and walked, as others did, too, on a slant along the
slippery bank. And thus I arrived at the little wooden bridge, covered

with fanciful craftsmen's ornaments, which led to the open space where the temple was. Yes, the temple was neither old nor particularly hand-some. People were scattered about the open space, tramping in the mud and walking around the temple, stopping in front of the statue of the divinity to pray and lay down their offerings. Like all the other temples and shrines, this one was full of little bronze bells, and people shook them, making them ring, sharp and deafening. I, too, went around the temple with the groups of pilgrims. The countryside was wet, gloomy, and black. When I returned to the front of the temple, rather than cross the little bridge again I stopped for a moment at the edge, beside a large bare bush surrounded by very tall reeds. I had been there for a few min-utes, always with my tape recorder raised (the music that continued in-cessantly was mixed with the irregular ringing of the little bells), when, behind me, I seemed to hear a cry. I strained my ears to listen, as far as it was possible to do so in that din. It was indeed a cry, a human cry. It came from behind the bush, among the reeds. I pushed my way into the tangle—around it, among other things, the persistent smell of infant shit was sharper—and I saw, lying in the mud, a human body; from the large dimensions and the clothes, I realized it was a man, a European. I leaned over and raised his head, which was horribly filthy with slime. It seemed to me that his mouth was bloody. He spoke to me in a thread of a voice. But at that moment the burst of bells was such that I could not hear his words. But after a while I began to grasp the sense of them. He spoke in English. He must have been American. However, when he re-alized from my pronunciation that I was Italian, he began to speak in Italian, almost perfectly. He had a long face, thin and yellow. The long hair fashionable among young men (though he was around forty) fell abjectly to his shoulders. He had the appearance of a drug addict who does not know if he is searching for the eyes of the next accomplice, for-giveness, or admiration. Anyway, on his face was stamped a sort of smile, disfiguring and constant, the smile of one who, lost or disgraced, is harmless. But that man was dying. Everything that I, seeing and hearing him, came to know of him was something unforgettable that, however, was about to be forgotten. Yet how could it be otherwise? Like everyone else, he, too, remained himself until the end. He told me, in the toneless voice of one who feels within himself the emptiness of a mortal trauma, how it had happened. 'Those men there,' that is, the poor citizens of Bhaktapur, all involved in their peasant festival, 'had murdered' him. Apparently by beating him; a few hours before, when it was still day, he had been there with his movie camera (I noticed it; it was on the ground near him in the stinking mud) to shoot the rather shabby preparations for the ceremony in that open space. Some boys had insistently placed themselves between the movie camera and the things to be filmed. He had begged them repeatedly to move, but they, perhaps because of their utter inability to understand his needs, did not move; then he, as he put it, 'gave one of them a kick in the ass.' I looked at him. How ever could such a man, reduced by degradation to meekness, have been able to give someone a kick in the ass? A question that remained without answer. The fact is that the child who had been so harshly treated ran crying to tell the old men. They intervened angrily, perhaps after a brief consultation. Certainly their reaction was collective. They arrived in a tight group, offended to the point of frenzy. They demanded that, to be forgiven, the guilty man must kneel before the oldest of those present and kiss his feet. One also had to wonder how men as mild as the inhabitants of Bhaktapur could become so excessively worked up. But this, too, was a question destined to remain without an answer. The guilty man did not feel like kneeling before anyone or kissing the feet of anyone. Then they began to beat him and in short lynched him. Now he was dying, there behind that bush, in the mud, while the festive bells of the temple kept ringing, closer together and more deafening. I understood that he was hurriedly preparing to tell me his last wishes. But it was not exactly a matter of last wishes; rather, it was a kind of confession that he made to me because I was Italian. He didn't want to be helped, taken to a hospital. The important thing was that he should speak to me. There he had a kind of impatient compassion in regard to me, observing that I was lying to make him believe there was still some hope for him. In this he behaved like the perfect Anglo-Saxon \bourgeois\. Only a little later did I learn that he was of Italian origin (but with an Anglo-Saxon mother) and that he belonged to the Mafia. What he had to confess to me was what he knew. His guilt, therefore, consisted in knowing. Perhaps, like those peasants who had beaten him to death, he believed in God and wished to pass on to the other world unburdened. Who knows. Or wished to take revenge on someone. What he told me covered a brief period of recent Italian history (exactly six years). My Nagra was running. Therefore everything he told me is recorded on a tape, mixed with the obsessive ringing of those bells and the Nepalese music, which continued to echo in that cold, dark stretch of countryside under the looming mountains."

[The story of the dying man is in the first person: a long story that begins in America—murder of Kennedy—arrival in Greece—Italian Fascists, etc.

The dying man tells what he knows; but also what he has learned from other dying men (three or four[55] who in their turn, before dying, tell him what they know.

The dying man of Nepal is therefore the last in chronological order. A suspicion that he was not murdered by the good Nepalese. Anyway he (metalinguistically) insists on saying that there are *two* phases of the slaughters, *two*, and the narrator repeats it to his listeners: *Two* phases, there are *two*]

NOTE 103A
An /uncertain/ basic point

I do not know if a formal structure really contains the entire reality of a book. On the identification of form with content I would not have Shklovsky's certainty, because every "unity," apparently, turns out to be "ideal." But there is no doubt that an identity of linguistic forms implies an identity of nonlinguistic forms. For example, this entire work is clearly divided into two parts (in a structural sense, because, I repeat, I am not writing a real story but creating a form): the first part is a "political bloc" based on the struggle of those in power against the Communist opposition; a real struggle, with real tension; the second part is a "political bloc" based on the struggle of those in power against Fascist

---

[55] One of them falls at night from the fourth floor of a clinic, right in front of him (D'Ambrosio). One dies falling down an elevator shaft.

subversion: struggle, on the other hand, as a pretext, with the tension of a pretext. A division of form that exactly reproduces that of the last story inserted into the text and attributed to an anonymous narrator in a circle of cultivated persons. This "transfer of meaning" in a work between compartments that should be watertight, < ... > † can certainly make the reader uncomfortable. And I, like the Marquis de Sade, think that *"Le lecteur a le droit de se fâcher quand il s'aperçoit que l'on veut trop exiger de lui . . ."* It is for this reason that I have generously set out the dilemma for him in almost elementary terms.

/IN PLACE OF THE ZEN STORIES/

Two stories about the Epoche: a complete change in the story

1) The story of discovering an artistic personality (a nobleman discovers a poor painter; a poor man discovers a noble painter; a petit bourgeois discovers a petit bourgeois painter [he disappears into a concentration camp]; but then comes the Epoche, and painters can no longer be discovered]

2) The father and his two daughters (holy and worldly); when he is about to reach his goal, the Epoche arrives and transforms values

(comments of the narrators and the listeners follow)

3) Story of the Infant-Shit‡

(May 1974)

4) A character created by dividing a person in two.
A character created as the synthesis of an infinite number of people or an infinite number of people created from the pulverization of a single one. In the first case there is order (which can therefore originate in separation) and death; in the second case there is disorder and life.
In an intermediate case there is a block: that is the Epoche.

(June 4, 1979)

NOTE 102
The Epoche: Comments in the living room

1) New era (of "Communes," etc.)
2) End of the Church
3) End of classical Fascism, etc.

Note 103—Search for a new Carmelo
             Pisa
   "   104—Return to Turin
   "   105—Turin station, Pensione Sicilia: the 20
   "   106—Episode of the twenty
   "   107—Disappearance of the twenty, their meeting with twenty Fascist Spirits
   "   108—The bomb
   "   109—Vision of the slaughter

NOTE 103
The impossibility of describing an anxiety
\A literally indescribable anxiety\

While around /him/ in the background the buzz of the Festival of the Quirinal continued and close to his ears the cultured discussion, like a living bas-relief on a heavy, overhanging rock, Carlo felt stabbed to the heart by the loss of Carmelo or whoever had been in Carmelo's place. The desire to find him again took away his breath; and the fatalistic feeling that told him clearly that he would never again find him was like a physical pain that < ... > everything mortal in him. In that condition—it was like being in a pit where he had the time and the means (like a daydreamer) to look out over the edge and cast a glance at the world around him; /he recognized it, and this only increased his despair. How real they were < ... > all those around him, who were speaking, smiling, looking for one another, avoiding one another, in the sarabande of life and of an old political struggle, which was, moreover, bleeding with innovations as if they were wounds!/ There in the midst, the memory of Carmelo's sex, enormous as the grappling iron of a pirate ship, of an implement found on peasant threshing floors, on ox-carts, and at the same time < ... >, almost silky, tender, in its hardness—it made him stagger, with his heart in his throat. And here I must point out that behind Carlo's desire and his pain there is nothing; there are neither equivalents nor precedents nor examples nor codes. What had bound Carlo to Carmelo so deeply that Carlo was ready, so to speak, to give his life for that bond was something completely arbitrary and groundless: something found neither in books of religious history, nor in books of ethnology, nor in books of anthropology, nor in books of psychology or psychoanalysis, not even in novels and memoirs; that is, in all /the knowledge/ that—even if it were arrayed in an immense, unlimited library—/I could/ consult to /help me/ in the task of describing precisely Carlo's desire and his pain.

At this point I feel it's necessary to make an observation, above all for myself. The stylistic system of my book prevents me < ... > from inventing a character whose final departure or death can be moving or can even (as I have no shame in considering natural) give rise to the divine \the ancient, human\ wish to cry hard, inconsolable as much as consoling.

POLITICAL BLOC I

[The sources—Appendices on yellow paper]

[The things that must be known]

*First phase—experienced by Carlo I half-consciously (?)—of the government's (State's) arrangement of slaughters as an anti-Communist function (cf. notes)

PETROLIO

/ (SECOND PART) / †

NOTE 103B
Second political bloc (Preamble)

What I am about to narrate in this book is, still, "something written." But "something written" that now refers exclusively to the previous "something written."

Only the *initiated* reader—*initiated,* that is, into the writing of this book—can perhaps claim to understand the column of signs printed on the page he is about to read.

The previous "something written" told of the genocide carried out by those in Power against the working class and therefore the poor, through the imposition of new Models (which, by radically transforming the workers and the poor, had made them literally disappear from the face of the earth).

The "something written" now recounts, literally, a criminal enterprise of those in Power (to be precise, in the Government).

Now, the criminal enterprise undertaken by power in its bureaucratic government form consists of a violent form of anti-working-class and, to be exact, anti-Communist conflict.

The question, then, is what is the meaning of all this, if, as we have seen in the previously cited "block of signs," the working classes, or anyway the poor, have in reality "disappeared from the face of the earth"? How is it possible, even conceivable, to struggle against someone who is no longer there?

Of course there is always an explanation. In the present case—which I have laid out artificially—the explanation is this: power is always, as they say in Italy, Machiavellian; that is, realistic. It excludes from its activities everything that can be "known" through Visions. Now, the Vision that describes the violent end of the working class is found in this novel, is included "in the domain of this writing"; and so it is only here, in this very place, that the mind of those in power has to take the Visions into account.

Now, since, apparently, it does not do that, it appears to be feeble, ineffectual, obtuse, fearful, pitiless, criminal. Yet—as we shall see later on in a third "block of signs," a third *laisse* of the "something written"—it is not. The stupid behavior of those in Power (in /assembling/ an enormous machinery, made up of a chain of common crimes, to destroy something that Power itself has already destroyed by other means) is really, at least in this context, enigmatic. The light of history needs a calendar; upset the chronological sequence of events just a little—perhaps breaking them down into their elements—and look, the light of history goes out and no longer explains anything.

Placing a series of (realistic) crimes after a Vision—a placement that mocks the logic of Machiavellianism or of political realism, making it extremely antiquated—is, moreover, still (let it be clear) an accusation. Because political men, besides not being assassins, must be able to have Visions.

/—Note on The Shit's fainting (<?>)
—The monument "for laughing"
—Note on "   "   "   (task undertaken with the reader to guide
   him)/

PART I

—Julia Mikhailovna's party (Carlo = Stavrogin = Tagore) brazenly Giulia Miceli (eternal feminine) <?> of Dostoyevsky—parasitical moment— "rewritten" with analogies, correspondences, etc., present world (feminists instead of governesses, *but* cf. always *The Possessed*)—Also literary men— also literary quadrille—etc.

———————

———————

PART II [*expectation* of scandal] [unusual and very significant physical aspects of C.]

—All paraphrased from Dostoyevsky because C. is falling apart, etc., *but* not with a disaster (fires or crimes) *but* with the scandal of the two coups de théâtre having to do with C.

1) He expresses his fear of a new anti-Fascism, and it is he who prosecutes and resolves the Fanfani cataclysm (heralding the "cosmic crisis" that will burst forth at the end of the novel)

2) Religious paradoxes
   (Possibly insert a love story)

———

———

—Journey to Edo—<?> for symmetry with the first journey—all telegraphic, etc.—then onward from the apparition and the suggestion for the journey from Cornelio

Nov. 11, 1974

FINALE

*<u>Cosmic crisis</u> (end of oil, water, air)

—Gods—not Gods[56] who relive the scene of the original cosmic crises (instead of the present, the most ancient crisis is evoked—which in effect is repeated, always the same: anasyrma, laugh, <?>, picking up the course of the story)

—Laughs, etc.

—it's a matter of deciding how—meeting—everything as before.

NOTE 103C
The lawn around the tower of Pisa

(This is a chapter analogous to Chapter 51a, "Bullicame." Carlo inspects the young students who are hanging around, stretched out, etc., on the vast lawn. Their physical and moral characteristics totally legible, totally different from those of the young men of Bullicame. There has

---

[56] Arriving, they see the new face of the disfigured, polluted earth—water, animals, vegetation, wastes <?> and plutonium dumps—thermonuclear power plant funeral monuments (in addition to the twisted ruins of everything having to do with oil, from refineries to gas station attendants).

been a gap of an era, but that has not yet come into Carlo's consciousness—while the other Carlo has already experienced it completely, etc.—and so he looks at them as if he were in a painful nightmare of impotence on both his part and theirs, etc.)

NOTE 104
The places of vice

From Pisa, Carlo returns directly to Turin. I spare myself, and spare the reader, the description of his "unknown" pain. He carries himself around like a sack that contains a gagged and bleeding man. He is tormented by a desire whose realization he considers impossible. Of this he has had a single experience, which has remained unique, isolated, abstract. It was when he was a boy and from his school companions had learned that "places of vice" existed. They spoke of those places among themselves quite naturally; but from that moment he buried within himself the knowledge of such a phenomenon. Then for his whole life the work of burial had continued. Now, however, if the knowledge was so deep inside him that he despaired of its ever again returning to the light, the "memory of it," on the contrary, had remained vivid in him, as if recent and glowing bright. He recalled in perfect detail what these places of vice were and what one did there.

He had been a slow, awkward boy, unbearably ridiculous and timid \cowardly\, with knee-length trousers, English style, tight over a crotch as empty as a woman's. He did not have the grace of timidity at all. He secretly grabbed everything to which he had a right, like the others. He was not a "different" sort of hopeless person. The fat, shapeless peasant cheeks, the small eyes, expressionless (except when charged with an indecipherable look of defensiveness and < ... >), the short neck packed between narrow, round shoulders, the fat, high rear, the puffy legs in the shape of xxx: all that made him an unattractive but perfectly normal boy.[57]

Now, as an adult, he was not much changed. In fact, he had remained curiously identical to what he was then. Greedy, sensual, and blindly convinced that not saying things ensured them a complete and lasting secrecy: as then.

All right. He now returns to Turin to look for those "places of vice" that were the only ones he had some knowledge of and to which he therefore attributed a particular, "solid" kind of validity: in some sense "traditional"! I repeat, they were the only ones he knew; and that made them "the places of vice" par excellence, absolutely the only ones.

—gets off the train in Turin

—evening (sinister half-light, *legal* dinner, everything too clear, etc.

—First "visions"—prostitutes
                           transvestites

—Bar—Customers in the Bar

—Acquaintance with Pambo

—Appearance of people with beards and a lot of hair who remember the writer whose name ends in -*trini*. It is impossible to tell whether they are Fascists or Communists and their mysterious attitude (drugs, bombs, etc.)

—Meeting with Teodoro (Fedka), retracing the meeting between Stavrogin and Fedka; but the latter is <?> who blackmails Carlo about nothing. Carlo is a man of power (or has been) and does not let himself be blackmailed

—<...> Fedka as a pimp—and it will be he who takes him to the Pensione Sicilia (where there is a throng and swarm of immigrants, of new men. A company that breaks up and is re-formed)

[57] *"Votivus puer"* precisely as *"perversus puer,"* and vice versa, to adopt <...> the language of Pietro da Eboli and Gioacchino da Fiore, who naturally refer to a son of the powerful (Frederick II).

NOTE 105
Preamble to the great Digression

But . . . for all the effort it takes and the qualms I have regarding the "disappointed expectations" of the reader, I must at this point interrupt the trajectory that was so decisively carrying Carlo toward the realization (even if it was < ... > unsatisfying and conventional) of his new desires and begin to follow another. This new narrative leap, however, has nothing to do with Carlo, at least for the moment, but concerns a series of characters who have not been "introduced," who are absolutely new and therefore justly suspect and off-putting. Moreover, the story that involves these new characters is not even original. It is "remade," parasitic; in addition to following a technique completely unknown to the narrator I take as my model (who is considered inimitable). That Carlo is a Stavrogin cannot be absolutely or even distantly true. There is no doubt, however, that he is precisely the *Stavrogin that Dostoyevsky had planned to create* (yet in fact did not create: for the simple reason that he could never have endured spending two years of his life, 1868–69, with such a person). /That is, Carlo is a person who is *truly* "tepid."/ It's also true that Stavrogin—as Dostoyevsky declares—is neither "ardent" nor "cold." < ... > He is both at once; but that does not in the least mean that he is "tepid." "Ardor" and "coldness" put together produce something other than "tepidness," that is, mediocrity, as Dostoyevsky claimed verbally. "Ardor" and "coldness" taken together produce ambiguity: experienced < ... > dramatically, but without explicit conflict. An ambiguity that is fixed, therefore, in the image of the enigmatic. I have already observed, I think, in the course of this work, that Carlo's carnal sins, precisely because they are infinitely repeated, do not even dimly approach Stavrogin's few terrible sins.

In brief, to conclude, Carlo is a Stavrogin as he should have been, that is, *truly* "tepid" (horrible for Dostoyevsky; and also for me); and if he is provided with a double life, that means, in our case, that it's a matter of two tepid lives.

Like Stavrogin, who committed his sins in the capital or outside the country, Carlo had an authoritative mother, a member of the establishment of "our city," that is, Turin. And his mother—who, in fact, was called Barbara—also had a powerful friend-rival, who had been settled in Turin for a while and was similar in every way to Julia Mikhailovna, and whom I will have the impudence to call, for convenience, Giulia Miceli. Certainly, her "eternal feminine" frightens me not a little; but I will try to measure up to it, even if, as I say, I have to paraphrase.

NOTE 106A
The great Digression begins

Barbara (Varvara Petrovna), the mother of our Stavrogin Italian style (a definition or identification that is not really accurate; or accurate *only in part*), in these last years had almost completely left her Skvoreshniki in the Canavese to establish herself in the city. She wished to be present. She was (as we know) a political woman. And furthermore she was of the left. Certainly, for example, farther to the left than Saragat, whom she had known when they were both young. < ... > She had developed in the ideal Turinese environment, whose immediate progenitors were Gobetti and Gramsci. Her ambition (which she had not confessed to anyone and was probably known only to me) was to resemble, "on a grand scale," the mother of the Pajettas. In her time she had been a good friend of Pavese (although he—at least it appears from documents— was not aware of it). She had decided to invest her progressivism of the left in the Christian Democratic Party, because she would then feel freer (from possible conformity with the left) and also, above all, more useful (so the period of John XXIII and the Catholicism of dissent arrived just in time). In any case, on one point she was unyielding: her anti-Fascism and her faith in the values of the Resistance. Thus she sincerely confused her desire to be preeminent < ... > with /having the right credentials/. In the period of Carlo's return to Turin (not as a prodigal son) some events very important to Barbara had recently occurred. An old school friend of hers had been transferred from Rome to Turin, as the wife of the new prefect. But, as often happens in such cases, especially in novels, in reality she was the Prefect.[58] She had married a poor devil of a bureaucrat, who nevertheless, by the inert force of promotions, had made a sort of career in the Ministry of Defense. < ... > He was originally from the Marches and was, by nature, on the one hand uncertain and neurotic, and on the other peaceful and without real ambition. But by chance he had been in Piedmont during the war and there, also by chance, had participated in the partisan war. To Barbara's old school friend, this had seemed a decisive reason, among others, to marry him, take him out of the Roman bureaucratic routine, and manage to have him appointed Prefect of Turin. It was the first time the Prefect of a big industrial city had come from the Resistance; and was therefore of proven anti-Fascist loyalty. Thus he seemed to initiate a new system—a prospect of tolerance—in the government and the administration. And so Barbara, as an old /frontline soldier/, suddenly found herself in the avant-garde. < ... > But there was a shadow: the shadow of Giulia Miceli. As a result, between the two rivals there could arise only a passionate alliance. And so it was.

< ... > Having given all this unbridled information, which seems to be obligatory in a story, I come rapidly to the kernel; that is, to the xxx of facts, intrigues, xxx xxx in which Carlo found himself (to his complete indifference) upon his arrival in Turin.

NOTE 106B
The great Digression continues

---

[58] By analogy with the Governoress, that is, of *The Possessed*.

NOTE 107
Meeting with "Fedka"

* Introduce the father figure Carmelo \Pambo\ (old Sicilian fag, giant) and reintroduce the figure of the writer whose name ends in -*on*—in a context of Marxist-Leninist and Feltrinellian divisions at the edge of the criminal world (which then *changes color from red to black,* etc., in the episode of the slaughter, which links that same criminal world [Pensione Sicilia] to the Communist extremists).

* The anonymous face "typical" of an enigmatic youth (neither Fascist nor anti-Fascist, neither conformist nor anti-conformist; perhaps imbecilic, perhaps criminal, etc.).

  A face that remains *imprinted* in Carlo's memory among all his "degrading" adventures.

* The hit men or allies of the underworld (or of the chaos in Italy) explode the bomb with the two million lire given by Carlo to the "prostitutes" at the Pensione Sicilia.

NOTE 110
The Godoari

Carlo went toward the back of the station. The walls, in some places collapsed, in others still standing, but with enormous cracks that split them obliquely or made huge gaping holes, looked like ruins. The dust had settled, and only the fresh piles of rubble all /around/ bore witness to the recent disaster. But the shape of the wreckage, the jagged profile of the xxx, because of the solidity of the construction, out of a material still in use at the beginning of the century, gave those destroyed walls the look of noble ruins: of a temple, for example, or an abandoned seventeenth-century church in the middle of the countryside, among tangles of nettles and feeble ivy, among bluebells and thistles, its arches open to the sky and the distant horizon. . . . In fact, mysteriously, the gaps and fissures in the Art Nouveau station let in the celestial (to say the least) light of the countryside, as if the city, in the background, had dissolved. /The gaps and fissures opened directly to the sky, from which came that light which can be the light of early morning, when it has just lost the tenuousness of dawn and life has already begun— or the light that precedes a summer twilight, when evening is still distant and in its ripeness there is something fresh and deathlike at the same time./ Entering, in any case, as if from a blue background, or from a marine horizon on which the sea was not visible, that light took on the monstrous shapes of the cracks and holes through which it penetrated, but it fell on the floor with an extraordinary and reassuring lightness: a real return of life (which, to tell the truth, had never, even for an instant, been suspended). But what had happened to those long reddish streets of the suburbs, lined with palazzos from the time of Umberto I, and tall porticoes, and with tram tracks embedded in the smooth pavement? < ... > Was it possible that the explosion could have razed to the ground the entire neighborhood around the station?

NOTE III
The Godoari (continued)

With the caution of a sedentary man, Carlo approached the piles of rubble, climbed over them, and, slipping and sliding, finally managed to get near a break in the wall and look out. In fact, the city was no longer there. The station building /rose/ in the middle of an immense desert,

exactly like an ancient church reduced to solitary ruins invaded by nettles and sun.

With difficulty Carlo climbed onto the sill of a blown-out window,
reduced to the solemn misery of an arch eaten away by the centuries.

The desert before him was a kind of green plain, with embankments
here and there and small groves of deciduous trees—stunted alders and
leafless acacias. Wild, scrubby grasses had grown up everywhere, there
were no traces of roads or paths. Certainly for years there had been no
reaping or haymaking; the more delicate grasses had disappeared or become rare, while the tougher weeds, fennel, xxx, xxx, persisted, grew
abundant, with their harder, calluslike stalks.

Carlo went out into that Piedmont plain, went in the direction of the
mountains, which, gray or /bluish/, like clouds, obstructed the sky; only
a white thread of snow marked their profile, distinguishing their hazy
outlines from the scarcely more transparent haze of the summer sky.

As Carlo went on, the earth gradually became less dry and barren;
perhaps he was approaching a series of springs, whose waters, arriving
underground from the snows on those milky \hazy\ mountains, were
emerging and, no longer confined by banks, were spreading over the
plain, making it green.

NOTE 112
The Godoari (III)

It was more difficult to walk through those /verdant/ places. It was no
longer a desert but a savanna, the edge of a forest. His legs sank into
grass so thick that neither earth nor mud could be seen at its roots. All
around, the woods became denser: elders with hard, dry leaves and slender branches; blackberry bushes; wild figs: now in a hollow where the
grass was even more /luxuriant/ and the ground was muddy, now on one
of the /plateaus/ that, from their regularity, seemed to have been dikes
once. Although every blade of grass, every little leaf was familiar and

there was not a single tree whose form had not been known forever to those who had never set foot outside the plain of the Po, the sun and the silence spread something wild and terrifying over it all. Where the trees became thicker, surrounded by dry shrubs that seemed to be nourished more on air and sun than on water, the cicadas did not chirp but raged. /Their concert was deep, monotonous, deafening, and powerful, as it had been among the fields of grain on the shores of the stream near Athens where Socrates and Phaedrus walked one afternoon thirteen centuries ago./ And the birds had returned, masters of the sky and the plants. Sometimes they were so many that the sky appeared to be swarming. And so, too, the creatures of the earth: reptiles, lizards, snails, beetles, flies. Behind the barrier of a hedge that looked like marble, among cypresses encircled by ivy dotted with bluebells and some low medlars that had grown up by chance, there was a canal, fed by a stream of deep green water, more transparent than crystal; into those depths the sunlight penetrated obliquely, mottling the stream and its banks. Hundreds and hundreds of bees had gathered around a pool and were drinking \quenching their thirst\. /It was like a Homeric fountain. Or perhaps the shifty eyes of Salimbene of Parma had also seen it. Surely some traveler/ must have passed there and forgotten it, like so many other familiar things. But there was not a trace of any passerby. The only sign of life was those golden bees on the still, slightly putrid water.

NOTE 113
The Godoari (IV)

Then the savanna began again, with its poplars that, once cultivated, had grown up thicker and thicker until they became a true wild forest. Yet along the edge of that forest the grass was short and thin and the ground hard, so that one could even run. The long, smooth trunks, clothed in sunlight that was already slanting a little, cast long, thin, even shadows, closer and closer together, on the dry leaves carpeting the ground.

The poplars ended, and the plain began again; but not as green—almost barren, as it had appeared in the beginning, around the ruins of the station.

The grass became yellowish and stiff and more sharply scented with fennel, chamomile, and mint. And it became thinner, laying bare the hard, rocky ground.

Finally, on the horizon, behind thin stands of the usual trees, a kind of gap appeared, a uniform expanse against the limitless horizon that ran clear below the dark, cloudy base of the mountains. It was a river; or rather a huge torrent, at least a kilometer wide and gleaming with pebbles just carried down from the mountains: clear, or white as eggs, or tender pink or gray.

Streams flowed over that desert of pebbles, now branching off and now reuniting; the water was turquoise, darkening just slightly at the deepest points, in the hollows, but remaining perfectly transparent, so that the color of the rocks on the bottom would be seen.

Within the boundless expanse of rocks—edged /in the background/ by a diaphanous barrier of trees and bushes, tiny in the distance—in the midst of those rapid greenish blue xxx, /sharp-/scented low bushes were growing: osiers, red-veined, almost lacquered, in whose shadow—on a bit of dusty ground—< ... > were some little yellow flowers, the poorest yet most precious products of summer, which could be felt there on that immense shore in all its lingering but powerful heat.

NOTE 114
The Godoari (V)

Beyond the shore the uncultivated land began again, grazed by the light of the sun, so that the line of the horizon was clearly drawn against the distant dark overhang of the mountains.

The silence—if it could be called silence, with the screech of cicadas as stupefying as that of the swallows or the twittering of the other birds—was absolute. There was no sign of human life.

When suddenly there appeared < ... > a patch of grass that seemed to have been mowed; yes, the bristling, cutoff stalks of the xxx xxx xxx were clearly visible. But nothing else around, except that precise evidence, indicated any other peace than that of the wildness of nature abandoned to itself.

The fruit trees, unpruned for decades or centuries, had tough, twisted branches, too many leaves, small unrecognizable fruits; they grew haphazardly among the brambles, which, along with nettles and xxx, appeared to be gradually covering the whole countryside. And yet beyond a dense thicket of iron-hard brambles and a plot of short green grasses—probably with some lettuce and chicory mixed in—appeared a second sign; and it was something that could not but give the heart a /jolt/ and bring unrestrained tears to the eyes: it was a little field of wheat, with a few rows of vines in the middle, in which the . . . of a human hand could be clearly discerned.

NOTE 115
The Godoari (VI)

Indeed, a little farther on, the traces of a path, or track, of beaten earth appeared among the grasses.

Passing now through fields of alfalfa, now through thickets of limes and acacias, the track led to a broader road, though it, too, was of beaten earth, like brown mud hardened by many days of good weather.

Along the edge of the road ran a canal, whose swift water was green and miraculously transparent.

The /mime leaf/ of the aquatic grass that grew on the bottom was visible, long leaves now ruffled by the current, now of a mossy, deep green compactness.

After a while, there was a little bridge over the canal, which, parallel to the road, was bordered by a tall hedge of limes and acacias.

The surface was of beaten earth, but the low-arched vault underneath was of brick. The current rushed through with a wonderful freshness; no longer in perfect solitude, however, because on the bridge, on the verdant banks, and in the water were ducks intent on their business, determined not to let anything disturb them. Every so often they beat their stubby wings, white, pearl gray, mouse gray, and their little blue heads had /sapphire/ highlights around the eyes.

NOTE 116
The Godoari (VII)

Evening had fallen almost suddenly; or at least twilight, < ... > which seemed darker there, at the edge of those watery thickets of plants. It was the hour when bells should begin to ring in the neighboring villages < ... >. Across the bridge, the long wall of limes and acacias ended, and behind it could be seen a high brick wall with a door in the middle. It was half closed. As one came nearer, there was an echo of voices in the air—or at least so it seemed—from within the farmyard. The words could not be distinguished, only the inflections. A woman's voice, very distant, perhaps from the far side of the farmyard, which must face the open country, said something loud and then continued more dreamy and muffled; probably the woman had drawn back into the house from the window where she had been leaning out. After a while a boy's voice rose, perhaps not responding to her directly but taking up the conversation she had begun, and on that was immediately superimposed the authoritarian voice of a man, certainly the father. The boy laughed and was silent. And a dog could be heard whimpering. Then the silence returned. It was the hour when the peasants returned home from the fields, put down their tools, went to wash up and comb their hair at the pump, with the large trough where the animals drank; and while the one whose turn it was looked after the livestock, the others went up to their rooms to change, getting ready perhaps to go into town on a bicycle or perhaps, clean and combed, to pass the evening in the courtyard with friends from the other farms. And it was the hour when, all at once, women began to prepare supper; through the windows fires could be seen shining on the dark hearths; there was a strong odor of roasting grains, and children, who waited just for that moment to make nuisances of themselves, were called by their mothers and sisters or quarreled among themselves. . . .

< ... > Just a push on the half-closed door was enough to enter that farmyard beyond the bridge. But a gap between its big, heavy, worn panels revealed behind the door something that was, in a way, miraculous: in the middle of the courtyard was an enormous mulberry tree, at least three or four times as big as the little mulberries that used to be planted in rows in the fields or were used to hold up the vines. Its thick leaves, massed in a round xxx, were of an intense, profound green, /blindingly bright/. Perhaps all the last light of the sun was concentrated in \was absorbed by\ that xxx and diffused through the courtyard, with its porches and its shed roofs, its brick paving already lost in shadow.

NOTE 117
The Godoari

Certainly the voices had been an illusion; perhaps they were the voices of birds or of other animals, because inside the farmhouse there was not a soul \living soul\. Like the big outer door, all the doors were ajar; indeed, some were even pushed in, and the thresholds were like dark mouths. The kitchen, as big as a barn, was empty; the hearth was on the outside house wall that faced the country, and through two windows, to the left and the right, entered a last green glow of twilight; the brick floor was uneven; the ceiling xxx. The upper rooms were reached from the outside by a wooden staircase that led to a long balcony; but the steps of the staircase were rotted, and one could not go up. In a corner of the courtyard was the wall of a church, with a pointed pediment, a small, fine fifteenth-century door, and, above, a small rose window, primitive and precious. There, too, the door panels were rotted and gaping, the bolt dangling. Inside, it was dark; there was only that weak greenish light of the countryside beyond the farm, which must face west.

As one's eyes became accustomed to the shadows, still tinged with the thin, cheerless gleam of sunset—which, in the rare clarity of the sky, faintly lit at the horizon, promised in vain a series of beautiful days— the dim remains of frescoes could be discerned on the walls. They must have been destroyed a long time ago; but still, after the final destruction, some fragments were visible: the face of a foreshortened saint with high cheekbones who looked out with a dark, noble gaze, perhaps from /the south, or at least from that school/; the headless body of a Madonna, the fabric of her Prussian-blue mantle faded on her knees and falling on either side in symmetrical folds; some sheep and a dog in a patch of green meadow, with the face of a donor in the foreground: this one was not from the south but, humble and crude, from the Po valley. In the apse one could distinguish only a layer of paint that was nearly black, with some big stars and the knobs of the back of a throne.

NOTE 118
The Godoari

—Looking for a place where he can go to sleep, *Carlo* (renamed) sees some fresh feces (because of the flies)

—He sleeps (in a bed filled with old peasant odors) in a nightmare: the one who produced the feces may be a hostile presence, kill him, etc.

—He falls into a profound sleep and in the morning wakes as if the nightmare had come true—There is a boy of 15 or 21–22, etc., etc., Tunin (in Piedmontese)—He becomes Carlo's guide to Turin—does not speak does not understand is half mad (like boys in institutions), etc.

NOTE 119
The Godoari†

The next morning everything was sparkling with icy dew; even among the summer acacias, mist hung suspended. Following the dirt road, one came first to fields of wheat; then again to uncultivated countryside. And again the desert: land that men had never reached or that they had abandoned.

The remains of formerly cultivated plants had grown wild and formed a tangled forest. The plots of land had not completely disappeared; nor had the regular shapes of vineyards and poplar groves or the system of canals or the long lines of the dikes been completely erased. But this made the primordial desolation that the old plain—so familiar a short time before—had been thrust back into even more desperate.

The plants that for so many centuries men had fought victoriously, confining them to useless corners, where, in close alliance with the dusty sun, or with shade and mud, they had preserved their invincible vitality, now, slowly, had resumed their true life, had proliferated everywhere in a kind of evil triumph, which only immensity and silence contained, in a kind of solemn self-restraint. Nettles and weeds, xxx and xxx, extended as far as the eye could see, choking what had once been fruit trees or vegetables; they had the same grandeur as the morning and its white light.

The lifeless forest that had grown from the old Po vegetation opened up in the direction of the not so distant edge of a river or a chain of hills; but one felt—as if in the heart of Africa—that everything would continue on in the same way, in the same icy utter solitude, even beyond the line of the horizon. A sinister tangle of plants that here and there, by chance, preserved, like traces of a dream, the designs of long ago— the sublime ornament of a grapevine; the umbrella of an oak among nut trees; a willow among the reeds; a hillside black with chestnuts against the intense, clear blue of the distant flank of a mountain chain; a yellow ridge against brown rocks and thick green grass—appeared endless before the eyes wherever one stopped to look for the reality of the past. One felt that this desert did not end among the hills of Vezzolano or Moniglio, nor at the plain of Poirino, Carmagnola, Carmignano, or Airasca, nor at the first, obliquely lighted slopes of the Alps, above Giaveno, Avigliana, or Viu; but that it continued unchanged for tens and hundreds of kilometers more, along the Chisone or the Dora Riparia, as far as the glaciers, or along the Varaita and the Maira to Cuneo and then, < ... > the Stura, as far as Liguria and the sea; and still—beyond Monferrato—as far as /the place/ where Alessandria, Novi, Tortona, or Piacenza once rose, from Bormida to Staffora, embracing in its immensity only, perhaps, some Romanesque ruin that had already existed for centuries before the civilization that had been buried by a desert reborn in a return to its origins.

NOTE 120
The Godoari (IX)†

< ... > /Slowly, however, that wasteland, which at first had had a form,/ became formless. It was no longer anything. It was pure presence, matter, extent. An anonymous land of weedy grass, of bare, stunted trees unable to be < tragic > in their poverty; rivers as if with just enough definition so that the water could flow in them, great plains, boundless and yet as if without space, mounds of fresh earth abandoned before taking on any function, embankments built up and left half finished. Finally, an immense pile of trash appeared, in a sort of large hollow in the earth, with an /unbreathable acid/ odor and the sparkle of tin

and the more <opaque> sparkle of plastic; part of the trash had been burned, leaving a barren expanse of ashes; the rest was burning. The fires hissed, faded, or flared up suddenly, fed by the polluted wind, in the most absolute solitude.

Then, at the edge of that vast garbage heap, there was a square little mountain† of coal or slag; it was partly black, partly whitish; perhaps it depended on the different exposure to the light; whatever it was, the color was the color of death but, I repeat, of a /true death/, without any shape.

/From the top/ of that plateau one could see the expanse of Turin, pushing unconfined almost to the foot of the mountains, which made a dark background for the ancient white /of the cities/ that appeared to the caravans.

NOTE 121
The new periphery

The first houses were placed on that formless plain: they were huge, white, geometric; the walls, beaten by the /rising/ sun, were blinding, and the endless succession of identical balconies speckled them with identical small, dry, pitiful shadows; the walls in shadow were black and smooth, gigantic rectangles. These big apartment buildings, arranged in asymmetrical but regular groups around walled courtyards, were in pairs. Repetitions of a single form; which, moreover, was repeated exactly in other nearby groups. These groups of dwellings that looked like constellations advanced from the desolate desert toward denser constellations. But the silence was no less profound than in the desert. In the huge courtyards, which were built of cheap materials—concrete sprayed to look like marble, fake-looking brick—the emptiness was complete. Only in a few two or three women had gathered, darkly outlined against the /metallic walls/, with bags of semitransparent white plastic in their hands. There were also some children, silent in the distance; mostly they were outside the courtyards, between the boundary walls and the ditches, which were dry and overflowing with garbage; beyond them stretched the desert.

NOTE 122
The new periphery (continued)

Before the citadels made up of the succession of buildings began to co-alesce definitively into the city that was emerging in the gray light of the sun (which, as it rose, slowly lost light and intensity), they became sparser for a distance, and the desert recommenced. It's true that this desert was traversed by a wide asphalt road. But its edges were chipped and strewn with garbage and the dirt of that formless plain. Occasion-ally the road was intersected by a canal full of fetid black water, on whose steep banks the garbage seemed to have been piled by a hand de-termined to create a sense of solidity, of eternity: bold on the bank where the sun struck, melancholy on the side in shadow. Some teenage boys had stopped on one of the bridges on the road that crossed the last strip of desert and were leaning on their motorcycles; they wore pants and shirts in lively /artificial/ colors, as if for a celebration. Then they all moved off together, revving their motorcycles angrily and raising the front tires, as if to make their mounts rear up. But their faces were ab-sent, pale, their gazes twisted or turned away. Their hair, cut short on the forehead and left very long behind the ears, so that it hung down to their shoulders, made them look like absurd, sinister \monstrous\ fe-male fetishes. Soon they disappeared; and in that last stretch of desert only the solitude remained, filled with the unbreathable stench of garbage. A little farther on, there was another constellation, but mixed in with it, like ruins or structures from another universe, were some old, run-down farm buildings. They were stuccoed in an orangey red, now faded and chipped; the tile roofs were speckled with moss, and on the inside wall, facing the farmyard, reduced to a little field where the grass was strangely green against the hard white earth, there was a wood-and-iron staircase that led to the upper floors, continuing in a balcony that ran the length of the entire house. The doors that opened onto the balcony were closed; but those old buildings were not abandoned. Some children were playing on the grass, and an old man was sitting on the balcony; his skin was dark, and his squinting eyes sparkled. Between clenched jaws was a sensual mouth, and white down covered the dark skin. His body was small but still lean, hardened by work. The light of his gaze was almost too expressive, even in that moment of solitude; its brightness was due, perhaps, to the gaiety with which a person who regards himself as inferior considers the misery of his own presence; or to the winning smile with which an unwelcome or pitiful guest, incapable of grasping the customs of a place, begs for understanding with a joke; or perhaps, even, the light in his eyes was threatening, vulgar, the look of a young outlaw who is suddenly old but will not give up his authority, which has become that of a father, of a poor patriarch, who no longer speaks and whose silence says nothing of things the world shouldn't know.

NOTE 123
The new periphery (III)

The end of the first bus route came into view, something by now quite \rather\ old in the world. But the conductor and the driver, awaiting their shift, did not joke the way men of the people usually do. They stood stiff as bureaucrats beside their big new shiny bus. Indifferent to the stink of garbage that reached even there—from the banks of a canal that ran behind an old yellow tollbooth, now abandoned and crumbling—the two were smoking, pale and withdrawn, their long hair falling onto their necks from beneath old work caps. Their real life—they seemed to be saying—was in some other place. It had refinements, claims, and troubles that had nothing to do with work. And the people who crowded around waiting for the bus to arrive or depart had the same hostile attitude. The intensity with which they accepted the burden of their day declared the irreplaceable totality of it. They were employed in jobs that gave them a dignity for which they were completely unprepared, so that it had the characteristics of a betrayal, however innocent; the humility of killers had been transformed in them into complicity, which made them arrogant and insensitive. Some young people arrived, men and women mixing together in a comradely way; and with them noise and happy laughter. But it was all conventional, learned /from television/. In fact, one of them was posing beside a small economy car, shiny /as a mirror/, the way young men do in ads for automobiles or for clothes or some accessory. He had in his eyes the same total happiness that prevented the /access/ of any feeling that did not correspond to a cherished model, without alternative; but since this total happiness was, of course, false and unnatural, a shadow of shame and fear remained in the depths of his eyes. The happy words were forced. But no one realized it. And so the performance was perfect on everyone's part.

People like those at the bus stop were the model that would be repeated not ten, not hundreds, not thousands, but tens of thousands of times on the journey into the city.

The constellations of apartment buildings were embedded one inside the other, and the only openings \breaks\ in that compact surface were the overpasses, observatories onto the disorder, that thousands of cars and trucks were crossing furiously. The morning was already advanced, and the sun had disappeared behind a kind of veil.

NOTE 124
The new periphery (IV)

Almost all those people (to one who did not share their interests they appeared as if in a sort of exposed reality) were going to the center of the city, drawn by the jobs that brought them prosperity and, as a result, that dream quality. One who was not in the same hurry but was going in their direction could easily see how the dream in which they were sunk really worked and functioned. It was a matter of an action and a function definable in essence through a series of negations: those people were *no longer* the people of a former time, those people *no longer* had the purity (even if forced on them) of poverty, those people *no longer* had the old respect, those people *no longer* had the old anxiety about blackmail, those people *no longer* created their own human model, those people *no longer* set their culture against that of their bosses, those people *no longer* knew the sanctity of resignation, those people *no longer* knew the silent will of revolution. All these negations were indispensable to one another.

This was expressed by the physical presence of those people, by their attitude: by their bodies. Suddenly there was an opposing surge, an invasion, which moved from the center of the city toward the periphery, or from one periphery to the other. It was the workers coming out of the factories. Sirens wailed; a few surviving bells tolled the arrival of noon.†

/NOTE 125
A Fascist demonstration/

<Carlo goes home. The first floor of a building on Via xxx. His mother and his sisters, Chiara, Emilia, Natalia, are to him like anachronistic shadows. The incest that took place with all of them is remembered now as an event in a dream, and he has practically abolished them from reality. They belong to another, purely social order. Besides, for Carlo being at home is like being in a hotel. He has breakfast, he sleeps. He goes out (available again, with no engagements, as when he was a boy). He goes to the café where his friends meet (thirteen years older than when he last saw them). He arrives there like a sleepwalker. To the others he is a man of power; he has reached the highest pinnacle of his profession. Qualities of an inhuman order are attributed to

him. As though he belonged to a theophany. His friends, who have had modest careers in the city (yet which in the sphere of the city have proved to be high-ranking, respectable; in a certain sense more respectable than Carlo's, which is not unconnected to the idea of something adventurous, unstable, bound to the corrupt capital, and of a socially inferior quality), welcome him with respect disguised—without any effort and, in fact, with surprising naturalness—by familiarity and cordiality. Their experience, philosophical, restricted, conditioned by a life without alternatives, has, however, a perfection of its own. In their knowledge and their cultural attitudes they very much resemble one another; but what truly unites them is a shared form of humor, very warm and vital, which Carlo is unused to. Political men who are successful—even if they come from environments like that, xxx, from cafés like the one on Via xxx—are infinitely poorer, duller, more provincial. A discussion begins among the old friends—one of those discussions that in Rome, particularly in the world that has become Carlo's world, are impossible (except in bad faith). The political big shot can't help but *always* be a demagogue and a liar; the one who holds true power—who is publicly less well known and has no need to beg continually for popularity, strutting like a peacock, but is cold and totally cynical—relaxes a bit and becomes a boy only in his hobbies. The old Turinese friends, who have spent their entire lives where they were born, can also still enjoy, it seems, besides good food and good wine, a disinterested intellectual discussion (which spawns practical initiatives parallel to power, but in a Calvinistic—as far as that may be possible in Italy, and particularly, surely, in Turin—polemic with power). In a discussion of this kind Carlo uses ideas that are worthless in the sphere of power, where, for something to be made concrete, realized, purely formal notions are needed, that is, notions that can be directly translated—and without the oppositions of pure reason—into actions, into deeds. For a political man, to have real conversations is to be an academic. But Carlo regressed to his earlier cultural state and got used to it again sincerely, like his other friends, more accustomed to it than he and therefore more detached (ready to stop the discussion for a joke that's part of their tradition as a group, or to go and eat).

Carlo, quoting Auden during a pause in a discussion on the immediate future of Italian society (seen from the inside; that is, through the best bourgeois consciousness), sighs, certainly not like a man of power: "Happy he who hopes for better, what awaits Her may well be worse . . ."

"What fun and games," quoted xxx, a grizzled man, his hair almost white, who also happened to know that poem of Auden's, "what fun and games you find it to play Jeremiah-cum-Juvenal: Shame on you for your *Schadenfreude*!"

"My God," said Carlo, continuing the quotation, "now you're giving me a moral! Would I be a man in the street? Let's suppose that I am, what does it matter if my words are true!"

The voice of a third friend interrupted from a nearby table, laughing (he, too, knew *City Without Walls*. Perhaps it had just been published by Einaudi): "Let's go eat, for the love of God! You will all feel better after eating." >

These remarks—the only ones in this novel, if I'm not mistaken (except in the stories incorporated into it)—were immediately belied by something odd at the end of the street, like a sudden gust of wind that makes shutters bang and women cry out. Life seemed to come to a halt, and a sort of question fell over all things and all faces. There was the sound of thuds; and high, isolated voices became denser, a confused shout of alarm. Cars began stopping and soon were backed up, blocking the entire street. From the direction of the voices and cries people began to arrive, running; some of them then stopped to wait under the portico of the great square, which looked Neapolitan because of the majestic town hall from the time of the Enlightenment. And there at the end of the street appeared a line of people, arms linked, holding, in whatever way they could, flags, placards, banners; behind that line was another line. There was a river of them.†

NOTE 126
A Fascist demonstration (continued)

\The new center\

It was a Fascist demonstration. In big letters and with slogans that imitated those of the New Left the placards praised Almirante and Birindelli. Some asked peremptorily for freedom for a certain xxx: FREE xxx. Perhaps it was for this reason that the demonstration had been organized and authorized. Carlo, with a small group of people (ordinary citizens who disapproved), was observing the demonstrators (who passed quickly on the cobblestones of the old street) from beneath a tall portico.† The moment was favorable for contemplation. Chance placed Carlo above the fray. He could look at those people as if they had nothing to do with him; or as if he himself were a stranger. But was it really chance? Was that situation really reducible to an ordinary moment in which a man (outside his public figure, momentarily anonymous) encountered some other men (who, on the other hand, were publicly demonstrating, like protagonists, what they were and wished for)? Perhaps, instead, it was a matter of the sudden radicalization and crystallization of something that had been developing for a long time: a definitive separation of good from evil; or, rather, of a phenomenon that was neither good nor bad from another phenomenon that was neither good nor bad. Among the demonstrators were middle-aged men (and also young men) in black shirts; some made (at the photographers) a provocatory Fascist salute; some were waving "pennants."‡

But that did not prevent Carlo, with the greatest lucidity, from drawing his own "inspired" conclusions, which were more or less the following.

No. These are no longer Fascists. Among them are some "old-timers" who are the classic Fascists, but they no longer count (or they count as survivors do in a new historical /context/). The disappointment is tremendous. The end of Fascism marks the end of an epoch and of a universe. The peasant world, the world of the people, is finished. It was from the poorest /parts/ of this that Fascism drew its bands of innocent, manly killers. /It's also the end for/ the middle /classes/, whose bourgeois culture was still based on popular culture (similar to that of the killers): peasant, pastoral, seafaring, poor. Distinct (from region to region, from city to city, from center to periphery). Singular, particular. Therefore *real*. After the war, the new power (which Carlo was directly a part of) relied on these cultural forms, which were *real* but electorally /reactionary/. That is, it did the same thing Fascism had done. But then slowly, imperceptibly, the nature of that power changed *radically*. The Church, having assumed all the common characteristics of those /various particular and real/ (electorally reactionary) /popular cultures/, had been of use to those in power in a /definitive/ way. Now, suddenly, the Church appeared obsolete, abandoned, useless, superfluous. The real (particular, popular) cultures had disappeared (or were in the process of disappearing). It was the power itself that had destroyed them; and with them had destroyed the Church. The life style preached by that power (every day, every hour, every moment of life) was completely unreligious. Nothing in the world—throughout all those years—could be considered more unreligious, for example, than television. It's true that television often showed official inaugurations, with a ridiculous bishop present; even more often, it showed religious ceremonies, /with the Pope himself/, etc. But all that was only an image of the parades of power: the religion of the State. In reality television preached pure hedonism, every day, hour after hour; its thrust was totally in the direction of prosperity and consumption. And the people had learned the lesson in a radical way: palingenetic (for the first time in history). They had mutated. They had made their own new human models, proposed by the culture of those in power. They had abandoned their traditional models. Existentially they had experienced new values, which they were still only nominally conscious of. Life was in advance of consciousness. Indulgence, necessary to the hedonistic ideology of consumption, imposed new duties: those of being equal to the new freedoms that, unnoticed, had been granted from above. Inevitable causes of neurosis. On the other hand, to experience new values existentially without knowing them was in turn a good reason for neurosis. The peasant world had crumbled. The countryside (and the seminaries) was full of vipers. That world had lost its own traditional and real values, along with the conventional ones imposed by the official religion. What replaced those values? And what, too, were the values of the petite bourgeoisie? No one—of those in power—had ever told the truth; that is, that the new values were those of excess, a fact that made lives superfluous and thus hopeless. So one pretended not to know. Carlo looked at those Fascists who were passing before him. They had to be the real people wanted at that moment by power (history). The classic slogans in their minds, like "God, Country, Family," were pure raving. They were the first not to *really* believe in them. Perhaps, of the old watchwords, the one that still made sense was, precisely, "Order." But that was not enough to bring about Fascism. The people who were passing before Carlo were poor citizens who had now been taken into the orbit of the anguish of prosperity, had been corrupted and destroyed by the extra thousand lire that a "developed" society had put in their pockets. They were uncertain men, gray, fearful. Neurotics. Their faces were drawn, twisted, and pale. The young men had long hair, like all the young consumers, with straggly curls and seventeenth-century ponytails, nineteenth-century beards, Art Nouveau–style curls; tight pants that covered pitiful balls. Their aggressiveness was /stupid/ and fierce—heartbreaking. They were pathetic, and nothing is less aphrodisiac than pathos. Their destiny called them to jobs that were better paid than in the preceding decades and to /weekends/ that were a little more bourgeois; the demonstration was a diversion from all this. The Spinolas are worse than the Caetanos. Caetano's hit men could still believe in their values, which were in part false, in part true: asceticism and virility had been real, practiced. Now they were only painful phantoms whose right to parade through the city was probably solely the result of a decision by the CIA. In fact, the true Fascists now were the anti-Fascists in power. Carlo was the powerful one, not those stupid crying children who did not know the origin of their pain.†

In the faces of those old Italians, disguised by prosperity, what was not neurosis was vulgarity: they had thick black eyebrows above weak eyes, /pale/ cheeks, they were repellently, aggressively fat, with buttocks like beasts of burden. Vulgarity, too, is /violently/ anti-aphrodisiac. That mass of people was swarming through the old street but without the least physical authority, in fact physically it was pitiful and disgusting. They were a petite bourgeoisie without destiny, put at the margins of the history of the world at the very moment when they became like everyone else.†

NOTE 127
Fourth fundamental moment of the poem
(from the "Mystery")

As soon as the last of those creeps had passed, dragging their swollen feet and xxx, in their harsh voices, the songs that the first were about to finish, Carlo felt a sudden, frightening pain in his stomach, and he went suddenly pale, the blood drained from his face, which is what always happens in such cases after the first < ... >. The pain seemed to subside for a moment, /but then/ < ... > recurred more sharply, an unbearable stabbing. Carlo could not keep from pressing his hands against his stomach, bending < ... > over on himself. It was now unmistakable. His eyes /clouded/ with pain, Carlo looked around, searching desperately for some salvation; even a corner behind a door would be enough. But there instead, there at the end of the square with its familiar gray cobblestones, within the cool porticoes, was the Caffè xxx, the café of his youth. Still pressing his hands against his stomach, Carlo reached the café quickly and crossed the threshold. It was full of people. Undoubtedly even some of his acquaintances were among them. But with a superhuman effort he pretended to be carefree and lighthearted and, passing the cashier, ordered a cup of tea as if nothing were wrong; then went on, without slowing down and apparently in the best of spirits, toward the toilet. He entered and closed himself inside, seized by an uncontainable joy; uncontainable to the point where he sang to himself, in a low voice, a thanks to God.

But something else was added to, or rather superimposed on, his situation, which was already in itself so fantastic.

All of human history, so it seems, does nothing but repeat one thing: there *is* only what *has been*. And in fact Carlo, undressing, saw *that what had already happened to him was happening to him*. He quickly completed the *anasyrma*, and there in the < ... > mirror of the men's room, which had reflected him as a student, he saw Polyhymnos again, rather than Polyhymnia, or, if you like, Baubo rather than Baubon. Polyhymnia or Polyhymnos, Baubo or Baubon, it does not, in truth, matter much. It's cause for laughter—perhaps sacred and with melancholy allusions—both for the child and for the cosmic divinity, as the reader knows better than I. Which does not take away the fact that it was with profound emotion that Carlo—in the old mirror in the men's room—saw that his chest was a flat chest, without breasts; and, pulling down his pants and underpants—exactly according to the rite of *anasyrma*, except that in this specific case no one was laughing—saw that dangling down below his belly again, under the thin hair, was his old penis.

NOTE 128
Before enlightenment and wordplay

"Do not be amazed that I know all languages, because I know that which is not said by men."[59]

Moreover: "Anyone who has eyes to see and ears to hear can be convinced that no mortal man can keep a secret. If his lips are silent, he speaks with the tips of his fingers: betrayal oozes from every pore."[60]

Naturally, the Carlo of Literal Reality spoke to no one about what had happened to him for historical reasons; and with such great simplicity (*"Verbum infans," "Dei dialectus solecismus"*).

[59] Apollonius of Tiana.
[60] Sigmund Freud.

In the world of power certain historical causes are not understood on principle, much less the simple language of symbols, which are always flesh or body. Having said this, I will relate in all simplicity how "the first coup de théâtre" (that is, the recovery of the penis—which occurred, moreover, < ... > as a mirror image of Carlo of the Time of the Dream's recovery of his penis; but not brought up to date, not repeated sacredly: pure repetition, rather, in two historically different situations)[61] was almost immediately succeeded not only by "a second coup de théâtre" but also, indeed, by a "third."

NOTE 128A
A brief word before taking up the great Digression

As soon as he regained possession of his penis (a restoration paid for by the loss of the breasts, of course), Carlo immediately thought of taking his place in the world again. That world (as we will soon see more clearly) was *this one here.* And it is pointless to say that he could not even conceive of reentering that world except at the highest level, where Power is not only the source of meaning but also the exercise of itself.

It was clear to Carlo, however, that he would never be able to begin again from the point at which he had left off. What he had experienced in that period had not entered only into his consciousness, a place in which it is generally easy to rid oneself of everything that can be annoying. Besides, he wouldn't even have been able to say what was *truly* new, that is, experienced in the immensity of his unconscious life: "The Tao that can be named is not the eternal Tao."

But let's get to the big chapter at the end of which will occur the two new "coups de théâtre" that I have announced and whose repercussions will be fundamental to the rest of our story.

---

[61] In that consists the complete originality (the joke) of this poem.

NOTE 129
The anti-Fascist reception

The reception took place, in spite of all the uncertainties of the previous "hot" day. I believe that even if Vice President Miceli had died that night, the reception would have taken place in the morning just the same; such a special meaning did Giulia Miceli attribute to it. It was affecting how blind she remained to the end, not perceiving the mood of society. At that point, no one believed that the solemn day would pass without some unforeseen excitement, without a real "disaster," as some put it (they were, however, destined to be disappointed, though their prediction was accurate). Many, it's true, tried to assume a look as severe and "politic" as possible; but, in general, we all know that the Italian male delights immeasurably in every scandalous upset of society. It's also true that there was in public opinion something much more serious than the simple thirst for scandal. There was a general irritation, an implacable anger. Apparently, everything had become terribly boring for everyone. A kind of confused cynicism spread, a kind of forced, reluctant cynicism (it was the final legacy, left by youths to adults, of 1968). Only the women, the eternal women, were not confused, and even in their case it was only on a single point: in the impotent hatred they felt toward that *flatus vocis* of our poem that is Giulia Miceli. There the attitudes of all the women were in agreement. While the poor thing did not even distantly suspect it: she persisted to the last moment in the conviction that she had a "following" and that everyone was still "fanatically devoted" to her.

I have already mentioned the fact that in those years a good deal of "riffraff" had appeared in society. Always, everywhere, in tumultuous periods of fluctuation and transition, that "riffraff" turns up. I am not speaking of those who, in general, always try to stay ahead and thus have a purpose, which, even though it's often utterly stupid, at least is more or less logical. No, I'm speaking—as Dostoyevsky says, and as I would not dare to say—of "scum." In every period of unrest followed by transition it comes out in full force, with, in particular, an immense capacity for blackmail and terrorism, this "scum," which in its potential state (and in that state it could be doing anything), is evidently rife in every society. And it appears not only without any logical goal but without even the shadow of an idea: merely expressing with all its strength the general disquiet and restlessness—the anxiety, in fact.

First of all, this particular "scum," having emerged in '68, almost always, without even being aware of it, follows the orders of that small group of "progressives" who act with a logical purpose (and also whose revolutionary intentions, I wish to add, are honest and noble even if at the same time improvised and childish). It was clear that the general inspiration was indeed revolutionary and Marxist, and, as far as regards our reception, Giulia Miceli was inspired by her revolutionary and Marxist young men. How (and what) happened in that period, few would be able to say (as for my reader, he is referred to Note 43: "*Linkskommunismus*"). The fact is that the more despicable "scum" (with a lot of whiskers, sideburns, shoulder-length hair) had got the upper hand, had begun to criticize everything "that is held sacred," whereas before they had not even dared to open their mouths; and the people of the first rank, who until that moment had so blissfully dominated, had suddenly begun to listen to them and were silent. Others in fact jeered in scorn "most shamefully." The revolutionary "scum" had gained the upper hand over not only our good bourgeoisie, professionals, high-level bureaucrats, industrialists, military (an unmentionable subject); but also the petite bourgeoisie, which had always been restless, and indeed the parties of the left, with their assertive politicians and their blameless intellectuals. If even Barbara xxx Valletti—until the moment of the catastrophe of her Carlo—had, so to speak, become an errand boy for all that "scum," the aberration at the time of the other local ladies is in part forgivable. Now everything is attributed to the Extremists and in particular—and also objectively, as regards the facts of our story—the Reds. Of course: there was also, among our good bourgeoisie, conservative or progressive, a small number of people who kept aloof from the beginning, who even locked themselves in. But what lock can resist the law of nature? Even in the most dignified families there are girls who want to go dancing. And look how all these people, too, end up in favor of supporting the feminists. And then such a grand, brilliant dance was expected; marvelous things were said; the participation of politicians who had come from the Resistance was mentioned, and, in bold contrast, of ten "bachelors" of noble family, of patrons from Rome; of the writer F., who, to increase the proceeds, had agreed to read his essay "Merci" (with its ambiguity between the French *merci* and the Italian word *merci*). It was said that there would be a "literary quadrille," in which different costumes would represent different literary movements. How was it possible not to subscribe? Everyone had subscribed. In spite of the fact that immigration from the South had transformed it into a metropolis, Turin remained a small provincial capital: a town within the megalopolis.

NOTE 129A
The anti-Fascist reception (continued)

The festivities were divided into two parts, according to the program: a literary matinée from noon until four, and then a ball from ten through the night. But in that very arrangement the germs of disorder were already concealed. Above all, at the very beginning a rumor had taken root among the public that there was to be a lunch immediately after the literary matinée, or perhaps during the matinée itself, in an intermission specially for that purpose; a free lunch, it should be understood, that was part of the program; and with champagne. The high price of a ticket—thirty thousand lire—encouraged the spread of the rumor. The idea seemed utterly logical. It must be said that Donna Giulia herself had, by her own thoughtlessness, helped to plant this disastrous rumor. About a month earlier, still in the heat of her first enthusiasm for the great idea, she had written to one of the newspapers of the capital (in a retort to a reader who had written a letter to the editor) that some toasts would be offered during the festivities. Then these toasts (political, of course) seduced her; she herself wanted to propose them, and meanwhile she continued to compose them herself. But for toasts (even if they were political) champagne was necessary, and since champagne cannot be drunk on an empty stomach, food also became indispensable. Then, when, through her efforts, the committee was established and considered the matter more seriously, it was made clear to her that if they dreamed of banquets, very little would be left for the Russian exile writers, even if they realized a very handsome profit. Two solutions to the question immediately presented themselves: a nabobs' feast, with toasts, and around nine hundred thousand or a million lire for the Russian writers in exile, or realizing a sizable profit with a party that would be, so to speak, pro forma. The committee, however, only wanted to frighten her, for it had, naturally, thought of a third solution, which was a reasonable compromise—that is, a fairly decent party in all respects but without champagne, so that a considerable sum would be left, rather more than nine hundred thousand lire. But Donna Giulia Miceli did not agree; her character despised the bourgeois middle road. Right away she declared that if the first idea was impossible they must throw themselves, immediately and wholeheartedly, to the other extreme— that is, realizing a colossal profit and giving it to the exiles with great fanfare. In a heated speech to the committee she maintained that the public ought to understand that the achievement of political goals is infinitely superior to the momentary pleasures of the body, that the party was essentially only the proclamation of a great anti-Fascist idea, and that they should therefore be content with the Four and All band if it was not possible to do without that intolerable ball. To such an extent had she suddenly, nobly, come to hate it. But finally they calmed her. It was just then that they came up with the anachronistic but kitschy idea of the "literary quadrille," along with other aesthetic items, to replace the pleasures of the body. And it was also just then that the writer agreed definitively to read his *Mercí* or "Merci" (while until that point he had been putting them off, wavering), thereby destroying the very idea of food in the mind of the intemperate public. Thus the fête was again presented, correctly, as a political fête. But so that it would not become completely austere and abstract, they decided that at the beginning of the ball some alcoholic beverages would be served, and perhaps also some ices.

While for those who inevitably, always, everywhere, get hungry and especially thirsty, a special buffet would be set up at the back of the suite of rooms, with Pandimiglio Fioretto, the Micelis' cook, whom Donna Giulia would make available, in charge; at the buffet, to be rigorously supervised by the committee, the guests could have anything they liked, but for a charge, and so there would have to be an appropriate written notice at the door of the room to the effect that the buffet was not part of the program. But then in the morning they decided not even to open the buffet, so as not to disturb the reading, despite the fact that the buffet would be set up five rooms away from the White Hall in which F. had agreed to read "Merci." It is curious that the committee and even the most sensible people would attribute such enormous importance to this event, that is, to the reading of "Merci." As for sensible people, in addition to lovers of culture, Signora Casalegno, for example, the wife of the assistant editor of *La Stampa,* said to F. that after the reading she would have fixed to the wall of the room a marble plaque with gold lettering, to the effect that, on that day of that year, there, in that very place, the great Italian and European writer had read what would be, publicly, his last work. What is known for certain is that F. demanded expressly and insistently that during his reading, in the morning, there be no buffet of any kind, no matter how compelling the need for nourishment and thirst quenching.

Thus matters stood, while the public continued to believe in the Pantagruelian banquet; that is, the buffet at the expense of the committee. They believed it until the last moment.

NOTE 129B
The anti-Fascist reception (III)

The literal identification of a scene or episode with its archetype, which, as the expression goes, has to be immensely anterior in time, can be bewildering and above all unreliable. This archaic Turin is no longer literally believable; it almost succeeds in creating panic. I realize this. But it is panic, precisely, that I want. And a panic that's totally anomalous, unjustifiable; and moreover irritating, because it's "not successful." I, too, am a troublemaker. Grant me that just this once. I do not have practical goals, like the provocateurs (of the right or the left) who surrounded Giulia Miceli. My goal is aesthetic. As we will see, in fact, a religious shadow looms over the story I'm telling. So it's logical that the stylistic equivalent < ... > should be characterized by unreliability, awkwardness, false notes, confusion. In fact, it's not, as will soon be clear, a matter of a confessional religion or even, probably, of an existing religion. Thus I've got away with remaking an archetypal episode and absurdly showing Turin back in the fifties, not to say the forties or even the thirties.[62] In the parties that are no longer held there is a supernatural < ... > sadness. < ... > On the other hand, the beginning of the party, given its mimetic origins, could lead only to a catastrophe of spectacular proportions—the burning of an entire neighborhood by the extremists, the murder of the probable wife-to-be of the protagonist (a horrible \hair-raising\ murder, as if from a crime story), and therefore to the debasement of the party, which ends in < ... > /shit/, with some drunken southerners who trample and befoul parquets and draperies, peeing, shitting, and vomiting everywhere. But this is not how the party in the present story ends. The party in the present story *desinit in piscem*. The scandal is an inner scandal that, for some minutes, flashes and /shud-

---

[62] And then who knows what I mean in backdating by so much the "anti-Fascist reception."

ders/ in public (as we will see). < ... > Thus the disproportion between the beginning and the end is more than evident. But this disproportion is also explained by the religious character that our story is about to /assume/: a religious character that itself colors the political moment immediately preceding it. Anyway, from this point on I will leave my model; and rather than reproduce it to the letter—with results of dismaying xxx—I will "adapt" it to the real time in which our story unfolds and to the inviolable characteristics of its surroundings. Therefore, when the prefect Miceli and his lady had taken their places in the improvised stalls, dispelling the rumors and /allowing/ the truth to be seen, the public appeared to "settle down."

NOTE 129C
Elements, it must be said, that cause delay

The prefect himself seemed to be in perfect health. Moreover, few suspected that he was ill and that in a few days that illness would send him to a nursing home in Switzerland—that is, practically to a madhouse. Besides, everyone found his actions of the day before, in regard to the Fascist demonstration, perfectly normal and for the most part, in fact, approved them unconditionally. Everyone agreed that, if anything, such action should be taken from the start, contrary to what the radicals maintained, who did not realize that their democratic insistence on legal means, on principle, their poetic formalism, would in the end turn against them. If anything, it was thought that the anti-Fascist prefect should have behaved a little more cold-bloodedly (and it is natural that the old Turinese bourgeoisie should think so). With a similar curiosity, eyes also turned toward his consort, Donna Giulia. Certainly no one has the right to claim from me—as narrator—precise details on a certain point: there is a mystery here, there is a woman. But I do know one thing: the evening before, she had gone to the study of Francesco Paolo Miceli and had remained there well beyond midnight. Francesco Paolo was charmed and soothed. The spouses agreed on everything. I will not enter into their nocturnal effusions. The fact is that the anti-Fascist prudence of the prefect was completely defeated. Everyone now saw happiness on her face. She had come before the crowd with an open gaze and a magnificent dress (a long gypsy- or peasant-type skirt and necklaces as if from a junk store, like a "hippie," but all in moderation, within the appropriate dimensions, and, of course, expensive). She seemed to be at the pinnacle of her ambition: the celebration—the goal and crowning moment of her politics—had been reached.

Taking their places together, just in front of the stage, the Micelis bowed and responded cordially to the greetings. Many women, among the most influential of the city, "corrected" by the presence of their children of the extreme left, rose to welcome them. . . . But here an unfortunate mistake occurred: the Four and All suddenly began to play; and not a "shake" but one of those old marches, perhaps Tyrolese or Bavarian if not Anglo-Saxon, that used to be played when toasts were drunk, especially around Christmastime or the annual celebration of some national holiday. Later people knew that the writer friend of the Venetian writer with the name ending in -*on* (who, as we have seen, after ten years, having become southernized, had taken a name in -*elli*) had been responsible for this: a certain Balestrini, who was quite good-looking, with teased hair of a color between yellow and pink. Of course, this Balestrini could always have justified himself as having done this through stupidity or too much zeal. . . . Unfortunately, however, the reality was that the moment for justification had passed; and that he had decided to go right to the end. /No one ever knew if it had been directed against the anti-Fascism of Signor Francesco Paolo Miceli and his consort Donna Giulia—that is, by the Fascists—or against the tepidness of that anti-Fascism: that is, by the "Reds."/ Everything remained ambiguous in a way that was, among other things, rather demoniacal—it should be said, in this context—and also terribly refined. This Venetian writer in -*on,* later in -*elli,* must have been quite a notable type: he and his companions. Besides, the ambiguity was characterized by the fact that it was not the only ambiguity originating in the theory of opposite extremisms. In a case like that of the reception for the anti-

Fascist exile writers, the extremes were certainly (and, furthermore, always had been) distinct and separate. Extremists naturally—that is, by their nature—always hasten to say what color they are. But this distressing and *perhaps,* but only *perhaps,* mocking situation did not end with the march. Suddenly, in the midst of some irritation and perplexity, and smiles among one part of the public, loud cheers were heard at the back of the room and in the stalls. It was clear that they were exaggerated cheers, which with their racket and mocking tone went beyond the bounds. But no one could swear that it was so. Indeed, were those cheers xxx the work of Fascists or of anti-Fascists (who had, in either case, come there to ruin everything)? Donna Giulia's face was alight, her eyes flashed. Dr. Miceli stopped at his seat and, turning in the direction of the shouts, gravely and severely looked around the room. . . . Over his face drifted a kind of dangerous smile that anyone with the least psychological insight could not help but observe with terror. There was in it something sinister but also, worse, something comical. . . . With a hurried nod Donna Giulia summoned one of the young men of the left, the son of one of the ladies on the Committee, to go quickly to F. and beg him to begin reading his poem immediately. But just then another disgraceful incident, even worse than the first, occurred.

At that moment, Carlo entered the room: in all the objective authority and prestige of his person. No one knew anything *about what had happened to him.* Only the staff of Einaudi, if it had interrupted, would have had the same prestige (being similarly above the fray) and the respect of both the probable sides. The "disgraceful thing" that was happening when he entered (and still no one knew that he would be the protagonist of that "matinée") was this. On the platform—on the empty platform that awaited the writer F. and Signora Antonietta Carinella, president of the famous "literary Wednesdays," who was to introduce him—on the empty platform where there was only a small table with a chair in front of it, and on the table a glass of water on a small silver tray—suddenly appeared the colossal, unmistakably Sicilian figure of Father Pambo. It's true that this is an acquaintance who is exclusively ours, that it's unlikely that he was known to more than one or two people (homosexuals, obviously) in that audience. Thus he was an apparition in its purest form. He did not have connections and references that were in themselves scandalous. Anyway, Father Pambo caused such a commotion that he did not have to be previously known to be revealed immediately for what he was. Gigantic, like a Norman statue, with a round face, sparkling little round eyes, long hair hanging in two big tufts on either side of his head, a small, fleshy mouth, half closed and foaming in an irresistibly narcissistic but untamed smile of satisfaction, he seemed much more like a character from the circus than like a priest and, moreover, a Jesuit. One expected him to roll up his sleeves and reveal monstrous biceps, emphasizing his triumphant infantile smile of self-love, and to pick up a rock in his teeth. Therefore the priest's robe on that body had a strange effect. Especially since Father Pambo was obviously drunk: he had that flabby, disordered, soup-stained, ragged, and presumably foul-smelling look that drunks have in the morning. < ... > † All this if, of course, one had had time to observe it; but never is the testimony of God so scandalous /as/ it is swift. Strong hands, evidently ready, immediately took care of removing him, and he, swaying gently, obeyed. It was therefore little more than a flash, a quick spin around himself. But the image of Father Pambo at that moment could not but remain ineradicable. Physically in his place appeared the writer with the name in *-trini* (the one with the teased hair of a color between yellow and pink), excited and conciliatory, although with a great show of embarrassment and quivering modesty—along with a subtle hint of complicity, refined and vaguely in sympathy with the entire audience. He was wearing a tie and a jacket with tight shoulders and wide lapels and xxx pockets. With an air of embarrassment he asked for silence, pointing out that Father Pambo was a Jesuit, an anti-Fascist, a friend of the poor, and a priest of dissent, and that he had come simply to bear witness. Circumstances did not permit him, being morbidly timid, to read his work, so he, the writer whose name ended in *-trini,* had taken it upon himself. He cleared his throat, took from his pocket a piece of paper that to the relief of everyone appeared to be single and very small, and began to read the following verses, whose title, spoken in a loud, dry voice as he stared, a little threateningly, at the audience, was /"Dirge"/:

flotsam an jetsam
are gentlemen poeds
urseappeal netsam
our spinsters and coeds,

thoroughly bretish
they scout the inhuman
itarian fetish
that man isn't wuman

vive the millenni
um three cheers for labor
give all things to enni
one bugger thy nabor

eneck and senecktie
are gentlemen ppoyds
even whose recktie
are covered by lloyd's

No one in that entire audience, of course, realized that it was one of those amazing texts that Ezra Pound—and only he—manages to quote with such naturalness in his writings about poetics, and with perhaps sublimely didactic claims. Yet even if someone there had known that "untranslatable" text, undoubtedly worthy of the *saevitia catulliana,* he would still never have recognized it there, in that context, given the pronunciation of the writer in *-trini,* who for one thing didn't know English. So it was startling when, from far back in the audience, as if from a celestial shadow, a voice growled incomprehensibly, just like a dog, and then succeeded in pronouncing intelligibly the word "Pound!" Since that "Pound" sounded roughly like "pand," it said nothing about nothing to the audience. But the writer in *-trini* cast a "demonic" and encouraging glance toward that "youth" (because such it must perforce be) who was interrupting from the depths of anonymity, from the imaginary gallery, where xxx xxx authentic. All eyes were fixed, excited, their hopes kindled, in his direction. He was not exactly a youth, he must easily have been in his thirties; he had an unruly beard, similarly unruly sideburns, and unruly hair that came down to his enormously thick neck; and he also wore thick spectacles flashing over a reddish nose. So his face could not be seen; but in a very loud, barklike, accusing voice from within that mass of tawny hair he finally managed to get something intelligible out, which proclaimed, as if Pound were its author as well, the following passage: "A thousand candles together create brilliance. No candle's light injures the light of another. Similarly the freedom of the individual in the ideal Fascist state." The title of the fragment was FASCIO. The whole thing was underlined "meaningfully" by the person who had interrupted.

What was the significance of this "meaningfulness"? Did he want to create neo-Fascist propaganda, dusting off a spiritual and monetary grandeur debased, in fact, by Pound? And in that case why had Father Pambo and the writer in *-trini* laid themselves open, pulling out that extraordinary poem from the Poundian universe at an anti-Fascist celebration? Perhaps (and, although this hypothesis was frightening, it, too, was not illogical) they were in league with that "student" who had interrupted? But the explanation could also be diametrically opposite: that is, the "student" who had interrupted could have been quoting Pound "negatively" and therefore disparagingly, for the purpose of underlining the criminal triviality of the anti-Fascism of that gathering. In that case, however, perhaps Father Pambo and the writer in *-trini* agreed with him and had provided him with the occasion for the interruption, which, then, was not Fascist but anti-Fascist: a vicious and extremist anti-Fascism, obviously. Nothing could be understood from the attitude of the writer in *-trini,* who had remained there like an idiot, his piece of paper nervously in his hand, looking embarrassed and at the same time xxx. In his little doll-like eyes shone the light of one who is enjoying a failure, the astonishment of one who hears a revelation that makes him feel guilty. With that extremely ambiguous light in his eyes, the writer in *-trini* withdrew from the stage. As for the interrupter, he had vanished into the depths where youth and < ... > class struggle lurk. But the truth, I insist, is that there was nothing about him that could clarify the subtle enigma of whether it had been a Fascist provocation or an anti-Fascist provocation. Moreover, it could very well have been neither the one nor the other, and that redheaded mercenary might be simply a Pound scholar or perhaps an employee of the publisher Scheiwiller.

There was not long to wait before the next delay. Signora Giulia Miceli had not yet put aside the expression of bright, frantic curiosity that had made her rise in her chair, vivaciously, and turn her gaze hurriedly back and forth from the writer in *-trini* to the distant interrupter as if she were ecstatic at the surprises that democracy and public debate hold in reserve, when, as she firmly xxx (in reality she was trembling, seized by a panic equal only to that of her consort, who had been left alone in his chair); and there on the platform were the writer F. and the beaming Antonietta Carinella, who was to introduce him.

They took their places behind the table that was too small, leaning against it so that the glass began to jingle on the silver tray. That jingling would not stop for the entire duration of "Merci." Applause welcomed them. But it must not have been the applause the writer F. expected; in fact, he pretended to be impatient with it, to consider it anti-democratic foolishness: while he was clearly the first to want to discredit the cult of his own personality. He sat down, trying to be as expressionless as possible, while Signora Carinella, in the voice of a girl, read her little exercise, full of compliments, whose essence was this: to introduce the writer F. is pointless since everyone knows who he is. Then the writer F. pulled out his bundle of pages and began to read.

There continued to be, as if suspended in the air, something ominous in the room. Let me say at once: I bow before the greatness of genius; but why do our geniuses, upon reaching an advanced age, which should be the age of wisdom, behave like little boys? Who doesn't know that it is impossible to keep an audience like ours (a Turinese audience) entertained for an entire hour with one article? In general I have observed that even a supergenius cannot with impunity keep the audience at a public reading interested for more than twenty minutes by himself. Besides, that audience was particular, like all the audiences of those years of transition; if the frontal assaults and the derision of '68 were by now temptations succumbed to only rarely, the recovery that took their place was far from stable. As I've said: the appearance of the famous writer had been greeted with considerable respect; even the most severe of the wise old men displayed signs of approval, and the ladies a certain enthusiasm, although it was self-mocking. The applause, however, was brief and as if scattered, confused. And in the back rows, in the deep shadow, if no one applauded, at least no one whistled; and even when he began to read nothing particularly unpleasant happened; /but it was/ like a misunderstanding. The writer F. had a shrill, rather feminine voice and spoke with a kind of excessive naiveté. As soon as he had uttered a few words, suddenly someone let out a laugh, probably some uneducated boor, perhaps a southerner, who had never attended a cultural event and had, besides, a natural weakness for laughter. Still, that was not the tinder that was to light the fuse; in fact, he was hushed. Very soon, meanwhile, it was clear that "Merci" was not the French word meaning "thanks" but the Italian word meaning "wares," the plural of "ware." And that these "wares" were literary works and artistic works in general. The article the writer F. had begun to read consisted of twenty typewritten pages, terrifyingly dense; in addition, the speaker read in an appropriately dull, serious, unyielding voice, completely caught up in the intellectual heights of his discourse, as if he were on purpose "offending" the audience, but adopting for his "offense" a technique completely opposite to that of the provocateurs. He "offended" by the rigor of culture, not by the terrorism of the subculture. It was clear.

The theme . . . But who could understand it, this theme? Certainly not the ladies, the heroic ladies, who had so tenaciously survived everything and were ready for anything, poor things: even for a revision of Hegelian logic, if the possibility occurred. Certainly not the sly old foxes of the bureaucracy, of politics and journalism; though of course they would never admit that they didn't get it and in fact would later /pronounce/ some suitable "catchwords" (already tried out on other occasions) that, good-naturedly and sympathetically, would destroy < ... > /everything/. Certainly not the young zealots, who were "integrated" and, being fresh from their studies, were naturally unwilling to renounce the truth and legitimacy of what they had just learned, and with such great enthusiasm (for example, Hegelian logic itself, the basis of progressivism). Certainly not the young protesters, who raised such defense mechanisms against everything that they were not even listening, for already in their hearts they were accusing everyone at the least of revisionism (criticism of Hegel, then, could in a correct Marxist-Leninist context be only a reactionary blasphemy). Certainly not any of the other intellectuals present, who were sitting among the young men, in fact camouflaged among them, with the same beards, the same whiskers, the same sideburns and the same permed hair; and who, if there had been an opportunity to criticize, for example, Hegelian logic, would have been the ones to do it, and with more balls than old F. So that old F., in his stern, dramatic voice, began to recite into the void his encyclical on thesis, antithesis, and synthesis: an encyclical in which, furthermore, he invoked—partly in jest and partly not, and thus provocatively—the lost possibility of a "duadic" logic in which everything remained coexistent and not "obsolete" and contradictions were only "oppositions"; in which case history would no longer be the linear and sequential history originating, as we all know, in the reformist exegesis of the Old and New Testaments and the letters of Saint Paul. On that all modern Western rationalism was founded, and yet science proved that time was not based on linearity and sequence and in fact did not really exist, since everything was present (as the Dravidian religions had already learned).

It was more or less at this point that from the shadows, where the people, in safety, were concealed, arose a loud naked cry of "Enough!" It was a demand from the people, peremptory, threatening; there was something cosmic about it. In fact, the passing of time, even if it is illusory, determines both the end of a historical period and the end of life. The one who had cried "Enough!" knew that: knew how to do injury, not merely express a just political demand. What again remained uncertain was whether the person who had shouted was simply a tired member of the audience or a Fascist to whom Pound as an intellectual, perhaps with Èvola, seemed more than enough, or even a Marxist extremist, who simply found any proposition reactionary that brought about a crisis in the concept of history. Whatever it was, panic made the audience turn pale, so to speak, as a sudden wind from the southwest makes the sea turn suddenly livid, dangerous, transparent. But it was only the first sign. The restrained portion of the audience—which still seemed to be the uncertain majority—prevailed, silencing the speaker. Who for the moment was mysteriously silent. Old F. was not really so old; in fact, he had the air of a young man. Naturally he had come there to read his work; only after endless vacillation had he yielded to the entreaties of his friends, though with a great deal of anguish and many remaining qualms. He cast an ironic glance in the direction of the intrusion: a glance in which sparkled a kind of admiration in the form of complicity. Then he lowered his eyes to his paper and again began to read. Works as "merchandise"—he maintained—present an insoluble form of ambiguity; the "linguistic" is not contradicted by the "nonlinguistic" (that is, the moment of commercialization) following the traditional rules of Hegelian logic; there is no possible synthesis, in a work, between "linguistic" and "nonlinguistic." Thus it would in fact be more precise to speak of "opposition" rather than of "contradiction," <...> /which/ produces an ambiguous amalgam rather than a synthesis (the work). Now, this problem has always been resolved idealistically; that is, by postulating the innocent unity of the work. It's true: in the work there is the moment of unity, of total autonomy, in that it is a form self-constituted by means of rules that are, furthermore, self-sufficient. But that is in the laboratory. In the laboratory of a formalist or a structuralist, for example. As long as it's a technician who is postulating the innocent unity of art—who examines "how it's done," "how it functions," etc.—everything is fine. But if it's a philosopher postulating the innocent unity of art, then he is tainted by the unforgivable sin of irrationalism and idealism. In the materialist field (at this point— that is, the moment when F. uttered these words—whistles were heard here and there, and no one could shut them up, because it was impossible to tell if those whistles were a conditioned reflex on the part of the Fascists <...> or a protest of extremist anti-Fascists who would not grant F. the right to speak about materialism); "in the materialist field," therefore, it was necessary to demystify the unity and innocence of art, just as Marxism had demystified social man and psychoanalysis inner man. Marxism had revealed to man that man, contrary to his own false idea of himself, is divided (according to class), and that makes him guilty (exploitation of man by man). Similarly, psychoanalysis had revealed to interior man that he (always contrary to his own false idea of himself) is divided (Ego and Id, conscious and unconscious), which makes him guilty (the innumerable, unnameable filthy sins that man, in a hallucinatory way, never ceases to commit or to desire). As for art, it would take a Third Jew to come and prove that it is neither "innocent" nor "one" . . .

At this point the whistles burst out again, and this time it was the end. Two factors played together, marvelously together \in harmony\: political criticism (still not very clear; and yet having reached, apparently, the limit of endurance) and the ordinary tiredness resulting from the unforgivable length of the /thought/. The effect of those two factors, marvelously in harmony, was first of all to make Signorina Carinella cry (though she cried easily) and then to break up the "debate" without further delay—a point that everyone was impatient to arrive at in a common, unified, irresistible condemnation of every personal reference, every paternalism, every *ex cathedra* preachment, every suppression. F.'s weak invitation—regarding the hecklers—to express their opinions somewhat more rationally than blackbirds was for the moment not welcomed. It made Signorina Carinella smile a little between her tears, but it was clear that no one wanted to come to any terms with F.

—Introduce into the preceding section (128) a synthesis of the new Italian political situation: that is, the reasons that pushed Cefis from ENI to Montedison and to the presidency of Edison with the help of the Fascists (<?>, etc.)

—That "historical situation"—which Carlo I overcomes by launching a new type of revolutionary anti-Fascism beyond Cefis and following the transnational line of Cefis—is then experienced and brought down by Carlo II, who therefore "regresses," practices some realpolitik (alliance with the Fascists, etc.)

Chia, end of August 1974

NOTE 128C
Resumption of "Before enlightenment and wordplay"†

< ... > He co-opted honesty, involving it in the calculation: < ... > /of which he made a tomb/ (not, however, for Apollonius, the one from Tiana, or, as usual, for Freud). /He would only partly transform his anti-Fascism and his relation with Fascism./ He would *name* only certain aspects or elements of that something *unnameable* that was the real new Power; that is, he would create a *nominalism,* perhaps with a liturgical character and structure. For example, regarding development and its relation to progress (prudently called "civil development," however), here is an excerpt from his notes, corresponding perfectly to a catechismlike "cursus": < ... >

"The damage to the country originating in the failed connection between a *program of civil development* and an *economic program* having been ascertained, we have drawn two conclusions: first, the parties that assume responsibility for the government of the country must, without being impatient in the limited time, try together to define the inspiration, the objectives, the means, the duration of a *program of civil development,* whose highest purpose should be the expansion of the personality of every citizen in a democratic society by means of wide civic participation and strong community bonds and which as a result cannot be a program of brief duration. Second, the governing parties must define an *economic program* consistent with the program of *civil development.* The shortcomings recorded up to now by the politics of economic planning having been ascertained, we have deduced from them that an economic program today, using all the natural resources, the technical capabilities, the available human energy—and thus eliminating the waste of inadequate research, the flight of brains and capital, emigration—must set the conditions for a modern, balanced development . . ."

In which the reader is desired to note the euphemistic value of the ablative absolutes ("the damage having been ascertained, etc." and "the shortcomings having been ascertained, etc."). The linguistic dignity "squeezed" out of the Latin in a pedantic spirit confers on the material the official stamp that an examination of the facts would undoubtedly find totally lacking in them. Outside the ablative absolute, those "damages" and those "shortcomings" are /undoubtedly/ criminal; within the ablative absolute, on the other hand, they are normal, they become moments, however deplorable, of necessary or inevitable "negativity." The euphemistic element of the style becomes explicit in the expressions "without being impatient in the limited time" and "cannot be a program of brief duration." That is, the criminal acts can still be perpetrated. I beg the reader to notice the "lists" in the loveliest—almost singing—didactic cadences of the liturgies: "define the inspiration, the objectives, the means, the duration of *a program of civil development*," "all the natural resources, the technical capabilities, the human energy," and finally "the waste of inadequate research, the flight of brains and capital, emigration": lists that have the liberating power of the "Act of contrition" uttered in the confessional in a monotone official voice, since, in making nominal, in the "codified, official" moment of repentance, the sins committed, it cancels them out; and does so, in this case, through a mnemonic device.

But above all I would beg the reader to meditate on the inspired invention of the government expression "program of civil development" to replace the expression typical of the left: "progress." There's something diabolical here. That is, the almost magical trust in the power of names, which conceals: first, the Fascist character of "economic development" that does not include "progress"; second, the change in that Fascist character, as brought about specifically by means of "economic development" and not by classical conservative violence; third, the abandonment of traditional values symbolized (and certainly not only platonically) by the Church in favor of assuming new values (for example, the hedonism resulting from "economic development"), which changes the reality of the power we are to serve. But these hidden concepts are not *named* precisely because the style of that "soul-searching" is completely and uniquely *nominalist*!

/The liturgy continues/ to advance, according to the plan drawn up in the heart of our new Christian Democrat, who, liberated from one fascism, does not intend (in words \at least in part\) to fall into a new fascism, which is unnameable. This time it's a "soul-searching" carried out inside one's own being; a "self-criticism" whose object is "parasitism," which is a problem typical exclusively of those in power: for the convenience of the reader I transpose the prose into its actual scheme of a "cursus" to be recited according to the model of the homily, or of the "Mystery":

The phenomenon of the parasite concerns all those who
from time to time
in exchange for a predetermined profit receive goods
or services that are worth somewhat less,
or directly pocket without giving up anything at all what they make:
by exploiting either particular positions of monopoly or near monopolyyyyy,
or difficult tiiiiimes,
or the pressing needs of othersssss,
or ignorance of the applicantsssss,
or lack of vigilance by overseeeeers,
or negligent performaaaaance,
or lack of respect for workdays and work scheduuuuules,
or fraudulent practiceeeees . . .

To which I cannot resist adding the seal of an "Aaaamen," chanted /in a loud voice/, which dates this < ... > "Parasitism" back conclusively to the formula of ritual or to the /half-consciousness/ of memory.

The same further on: when the moment comes to protest the firm (but not reckless) desire to assure the continuity of *economic progress* that is not separate from *civil progress:*

But at the same time an anti-recession politics consisting
of measures against inflation is carried out,
acts to reduce unnecessary demand,
rumors of deterioration in the balance of payments,
the abundance of money in circulation,
the flight of capital,

fiscal evasions,

the imbalance of public budgets—

and made up also of measures for an increase in or at least the preservation of

the rhythm of production,

the level of employment,

the volume of exports,

with qualitative and quantitative control of crediiiiit,

with measures for providing incentives,

with protection from the demand coming from lower-income claaaaasses,

with facilitation of supplying products

and services for foreign markeeeets . . .

"Aaaaamen." The cadence of the voice reciting the "Mysteries" here clearly inclines toward the inflections of the "Rhythms" of student songs, and a sense of sacrilege and obscenity is incumbent.

In any case, *his fretus,* that is, with his notes in his pocket, < ... > Carlo made his official reappearance in society on the occasion of the Auto Show—since he was in Turin, recuperating, according to an interpretation that might be completely believable, in a return to his Lares. Things were now in full recovery, with respect to '68, and no threat of recession was imminent.[63] Clothes had returned more or less to normal, at least for old people. And language, too. It was otherwise that Carlo /intended/ to cause a scandal, to put himself forward as "a new man."

The reader realizes that this is all a pretext. Furthermore, Carlo was preparing (in reappearing in society) to play a role; and so whatever the content of or script for that role was, in reality it was nothing but a "process of discharging masturbatory fantasies," as either Klein in *Psychoanalysis of Children* or Fenichel in *The Psychoanalytic Theory of Neurosis*—I don't remember which—puts it. And the rule for masturbation is in its turn a pretext; it, too, finally, when it has been articulated, belongs to the world of the Letter. While Allegories—like this one—are not scientific.

The fact is that Carlo appeared at the Inauguration of the Show—a completely pedestrian official act—/in the fullness of his/ virility and in

---

[63] The time frame of this book is not linear.

the perfect frame of mind for one who accepts the Game of Power. What happened in Turin was in fact to be "taken up" in Rome, and become a political act.

But right here, at this point, comes the "second coup de théâtre."

NOTE 129
The fateful proposition (from the "Plan")†

Carlo found himself in the midst of a dense throng of invited guests (the privileged), in a little group made up mainly of women who were indignantly discussing the Fascist demonstration of the day before. They were all very elegant. Carlo, too, was very elegant. Tall, rather florid, like a man who in his youth had been a swimmer, with a fixed, blissful smile in his pale eyes, a full mouth, the upper lip slightly protruding (which emphasized even more the suggestion of the youthful swimmer), the humble, slightly slouching pose, as if he did not want the sense of authority emanating from his entire person to be too weighty, wearing a light gray suit, he listened in silence to the conversation of his friends; although he kept it to himself, in his silence he urged and < ... > an ironic patience: an irony due evidently to the pretextual and elusive but now open and almost scandalous character of the indignation against *those* Fascists. When an old waiter passed by with a tray of sparkling glasses, Carlo as if mechanically reached out a hand to take a glass of whiskey. It was at that point that he woke up.

NOTE 130
Enlightenment and wordplay (from the "Plan")†

Often in Carlo's dreams (as we have said) a mute character appeared.[64]

The moment Carlo woke up, this personage unexpectedly began to speak (making use, naturally, of Carlo's mouth).

The words came thickly, without stopping, like a cataract that was finally able to plunge down, < ... > in an almost aphasic, utterly joyful frenzy < ... >; in fact, everything that that person said through Carlo consisted of puns, plays on words, linguistic jokes, neologisms, slips of the tongue or of memory. In Turin that utterly exceptional—/one might say/ epiphanic—performance is still remembered. Apart from the highly amusing descriptions that he gave of people, based on exchanges of syllables or distortions of clichés or titles of literary works (regarding himself he spoke of "Il Carriera della Sera"), some of the aphorisms that Carlo improvised /that evening/ remained impressed in the memory of Turinese society: "While you are alive, be a dead man," "He who enters into the kingdom of God must first enter into his mother and die," "If the material is nothing, we are materialists," "Instead of vanity, inanity," "Having found himself in the mold of a human being, he emptied himself" (this was reminiscent of Saint Paul, I think the Letter to the Philippians), "You will hear me and not understand me," "What always speaks silently is the body," "It is the foolish King Lear who asks his daughters how much they love him, and it is she who loves him who doesn't speak." And also "On Lifu, one of the Loyalty Islands, the sexual organ is called *one's word*,"

"Don't be at home anywhere," "To teach is not to speak, it is to not speak of the obscure,"

---

[64] "In dreams muteness is often a familiar representation of death" (Freud).

"God did not know how to lie: and so he did not deceive the citizens,"

"If the truth isn't new, it doesn't exist,"

"Meaning is not in things but in means" and "If it's not vanishing, it doesn't exist,"

"Freedom is violence,"

"Seeds must be sown prodigally: if there aren't too many, there aren't enough,"

"Bring meaninglessness back to words,"

"Admit the void: accept the loss forever."

But I who am reporting all this am "over here." With respect to Carlo's point of view, I am at the mercy of "civil objectivity," which "is the consciousness apart," "consciousness as separation, dualism, distance, definition," alas. I am a slave to the Letter. My words are literal, and so they always define properties; these are within the reality and reification principle and therefore false. Yet it turns out (and I can report only in my own words) that at the end of his verbal delirium—and many of the fine Turinese bourgeois present would be ready to swear it—Carlo had become "brilliant" not only in his discourse but also in his appearance, his body. Those who were present said "brilliant"; but it would perhaps have been truer to say "luminous."†

All the preceding sections go together in a single big chapter (Note 129) that has as its centerpiece Signora Giulia Miceli's reception, etc., etc.

(cf. 1st note preceding Note 110)

NOTE 131
A new gloss

At this point in my omniscient and also somewhat pedantic management of my "Legomenon" (even if, at least in part, it is roughly abandoned to its crude approximation of the "Dromenon"), I am forced to find the proper distance from my material; and so report the facts with that dose of incredulity which allows me not to compromise too much with something utopian that—from now on—the reader will be able to recognize.

Furthermore, I would advise the reader to reread Note 37, entitled "Something written," and, at the least, Notes 22i ("Continuation of the *puzzle,* etc."), 3c ("Postponed preface [III]), and 103b ("Second political bloc [Premise]"): where I speak of my ambition to construct a form /with its own self-supporting/ and self-sufficient /laws/ rather than write a story that explains itself through correspondences, more or less *à clef,* with a very dangerous reality. (In this regard, the reader may also remember the tale "The story of a man and his body," which constitutes Note 98.) It's not without some pride that I recommend these internal references to my work. What I wished to do is realized precisely by creating and explaining the work in terms of itself, even literally.

The extreme case—which is justified by Note 3c—that is, an entire section written in Greek, or neo-Greek, letters, practically illegible and therefore constituting no more than "something written"—is now about to be repeated. This time the characters are Japanese. Here pure ideograph and meaningful illegibility are, obviously, expressed /even better/.

But while the first insert of "pure writing" (in neo-Greek)—for all that it was extreme and anomalous with respect to the strict rules that I imposed—was nevertheless justified, this second insert (in Japanese) is undoubtedly less so; in fact, it really risks being repetitious and superfluous.

Certainly the reader has heard talk of symmetry. Well, I *could not* resist the temptation to construct this second, architecturally "symmetrical" body. Besides, Cathedrals and Allegories are based on symmetry, even when they later become magmatic, out of proportion, and abnormal.[65]

---

[65] Moreover, the cultivated reader will have realized that other, similar "architecturally symmetrical bodies" exist in the work; except that they are texts recorded in Italian and in normal alphabetic characters (cf. Notes x, y, and 129–30).

NOTE 132
Toward Edo: planning the trip

The "mute personage" of Carlo's dreams separates from Carlo and acquires a body—He acquires a name as well: the onomasiologically joking name, in accordance with his character, of Cornelio—His typical
irony, somewhat ambiguous and "toying"—He observes that Carlo has,
yes, "awakened" but that, nevertheless, he does not know in a practical
sense what to do.—Enlightenment comes, as usual, when it likes and
pleases—In Carlo's case it came to one who had in no way looked for it
(and was not at all prepared for it—Once he is satisfied by his choice, he
does not know how to behave at all—He, Carlo, is not one of those boring monks who wait for perhaps their whole life and then, when enlightenment comes, know immediately what to do—Laughter (sacred?)
of Carlo and Cornelio—The need for a new culture and a new model of
behavior for Carlo—Cessation of logic in the conversation of Cornelio—Transfigured but still smiling, or rather winking, he points to
where, just then, the sun is rising—Six in the morning in Turin—
Cornelio pronounces the word "Edo"—Cornelio slips away—Carlo's
meditation—His unpleasant frame of mind—Impression "on his return" that Cornelio resembles a drugged, stupid "hippie"—Perhaps
also very ignorant, and Italian besides.

(Japanese text)

NOTE 133
Mockery (from the "Plan")

Carlo, back in his own country, had only to profit from the precious teaching he received in Edo, to live it fully. Meanwhile he had built, in the Canavese, along the rocky and deserted Adda (?), a villa with the aspect of a little hermitage, in the shape of the temple in Edo: doubtless, this frame seemed to him necessary. There solitude, meditation, withdrawal:

> *I am happy. My life is so much*
> *the same as my dream: a dream that doesn't vary:*
> *to live in a villa, solitary,*
> *without the past, without regret:*
> *to belong, to meditate. . . . I sing*
> *of exile, of renunciation that is voluntary.*[66]

It was the cult of the "idle God," practiced through idleness, or, in another sense, the cult of the "joking God," practiced through playing: the God who plays at hiding himself, the God who expresses himself in puns and wordplay, like a madman, and who, casually strolling here and there with unexpected agility, demonstrates that "in stupidity is wisdom" and that, fortunately, "the world cannot be made safe for democracy or any other thing." But that cult, while it kept Carlo from having normal relations with men—mockery of whom was justly the highest form of love toward them—did not keep him from having some commerce with those Gods to whom the first God, the idler and joker—

---

[66] Guido Gozzano, "Un' Altra Risorta."

perhaps he was even asleep beyond the heavens[67]—had entrusted the management of this world.

Carlo I becomes a saint in the search for Carlo II, etc., in his "stoical" social struggle, etc., etc., a supernatural aid, etc., achieves

A DESCENT INTO HELL

which is depicted as a classical voyage, according to the mythological and medieval models, including Dante. But it's only a chapter (as for Ulysses) and much simpler, more direct, etc.

What is this Inferno today, for a man like C.: it is the place of dreams, or the unconscious (the personal Girone and the Girone of the Massenpsyche, or collective Unconscious), with all its symbols. An "Ideal Dream," which synthesizes all possible dreams, with all their possible symbols; the dream of dreams, having become an archetypal commonplace, crystallized in a series of didactic visions. Reaching the lowest point of this Inferno and faced with the primal Scene (which can be invented, overturning all the hypotheses of the scholars; and reduced to an act that is irrelevant and disappointing, and thus extremely significant, as if a glass placed on a tomb under which the true Region of the Dead, etc., extends were to be overturned), C. performs the ritual liberating gesture—which liberates him from sense and mechanical logic (even from the logic of dream symbolism). Of course, the "Descent" is fictionalized. E.g., reappearance of the sexual organ, in the Vision of the Centaur with the enormous prick between his front legs rather than hind legs, etc.; "architectural" visions of a city. But the real fictionalized Story of this descent concerns not C. but a person whom he in reality *accompanies* on the Descent and who must repeat the mythic undertaking, reestablish a relationship with one of his peers, a companion—like Orestes and Pilades, etc.—who died before him (some centuries earlier). An Alexandrian myth (again, like the Argonauts of Apollonius Rhodius) concerning deeds that occurred in the classical world, although everything refers back to the earliest beginnings. Thus I could rework a prim-

---

[67] That, at least, is the conviction of the Kai, a small population of New Guinea, who grow tubers: they believe that the Creator, Malengfung, after creating the cosmos and man, withdrew to the end of the world, to the horizon, and there went to sleep. But one day he will wake up, rise from his pallet, and destroy everything he has created.

itive myth, Indian or African or Polynesian, in which, roughly, the elements of the Mediterranean and Christian myth are found, etc.

—Tracking shot backward in which Carlo is looking at the mythical hero's deeds—Only at the end the protagonist becomes Carlo—The tracking shot is analogous to that of the Vision in the "Shit" section.

Chia, 16 August 1974
(Dreamed during the night)

<?>

—Explain the anomaly of Polis and Tetis, along with the meaning of the *scheme* of their stories—
Note that the secrets they confide to the men who are chosen is the story of Carlo Valletti—
Other sections about Carlo: "The prefatory folly continues"

* All the inserted stories are the concrete and living representations of facts or characters that in the text are the product of pure abstract distortion.

    1) E.g., the first group of stories "represents" the political types who in the text <?>—abstractly—the politics of development and the two groups of political massacres—
    Only one of the narrators—at the end—tells a true story—He omits names—but gives the concrete *facts,* that is, of the massacres he committed, in their historical setting (he pretends that a CIA agent on the point of death confided everything to him)—*This is also the thesis of my book (do not say this explicitly but let it be understood, saying that this is also the *outline* of his book)

    2) In the group of stories of the Epoche failed "coups" are hinted at: to them is opposed historical reality, symbolized by natural apocalyptic upheavals—*mud*—*fire*—etc. (the mud in the story of the aristocratic Roman and his two daughters)—(The *fire* will recall the fire in the story of Bihar)

* For the story of the father who gives birth to the son-shit—

    —At the same time as the fat millionaire bourgeois, a man of the people in the center-South also shits a son—The matter is taken under consideration by a scientific luminary, etc., who welcomes the man giving birth to the same

luxurious clinic where he has also welcomed the son of the great bourgeois—The two shit-children are mixed up—The fathers therefore exchange them—Thus the shits that are alive have a universality that is also
classist, etc., etc., they are interchangeable, etc.

—prefinale: sunny summer day, after some days winter returns—New men,
new spirit—End of a world, of a hairstyle—Naiveté, <?>—everything concentrated in the figure of a young man (the decline of the
crisis and of poverty creates a *novelty*)

* —The divinities who help resolve the cosmic crisis are, of course, peasant gods
* (Baubon or the Japanese divinity, etc.). That is inserted into the reorganiza-
tion of agriculture and the crisis of the peasant world (cf. also the caricature
of Fanfani's discussion with Carlo at the Turinese reception)—The cortege
passes through a country landscape surrounding a nuclear power plant
graveyard

END NOTES

xi †Note in the margin between this paragraph and the next, marked to be inserted: "long description the impossibility of his getting ahead."

xvi †Note in the left-hand margin: "Bologna hills."

xvii †Note above "Central Station": "Bologna."

xix †Note in the space between the lines: "<?> Pisa."

xxi †Marginal note: "link the blackmail of Carlo II and the punishment of Carlo I."

Note 2

4 †Question mark after the title.
‡Note: "Another chapter."

Note 3

8 †Note: ["indirect discourse"]; the word "that" at the beginning of the two preceding paragraphs, "This Body" and "No, because . . . ," indicates that they were also to be changed to indirect discourse.

Note 3b

11 †An indication that the entire section was to be moved "to a note."

Note 3d

15 †Note planned but not written.

Note 5

24 †Note planned but not written.

Note 6

25 †Originally "Carlo the Second" throughout the note, later altered to "Karl," with a black pen, and finally, starting from the third paragraph, but intermittently, to "the second Carlo," with a blue pen.

Note 6b

29 †An asterisk in the left-hand margin, probably referring to the material between dashes that begins "a 'movement' . . . ," refers to a note at the bottom of the page: "add these lines to Note 3c (Postponed preface, III)."

Note 6 *ter*
31 †Question mark after the title.
32 †A page and a half that has been crossed out concludes with the following note: "describe in detail the various exhibitionistic acts, etc."

Note 6 *quinquies*
34 †Question mark.

Note 9
51 †At the top of the page: "insert two chapters on exhibitionism in the
country, in the town"; arrow from the title to the right-hand margin.

Note 10
52 †Arrow from the title to the right-hand margin.

Note 17
67 †Title added in the space between the lines, with the marginal note:
"New chapter."
†Note: "shadow and light."
‡Note: "(Carlo's distress)."
§Note: "(Carlo's distress)."
‖Note: "(Carlo's distress)."

Note 22h
95 †Handwritten note for which the corresponding reference to the text was
not inserted.

Note 31
99 †The preceding page is missing, and the text begins in the middle of a
sentence: "themselves, good feelings, obedience, grace, interest from inferiors in everything that is discussed—all has been said," followed by a
question mark. The rest of the page is circled and preceded by a note:
"(to be revised)."

Note 32
100 †Note at the top of the page: "rewrite all 'as seen by' Carlo, who goes
into the living room, where someone is telling a story," and, on a new
line "(then a series of stories)."

Note 33
106 †Question mark; eleven typewritten lines that have been crossed out.

Note 34 *bis*
106 ‡Arrow to the preceding page.
114 †The word "Dialect," followed by a reminder for a note planned but not
written.
114 ‡"I put it on my face" refers to "a mask," later replaced by "simply an
aspect."

Note 41

139   †Note planned but not written.

Note 42

150   †The end of the sentence, from "was having," added in pen and left hanging.

Note 43

151   †Initially "Note 41," then corrected to "43," with an arrow pointing to "end of 42."

Note 43a

156   †Notation for an insert, referring to a note written at the top of the page: "an example 'I was licking her cunt.'"

Note 55

190   †Note at the start of the paragraph: "IX."

195   †In the space between the lines the beginning of a correction: "as."

Note 61

200   †Thus in the manuscript.

200   ‡The entire paragraph was originally in Note 62, cf. the following note.

Note 62

201   †Two arrows indicate that the paragraph beginning "The first solution Carlo . . ." was to be inserted after this paragraph; the paragraph that originally followed is circled in pen and, in accordance with the marginal note "Karl is gone (in conclusion)," has been moved to the end of the preceding Note 61.

Note 65

211   †"he meets an Angel" is underlined and an arrow points to the note "Dmitri = Demeter (drunken confusion)."

Note 65 *bis*

212   †"was Providence" is circled in pen and linked by an arrow to the end of the paragraph.

215   †Between the lines is the note "Heroism <Humility> and Resignation."

215   ‡Note planned but not written.

Note 67

224   †Note planned but not written.

Note 62

254   †Reference to a preceding passage that was later deleted.

254   ‡Note: "Hospital ('Eh, how many have died!')."

Note 63a

262   †The beginning of this Note, originally part of Note 62, is circled;

"Note 63a" is inserted in the space between the lines.

263 †Note, circled: "—motorboat—embarkation/—Charon/—disappearance at the horizon into the lights."

Note 63

268 †Note planned but not written.

Note 65

276 †Note planned but not written.

Note 71u

310 †Two question marks in the left-hand margin.

Note 71z

318 †Note planned but not written.

Note 72f

327 †Three typewritten lines, crossed out and replaced by a note: "< ... > Lack of initiation: the Pattern acts immediately even for prepubescent children—there is no training or *brimade* (except genocide, also slaughter of the innocents)."

Note 74

331 †Arrow pointing to the preceding page.

343 †Note: "30 Zen stories; at a sophisticated reception (Oct. 2, 1973)"; "30 Zen stories" is circled; above it are written a question mark and "foll. page."

344 †An arrow indicates that the circled note "Enlightenment (Zen)" is to be inserted between this sentence and the next.
‡Note in red pen: "Journey to Edo."

Note 100

344 §The title is circled and an arrow points to the following pages; notes follow that have been crossed out.

Note 97

345 †Note at the top of the page, with an arrow pointing to the text: "All seen with the 'lucidity of mortal melancholy' of Carlo 'changed into another.'"

Note 98

356 †This paragraph is on a page by itself; it is connected to Note 98, but there is nothing to establish its position.

Note 101

371 †Arrow points to a note: "delaying element: meeting of 'scholars' in progress but which foreshadows the Epoche."

371 ‡Arrow points to a note: "situation of the scene: family meeting. The two girls think they haven't understood . . ."

Note 103

389 †Word to be inserted.

Note 103a

397 †Question mark follows.

397 ‡The phrase "3) Story of the Infant-Shit" is added in red; the number "3)," which originally indicated the following notes, is corrected to "4)"; an arrow indicates a further transposition of the episode of the Infant-Shit to follow those listed at point 4).

401 †The whole is circled, with a question mark.

Note 119

420 †Note next to the title, with an arrow pointing to the text: "All as seen by Carlo led by the boy."

Note 120

421 †Note next to the title, with an arrow pointing to the text: "idem," obviously referring to the note at the beginning of Note 119.

422 †"little mountain" is underlined, and a mark refers to a note at the bottom of the page: "at the foot of this little mountain the boy stops and silently turns back (crying) and leaves Carlo alone—who ascends and from the top sees Turin."

Note 124

426 †Note, preceded by an arrow pointing to the text: "VISION/as if for a publicity photograph, divided into three parts: silent majority, criminality, political and intellectual élites."

Note 125

428 †The first part of the note is crossed out; this last paragraph is circled, with a note: "new chapter."

Note 126

429 †Note in the space between the lines: "gray stone of his city."

429 ‡Reference to a note next to the title: "end the chapter with a visionary description of the 'misery' of these classic Fascists"; what follows, almost to the end of the note (cf. the following note), is circled and a marginal note, "Epoche," indicates that it is linked to the preceding section.

431 †The circled part described in the preceding note ends here.

432 †Notes with an arrow pointing to this paragraph: "incorporate in the visionary description" and "—a poor assassin (Di Lauria?) (Angels?)."

Note 129c

444 †Reference to a note at the bottom of the page: "his gestures like a female homosexual's."

Note 128c

452   †The title is circled, with an arrow pointing to the note at the bottom of
p. 673.

Note 129

456   †The title is circled, with an arrow pointing to the note at the bottom of
p. 673.

Note 130

457   †The title is circled, with an arrow pointing to the note at the bottom of
p. 673.

458   †Note at the bottom of the page: "Directing the 'Mystery,' omniscient
and wise."